WINNER OF
THE EISNER AWARD FOR
BEST LIMITED SERIES

———————⬦———————

WINNER OF
THE HARVEY AWARD FOR
BOOK OF THE YEAR

FEATURED ON
20+ BEST OF THE YEAR
LISTS INCLUDING:

———————————

"Astonishing... a perfect blend of genres and ideas,
and one of the best crime books out there."
— **MATTHEW JACKSON**, *SyFy Wire*

"Nuanced characters, gorgeously mood-setting art, and
an impressively layered story... the kind of textured plotting you
might expect from Raymond Chandler if he were writing today."
— **DUSTIN NELSON**, *Thrillist*

"A unique blend of old and new which elevates the medium
of comics... historical as well as political and touches on
hot button topics that are just as important in 2021 as they
were in the 1930s."
— **DALTON NORMAN**, *Screenrant*

"Dark and violent and beautiful."
— **JIM DANDENEAU**, *Den of Geek*

"This series — at once historical and timely — teaches as it stings. Its
furious didacticism invests the genre's usual damaged, conflicted
characters with new meaning. Gripping, nasty, powerful."
— **CHARLES HATFIELD**, *The Comics Journal*

"It's somehow gotten even better with time...
chock full of drama, intrigue, and noir."
— **DANA FORSYTHE**, *Paste Magazine*

One of the best pieces of art in any medium that debuted in
021. Arguably, it could be the single best comic of the year."
— **HANK REA**, *Lotusland Comics*

"This is the food you eat, which makes you tear up, as you
suddenly realize how truly starved you were, and how bad it
ally was before you got to eat it. We need this. We need more
people to read this. It's bloody brilliant."
— **RITESH BABU**, *ComicsXF*

"Dripping with noir-ish style... immediately engaging."
— **AVERY KAPLAN**, *Comics Beat*

"Compelling crime storytelling and stark mirror of the nation's
acist legacies... Definitely one of the year's best limited series."
— **PAUL LAI**, *Multiversity Comics*

"Emotionally raw, with complex characters and
tough moral quandaries."
— **JOHN MILES**, *Comic Book Resources*

"Impressive... breathe[s] new life into the
ground broken by Chandler and Hammett."
— **CHRISTOPHER FARNSWORTH**, *Book and Film Globe*

"From top to bottom this book sings: the characters, plot,
pencils, layouts, letters, and especially the COLORS! Top it off
with the most educational and personal back matter of any book
on the stands, and you have one of the best books of 2021."
— **FIRE GUY RYAN**, *ComicTom101*

THE GOOD ASIAN: 1936. First printing. May 2023. Published by Image Comics, Inc. Office of publication: PO BOX 14457, Portland, OR 97293. Printed in China. For international rights, contact: foreignlicensing@imagecomics.com.

Standard edition ISBN: 978-1-5343-2585-2
DCBS exclusive variant edition ISBN: 978-1-5343-2664-4

BOOK DESIGN BY
JEFF POWELL

THE GOOD ASIAN

AN EDISON HARK MYSTERY

PORNSAK PICHETSHOTE
WRITER

ALEXANDRE TEFENKGI
ARTIST

LEE LOUGHRIDGE
COLORIST

JEFF POWELL
LETTERER & DESIGNER

DAVE JOHNSON
SERIES COVER ARTIST

GRANT DIN
HISTORICAL CONSULTANT

ERIKA SCHNATZ
SERIES LOGO DESIGN & PRODUCTION

WILL DENNIS
EDITOR

BY DAVID CHOE

Fuck you chink

Go back to China

Go back to where you came from

I grew up with this

It hurt

It made me feel sad alone like an outsider like I didn't belong

But also a small % of the hurt was because it wasn't even accurate it was lazy if you did a little digging you'd know I was a gook

And if you went even further you'd see I was neither. My oppressors aren't going to take the extra time to get my ethnic background correct but neither did I. I was taught to be less than by outsiders and within my own community and my own family. Why speak up your voice does not matter

Why would I expect my oppressors to look deep when even I didn't look that deep because of laziness? Or something more resembling shame? Who would do the digging to get us those answers?

For anyone not Asian I'll briefly explain Asian culture

It's shut the fuck up and keep your head down, be invisible, you don't matter, the individual does not matter, the family is everything, image and how you make the family look is everything, sacrifice and martyr yourself for everyone but yourself, suffer silently, Never complain, let them curse you, beat you, harass threaten bully beat you down burn your stores, say nothing, smile and take it, take that anger and hatred, bury it deep and use it as revenge fuel, work hard, word harder than anyone and then become rich, own everything and then when you are on top serve the revenge very cold, fire everyone that ever fucked with you punish those who punished you and their entire families. That's why you never hear from us, stealth mode. We never forget. Success is the best revenge, get there quietly without ever complaining.

Art has always been the answer for me, it has saved me and the planet multiple times, it's as important as a doctor or lawyer because it changes culture and perception.

But try telling that to an immigrant parent that art is as important as medicine and law and you get the belt. Which is why Pornsak is an outlier an anomaly a treasure and a gift to me and the culture.

Because you've never heard a voice like his.

THANK GOD FOR PORNSAK, who by all accounts is a "Good Asian" but I see the truth. For Pornsak the writer to exist means he went against his culture, so he's a "Bad Asian."

Bad Asian is what I've been my entire life

Long greasy hair

Heavy metal

Poor grades

Criminal record

No piano

I've been called a Chigger before

So when I saw the title "GOOD ASIAN," I picked it up as a goof.

I looked at my friend Rhode and my brother Paul, what are the chances this is any good I asked.

And I was right... it's not good.

Its fucking great! I love this shit

I'm so happy, I cried.

This fucker this brilliant Pornsak fucker addresses all my baggage and all this heavy cultural shit in a trojan horse of a Chinatown murder mystery.

I learn facts and true shit every issue that I never knew (because once again no talking!)

I've only met Pornsak recently and have only hung out a handful of times, the first time we met, even though we live in Thaitown we didn't just have Thai food, we had northern Thai food from a very specific region, while we were bro'ing out his mom and his sister completely randomly drove an hour in traffic to eat here at the same time, very specific tastes. It runs in the family and this level of attention to detail is what he brings to his writing. This is the shit I love.

For all new Good Asian readers, the complex characters and well-crafted plotlines are self evident...

But Pornsak's incredibly thorough research with the goal of historical accuracy (regardless of the fictional storyline), the importance of not brushing this shameful/overtly-racist period under the metaphorical carpet, and not letting America/Americans remember itself/themselves with bullshit rose-colored glasses.

His level of dedication really shows; even in the post-comic wrap-up section! (if you finish the trade and you love it like I do go back and buy the individual issues, because there's so much great extra stuff in the letters column and the interviews in the back pages of the individual issues).

Alexandre Tefenkgi's art is solid. Initially, his style struck me as simplistic/minimal, but over time I found it deceptive because he fills the panels with mad nuance and subtlety. His artwork is a great match and complements the story very well. (Also big-up to Lee Loughridge's color work!)

I'm not an actor but the only reason I agreed to write this intro is so I can finally play a good Asian on the big screen when you know Hollywood eventually turns this into a movie.

The book is beautiful.

It's better than a movie. It's thrilling and makes you think and it's fun and entertaining.

But more than that

It's important and it matters

And it's brave enough to explore the question

Go back to where you come from

David Choe
2/2/22 Northern Thai Food Club

Long famous for his fine art which has garnered the respect and adulation of museums and fans around the world, iconoclastic painter David Choe is one of the few fine artists to successfully jump from the museum to the media world. Dubbed "the prince of all media" by Howard Stern, Choe has directed well-regarded music videos and has had his art featured on multi-platinum album covers. In 2021, his television show The Choe Show *premiered on FX.*

SPECIAL THANKS

Octavia Bray
Liz Choi Bubriski
Cliff Chiang
Jimmy Nguyen
Keith Chow
Tyler Jennes
Mel Judson
David Lei
Dawn Lee Tu
Cindy Wei

Jessica, Anaïs, Miles, Angelique,
Daniel, Leila, Steve, Niki, Eric, CC,
and our Moms for all their support
during a crazy pandemic

CHAPTER ONE

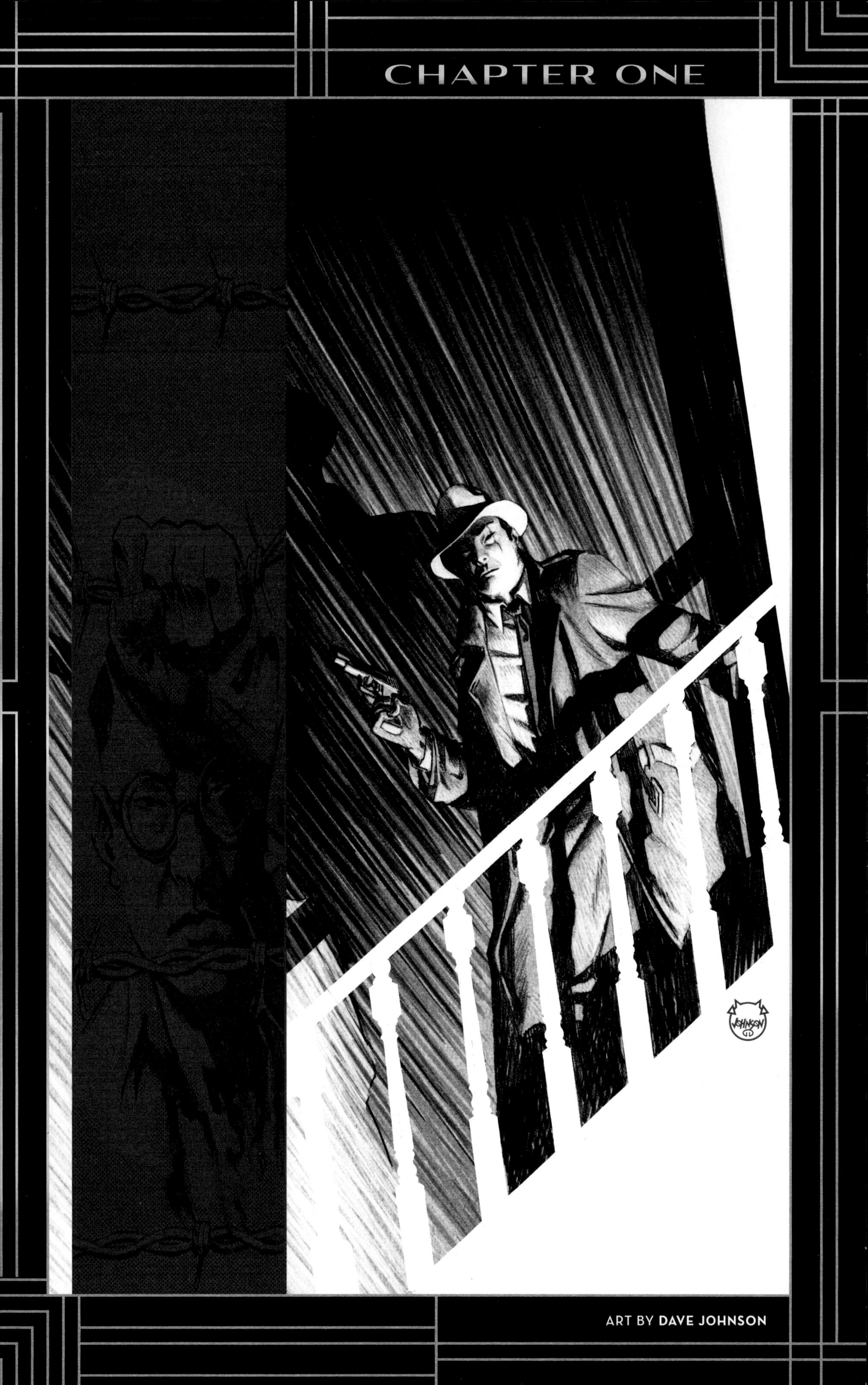

ART BY **DAVE JOHNSON**

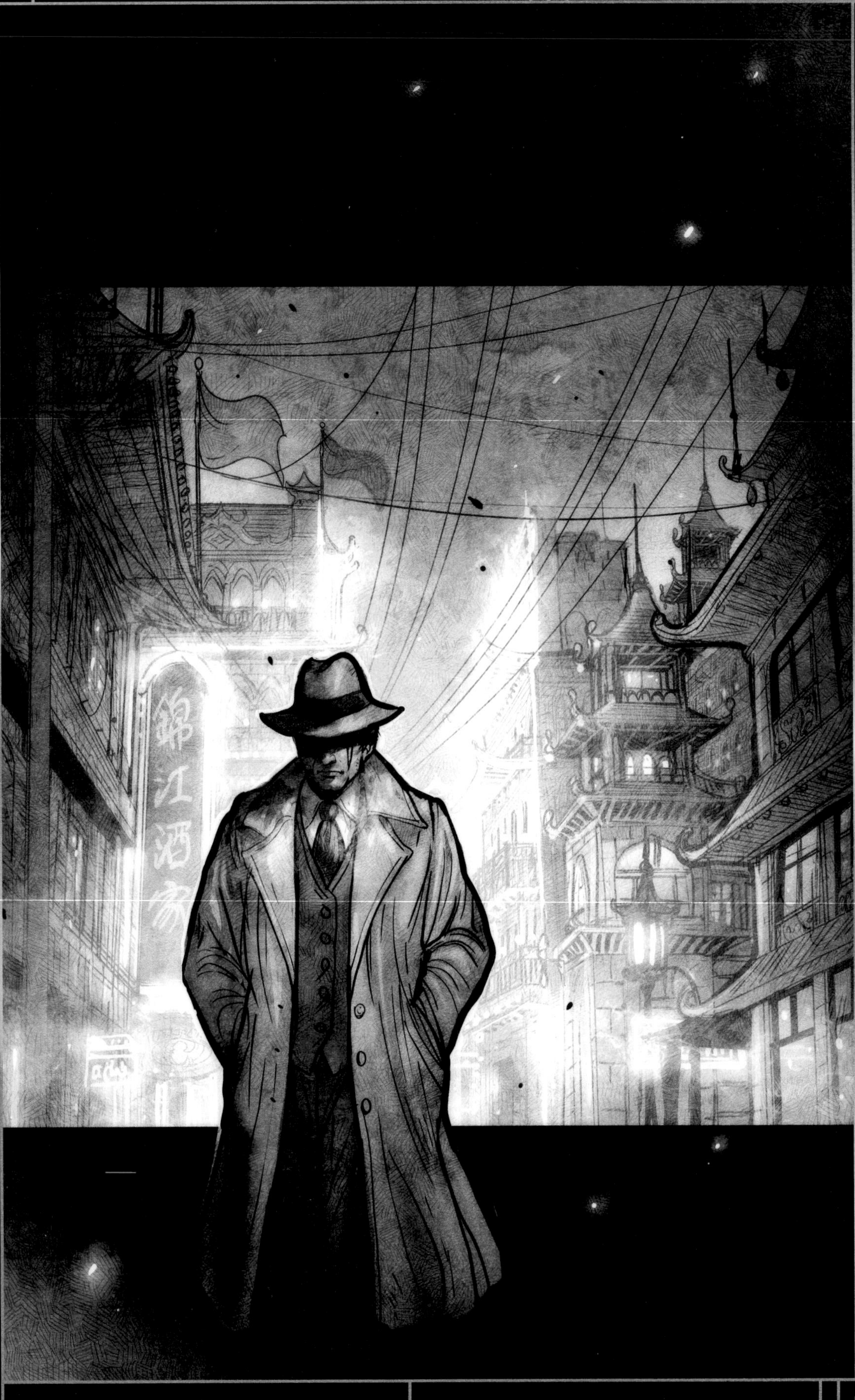
錦江酒家

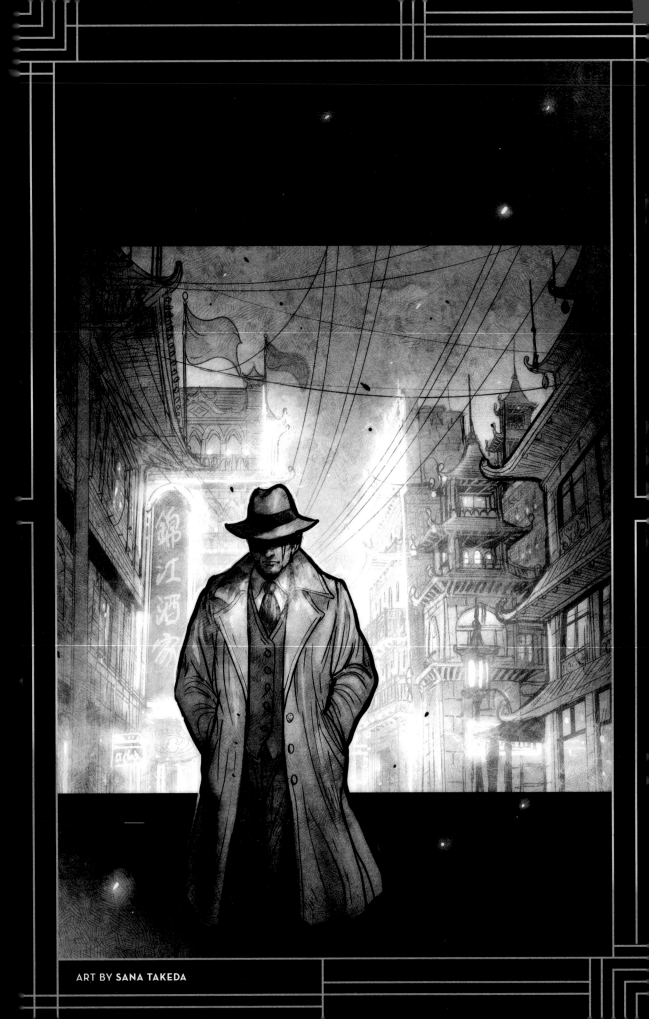

ART BY **SANA TAKEDA**

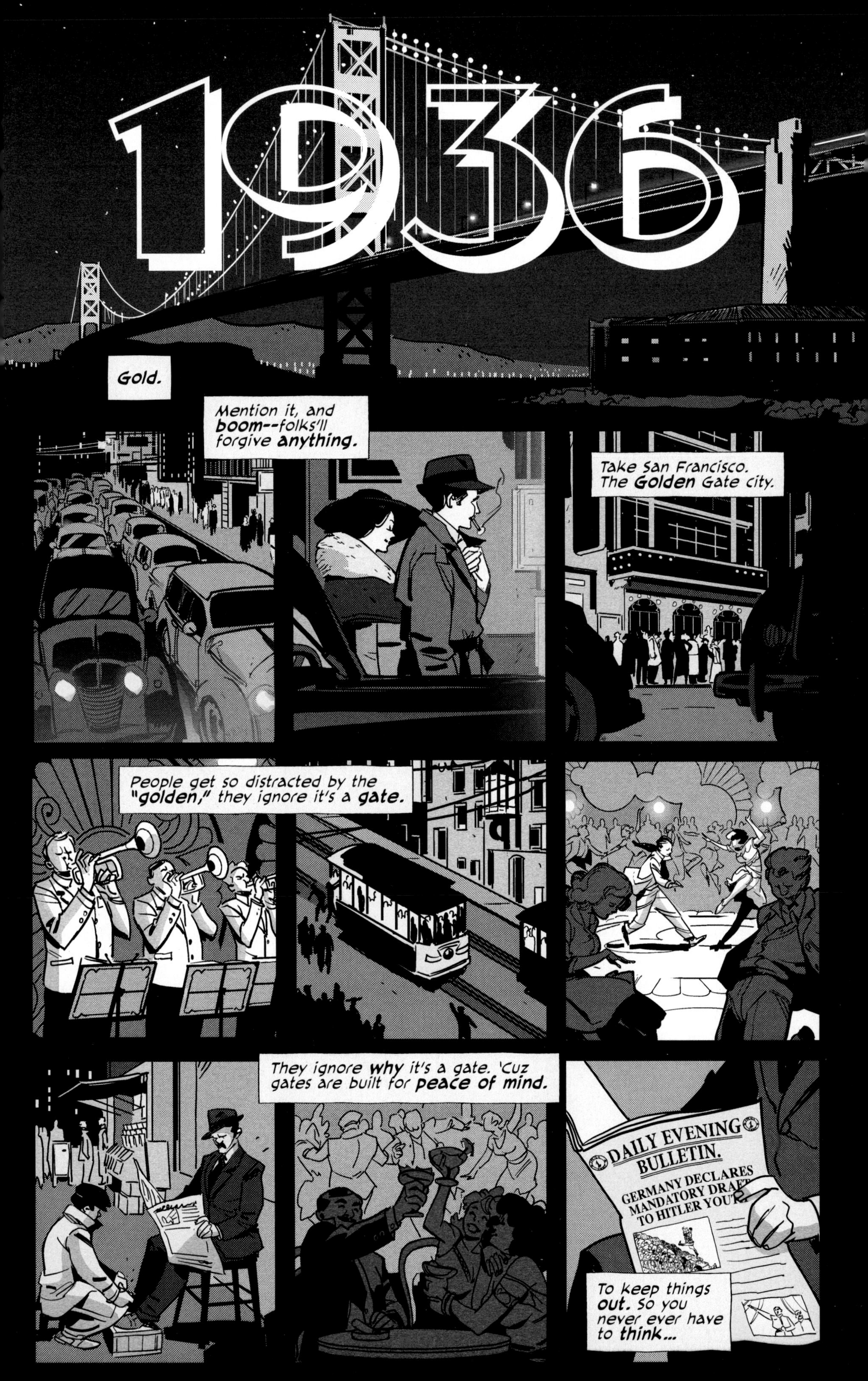
1936
Gold.
Mention it, and boom--folks'll forgive anything.
Take San Francisco. The Golden Gate city.
People get so distracted by the "golden," they ignore it's a gate.
They ignore why it's a gate. 'Cuz gates are built for peace of mind.
DAILY EVENING BULLETIN.
GERMANY DECLARES MANDATORY DRAFT TO HITLER YOUTH
To keep things out. So you never ever have to think...

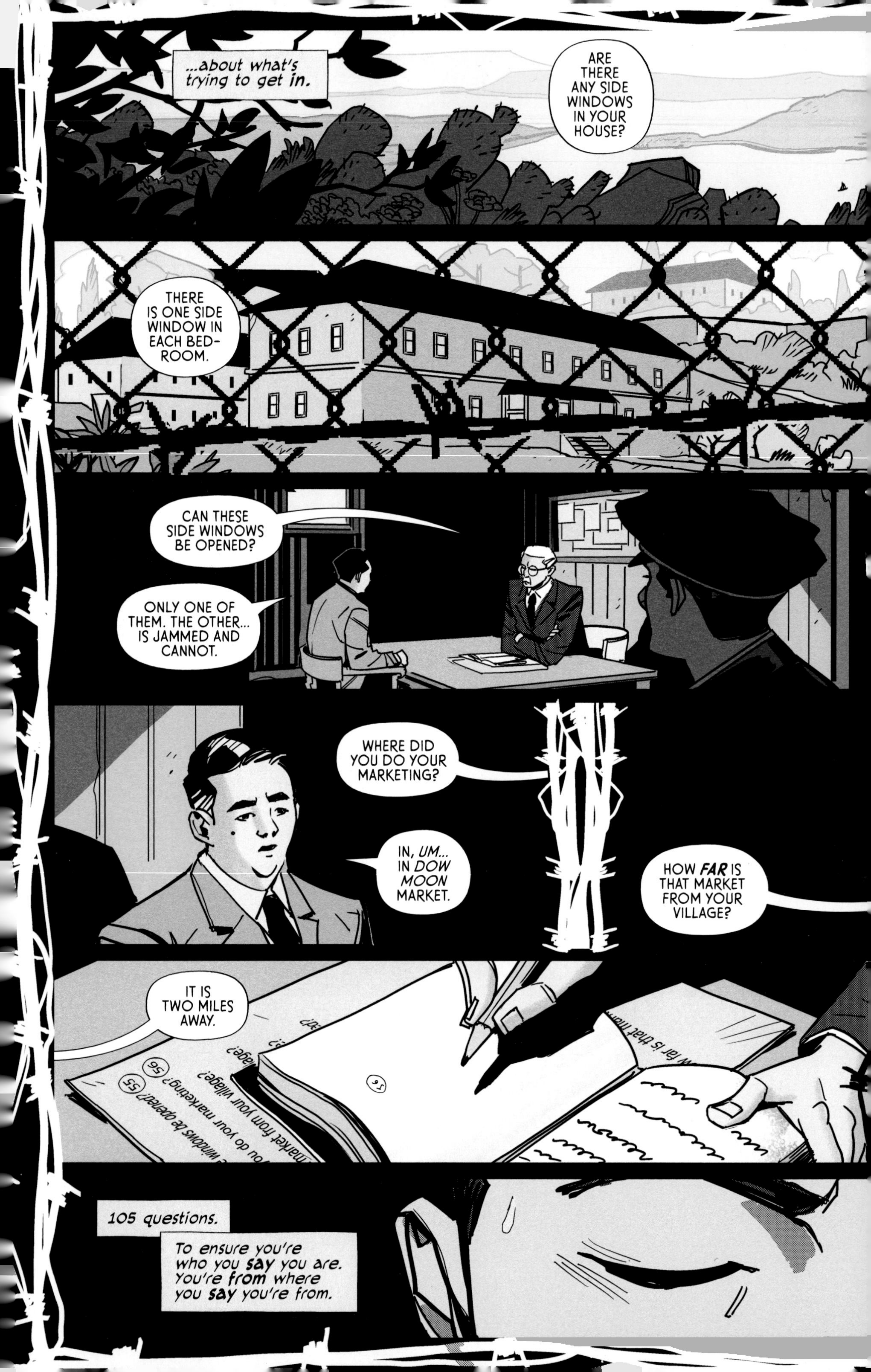
...about what's trying to get in.
ARE THERE ANY SIDE WINDOWS IN YOUR HOUSE?
THERE IS ONE SIDE WINDOW IN EACH BED-ROOM.
CAN THESE SIDE WINDOWS BE OPENED?
ONLY ONE OF THEM. THE OTHER... IS JAMMED AND CANNOT.
WHERE DID YOU DO YOUR MARKETING?
IN, UM... IN DOW MOON MARKET.
HOW FAR IS THAT MARKET FROM YOUR VILLAGE?
IT IS TWO MILES AWAY.
105 questions.
To ensure you're who you say you are. You're from where you say you're from.

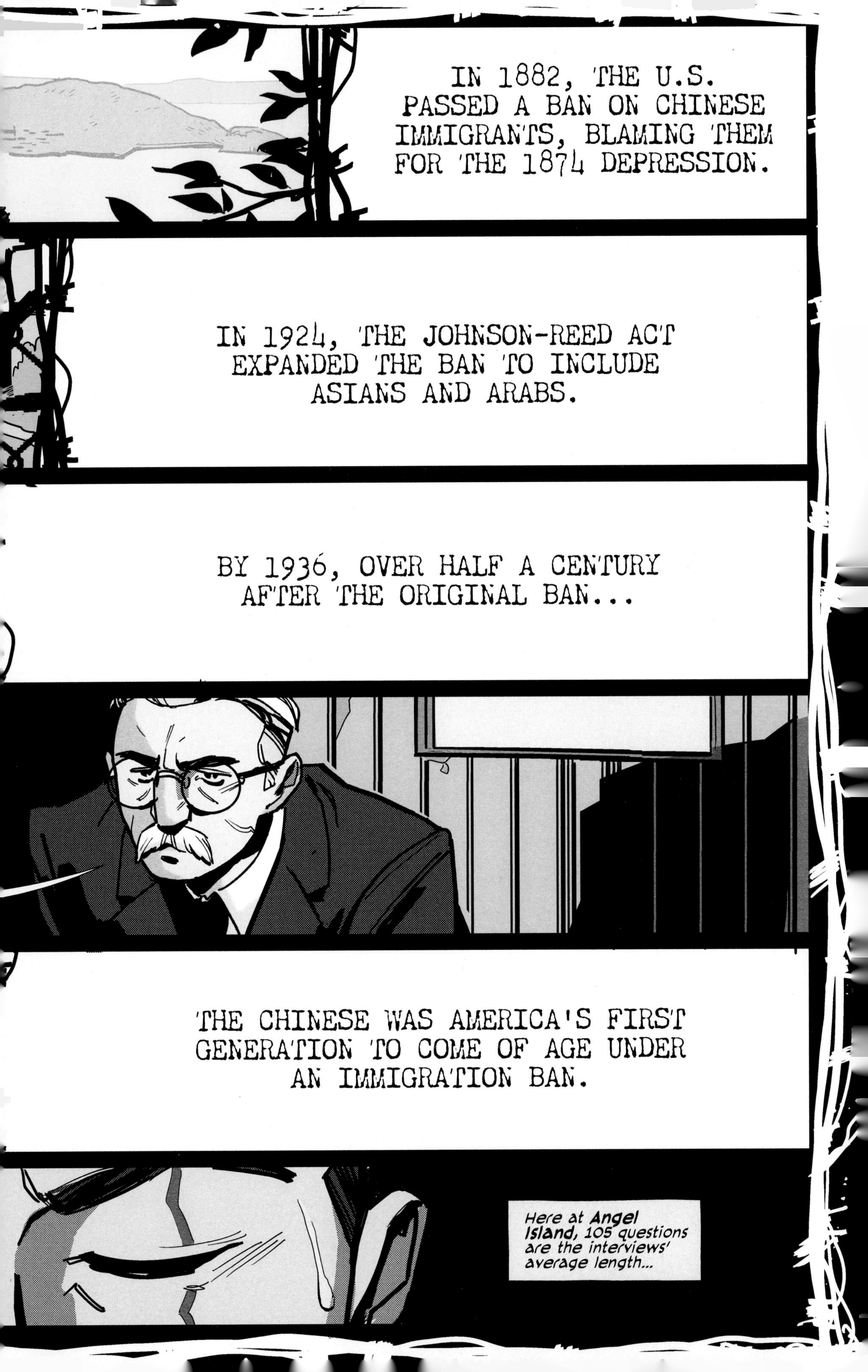
IN 1882, THE U.S. PASSED A BAN ON CHINESE IMMIGRANTS, BLAMING THEM FOR THE 1874 DEPRESSION.
IN 1924, THE JOHNSON-REED ACT EXPANDED THE BAN TO INCLUDE ASIANS AND ARABS.
BY 1936, OVER HALF A CENTURY AFTER THE ORIGINAL BAN...
THE CHINESE WAS AMERICA'S FIRST GENERATION TO COME OF AGE UNDER AN IMMIGRATION BAN.
Here at Angel Island, 105 questions are the interviews' average length...

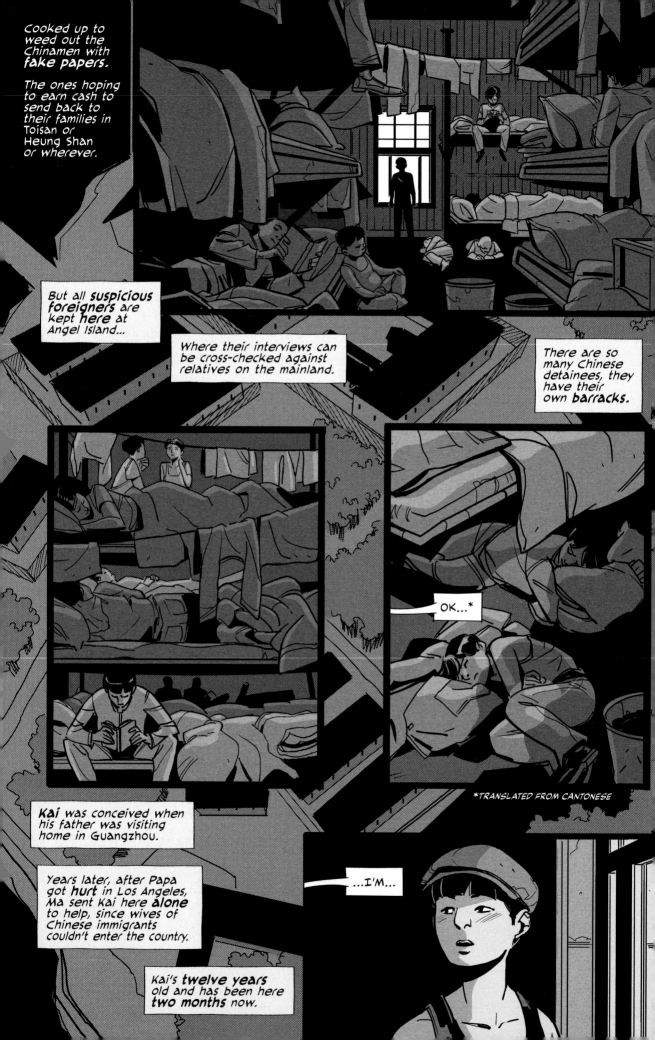

Cooked up to weed out the Chinamen with **fake papers**.

The ones hoping to earn cash to send back to their families in Toisan or Heung Shan or wherever.

But all **suspicious foreigners** are kept **here** at Angel Island...

Where their interviews can be cross-checked against relatives on the mainland.

There are so many Chinese detainees, they have their own **barracks**.

OK...*

*TRANSLATED FROM CANTONESE

Kai was conceived when his father was visiting home in Guangzhou.

Years later, after Papa got **hurt** in Los Angeles, Ma sent Kai here **alone** to help, since wives of Chinese immigrants couldn't enter the country.

...I'M...

Kai's **twelve years** old and has been here **two months** now.

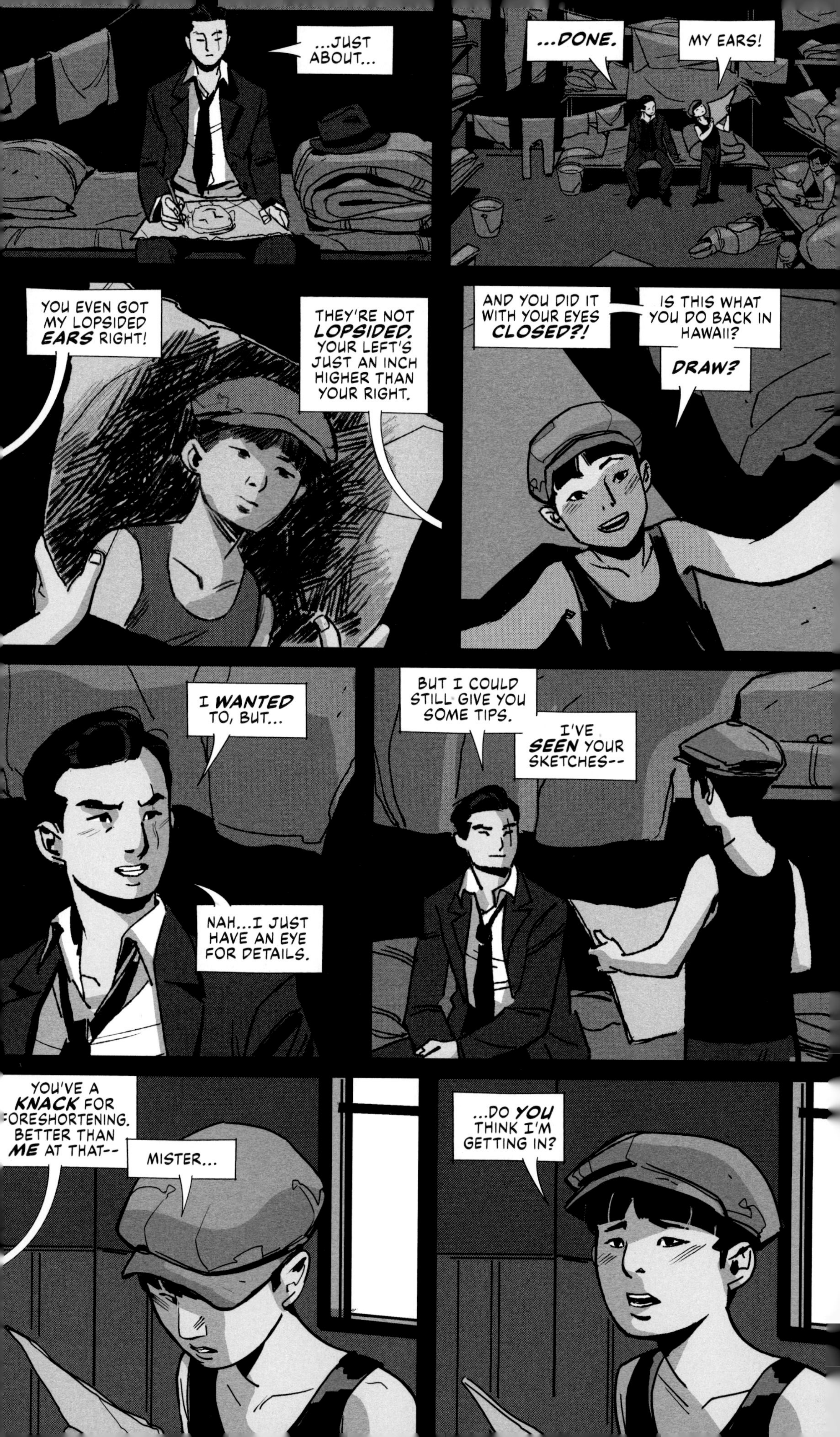
...JUST ABOUT...
...DONE.
MY EARS!
YOU EVEN GOT MY LOPSIDED EARS RIGHT!
THEY'RE NOT LOPSIDED. YOUR LEFT'S JUST AN INCH HIGHER THAN YOUR RIGHT.
AND YOU DID IT WITH YOUR EYES CLOSED?!
IS THIS WHAT YOU DO BACK IN HAWAII?
DRAW?
I WANTED TO, BUT...
NAH...I JUST HAVE AN EYE FOR DETAILS.
BUT I COULD STILL GIVE YOU SOME TIPS.
I'VE SEEN YOUR SKETCHES--
YOU'VE A KNACK FOR FORESHORTENING. BETTER THAN ME AT THAT--
MISTER...
...DO YOU THINK I'M GETTING IN?

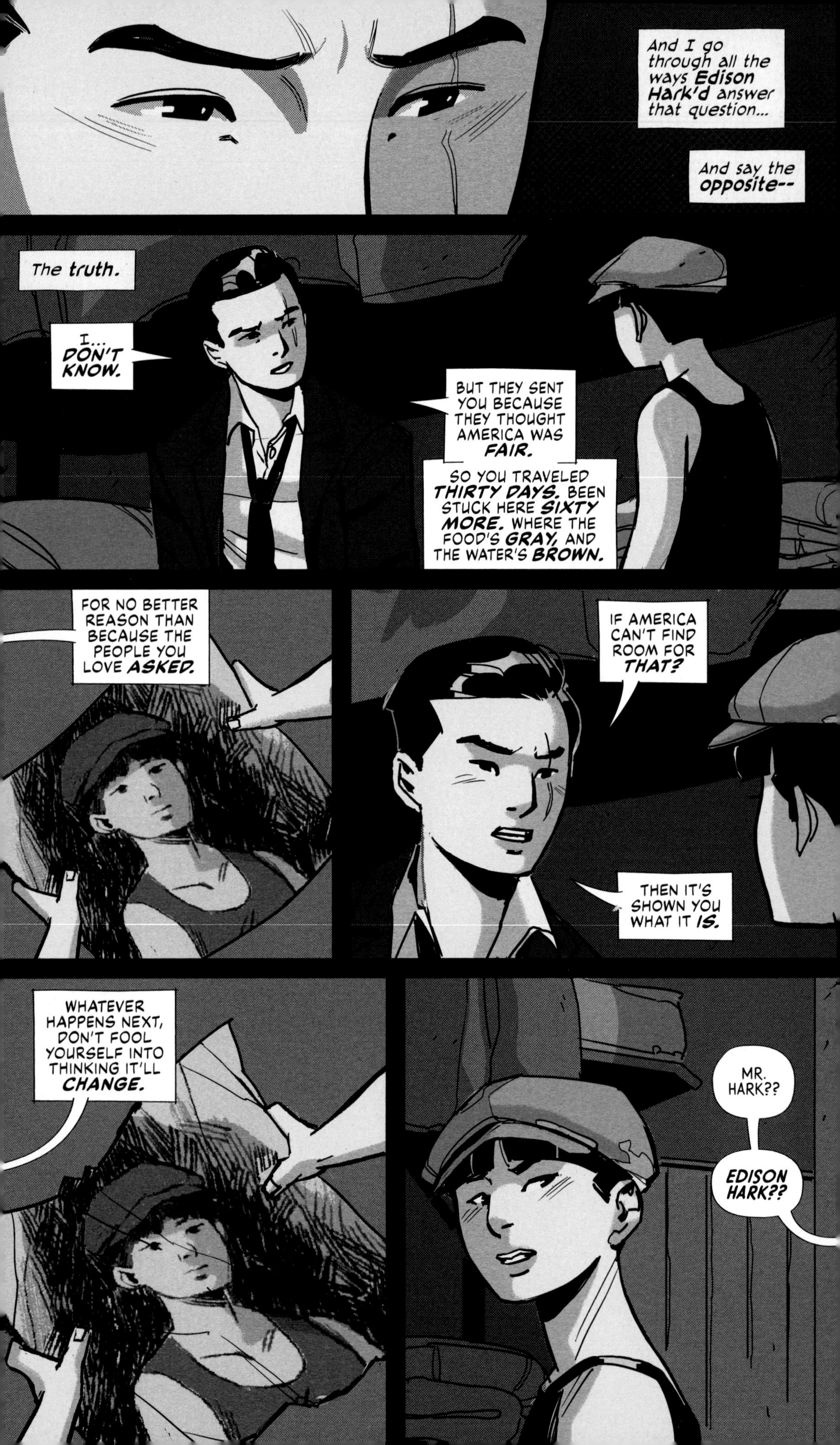
And I go through all the ways **Edison Hark'd** answer that question...
And say the **opposite--**
The **truth.**
I... **DON'T KNOW.**
BUT THEY SENT YOU BECAUSE THEY THOUGHT AMERICA WAS **FAIR.**
SO YOU TRAVELED **THIRTY DAYS.** BEEN STUCK HERE **SIXTY MORE.** WHERE THE FOOD'S **GRAY,** AND THE WATER'S **BROWN.**
FOR NO BETTER REASON THAN BECAUSE THE PEOPLE YOU LOVE **ASKED.**
IF AMERICA CAN'T FIND ROOM FOR **THAT?**
THEN IT'S SHOWN YOU WHAT IT **IS.**
WHATEVER HAPPENS NEXT, DON'T FOOL YOURSELF INTO THINKING IT'LL **CHANGE.**
MR. HARK??
EDISON HARK??

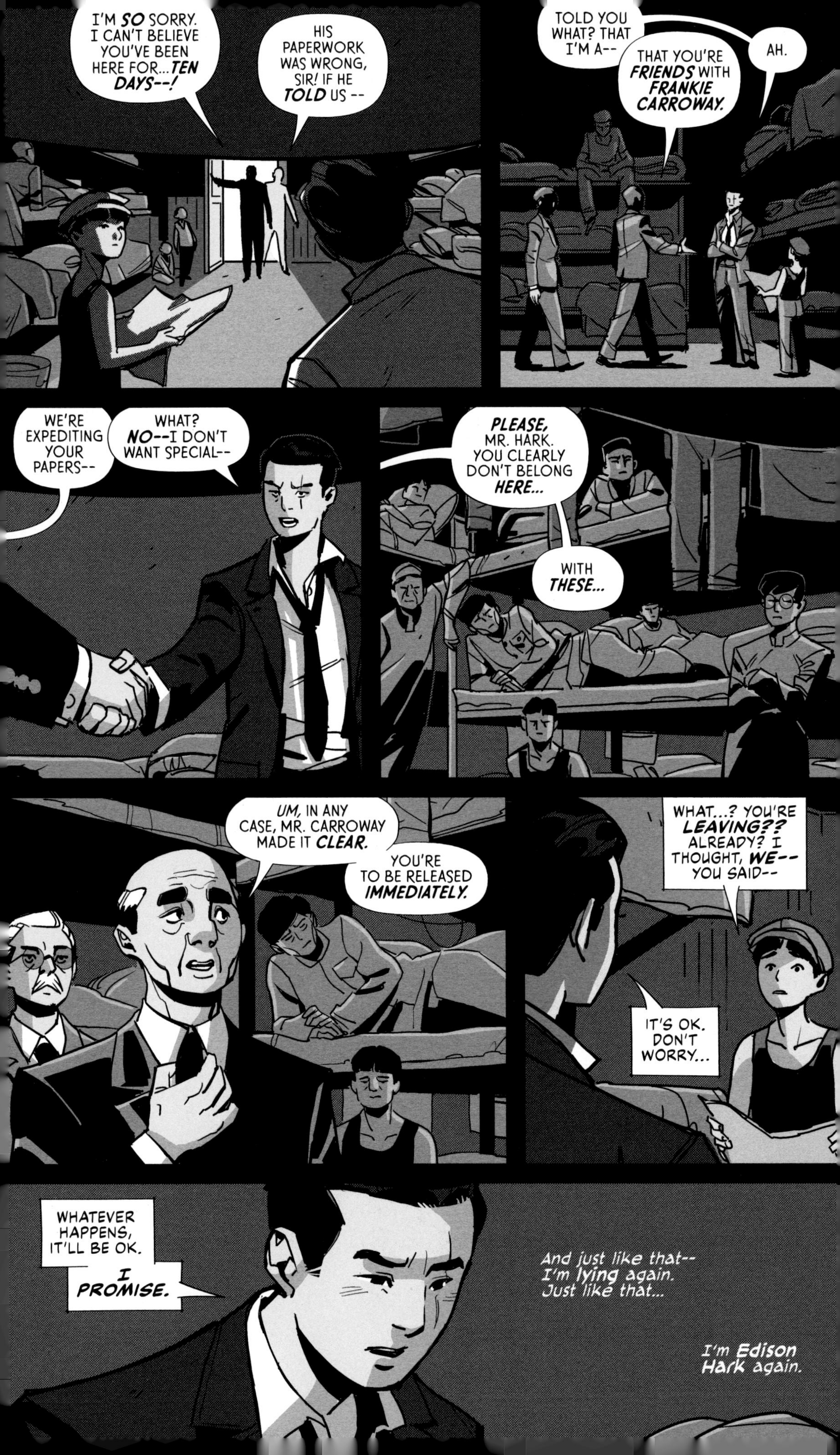
I'M SO SORRY. I CAN'T BELIEVE YOU'VE BEEN HERE FOR...TEN DAYS--!
HIS PAPERWORK WAS WRONG, SIR! IF HE TOLD US --
TOLD YOU WHAT? THAT I'M A--
THAT YOU'RE FRIENDS WITH FRANKIE CARROWAY.
AH.
WE'RE EXPEDITING YOUR PAPERS--
WHAT? NO--I DON'T WANT SPECIAL--
PLEASE, MR. HARK. YOU CLEARLY DON'T BELONG HERE...
WITH THESE...
UM, IN ANY CASE, MR. CARROWAY MADE IT CLEAR.
YOU'RE TO BE RELEASED IMMEDIATELY.
WHAT...? YOU'RE LEAVING?? ALREADY? I THOUGHT, WE-- YOU SAID--
IT'S OK. DON'T WORRY...
WHATEVER HAPPENS, IT'LL BE OK.
I PROMISE.
And just like that-- I'm lying again. Just like that...
I'm Edison Hark again.

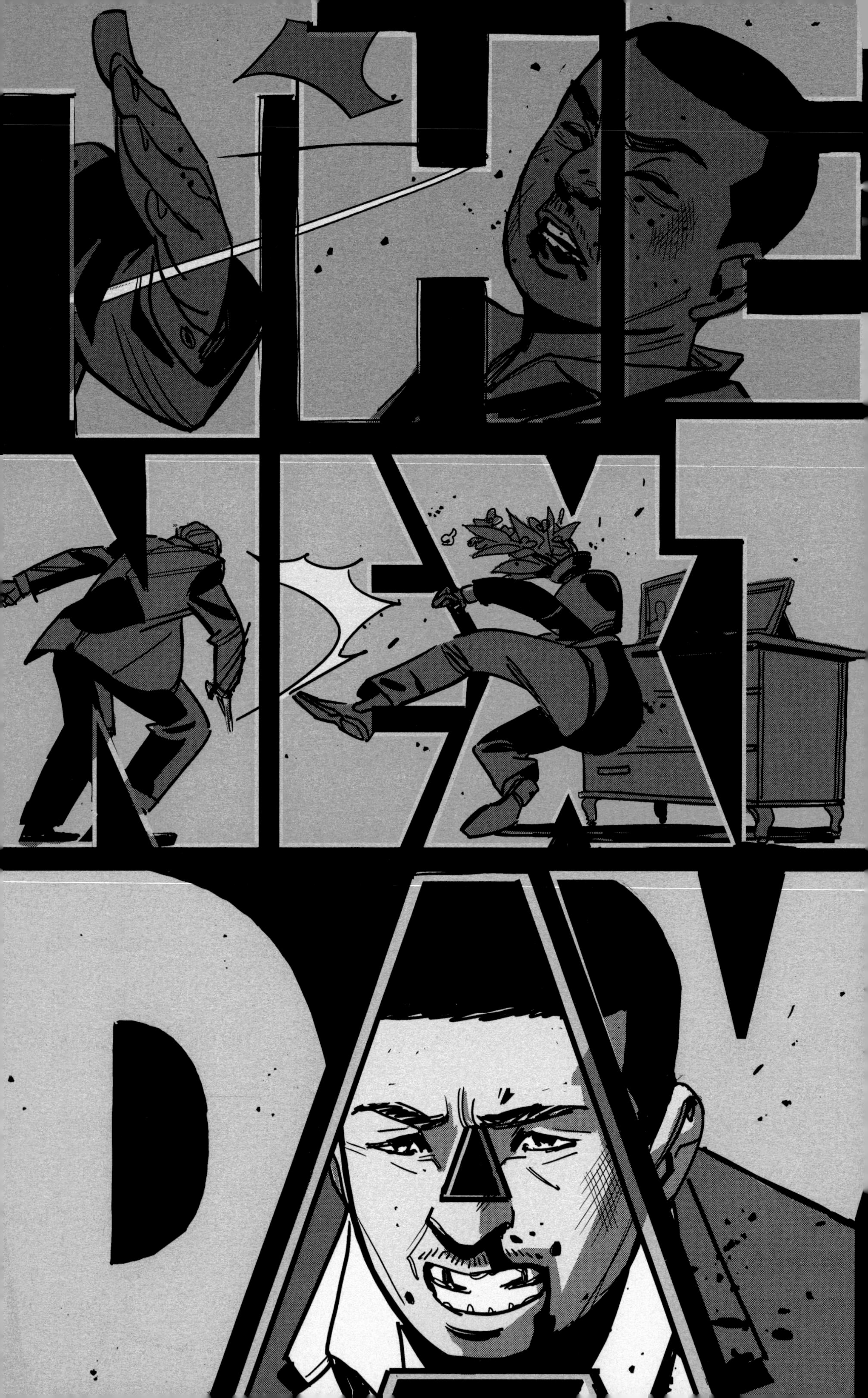
THE NEXT DAY

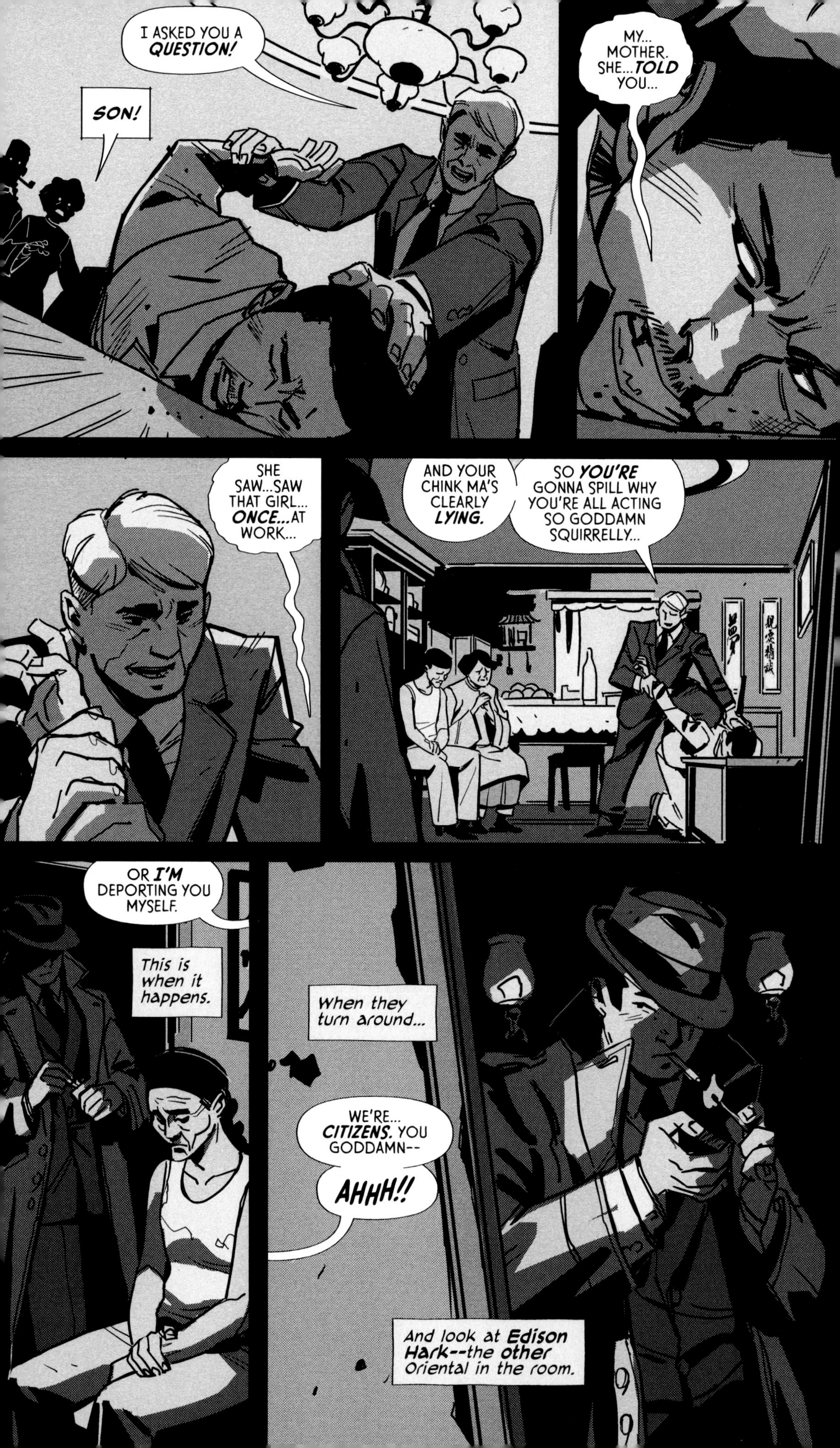

I ASKED YOU A QUESTION!
SON!
MY... MOTHER. SHE... TOLD YOU...
SHE SAW...SAW THAT GIRL... ONCE...AT WORK...
AND YOUR CHINK MA'S CLEARLY LYING.
SO YOU'RE GONNA SPILL WHY YOU'RE ALL ACTING SO GODDAMN SQUIRRELLY...
OR I'M DEPORTING YOU MYSELF.
This is when it happens.
When they turn around...
WE'RE... CITIZENS. YOU GODDAMN--
AHHH!!
And look at Edison Hark--the other Oriental in the room.

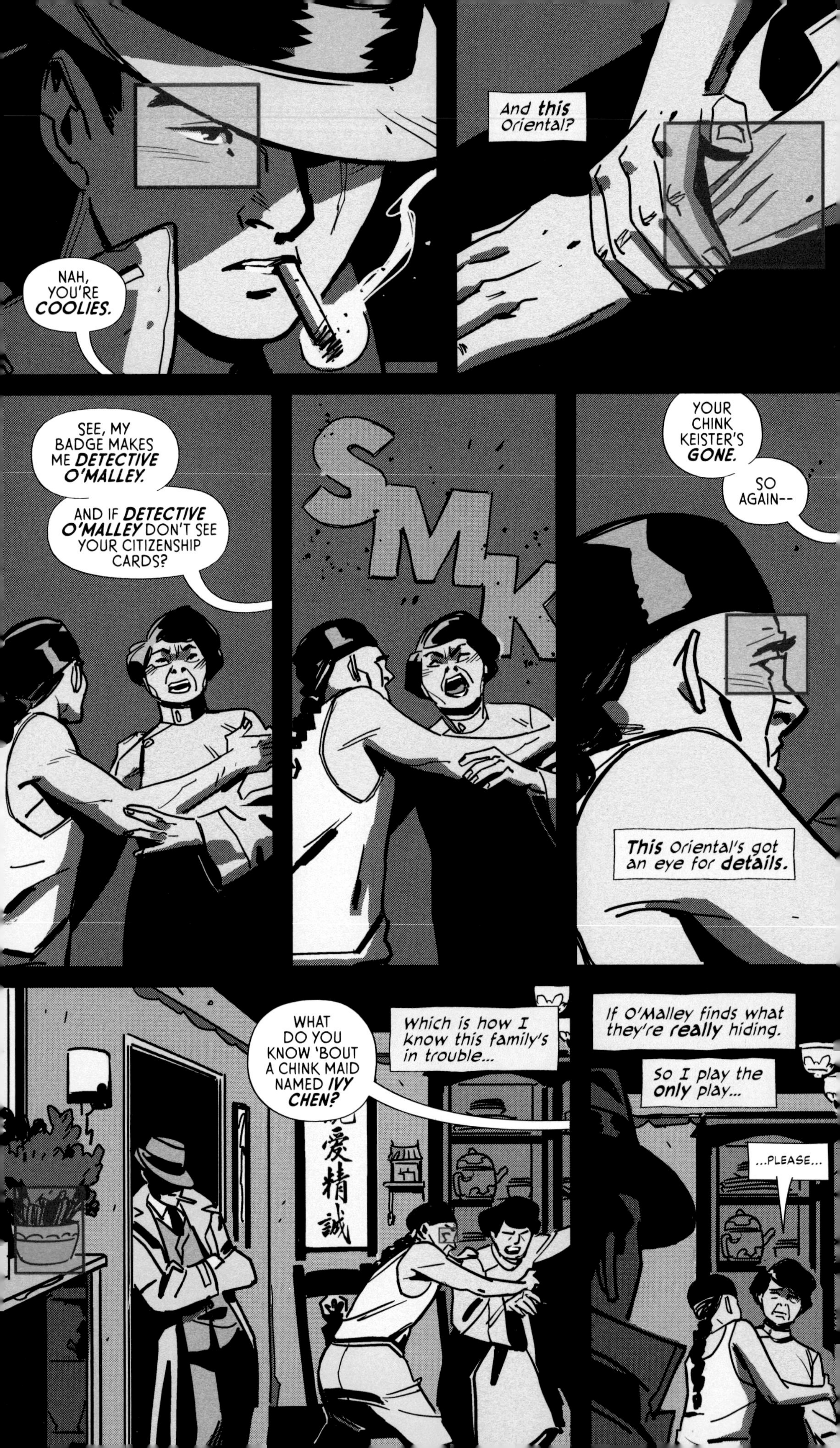
NAH, YOU'RE COOLIES.
And this Oriental?
SEE, MY BADGE MAKES ME DETECTIVE O'MALLEY.
AND IF DETECTIVE O'MALLEY DON'T SEE YOUR CITIZENSHIP CARDS?
SMK
YOUR CHINK KEISTER'S GONE.
SO AGAIN--
This Oriental's got an eye for details.
WHAT DO YOU KNOW 'BOUT A CHINK MAID NAMED IVY CHEN?
Which is how I know this family's in trouble...
If O'Malley finds what they're really hiding.
So I play the only play...
...PLEASE...

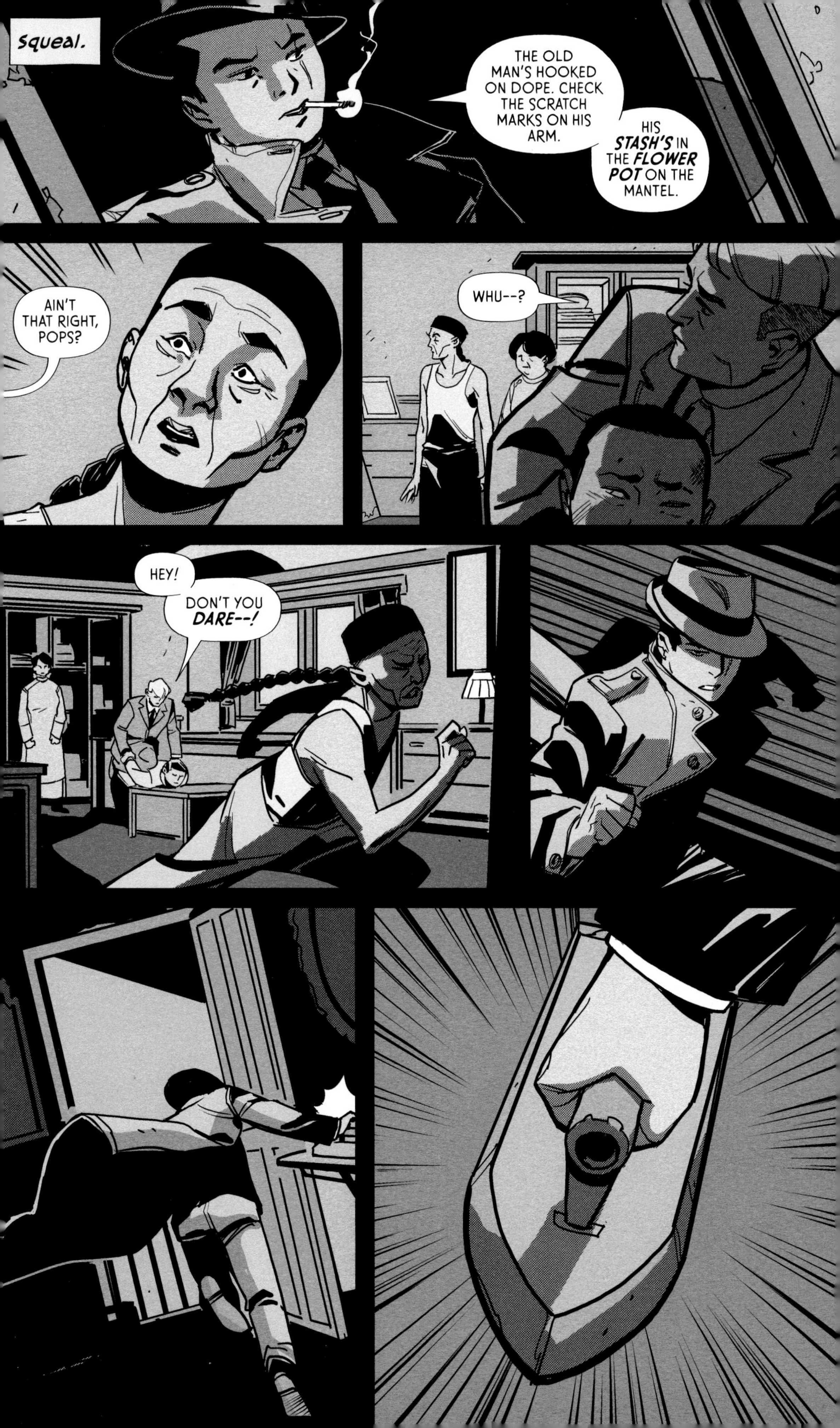
squeal.
THE OLD MAN'S HOOKED ON DOPE. CHECK THE SCRATCH MARKS ON HIS ARM.
HIS STASH'S IN THE FLOWER POT ON THE MANTEL.
AIN'T THAT RIGHT, POPS?
WHU--?
HEY!
DON'T YOU DARE--!

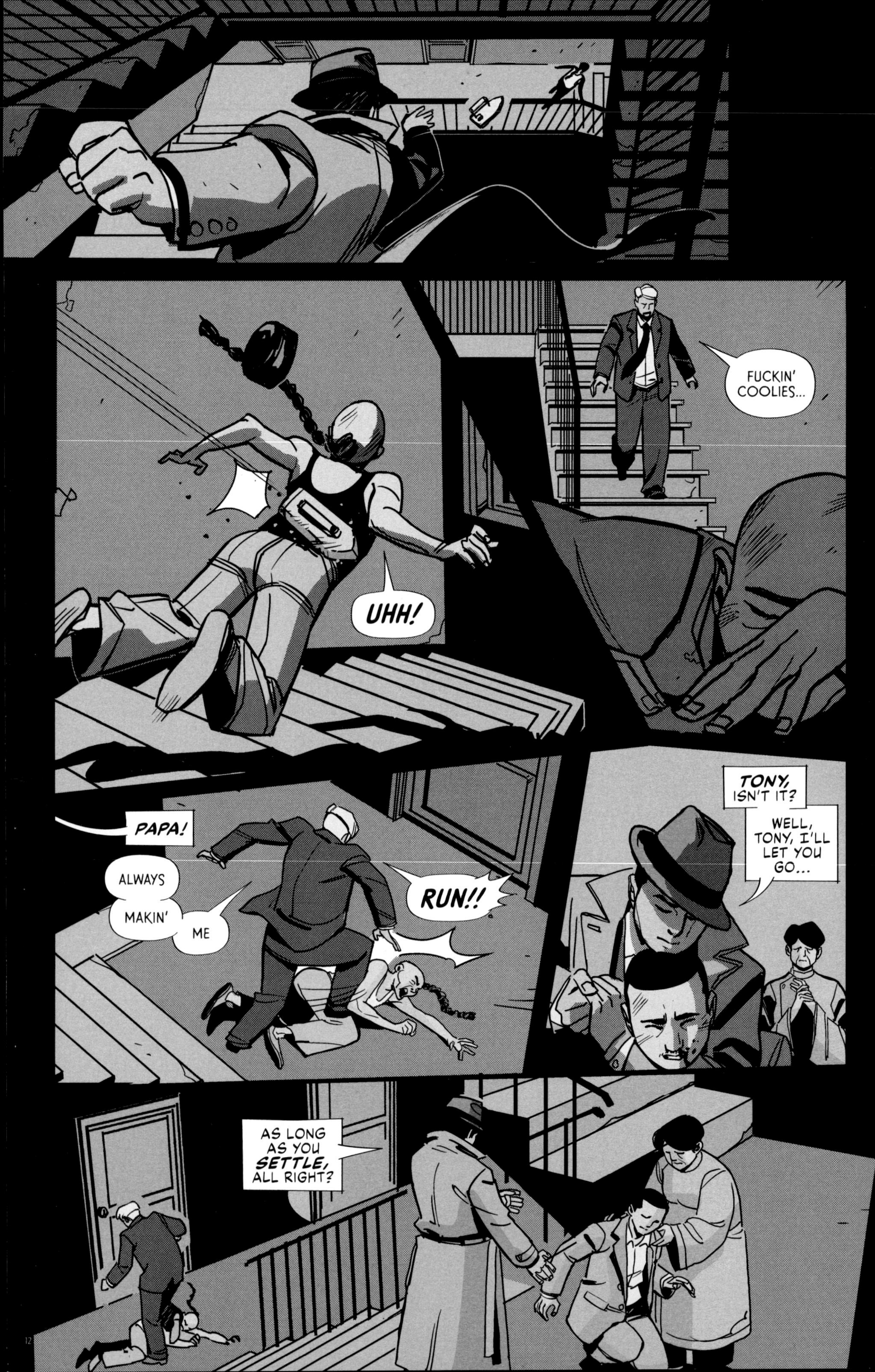
FUCKIN' COOLIES...
UHH!
PAPA!
ALWAYS
MAKIN'
ME
RUN!!
TONY, ISN'T IT?
WELL, TONY, I'LL LET YOU GO...
AS LONG AS YOU SETTLE, ALL RIGHT?

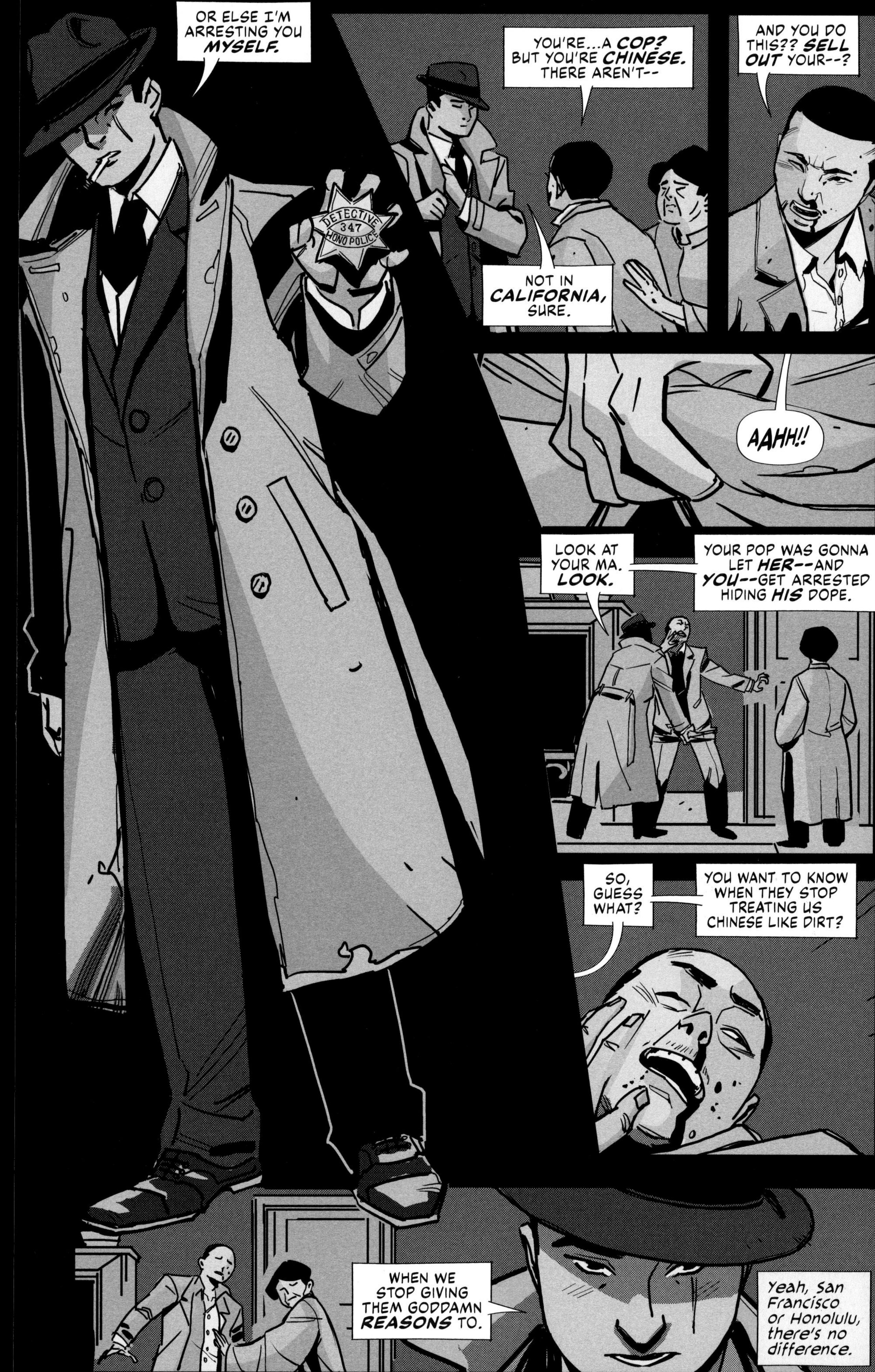
OR ELSE I'M ARRESTING YOU MYSELF.
DETECTIVE 347 HONO POLICE
YOU'RE...A COP? BUT YOU'RE CHINESE. THERE AREN'T--
NOT IN CALIFORNIA, SURE.
AND YOU DO THIS?? SELL OUT YOUR--?
AAHH!!
LOOK AT YOUR MA. LOOK.
YOUR POP WAS GONNA LET HER--AND YOU--GET ARRESTED HIDING HIS DOPE.
SO, GUESS WHAT?
YOU WANT TO KNOW WHEN THEY STOP TREATING US CHINESE LIKE DIRT?
WHEN WE STOP GIVING THEM GODDAMN REASONS TO.
Yeah, San Francisco or Honolulu, there's no difference.

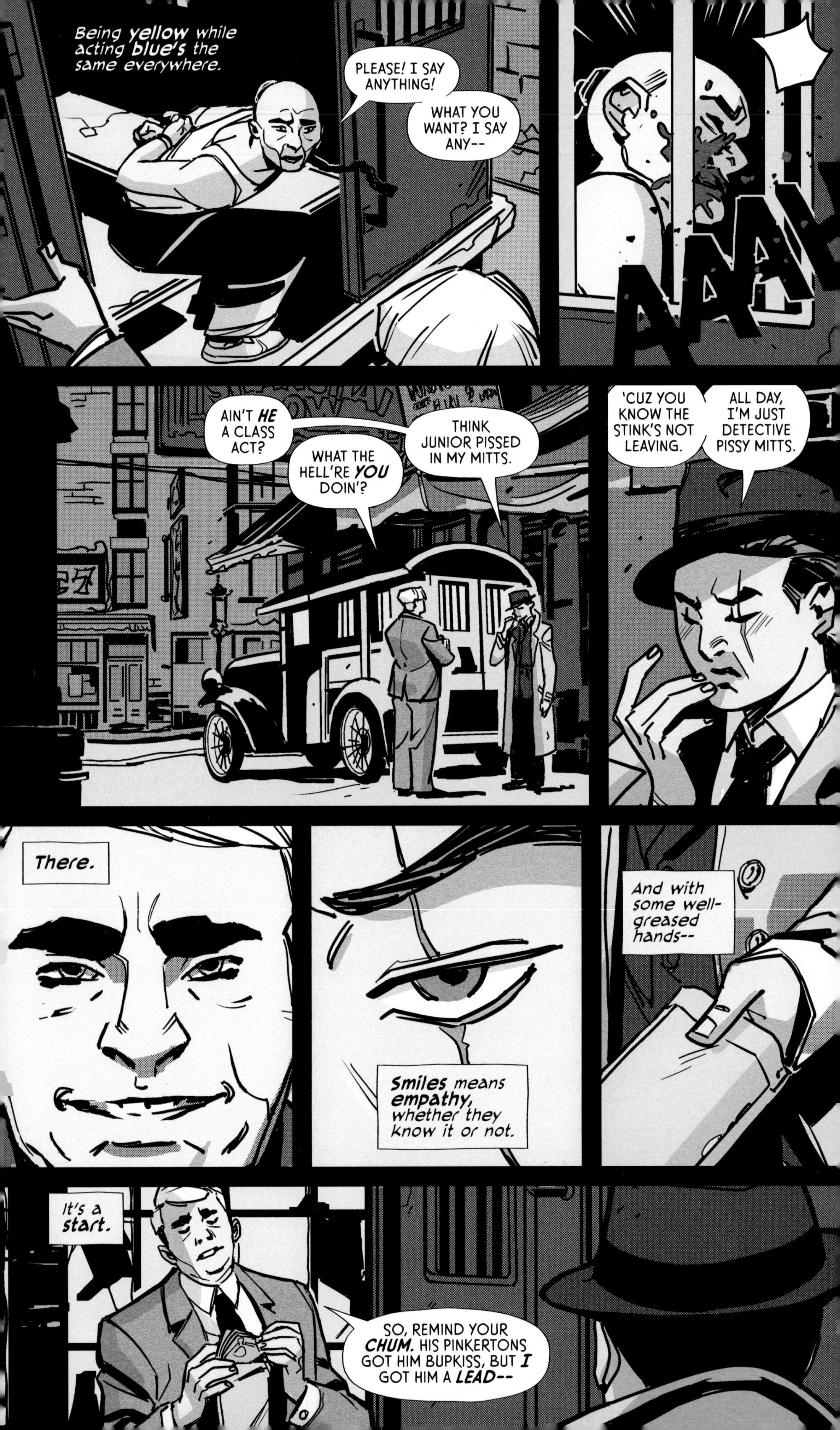
Being yellow while acting blue's the same everywhere.
PLEASE! I SAY ANYTHING!
WHAT YOU WANT? I SAY ANY--
AIN'T HE A CLASS ACT?
WHAT THE HELL'RE YOU DOIN'?
THINK JUNIOR PISSED IN MY MITTS.
'CUZ YOU KNOW THE STINK'S NOT LEAVING.
ALL DAY, I'M JUST DETECTIVE PISSY MITTS.
There.
Smiles means empathy, whether they know it or not.
And with some well-greased hands--
It's a start.
SO, REMIND YOUR CHUM. HIS PINKERTONS GOT HIM BUPKISS, BUT I GOT HIM A LEAD--

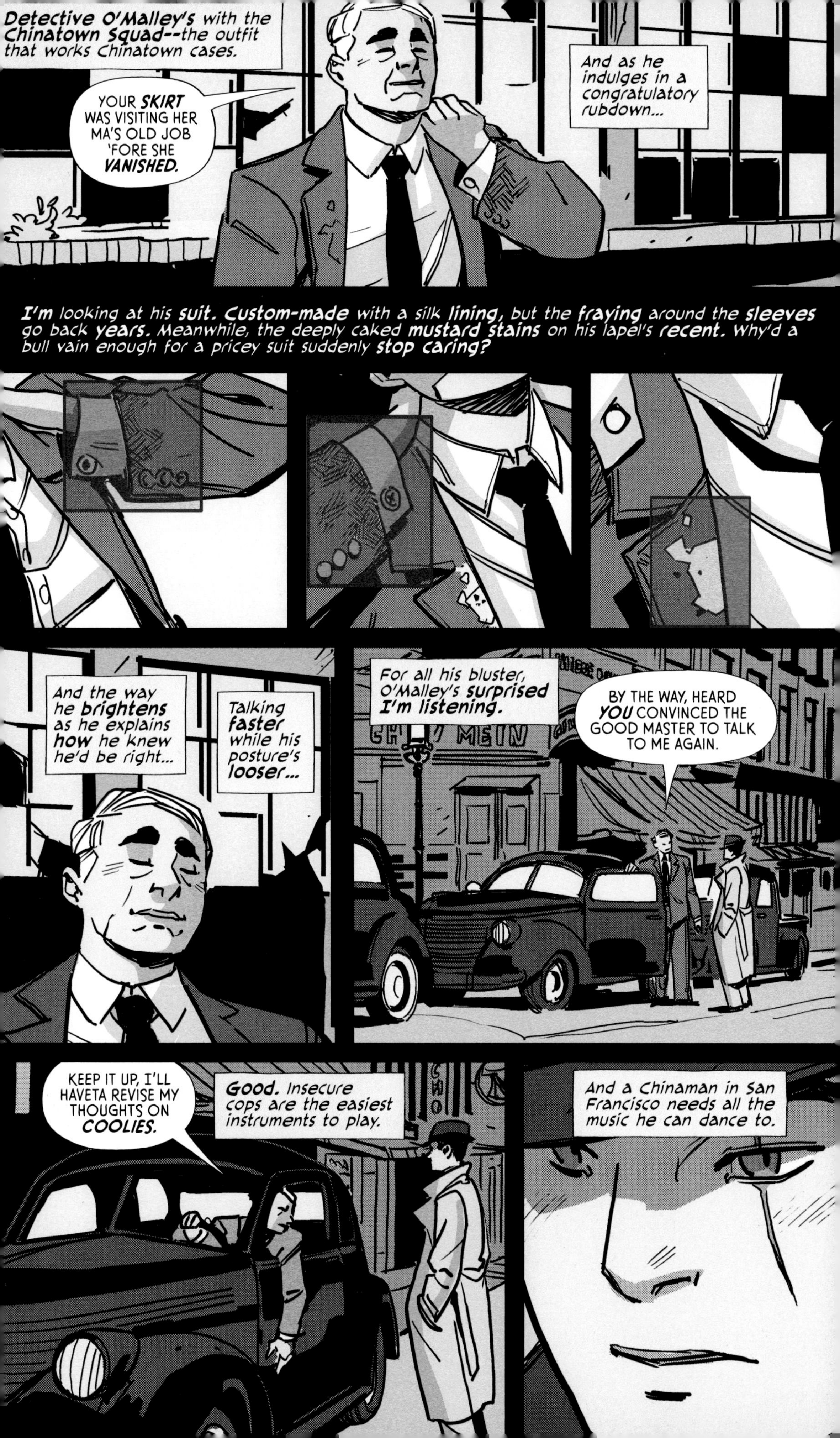
Detective O'Malley's with the Chinatown Squad--the outfit that works Chinatown cases.
YOUR SKIRT WAS VISITING HER MA'S OLD JOB 'FORE SHE VANISHED.
And as he indulges in a congratulatory rubdown...
I'm looking at his suit. Custom-made with a silk lining, but the fraying around the sleeves go back years. Meanwhile, the deeply caked mustard stains on his lapel's recent. Why'd a bull vain enough for a pricey suit suddenly stop caring?
And the way he brightens as he explains how he knew he'd be right...
Talking faster while his posture's looser...
For all his bluster, O'Malley's surprised I'm listening.
BY THE WAY, HEARD YOU CONVINCED THE GOOD MASTER TO TALK TO ME AGAIN.
KEEP IT UP, I'LL HAVETA REVISE MY THOUGHTS ON COOLIES.
Good. Insecure cops are the easiest instruments to play.
And a Chinaman in San Francisco needs all the music he can dance to.

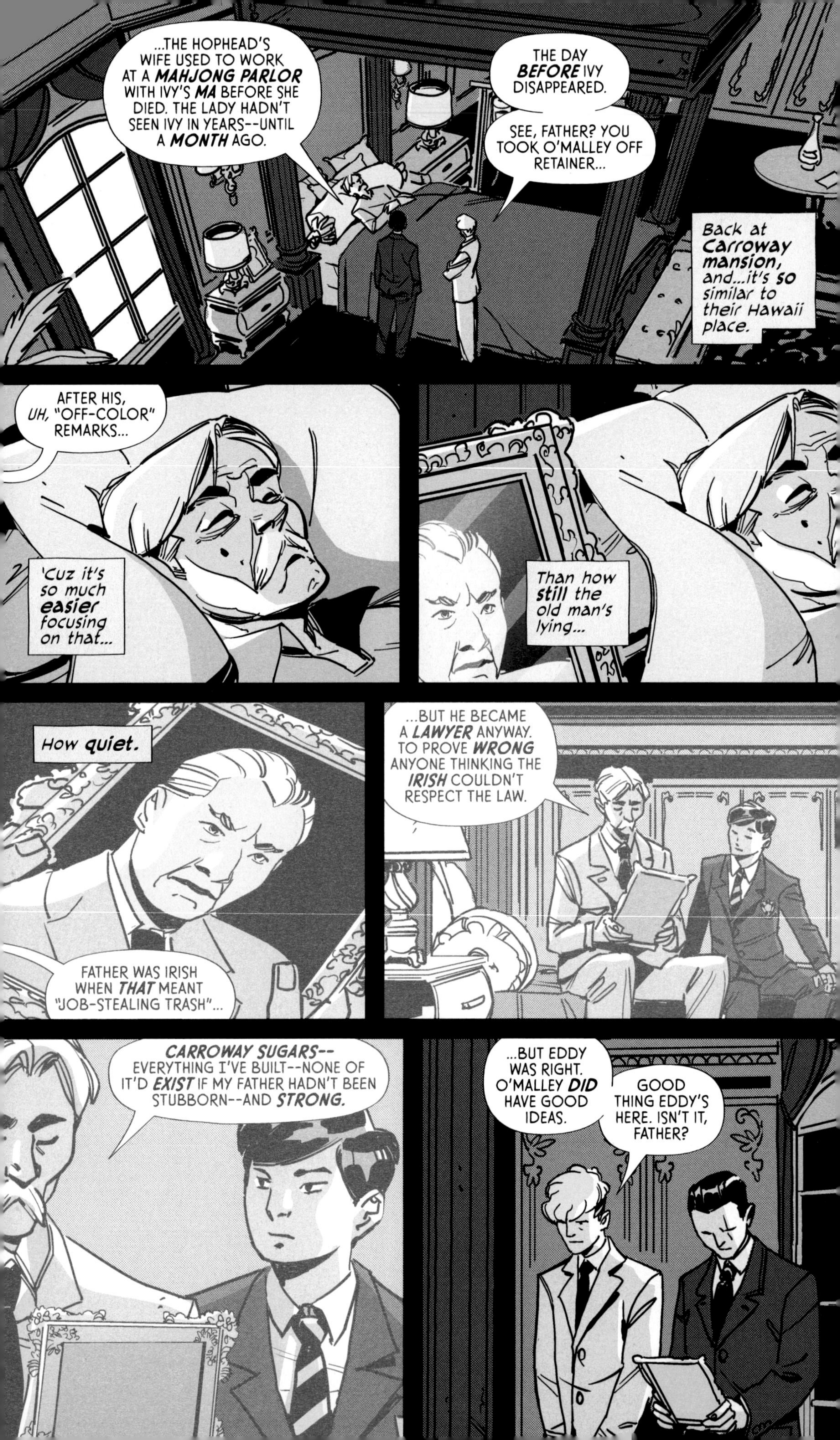
...THE HOPHEAD'S WIFE USED TO WORK AT A MAHJONG PARLOR WITH IVY'S MA BEFORE SHE DIED. THE LADY HADN'T SEEN IVY IN YEARS--UNTIL A MONTH AGO.
THE DAY BEFORE IVY DISAPPEARED.
SEE, FATHER? YOU TOOK O'MALLEY OFF RETAINER...
Back at Carroway mansion, and...it's so similar to their Hawaii place.
AFTER HIS, UH, "OFF-COLOR" REMARKS...
'Cuz it's so much easier focusing on that...
Than how still the old man's lying...
How quiet.
FATHER WAS IRISH WHEN THAT MEANT "JOB-STEALING TRASH"...
...BUT HE BECAME A LAWYER ANYWAY. TO PROVE WRONG ANYONE THINKING THE IRISH COULDN'T RESPECT THE LAW.
CARROWAY SUGARS-- EVERYTHING I'VE BUILT--NONE OF IT'D EXIST IF MY FATHER HADN'T BEEN STUBBORN--AND STRONG.
...BUT EDDY WAS RIGHT. O'MALLEY DID HAVE GOOD IDEAS.
GOOD THING EDDY'S HERE. ISN'T IT, FATHER?

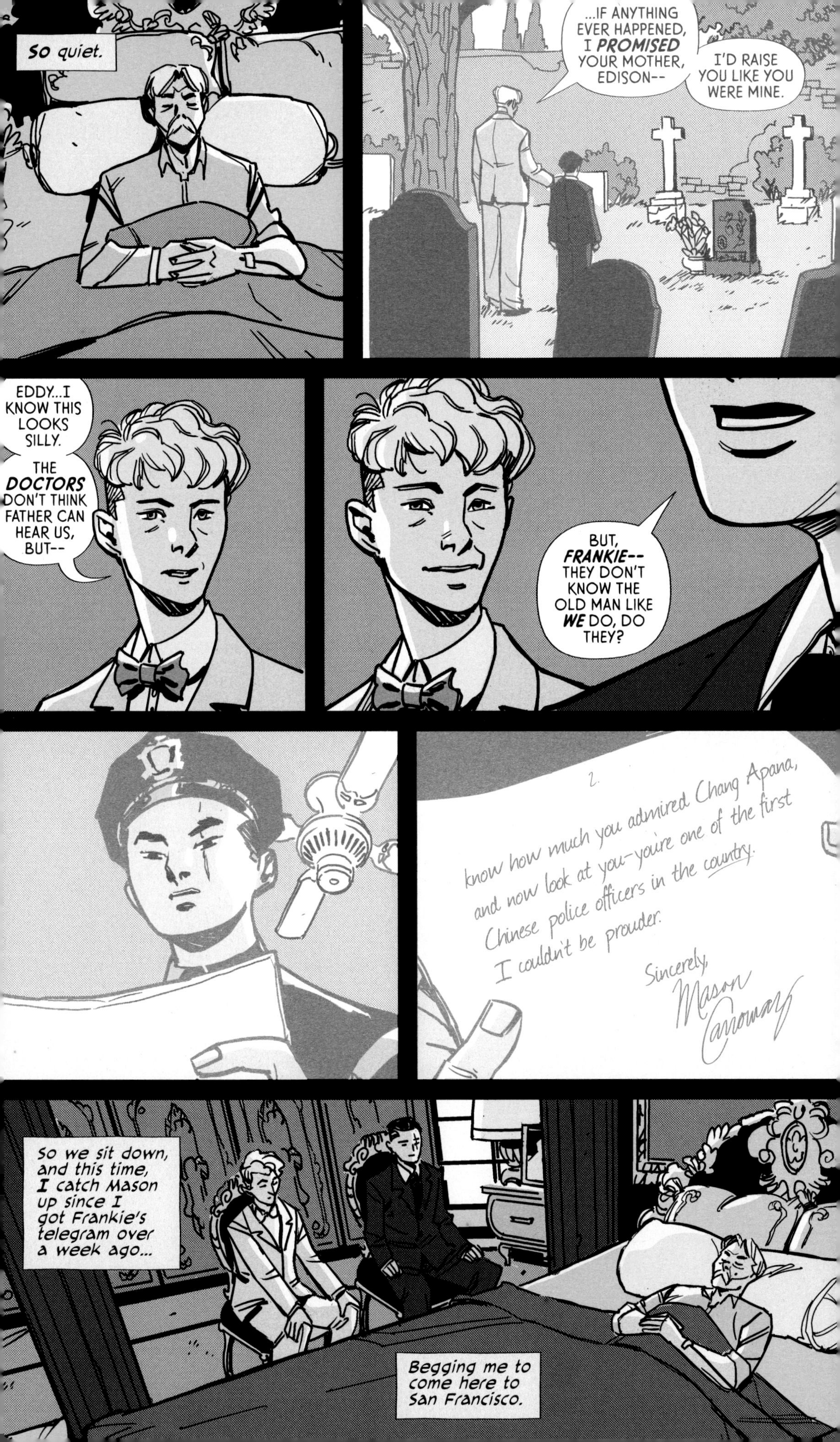
So quiet.
...IF ANYTHING EVER HAPPENED, I PROMISED YOUR MOTHER, EDISON--
I'D RAISE YOU LIKE YOU WERE MINE.
EDDY...I KNOW THIS LOOKS SILLY.
THE DOCTORS DON'T THINK FATHER CAN HEAR US, BUT--
BUT, FRANKIE-- THEY DON'T KNOW THE OLD MAN LIKE WE DO, DO THEY?
2.
know how much you admired Chang Apana,
and now look at you-you're one of the first
Chinese police officers in the country.
I couldn't be prouder.
Sincerely,
Mason Carroway
So we sit down, and this time, I catch Mason up since I got Frankie's telegram over a week ago...
Begging me to come here to San Francisco.

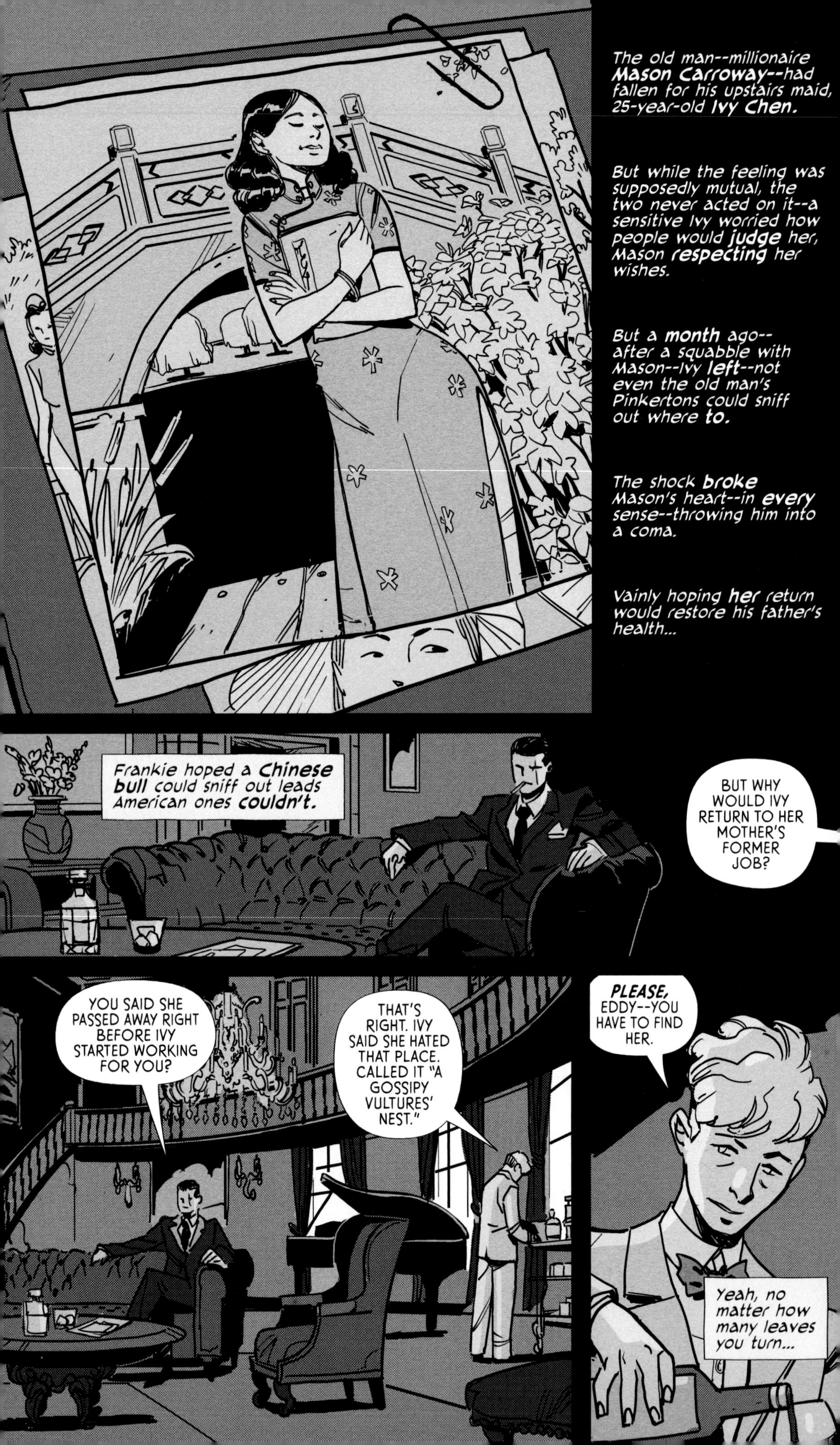

The old man--millionaire Mason Carroway--had fallen for his upstairs maid, 25-year-old Ivy Chen.
But while the feeling was supposedly mutual, the two never acted on it--a sensitive Ivy worried how people would judge her, Mason respecting her wishes.
But a month ago--after a squabble with Mason--Ivy left--not even the old man's Pinkertons could sniff out where to.
The shock broke Mason's heart--in every sense--throwing him into a coma.
Vainly hoping her return would restore his father's health...
Frankie hoped a Chinese bull could sniff out leads American ones couldn't.
BUT WHY WOULD IVY RETURN TO HER MOTHER'S FORMER JOB?
YOU SAID SHE PASSED AWAY RIGHT BEFORE IVY STARTED WORKING FOR YOU?
THAT'S RIGHT. IVY SAID SHE HATED THAT PLACE. CALLED IT "A GOSSIPY VULTURES' NEST."
PLEASE, EDDY--YOU HAVE TO FIND HER.
Yeah, no matter how many leaves you turn...

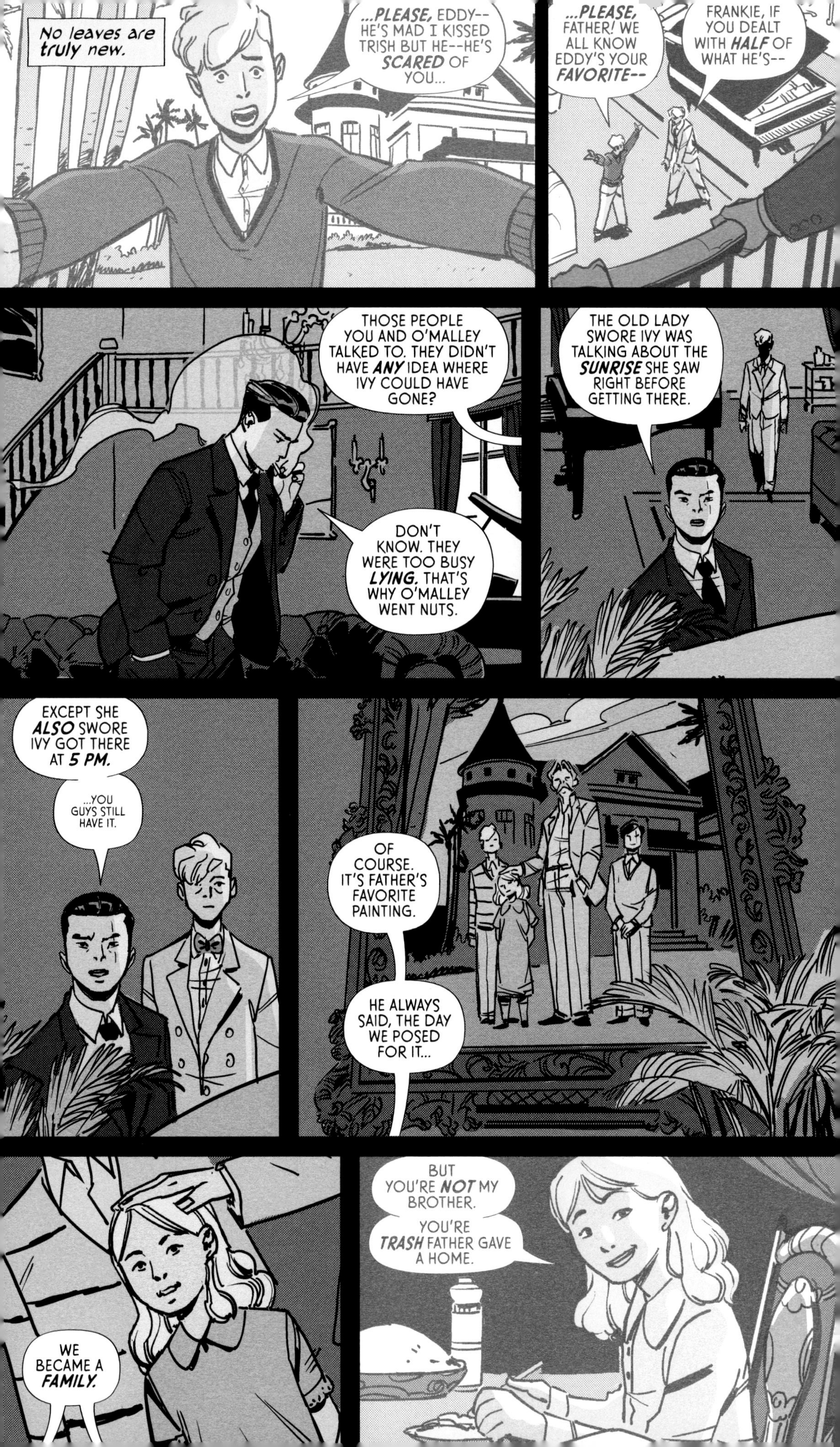
No leaves are truly new.
...PLEASE, EDDY-- HE'S MAD I KISSED TRISH BUT HE--HE'S SCARED OF YOU...
...PLEASE, FATHER! WE ALL KNOW EDDY'S YOUR FAVORITE--
FRANKIE, IF YOU DEALT WITH HALF OF WHAT HE'S--
THOSE PEOPLE YOU AND O'MALLEY TALKED TO. THEY DIDN'T HAVE ANY IDEA WHERE IVY COULD HAVE GONE?
DON'T KNOW. THEY WERE TOO BUSY LYING. THAT'S WHY O'MALLEY WENT NUTS.
THE OLD LADY SWORE IVY WAS TALKING ABOUT THE SUNRISE SHE SAW RIGHT BEFORE GETTING THERE.
EXCEPT SHE ALSO SWORE IVY GOT THERE AT 5 PM.
...YOU GUYS STILL HAVE IT.
OF COURSE. IT'S FATHER'S FAVORITE PAINTING.
HE ALWAYS SAID, THE DAY WE POSED FOR IT...
WE BECAME A FAMILY.
BUT YOU'RE NOT MY BROTHER.
YOU'RE TRASH FATHER GAVE A HOME.

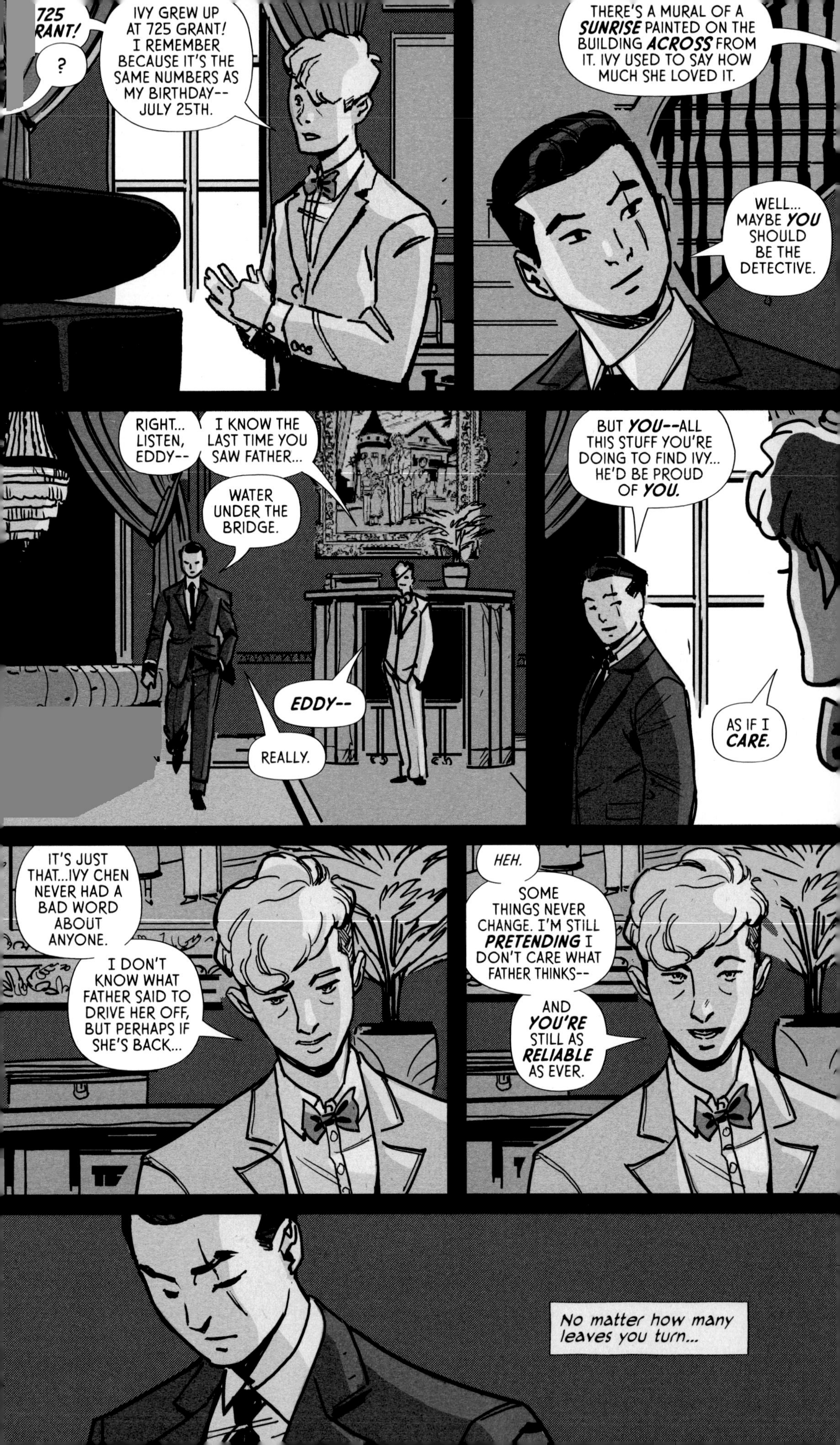
725 GRANT!
?
IVY GREW UP AT 725 GRANT! I REMEMBER BECAUSE IT'S THE SAME NUMBERS AS MY BIRTHDAY-- JULY 25TH.
THERE'S A MURAL OF A SUNRISE PAINTED ON THE BUILDING ACROSS FROM IT. IVY USED TO SAY HOW MUCH SHE LOVED IT.
WELL... MAYBE YOU SHOULD BE THE DETECTIVE.
RIGHT... LISTEN, EDDY--
I KNOW THE LAST TIME YOU SAW FATHER...
WATER UNDER THE BRIDGE.
EDDY--
REALLY.
BUT YOU--ALL THIS STUFF YOU'RE DOING TO FIND IVY... HE'D BE PROUD OF YOU.
AS IF I CARE.
IT'S JUST THAT...IVY CHEN NEVER HAD A BAD WORD ABOUT ANYONE.
I DON'T KNOW WHAT FATHER SAID TO DRIVE HER OFF, BUT PERHAPS IF SHE'S BACK...
HEH.
SOME THINGS NEVER CHANGE. I'M STILL PRETENDING I DON'T CARE WHAT FATHER THINKS--
AND YOU'RE STILL AS RELIABLE AS EVER.
No matter how many leaves you turn...

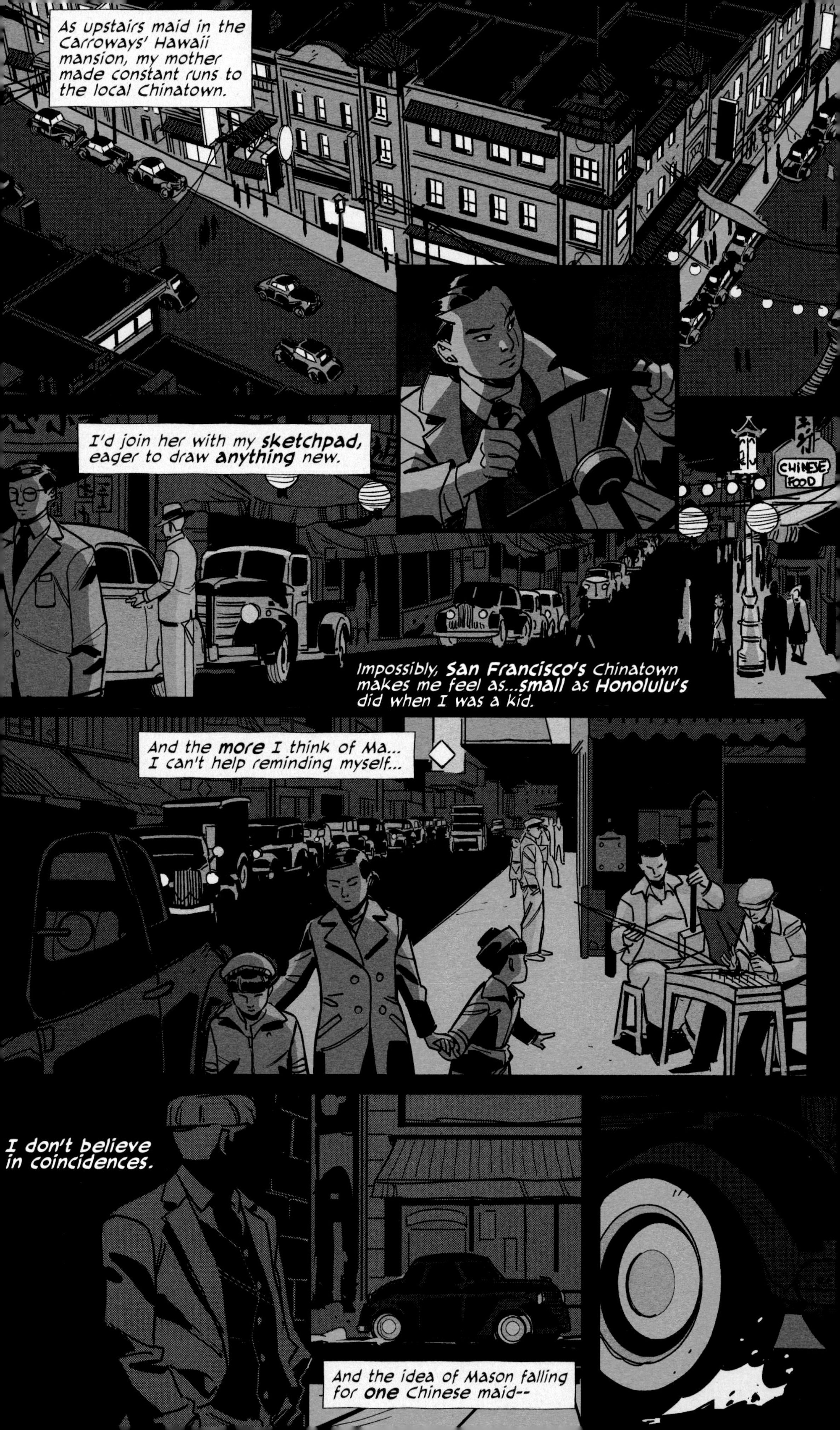
As upstairs maid in the Carroways' Hawaii mansion, my mother made constant runs to the local Chinatown.
I'd join her with my **sketchpad,** eager to draw **anything** new.
CHINESE FOOD
Impossibly, **San Francisco's** Chinatown makes me feel as...**small** as **Honolulu's** did when I was a kid.
And the **more** I think of Ma... I can't help reminding myself...
I don't believe in coincidences.
And the idea of Mason falling for **one** Chinese maid--

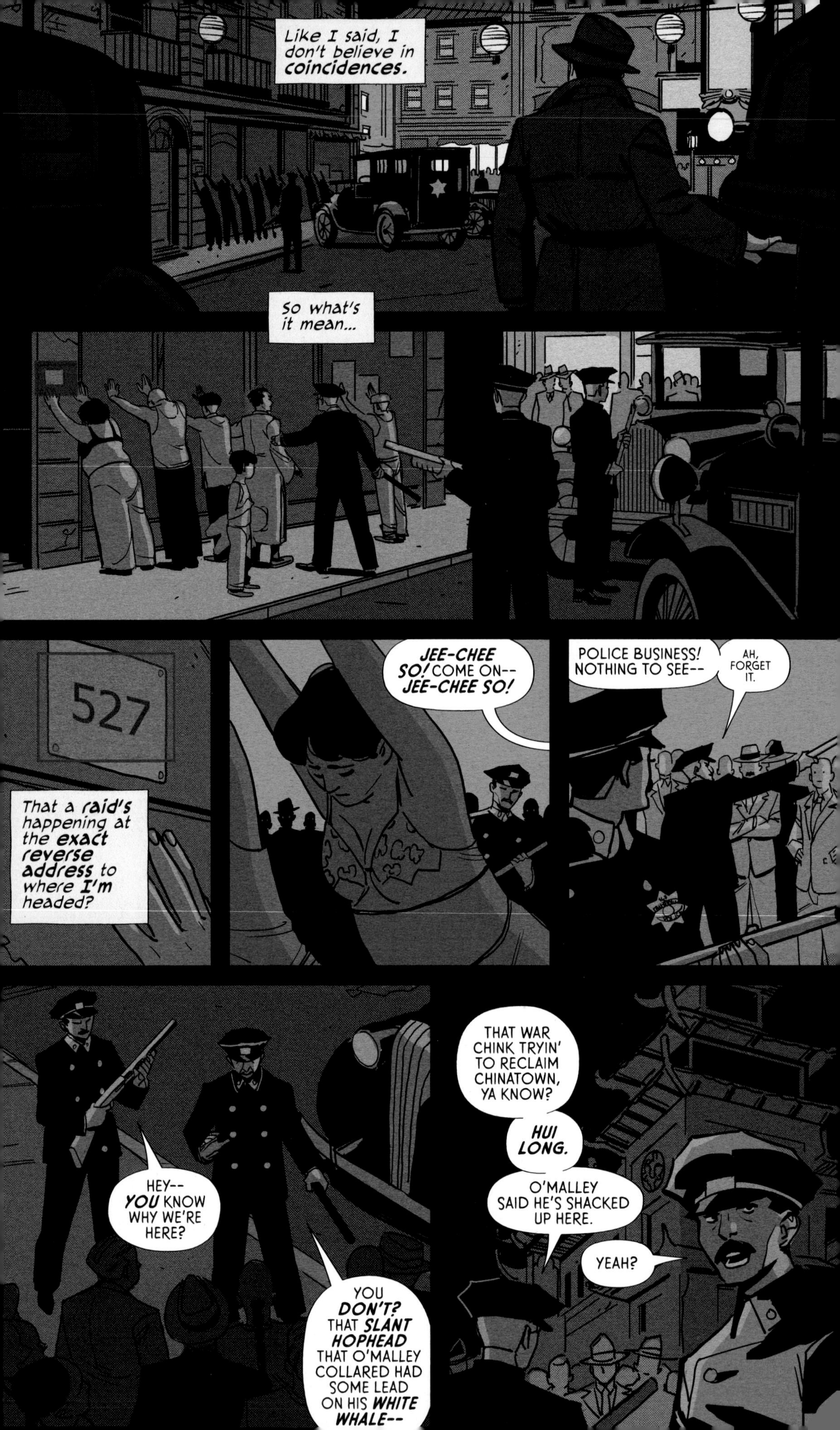
Like I said, I don't believe in coincidences.
So what's it mean...
527
That a raid's happening at the exact reverse address to where I'm headed?
JEE-CHEE SO! COME ON-- JEE-CHEE SO!
POLICE BUSINESS! NOTHING TO SEE--
AH, FORGET IT.
HEY-- YOU KNOW WHY WE'RE HERE?
YOU DON'T? THAT SLANT HOPHEAD THAT O'MALLEY COLLARED HAD SOME LEAD ON HIS WHITE WHALE--
THAT WAR CHINK TRYIN' TO RECLAIM CHINATOWN, YA KNOW?
HUI LONG.
O'MALLEY SAID HE'S SHACKED UP HERE.
YEAH?

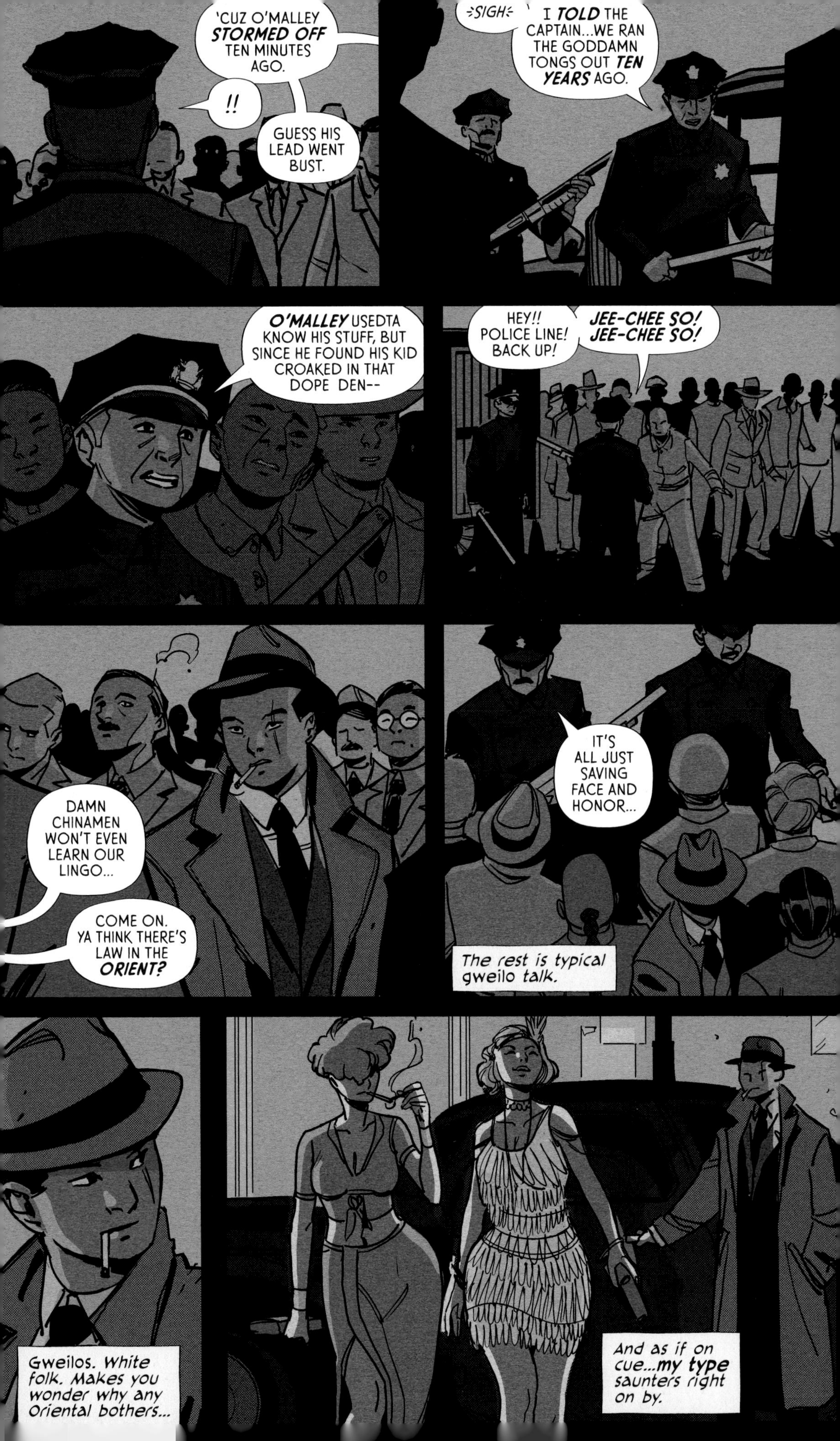
'CUZ O'MALLEY **STORMED OFF** TEN MINUTES AGO.
!!
GUESS HIS LEAD WENT BUST.
=SIGH=
I **TOLD** THE CAPTAIN...WE RAN THE GODDAMN TONGS OUT **TEN YEARS** AGO.
O'MALLEY USEDTA KNOW HIS STUFF, BUT SINCE HE FOUND HIS KID CROAKED IN THAT DOPE DEN--
HEY!! POLICE LINE! BACK UP!
JEE-CHEE SO! JEE-CHEE SO!
DAMN CHINAMEN WON'T EVEN LEARN OUR LINGO...
COME ON. YA THINK THERE'S LAW IN THE **ORIENT?**
IT'S ALL JUST SAVING FACE AND HONOR...
The rest is typical gweilo talk.
Gweilos. White folk. Makes you wonder why any Oriental bothers...
*And as if on cue...**my type** saunters right on by.*

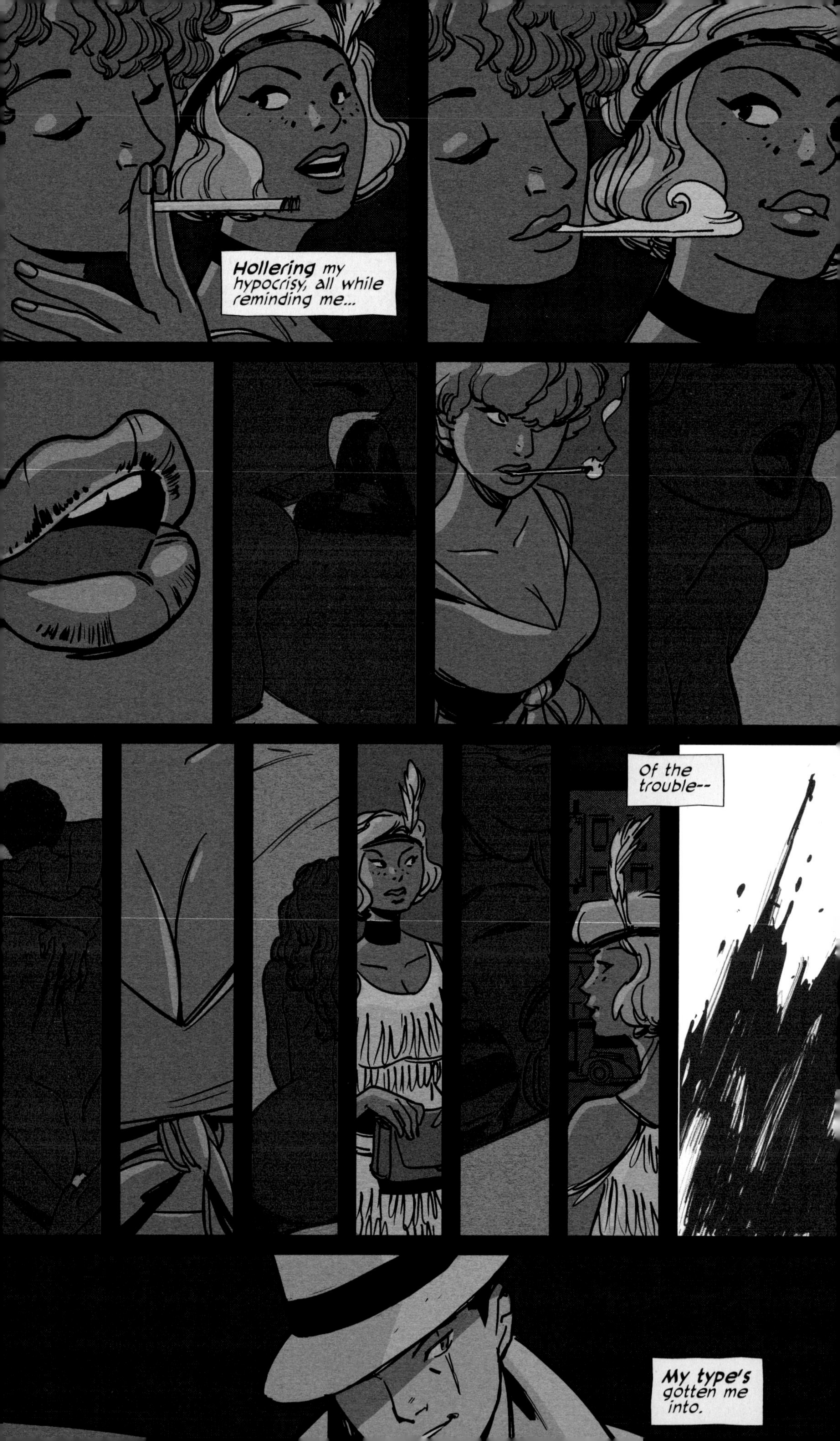
Hollering my hypocrisy, all while reminding me...
Of the trouble--
My type's gotten me into.

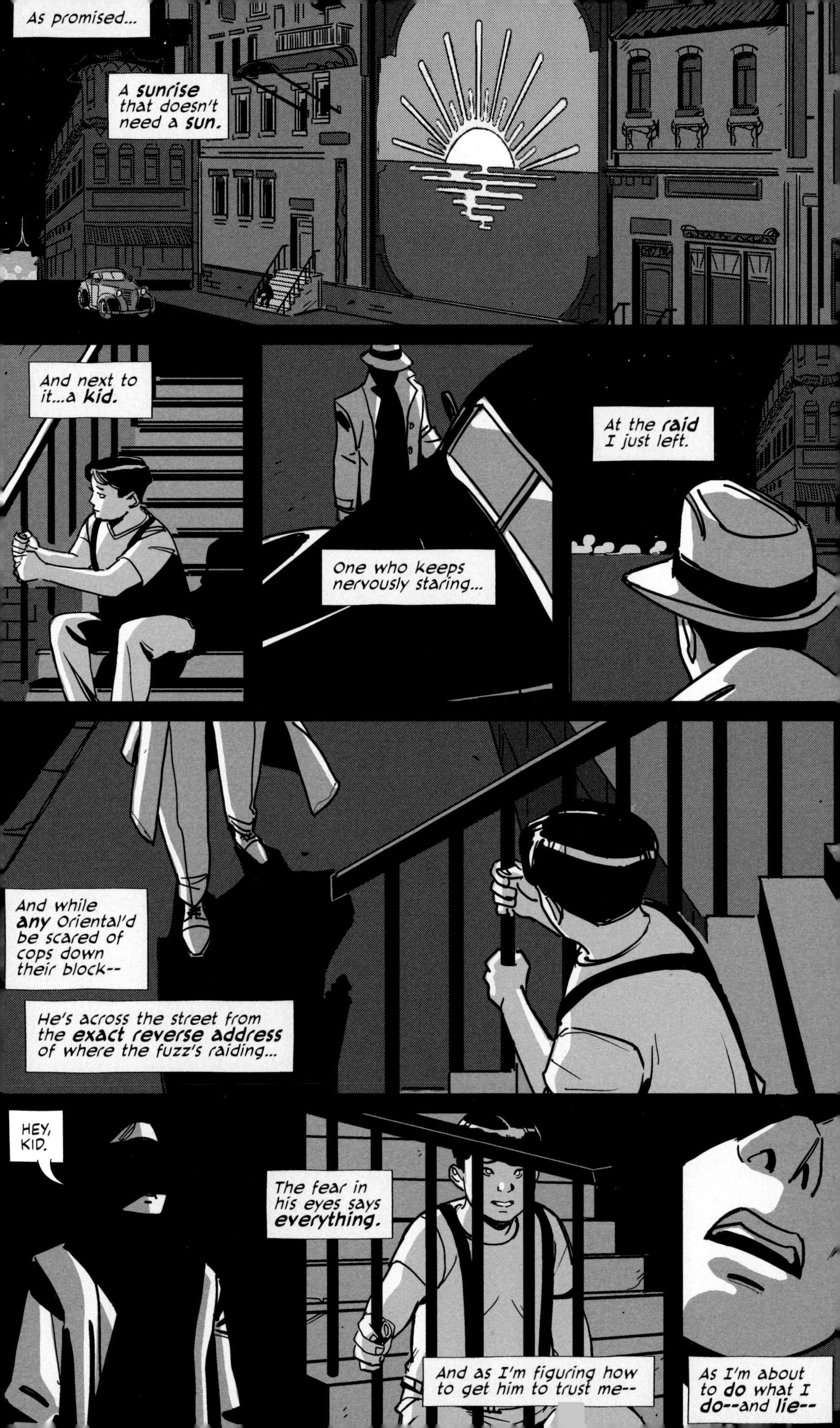

As promised...
A sunrise that doesn't need a sun.
And next to it...a kid.
One who keeps nervously staring...
At the raid I just left.
And while any Oriental'd be scared of cops down their block--
He's across the street from the exact reverse address of where the fuzz's raiding...
HEY, KID.
The fear in his eyes says everything.
And as I'm figuring how to get him to trust me--
As I'm about to do what I do--and lie--

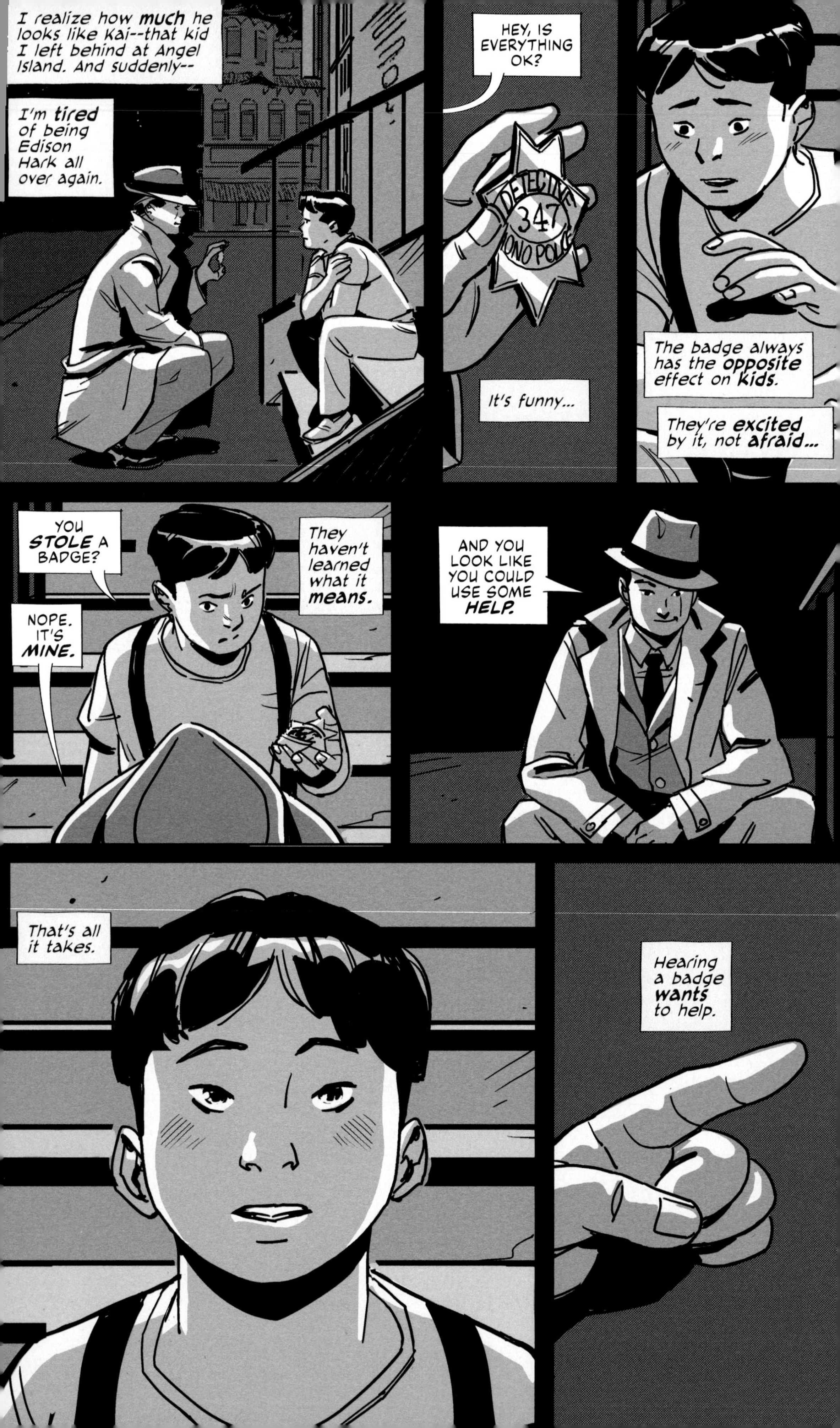
I realize how much he looks like Kai--that kid I left behind at Angel Island. And suddenly--
I'm tired of being Edison Hark all over again.
HEY, IS EVERYTHING OK?
DETECTIVE 347
It's funny...
The badge always has the opposite effect on kids.
They're excited by it, not afraid...
YOU STOLE A BADGE?
NOPE. IT'S MINE.
They haven't learned what it means.
AND YOU LOOK LIKE YOU COULD USE SOME HELP.
That's all it takes.
Hearing a badge wants to help.

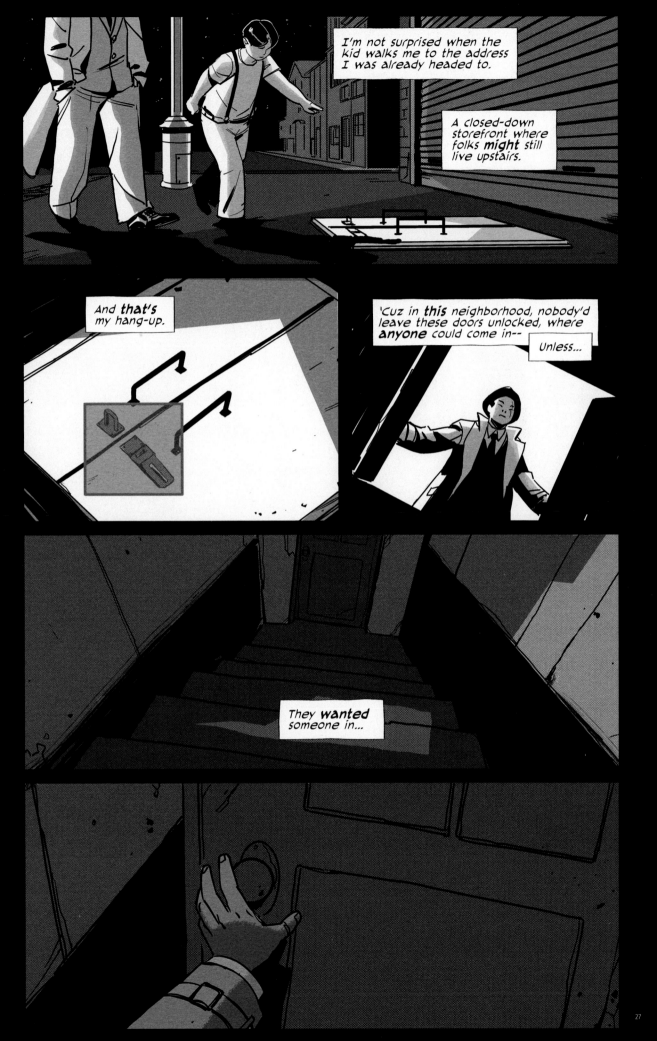

I'm not surprised when the kid walks me to the address I was already headed to.

A closed-down storefront where folks **might** still live upstairs.

And **that's** my hang-up.

'Cuz in **this** neighborhood, nobody'd leave these doors unlocked, where **anyone** could come in--

Unless...

They **wanted** someone in...

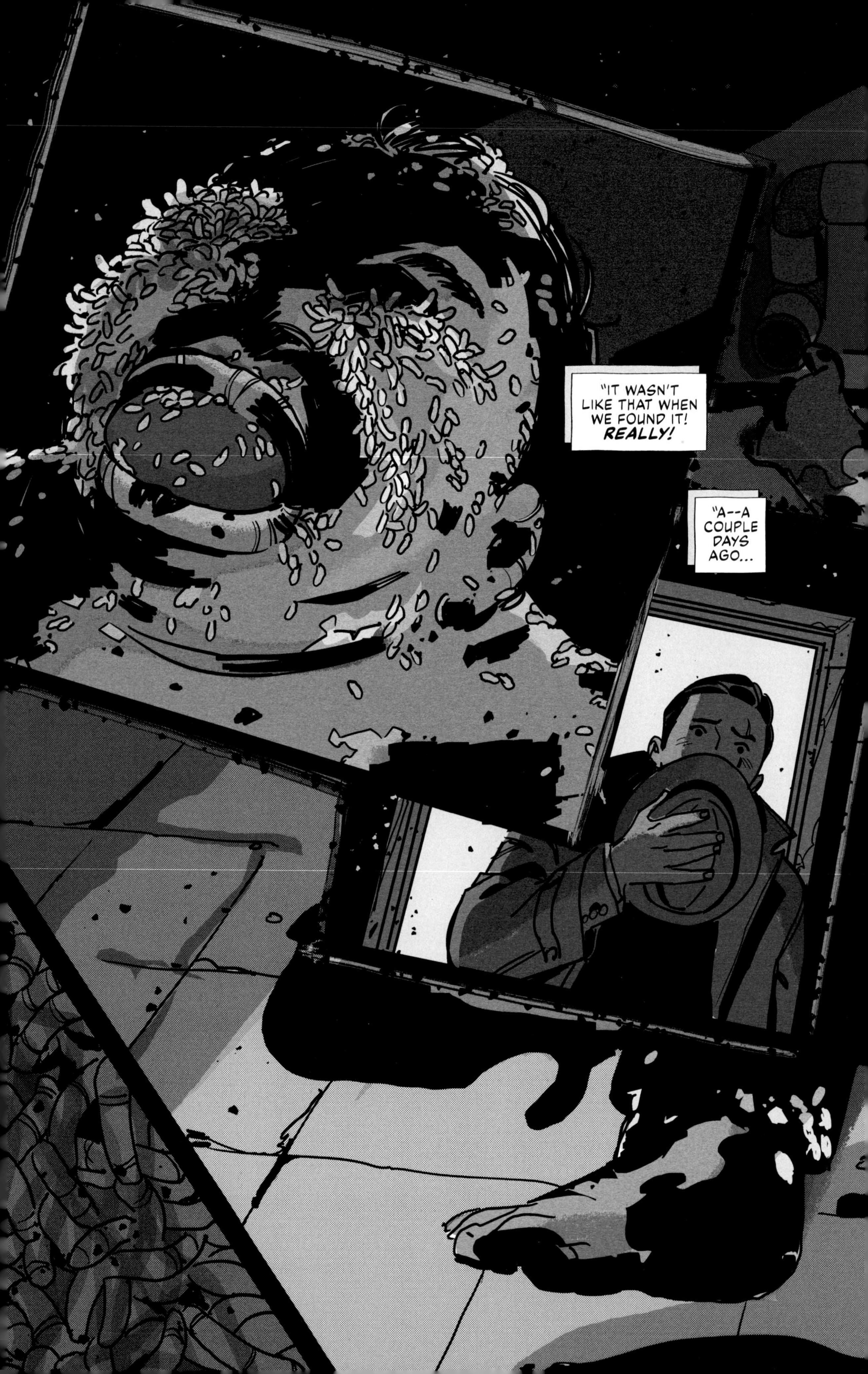
"IT WASN'T LIKE THAT WHEN WE FOUND IT! *REALLY!*
"A--A COUPLE DAYS AGO...

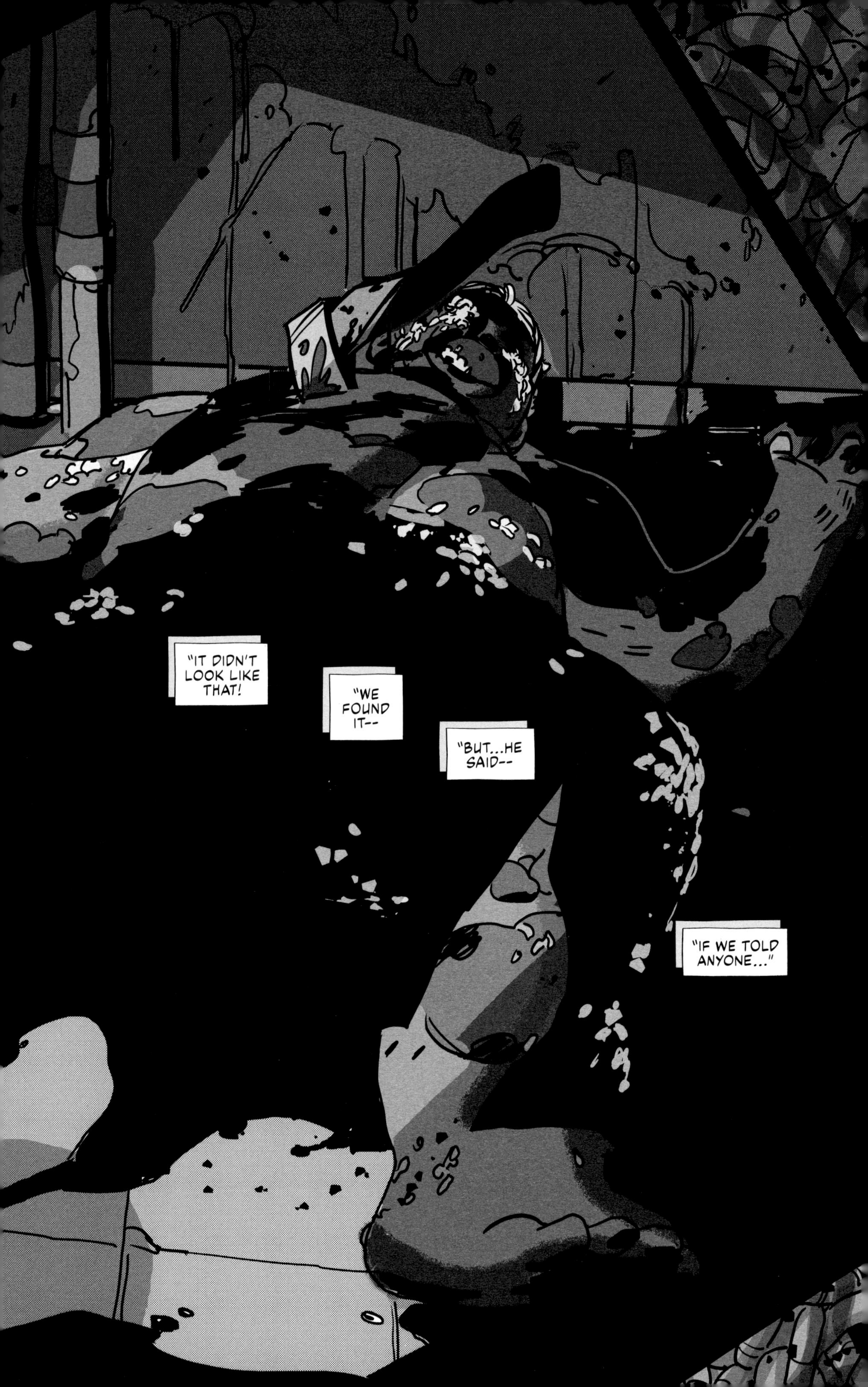
"IT DIDN'T LOOK LIKE THAT!
"WE FOUND IT--
"BUT...HE SAID--
"IF WE TOLD ANYONE..."

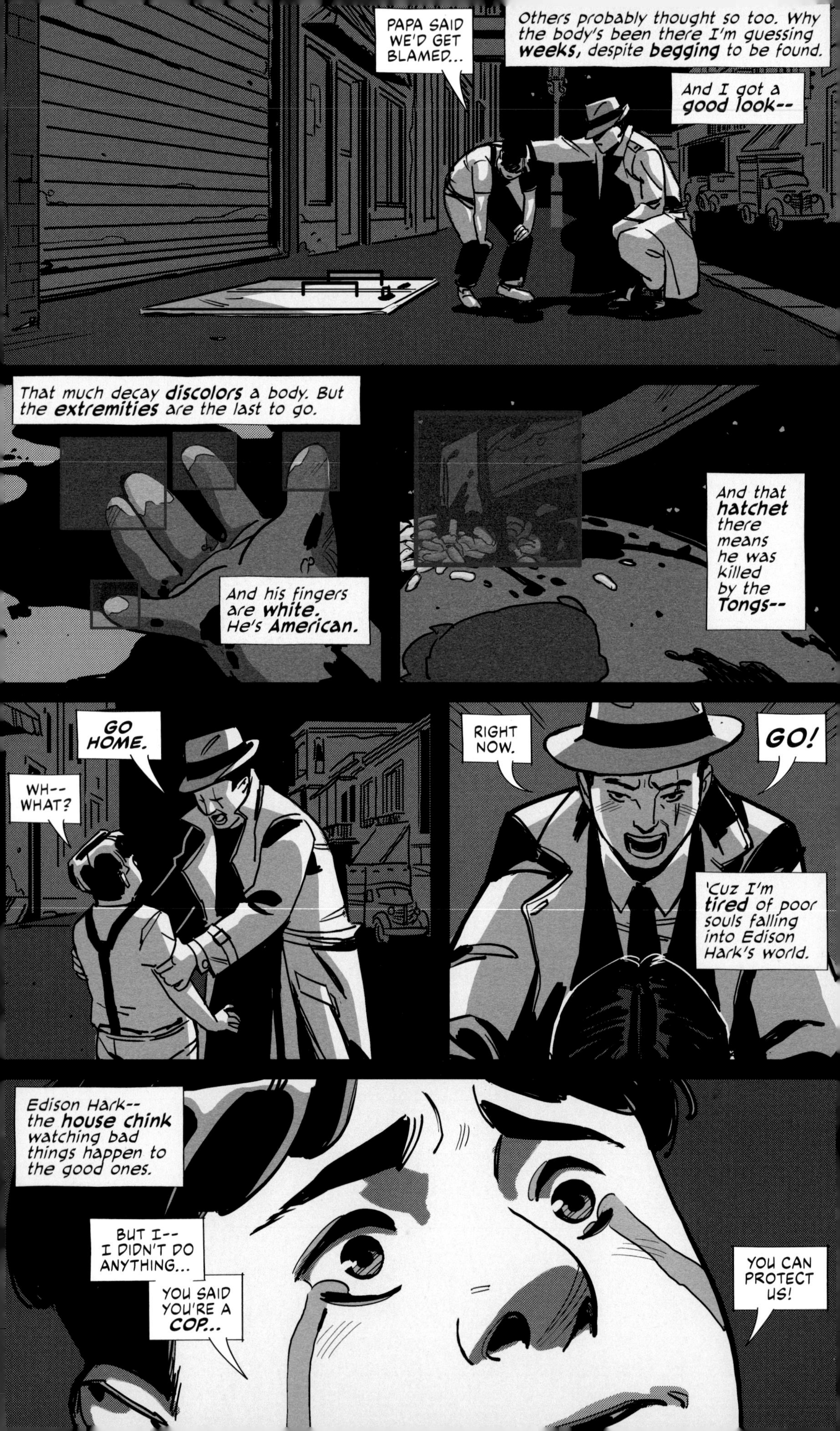
PAPA SAID WE'D GET BLAMED...
Others probably thought so too. Why the body's been there I'm guessing weeks, despite begging to be found.
And I got a good look--
That much decay discolors a body. But the extremities are the last to go.
And his fingers are white. He's American.
And that hatchet there means he was killed by the Tongs--
GO HOME.
WH-- WHAT?
RIGHT NOW.
GO!
'Cuz I'm tired of poor souls falling into Edison Hark's world.
Edison Hark-- the house chink watching bad things happen to the good ones.
BUT I-- I DIDN'T DO ANYTHING...
YOU SAID YOU'RE A COP...
YOU CAN PROTECT US!

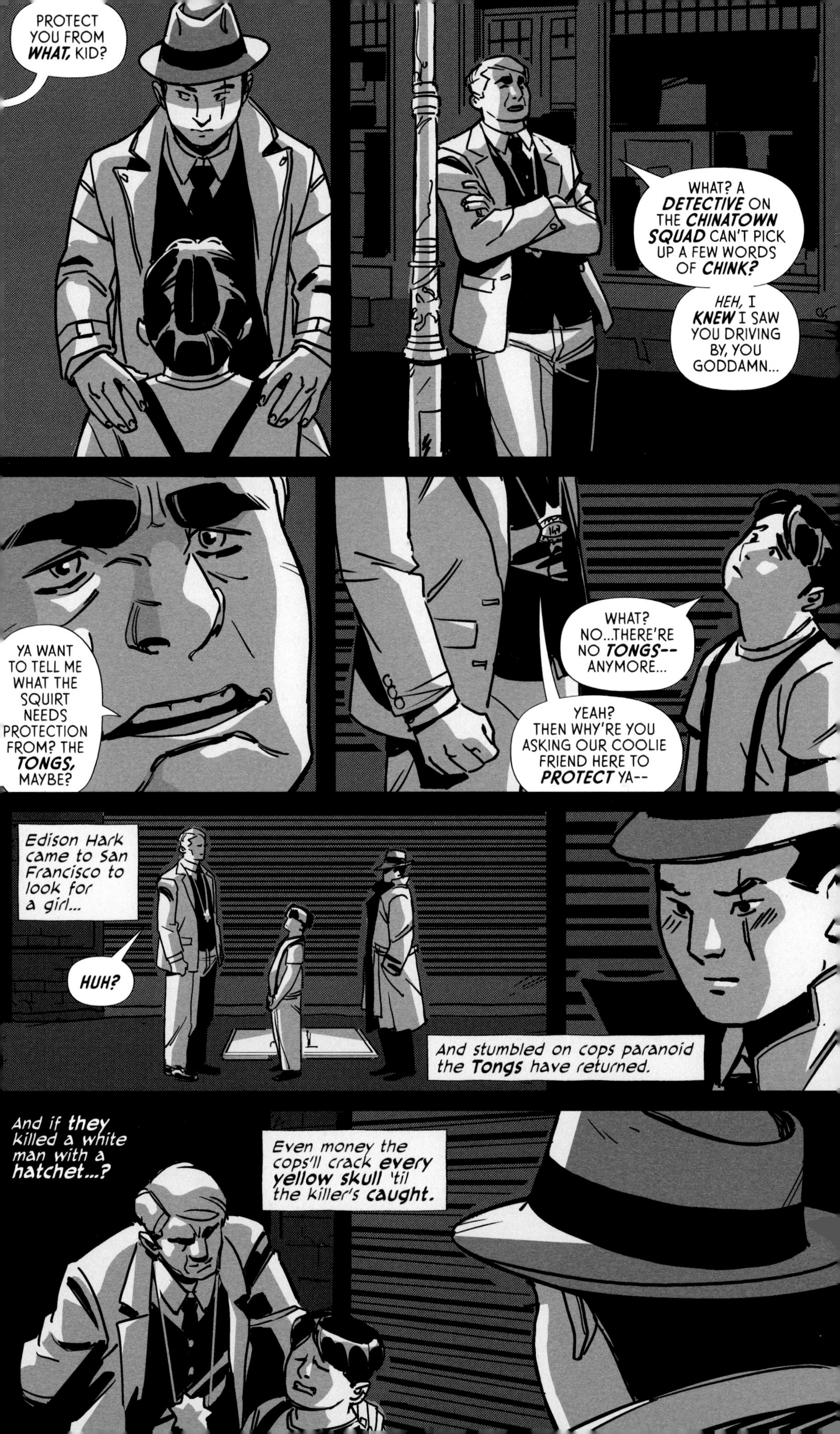
PROTECT YOU FROM WHAT, KID?
WHAT? A DETECTIVE ON THE CHINATOWN SQUAD CAN'T PICK UP A FEW WORDS OF CHINK?
HEH, I KNEW I SAW YOU DRIVING BY, YOU GODDAMN...
YA WANT TO TELL ME WHAT THE SQUIRT NEEDS PROTECTION FROM? THE TONGS, MAYBE?
WHAT? NO...THERE'RE NO TONGS-- ANYMORE...
YEAH? THEN WHY'RE YOU ASKING OUR COOLIE FRIEND HERE TO PROTECT YA--
Edison Hark came to San Francisco to look for a girl...
HUH?
And stumbled on cops paranoid the Tongs have returned.
And if they killed a white man with a hatchet...?
Even money the cops'll crack every yellow skull 'til the killer's caught.

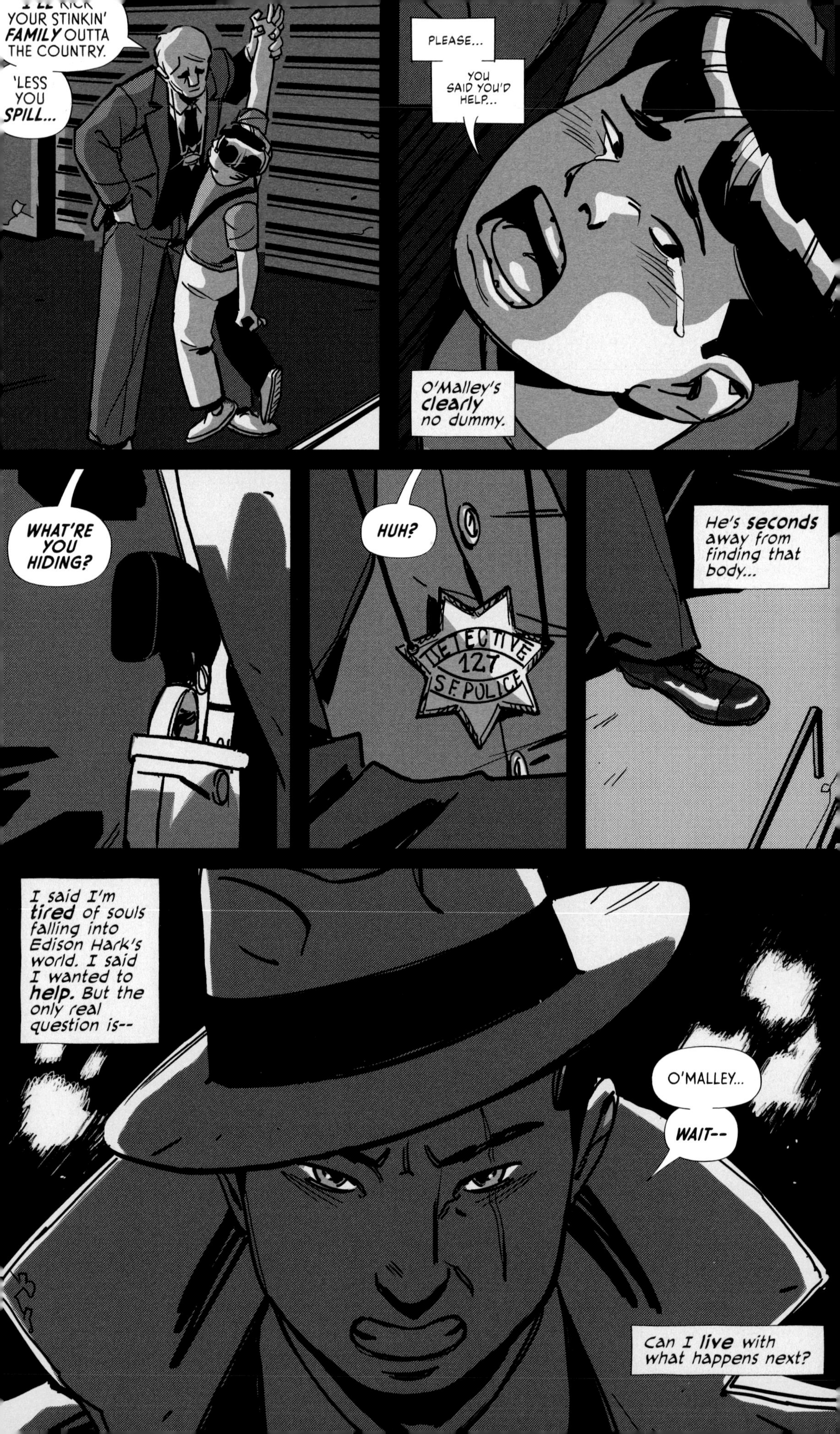
YOUR STINKIN' FAMILY OUTTA THE COUNTRY.
'LESS YOU SPILL...
PLEASE...
YOU SAID YOU'D HELP...
O'Malley's clearly no dummy.
WHAT'RE YOU HIDING?
HUH?
DETECTIVE 127 S.F. POLICE
He's seconds away from finding that body...
I said I'm tired of souls falling into Edison Hark's world. I said I wanted to help. But the only real question is--
O'MALLEY...
WAIT--
Can I live with what happens next?

CHAPTER TWO

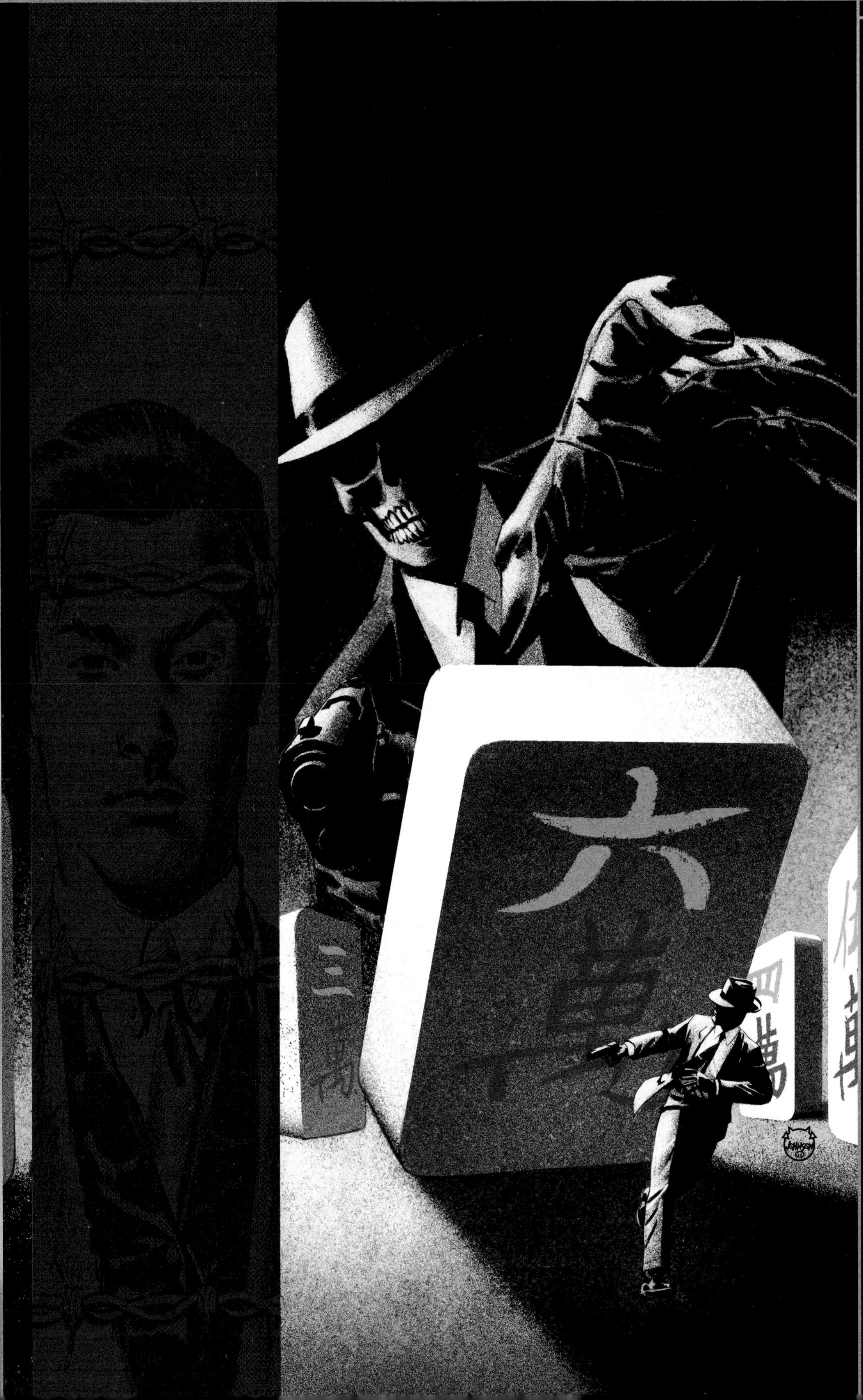
六
三萬
四萬

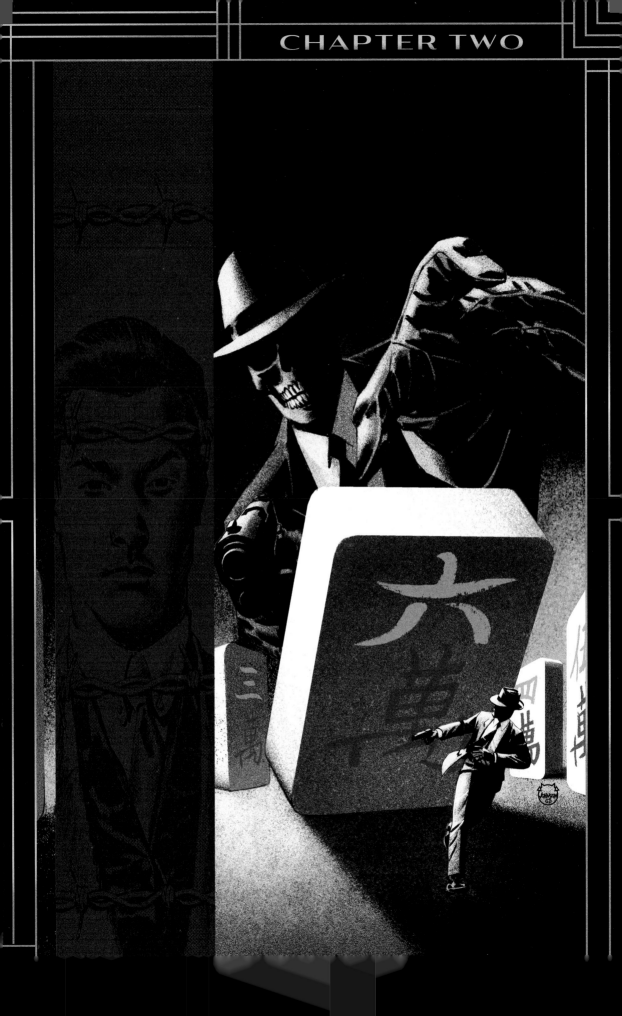

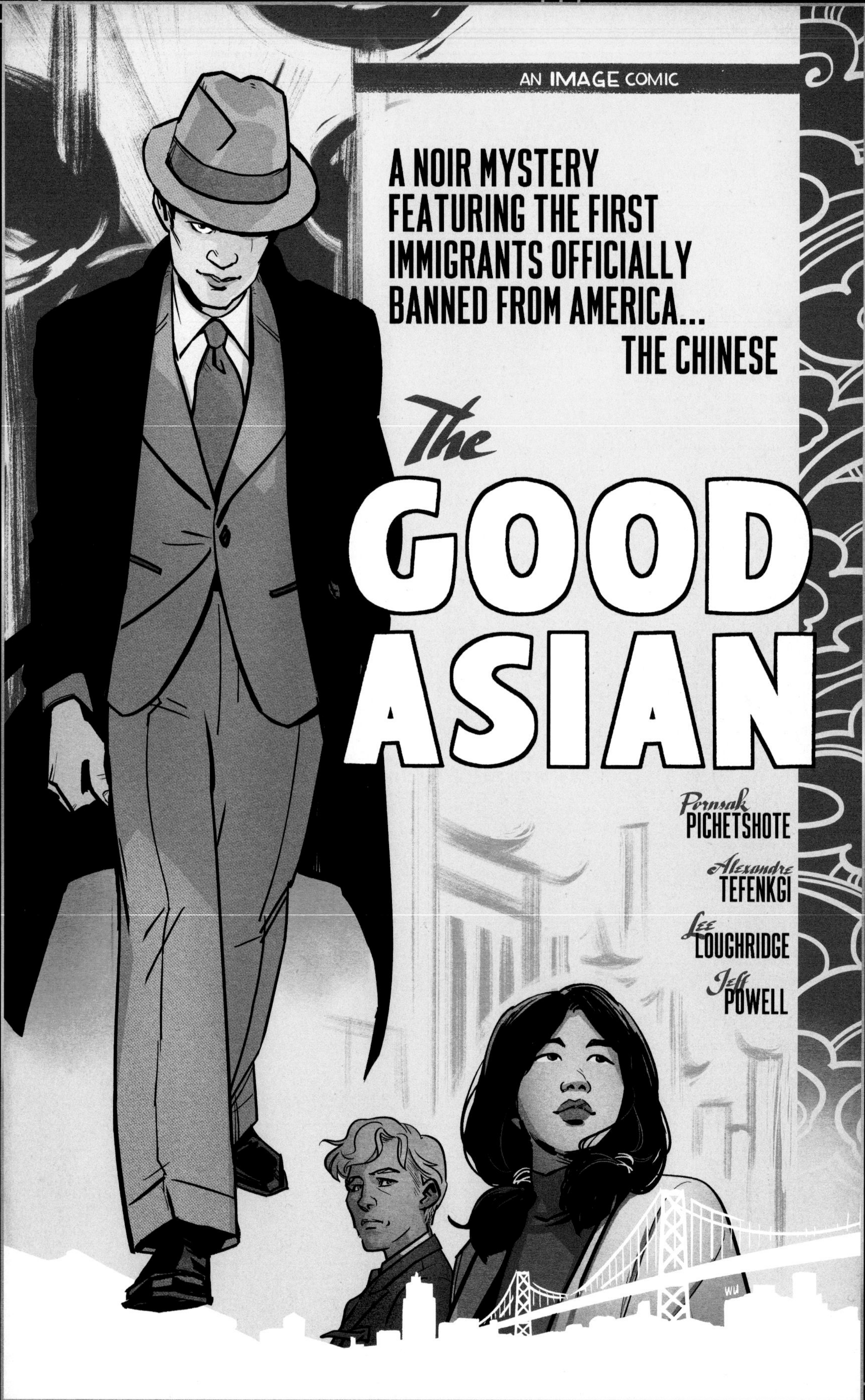

ART BY ANNIE WU

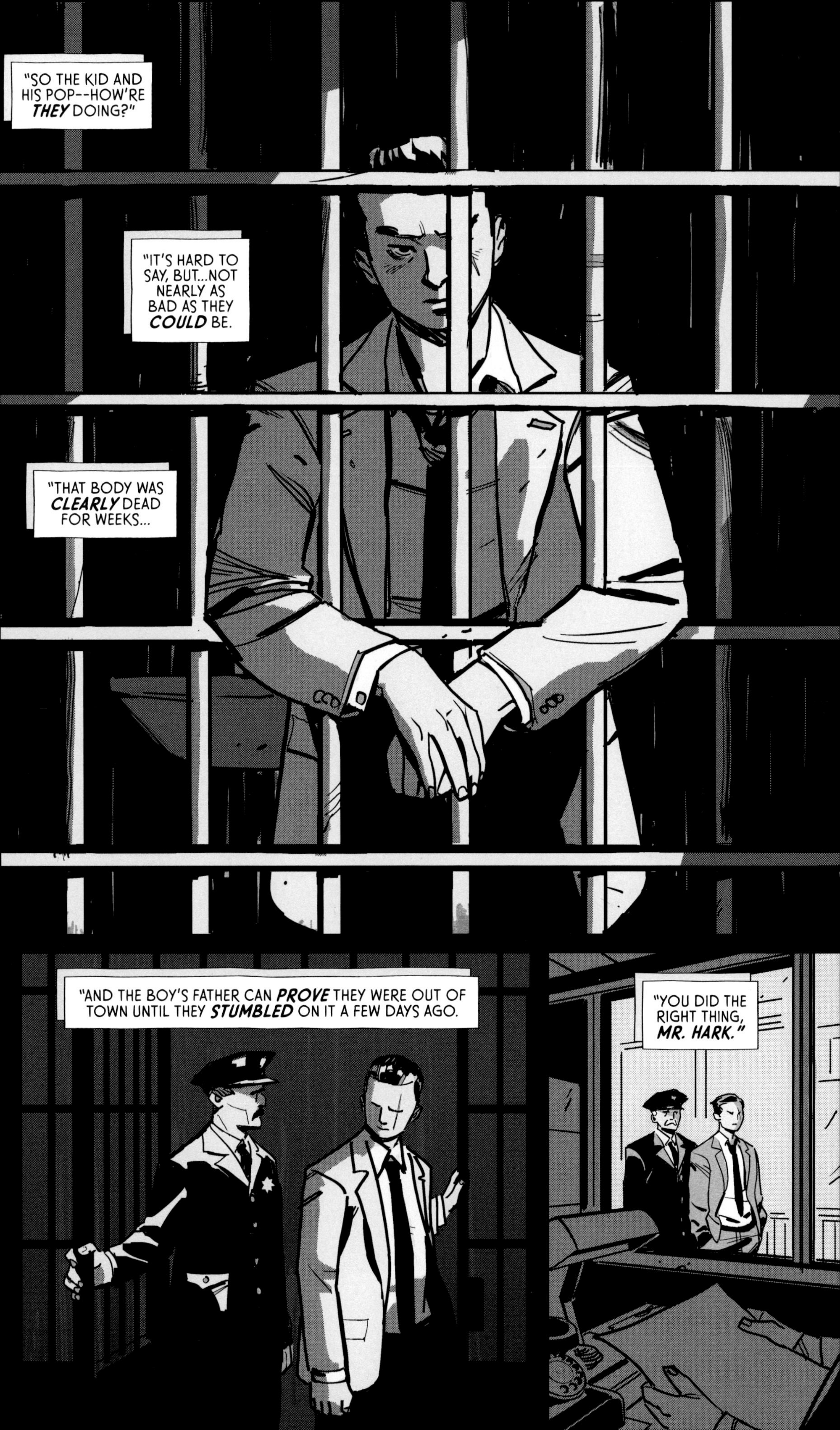
"SO THE KID AND HIS POP--HOW'RE *THEY* DOING?"
"IT'S HARD TO SAY, BUT...NOT NEARLY AS BAD AS THEY *COULD* BE.
"THAT BODY WAS *CLEARLY* DEAD FOR WEEKS...
"AND THE BOY'S FATHER CAN *PROVE* THEY WERE OUT OF TOWN UNTIL THEY *STUMBLED* ON IT A FEW DAYS AGO.
"YOU DID THE RIGHT THING, *MR. HARK.*"

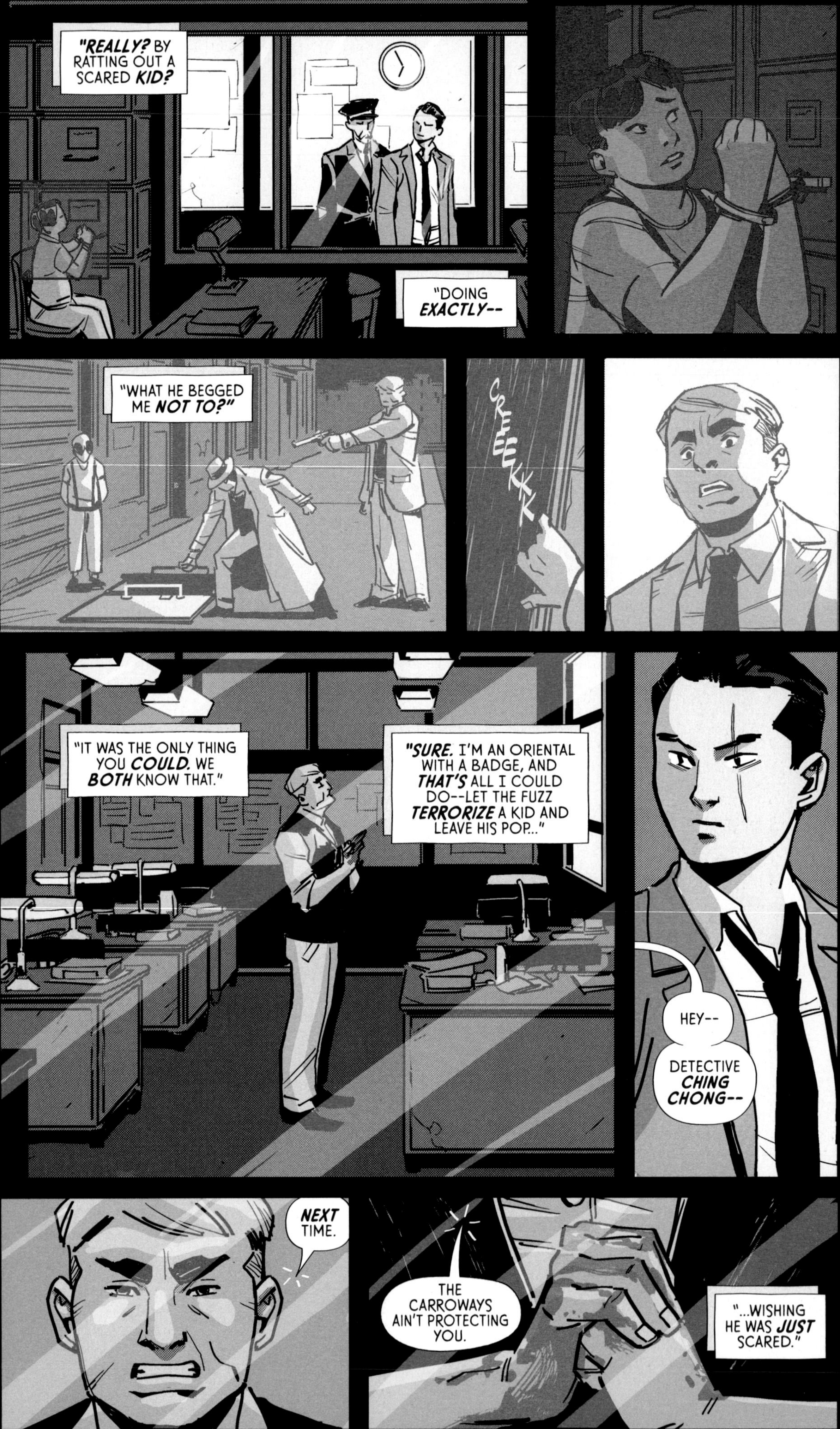

"REALLY? BY RATTING OUT A SCARED KID?
"DOING EXACTLY--
"WHAT HE BEGGED ME NOT TO?"
CREEKKK
"IT WAS THE ONLY THING YOU COULD. WE BOTH KNOW THAT."
"SURE. I'M AN ORIENTAL WITH A BADGE, AND THAT'S ALL I COULD DO--LET THE FUZZ TERRORIZE A KID AND LEAVE HIS POP..."
HEY--
DETECTIVE CHING CHONG--
NEXT TIME.
THE CARROWAYS AIN'T PROTECTING YOU.
"...WISHING HE WAS JUST SCARED."

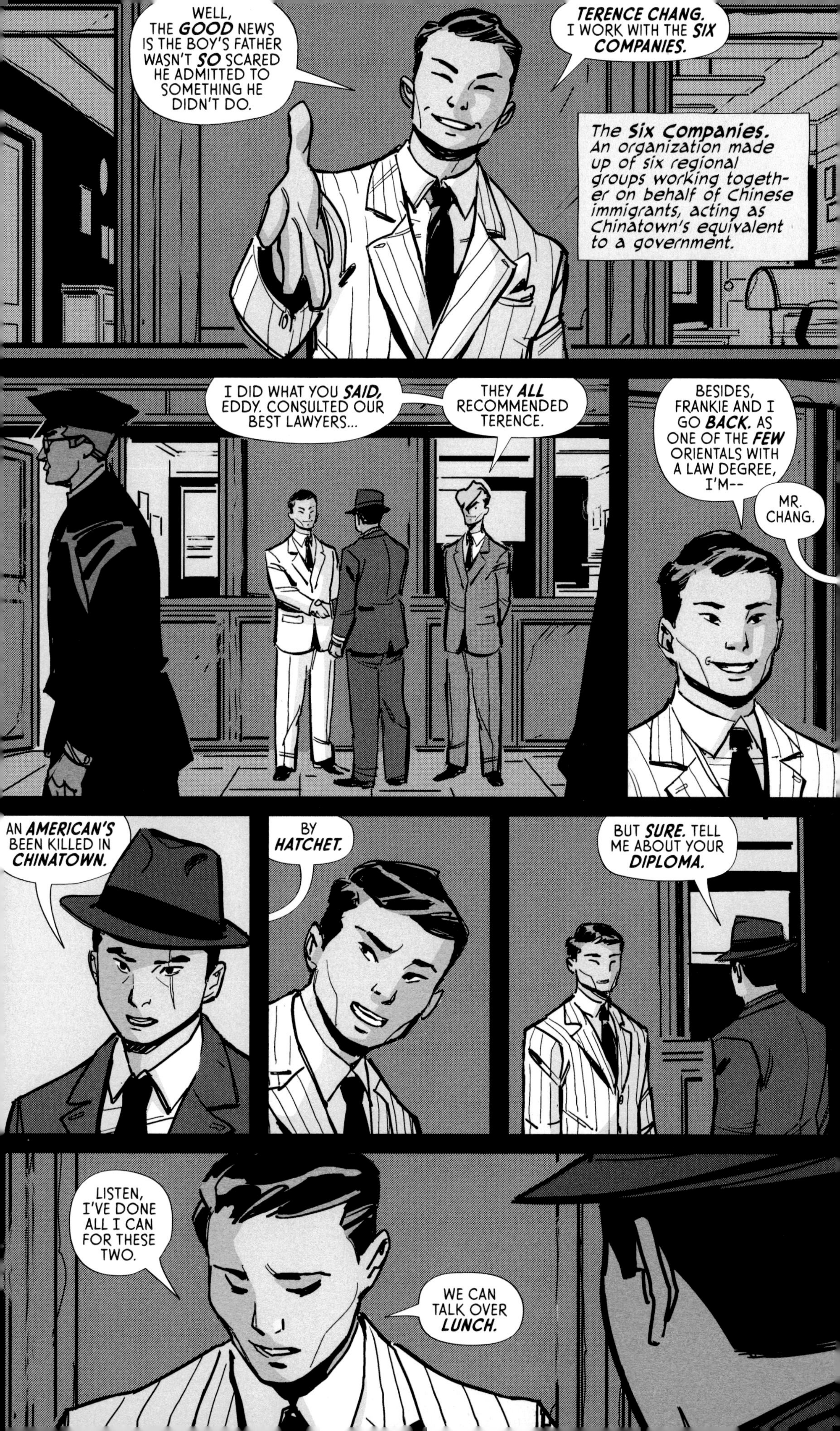
WELL, THE **GOOD** NEWS IS THE BOY'S FATHER WASN'T **SO** SCARED HE ADMITTED TO SOMETHING HE DIDN'T DO.
TERENCE CHANG. I WORK WITH THE **SIX COMPANIES.**
The **Six Companies.** An organization made up of six regional groups working together on behalf of Chinese immigrants, acting as Chinatown's equivalent to a government.
I DID WHAT YOU **SAID,** EDDY. CONSULTED OUR BEST LAWYERS...
THEY **ALL** RECOMMENDED TERENCE.
BESIDES, FRANKIE AND I GO **BACK.** AS ONE OF THE **FEW** ORIENTALS WITH A LAW DEGREE, I'M--
MR. CHANG.
AN **AMERICAN'S** BEEN KILLED IN **CHINATOWN.**
BY **HATCHET.**
BUT **SURE.** TELL ME ABOUT YOUR **DIPLOMA.**
LISTEN, I'VE DONE ALL I CAN FOR THESE TWO.
WE CAN TALK OVER **LUNCH.**

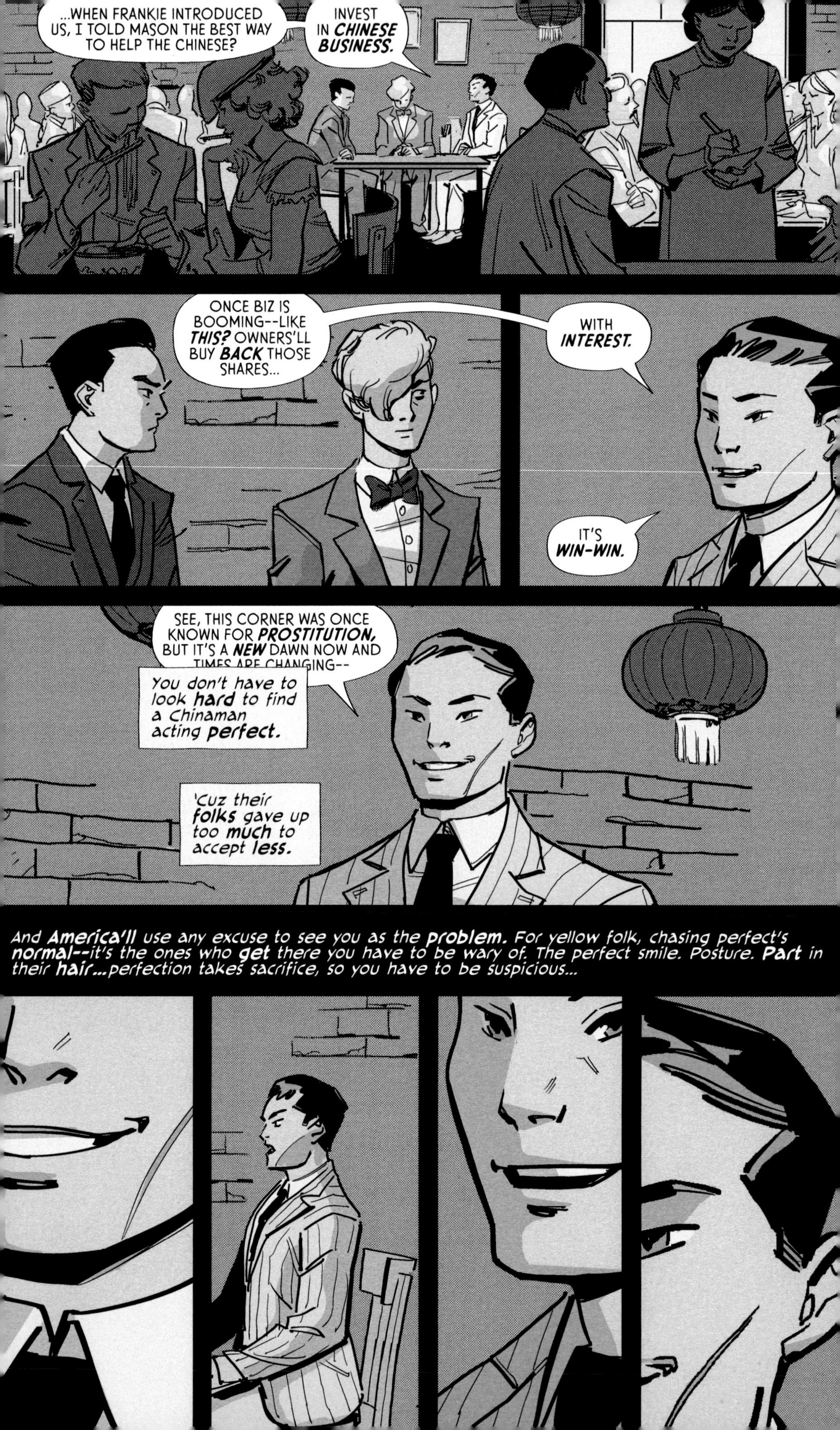
...WHEN FRANKIE INTRODUCED US, I TOLD MASON THE BEST WAY TO HELP THE CHINESE?
INVEST IN CHINESE BUSINESS.
ONCE BIZ IS BOOMING--LIKE THIS? OWNERS'LL BUY BACK THOSE SHARES...
WITH INTEREST.
IT'S WIN-WIN.
SEE, THIS CORNER WAS ONCE KNOWN FOR PROSTITUTION, BUT IT'S A NEW DAWN NOW AND TIMES ARE CHANGING--
You don't have to look hard to find a Chinaman acting perfect.
'Cuz their folks gave up too much to accept less.
And America'll use any excuse to see you as the problem. For yellow folk, chasing perfect's normal--it's the ones who get there you have to be wary of. The perfect smile. Posture. Part in their hair...perfection takes sacrifice, so you have to be suspicious...

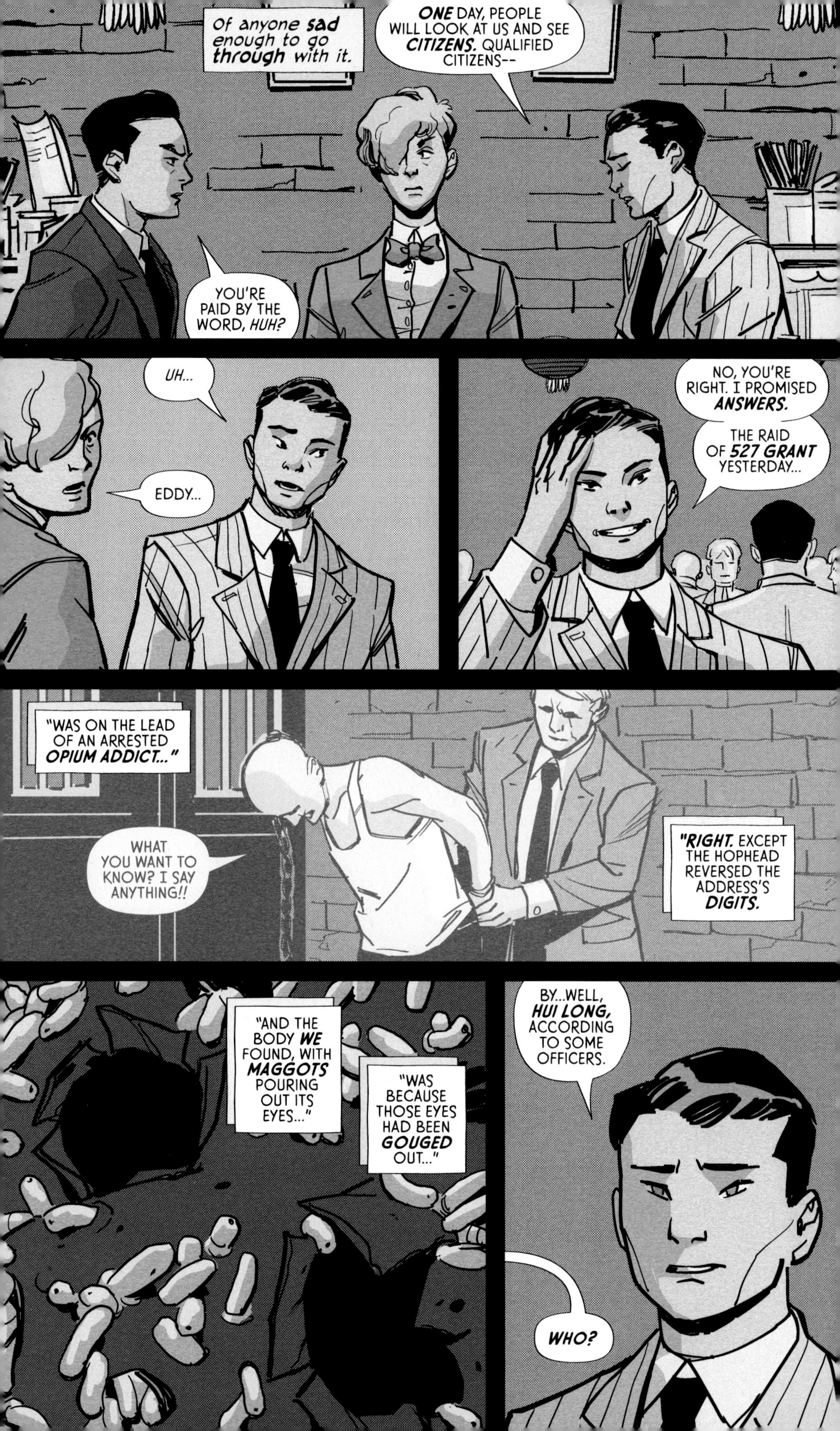
Of anyone sad enough to go through with it.
ONE DAY, PEOPLE WILL LOOK AT US AND SEE CITIZENS. QUALIFIED CITIZENS--
YOU'RE PAID BY THE WORD, HUH?
UH...
EDDY...
NO, YOU'RE RIGHT. I PROMISED ANSWERS.
THE RAID OF 527 GRANT YESTERDAY...
"WAS ON THE LEAD OF AN ARRESTED OPIUM ADDICT..."
WHAT YOU WANT TO KNOW? I SAY ANYTHING!!
"RIGHT. EXCEPT THE HOPHEAD REVERSED THE ADDRESS'S DIGITS.
"AND THE BODY WE FOUND, WITH MAGGOTS POURING OUT ITS EYES..."
"WAS BECAUSE THOSE EYES HAD BEEN GOUGED OUT..."
BY...WELL, HUI LONG, ACCORDING TO SOME OFFICERS.
WHO?

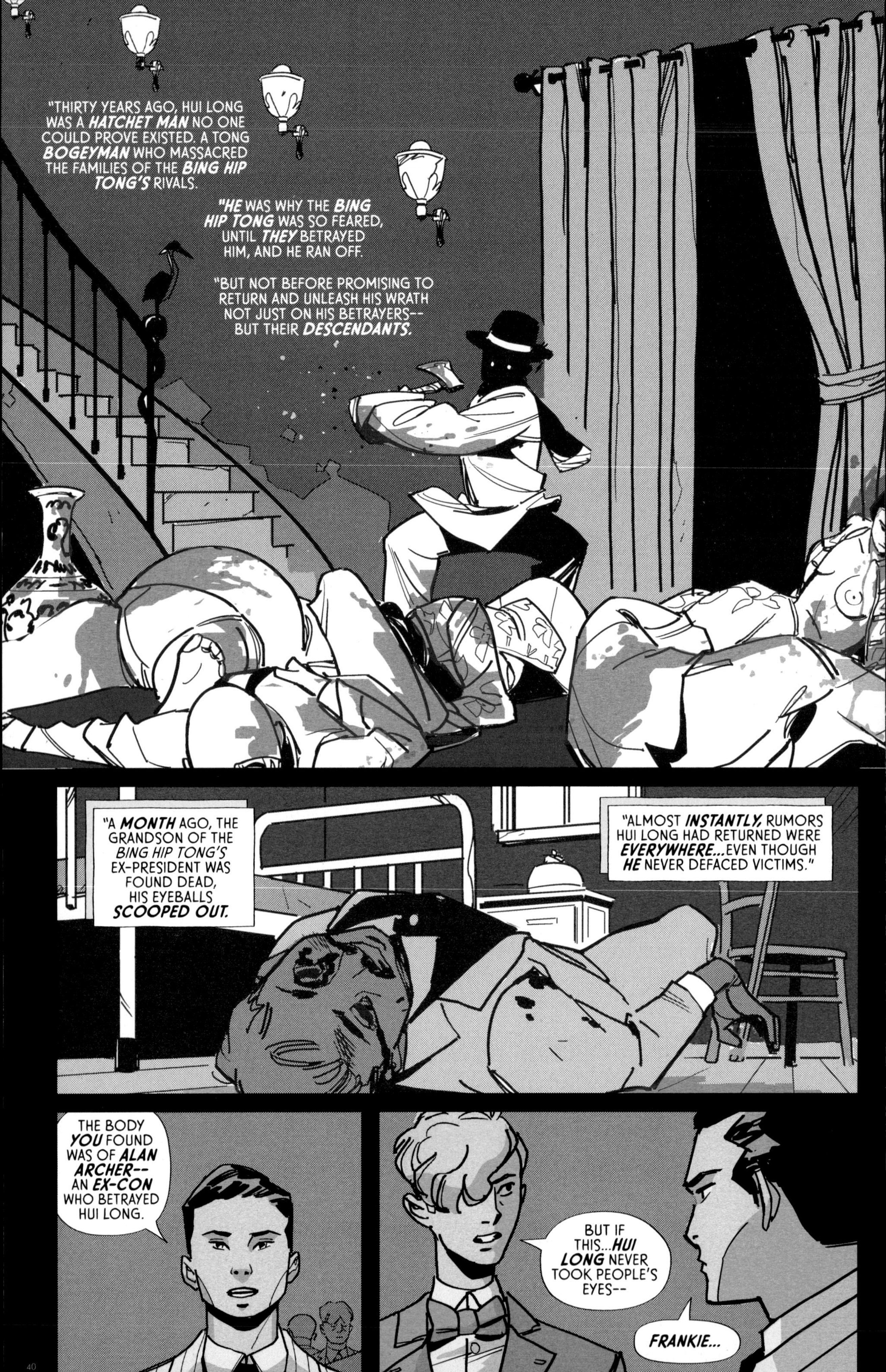
"THIRTY YEARS AGO, HUI LONG WAS A HATCHET MAN NO ONE COULD PROVE EXISTED. A TONG BOGEYMAN WHO MASSACRED THE FAMILIES OF THE BING HIP TONG'S RIVALS.
"HE WAS WHY THE BING HIP TONG WAS SO FEARED, UNTIL THEY BETRAYED HIM, AND HE RAN OFF.
"BUT NOT BEFORE PROMISING TO RETURN AND UNLEASH HIS WRATH NOT JUST ON HIS BETRAYERS--BUT THEIR DESCENDANTS.
"A MONTH AGO, THE GRANDSON OF THE BING HIP TONG'S EX-PRESIDENT WAS FOUND DEAD, HIS EYEBALLS SCOOPED OUT.
"ALMOST INSTANTLY, RUMORS HUI LONG HAD RETURNED WERE EVERYWHERE...EVEN THOUGH HE NEVER DEFACED VICTIMS."
THE BODY YOU FOUND WAS OF ALAN ARCHER--AN EX-CON WHO BETRAYED HUI LONG.
BUT IF THIS...HUI LONG NEVER TOOK PEOPLE'S EYES--
FRANKIE...

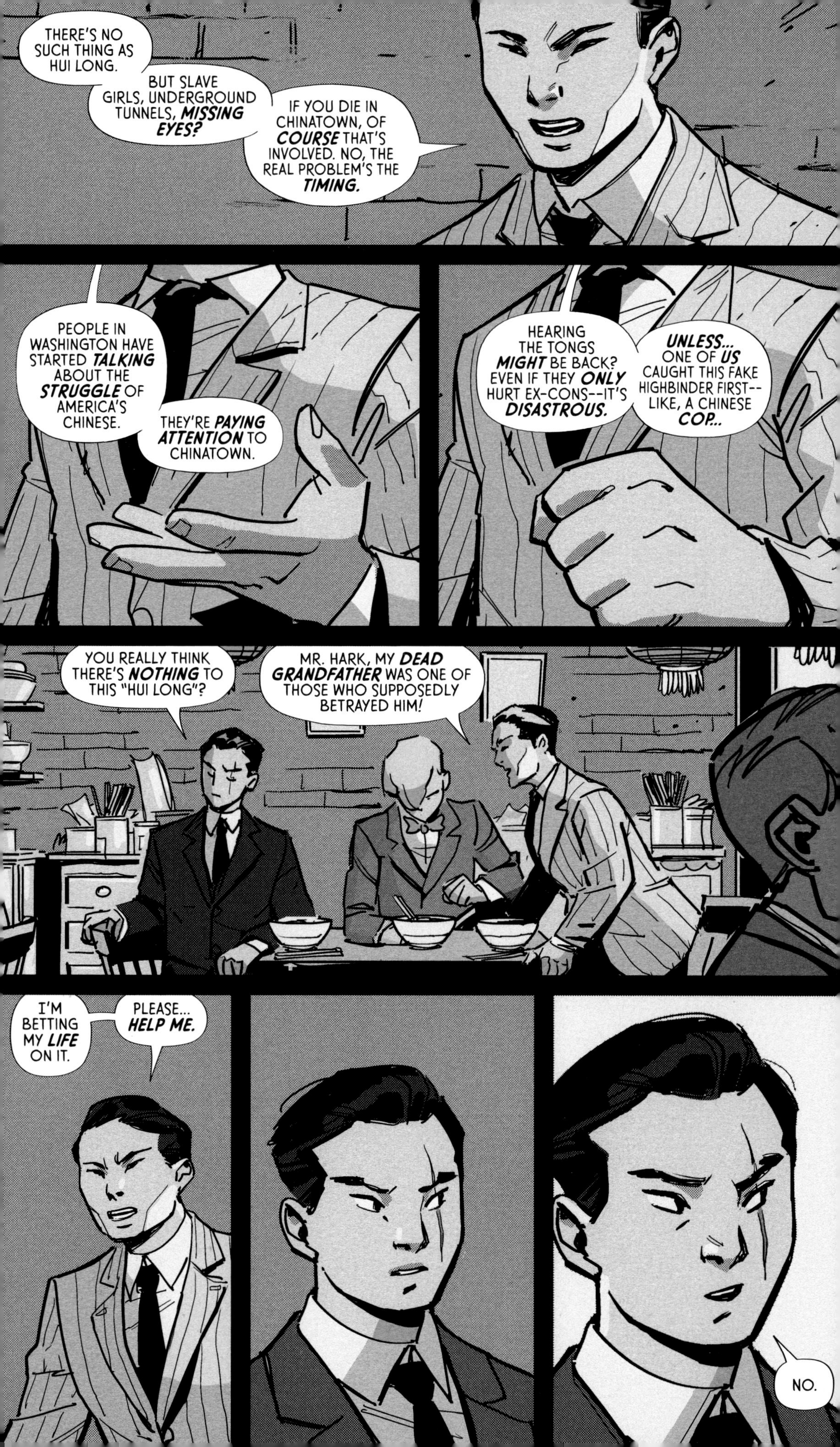

THERE'S NO SUCH THING AS HUI LONG.
BUT SLAVE GIRLS, UNDERGROUND TUNNELS, *MISSING EYES?*
IF YOU DIE IN CHINATOWN, OF *COURSE* THAT'S INVOLVED. NO, THE REAL PROBLEM'S THE *TIMING.*
PEOPLE IN WASHINGTON HAVE STARTED *TALKING* ABOUT THE *STRUGGLE* OF AMERICA'S CHINESE.
THEY'RE *PAYING ATTENTION* TO CHINATOWN.
HEARING THE TONGS *MIGHT* BE BACK? EVEN IF THEY *ONLY* HURT EX-CONS--IT'S *DISASTROUS.*
UNLESS... ONE OF *US* CAUGHT THIS FAKE HIGHBINDER FIRST--LIKE, A CHINESE *COP...*
YOU REALLY THINK THERE'S *NOTHING* TO THIS "HUI LONG"?
MR. HARK, MY *DEAD GRANDFATHER* WAS ONE OF THOSE WHO SUPPOSEDLY BETRAYED HIM!
I'M BETTING MY *LIFE* ON IT.
PLEASE... *HELP ME.*
NO.

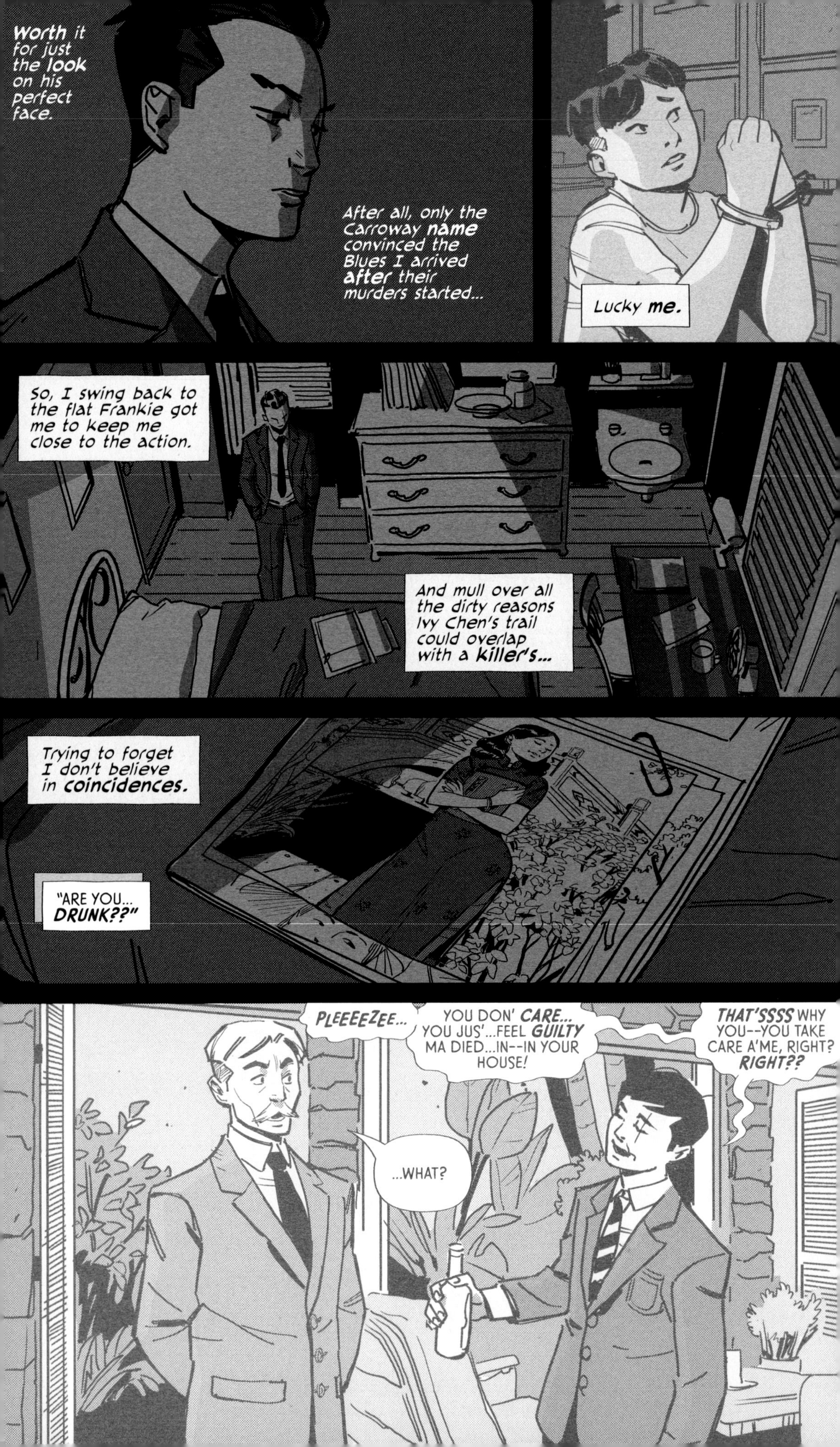
Worth it for just the look on his perfect face.
After all, only the Carroway name convinced the Blues I arrived after their murders started...
Lucky me.
So, I swing back to the flat Frankie got me to keep me close to the action.
And mull over all the dirty reasons Ivy Chen's trail could overlap with a killer's...
Trying to forget I don't believe in coincidences.
"ARE YOU... DRUNK??"
PLEEEEZEE...
YOU DON' CARE... YOU JUS'...FEEL GUILTY MA DIED...IN--IN YOUR HOUSE!
THAT'SSSS WHY YOU--YOU TAKE CARE A'ME, RIGHT? RIGHT??
...WHAT?

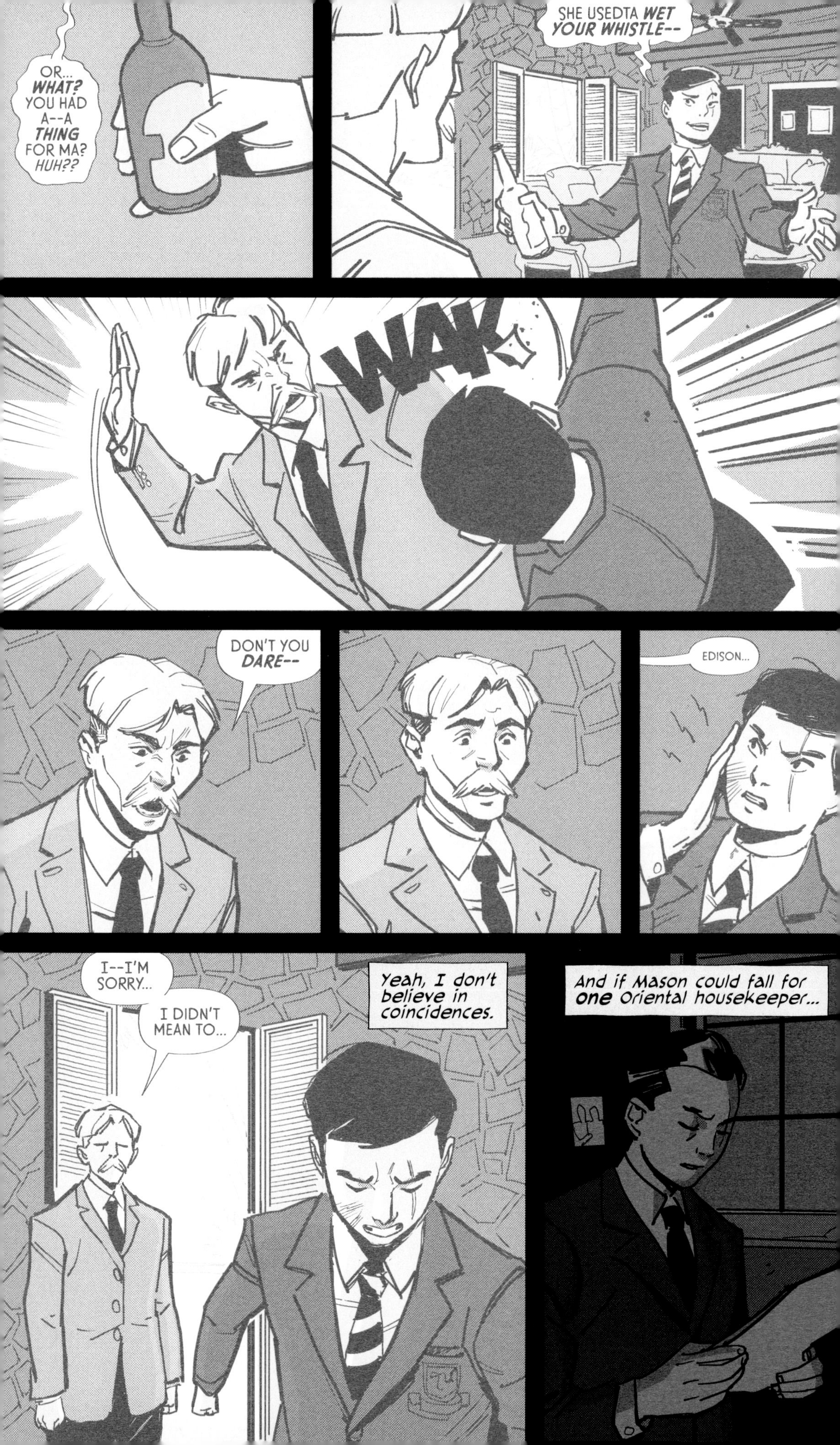
OR... WHAT? YOU HAD A--A THING FOR MA? HUH??
SHE USEDTA WET YOUR WHISTLE--
WAK
DON'T YOU DARE--
EDISON...
I--I'M SORRY...
I DIDN'T MEAN TO...
Yeah, I don't believe in coincidences.
And if Mason could fall for one Oriental housekeeper...

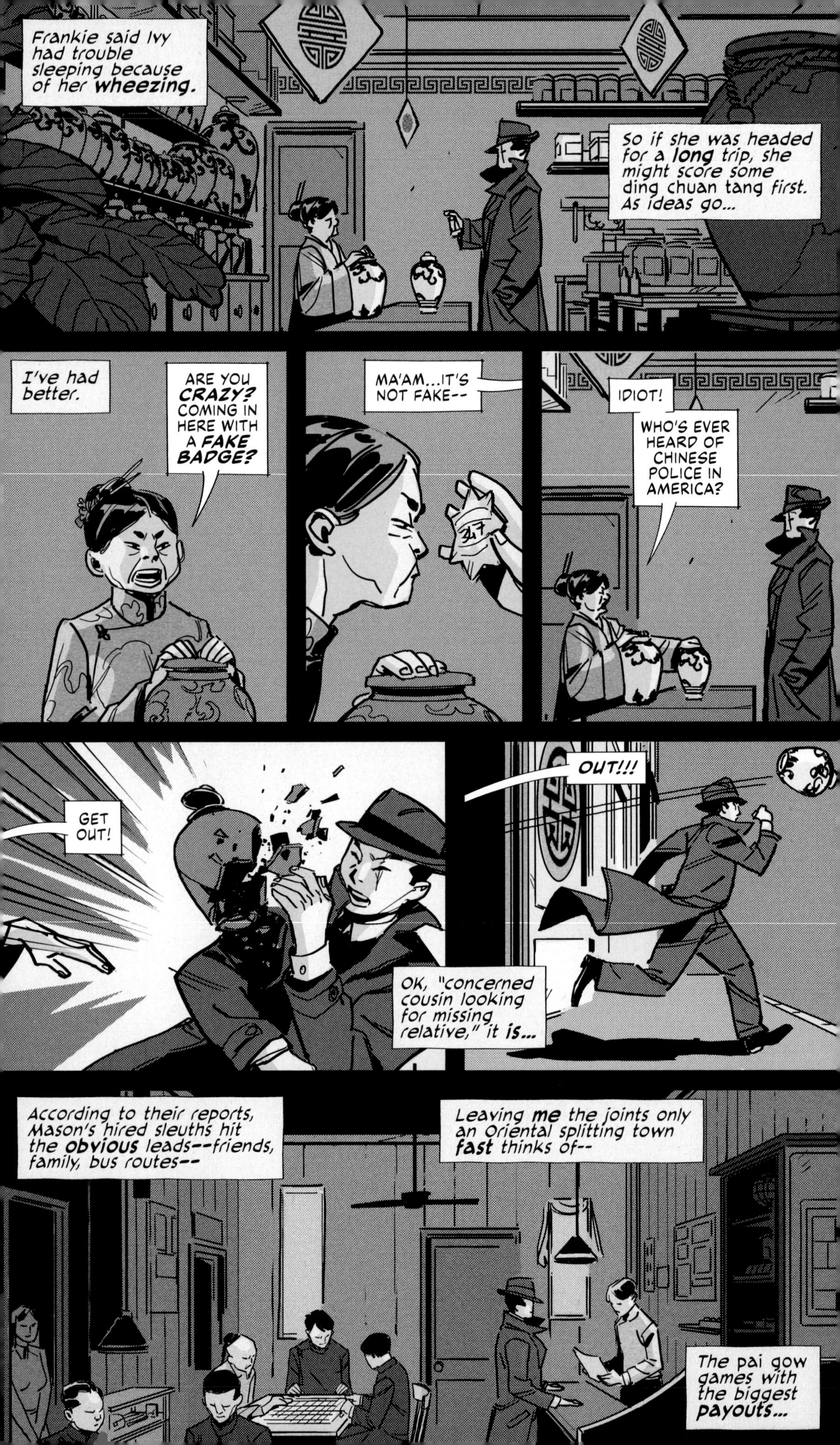

Frankie said Ivy had trouble sleeping because of her **wheezing.**
So if she was headed for a **long** trip, she might score some ding chuan tang first. As ideas go...
I've had better.
ARE YOU **CRAZY?** COMING IN HERE WITH A **FAKE BADGE?**
MA'AM...IT'S NOT FAKE--
IDIOT!
WHO'S EVER HEARD OF CHINESE POLICE IN AMERICA?
GET OUT!
OK, "concerned cousin looking for missing relative," it **is...**
OUT!!!
According to their reports, Mason's hired sleuths hit the **obvious** leads--friends, family, bus routes--
Leaving **me** the joints only an Oriental splitting town **fast** thinks of--
The pai gow games with the biggest **payouts...**

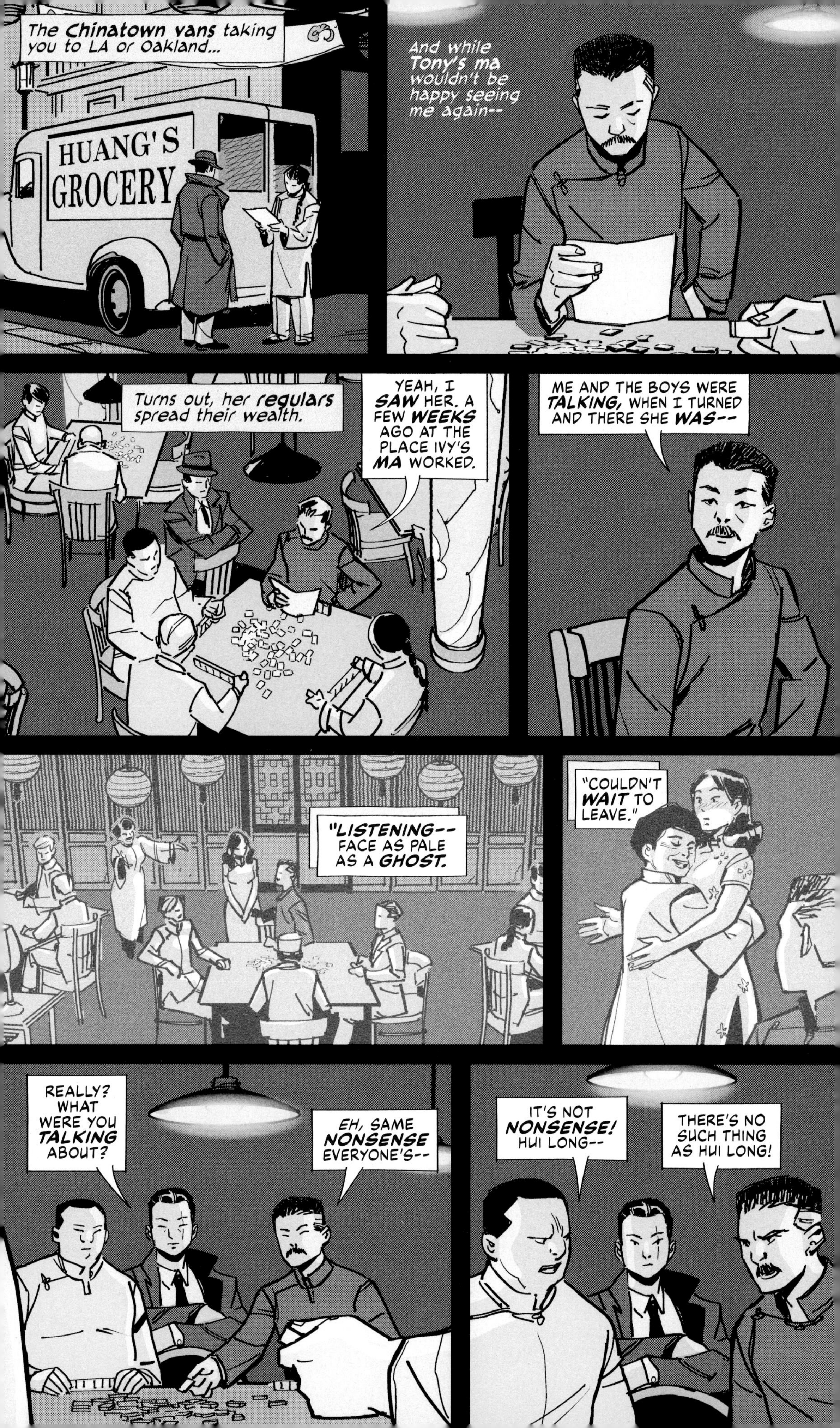
The Chinatown vans taking you to LA or Oakland...
HUANG'S GROCERY
And while Tony's ma wouldn't be happy seeing me again--
Turns out, her regulars spread their wealth.
YEAH, I SAW HER. A FEW WEEKS AGO AT THE PLACE IVY'S MA WORKED.
ME AND THE BOYS WERE TALKING, WHEN I TURNED AND THERE SHE WAS--
"LISTENING-- FACE AS PALE AS A GHOST.
"COULDN'T WAIT TO LEAVE."
REALLY? WHAT WERE YOU TALKING ABOUT?
EH, SAME NONSENSE EVERYONE'S--
IT'S NOT NONSENSE! HUI LONG--
THERE'S NO SUCH THING AS HUI LONG!

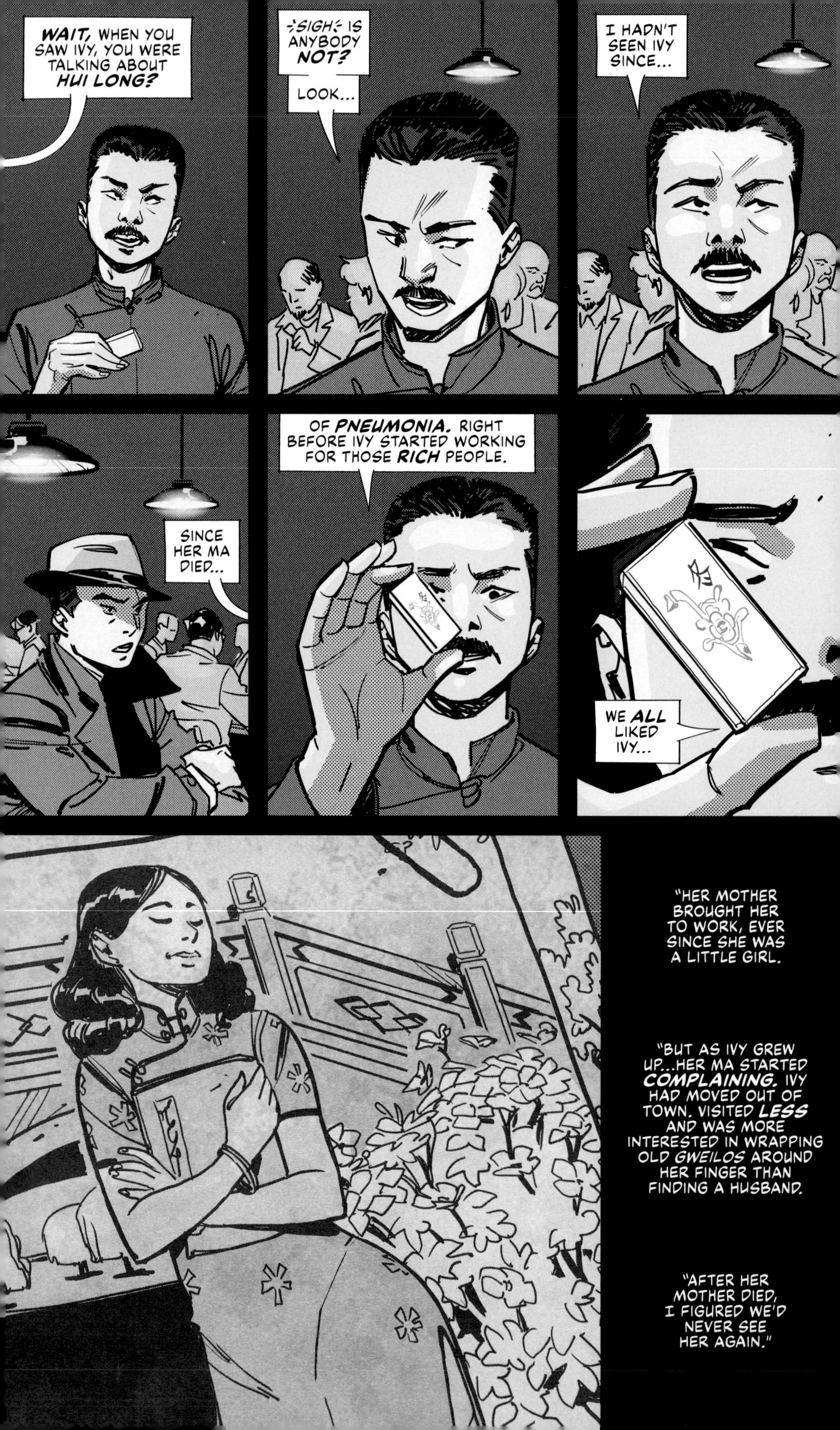
WAIT, WHEN YOU SAW IVY, YOU WERE TALKING ABOUT HUI LONG?
-SIGH- IS ANYBODY NOT?
LOOK...
I HADN'T SEEN IVY SINCE...
SINCE HER MA DIED...
OF PNEUMONIA. RIGHT BEFORE IVY STARTED WORKING FOR THOSE RICH PEOPLE.
WE ALL LIKED IVY...
"HER MOTHER BROUGHT HER TO WORK, EVER SINCE SHE WAS A LITTLE GIRL.
"BUT AS IVY GREW UP...HER MA STARTED COMPLAINING. IVY HAD MOVED OUT OF TOWN. VISITED LESS AND WAS MORE INTERESTED IN WRAPPING OLD GWEILOS AROUND HER FINGER THAN FINDING A HUSBAND.
"AFTER HER MOTHER DIED, I FIGURED WE'D NEVER SEE HER AGAIN."

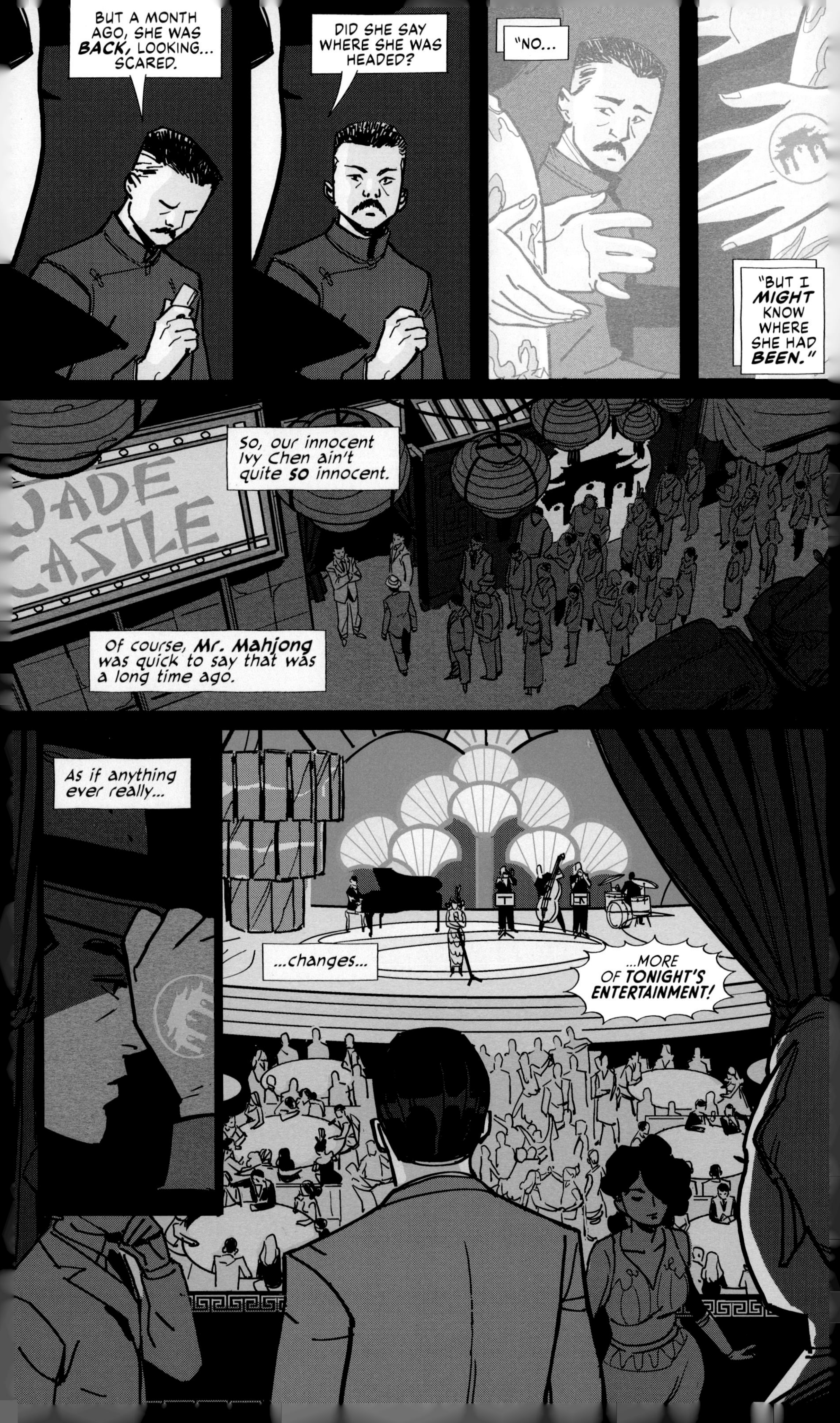
BUT A MONTH AGO, SHE WAS **BACK,** LOOKING... SCARED.
DID SHE SAY WHERE SHE WAS HEADED?
"NO...
"BUT I **MIGHT** KNOW WHERE SHE HAD **BEEN.**"
JADE CASTLE
So, our innocent Ivy Chen ain't quite **so** innocent.
Of course, **Mr. Mahjong** was quick to say that was a long time ago.
As if anything ever really...
...changes...
...MORE OF **TONIGHT'S ENTERTAINMENT!**

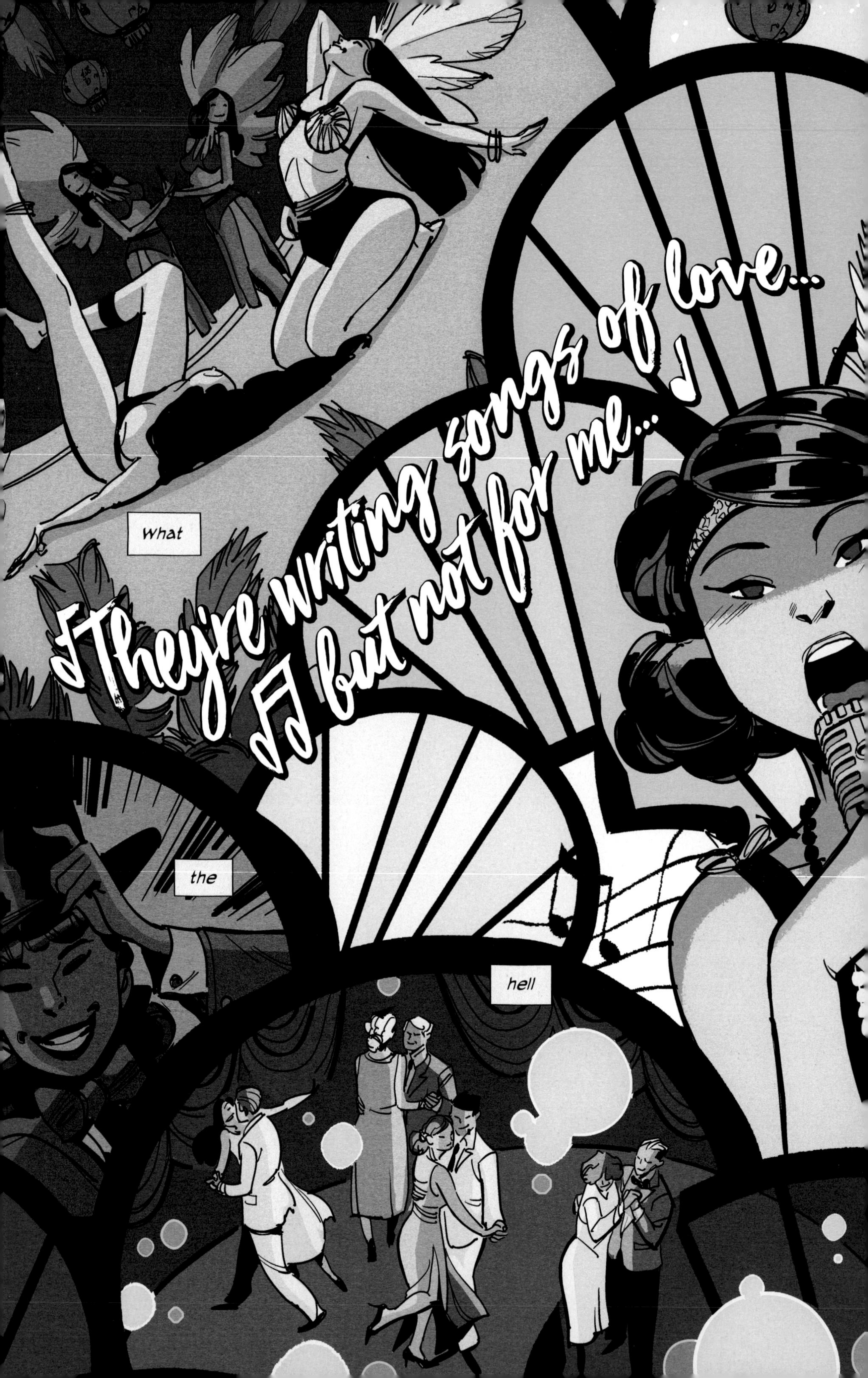

what
♪ They're writing songs of love... ♪
♫ but not for me... ♪
the
hell

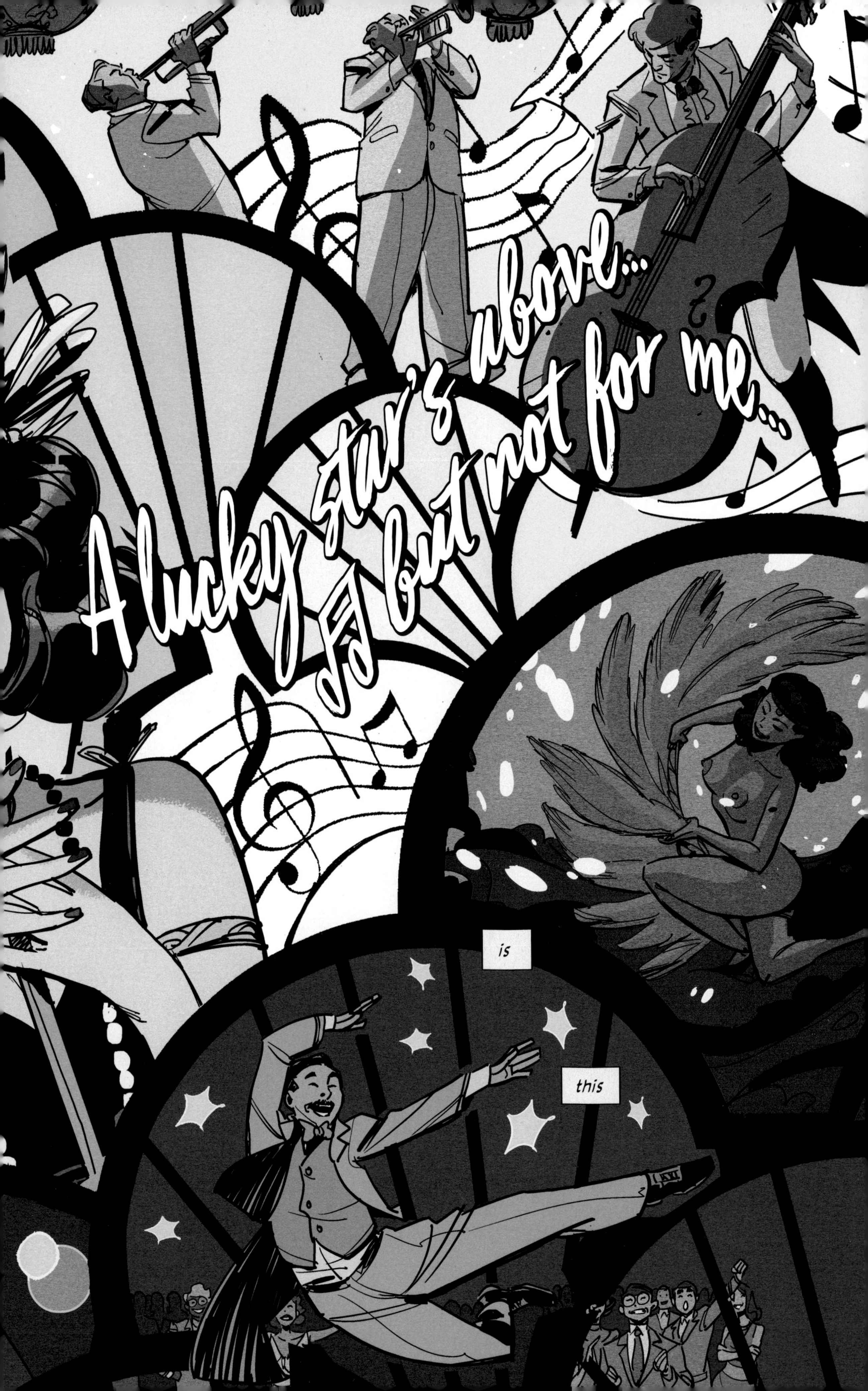
A lucky star's above...
but not for me...
is
this

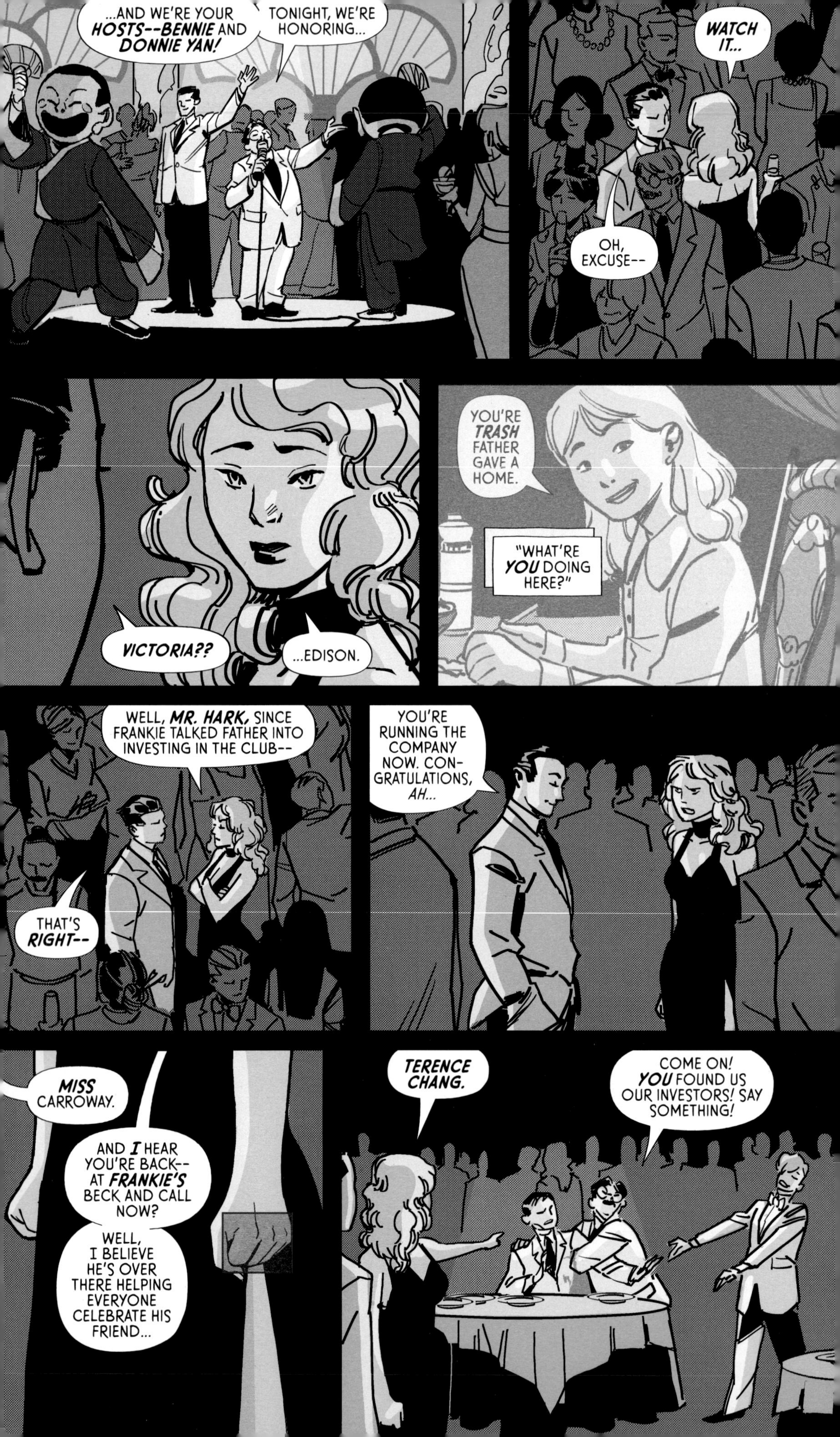

...AND WE'RE YOUR HOSTS--BENNIE AND DONNIE YAN!
TONIGHT, WE'RE HONORING...
WATCH IT...
OH, EXCUSE--
VICTORIA??
...EDISON.
YOU'RE TRASH FATHER GAVE A HOME.
"WHAT'RE YOU DOING HERE?"
WELL, MR. HARK, SINCE FRANKIE TALKED FATHER INTO INVESTING IN THE CLUB--
THAT'S RIGHT--
YOU'RE RUNNING THE COMPANY NOW. CON-GRATULATIONS, AH...
MISS CARROWAY.
AND I HEAR YOU'RE BACK-- AT FRANKIE'S BECK AND CALL NOW?
WELL, I BELIEVE HE'S OVER THERE HELPING EVERYONE CELEBRATE HIS FRIEND...
TERENCE CHANG.
COME ON! YOU FOUND US OUR INVESTORS! SAY SOMETHING!

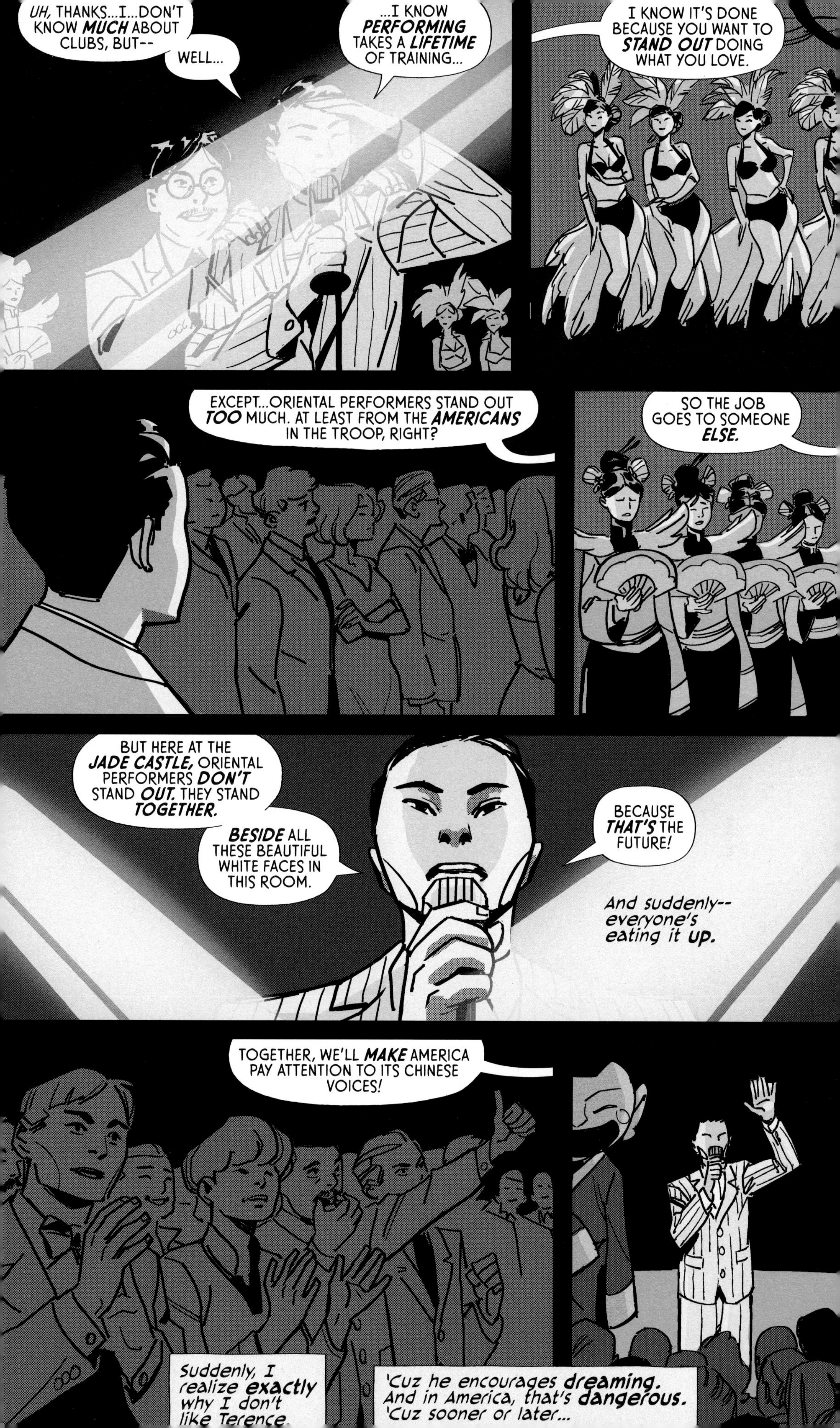
UH, THANKS...I...DON'T KNOW MUCH ABOUT CLUBS, BUT--
WELL...
...I KNOW PERFORMING TAKES A LIFETIME OF TRAINING...
I KNOW IT'S DONE BECAUSE YOU WANT TO STAND OUT DOING WHAT YOU LOVE.
EXCEPT...ORIENTAL PERFORMERS STAND OUT TOO MUCH. AT LEAST FROM THE AMERICANS IN THE TROOP, RIGHT?
SO THE JOB GOES TO SOMEONE ELSE.
BUT HERE AT THE JADE CASTLE, ORIENTAL PERFORMERS DON'T STAND OUT. THEY STAND TOGETHER.
BESIDE ALL THESE BEAUTIFUL WHITE FACES IN THIS ROOM.
BECAUSE THAT'S THE FUTURE!
And suddenly--everyone's eating it up.
TOGETHER, WE'LL MAKE AMERICA PAY ATTENTION TO ITS CHINESE VOICES!
Suddenly, I realize exactly why I don't like Terence.
'Cuz he encourages dreaming. And in America, that's dangerous. 'Cuz sooner or later...

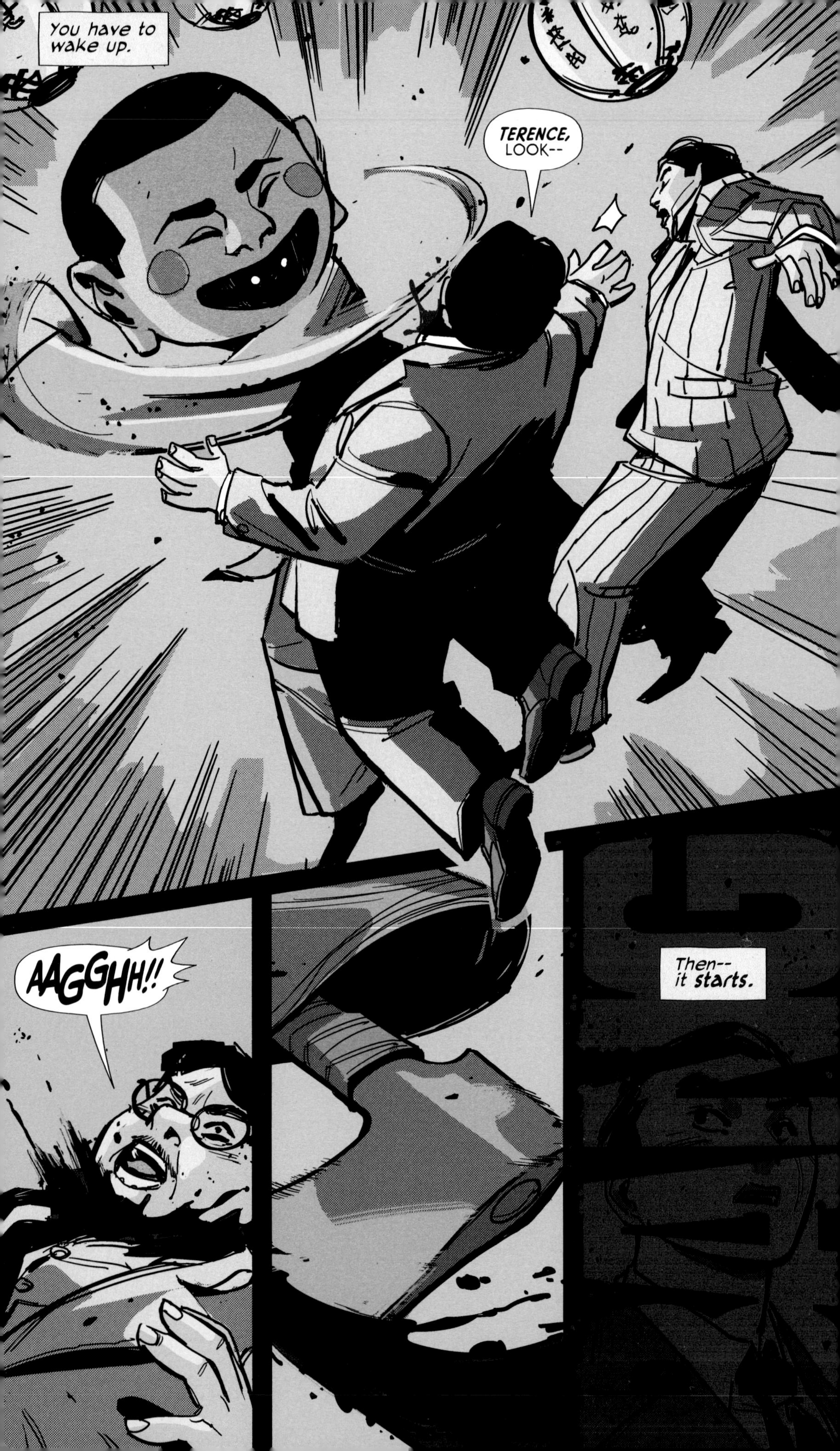
You have to wake up.
TERENCE, LOOK--
AAGGHH!!
Then-- it starts.

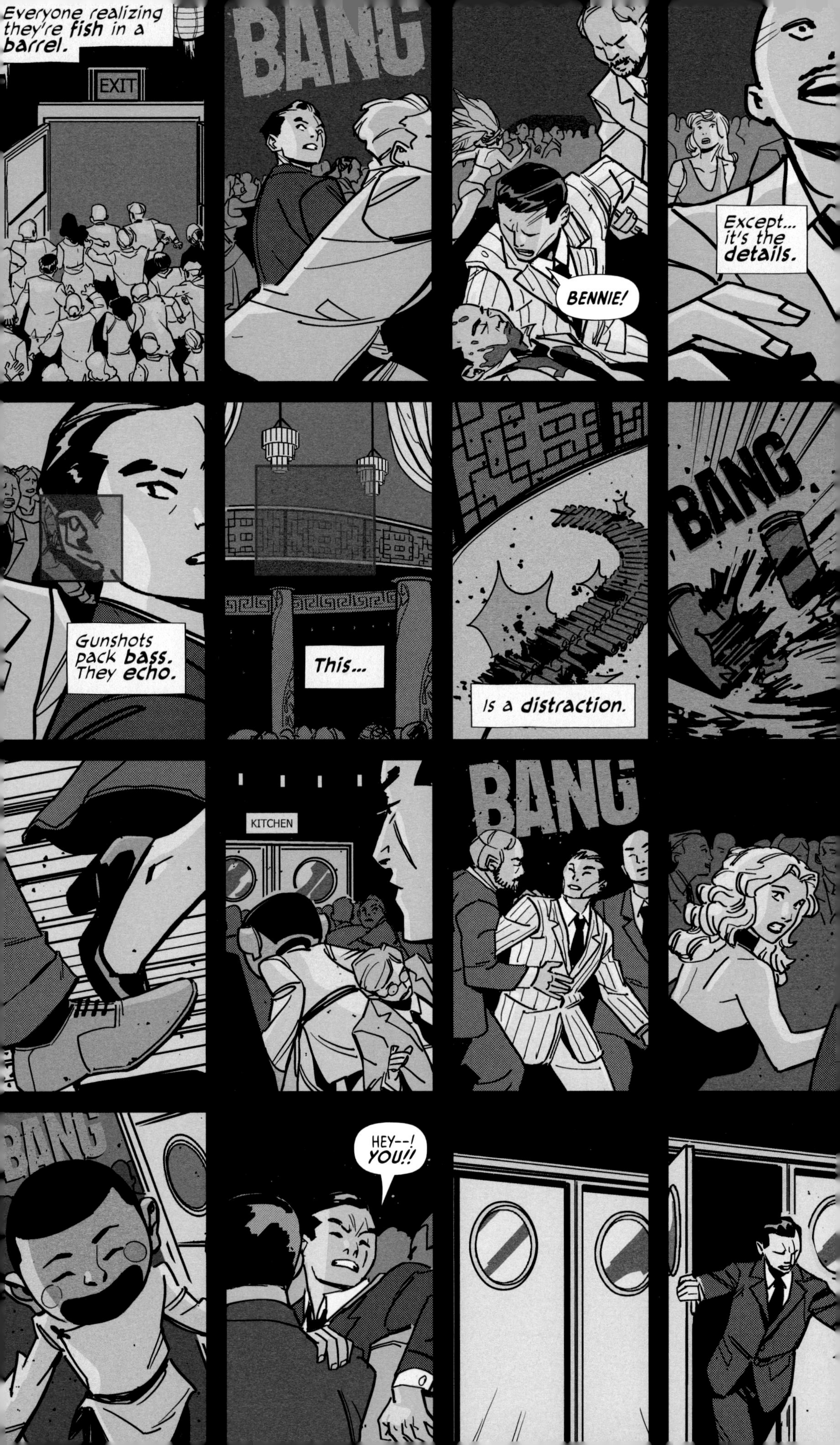

Everyone realizing they're fish in a barrel.
EXIT
BANG
BENNIE!
Except... it's the details.
Gunshots pack bass. They echo.
This...
Is a distraction.
BANG
KITCHEN
BANG
BANG
HEY--! YOU!!

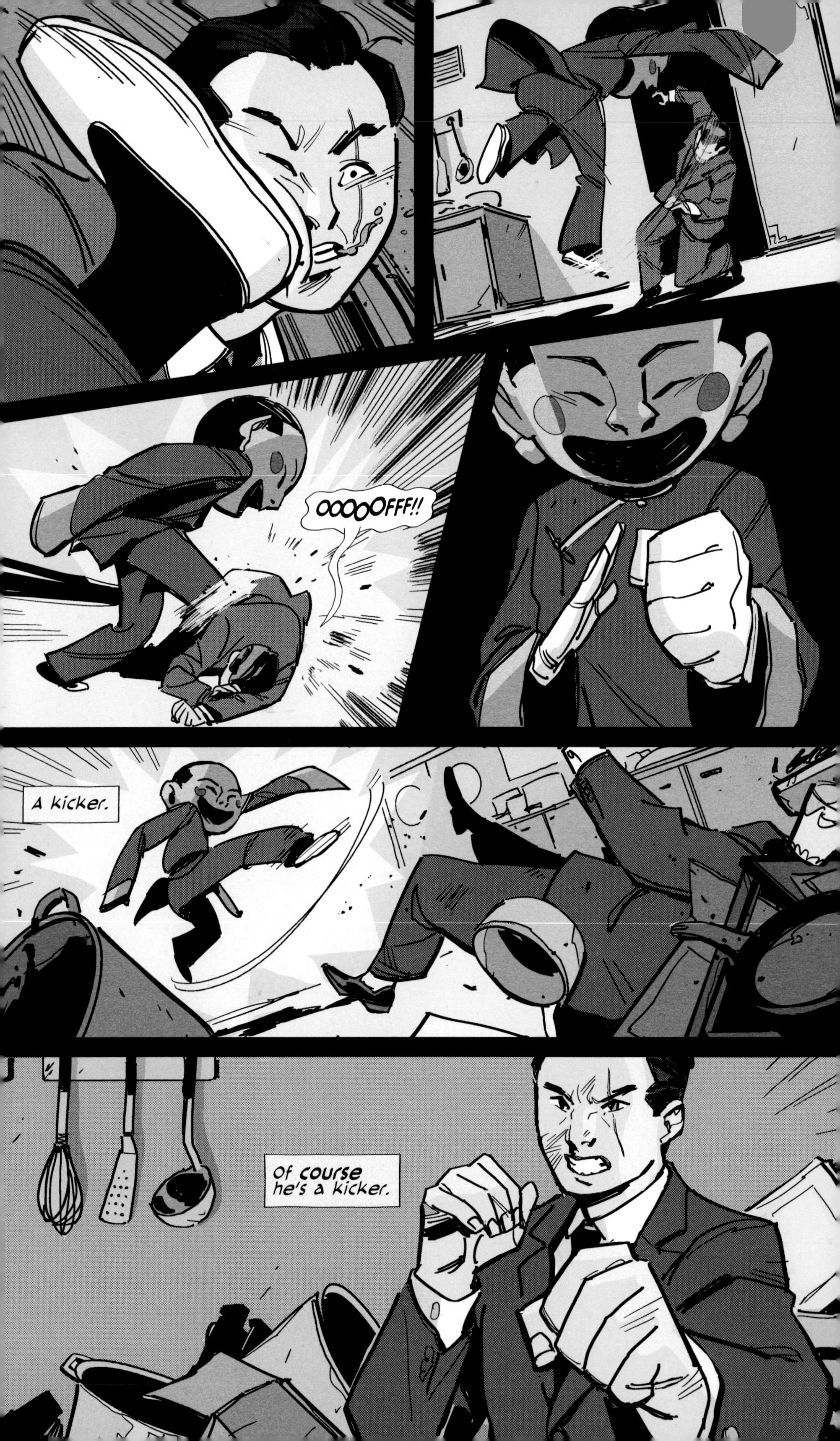
OOOOOFFF!!
A kicker.
Of course he's a kicker.

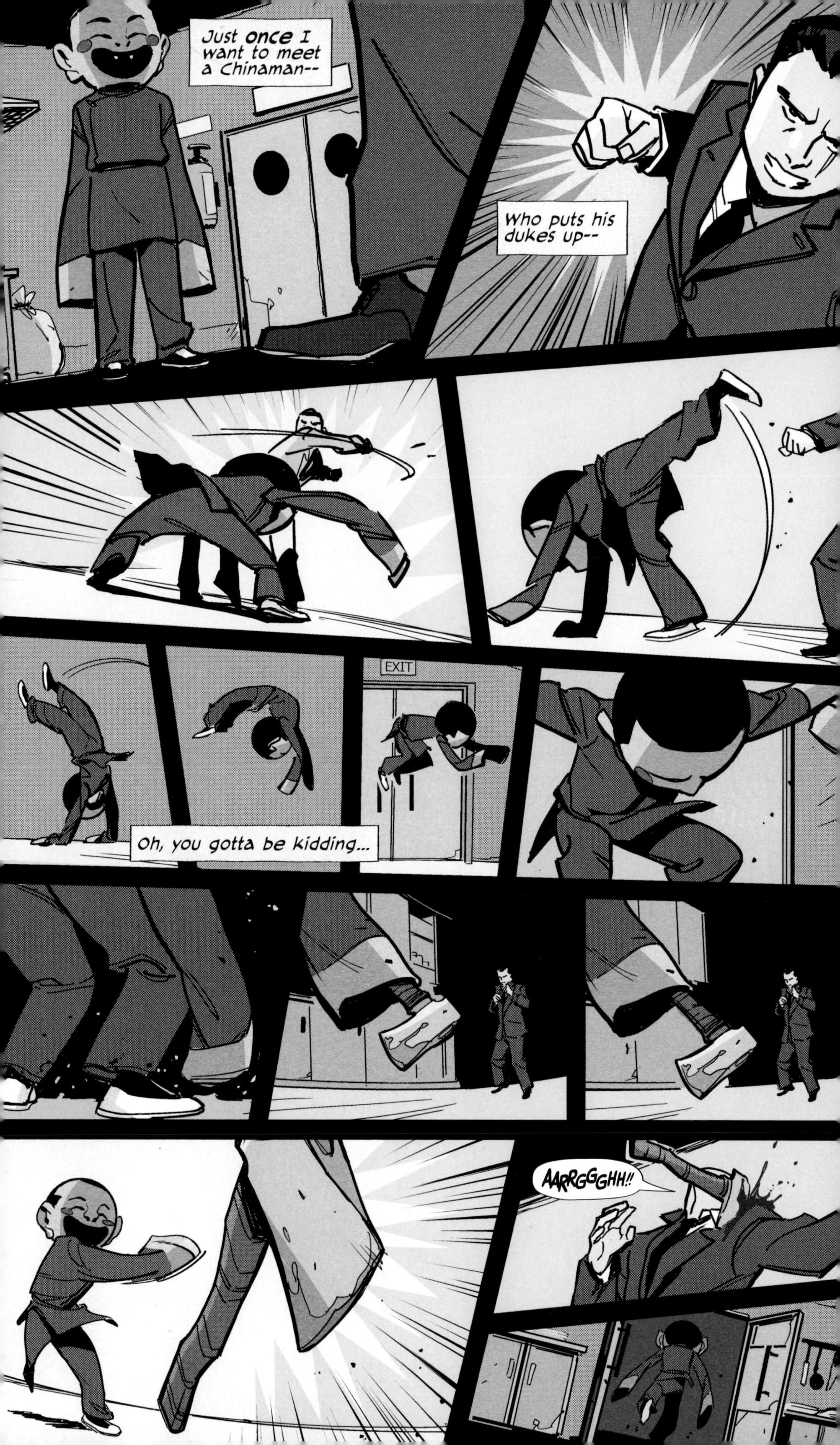
Just once I want to meet a Chinaman--
Who puts his dukes up--
Oh, you gotta be kidding...
AARRGGGHH!!

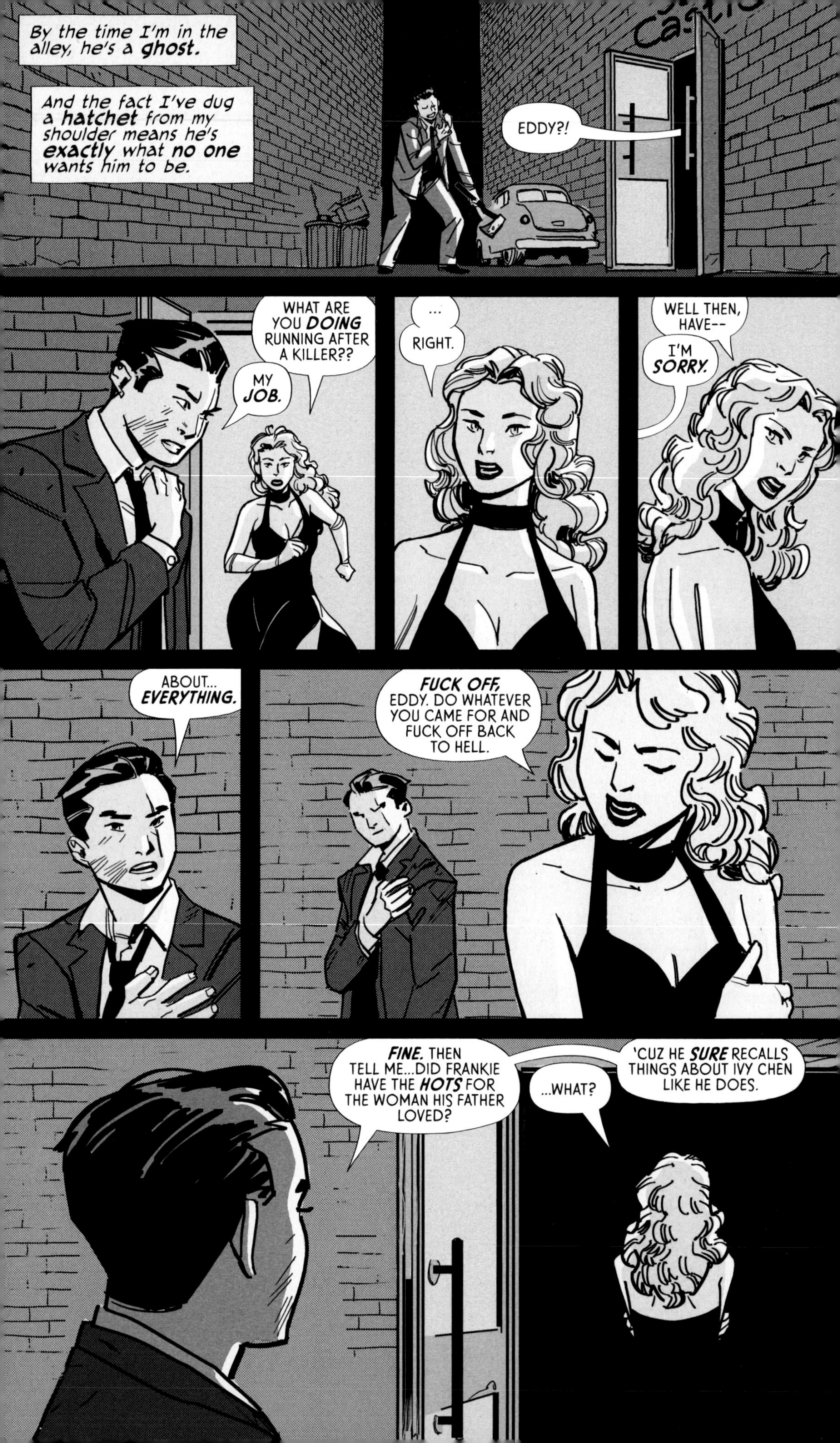
By the time I'm in the alley, he's a ghost.
And the fact I've dug a hatchet from my shoulder means he's exactly what no one wants him to be.
EDDY?!
WHAT ARE YOU DOING RUNNING AFTER A KILLER??
MY JOB.
...
RIGHT.
WELL THEN, HAVE--
I'M SORRY.
ABOUT... EVERYTHING.
FUCK OFF, EDDY. DO WHATEVER YOU CAME FOR AND FUCK OFF BACK TO HELL.
FINE. THEN TELL ME...DID FRANKIE HAVE THE HOTS FOR THE WOMAN HIS FATHER LOVED?
...WHAT?
'CUZ HE SURE RECALLS THINGS ABOUT IVY CHEN LIKE HE DOES.

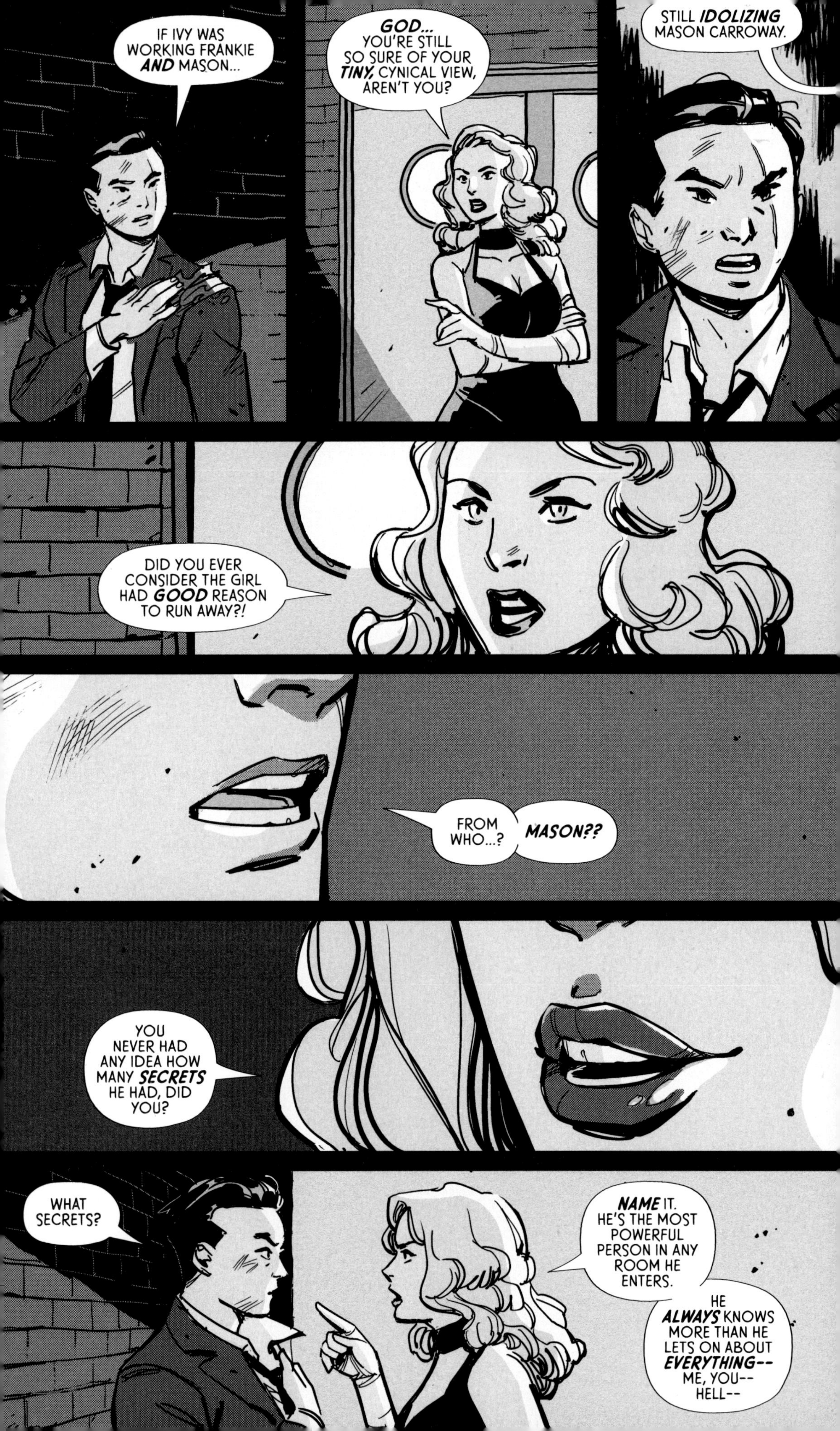
IF IVY WAS WORKING FRANKIE AND MASON...
GOD... YOU'RE STILL SO SURE OF YOUR TINY, CYNICAL VIEW, AREN'T YOU?
STILL IDOLIZING MASON CARROWAY.
DID YOU EVER CONSIDER THE GIRL HAD GOOD REASON TO RUN AWAY?!
FROM WHO...?
MASON??
YOU NEVER HAD ANY IDEA HOW MANY SECRETS HE HAD, DID YOU?
WHAT SECRETS?
NAME IT. HE'S THE MOST POWERFUL PERSON IN ANY ROOM HE ENTERS.
HE ALWAYS KNOWS MORE THAN HE LETS ON ABOUT EVERYTHING-- ME, YOU-- HELL--

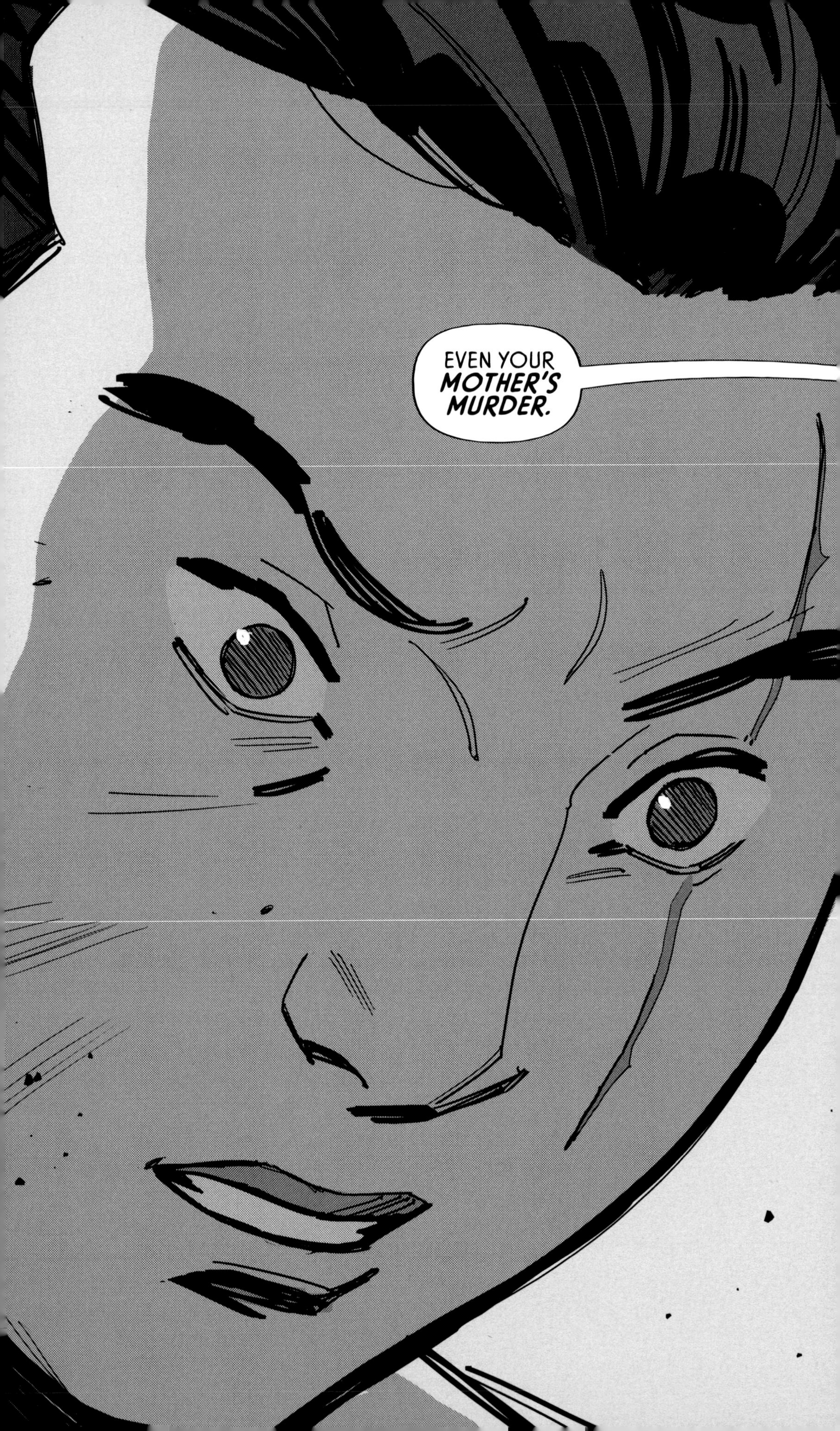
EVEN YOUR *MOTHER'S MURDER.*

CHAPTER THREE

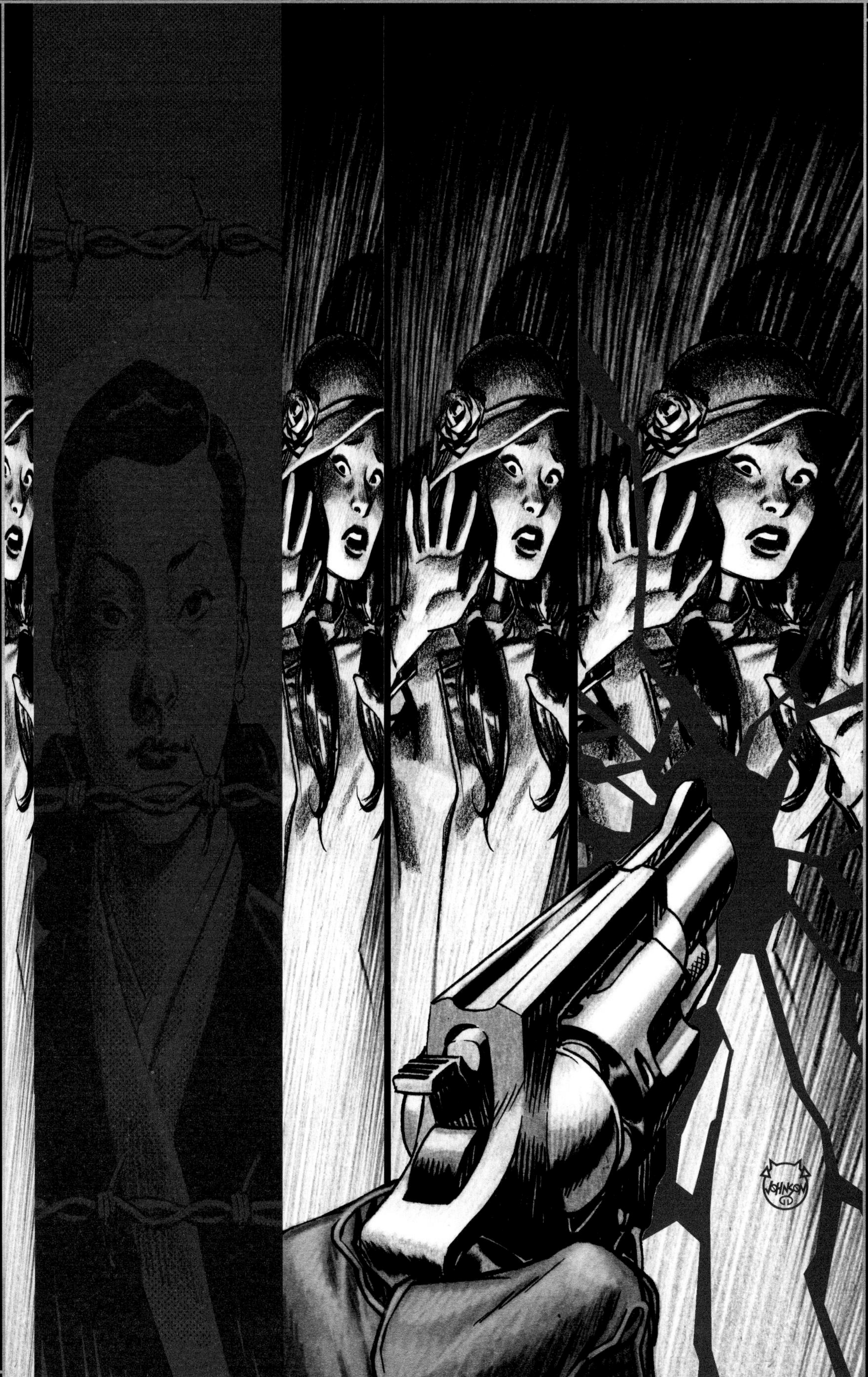
JOHNSON

ART BY **DAVE JOHNSON**

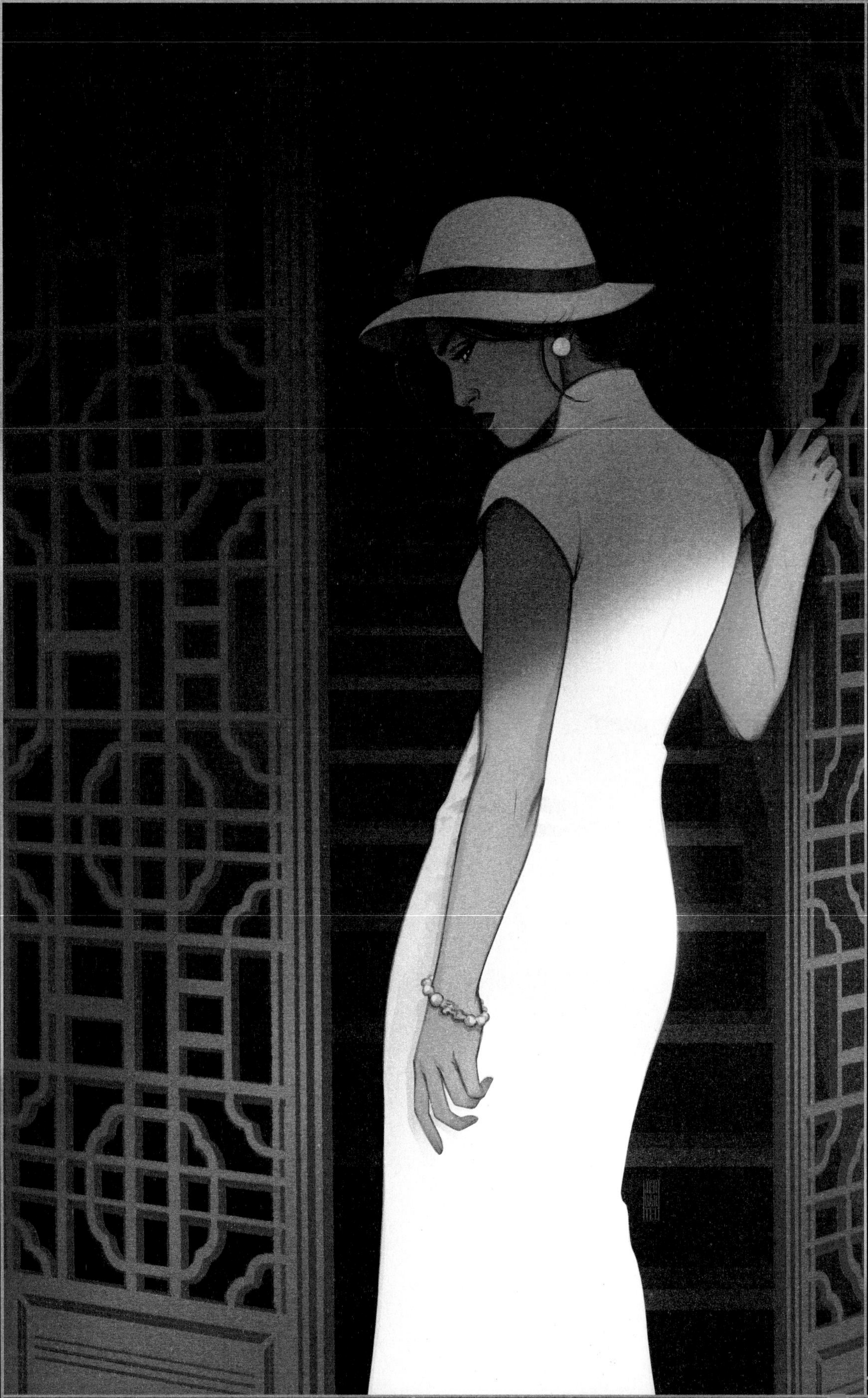

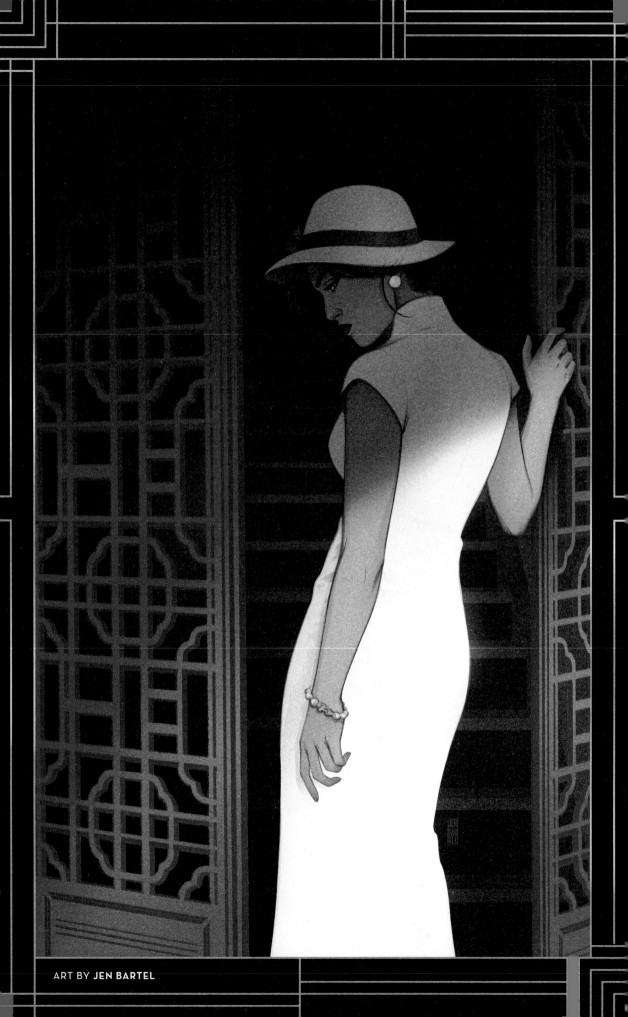

ART BY **JEN BARTEL**

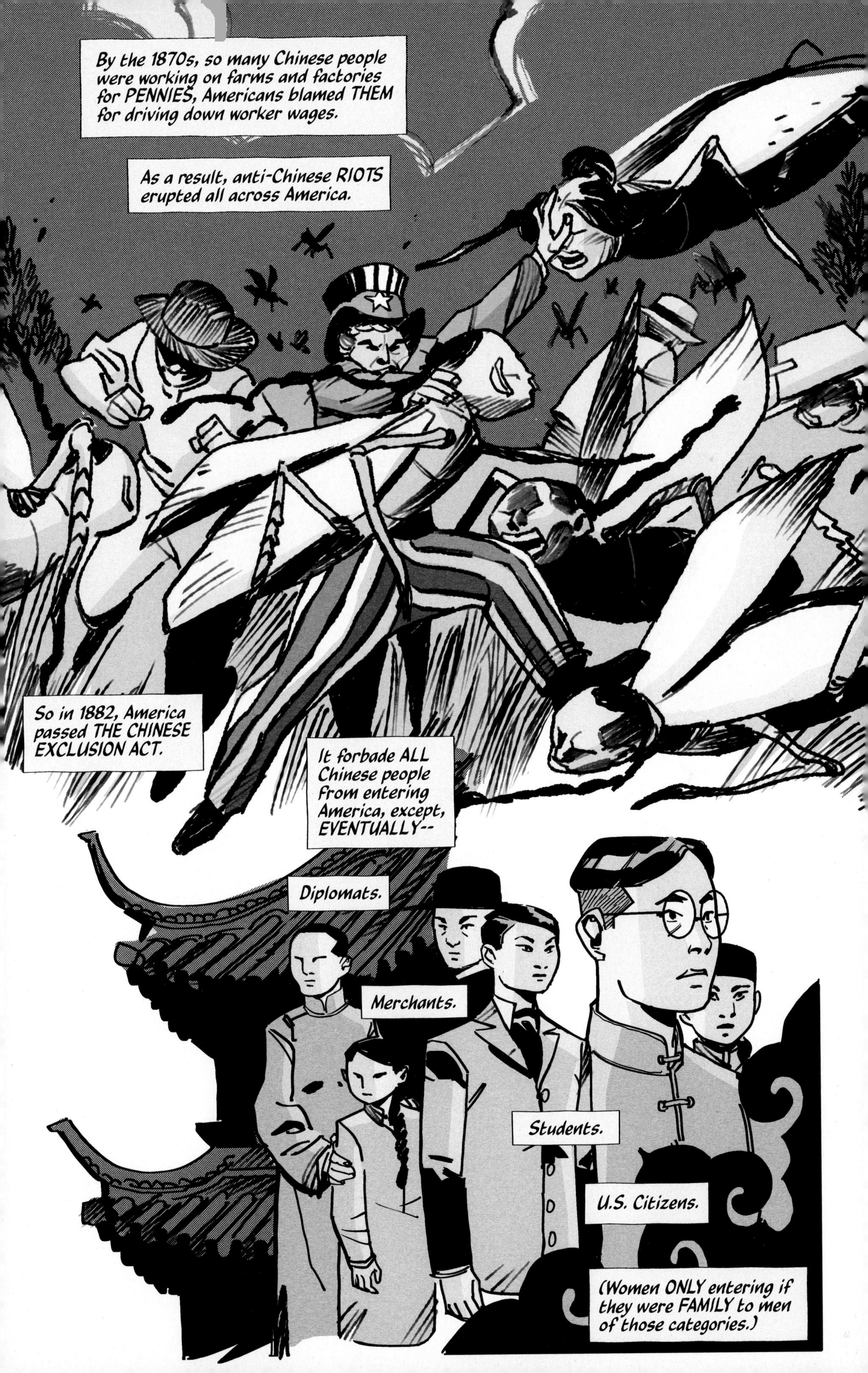

By the 1870s, so many Chinese people were working on farms and factories for PENNIES, Americans blamed THEM for driving down worker wages.
As a result, anti-Chinese RIOTS erupted all across America.
So in 1882, America passed THE CHINESE EXCLUSION ACT.
It forbade ALL Chinese people from entering America, except, EVENTUALLY--
Diplomats.
Merchants.
Students.
U.S. Citizens.
(Women ONLY entering if they were FAMILY to men of those categories.)

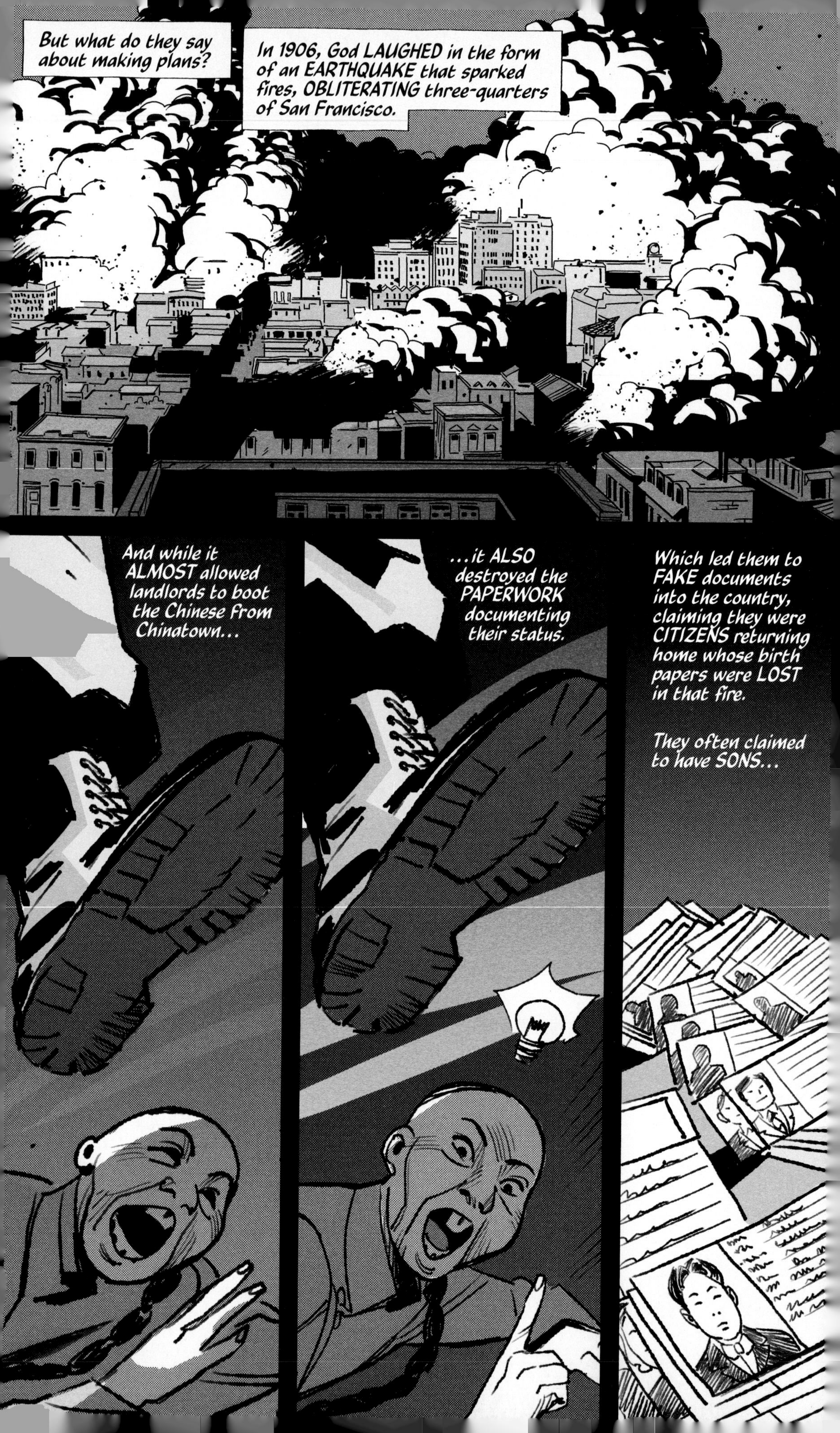
But what do they say about making plans?
In 1906, God LAUGHED in the form of an EARTHQUAKE that sparked fires, OBLITERATING three-quarters of San Francisco.
And while it ALMOST allowed landlords to boot the Chinese from Chinatown...
...it ALSO destroyed the PAPERWORK documenting their status.
Which led them to FAKE documents into the country, claiming they were CITIZENS returning home whose birth papers were LOST in that fire.
They often claimed to have SONS...

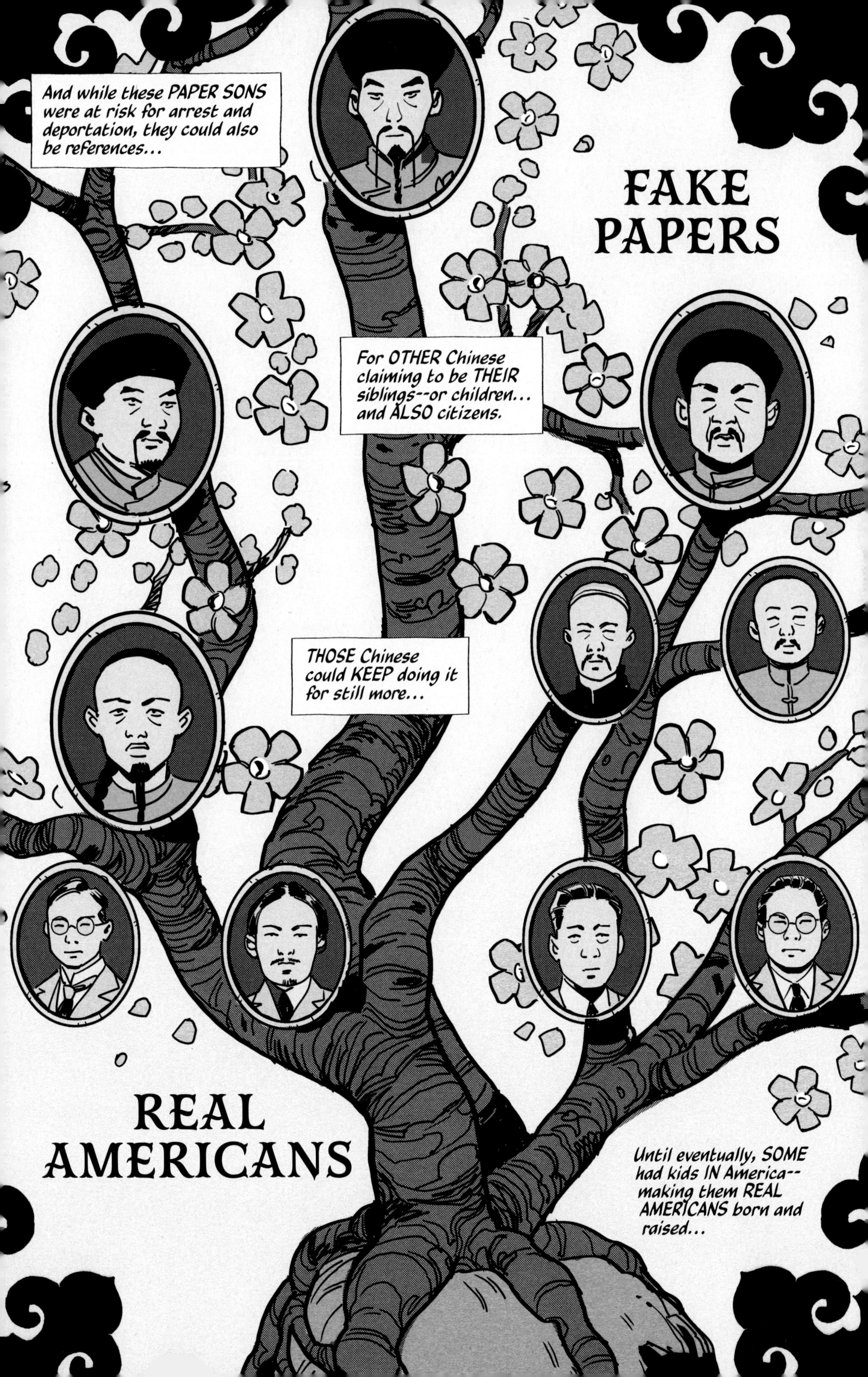

And while these PAPER SONS were at risk for arrest and deportation, they could also be references...
FAKE PAPERS
For OTHER Chinese claiming to be THEIR siblings--or children... and ALSO citizens.
THOSE Chinese could KEEP doing it for still more...
REAL AMERICANS
Until eventually, SOME had kids IN America--making them REAL AMERICANS born and raised...

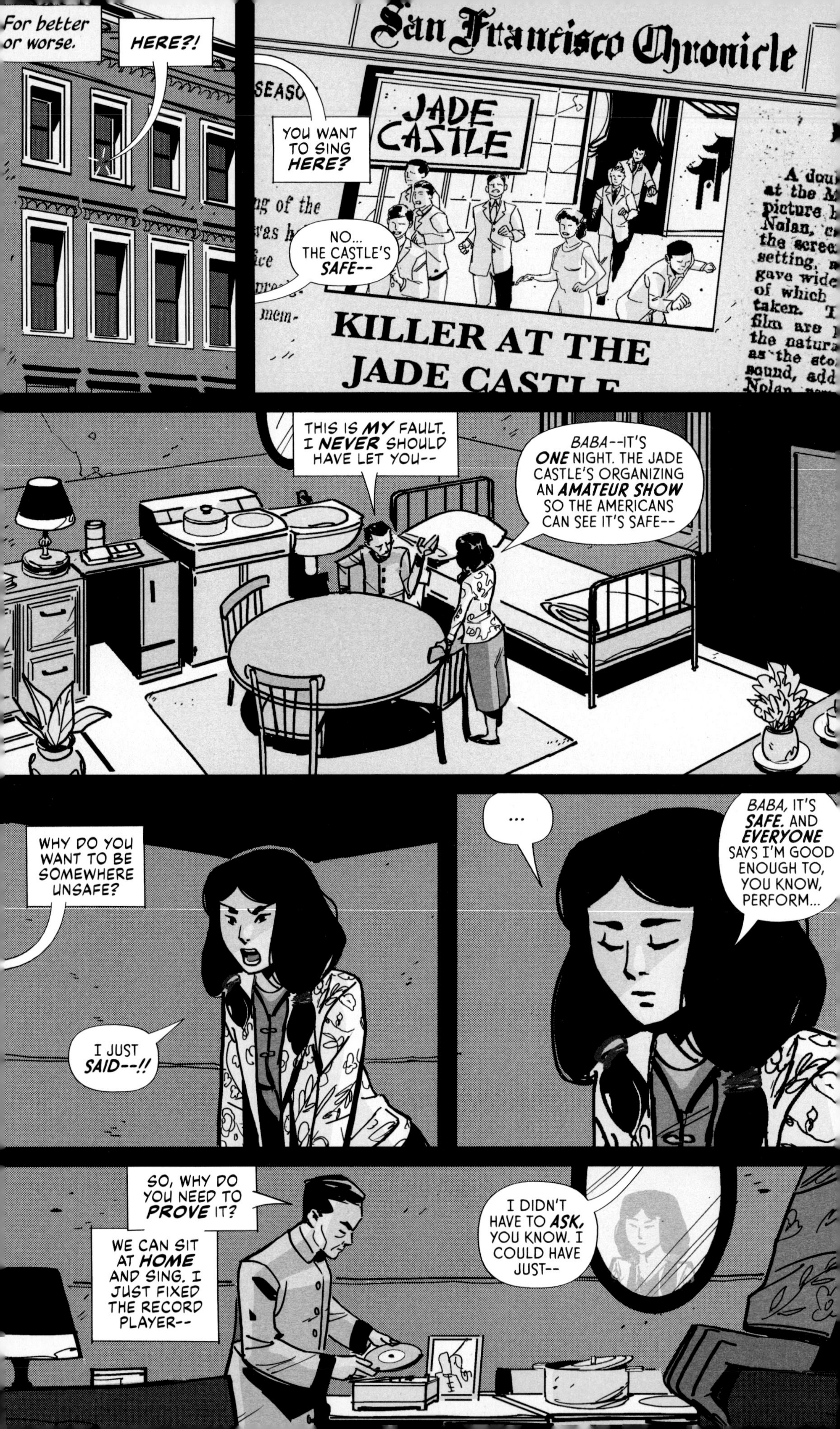

For better or worse.
HERE?!
San Francisco Chronicle
YOU WANT TO SING HERE?
JADE CASTLE
NO... THE CASTLE'S SAFE--
KILLER AT THE JADE CASTLE
THIS IS MY FAULT. I NEVER SHOULD HAVE LET YOU--
BABA--IT'S ONE NIGHT. THE JADE CASTLE'S ORGANIZING AN AMATEUR SHOW SO THE AMERICANS CAN SEE IT'S SAFE--
WHY DO YOU WANT TO BE SOMEWHERE UNSAFE?
I JUST SAID--!!
...
BABA, IT'S SAFE. AND EVERYONE SAYS I'M GOOD ENOUGH TO, YOU KNOW, PERFORM...
SO, WHY DO YOU NEED TO PROVE IT?
WE CAN SIT AT HOME AND SING. I JUST FIXED THE RECORD PLAYER--
I DIDN'T HAVE TO ASK, YOU KNOW. I COULD HAVE JUST--

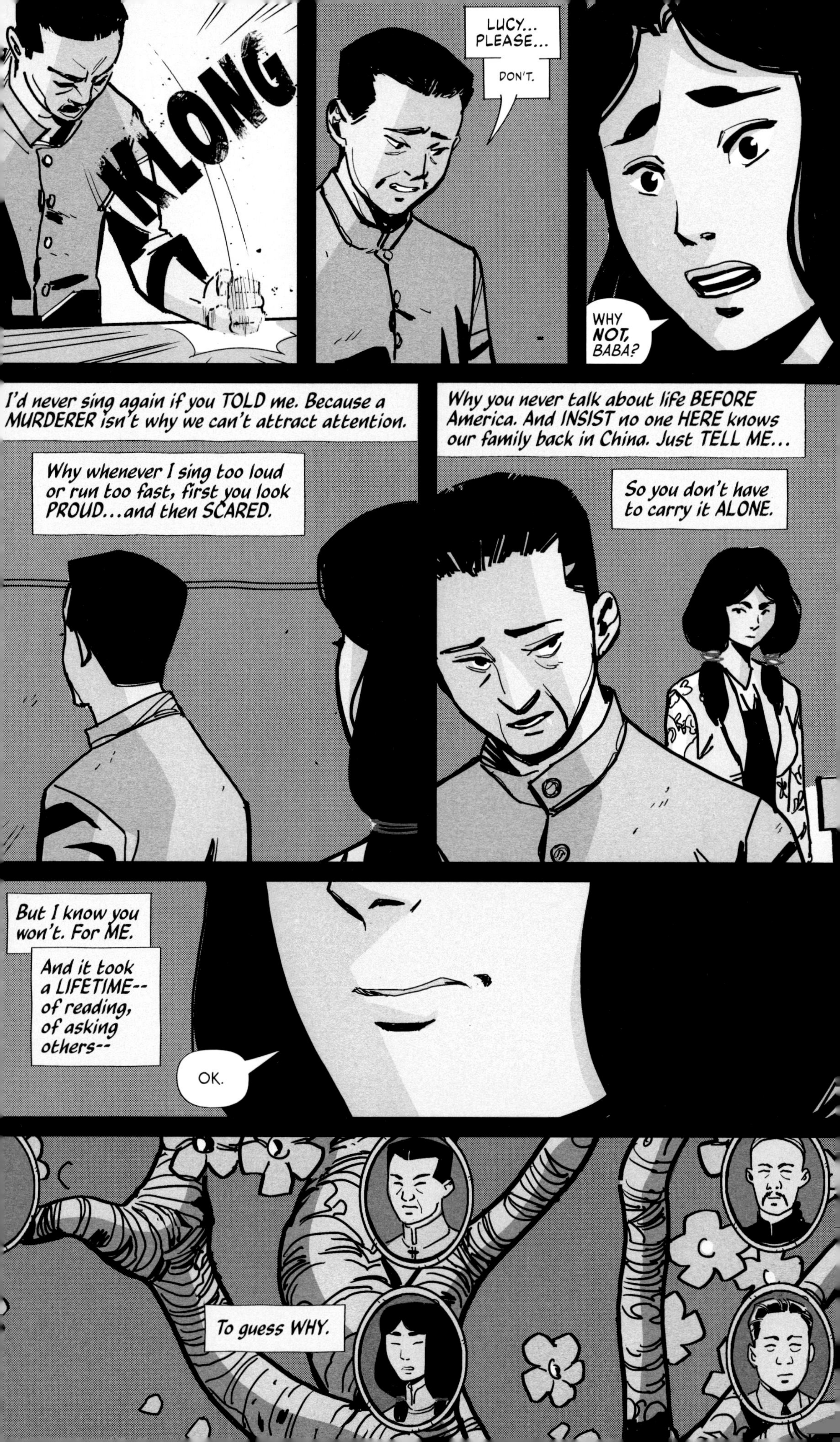
KLONG
LUCY... PLEASE...
DON'T.
WHY NOT, BABA?
I'd never sing again if you TOLD me. Because a MURDERER isn't why we can't attract attention.
Why whenever I sing too loud or run too fast, first you look PROUD...and then SCARED.
Why you never talk about life BEFORE America. And INSIST no one HERE knows our family back in China. Just TELL ME...
So you don't have to carry it ALONE.
But I know you won't. For ME.
And it took a LIFETIME-- of reading, of asking others--
OK.
To guess WHY.

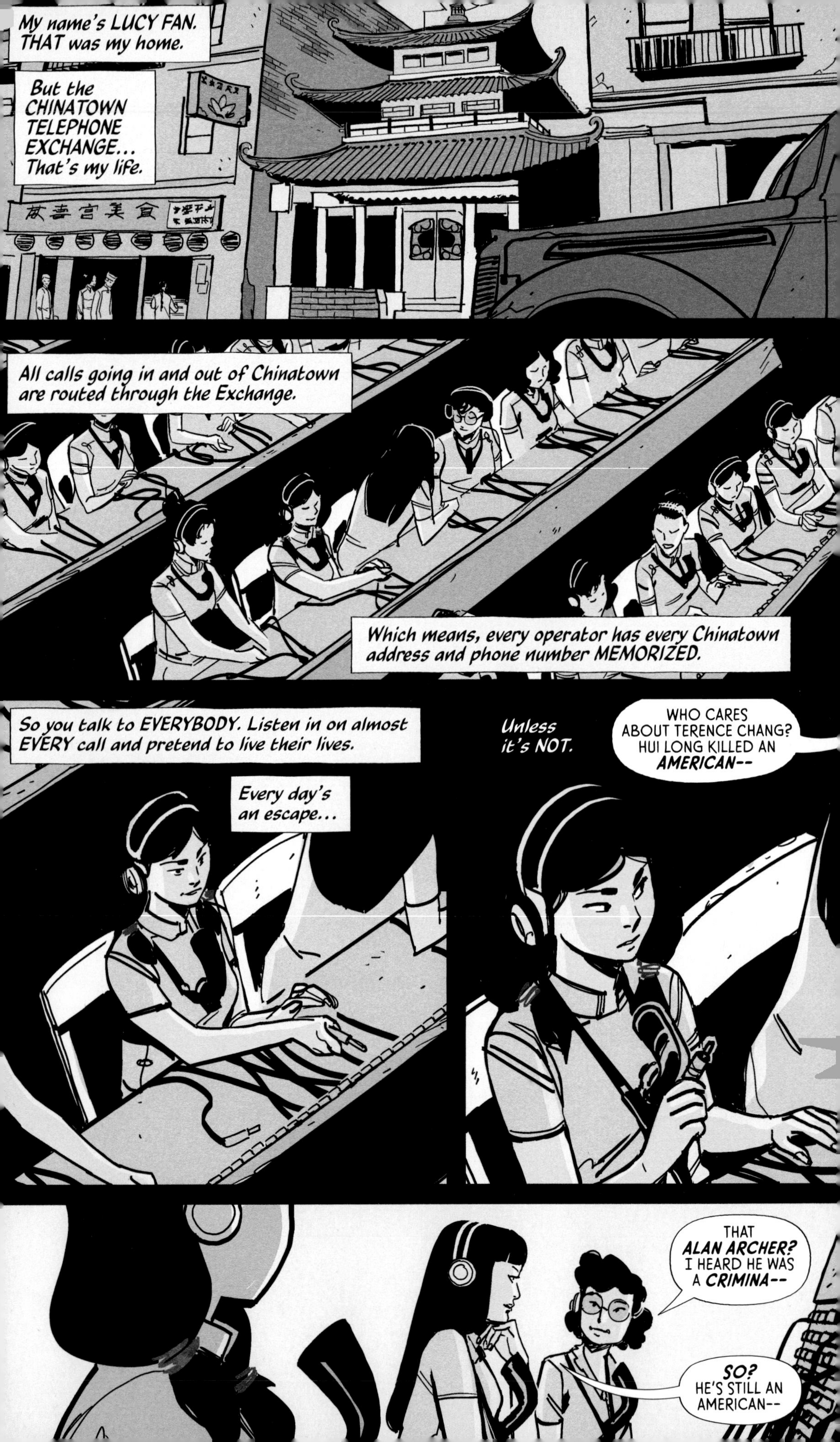
My name's LUCY FAN. THAT was my home.
But the CHINATOWN TELEPHONE EXCHANGE... That's my life.
All calls going in and out of Chinatown are routed through the Exchange.
Which means, every operator has every Chinatown address and phone number MEMORIZED.
So you talk to EVERYBODY. Listen in on almost EVERY call and pretend to live their lives.
Every day's an escape...
Unless it's NOT.
WHO CARES ABOUT TERENCE CHANG? HUI LONG KILLED AN AMERICAN--
THAT ALAN ARCHER? I HEARD HE WAS A CRIMINA--
SO? HE'S STILL AN AMERICAN--

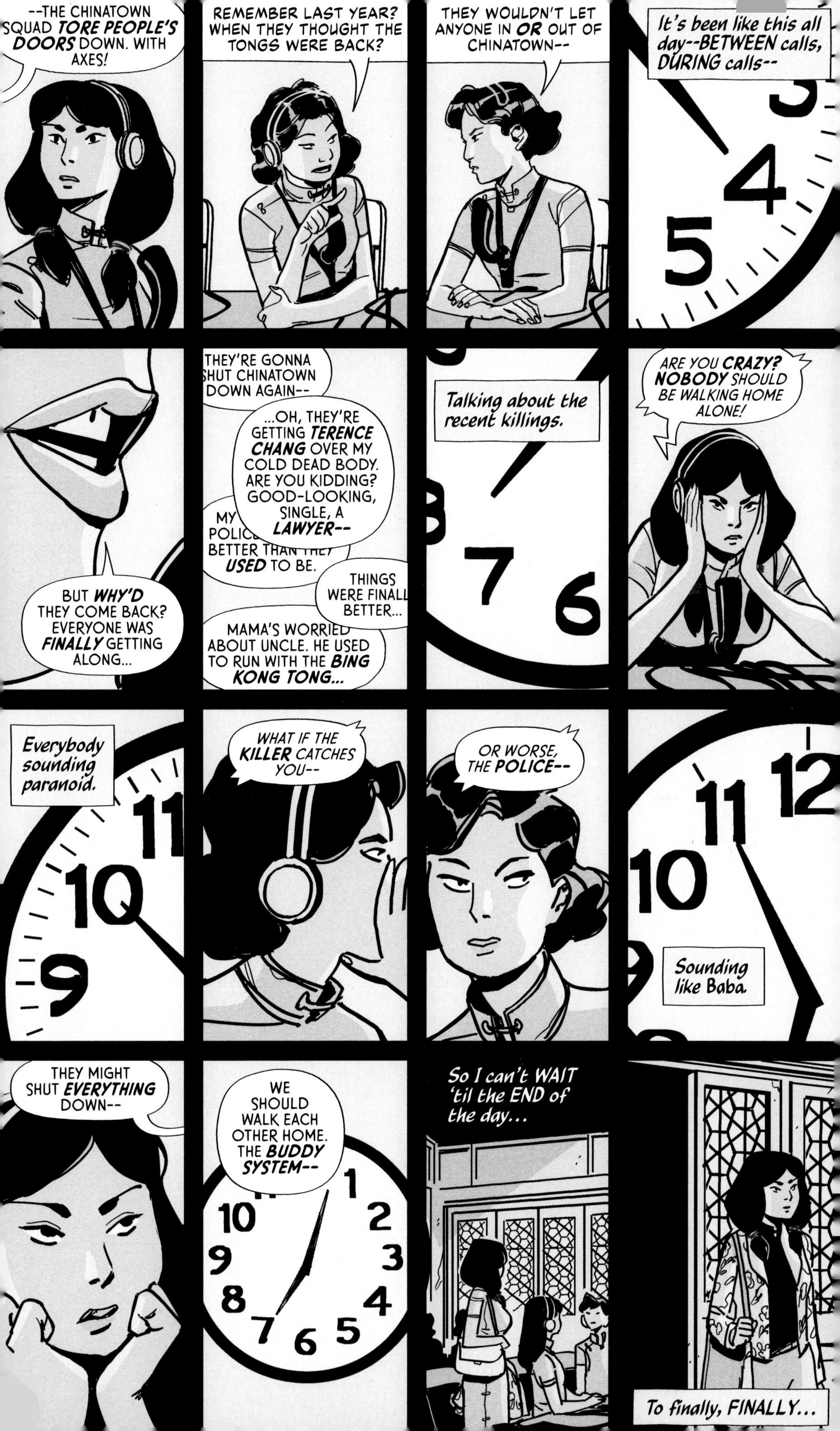
--THE CHINATOWN SQUAD TORE PEOPLE'S DOORS DOWN. WITH AXES!
REMEMBER LAST YEAR? WHEN THEY THOUGHT THE TONGS WERE BACK?
THEY WOULDN'T LET ANYONE IN OR OUT OF CHINATOWN--
It's been like this all day--BETWEEN calls, DURING calls--
BUT WHY'D THEY COME BACK? EVERYONE WAS FINALLY GETTING ALONG...
THEY'RE GONNA SHUT CHINATOWN DOWN AGAIN--
...OH, THEY'RE GETTING TERENCE CHANG OVER MY COLD DEAD BODY. ARE YOU KIDDING? GOOD-LOOKING, SINGLE, A LAWYER--
BETTER THAN THEY USED TO BE.
THINGS WERE FINALL BETTER...
MAMA'S WORRIED ABOUT UNCLE. HE USED TO RUN WITH THE BING KONG TONG...
Talking about the recent killings.
ARE YOU CRAZY? NOBODY SHOULD BE WALKING HOME ALONE!
Everybody sounding paranoid.
WHAT IF THE KILLER CATCHES YOU--
OR WORSE, THE POLICE--
Sounding like Baba.
THEY MIGHT SHUT EVERYTHING DOWN--
WE SHOULD WALK EACH OTHER HOME. THE BUDDY SYSTEM--
So I can't WAIT 'til the END of the day...
To finally, FINALLY...

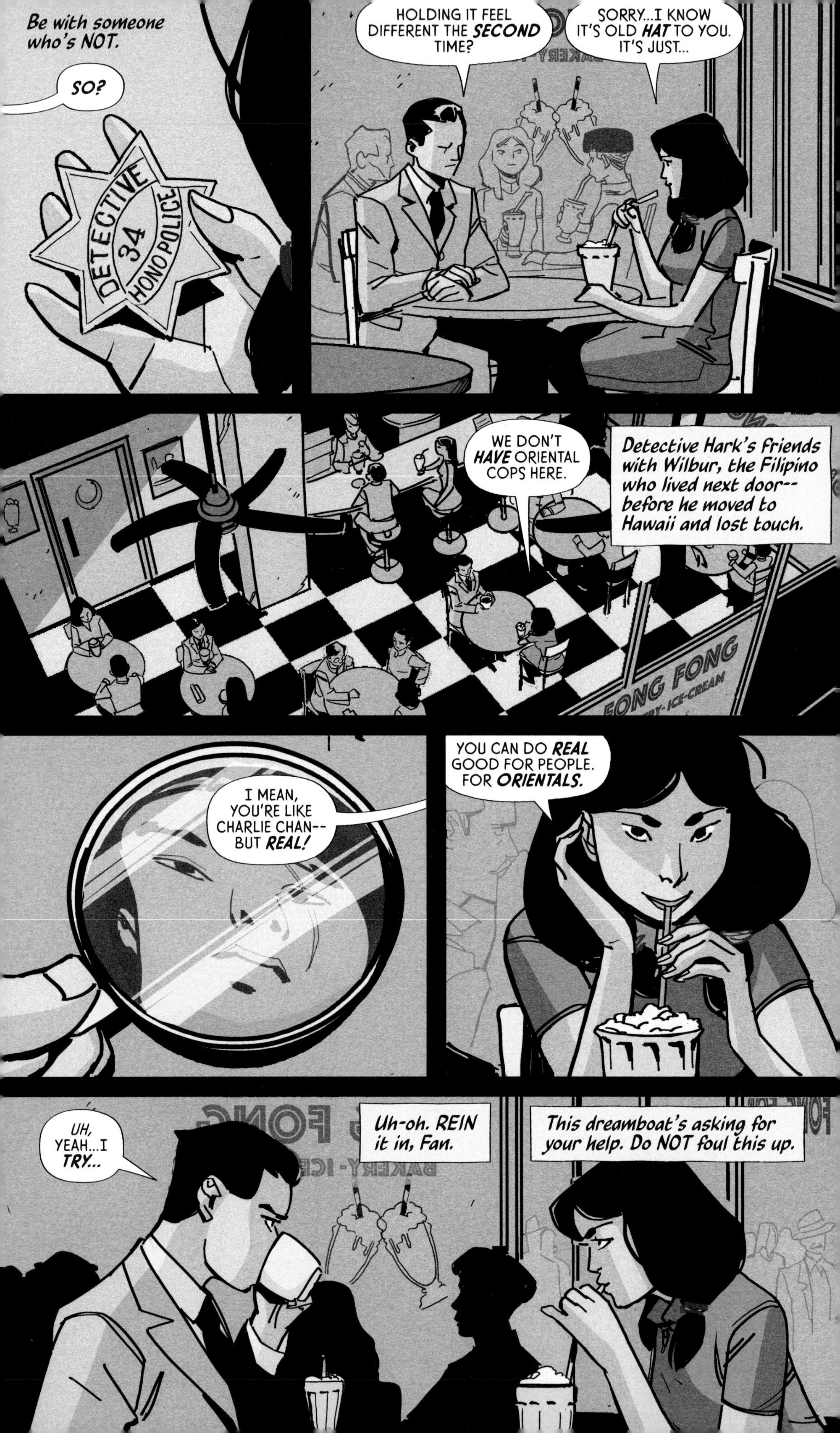
Be with someone who's NOT.
SO?
DETECTIVE 34 HONO POLICE
HOLDING IT FEEL DIFFERENT THE SECOND TIME?
SORRY...I KNOW IT'S OLD HAT TO YOU. IT'S JUST...
WE DON'T HAVE ORIENTAL COPS HERE.
Detective Hark's friends with Wilbur, the Filipino who lived next door-- before he moved to Hawaii and lost touch.
FONG FONG
I MEAN, YOU'RE LIKE CHARLIE CHAN-- BUT REAL!
YOU CAN DO REAL GOOD FOR PEOPLE. FOR ORIENTALS.
UH, YEAH...I TRY...
Uh-oh. REIN it in, Fan.
This dreamboat's asking for your help. Do NOT foul this up.

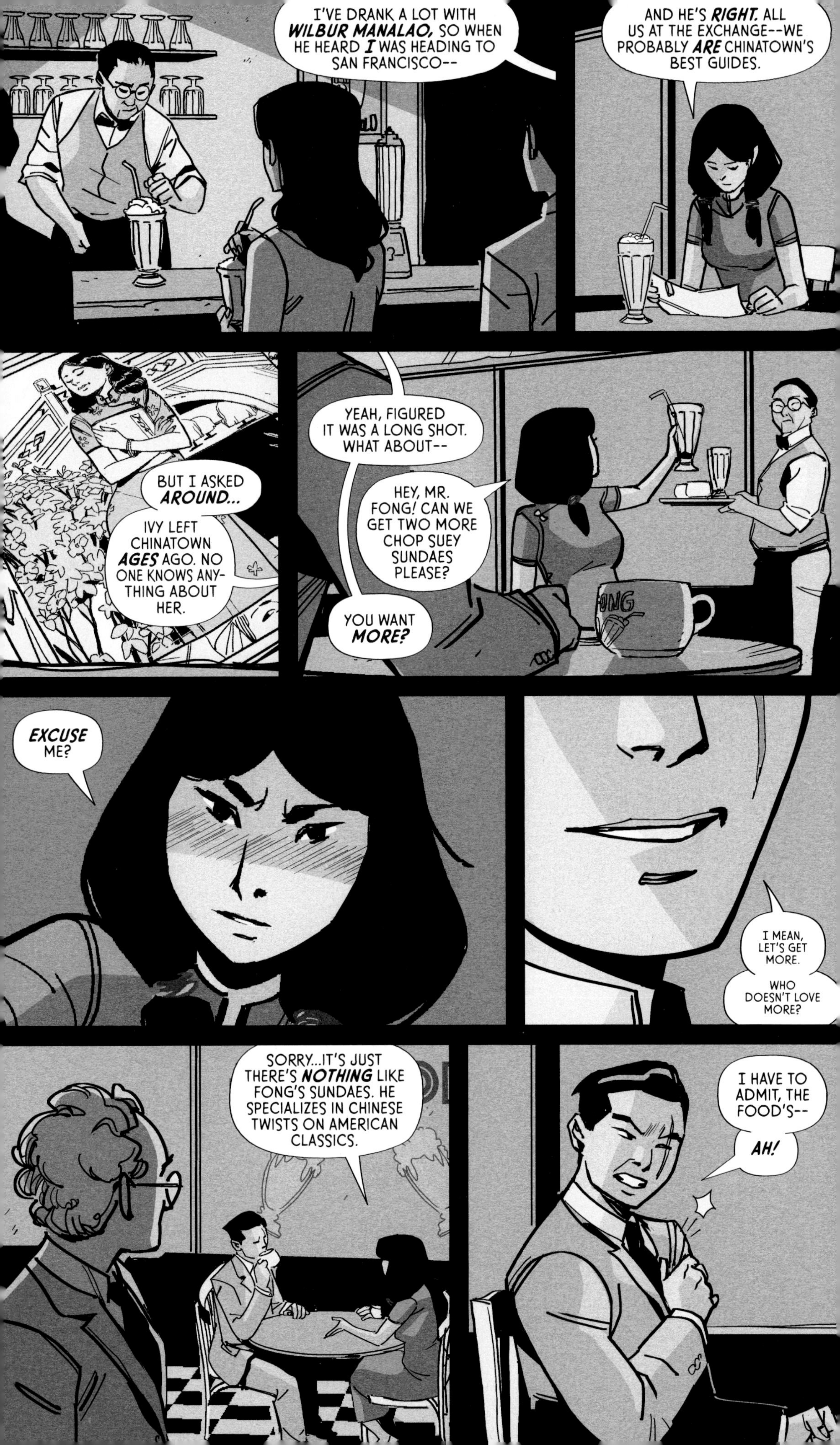
I'VE DRANK A LOT WITH WILBUR MANALAO, SO WHEN HE HEARD I WAS HEADING TO SAN FRANCISCO--
AND HE'S RIGHT. ALL US AT THE EXCHANGE--WE PROBABLY ARE CHINATOWN'S BEST GUIDES.
BUT I ASKED AROUND...
IVY LEFT CHINATOWN AGES AGO. NO ONE KNOWS ANYTHING ABOUT HER.
YEAH, FIGURED IT WAS A LONG SHOT. WHAT ABOUT--
HEY, MR. FONG! CAN WE GET TWO MORE CHOP SUEY SUNDAES PLEASE?
YOU WANT MORE?
FONG
EXCUSE ME?
I MEAN, LET'S GET MORE.
WHO DOESN'T LOVE MORE?
SORRY...IT'S JUST THERE'S NOTHING LIKE FONG'S SUNDAES. HE SPECIALIZES IN CHINESE TWISTS ON AMERICAN CLASSICS.
I HAVE TO ADMIT, THE FOOD'S--
AH!

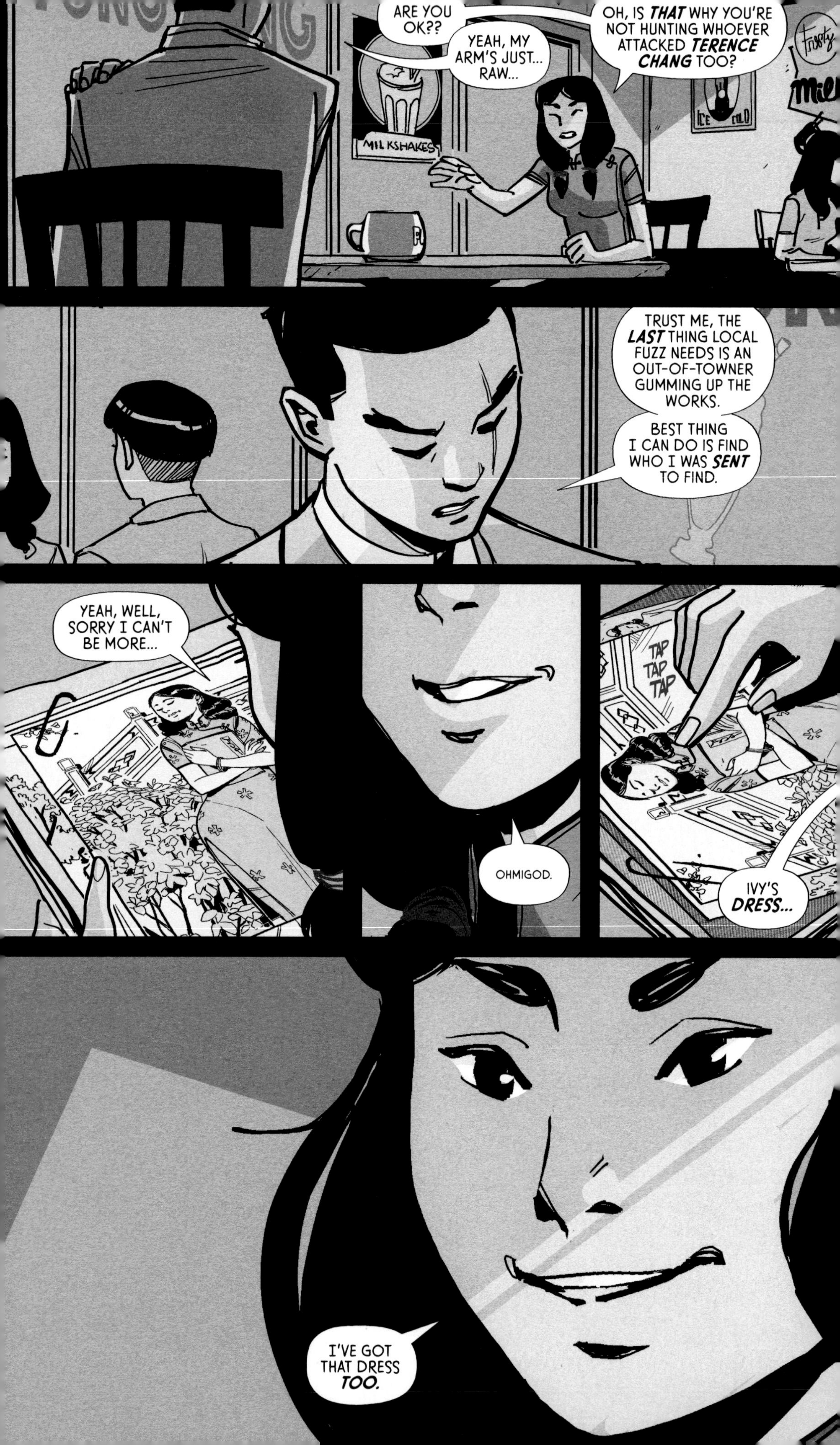
ARE YOU OK??
YEAH, MY ARM'S JUST... RAW...
OH, IS THAT WHY YOU'RE NOT HUNTING WHOEVER ATTACKED TERENCE CHANG TOO?
MILKSHAKES
ICE COLD
TRUST ME, THE LAST THING LOCAL FUZZ NEEDS IS AN OUT-OF-TOWNER GUMMING UP THE WORKS.
BEST THING I CAN DO IS FIND WHO I WAS SENT TO FIND.
YEAH, WELL, SORRY I CAN'T BE MORE...
OHMIGOD.
TAP TAP TAP
IVY'S DRESS...
I'VE GOT THAT DRESS TOO.

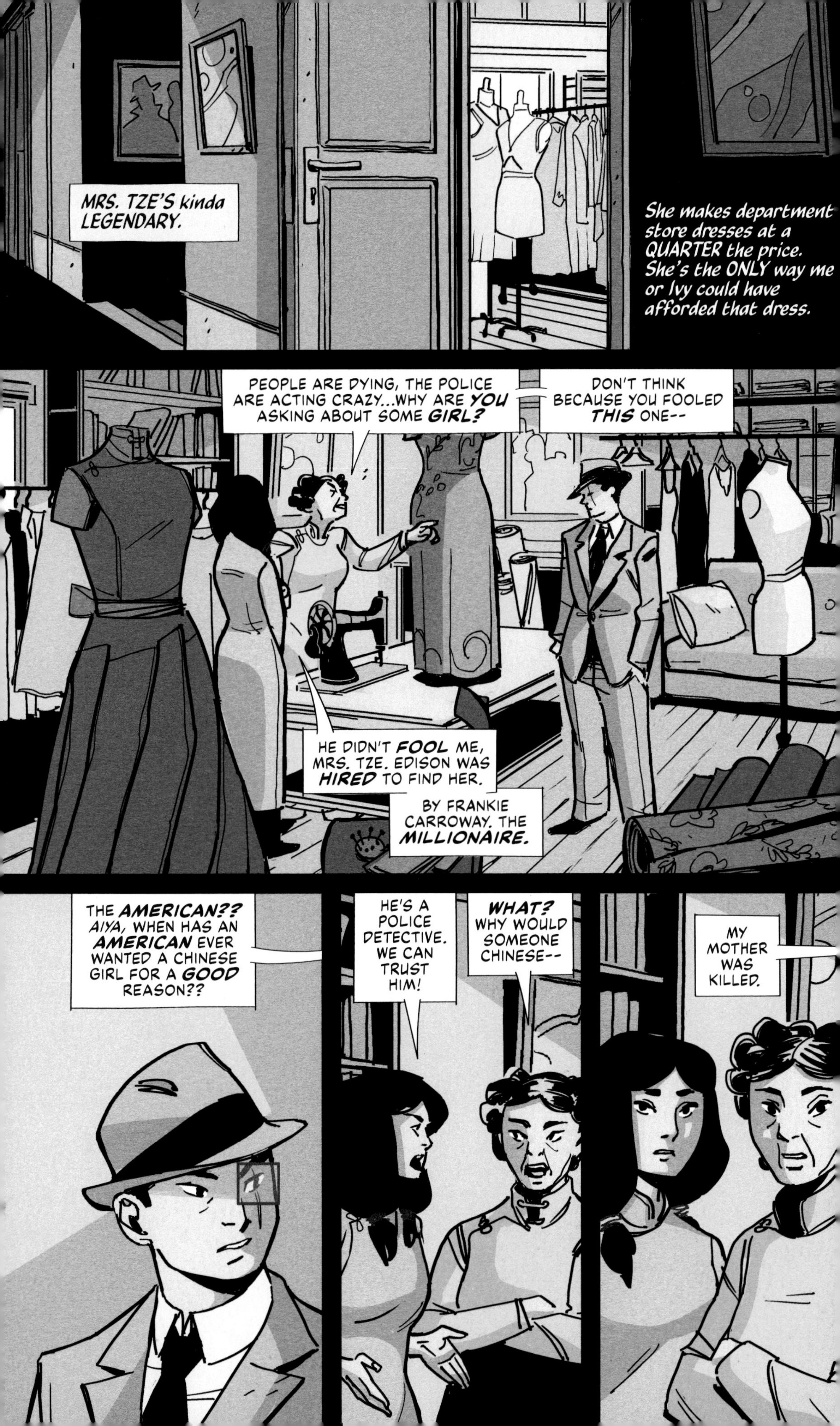

MRS. TZE'S kinda LEGENDARY.
She makes department store dresses at a QUARTER the price. She's the ONLY way me or Ivy could have afforded that dress.
PEOPLE ARE DYING, THE POLICE ARE ACTING CRAZY...WHY ARE YOU ASKING ABOUT SOME GIRL?
DON'T THINK BECAUSE YOU FOOLED THIS ONE--
HE DIDN'T FOOL ME, MRS. TZE. EDISON WAS HIRED TO FIND HER.
BY FRANKIE CARROWAY. THE MILLIONAIRE.
THE AMERICAN?? AIYA, WHEN HAS AN AMERICAN EVER WANTED A CHINESE GIRL FOR A GOOD REASON??
HE'S A POLICE DETECTIVE. WE CAN TRUST HIM!
WHAT? WHY WOULD SOMEONE CHINESE--
MY MOTHER WAS KILLED.

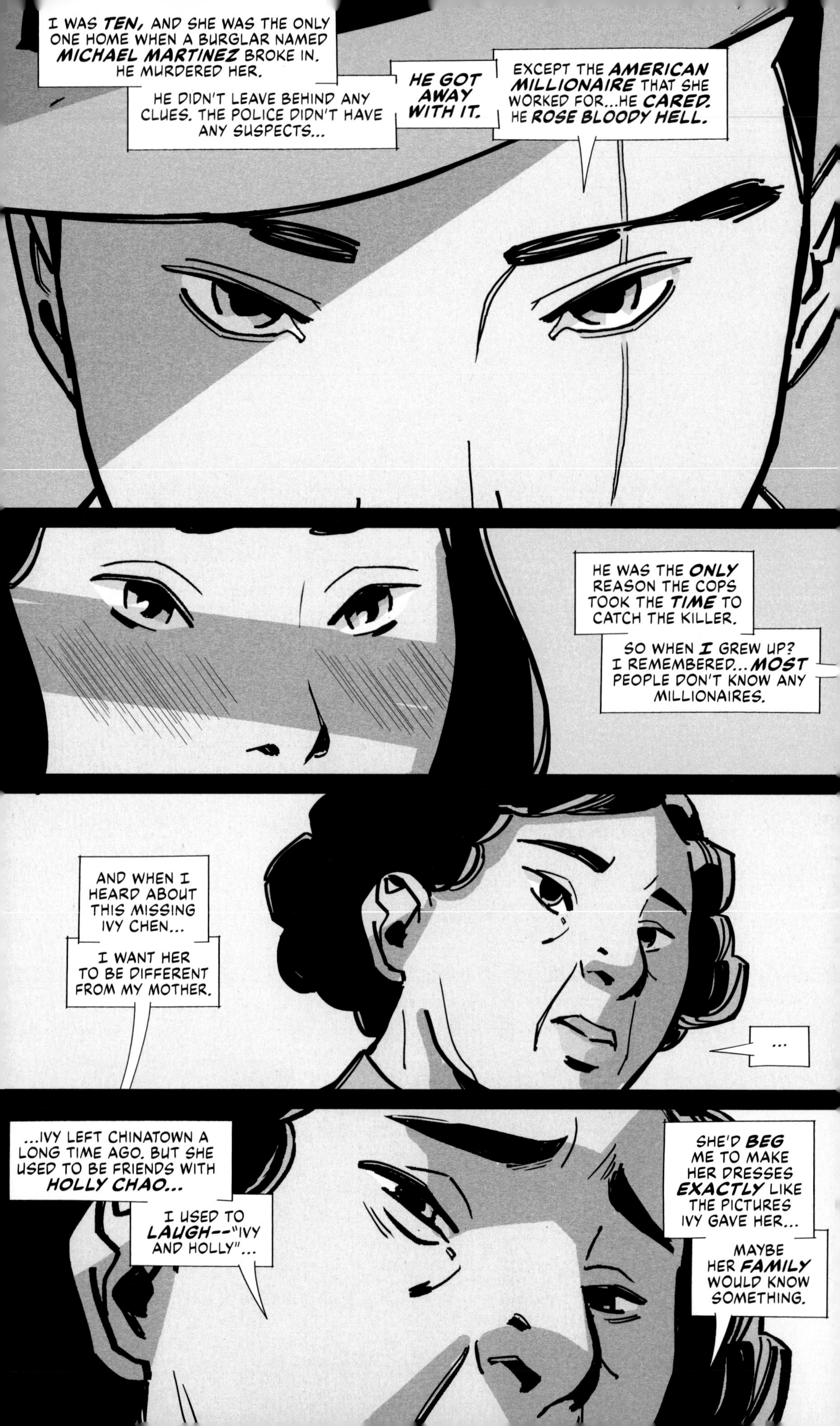
I WAS TEN, AND SHE WAS THE ONLY ONE HOME WHEN A BURGLAR NAMED MICHAEL MARTINEZ BROKE IN. HE MURDERED HER.
HE DIDN'T LEAVE BEHIND ANY CLUES. THE POLICE DIDN'T HAVE ANY SUSPECTS...
HE GOT AWAY WITH IT.
EXCEPT THE AMERICAN MILLIONAIRE THAT SHE WORKED FOR...HE CARED. HE ROSE BLOODY HELL.
HE WAS THE ONLY REASON THE COPS TOOK THE TIME TO CATCH THE KILLER.
SO WHEN I GREW UP? I REMEMBERED...MOST PEOPLE DON'T KNOW ANY MILLIONAIRES.
AND WHEN I HEARD ABOUT THIS MISSING IVY CHEN...
I WANT HER TO BE DIFFERENT FROM MY MOTHER.
...
...IVY LEFT CHINATOWN A LONG TIME AGO. BUT SHE USED TO BE FRIENDS WITH HOLLY CHAO...
I USED TO LAUGH--"IVY AND HOLLY"...
SHE'D BEG ME TO MAKE HER DRESSES EXACTLY LIKE THE PICTURES IVY GAVE HER...
MAYBE HER FAMILY WOULD KNOW SOMETHING.

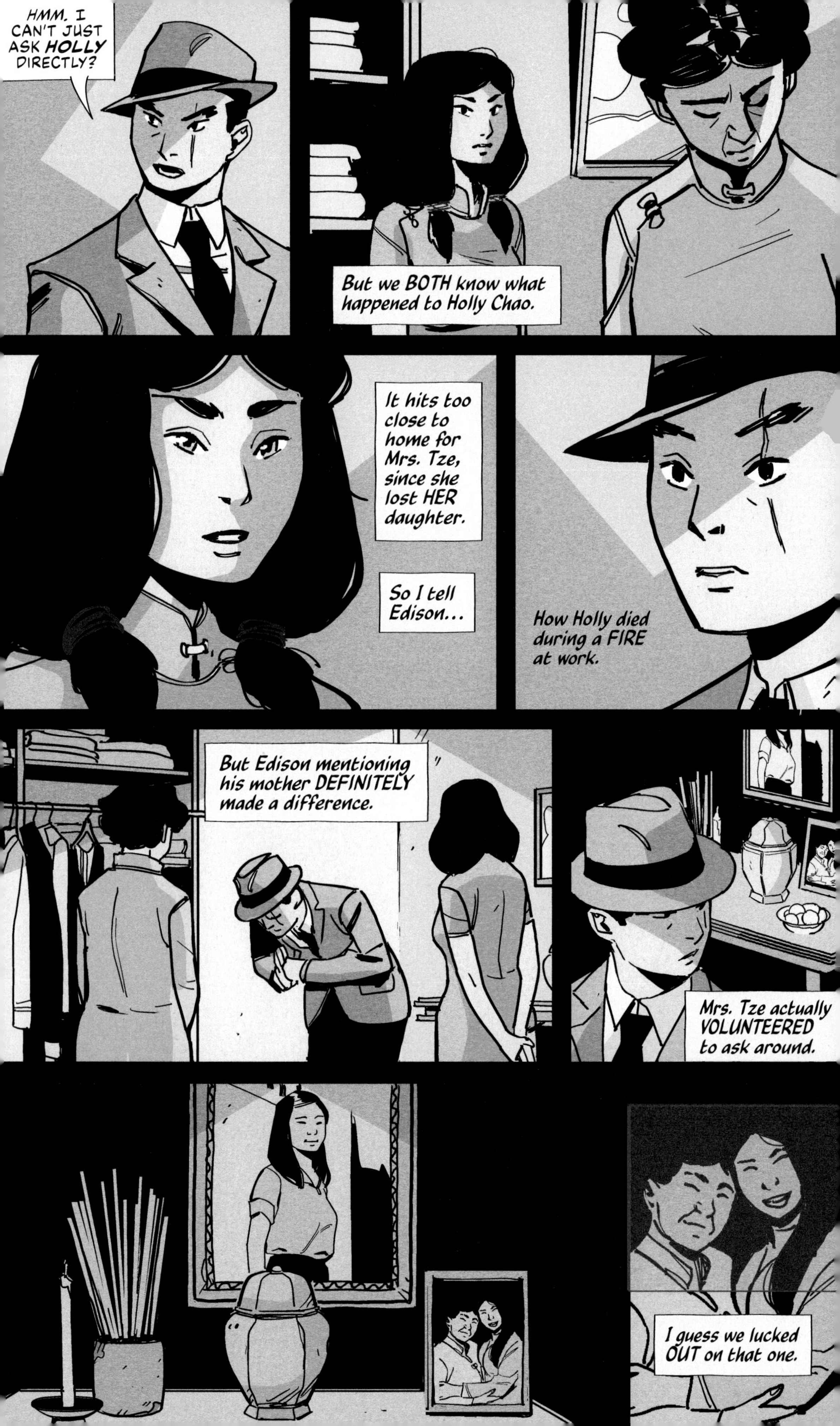
HMM. I CAN'T JUST ASK HOLLY DIRECTLY?
But we BOTH know what happened to Holly Chao.
It hits too close to home for Mrs. Tze, since she lost HER daughter.
So I tell Edison...
How Holly died during a FIRE at work.
But Edison mentioning his mother DEFINITELY made a difference.
Mrs. Tze actually VOLUNTEERED to ask around.
I guess we lucked OUT on that one.

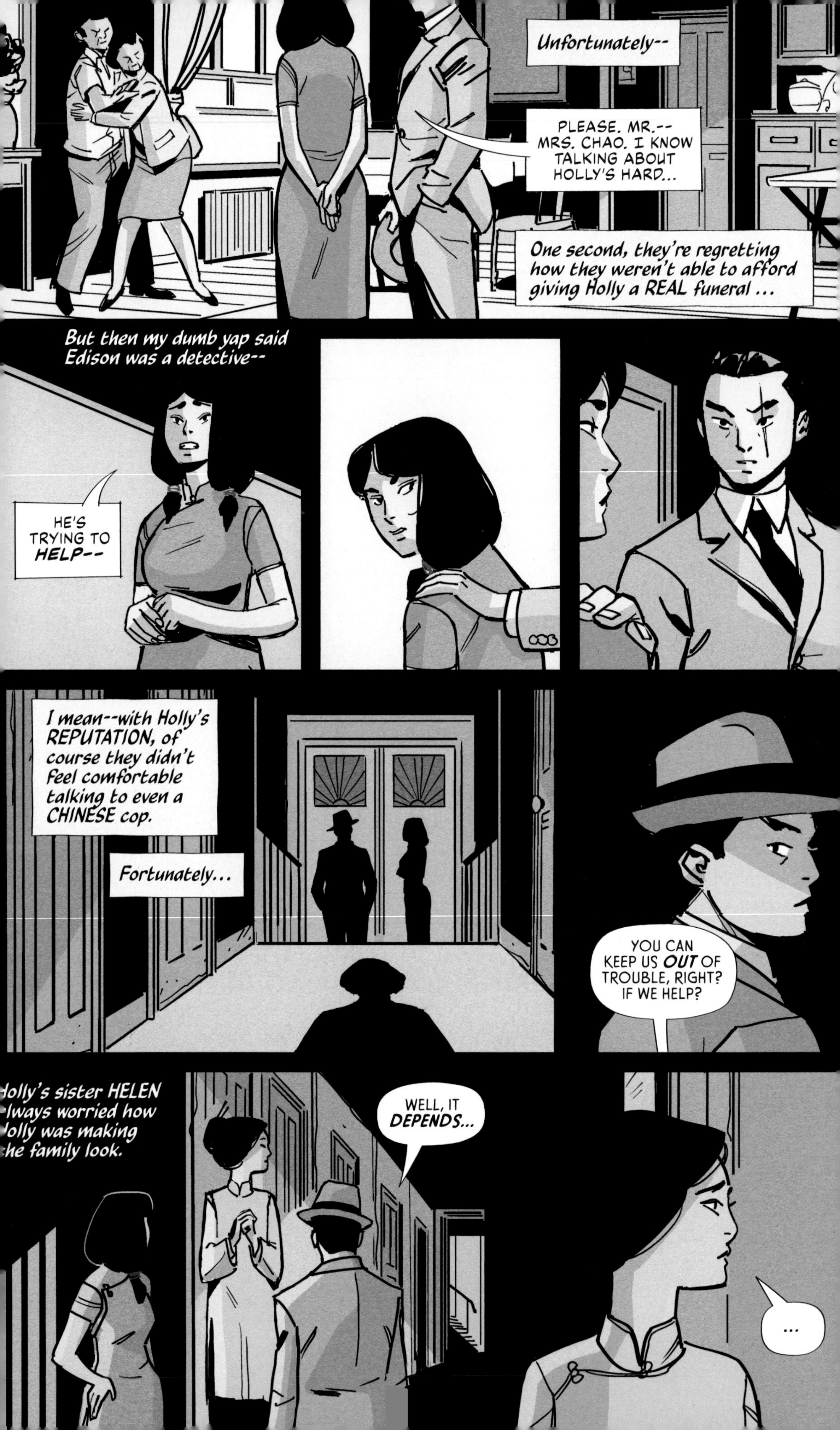
Unfortunately--
PLEASE. MR.-- MRS. CHAO. I KNOW TALKING ABOUT HOLLY'S HARD...
One second, they're regretting how they weren't able to afford giving Holly a REAL funeral...
But then my dumb yap said Edison was a detective--
HE'S TRYING TO HELP--
I mean--with Holly's REPUTATION, of course they didn't feel comfortable talking to even a CHINESE cop.
Fortunately...
YOU CAN KEEP US OUT OF TROUBLE, RIGHT? IF WE HELP?
olly's sister HELEN lways worried how olly was making he family look.
WELL, IT DEPENDS...
...

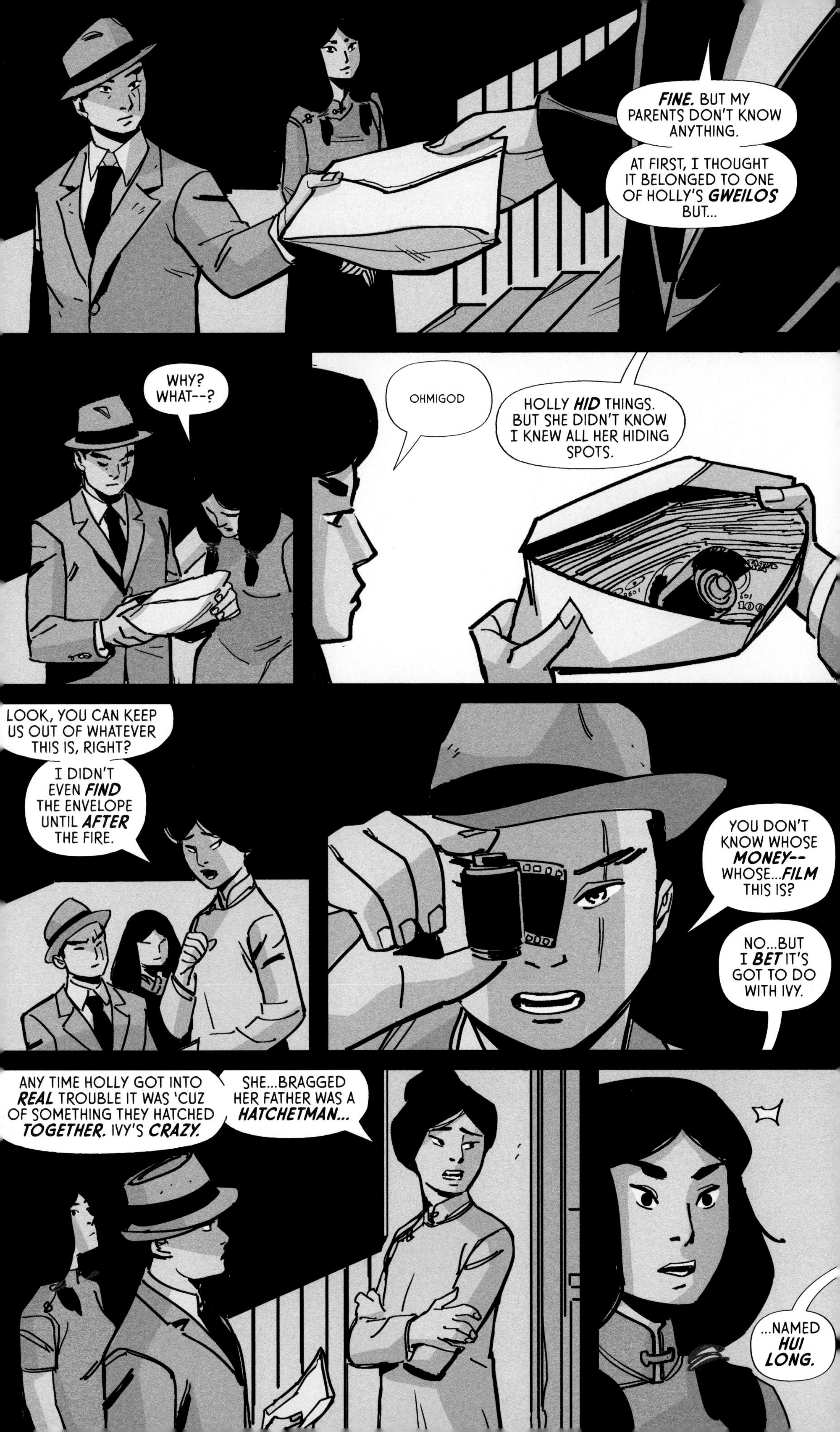
FINE. BUT MY PARENTS DON'T KNOW ANYTHING.
AT FIRST, I THOUGHT IT BELONGED TO ONE OF HOLLY'S GWEILOS BUT...
WHY? WHAT--?
OHMIGOD
HOLLY HID THINGS. BUT SHE DIDN'T KNOW I KNEW ALL HER HIDING SPOTS.
LOOK, YOU CAN KEEP US OUT OF WHATEVER THIS IS, RIGHT?
I DIDN'T EVEN FIND THE ENVELOPE UNTIL AFTER THE FIRE.
YOU DON'T KNOW WHOSE MONEY-- WHOSE...FILM THIS IS?
NO...BUT I BET IT'S GOT TO DO WITH IVY.
ANY TIME HOLLY GOT INTO REAL TROUBLE IT WAS 'CUZ OF SOMETHING THEY HATCHED TOGETHER. IVY'S CRAZY.
SHE...BRAGGED HER FATHER WAS A HATCHETMAN...
...NAMED HUI LONG.

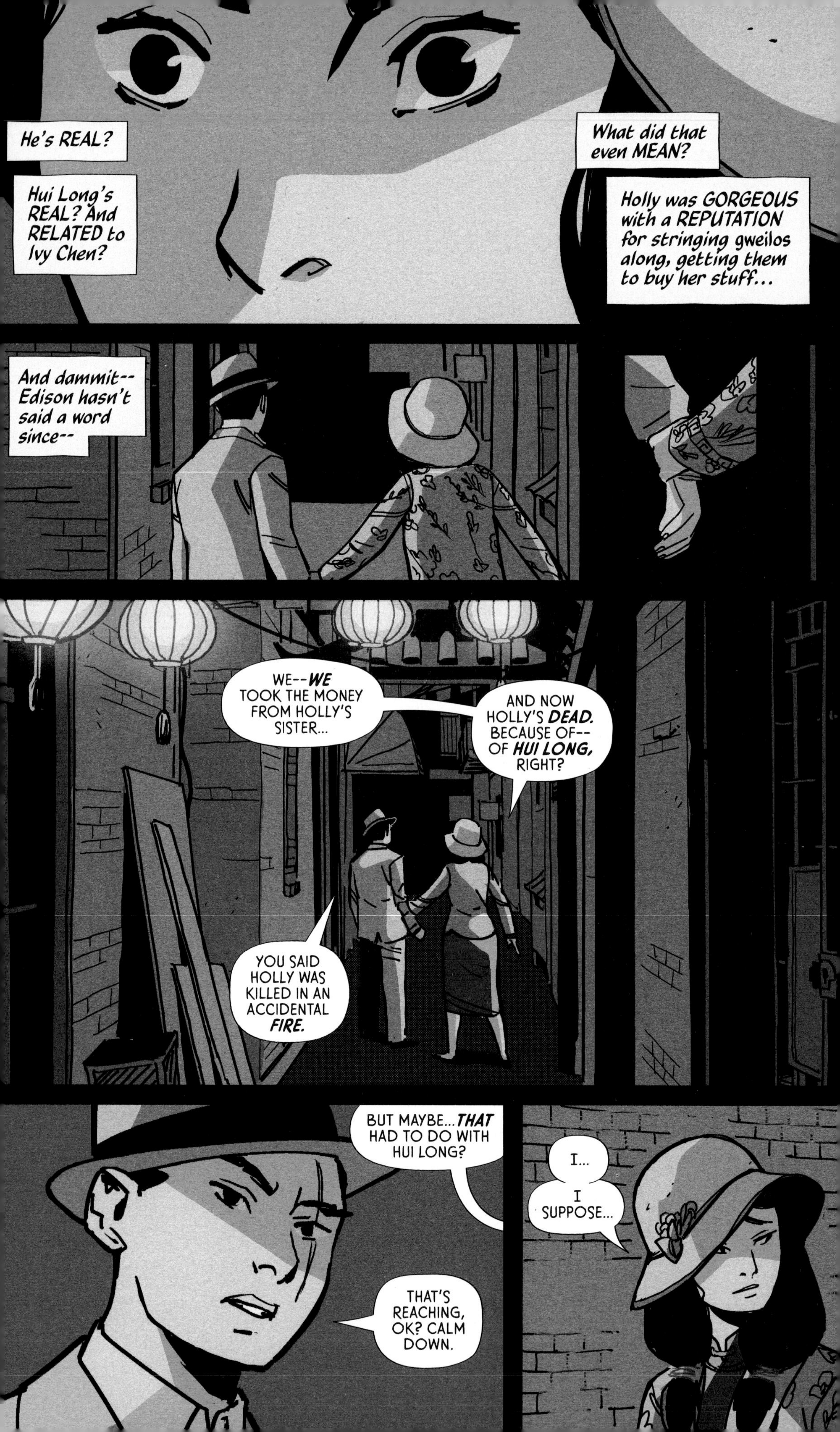
He's REAL?
Hui Long's REAL? And RELATED to Ivy Chen?
What did that even MEAN?
Holly was GORGEOUS with a REPUTATION for stringing gweilos along, getting them to buy her stuff...
And dammit-- Edison hasn't said a word since--
WE--*WE* TOOK THE MONEY FROM HOLLY'S SISTER...
AND NOW HOLLY'S *DEAD.* BECAUSE OF-- OF *HUI LONG,* RIGHT?
YOU SAID HOLLY WAS KILLED IN AN ACCIDENTAL *FIRE.*
BUT MAYBE...*THAT* HAD TO DO WITH HUI LONG?
I...
I SUPPOSE...
THAT'S REACHING, OK? CALM DOWN.

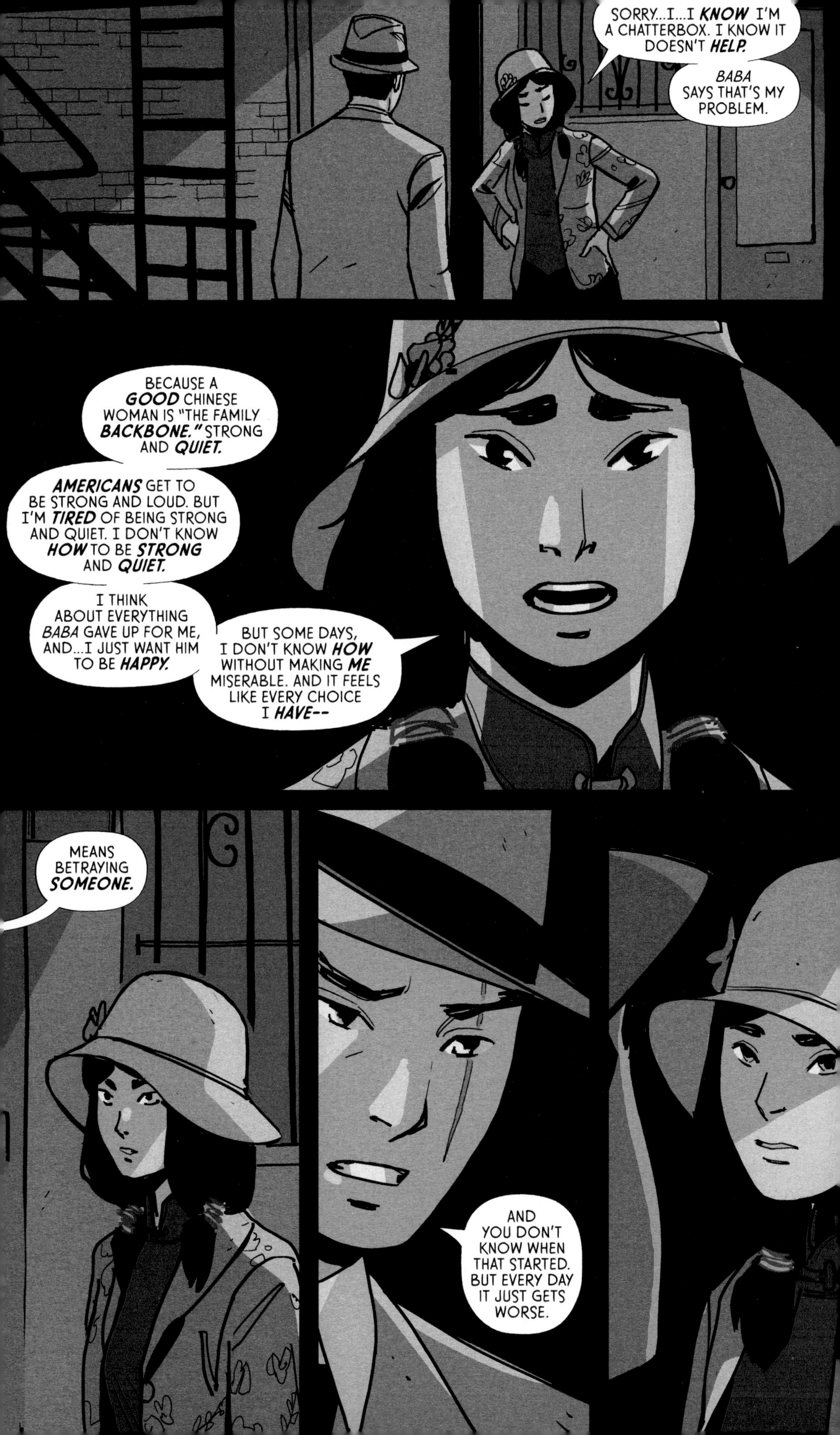

SORRY...I...I **KNOW** I'M A CHATTERBOX. I KNOW IT DOESN'T **HELP.**
BABA SAYS THAT'S MY PROBLEM.
BECAUSE A **GOOD** CHINESE WOMAN IS "THE FAMILY **BACKBONE."** STRONG AND **QUIET.**
AMERICANS GET TO BE STRONG AND LOUD. BUT I'M **TIRED** OF BEING STRONG AND QUIET. I DON'T KNOW **HOW** TO BE **STRONG** AND **QUIET.**
I THINK ABOUT EVERYTHING *BABA* GAVE UP FOR ME, AND...I JUST WANT HIM TO BE **HAPPY.**
BUT SOME DAYS, I DON'T KNOW **HOW** WITHOUT MAKING **ME** MISERABLE. AND IT FEELS LIKE EVERY CHOICE I **HAVE--**
MEANS BETRAYING **SOMEONE.**
AND YOU DON'T KNOW WHEN THAT STARTED. BUT EVERY DAY IT JUST GETS WORSE.

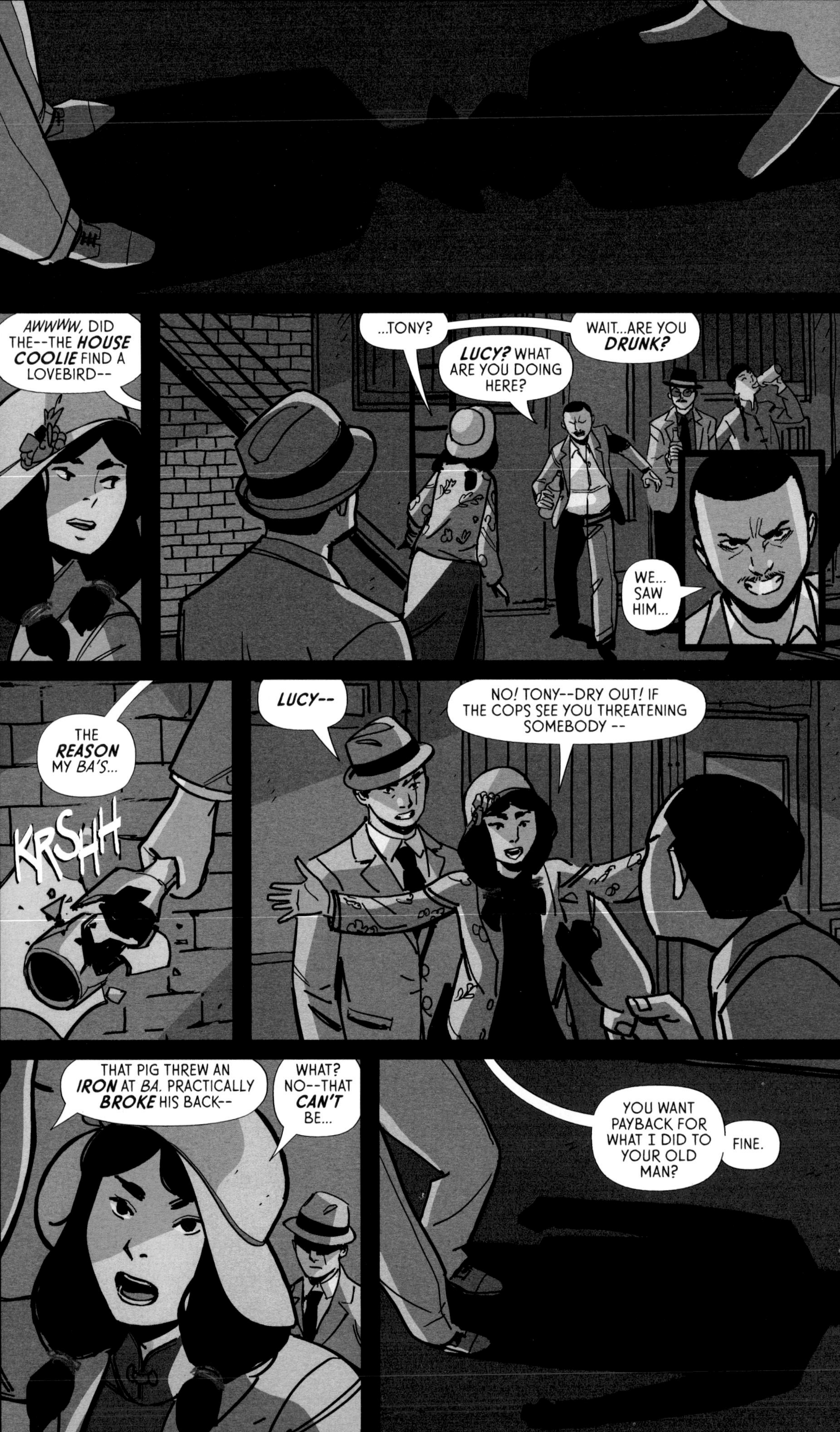
AWWWW, DID THE--THE HOUSE COOLIE FIND A LOVEBIRD--
...TONY?
LUCY? WHAT ARE YOU DOING HERE?
WAIT...ARE YOU DRUNK?
WE... SAW HIM...
THE REASON MY BA'S...
KRSHH
LUCY--
NO! TONY--DRY OUT! IF THE COPS SEE YOU THREATENING SOMEBODY --
THAT PIG THREW AN IRON AT BA. PRACTICALLY BROKE HIS BACK--
WHAT? NO--THAT CAN'T BE...
YOU WANT PAYBACK FOR WHAT I DID TO YOUR OLD MAN?
FINE.

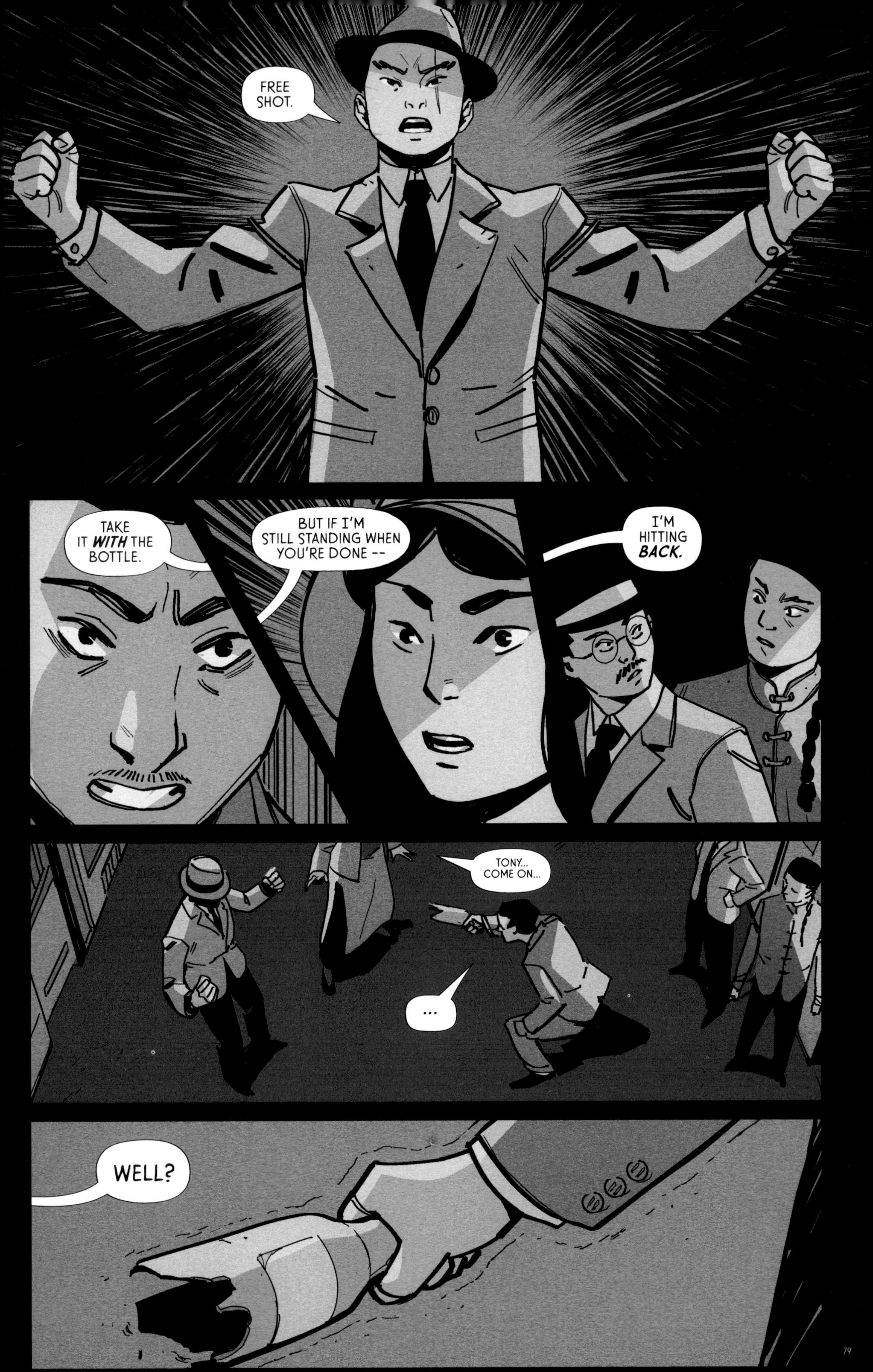
FREE SHOT.
TAKE IT *WITH* THE BOTTLE.
BUT IF I'M STILL STANDING WHEN YOU'RE DONE --
I'M HITTING *BACK.*
TONY... COME ON...
...
WELL?

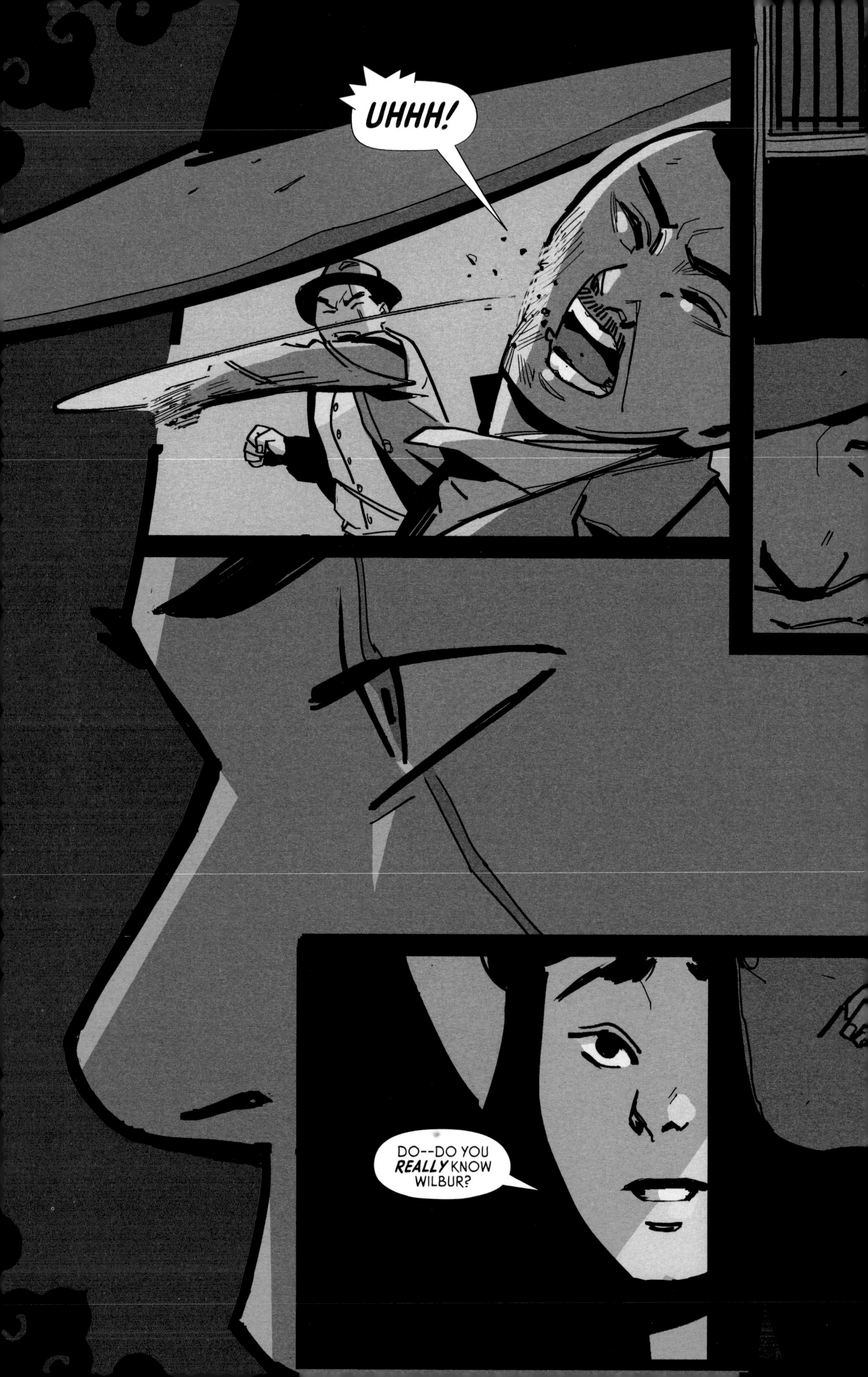
UHHH!
DO--DO YOU REALLY KNOW WILBUR?

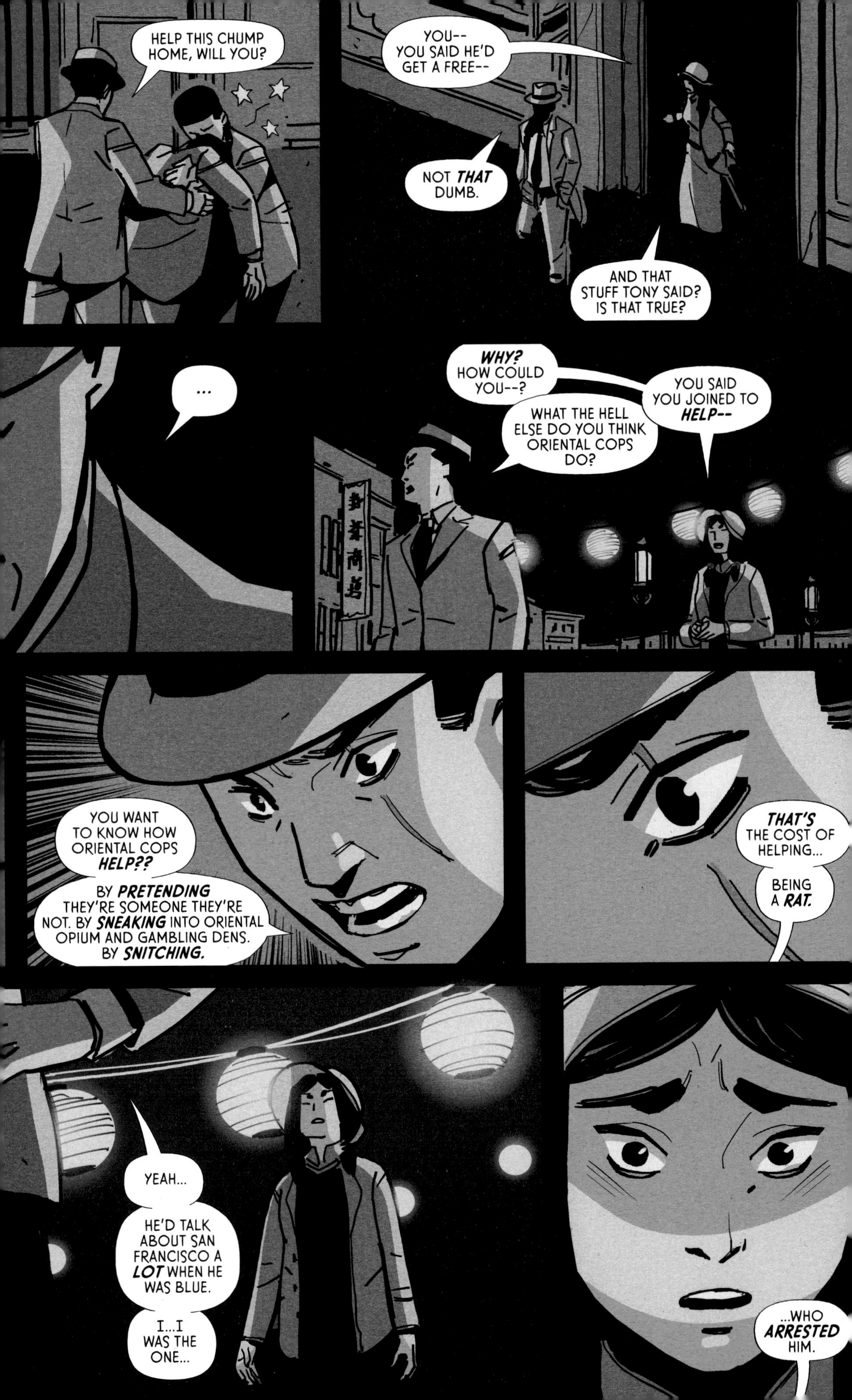
HELP THIS CHUMP HOME, WILL YOU?
YOU-- YOU SAID HE'D GET A FREE--
NOT THAT DUMB.
AND THAT STUFF TONY SAID? IS THAT TRUE?
...
WHY? HOW COULD YOU--?
YOU SAID YOU JOINED TO HELP--
WHAT THE HELL ELSE DO YOU THINK ORIENTAL COPS DO?
YOU WANT TO KNOW HOW ORIENTAL COPS HELP??
BY PRETENDING THEY'RE SOMEONE THEY'RE NOT. BY SNEAKING INTO ORIENTAL OPIUM AND GAMBLING DENS. BY SNITCHING.
THAT'S THE COST OF HELPING...
BEING A RAT.
YEAH...
HE'D TALK ABOUT SAN FRANCISCO A LOT WHEN HE WAS BLUE.
I...I WAS THE ONE...
...WHO ARRESTED HIM.

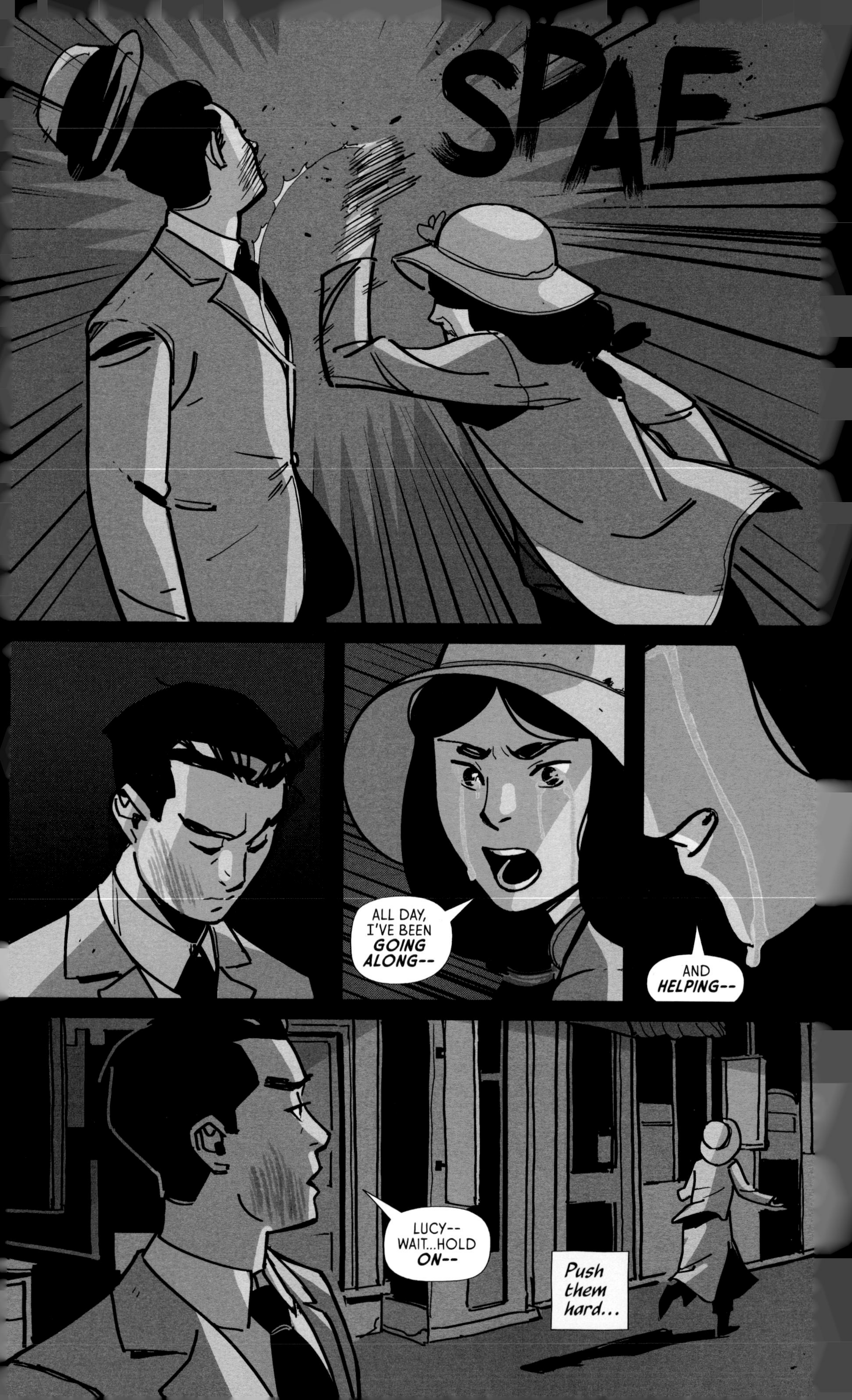
SPAF
ALL DAY, I'VE BEEN GOING ALONG--
AND HELPING--
LUCY-- WAIT...HOLD ON--
Push them hard...

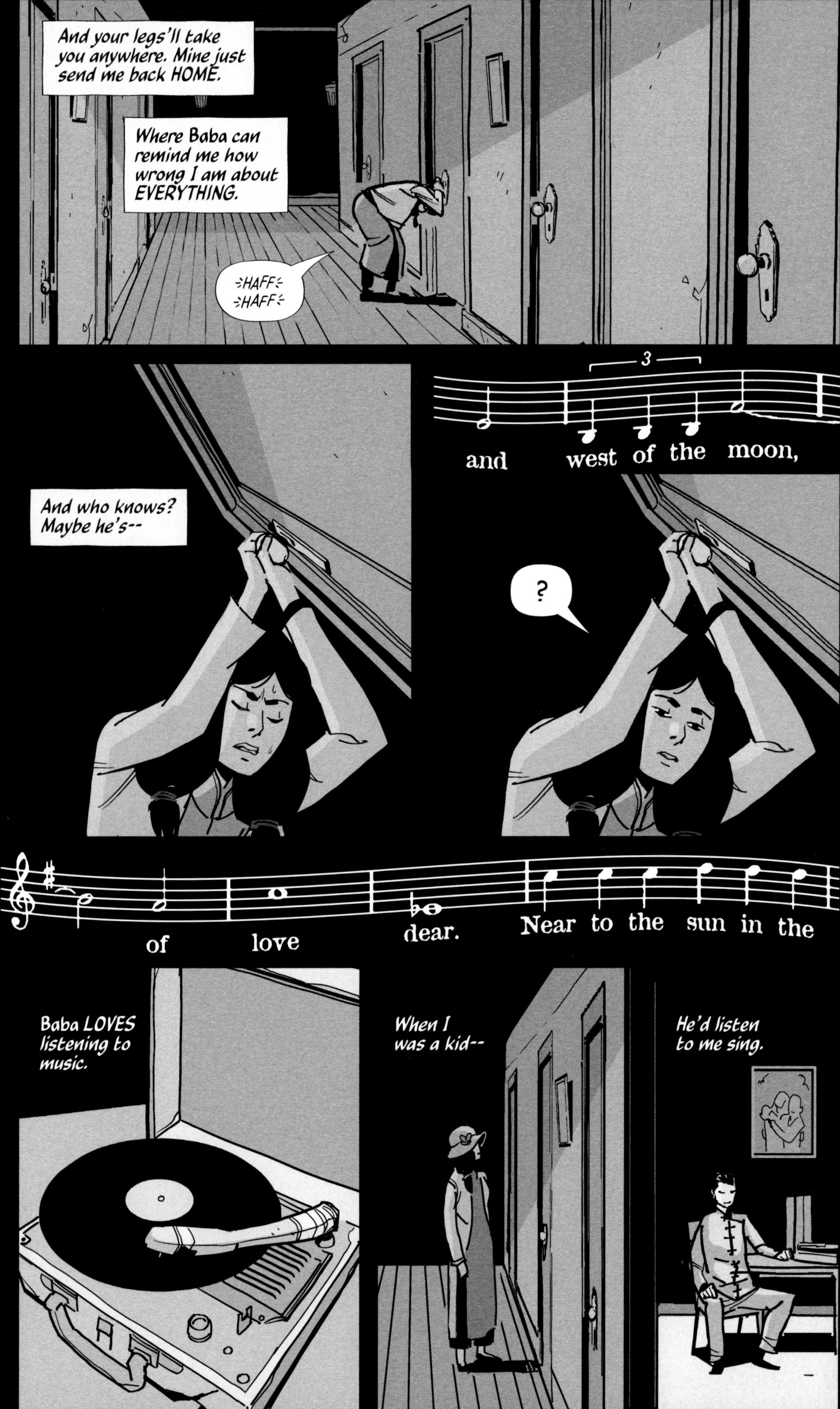

And your legs'll take you anywhere. Mine just send me back HOME.
Where Baba can remind me how wrong I am about EVERYTHING.
HAFF HAFF
And who knows? Maybe he's--
3
and west of the moon,
?
of love dear. Near to the sun in the
Baba LOVES listening to music.
When I was a kid--
He'd listen to me sing.

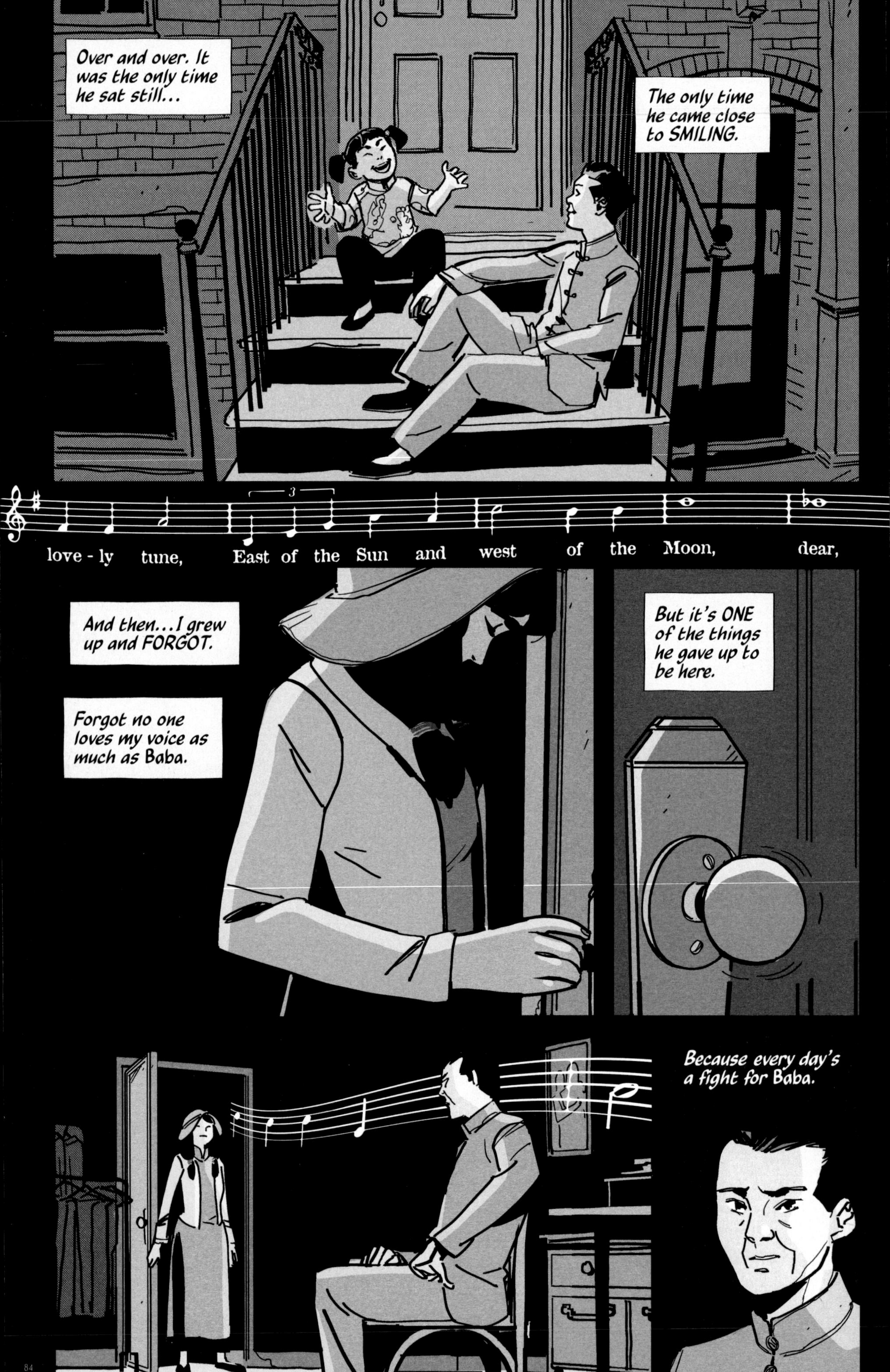

Over and over. It was the only time he sat still...
The only time he came close to SMILING.
love - ly tune, East of the Sun and west of the Moon, dear,
And then... I grew up and FORGOT.
Forgot no one loves my voice as much as Baba.
But it's ONE of the things he gave up to be here.
Because every day's a fight for Baba.

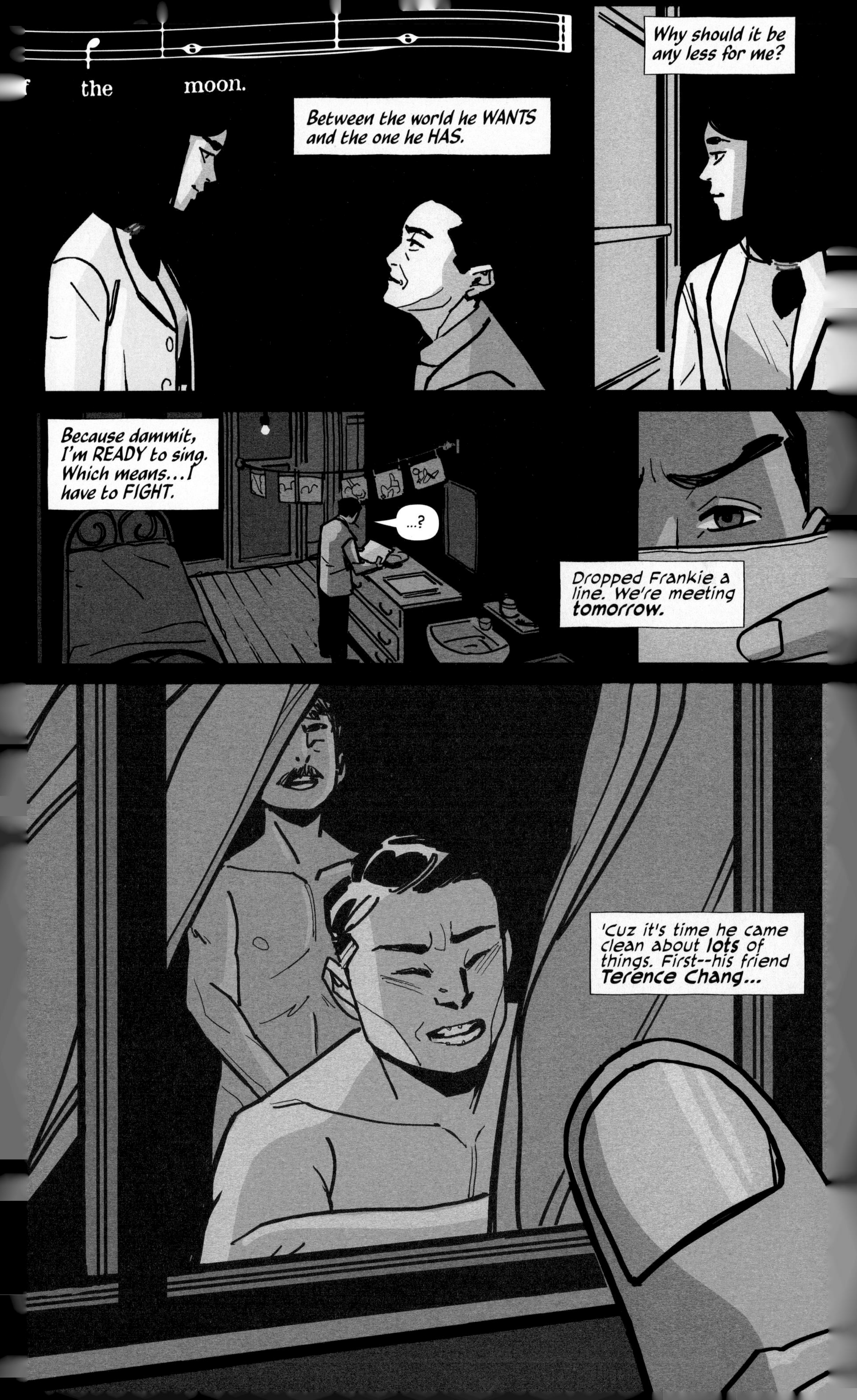

f the moon.
Between the world he WANTS and the one he HAS.
Why should it be any less for me?
Because dammit, I'm READY to sing. Which means... I have to FIGHT.
...?
Dropped Frankie a line. We're meeting tomorrow.
'Cuz it's time he came clean about lots of things. First--his friend Terence Chang...

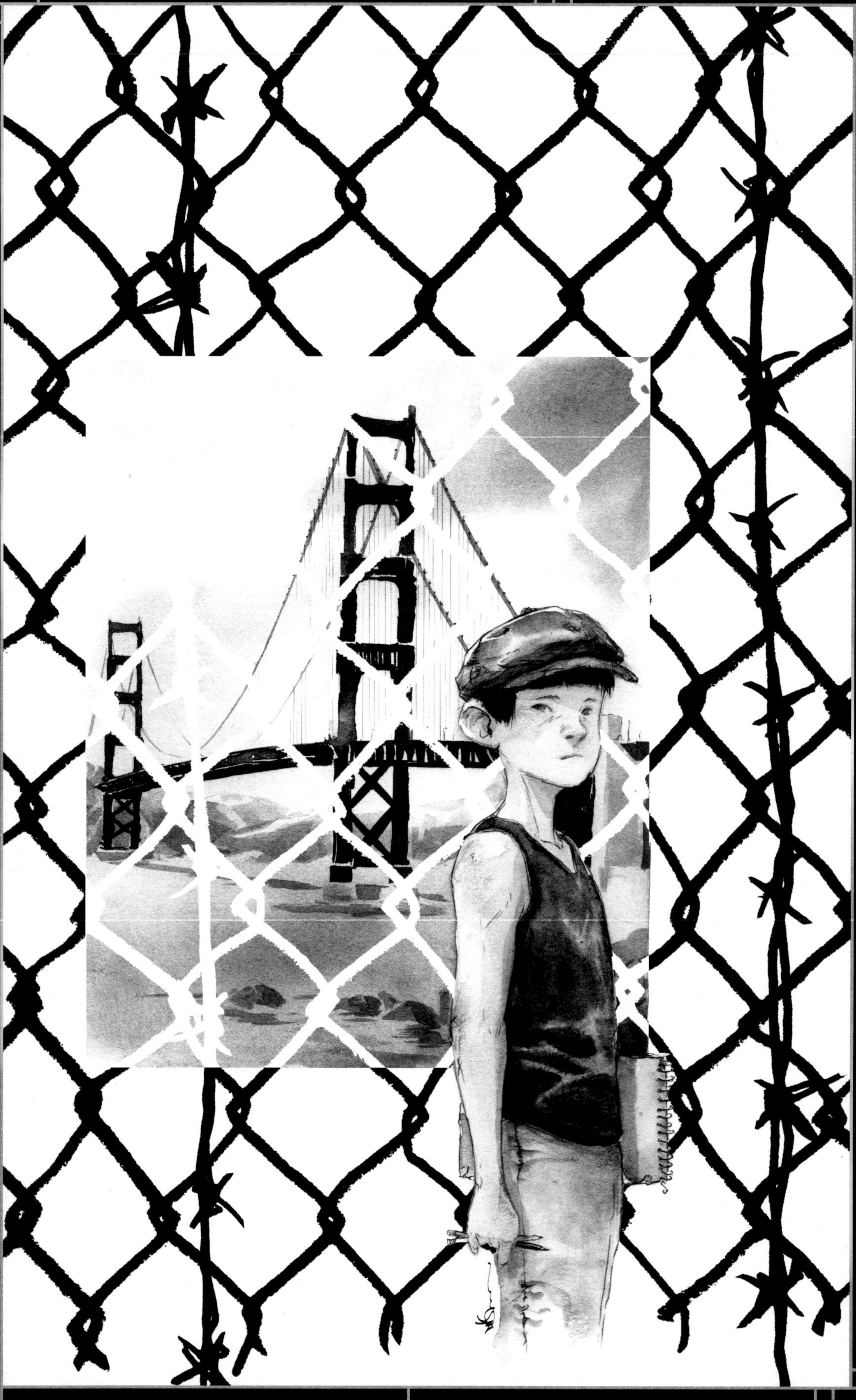

ART BY **DUSTIN NGUYEN**

CHAPTER FOUR

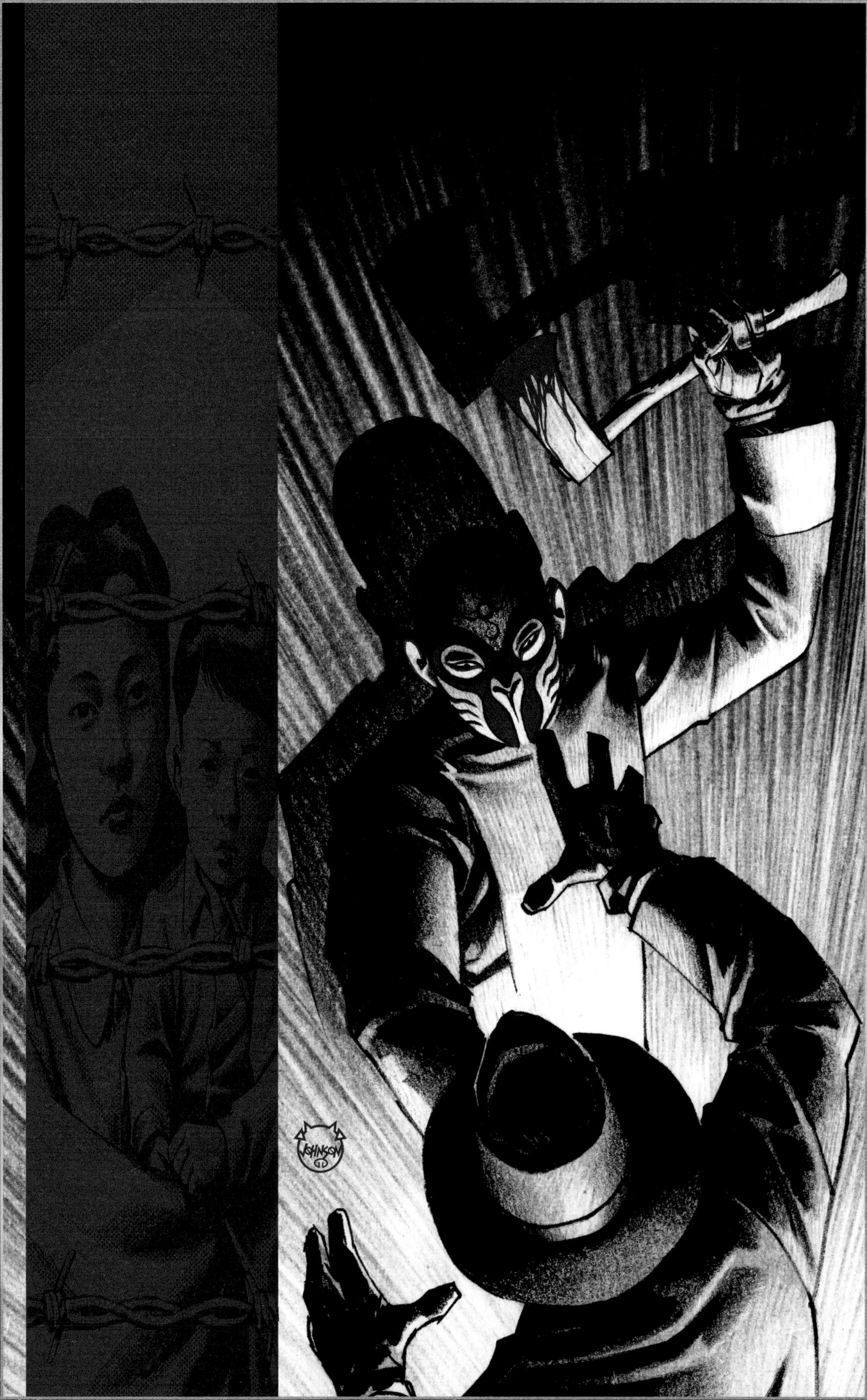

ART BY **DAVE JOHNSON**

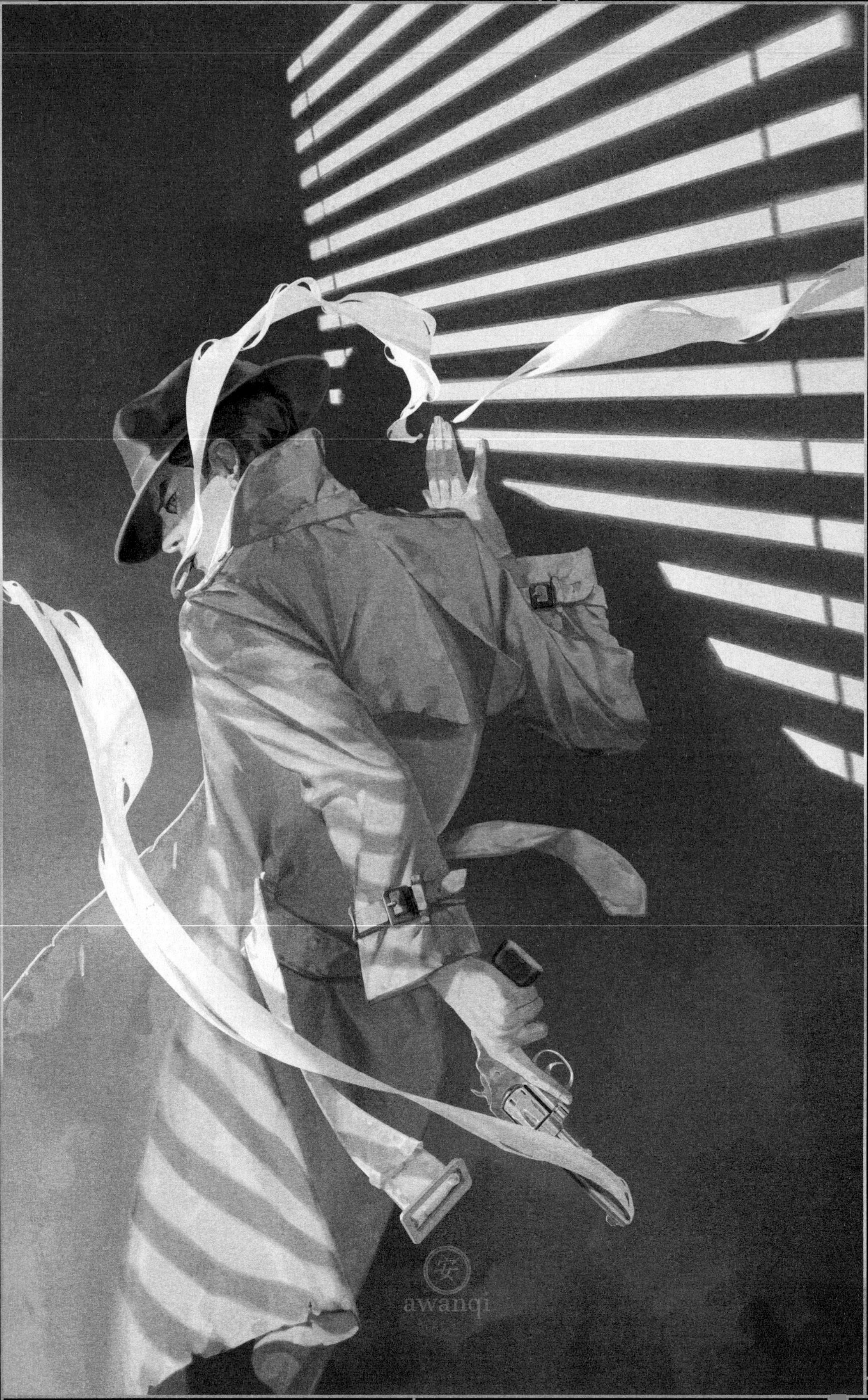
awanqi

ART BY **AWANQI**

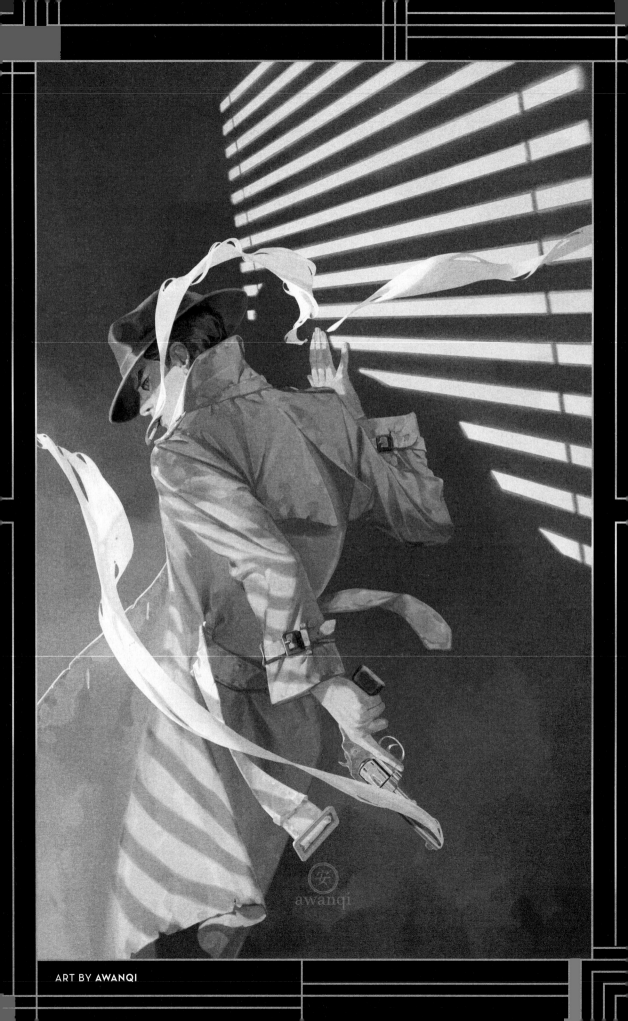

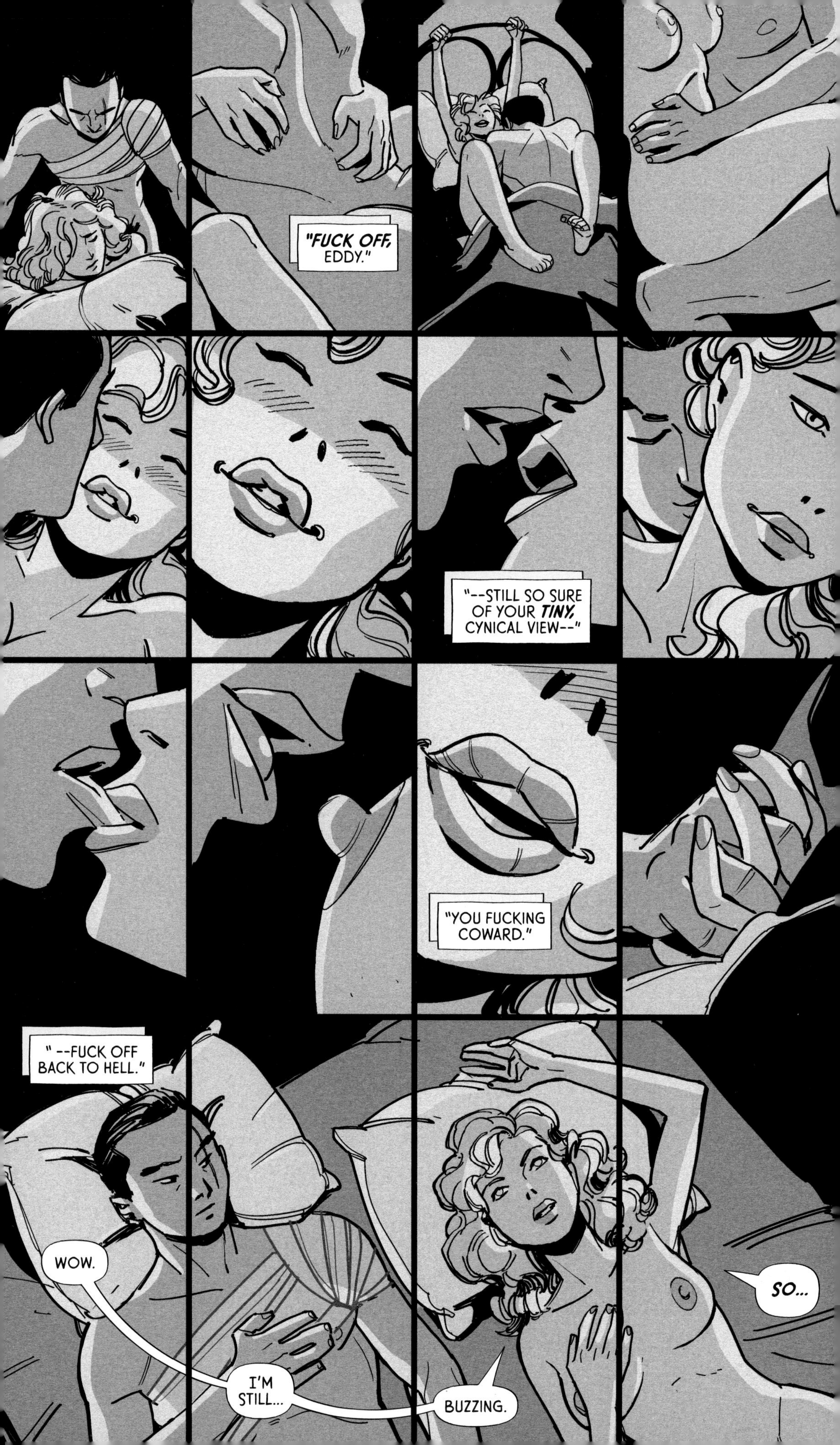
"FUCK OFF, EDDY."
"--STILL SO SURE OF YOUR TINY, CYNICAL VIEW--"
"YOU FUCKING COWARD."
" --FUCK OFF BACK TO HELL."
WOW.
I'M STILL...
BUZZING.
SO...

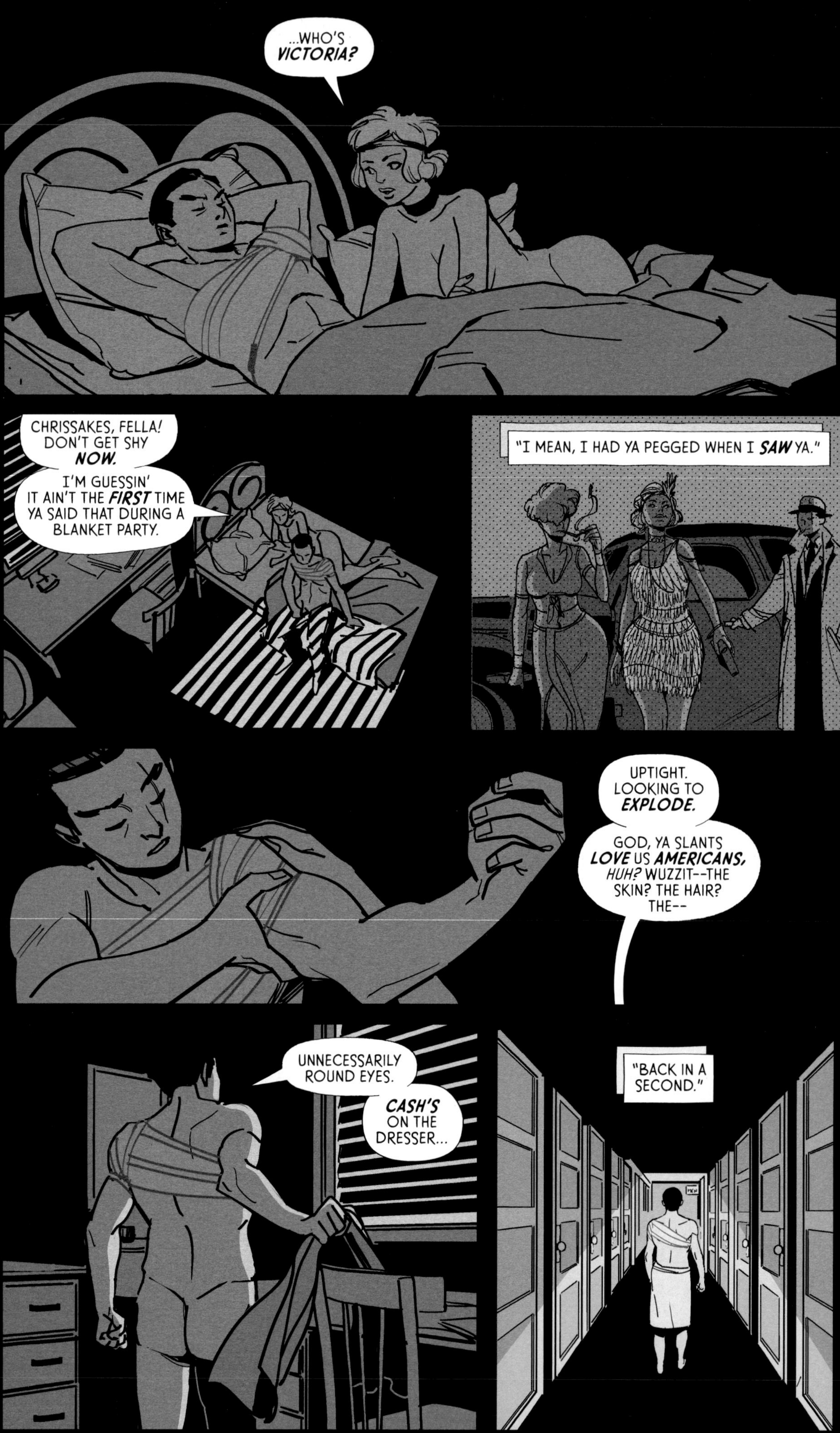
...WHO'S VICTORIA?
CHRISSAKES, FELLA! DON'T GET SHY NOW.
I'M GUESSIN' IT AIN'T THE FIRST TIME YA SAID THAT DURING A BLANKET PARTY.
"I MEAN, I HAD YA PEGGED WHEN I SAW YA."
UPTIGHT. LOOKING TO EXPLODE.
GOD, YA SLANTS LOVE US AMERICANS, HUH? WUZZIT--THE SKIN? THE HAIR? THE--
UNNECESSARILY ROUND EYES.
CASH'S ON THE DRESSER...
"BACK IN A SECOND."

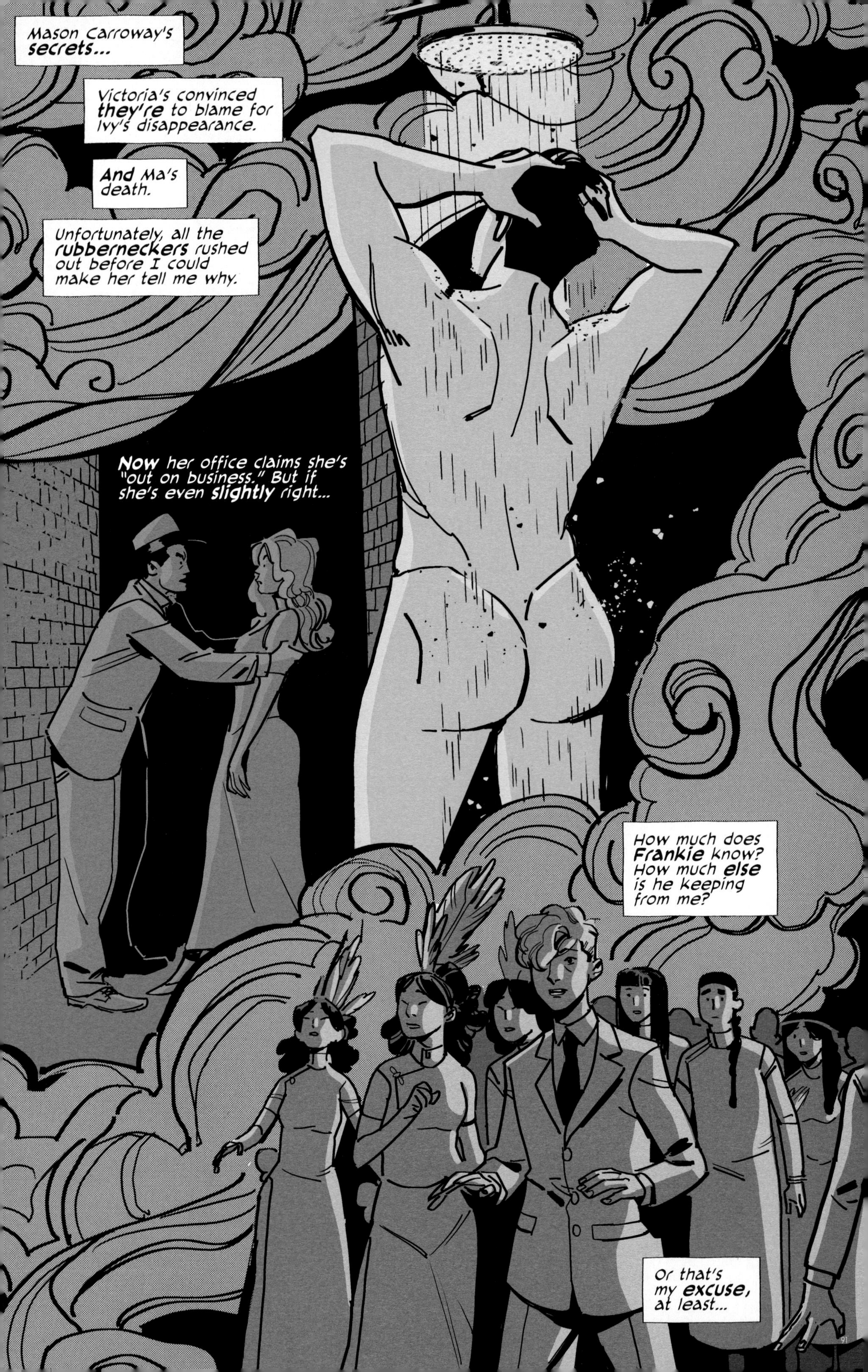
Mason Carroway's **secrets**...
Victoria's convinced **they're** to blame for Ivy's disappearance.
And Ma's death.
Unfortunately, all the **rubberneckers** rushed out before I could make her tell me why.
Now her office claims she's "out on business." But if she's even **slightly** right...
How much does **Frankie** know? How much **else** is he keeping from me?
Or that's my **excuse**, at least...

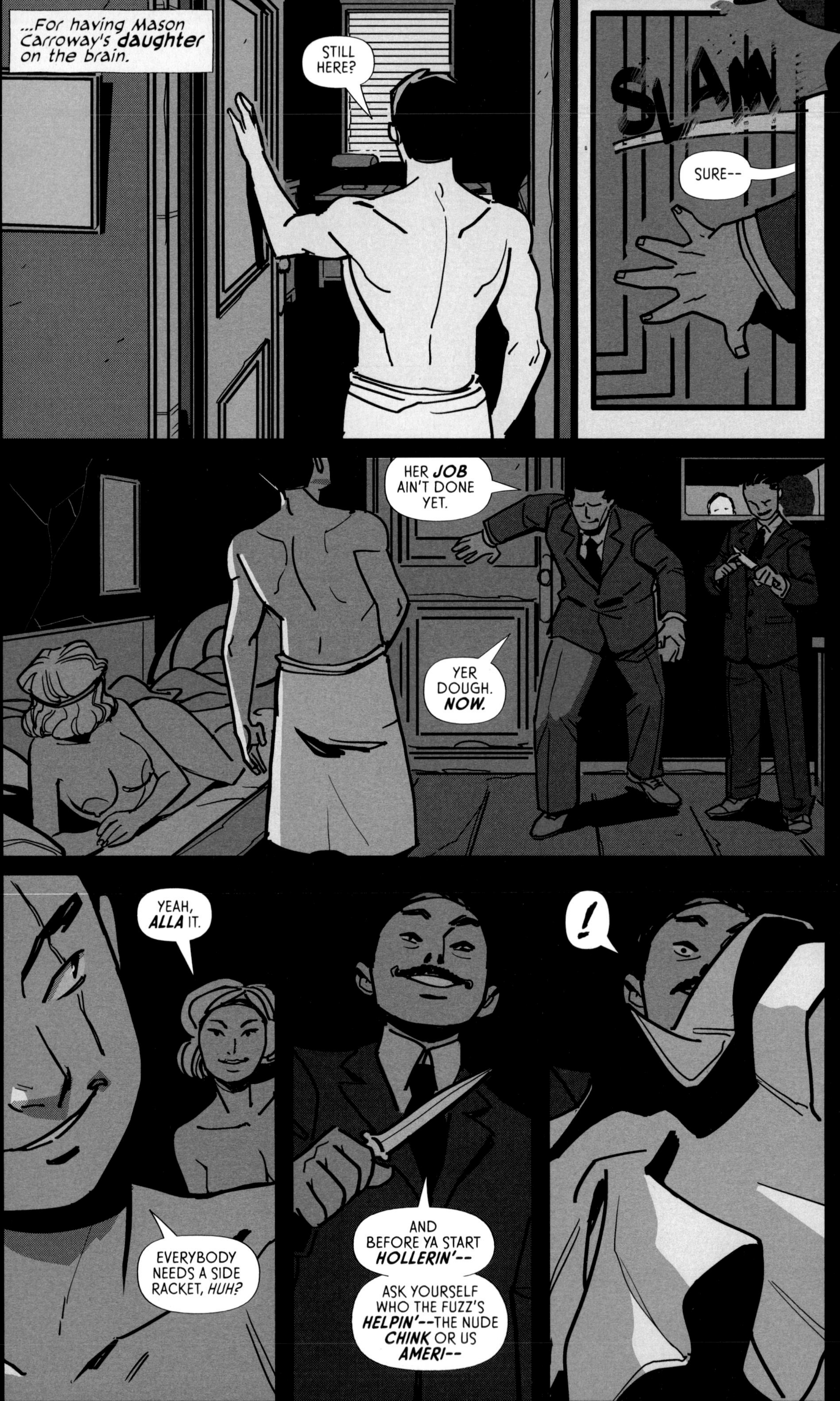

...For having Mason Carroway's daughter on the brain.
STILL HERE?
SLAM
SURE--
HER JOB AIN'T DONE YET.
YER DOUGH. NOW.
YEAH, ALLA IT.
EVERYBODY NEEDS A SIDE RACKET, HUH?
AND BEFORE YA START HOLLERIN'--
ASK YOURSELF WHO THE FUZZ'S HELPIN'--THE NUDE CHINK OR US AMERI--
!

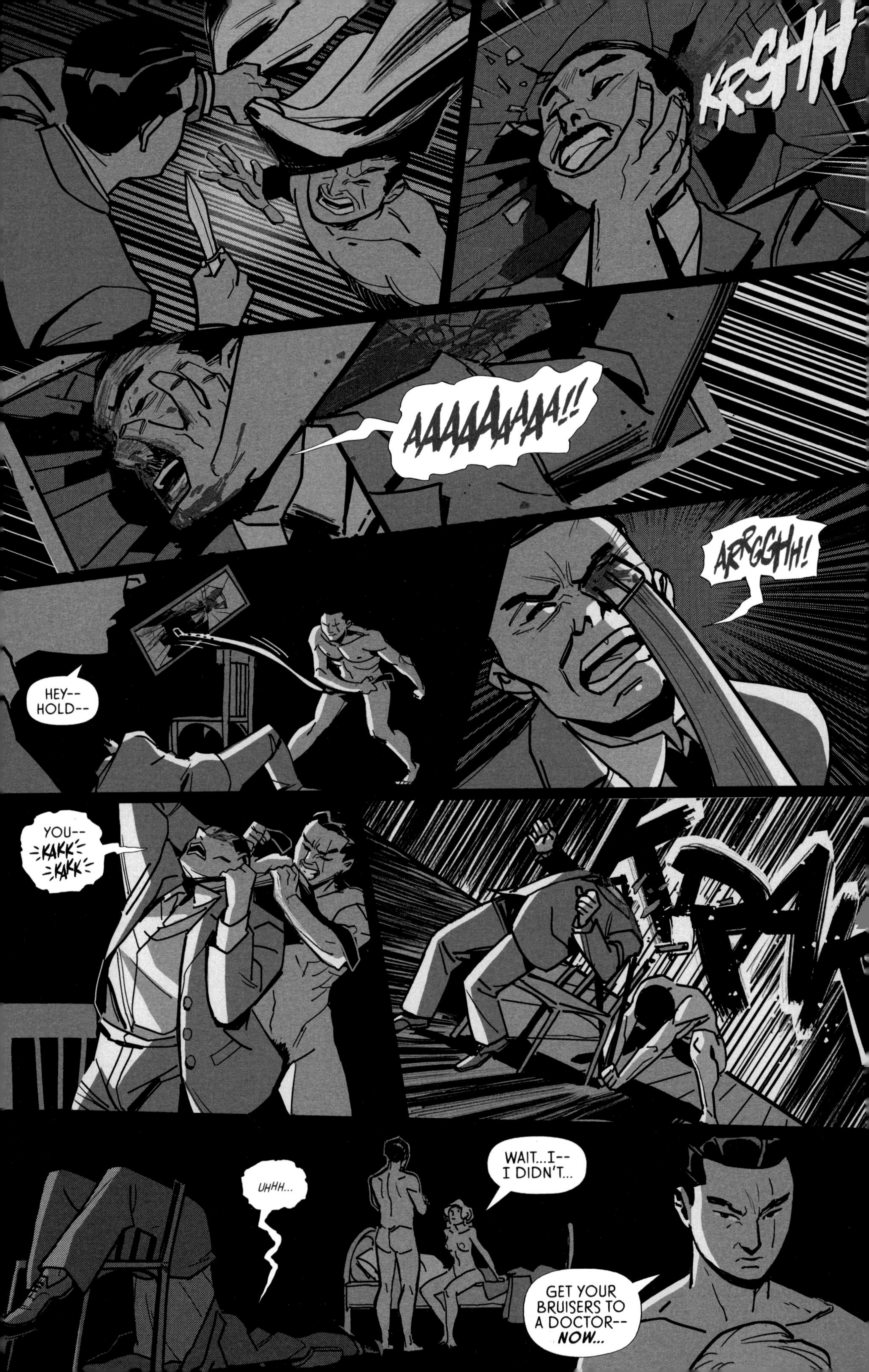
KRSHH
AAAAAAAAA!!
HEY--
HOLD--
ARRGGHH!
YOU--
KAKK
KAKK
UHHH...
WAIT...I--
I DIDN'T...
GET YOUR
BRUISERS TO
A DOCTOR--
NOW...

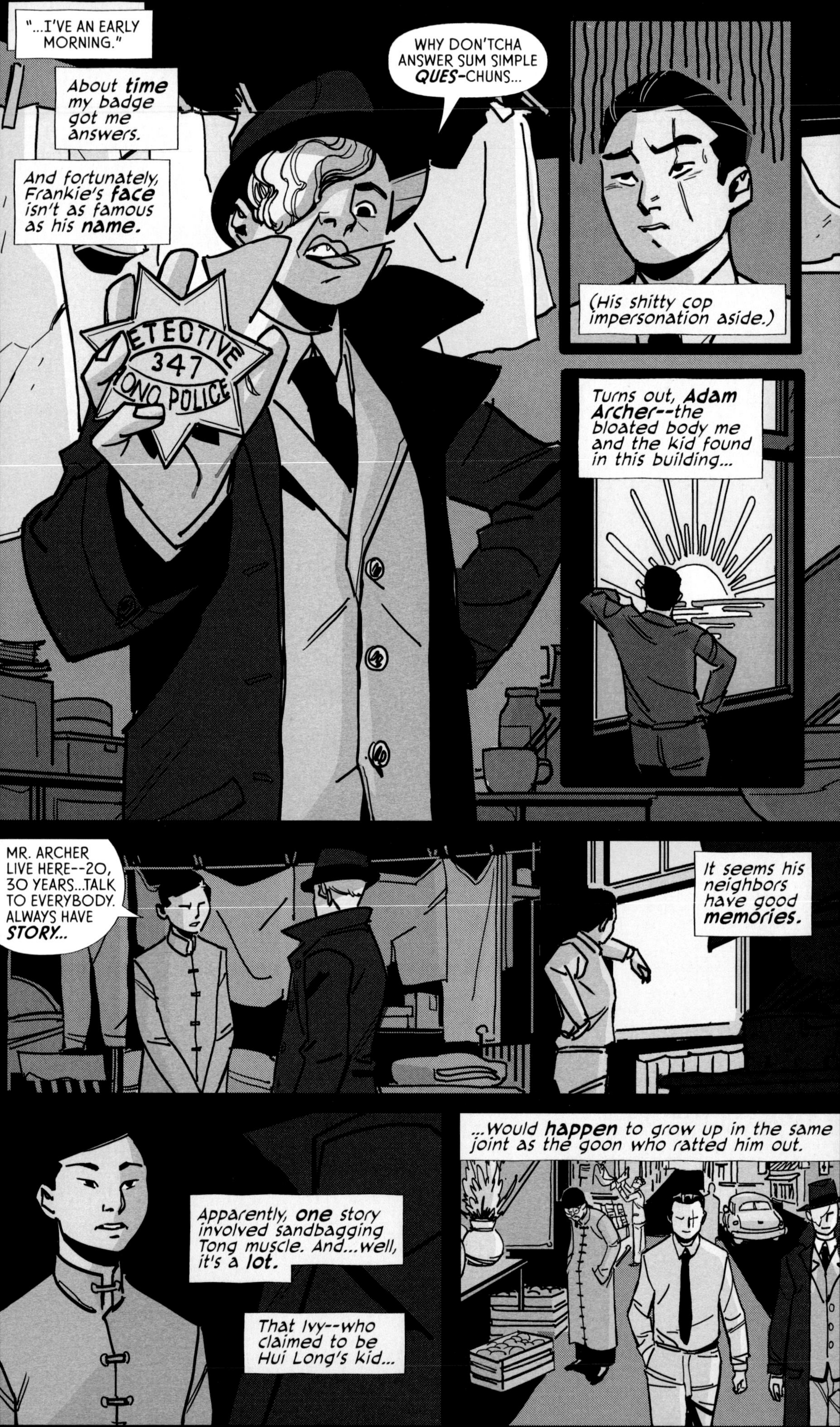

"...I'VE AN EARLY MORNING."
About time my badge got me answers.
And fortunately, Frankie's face isn't as famous as his name.
WHY DON'TCHA ANSWER SUM SIMPLE QUES-CHUNS...
(His shitty cop impersonation aside.)
Turns out, Adam Archer--the bloated body me and the kid found in this building...
MR. ARCHER LIVE HERE--20, 30 YEARS...TALK TO EVERYBODY. ALWAYS HAVE STORY...
It seems his neighbors have good memories.
Apparently, one story involved sandbagging Tong muscle. And...well, it's a lot.
That Ivy--who claimed to be Hui Long's kid...
...would happen to grow up in the same joint as the goon who ratted him out.

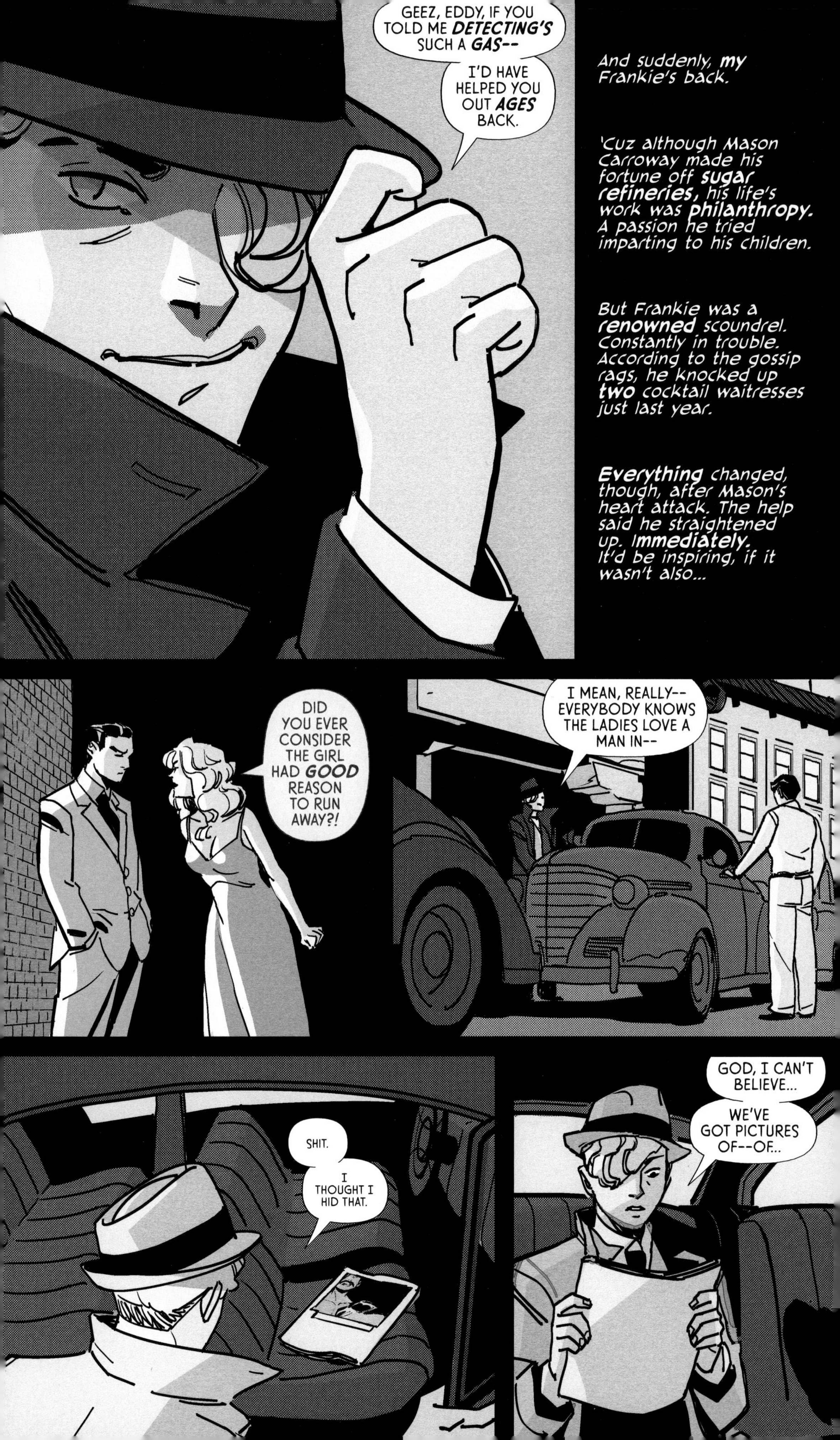
GEEZ, EDDY, IF YOU TOLD ME DETECTING'S SUCH A GAS--
I'D HAVE HELPED YOU OUT AGES BACK.
And suddenly, my Frankie's back.
'Cuz although Mason Carroway made his fortune off sugar refineries, his life's work was philanthropy. A passion he tried imparting to his children.
But Frankie was a renowned scoundrel. Constantly in trouble. According to the gossip rags, he knocked up two cocktail waitresses just last year.
Everything changed, though, after Mason's heart attack. The help said he straightened up. Immediately. It'd be inspiring, if it wasn't also...
DID YOU EVER CONSIDER THE GIRL HAD GOOD REASON TO RUN AWAY?!
I MEAN, REALLY-- EVERYBODY KNOWS THE LADIES LOVE A MAN IN--
SHIT.
I THOUGHT I HID THAT.
GOD, I CAN'T BELIEVE...
WE'VE GOT PICTURES OF--OF...

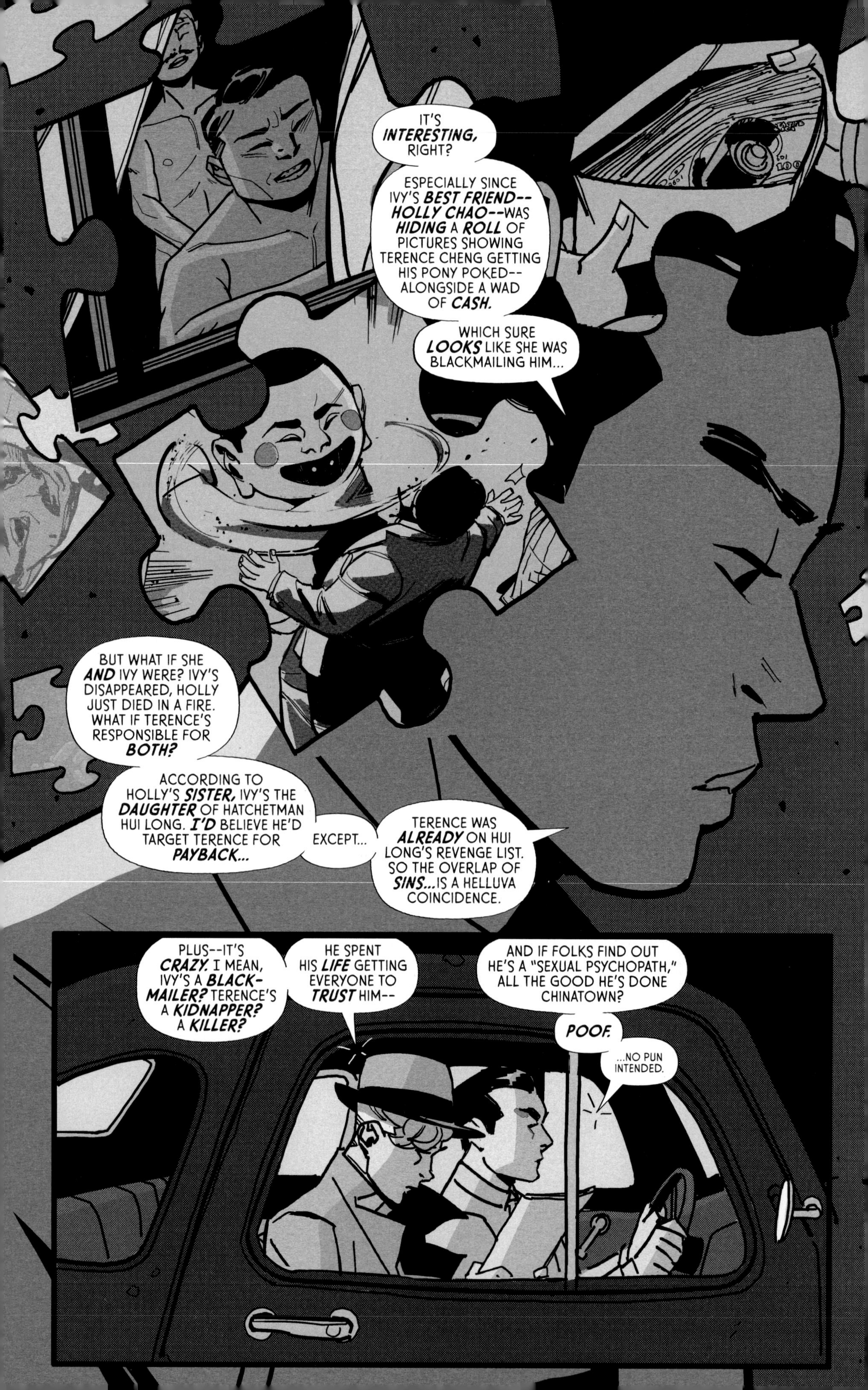
IT'S INTERESTING, RIGHT?
ESPECIALLY SINCE IVY'S BEST FRIEND--HOLLY CHAO--WAS HIDING A ROLL OF PICTURES SHOWING TERENCE CHENG GETTING HIS PONY POKED--ALONGSIDE A WAD OF CASH.
WHICH SURE LOOKS LIKE SHE WAS BLACKMAILING HIM...
BUT WHAT IF SHE AND IVY WERE? IVY'S DISAPPEARED, HOLLY JUST DIED IN A FIRE. WHAT IF TERENCE'S RESPONSIBLE FOR BOTH?
ACCORDING TO HOLLY'S SISTER, IVY'S THE DAUGHTER OF HATCHETMAN HUI LONG. I'D BELIEVE HE'D TARGET TERENCE FOR PAYBACK...
EXCEPT...
TERENCE WAS ALREADY ON HUI LONG'S REVENGE LIST. SO THE OVERLAP OF SINS...IS A HELLUVA COINCIDENCE.
PLUS--IT'S CRAZY. I MEAN, IVY'S A BLACK-MAILER? TERENCE'S A KIDNAPPER? A KILLER?
HE SPENT HIS LIFE GETTING EVERYONE TO TRUST HIM--
AND IF FOLKS FIND OUT HE'S A "SEXUAL PSYCHOPATH," ALL THE GOOD HE'S DONE CHINATOWN?
POOF.
...NO PUN INTENDED.

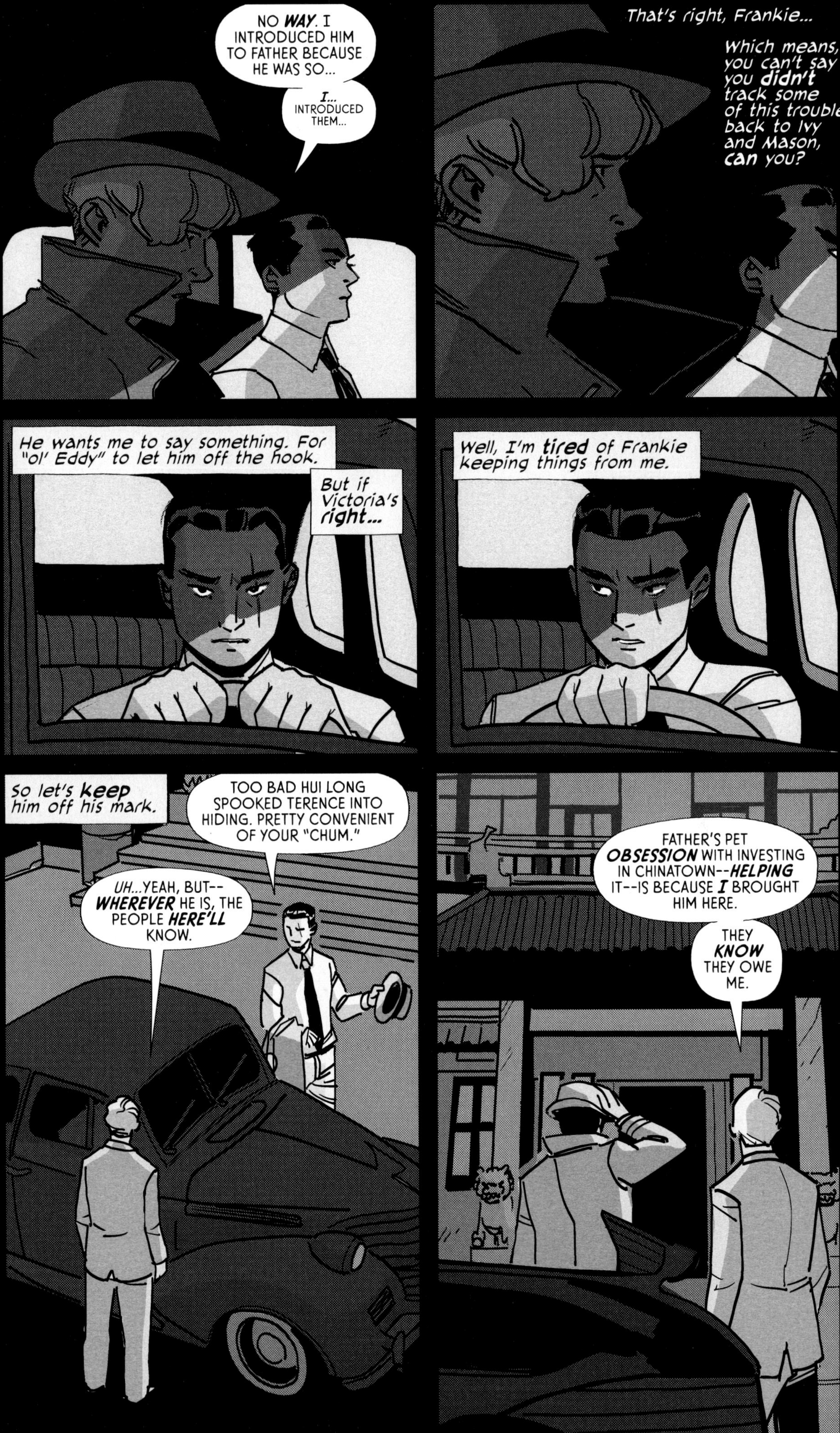
NO WAY. I INTRODUCED HIM TO FATHER BECAUSE HE WAS SO...
I... INTRODUCED THEM...
That's right, Frankie...
Which means, you can't say you didn't track some of this trouble back to Ivy and Mason, can you?
He wants me to say something. For "ol' Eddy" to let him off the hook.
But if Victoria's right...
Well, I'm tired of Frankie keeping things from me.
So let's keep him off his mark.
TOO BAD HUI LONG SPOOKED TERENCE INTO HIDING. PRETTY CONVENIENT OF YOUR "CHUM."
UH...YEAH, BUT-- WHEREVER HE IS, THE PEOPLE HERE'LL KNOW.
FATHER'S PET OBSESSION WITH INVESTING IN CHINATOWN--HELPING IT--IS BECAUSE I BROUGHT HIM HERE.
THEY KNOW THEY OWE ME.

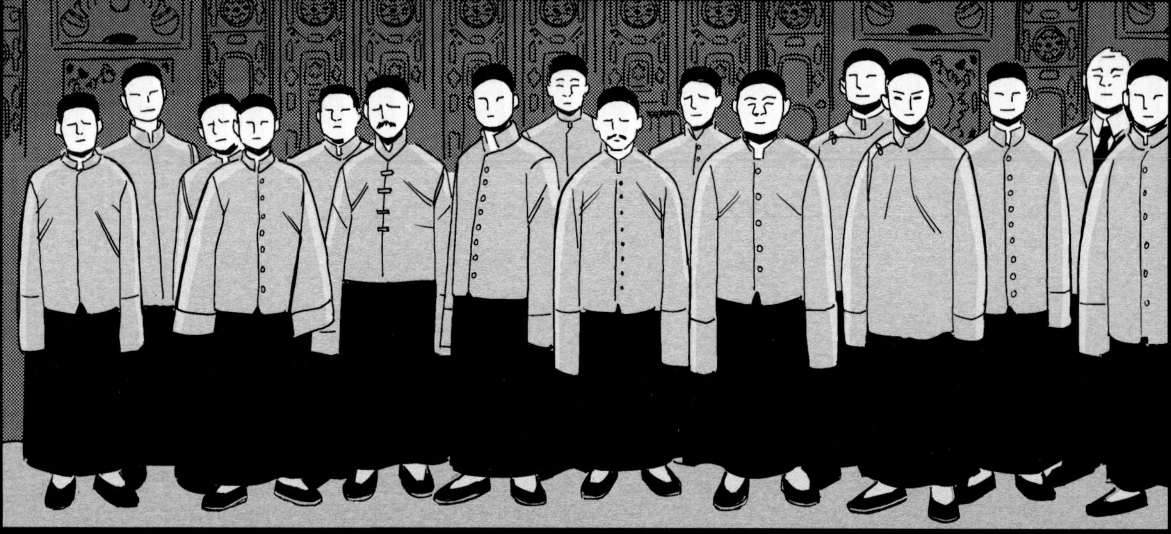

By 1882, after enough Chinese had come to San Francisco, the regional groups the majority of them belonged to banded together.

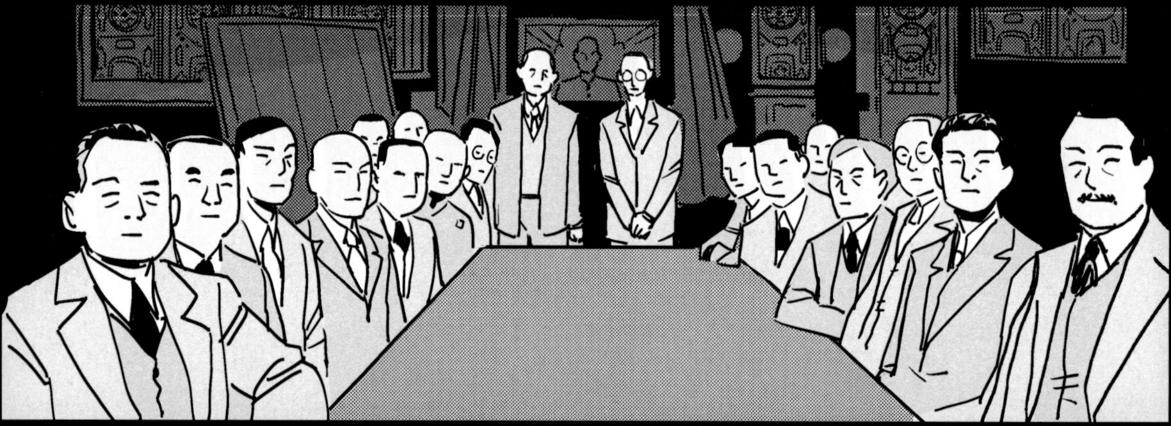

Those six Chinese companies united, officially organizing to help their members--and **all** of Chinatown's citizens.

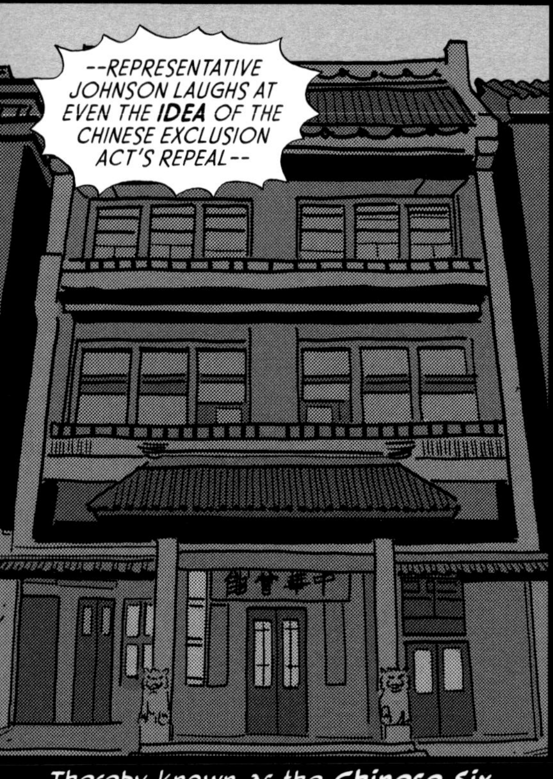
--REPRESENTATIVE JOHNSON LAUGHS AT EVEN THE **IDEA** OF THE CHINESE EXCLUSION ACT'S REPEAL--
中華會館

Thereby known as the **Chinese Six Companies,** they located their headquarters at 843 Stockton Street...

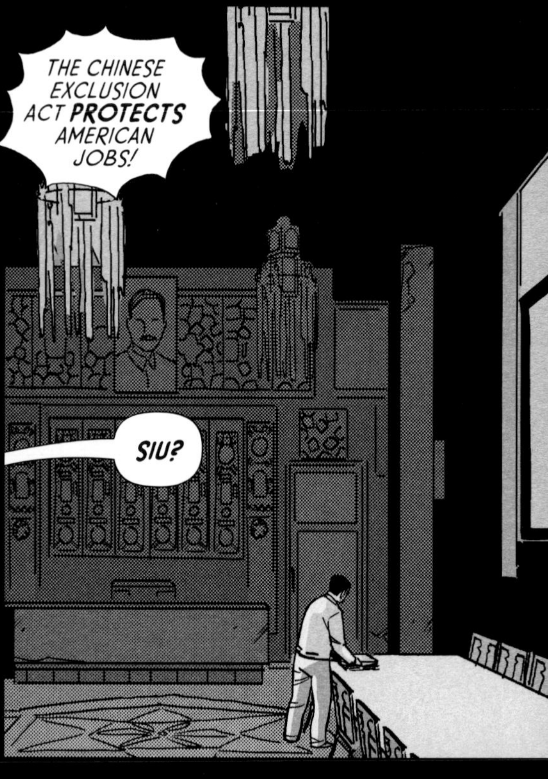
THE CHINESE EXCLUSION ACT **PROTECTS** AMERICAN JOBS!
SIU?

And might as well **be** Chinatown's governmen

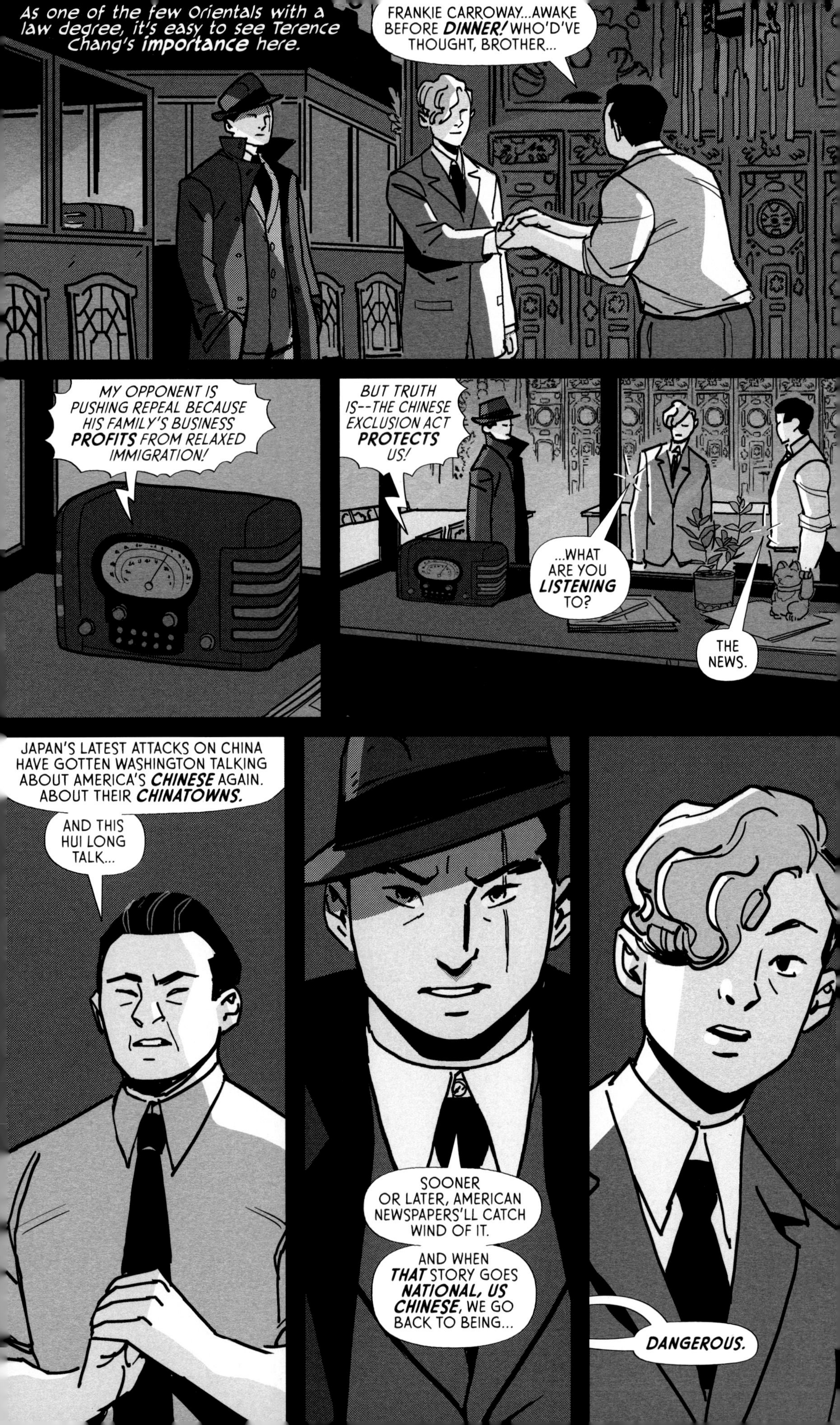
As one of the few Orientals with a law degree, it's easy to see Terence Chang's importance here.
FRANKIE CARROWAY...AWAKE BEFORE DINNER! WHO'D'VE THOUGHT, BROTHER...
MY OPPONENT IS PUSHING REPEAL BECAUSE HIS FAMILY'S BUSINESS PROFITS FROM RELAXED IMMIGRATION!
BUT TRUTH IS--THE CHINESE EXCLUSION ACT PROTECTS US!
...WHAT ARE YOU LISTENING TO?
THE NEWS.
JAPAN'S LATEST ATTACKS ON CHINA HAVE GOTTEN WASHINGTON TALKING ABOUT AMERICA'S CHINESE AGAIN. ABOUT THEIR CHINATOWNS.
AND THIS HUI LONG TALK...
SOONER OR LATER, AMERICAN NEWSPAPERS'LL CATCH WIND OF IT.
AND WHEN THAT STORY GOES NATIONAL, US CHINESE, WE GO BACK TO BEING...
DANGEROUS.

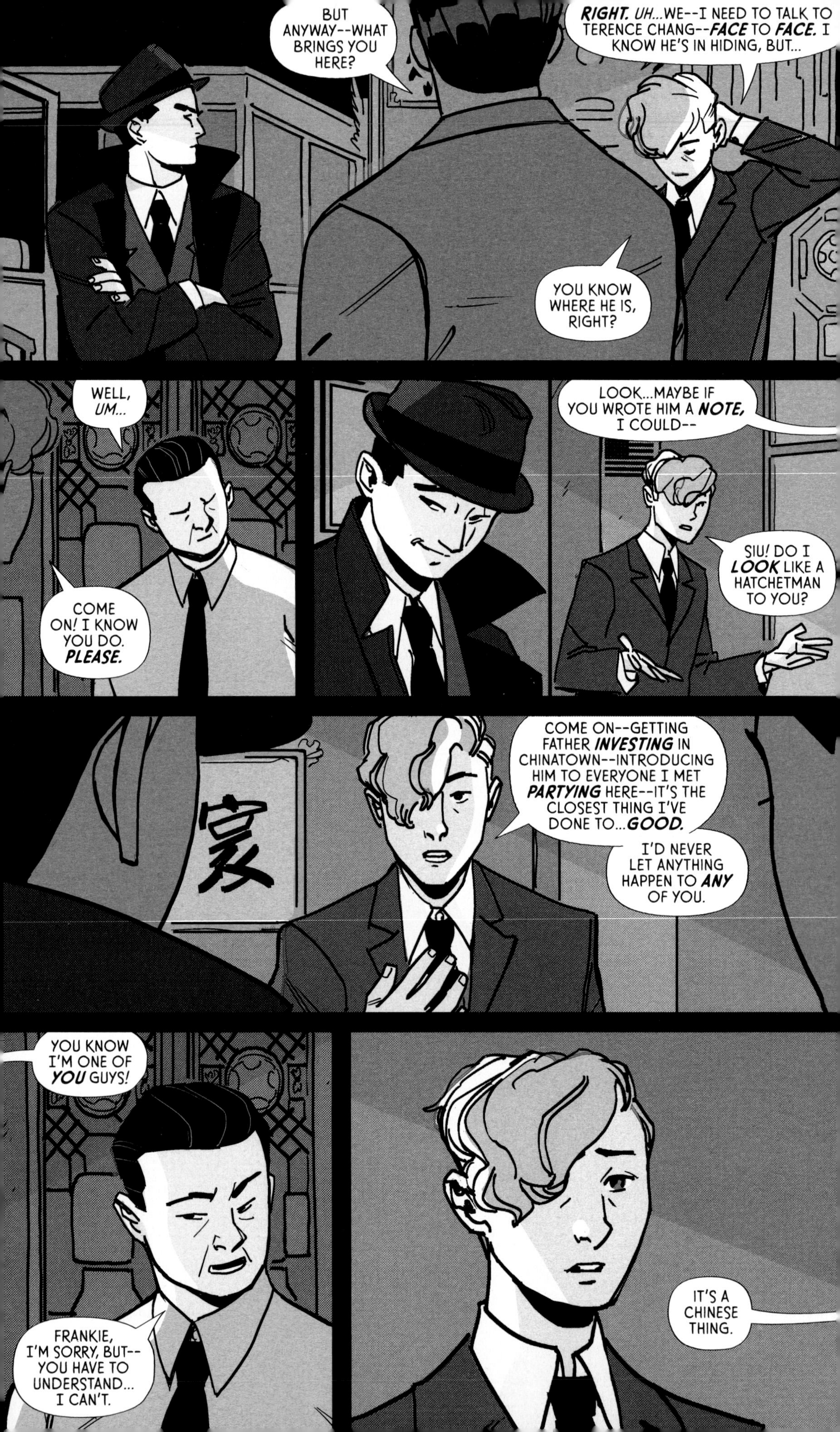
BUT ANYWAY--WHAT BRINGS YOU HERE?
RIGHT. UH...WE--I NEED TO TALK TO TERENCE CHANG--FACE TO FACE. I KNOW HE'S IN HIDING, BUT...
YOU KNOW WHERE HE IS, RIGHT?
WELL, UM...
COME ON! I KNOW YOU DO. PLEASE.
LOOK...MAYBE IF YOU WROTE HIM A NOTE, I COULD--
SIU! DO I LOOK LIKE A HATCHETMAN TO YOU?
COME ON--GETTING FATHER INVESTING IN CHINATOWN--INTRODUCING HIM TO EVERYONE I MET PARTYING HERE--IT'S THE CLOSEST THING I'VE DONE TO...GOOD.
I'D NEVER LET ANYTHING HAPPEN TO ANY OF YOU.
YOU KNOW I'M ONE OF YOU GUYS!
FRANKIE, I'M SORRY, BUT-- YOU HAVE TO UNDERSTAND... I CAN'T.
IT'S A CHINESE THING.

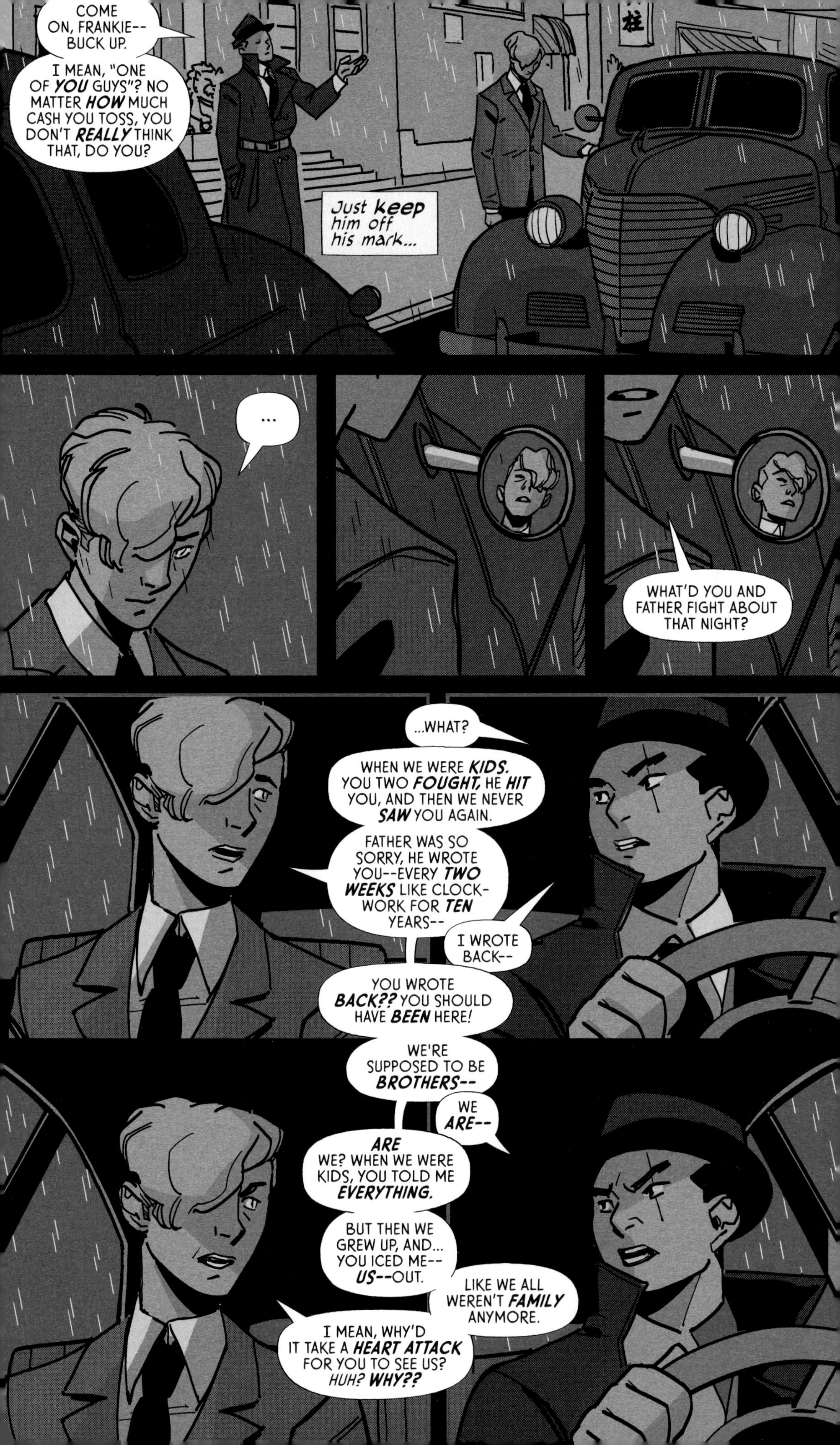
COME ON, FRANKIE-- BUCK UP.
I MEAN, "ONE OF YOU GUYS"? NO MATTER HOW MUCH CASH YOU TOSS, YOU DON'T REALLY THINK THAT, DO YOU?
Just keep him off his mark...
...
WHAT'D YOU AND FATHER FIGHT ABOUT THAT NIGHT?
...WHAT?
WHEN WE WERE KIDS. YOU TWO FOUGHT, HE HIT YOU, AND THEN WE NEVER SAW YOU AGAIN.
FATHER WAS SO SORRY, HE WROTE YOU--EVERY TWO WEEKS LIKE CLOCK-WORK FOR TEN YEARS--
I WROTE BACK--
YOU WROTE BACK?? YOU SHOULD HAVE BEEN HERE!
WE'RE SUPPOSED TO BE BROTHERS--
WE ARE--
ARE WE? WHEN WE WERE KIDS, YOU TOLD ME EVERYTHING.
BUT THEN WE GREW UP, AND... YOU ICED ME-- US--OUT.
LIKE WE ALL WEREN'T FAMILY ANYMORE.
I MEAN, WHY'D IT TAKE A HEART ATTACK FOR YOU TO SEE US? HUH? WHY??

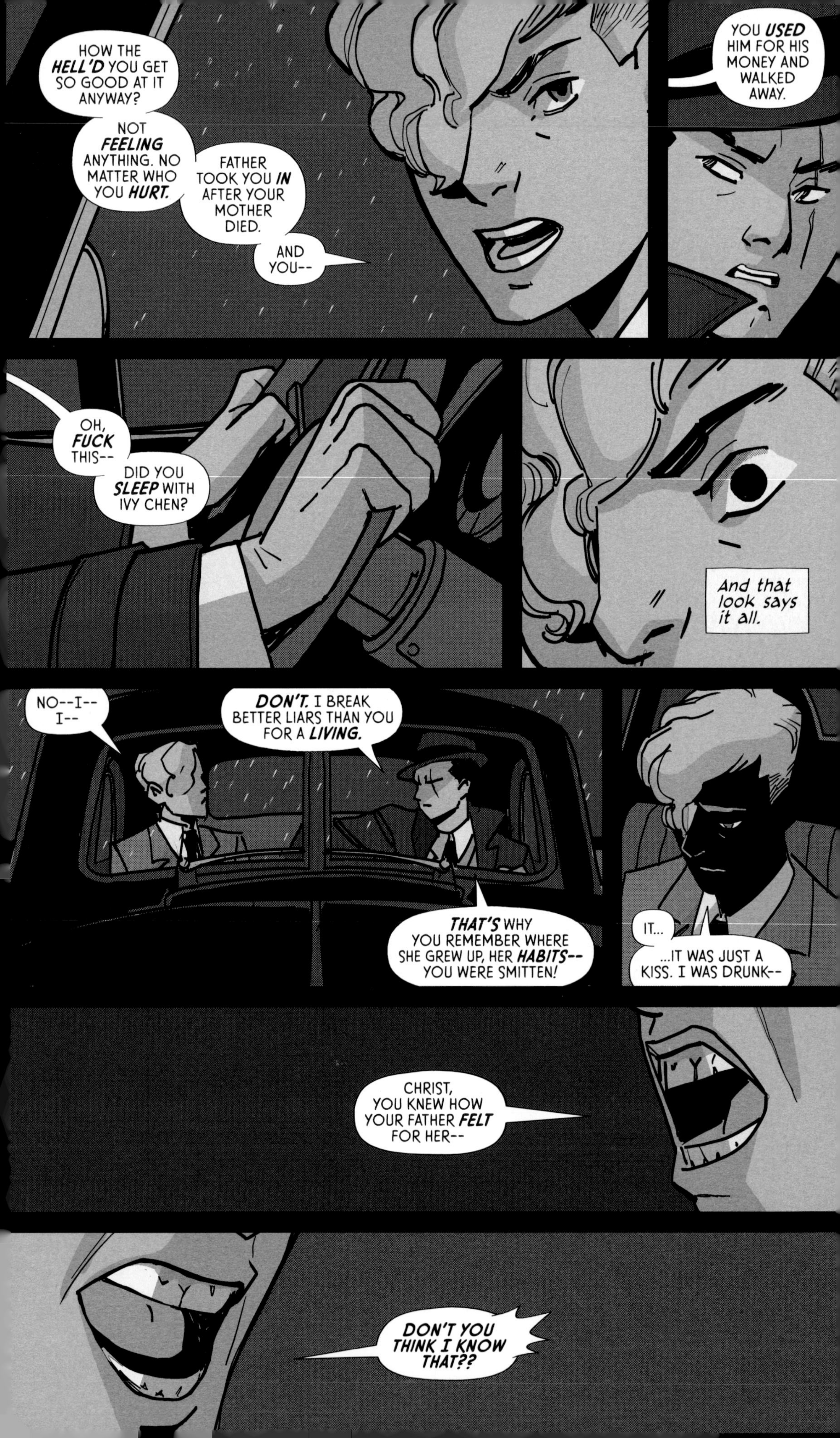
HOW THE HELL'D YOU GET SO GOOD AT IT ANYWAY?
NOT FEELING ANYTHING. NO MATTER WHO YOU HURT.
FATHER TOOK YOU IN AFTER YOUR MOTHER DIED.
AND YOU--
YOU USED HIM FOR HIS MONEY AND WALKED AWAY.
OH, FUCK THIS--
DID YOU SLEEP WITH IVY CHEN?
And that look says it all.
NO--I-- I--
DON'T. I BREAK BETTER LIARS THAN YOU FOR A LIVING.
THAT'S WHY YOU REMEMBER WHERE SHE GREW UP, HER HABITS-- YOU WERE SMITTEN!
IT...
...IT WAS JUST A KISS. I WAS DRUNK--
CHRIST, YOU KNEW HOW YOUR FATHER FELT FOR HER--
DON'T YOU THINK I KNOW THAT??

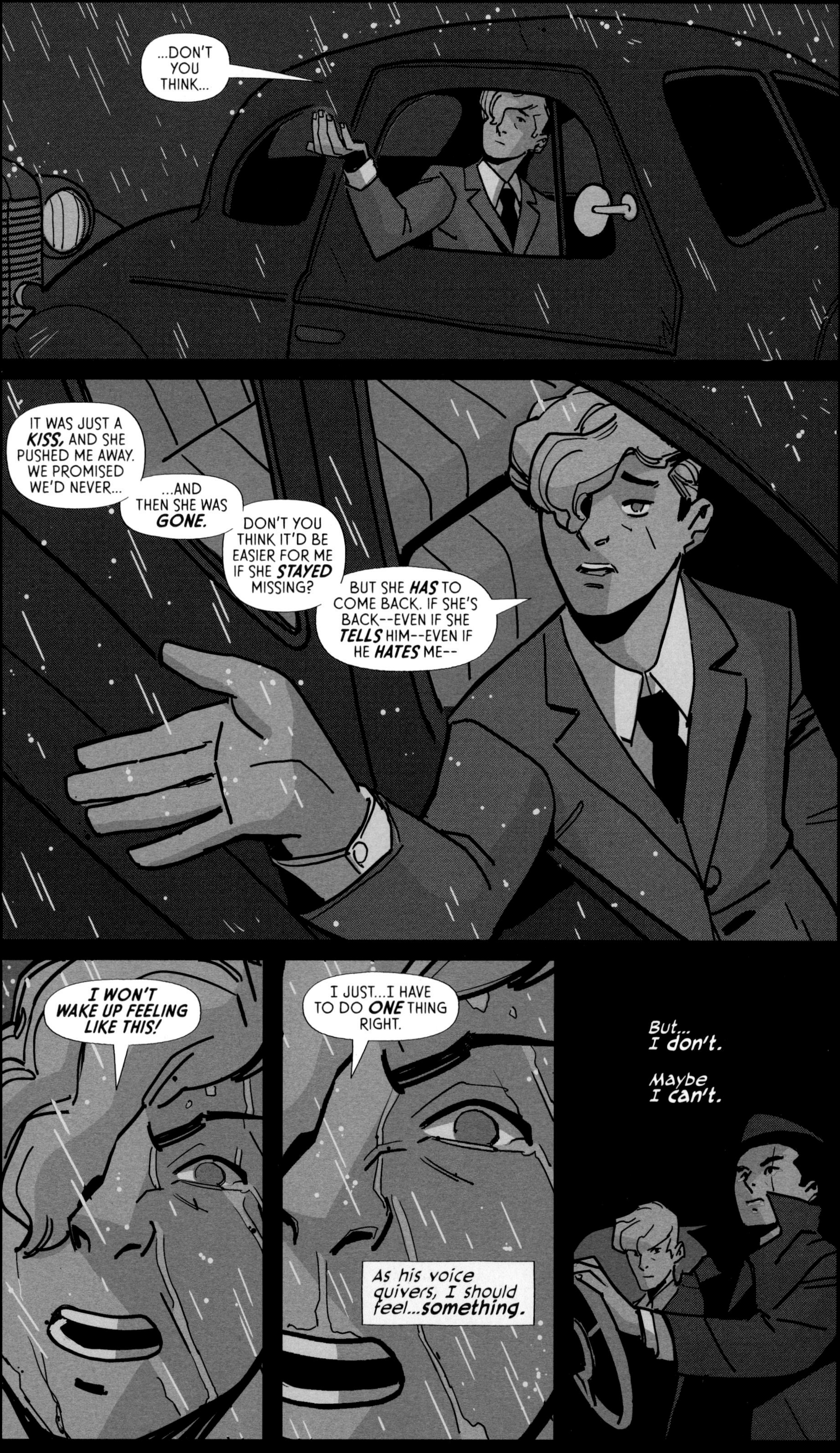
...DON'T YOU THINK...
IT WAS JUST A KISS, AND SHE PUSHED ME AWAY. WE PROMISED WE'D NEVER...
...AND THEN SHE WAS GONE.
DON'T YOU THINK IT'D BE EASIER FOR ME IF SHE STAYED MISSING?
BUT SHE HAS TO COME BACK. IF SHE'S BACK--EVEN IF SHE TELLS HIM--EVEN IF HE HATES ME--
I WON'T WAKE UP FEELING LIKE THIS!
I JUST...I HAVE TO DO ONE THING RIGHT.
As his voice quivers, I should feel...something.
But... I don't.
Maybe I can't.

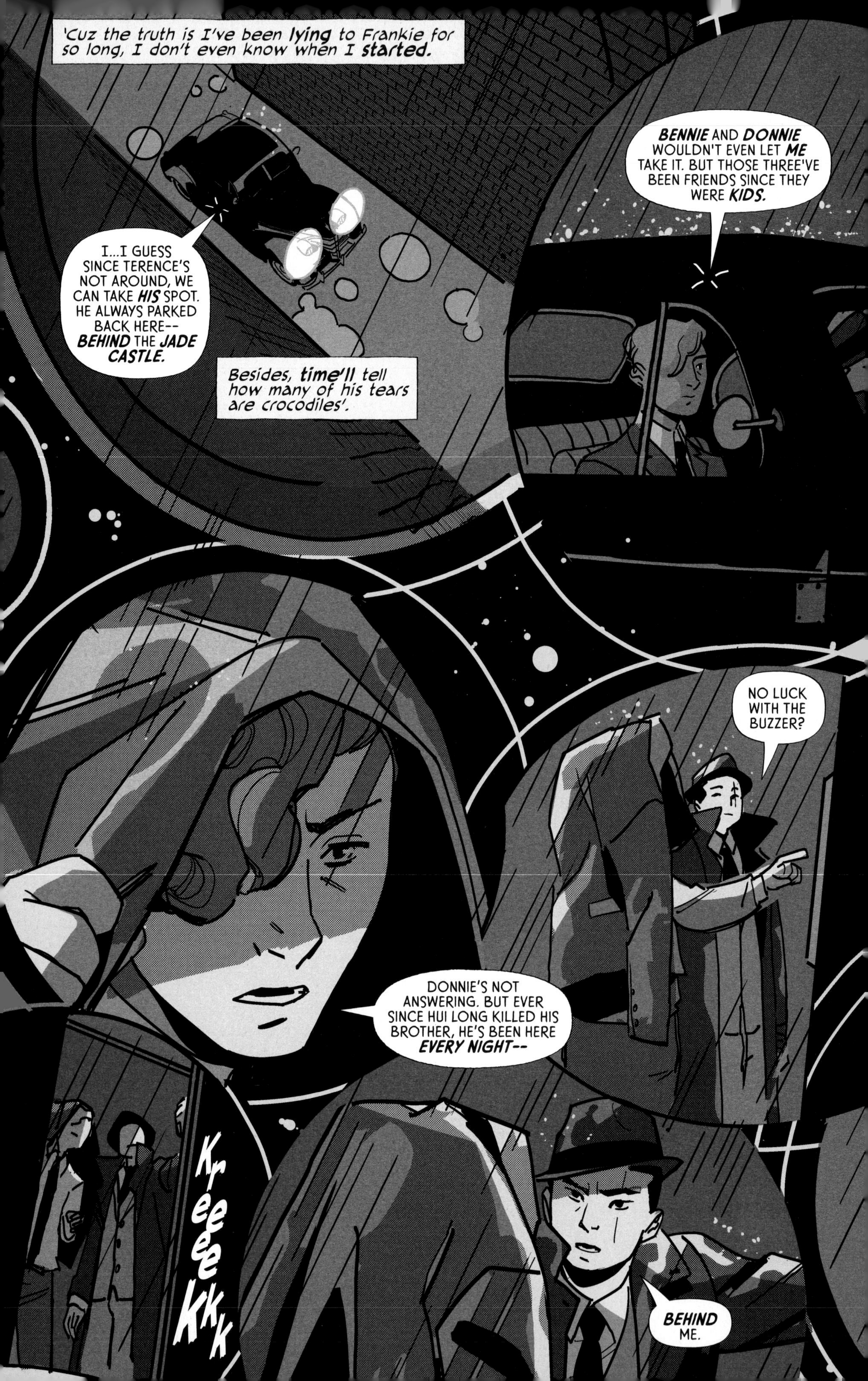
'Cuz the truth is I've been lying to Frankie for so long, I don't even know when I started.
I...I GUESS SINCE TERENCE'S NOT AROUND, WE CAN TAKE HIS SPOT. HE ALWAYS PARKED BACK HERE-- BEHIND THE JADE CASTLE.
Besides, time'll tell how many of his tears are crocodiles'.
BENNIE AND DONNIE WOULDN'T EVEN LET ME TAKE IT. BUT THOSE THREE'VE BEEN FRIENDS SINCE THEY WERE KIDS.
NO LUCK WITH THE BUZZER?
DONNIE'S NOT ANSWERING. BUT EVER SINCE HUI LONG KILLED HIS BROTHER, HE'S BEEN HERE EVERY NIGHT--
Kreeeekkk
BEHIND ME.

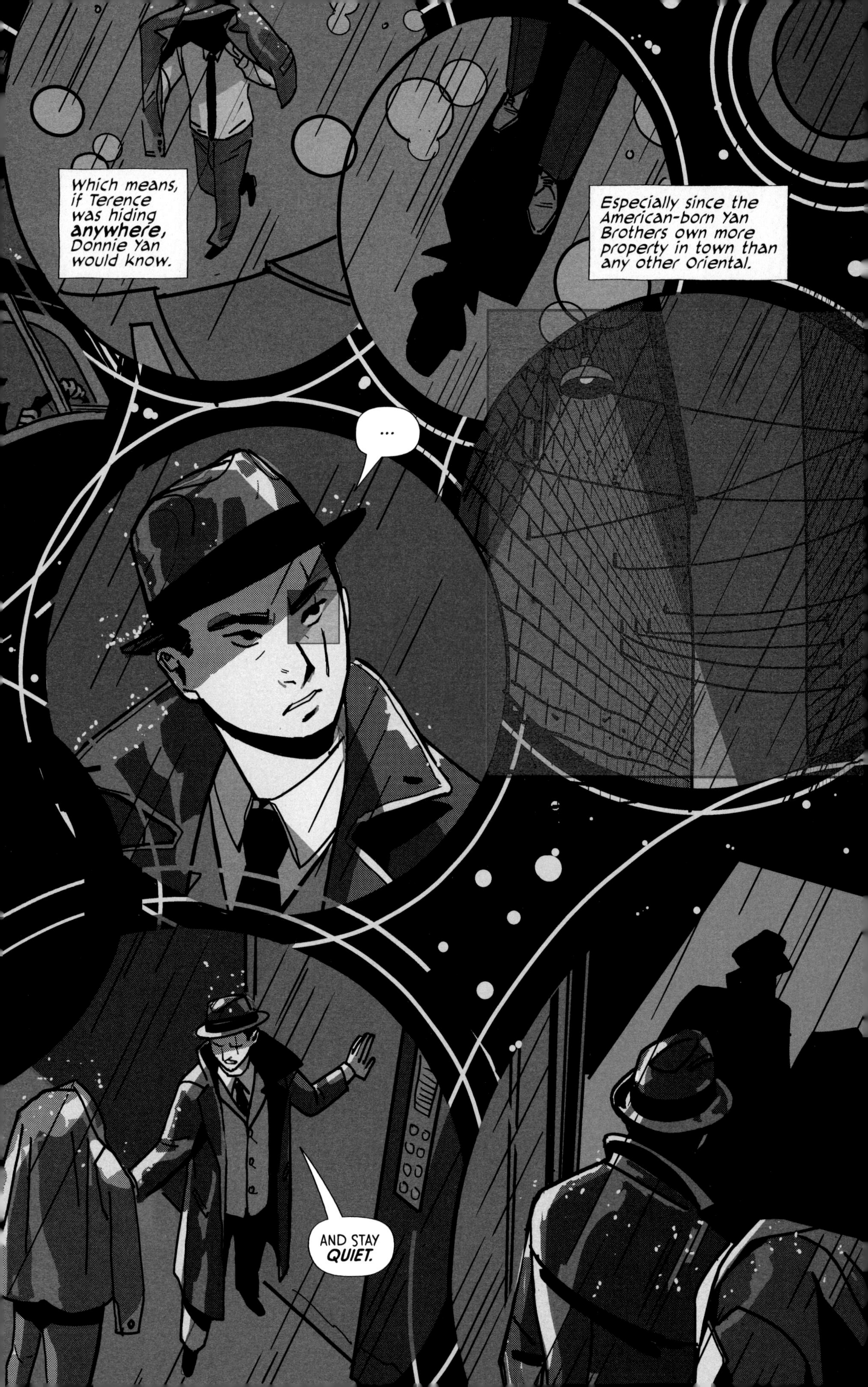
Which means, if Terence was hiding **anywhere,** Donnie Yan would know.
Especially since the American-born Yan Brothers own more property in town than any other Oriental.
...
AND STAY *QUIET.*

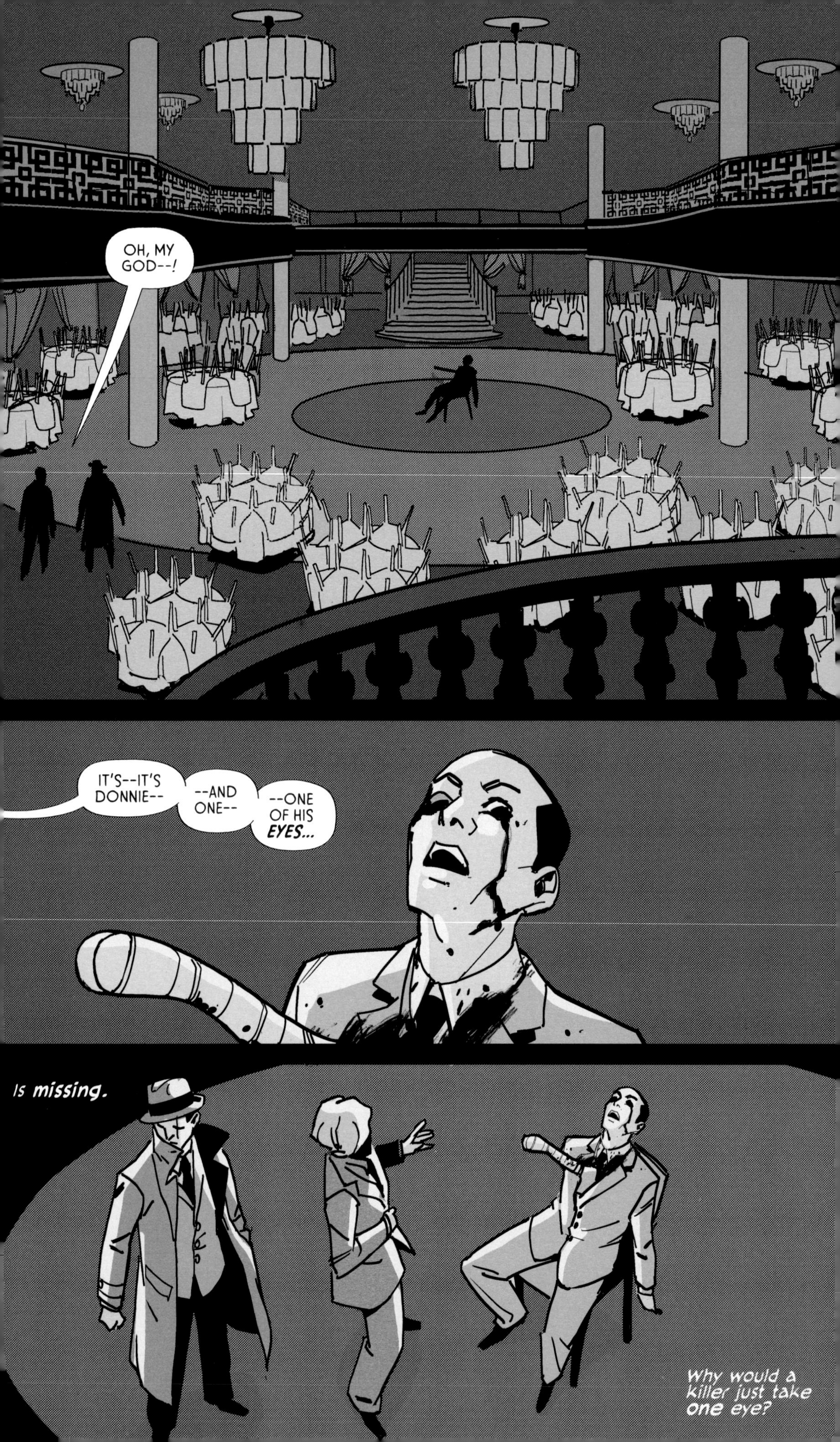
OH, MY GOD--!
IT'S--IT'S DONNIE--
--AND ONE--
--ONE OF HIS *EYES...*
Is *missing.*
Why would a killer just take *one eye?*

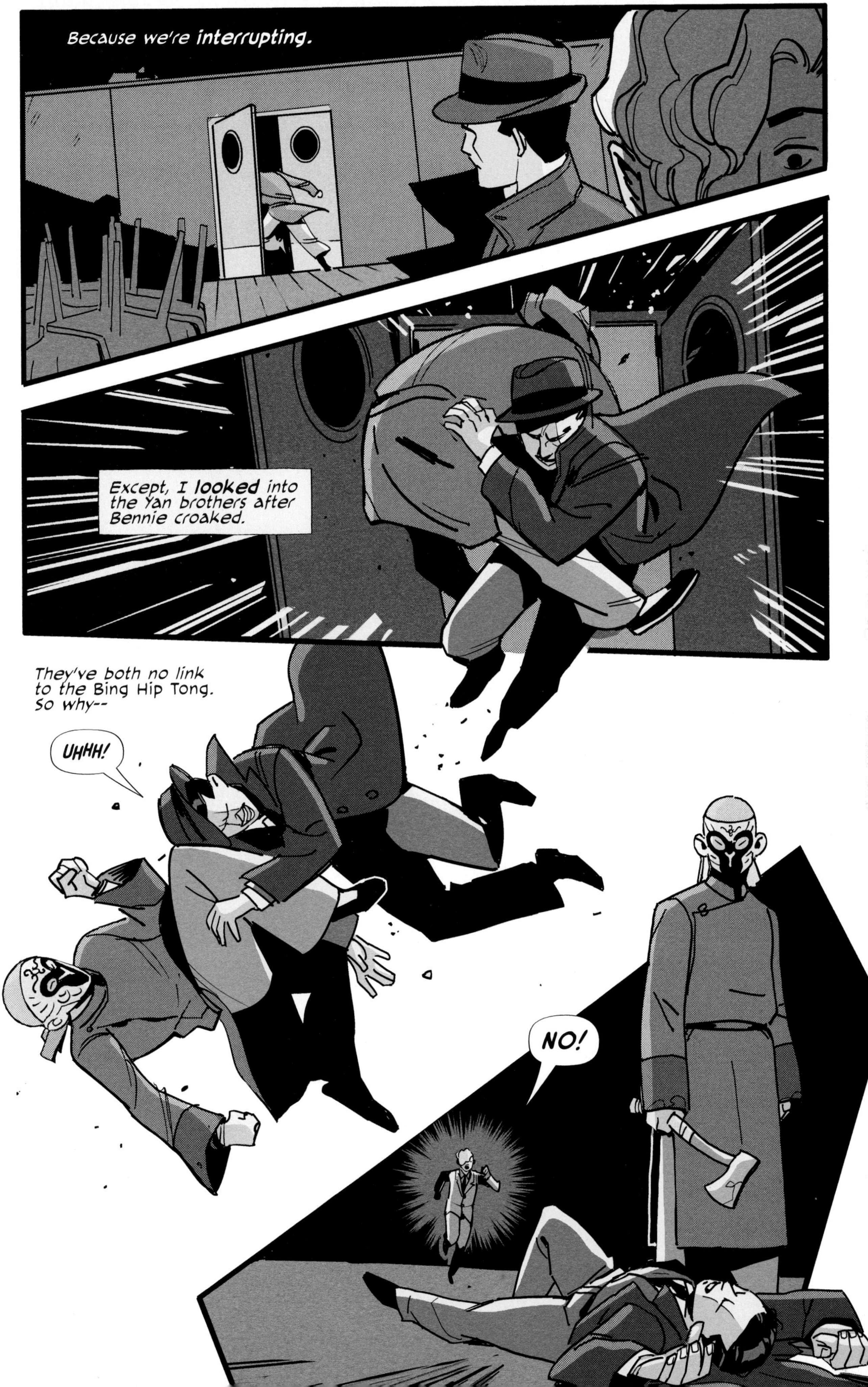
Because we're interrupting.
Except, I looked into the Yan brothers after Bennie croaked.
They've both no link to the Bing Hip Tong. So why--
UHHH!
NO!

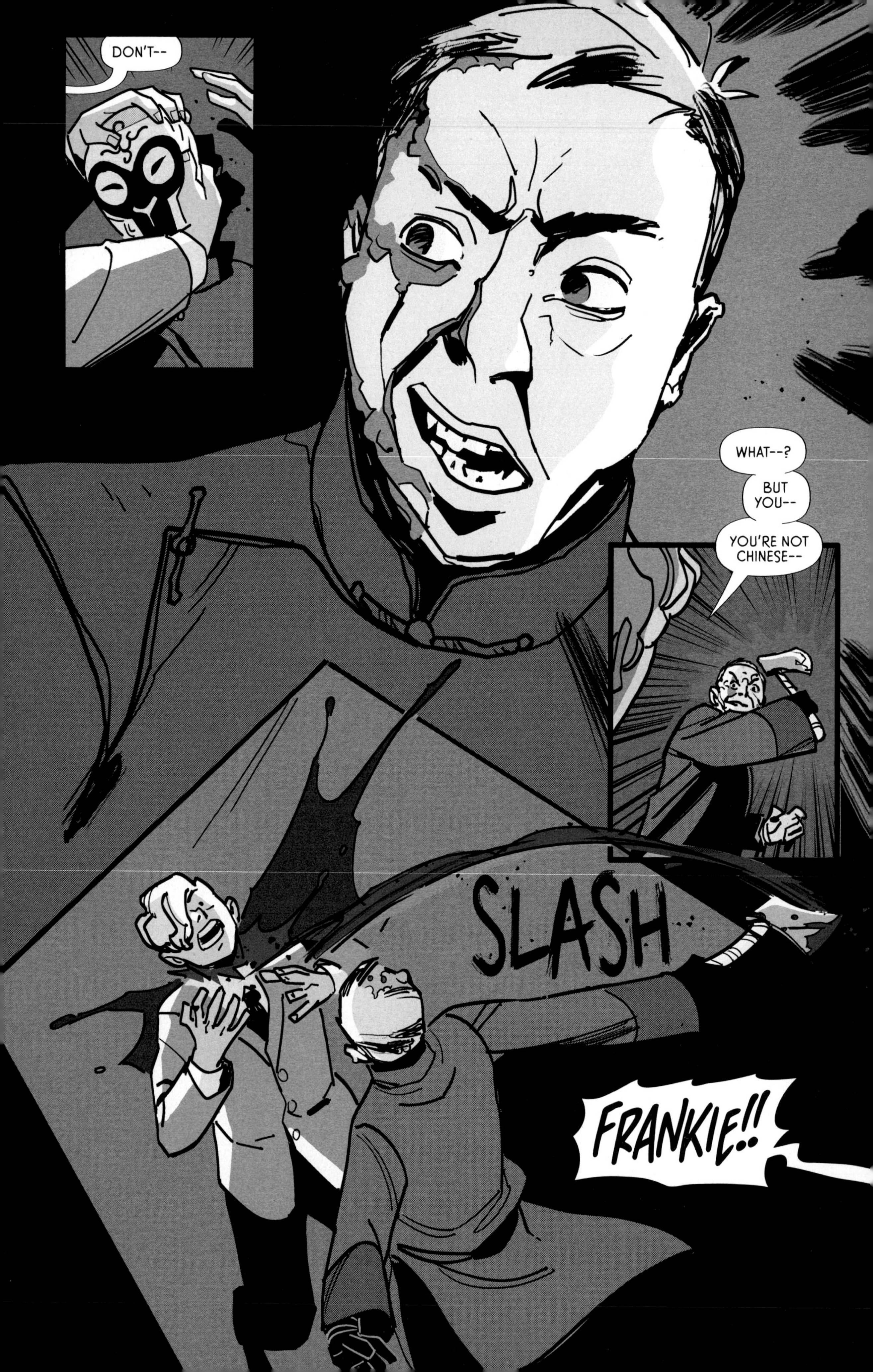
DON'T--
WHAT--?
BUT YOU--
YOU'RE NOT CHINESE--
SLASH
FRANKIE!!

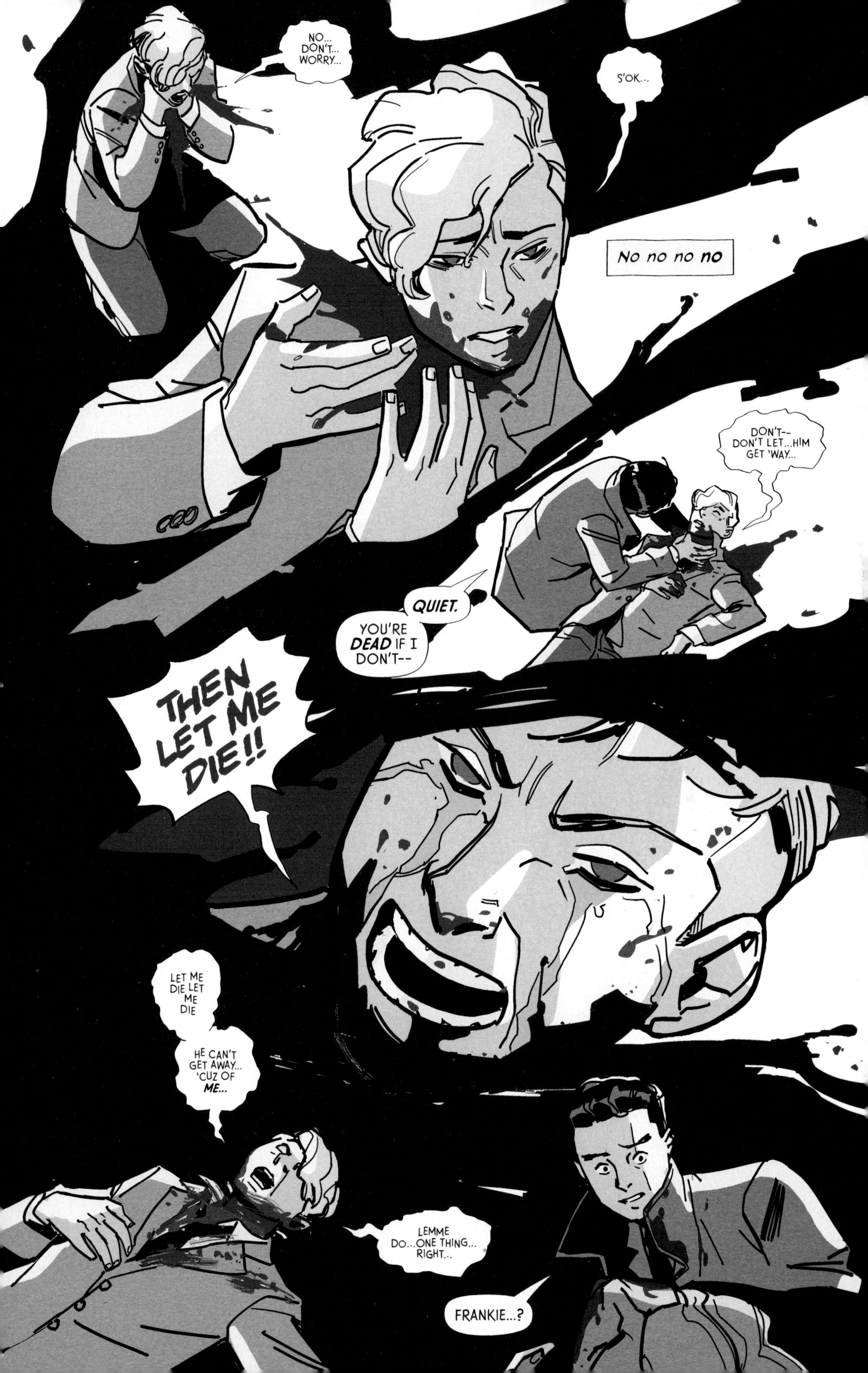
NO... DON'T... WORRY...
S'OK...
No no no no
DON'T-- DON'T LET...HIM GET 'WAY...
QUIET.
YOU'RE DEAD IF I DON'T--
THEN LET ME DIE!!
LET ME DIE LET ME DIE
HE CAN'T GET AWAY... 'CUZ OF ME...
LEMME DO...ONE THING... RIGHT...
FRANKIE...?

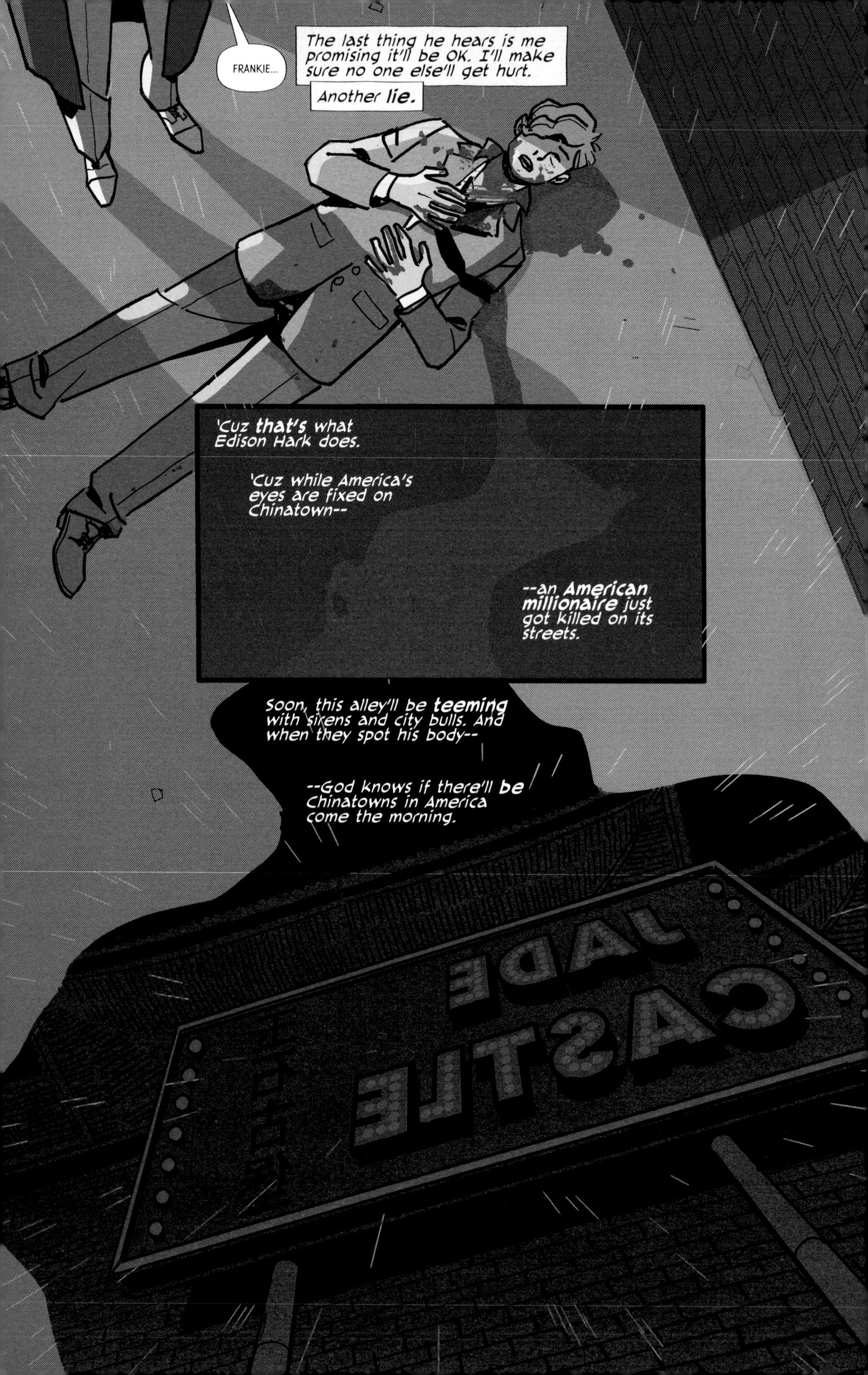

FRANKIE...
The last thing he hears is me promising it'll be OK. I'll make sure no one else'll get hurt.
Another lie.
'Cuz that's what Edison Hark does.
'Cuz while America's eyes are fixed on Chinatown--
--an American millionaire just got killed on its streets.
Soon, this alley'll be teeming with sirens and city bulls. And when they spot his body--
--God knows if there'll be Chinatowns in America come the morning.
JADE CASTLE

CHAPTER FIVE

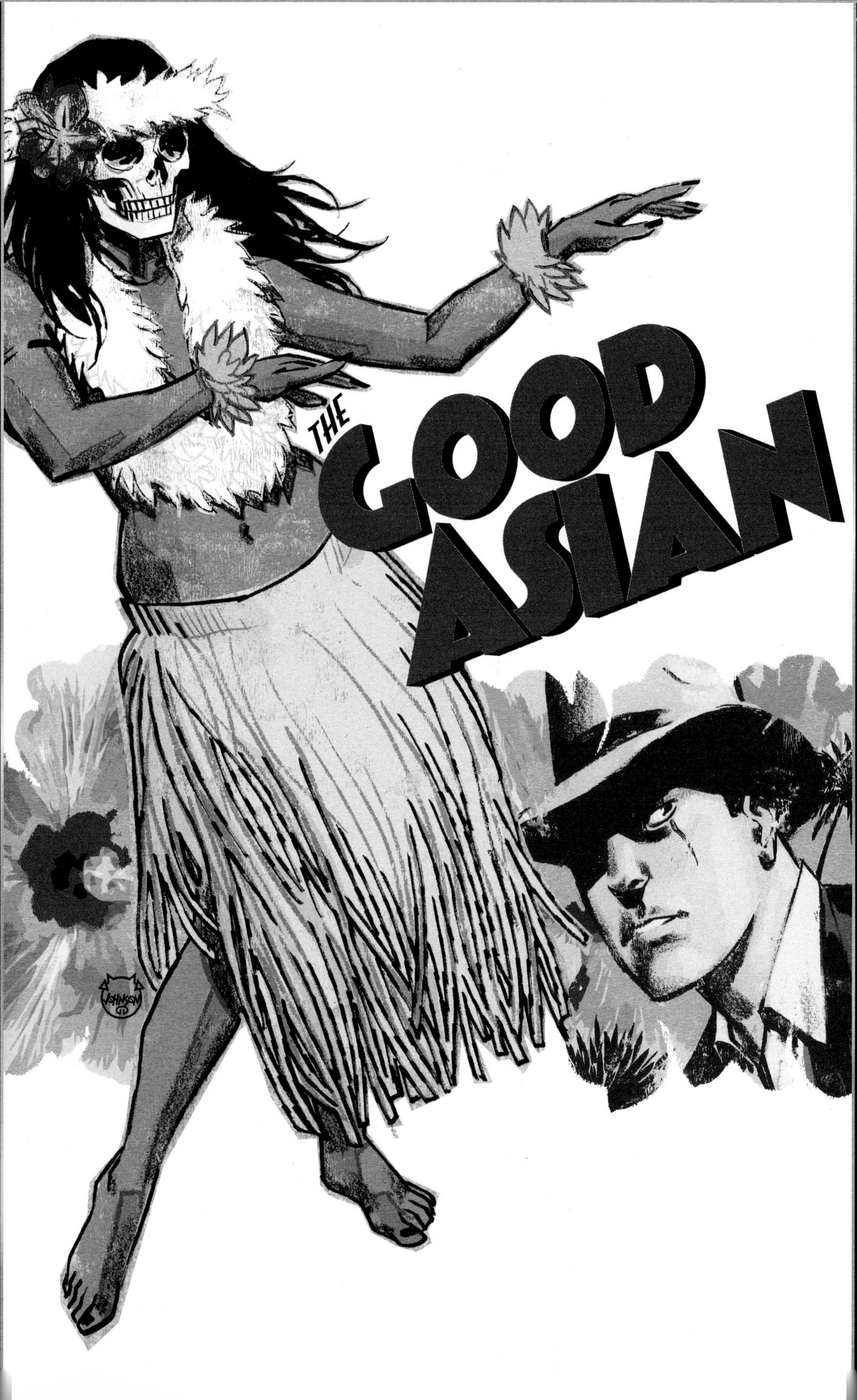
THE
GOOD
ASIAN

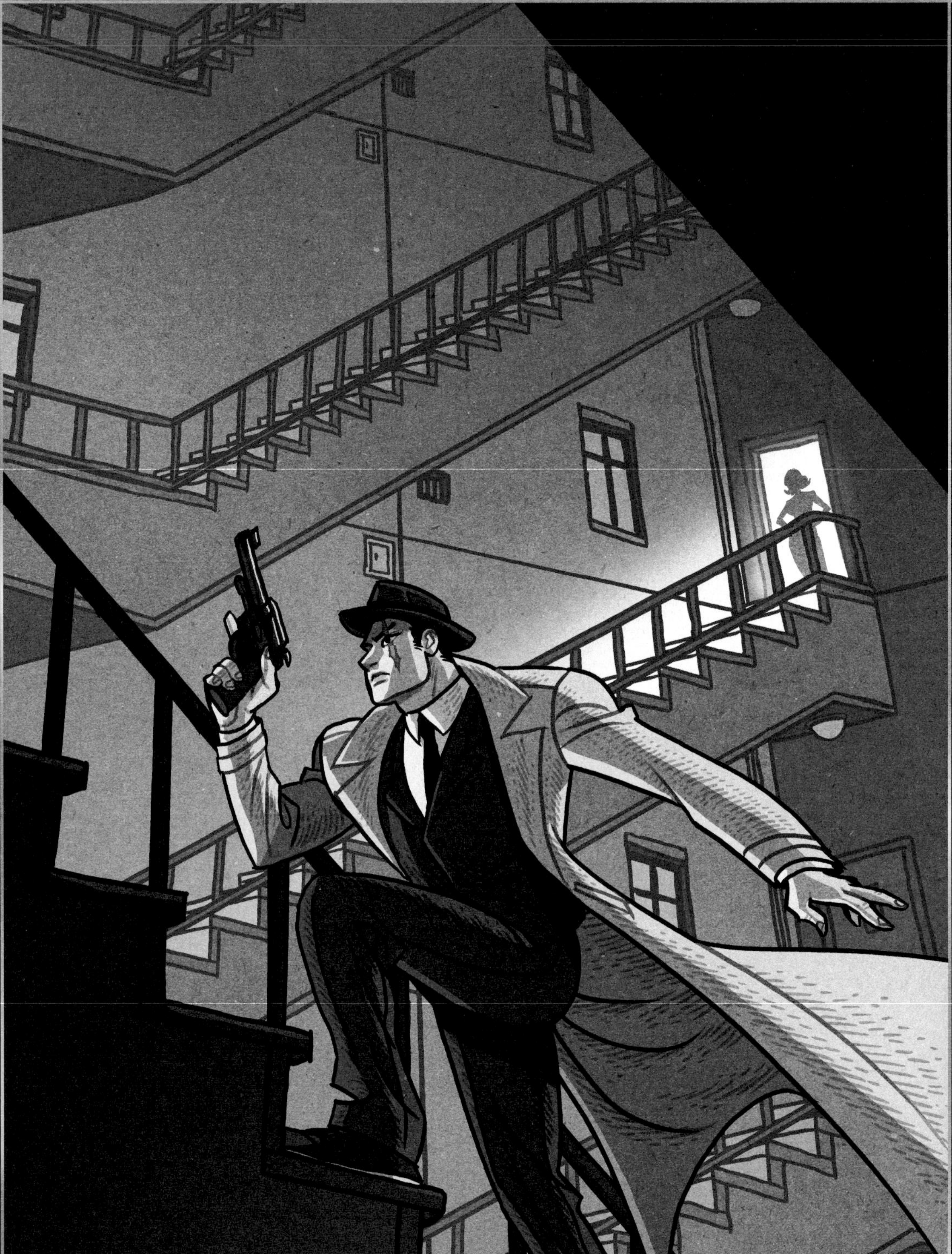
AFU
CHAN
2021

ART BY **AFU CHAN**

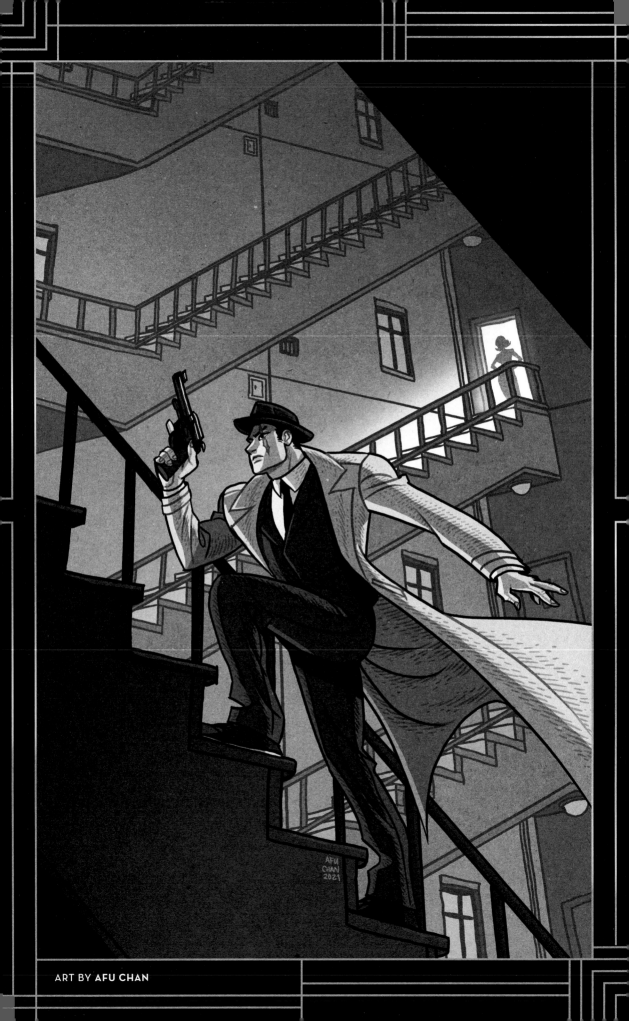

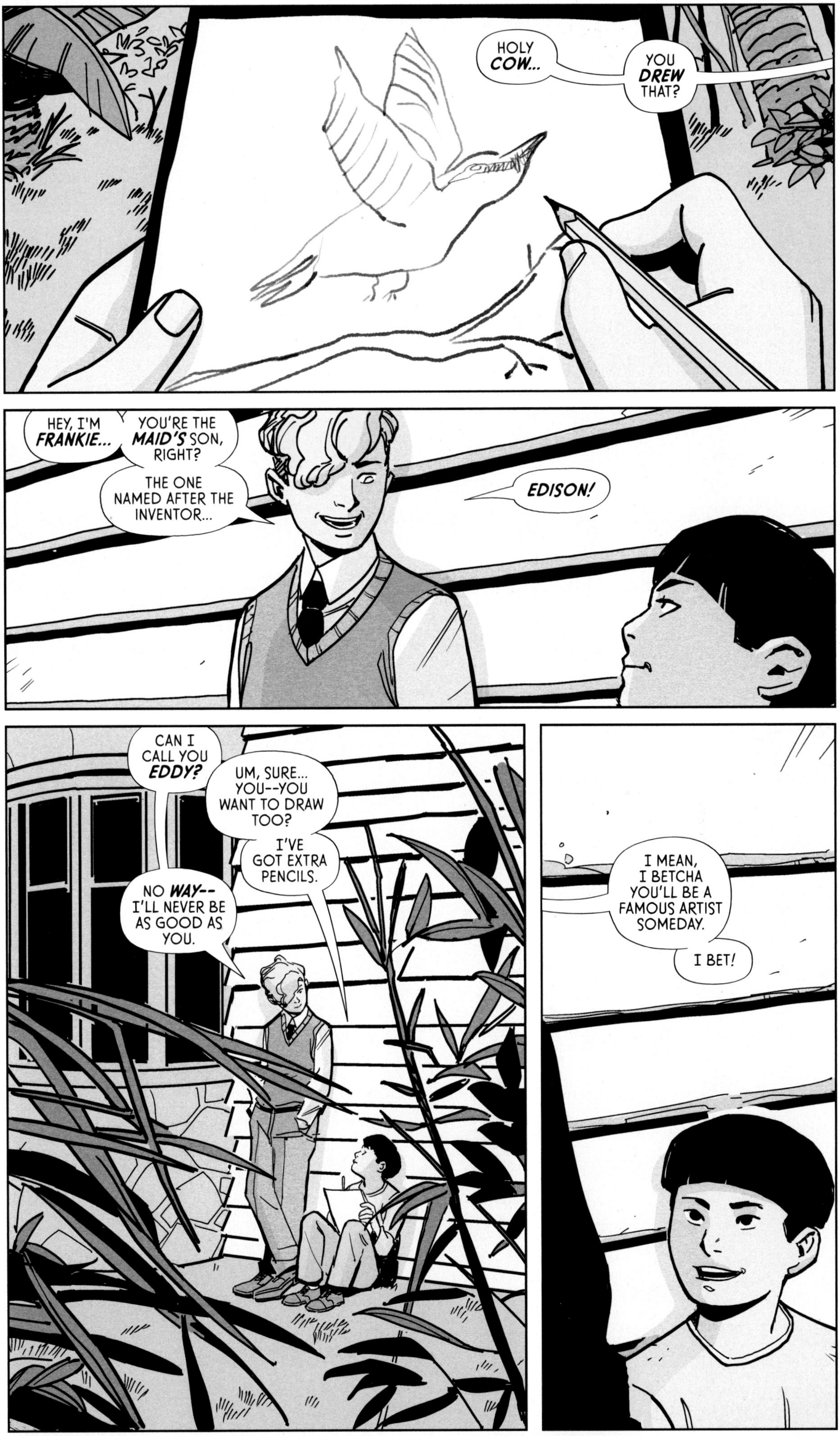
HOLY COW...
YOU DREW THAT?
HEY, I'M FRANKIE...
YOU'RE THE MAID'S SON, RIGHT?
THE ONE NAMED AFTER THE INVENTOR...
EDISON!
CAN I CALL YOU EDDY?
UM, SURE... YOU--YOU WANT TO DRAW TOO?
I'VE GOT EXTRA PENCILS.
NO WAY-- I'LL NEVER BE AS GOOD AS YOU.
I MEAN, I BETCHA YOU'LL BE A FAMOUS ARTIST SOMEDAY.
I BET!

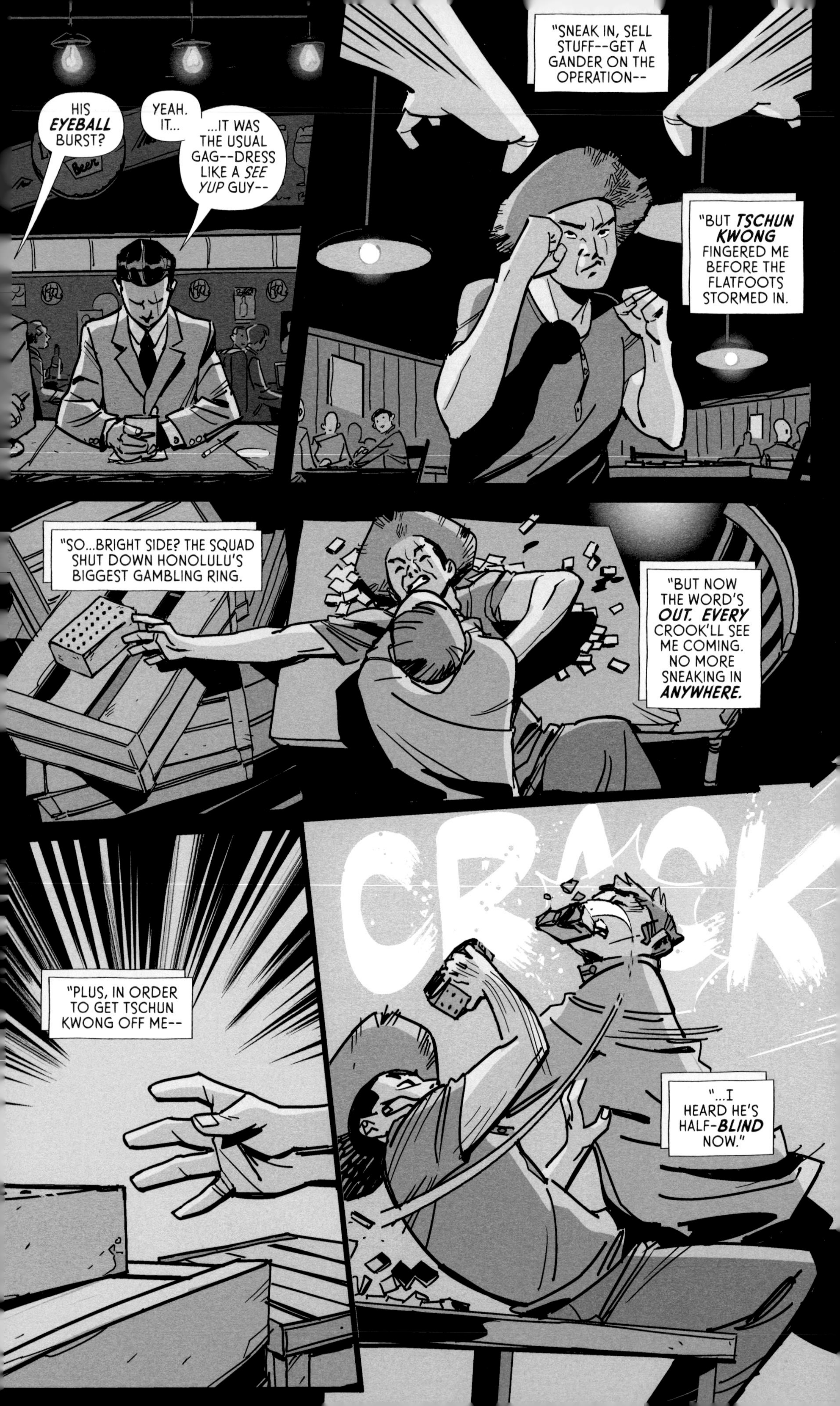
HIS *EYEBALL* BURST?
YEAH. IT...
...IT WAS THE USUAL GAG--DRESS LIKE A *SEE YUP* GUY--
"SNEAK IN, SELL STUFF--GET A GANDER ON THE OPERATION--
"BUT *TSCHUN KWONG* FINGERED ME BEFORE THE FLATFOOTS STORMED IN.
"SO...BRIGHT SIDE? THE SQUAD SHUT DOWN HONOLULU'S BIGGEST GAMBLING RING.
"BUT NOW THE WORD'S *OUT. EVERY* CROOK'LL SEE ME COMING. NO MORE SNEAKING IN *ANYWHERE.*
"PLUS, IN ORDER TO GET TSCHUN KWONG OFF ME--
CRACK
"...I HEARD HE'S HALF-*BLIND* NOW."

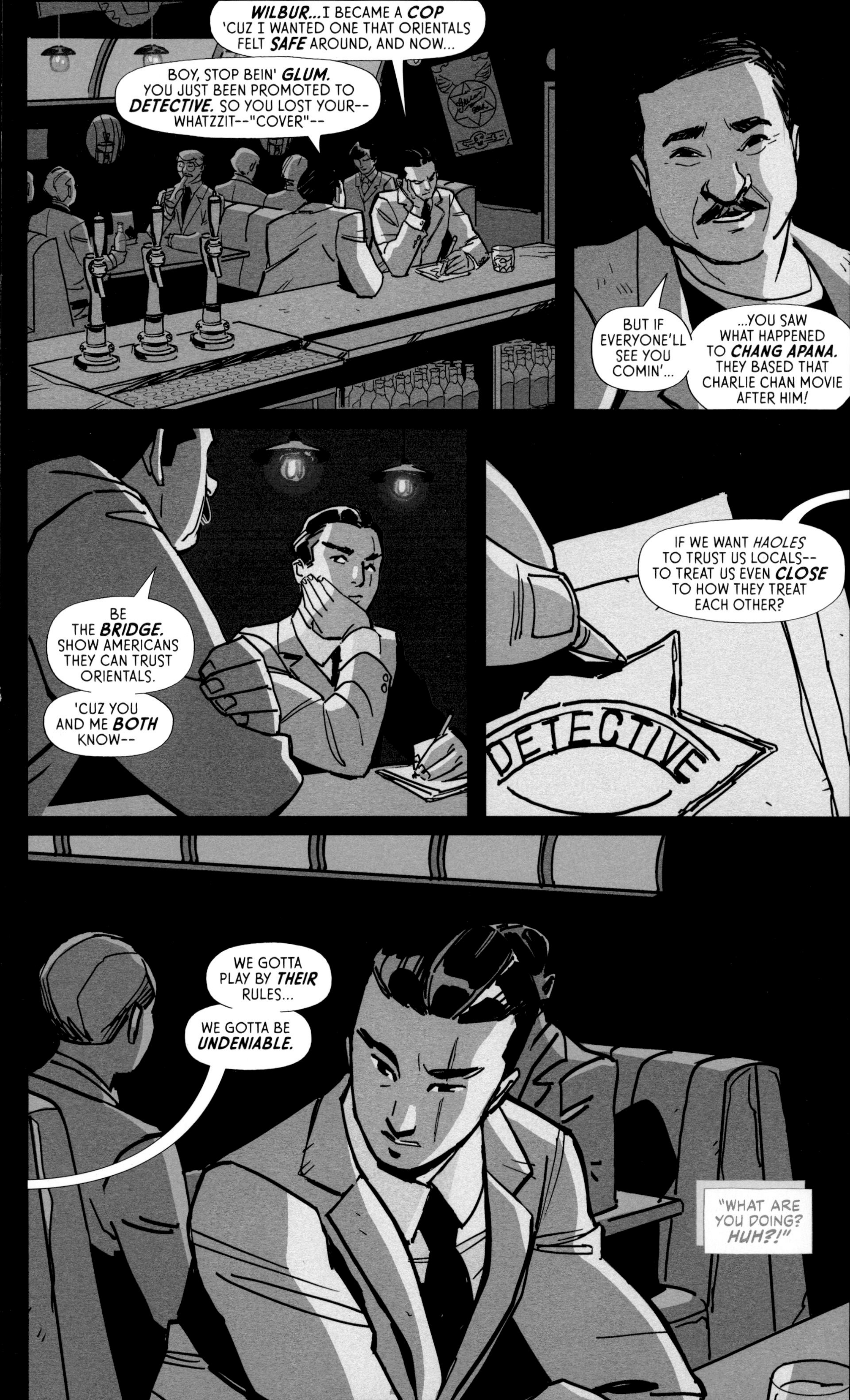
WILBUR...I BECAME A COP 'CUZ I WANTED ONE THAT ORIENTALS FELT SAFE AROUND, AND NOW...
BOY, STOP BEIN' GLUM. YOU JUST BEEN PROMOTED TO DETECTIVE. SO YOU LOST YOUR-- WHATZZIT--"COVER"--
BUT IF EVERYONE'LL SEE YOU COMIN'...
...YOU SAW WHAT HAPPENED TO CHANG APANA. THEY BASED THAT CHARLIE CHAN MOVIE AFTER HIM!
BE THE BRIDGE. SHOW AMERICANS THEY CAN TRUST ORIENTALS.
'CUZ YOU AND ME BOTH KNOW--
IF WE WANT HAOLES TO TRUST US LOCALS-- TO TREAT US EVEN CLOSE TO HOW THEY TREAT EACH OTHER?
DETECTIVE
WE GOTTA PLAY BY THEIR RULES...
WE GOTTA BE UNDENIABLE.
"WHAT ARE YOU DOING? HUH?!"

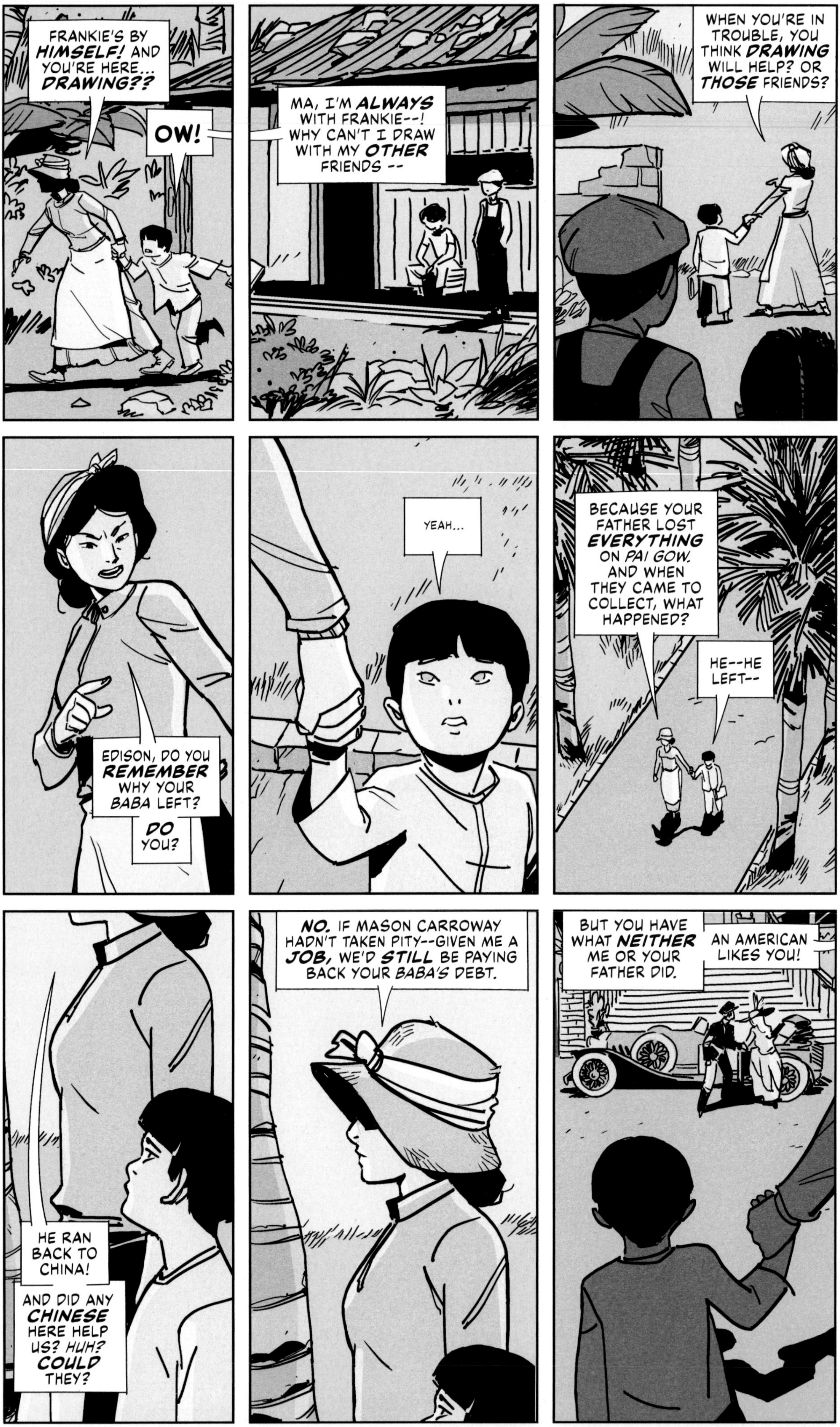
FRANKIE'S BY HIMSELF! AND YOU'RE HERE... DRAWING??
OW!
MA, I'M ALWAYS WITH FRANKIE--! WHY CAN'T I DRAW WITH MY OTHER FRIENDS --
WHEN YOU'RE IN TROUBLE, YOU THINK DRAWING WILL HELP? OR THOSE FRIENDS?
EDISON, DO YOU REMEMBER WHY YOUR BABA LEFT?
DO YOU?
YEAH...
BECAUSE YOUR FATHER LOST EVERYTHING ON PAI GOW. AND WHEN THEY CAME TO COLLECT, WHAT HAPPENED?
HE--HE LEFT--
HE RAN BACK TO CHINA!
AND DID ANY CHINESE HERE HELP US? HUH? COULD THEY?
NO. IF MASON CARROWAY HADN'T TAKEN PITY--GIVEN ME A JOB, WE'D STILL BE PAYING BACK YOUR BABA'S DEBT.
BUT YOU HAVE WHAT NEITHER ME OR YOUR FATHER DID.
AN AMERICAN LIKES YOU!

"FRANKIE ALWAYS SAYS-- EDDY *THIS!* EDDY *THAT!*

"YOU PAY ATTENTION TO THAT WHOLE FAMILY. YOU ACT LIKE *THEM*--"

MA, THE CARROWAYS ARE MILLIONAIRES! IT'S NOT THE SAME.

YOU MAY NOT HAVE MILLIONS, BUT YOU HAVE A *BRAIN*. YOU HAVE *EYES*.

"YOU *PAY ATTENTION.* WHEN THEY'RE *NERVOUS.* WHEN THEY'RE *RELIEVED.* ALL THE DIFFERENT WAYS THEY THINK THE WORLD OWES THEM *HAPPINESS.* THEY'LL TELL YOU *EVERYTHING* ABOUT HOW THEY WANT TO BE TREATED. YOU JUST HAVE TO *PAY ATTENTION.*"

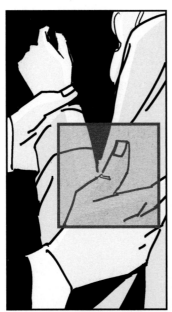

DO *EVERYTHING* RIGHT--

FOLLOW THEIR RULES.

DON'T GIVE THEM A *REASON* NOT TO HAVE YOU.

CAN YOU DO THAT FOR YOUR MA?

CAN YOU?

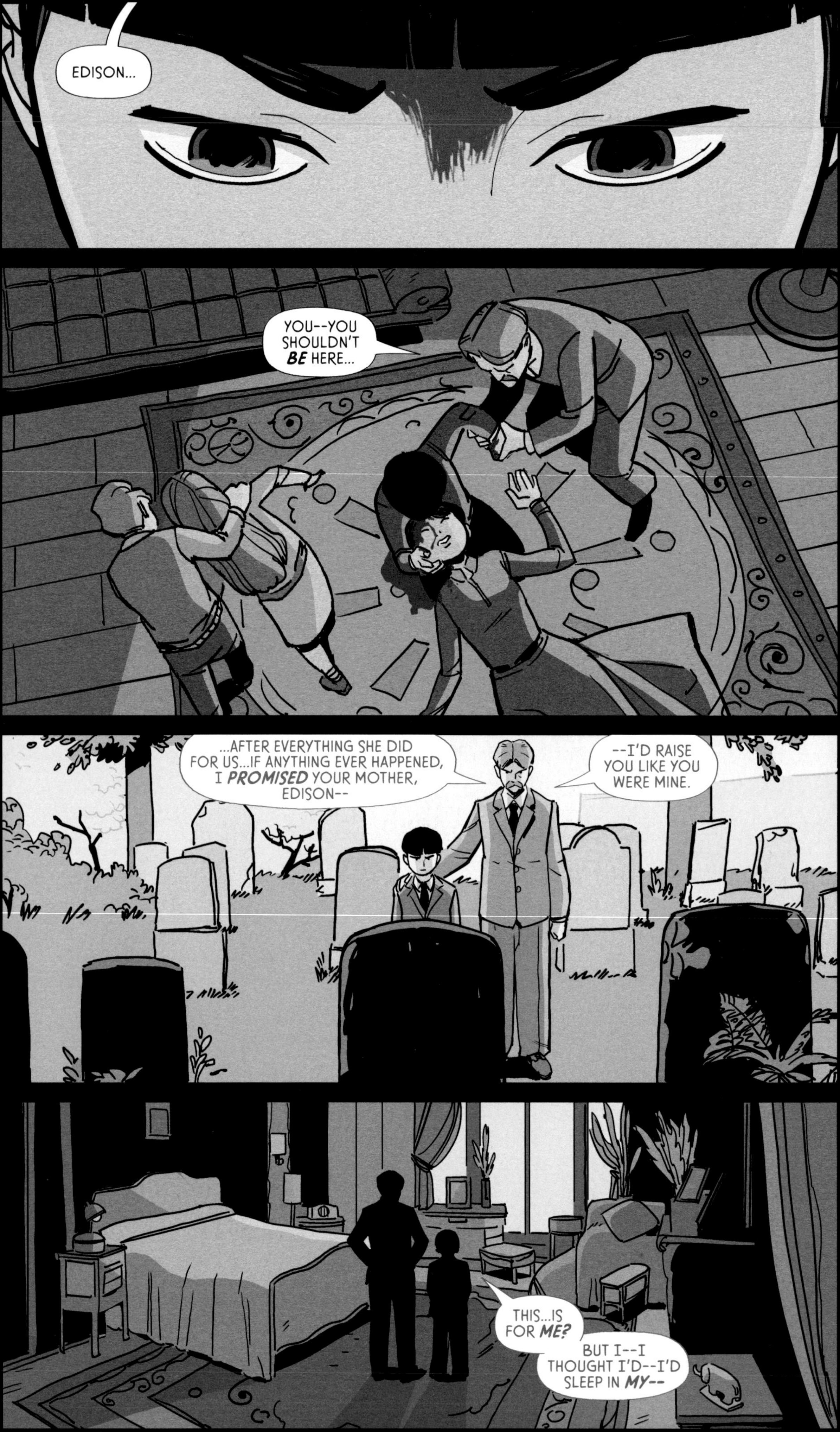
EDISON...
YOU--YOU SHOULDN'T *BE* HERE...
...AFTER EVERYTHING SHE DID FOR US...IF ANYTHING EVER HAPPENED, I *PROMISED* YOUR MOTHER, EDISON--
--I'D RAISE YOU LIKE YOU WERE MINE.
THIS...IS FOR *ME?*
BUT I--I THOUGHT I'D--I'D SLEEP IN *MY*--

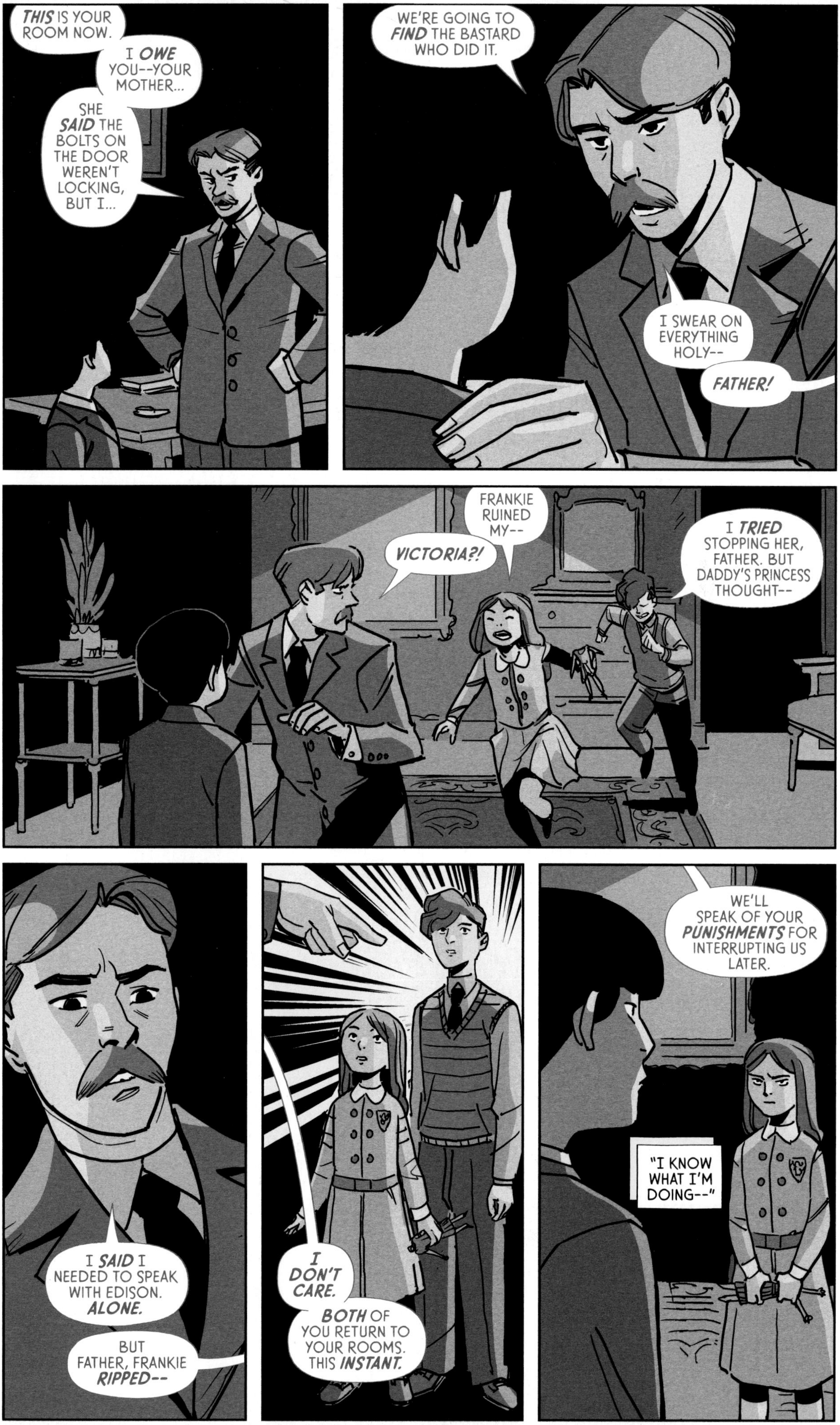
THIS IS YOUR ROOM NOW.
I OWE YOU--YOUR MOTHER...
SHE SAID THE BOLTS ON THE DOOR WEREN'T LOCKING, BUT I...
WE'RE GOING TO FIND THE BASTARD WHO DID IT.
I SWEAR ON EVERYTHING HOLY--
FATHER!
VICTORIA?!
FRANKIE RUINED MY--
I TRIED STOPPING HER, FATHER. BUT DADDY'S PRINCESS THOUGHT--
I SAID I NEEDED TO SPEAK WITH EDISON. ALONE.
BUT FATHER, FRANKIE RIPPED--
I DON'T CARE.
BOTH OF YOU RETURN TO YOUR ROOMS. THIS INSTANT.
WE'LL SPEAK OF YOUR PUNISHMENTS FOR INTERRUPTING US LATER.
"I KNOW WHAT I'M DOING--"

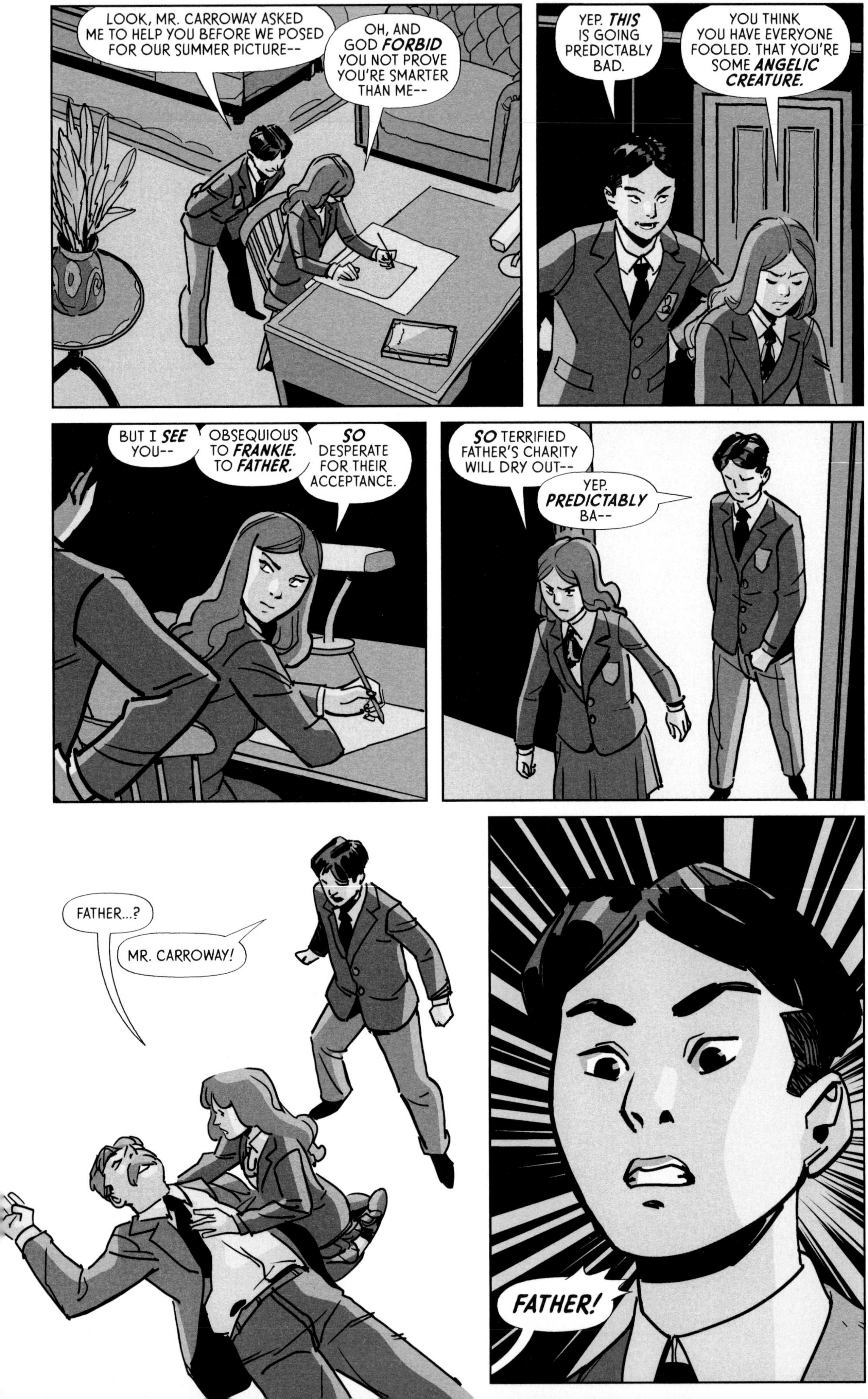
LOOK, MR. CARROWAY ASKED ME TO HELP YOU BEFORE WE POSED FOR OUR SUMMER PICTURE--
OH, AND GOD FORBID YOU NOT PROVE YOU'RE SMARTER THAN ME--
YEP. THIS IS GOING PREDICTABLY BAD.
YOU THINK YOU HAVE EVERYONE FOOLED. THAT YOU'RE SOME ANGELIC CREATURE.
BUT I SEE YOU--
OBSEQUIOUS TO FRANKIE. TO FATHER.
SO DESPERATE FOR THEIR ACCEPTANCE.
SO TERRIFIED FATHER'S CHARITY WILL DRY OUT--
YEP. PREDICTABLY BA--
FATHER...?
MR. CARROWAY!
FATHER!

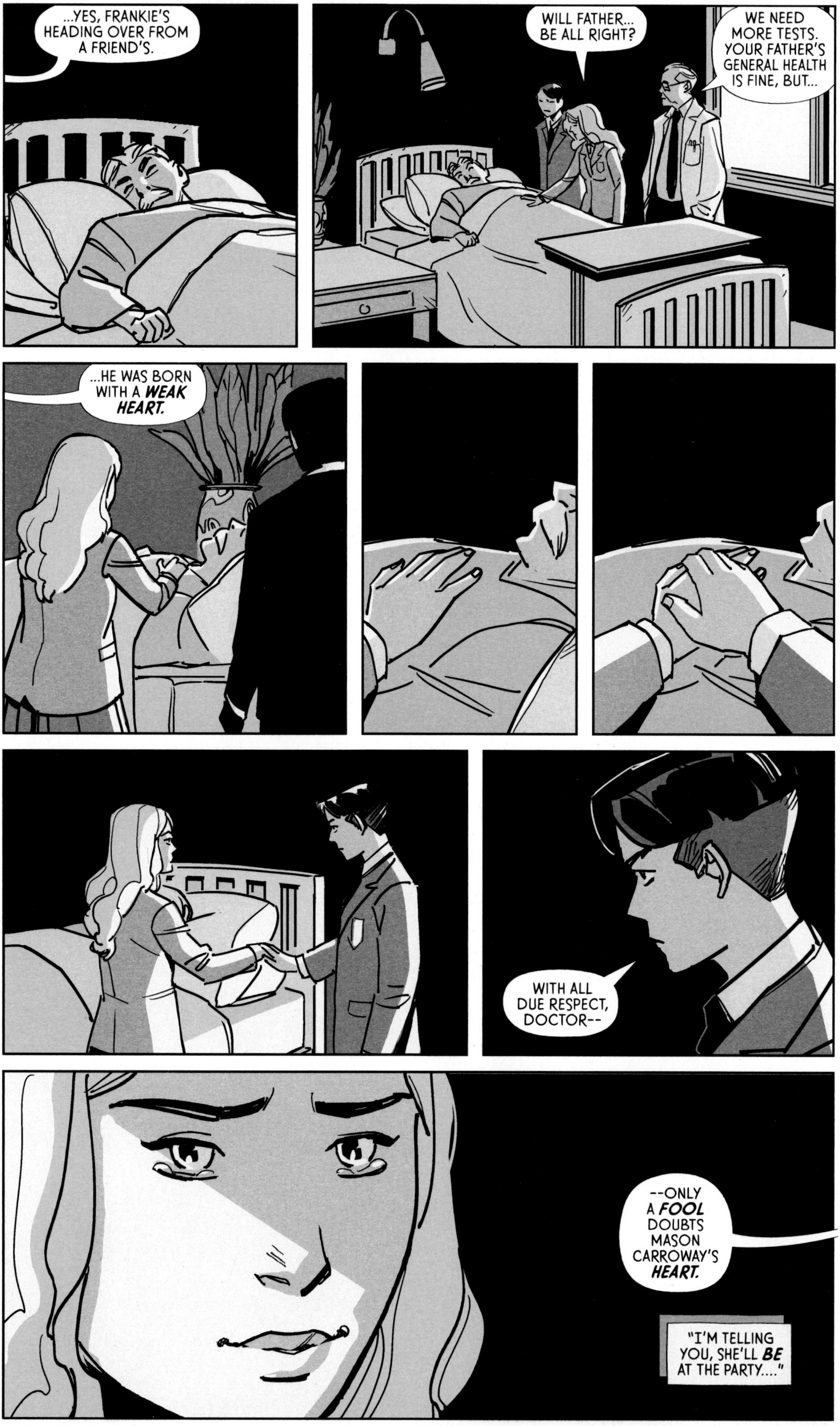
...YES, FRANKIE'S HEADING OVER FROM A FRIEND'S.
WILL FATHER... BE ALL RIGHT?
WE NEED MORE TESTS. YOUR FATHER'S GENERAL HEALTH IS FINE, BUT...
...HE WAS BORN WITH A *WEAK HEART.*
WITH ALL DUE RESPECT, DOCTOR--
--ONLY A *FOOL* DOUBTS MASON CARROWAY'S *HEART.*
"I'M TELLING YOU, SHE'LL *BE* AT THE PARTY...."

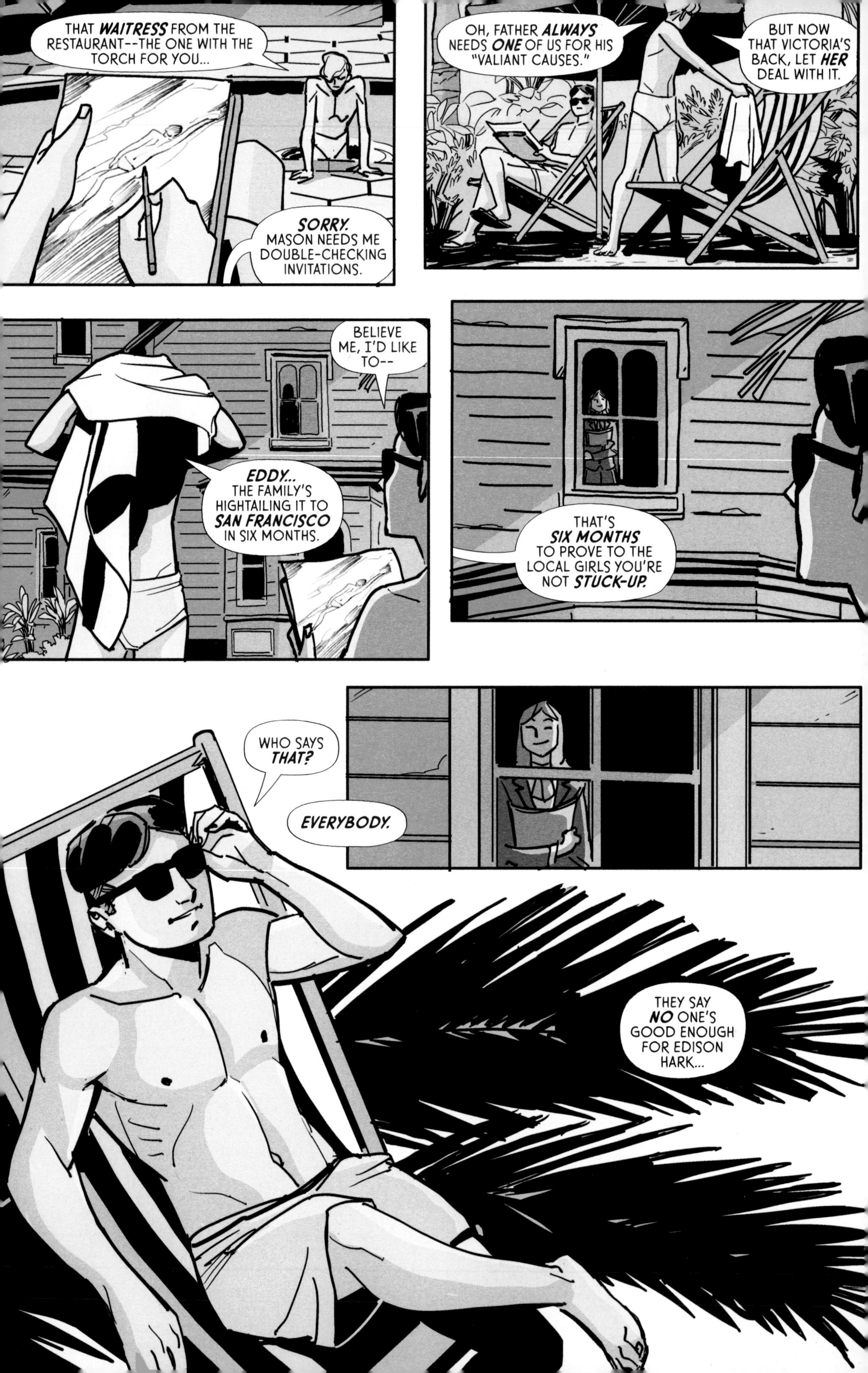
THAT WAITRESS FROM THE RESTAURANT--THE ONE WITH THE TORCH FOR YOU...
SORRY. MASON NEEDS ME DOUBLE-CHECKING INVITATIONS.
OH, FATHER ALWAYS NEEDS ONE OF US FOR HIS "VALIANT CAUSES."
BUT NOW THAT VICTORIA'S BACK, LET HER DEAL WITH IT.
BELIEVE ME, I'D LIKE TO--
EDDY... THE FAMILY'S HIGHTAILING IT TO SAN FRANCISCO IN SIX MONTHS.
THAT'S SIX MONTHS TO PROVE TO THE LOCAL GIRLS YOU'RE NOT STUCK-UP.
WHO SAYS THAT?
EVERYBODY.
THEY SAY NO ONE'S GOOD ENOUGH FOR EDISON HARK...

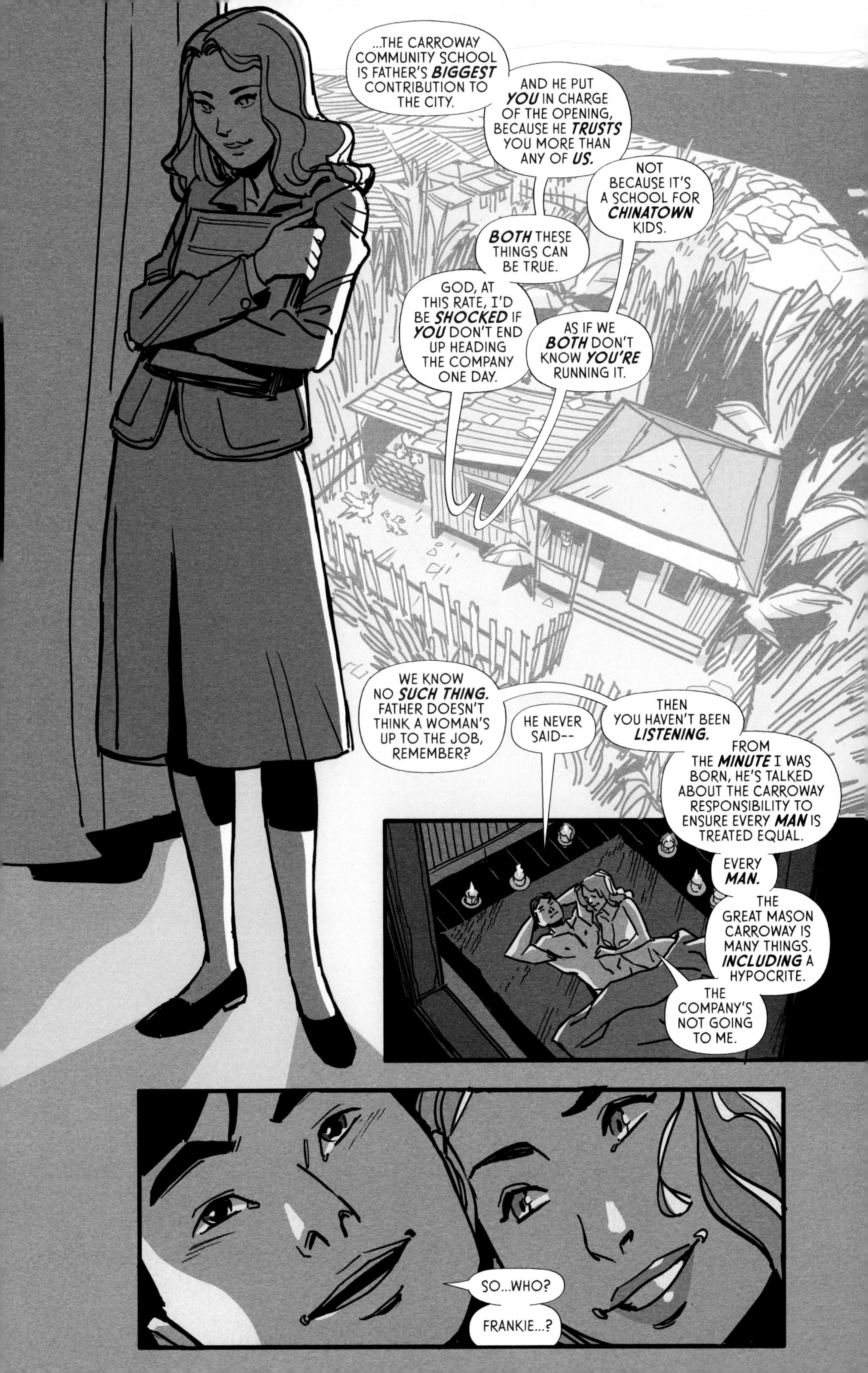

...THE CARROWAY COMMUNITY SCHOOL IS FATHER'S **BIGGEST** CONTRIBUTION TO THE CITY.
AND HE PUT **YOU** IN CHARGE OF THE OPENING, BECAUSE HE **TRUSTS** YOU MORE THAN ANY OF **US.**
NOT BECAUSE IT'S A SCHOOL FOR **CHINATOWN** KIDS.
BOTH THESE THINGS CAN BE TRUE.
GOD, AT THIS RATE, I'D BE **SHOCKED** IF **YOU** DON'T END UP HEADING THE COMPANY ONE DAY.
AS IF WE **BOTH** DON'T KNOW **YOU'RE** RUNNING IT.
WE KNOW NO **SUCH THING.** FATHER DOESN'T THINK A WOMAN'S UP TO THE JOB, REMEMBER?
HE NEVER SAID--
THEN YOU HAVEN'T BEEN **LISTENING.**
FROM THE **MINUTE** I WAS BORN, HE'S TALKED ABOUT THE CARROWAY RESPONSIBILITY TO ENSURE EVERY **MAN** IS TREATED EQUAL.
EVERY **MAN.**
THE GREAT MASON CARROWAY IS MANY THINGS. **INCLUDING** A HYPOCRITE.
THE COMPANY'S NOT GOING TO ME.
SO...WHO?
FRANKIE...?

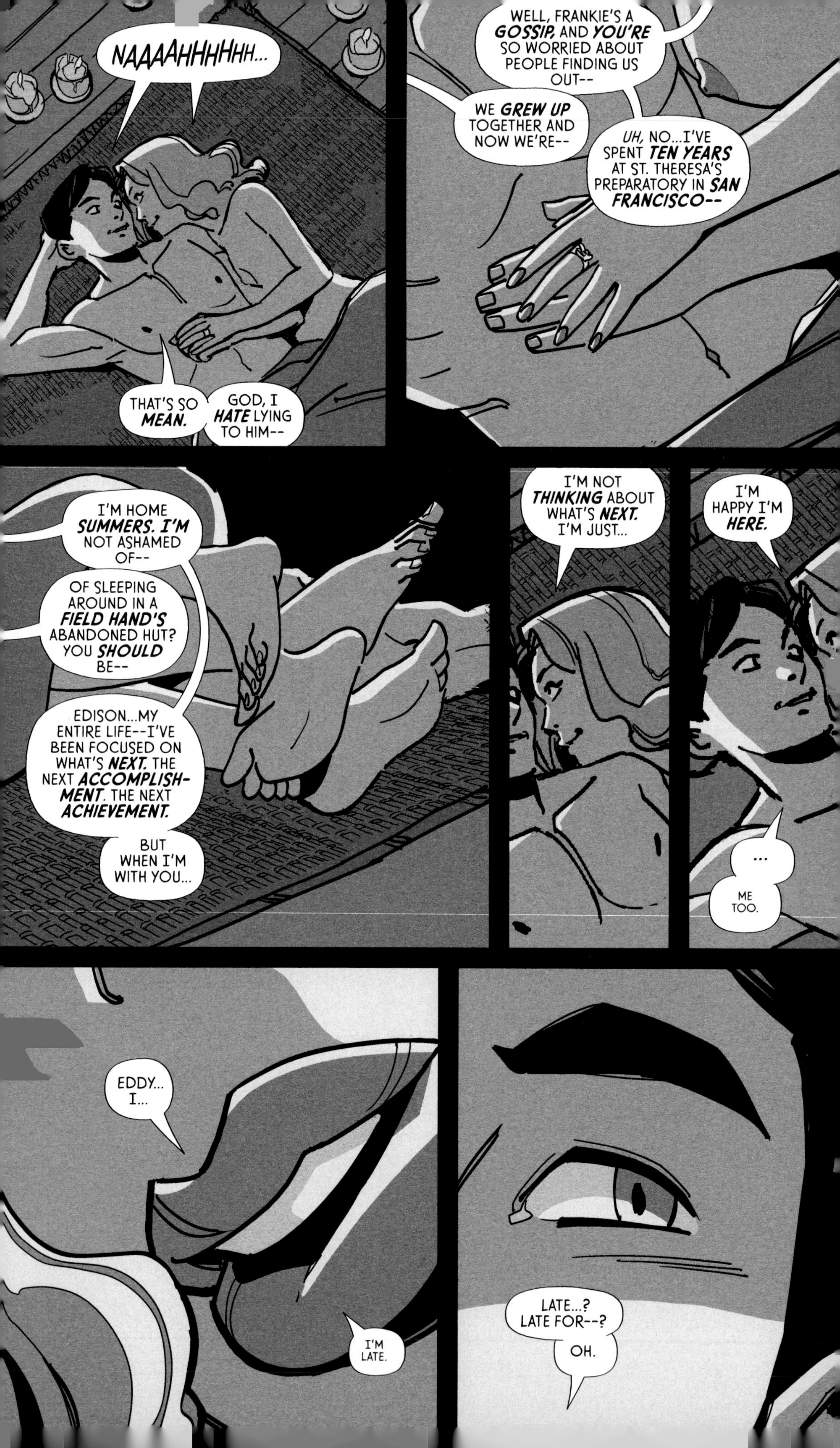
NAAAAHHHHHH...
THAT'S SO MEAN.
GOD, I HATE LYING TO HIM--
WELL, FRANKIE'S A GOSSIP, AND YOU'RE SO WORRIED ABOUT PEOPLE FINDING US OUT--
WE GREW UP TOGETHER AND NOW WE'RE--
UH, NO...I'VE SPENT TEN YEARS AT ST. THERESA'S PREPARATORY IN SAN FRANCISCO--
I'M HOME SUMMERS. I'M NOT ASHAMED OF--
OF SLEEPING AROUND IN A FIELD HAND'S ABANDONED HUT? YOU SHOULD BE--
EDISON...MY ENTIRE LIFE--I'VE BEEN FOCUSED ON WHAT'S NEXT. THE NEXT ACCOMPLISHMENT. THE NEXT ACHIEVEMENT.
BUT WHEN I'M WITH YOU...
I'M NOT THINKING ABOUT WHAT'S NEXT. I'M JUST...
I'M HAPPY I'M HERE.
...
ME TOO.
EDDY... I...
I'M LATE.
LATE...? LATE FOR--?
OH.

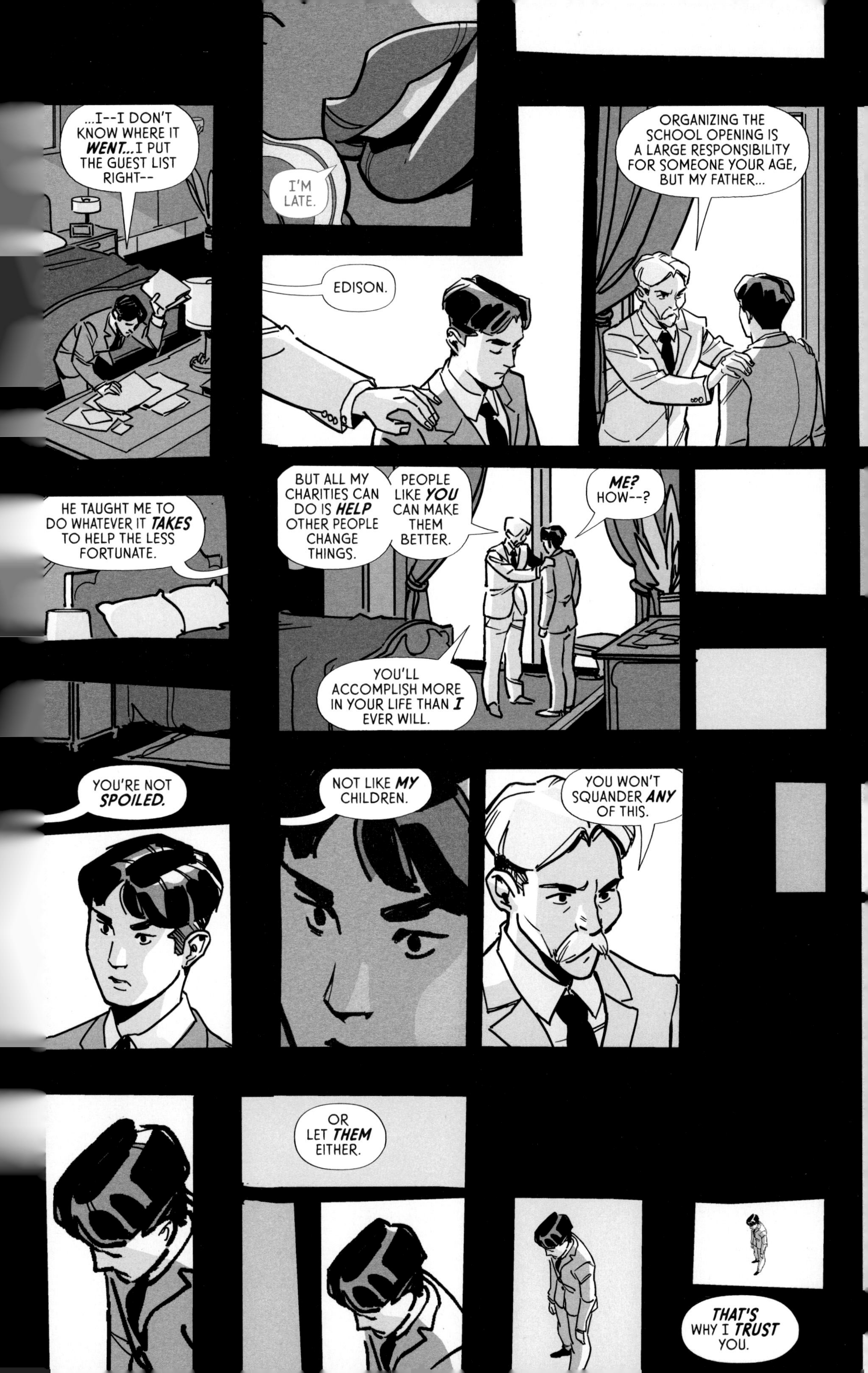
...I--I DON'T KNOW WHERE IT WENT...I PUT THE GUEST LIST RIGHT--
I'M LATE.
EDISON.
ORGANIZING THE SCHOOL OPENING IS A LARGE RESPONSIBILITY FOR SOMEONE YOUR AGE, BUT MY FATHER...
HE TAUGHT ME TO DO WHATEVER IT TAKES TO HELP THE LESS FORTUNATE.
BUT ALL MY CHARITIES CAN DO IS HELP OTHER PEOPLE CHANGE THINGS.
PEOPLE LIKE YOU CAN MAKE THEM BETTER.
ME? HOW--?
YOU'LL ACCOMPLISH MORE IN YOUR LIFE THAN I EVER WILL.
YOU'RE NOT SPOILED.
NOT LIKE MY CHILDREN.
YOU WON'T SQUANDER ANY OF THIS.
OR LET THEM EITHER.
THAT'S WHY I TRUST YOU.

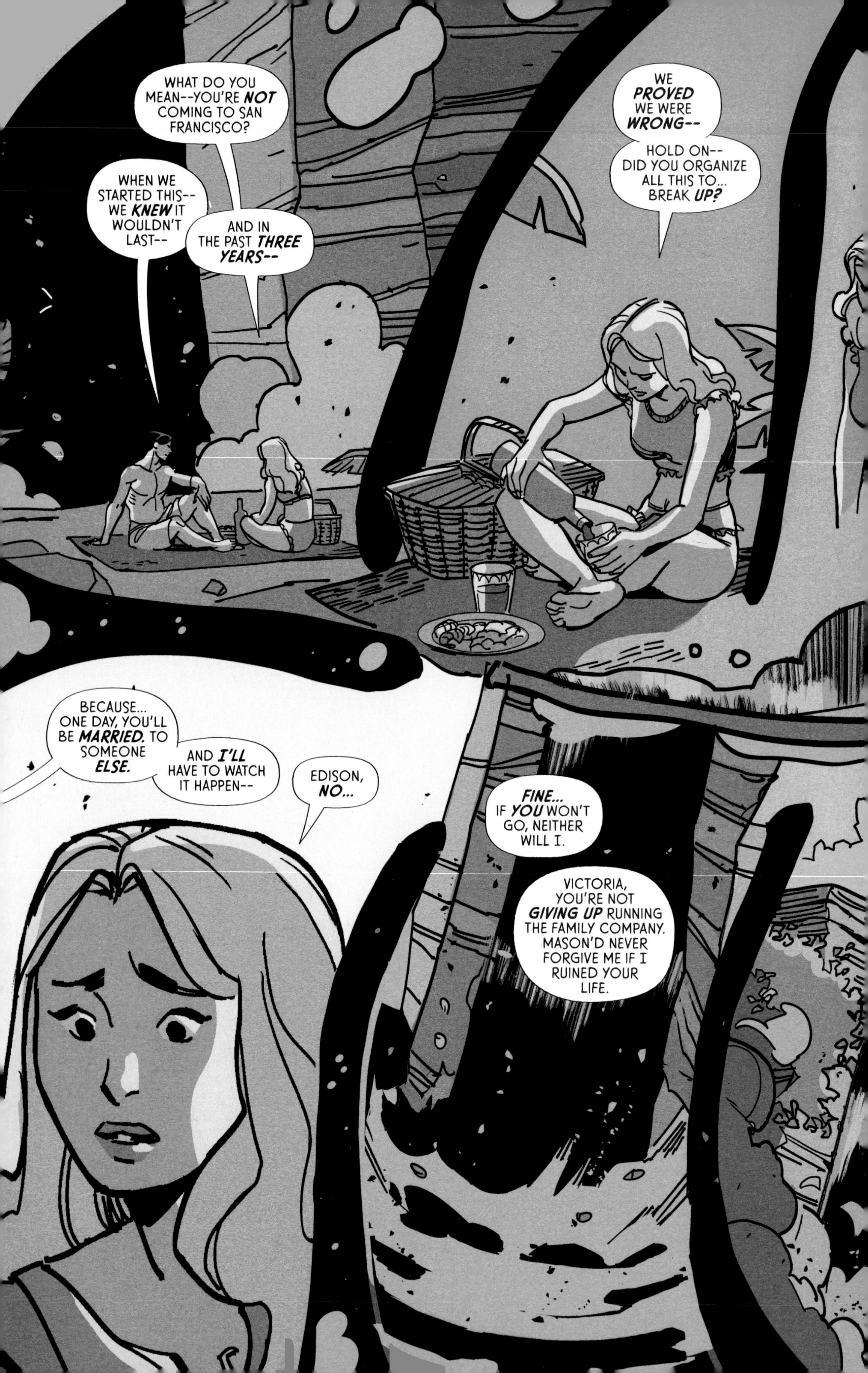
WHAT DO YOU MEAN--YOU'RE NOT COMING TO SAN FRANCISCO?
WHEN WE STARTED THIS--WE KNEW IT WOULDN'T LAST--
AND IN THE PAST THREE YEARS--
WE PROVED WE WERE WRONG--
HOLD ON--DID YOU ORGANIZE ALL THIS TO... BREAK UP?
BECAUSE... ONE DAY, YOU'LL BE MARRIED. TO SOMEONE ELSE.
AND I'LL HAVE TO WATCH IT HAPPEN--
EDISON, NO...
FINE... IF YOU WON'T GO, NEITHER WILL I.
VICTORIA, YOU'RE NOT GIVING UP RUNNING THE FAMILY COMPANY. MASON'D NEVER FORGIVE ME IF I RUINED YOUR LIFE.

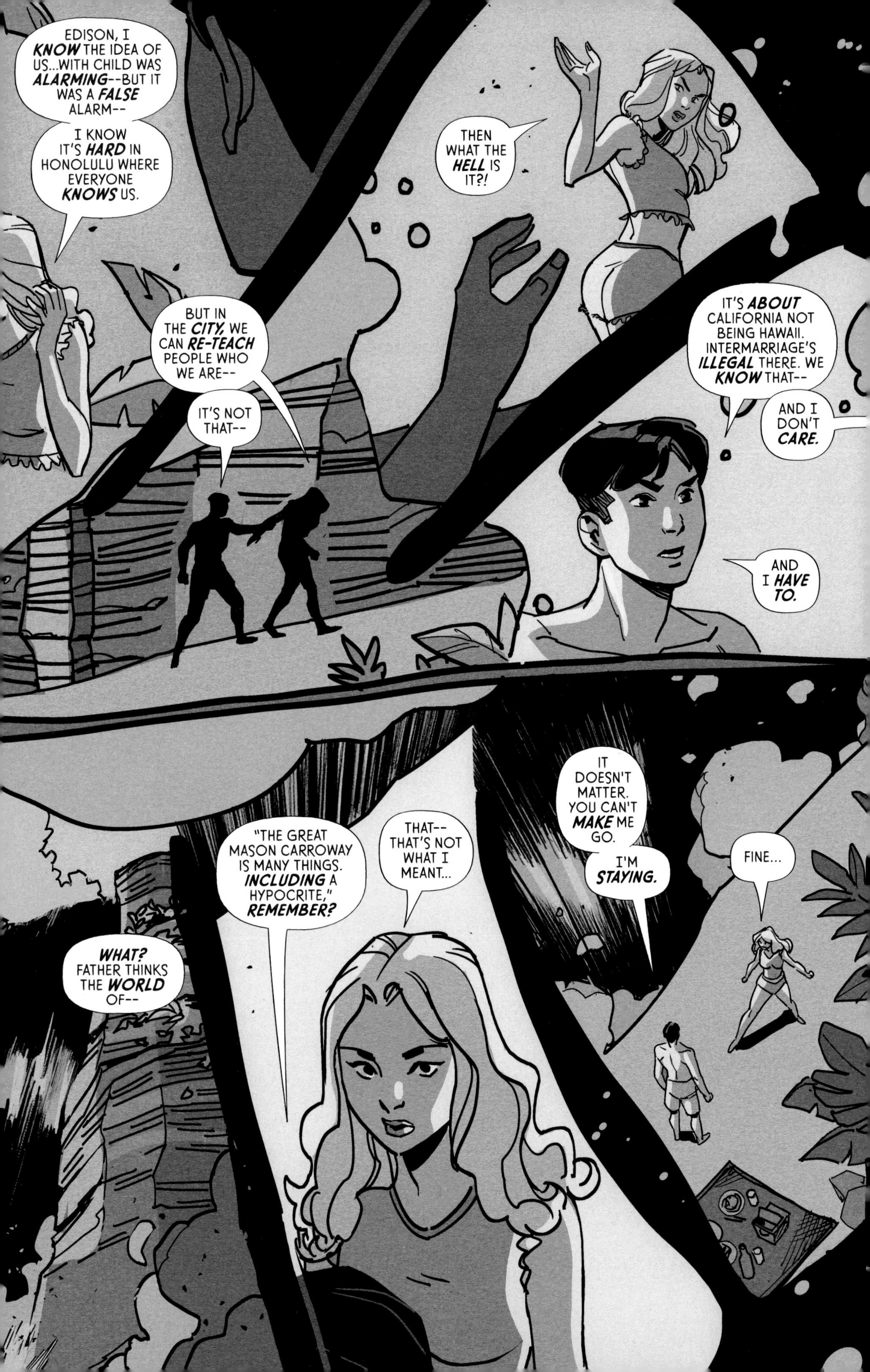
EDISON, I KNOW THE IDEA OF US...WITH CHILD WAS ALARMING--BUT IT WAS A FALSE ALARM--
I KNOW IT'S HARD IN HONOLULU WHERE EVERYONE KNOWS US.
THEN WHAT THE HELL IS IT?!
BUT IN THE CITY, WE CAN RE-TEACH PEOPLE WHO WE ARE--
IT'S NOT THAT--
IT'S ABOUT CALIFORNIA NOT BEING HAWAII. INTERMARRIAGE'S ILLEGAL THERE. WE KNOW THAT--
AND I DON'T CARE.
AND I HAVE TO.
WHAT? FATHER THINKS THE WORLD OF--
"THE GREAT MASON CARROWAY IS MANY THINGS. INCLUDING A HYPOCRITE," REMEMBER?
THAT--THAT'S NOT WHAT I MEANT...
IT DOESN'T MATTER. YOU CAN'T MAKE ME GO.
I'M STAYING.
FINE...

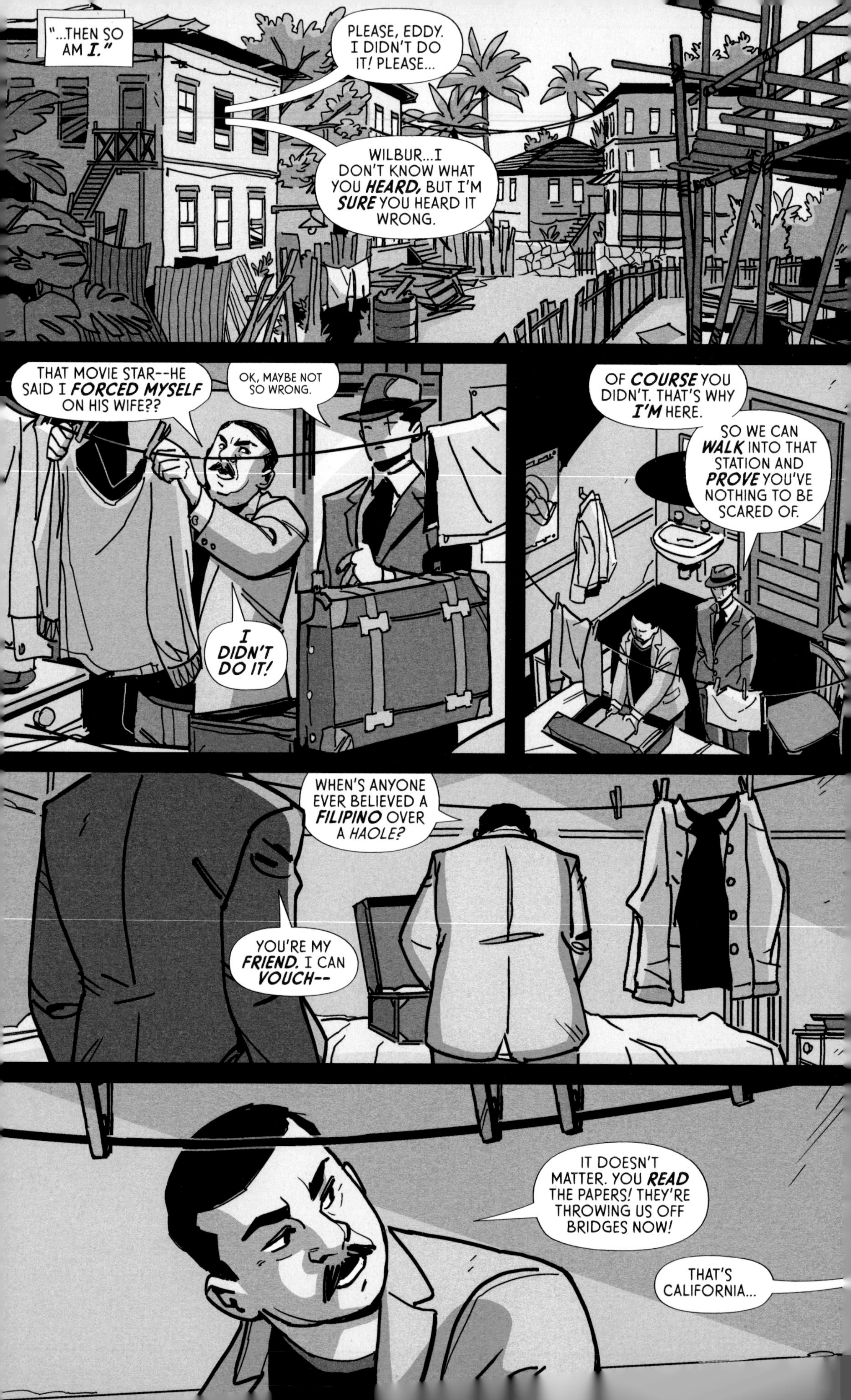
"...THEN SO AM I."
PLEASE, EDDY. I DIDN'T DO IT! PLEASE...
WILBUR...I DON'T KNOW WHAT YOU HEARD, BUT I'M SURE YOU HEARD IT WRONG.
THAT MOVIE STAR--HE SAID I FORCED MYSELF ON HIS WIFE??
OK, MAYBE NOT SO WRONG.
I DIDN'T DO IT!
OF COURSE YOU DIDN'T. THAT'S WHY I'M HERE.
SO WE CAN WALK INTO THAT STATION AND PROVE YOU'VE NOTHING TO BE SCARED OF.
WHEN'S ANYONE EVER BELIEVED A FILIPINO OVER A HAOLE?
YOU'RE MY FRIEND. I CAN VOUCH--
IT DOESN'T MATTER. YOU READ THE PAPERS! THEY'RE THROWING US OFF BRIDGES NOW!
THAT'S CALIFORNIA...

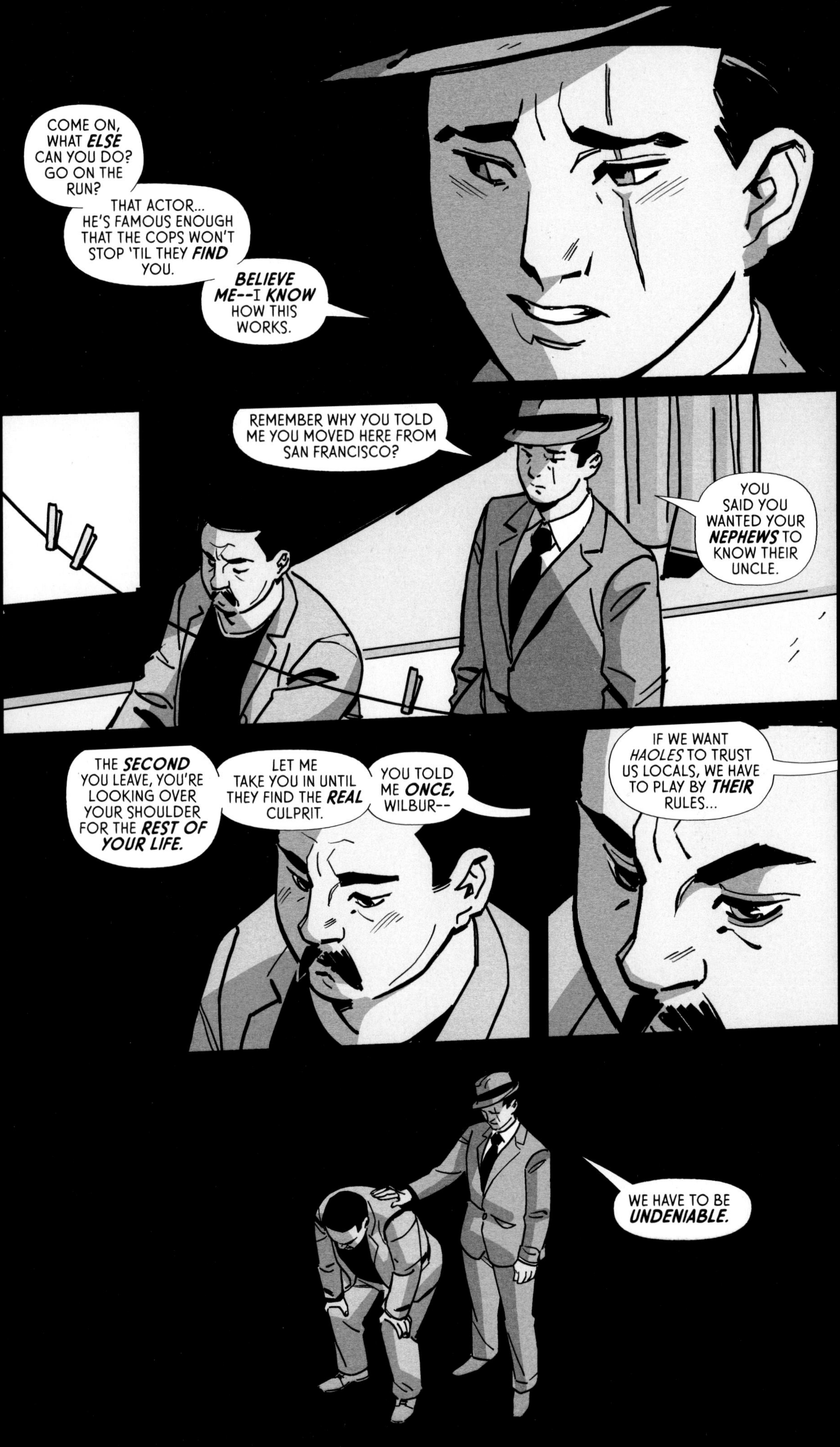
COME ON, WHAT *ELSE* CAN YOU DO? GO ON THE RUN?
THAT ACTOR... HE'S FAMOUS ENOUGH THAT THE COPS WON'T STOP 'TIL THEY *FIND* YOU.
BELIEVE ME--I *KNOW* HOW THIS WORKS.
REMEMBER WHY YOU TOLD ME YOU MOVED HERE FROM SAN FRANCISCO?
YOU SAID YOU WANTED YOUR *NEPHEWS* TO KNOW THEIR UNCLE.
THE *SECOND* YOU LEAVE, YOU'RE LOOKING OVER YOUR SHOULDER FOR THE *REST OF YOUR LIFE.*
LET ME TAKE YOU IN UNTIL THEY FIND THE *REAL* CULPRIT.
YOU TOLD ME *ONCE,* WILBUR--
IF WE WANT *HAOLES* TO TRUST US LOCALS, WE HAVE TO PLAY BY *THEIR* RULES...
WE HAVE TO BE *UNDENIABLE.*

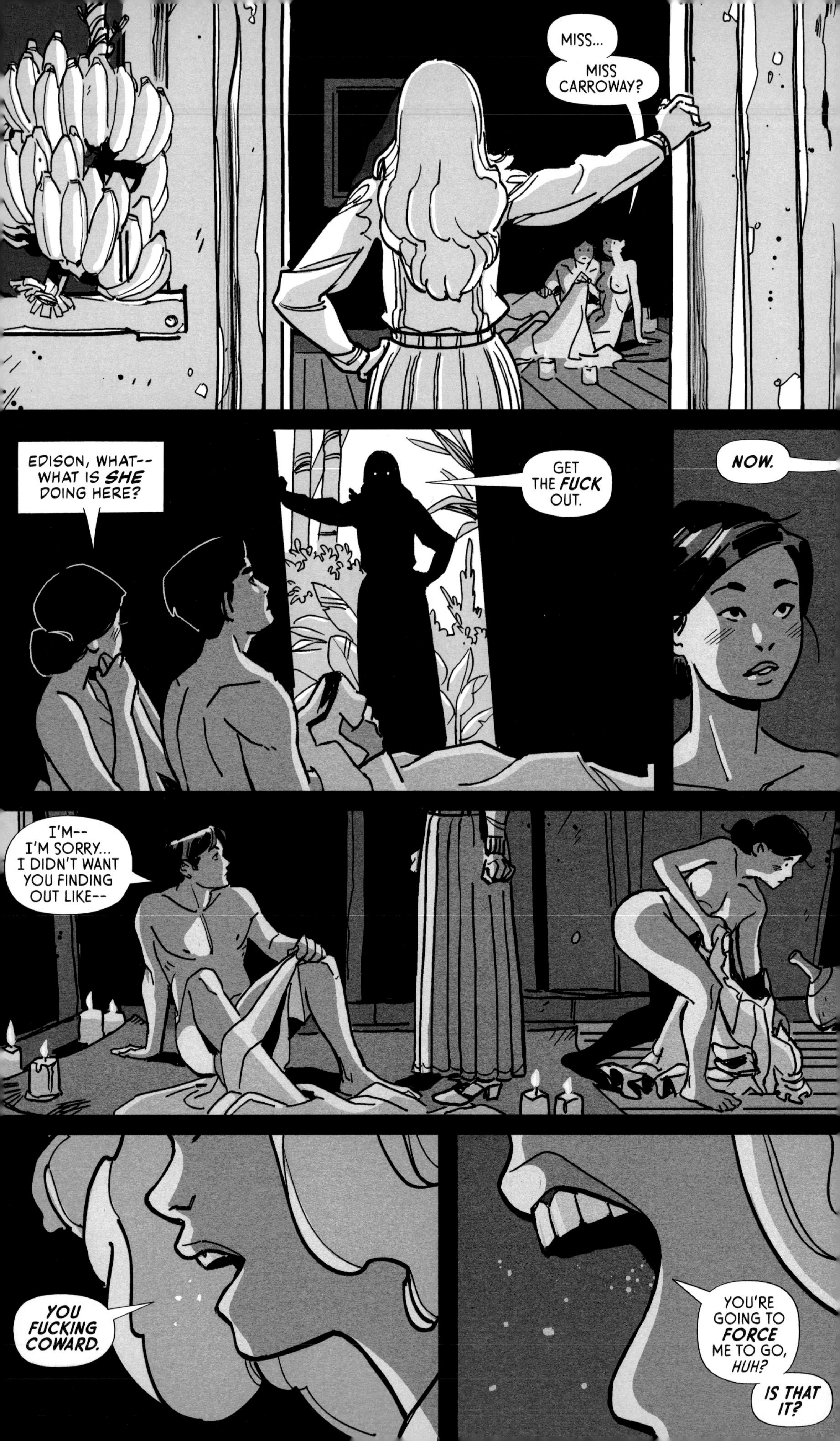
MISS...
MISS CARROWAY?
EDISON, WHAT-- WHAT IS *SHE* DOING HERE?
GET THE *FUCK* OUT.
NOW.
I'M-- I'M SORRY... I DIDN'T WANT YOU FINDING OUT LIKE--
YOU FUCKING COWARD.
YOU'RE GOING TO *FORCE* ME TO GO, *HUH?*
IS THAT IT?

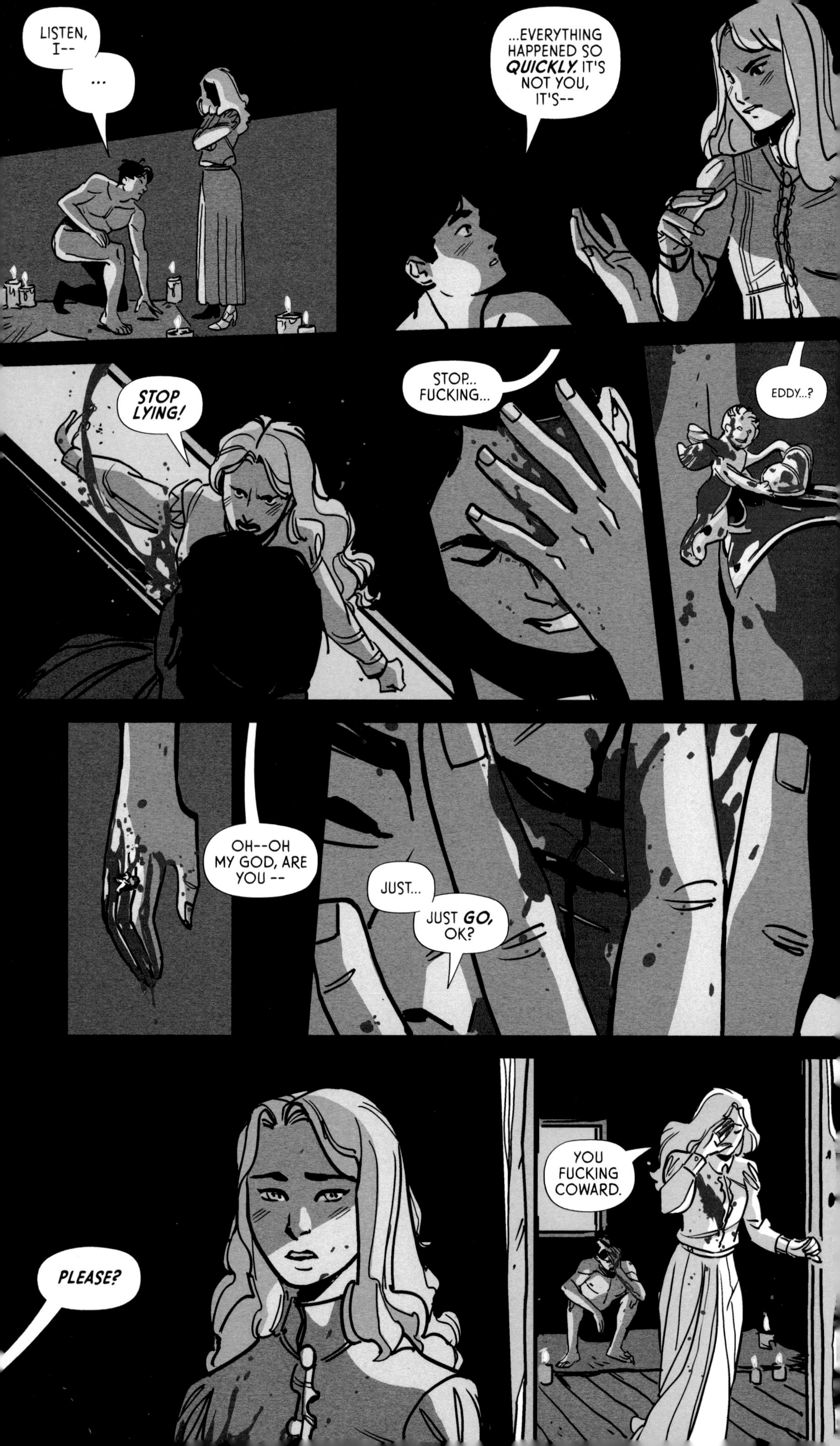
LISTEN, I--
...
...EVERYTHING HAPPENED SO QUICKLY. IT'S NOT YOU, IT'S--
STOP LYING!
STOP.. FUCKING...
EDDY...?
OH--OH MY GOD, ARE YOU --
JUST...
JUST GO, OK?
PLEASE?
YOU FUCKING COWARD.

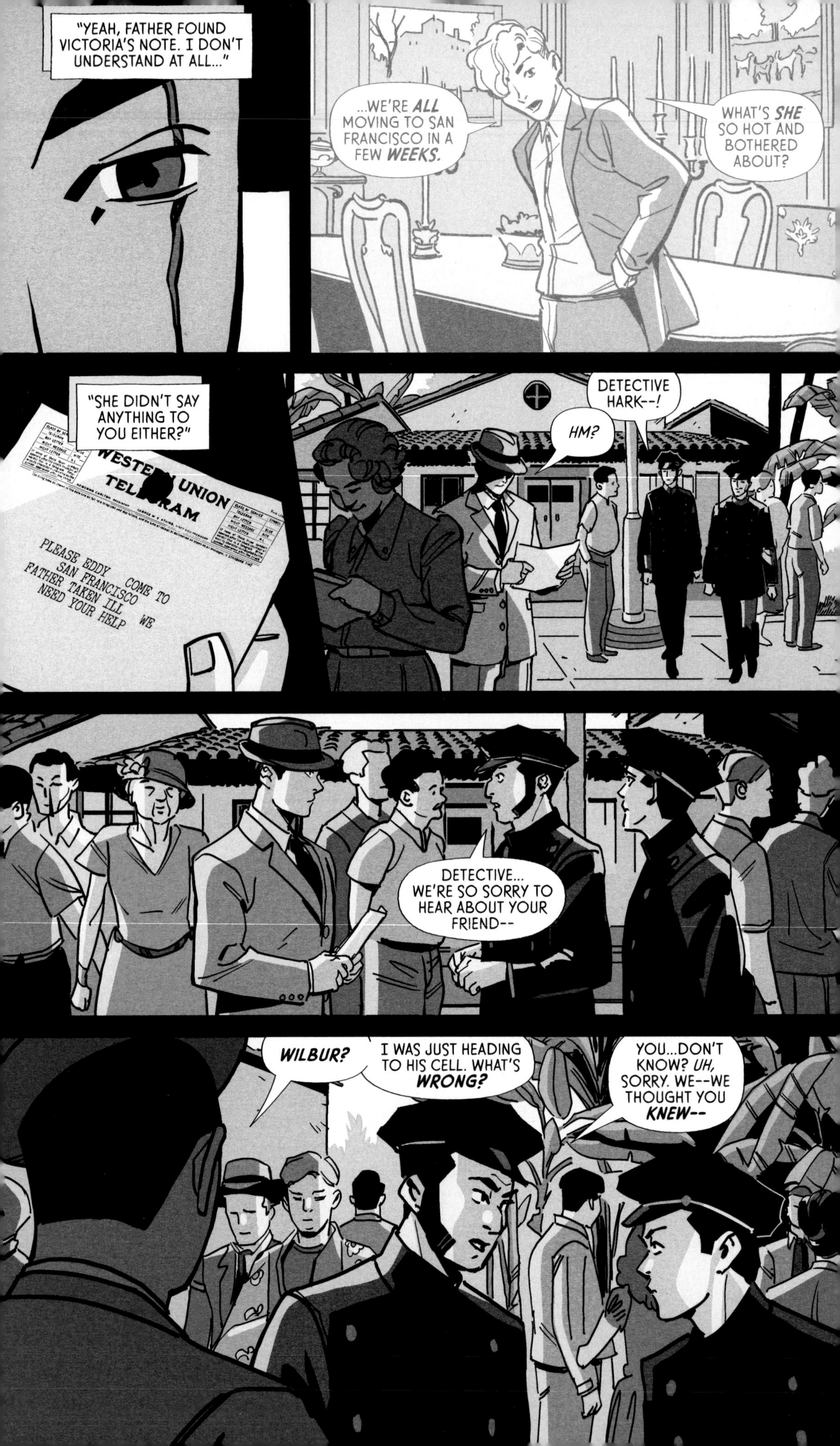
"YEAH, FATHER FOUND VICTORIA'S NOTE. I DON'T UNDERSTAND AT ALL..."
...WE'RE ALL MOVING TO SAN FRANCISCO IN A FEW WEEKS.
WHAT'S SHE SO HOT AND BOTHERED ABOUT?
"SHE DIDN'T SAY ANYTHING TO YOU EITHER?"
WESTERN UNION TELEGRAM
PLEASE EDDY COME TO SAN FRANCISCO FATHER TAKEN ILL WE NEED YOUR HELP
DETECTIVE HARK--!
HM?
DETECTIVE... WE'RE SO SORRY TO HEAR ABOUT YOUR FRIEND--
WILBUR?
I WAS JUST HEADING TO HIS CELL. WHAT'S WRONG?
YOU...DON'T KNOW? UH, SORRY. WE--WE THOUGHT YOU KNEW--

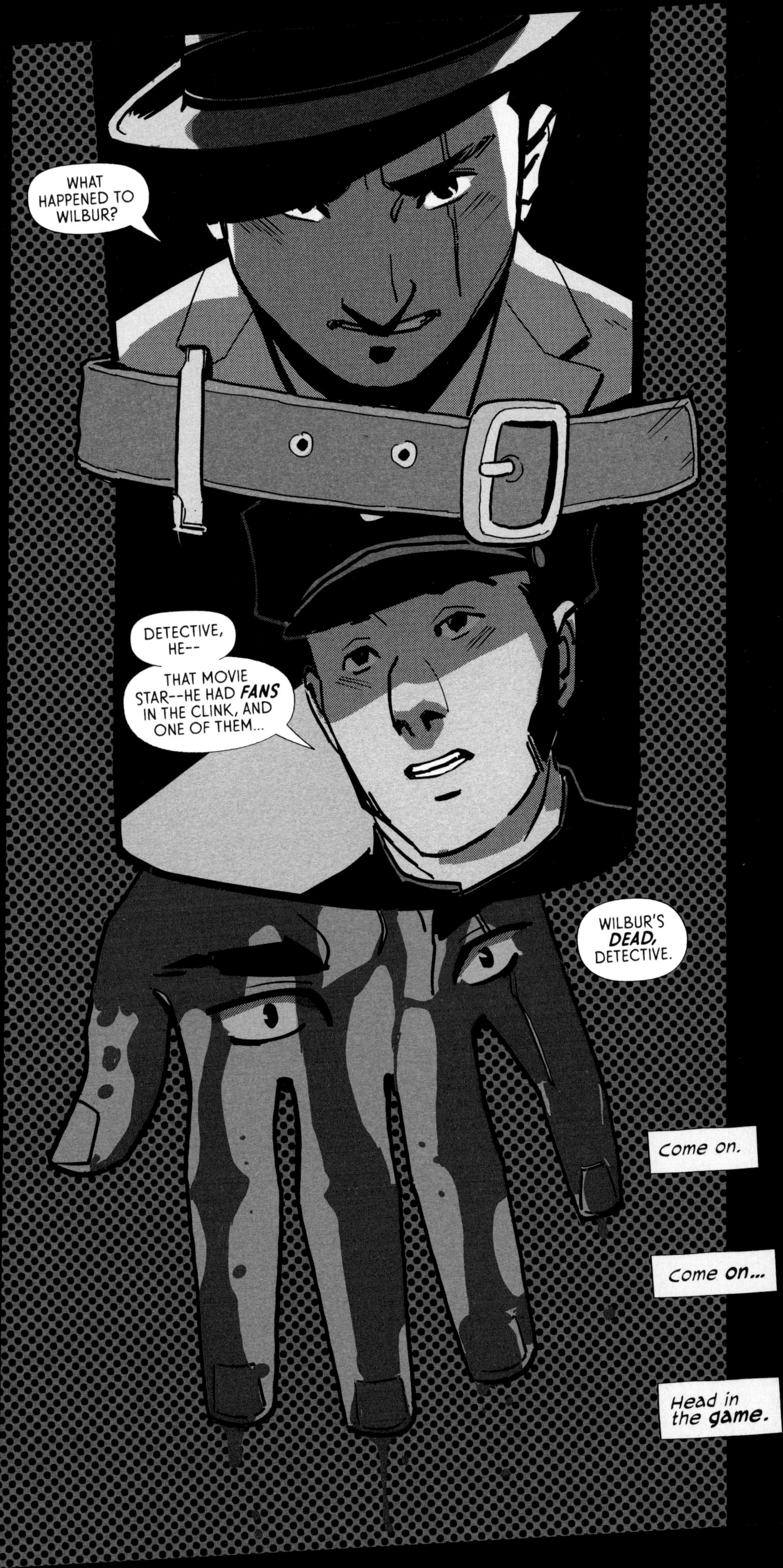
WHAT HAPPENED TO WILBUR?
DETECTIVE, HE--
THAT MOVIE STAR--HE HAD *FANS* IN THE CLINK, AND ONE OF THEM...
WILBUR'S *DEAD,* DETECTIVE.
Come on.
Come on...
Head in the game.

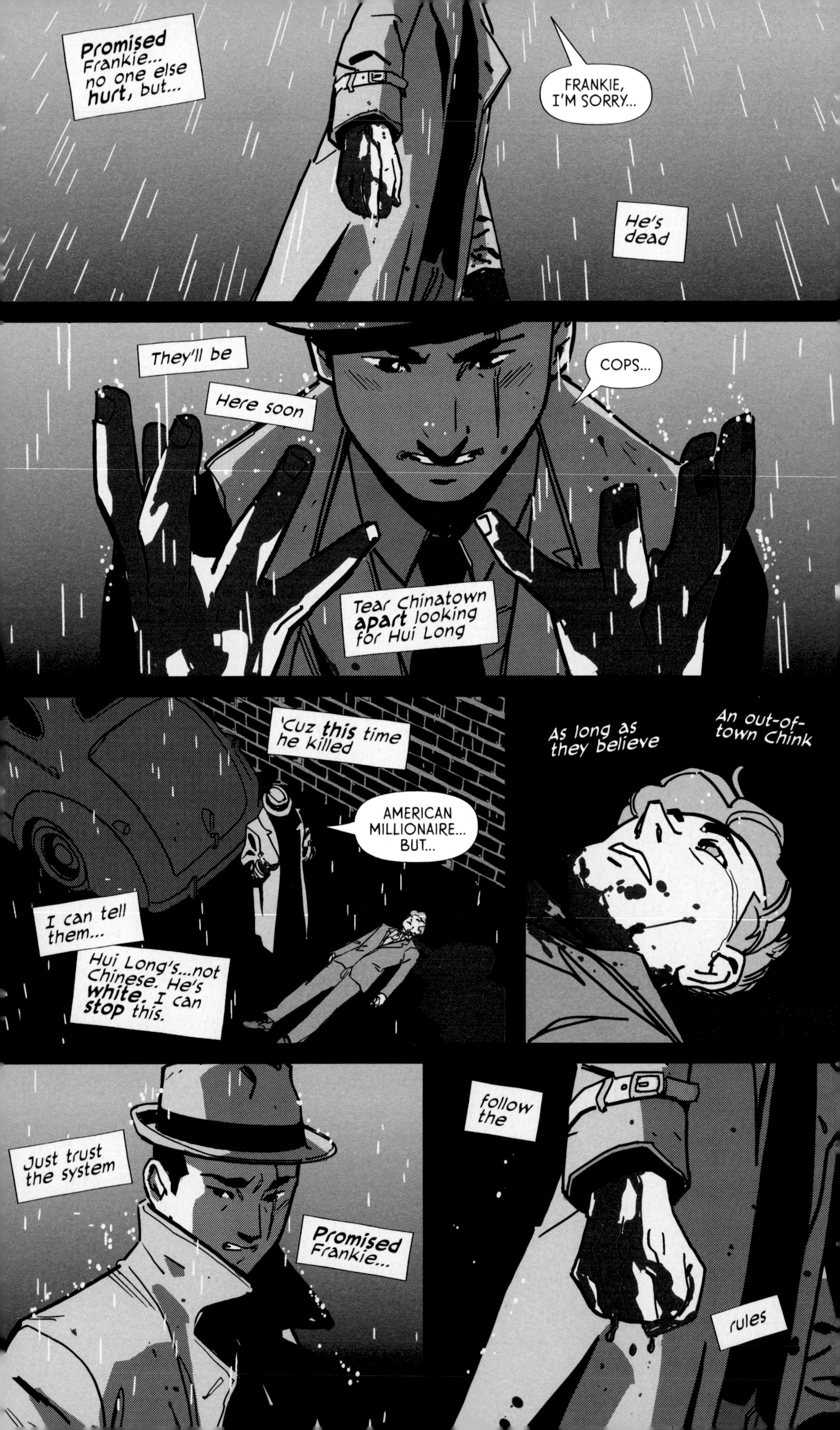

Promised Frankie... no one else hurt, but...
FRANKIE, I'M SORRY...
He's dead
They'll be
Here soon
COPS...
Tear Chinatown apart looking for Hui Long
'Cuz this time he killed
AMERICAN MILLIONAIRE... BUT...
I can tell them...
Hui Long's...not Chinese. He's white. I can stop this.
As long as they believe
An out-of-town Chink
Just trust the system
Promised Frankie...
follow the
rules

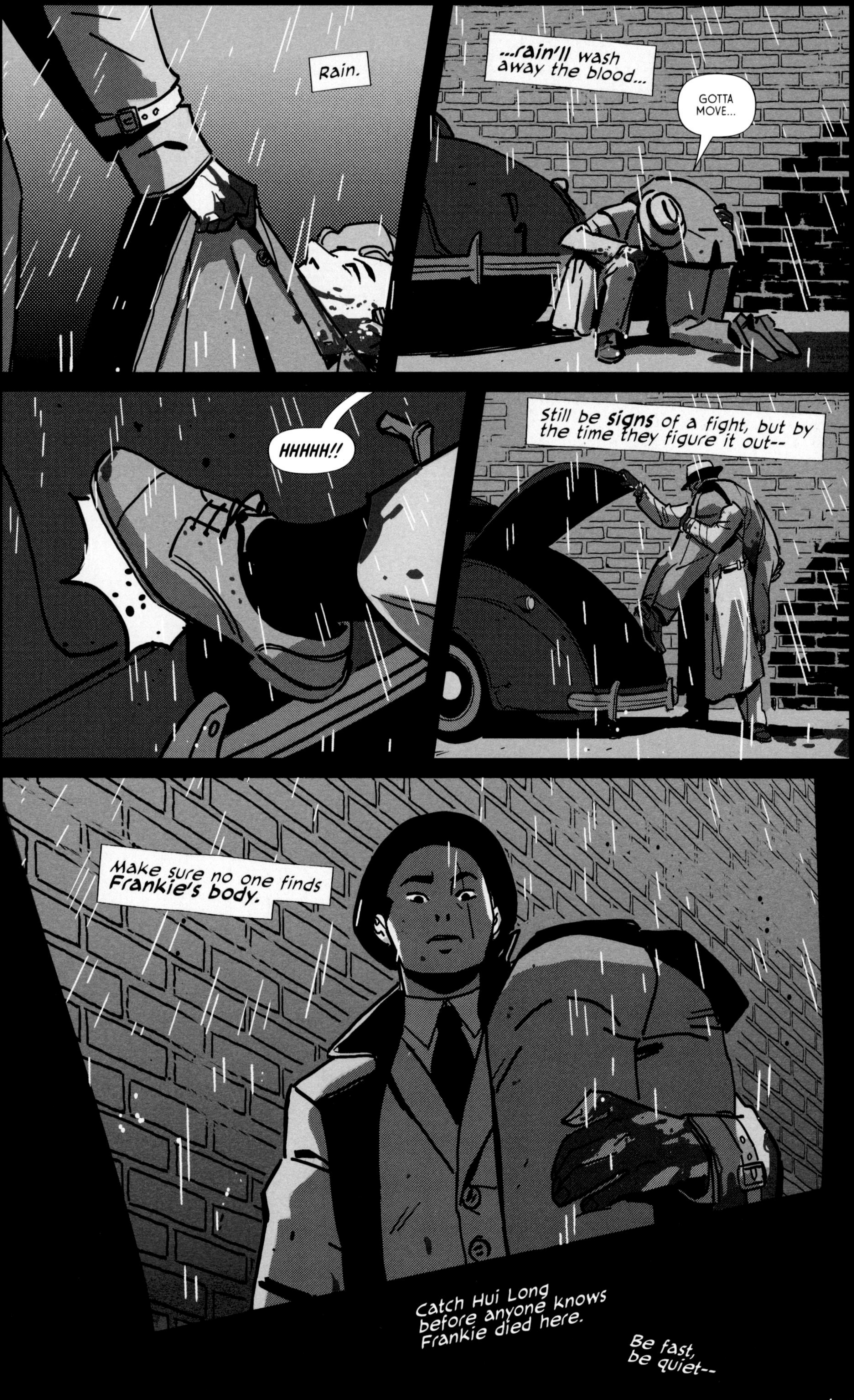
Rain.
...rain'll wash away the blood...
GOTTA MOVE...
HHHHH!!
Still be signs of a fight, but by the time they figure it out--
Make sure no one finds Frankie's body.
Catch Hui Long before anyone knows Frankie died here.
Be fast, be quiet--
Be perfect--

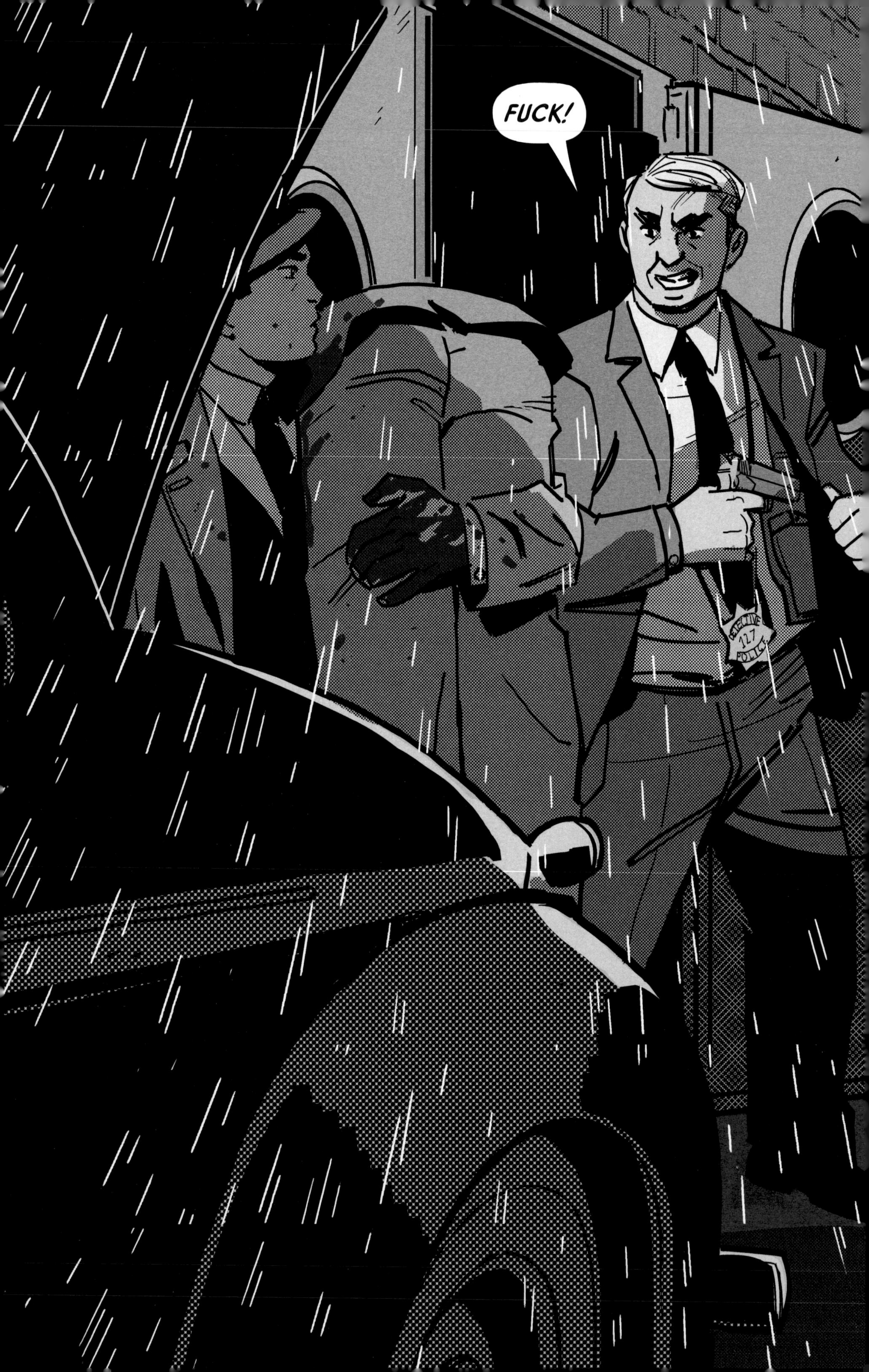
FUCK!
DETECTIVE
127
POLICE

CHAPTER SIX

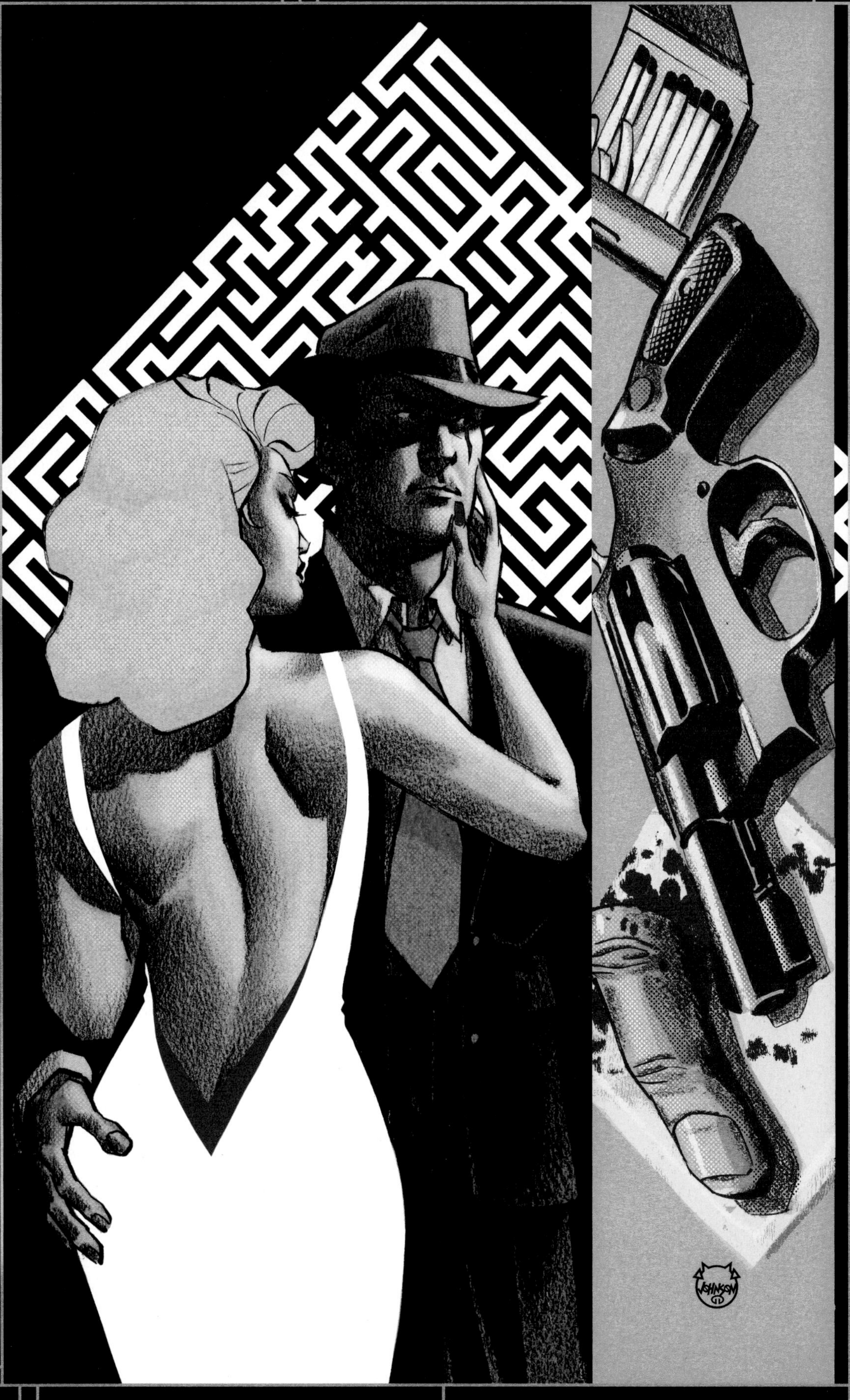

ART BY **DAVE JOHNSON**

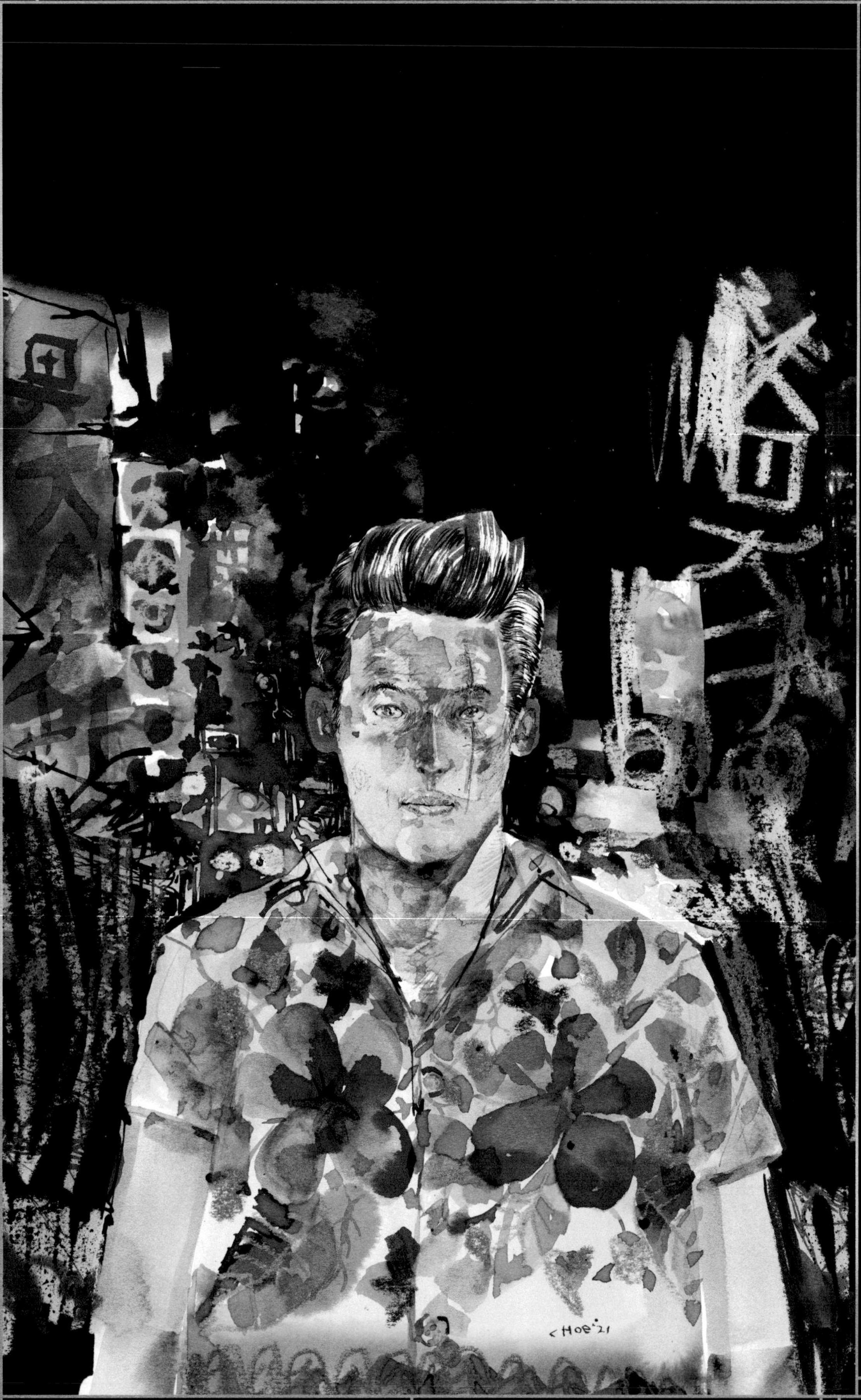

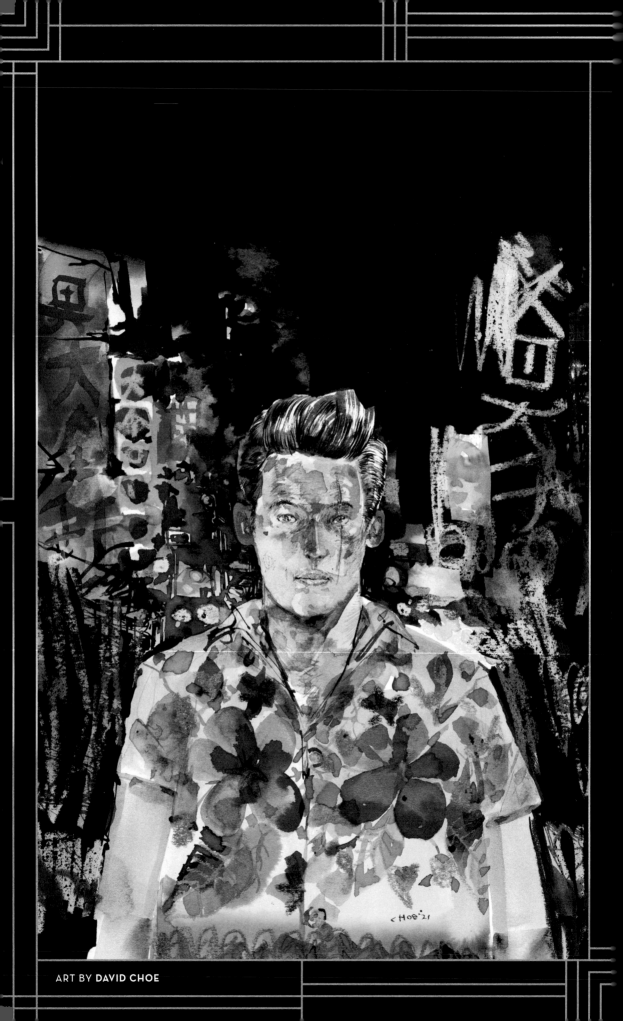

ART BY **DAVID CHOE**

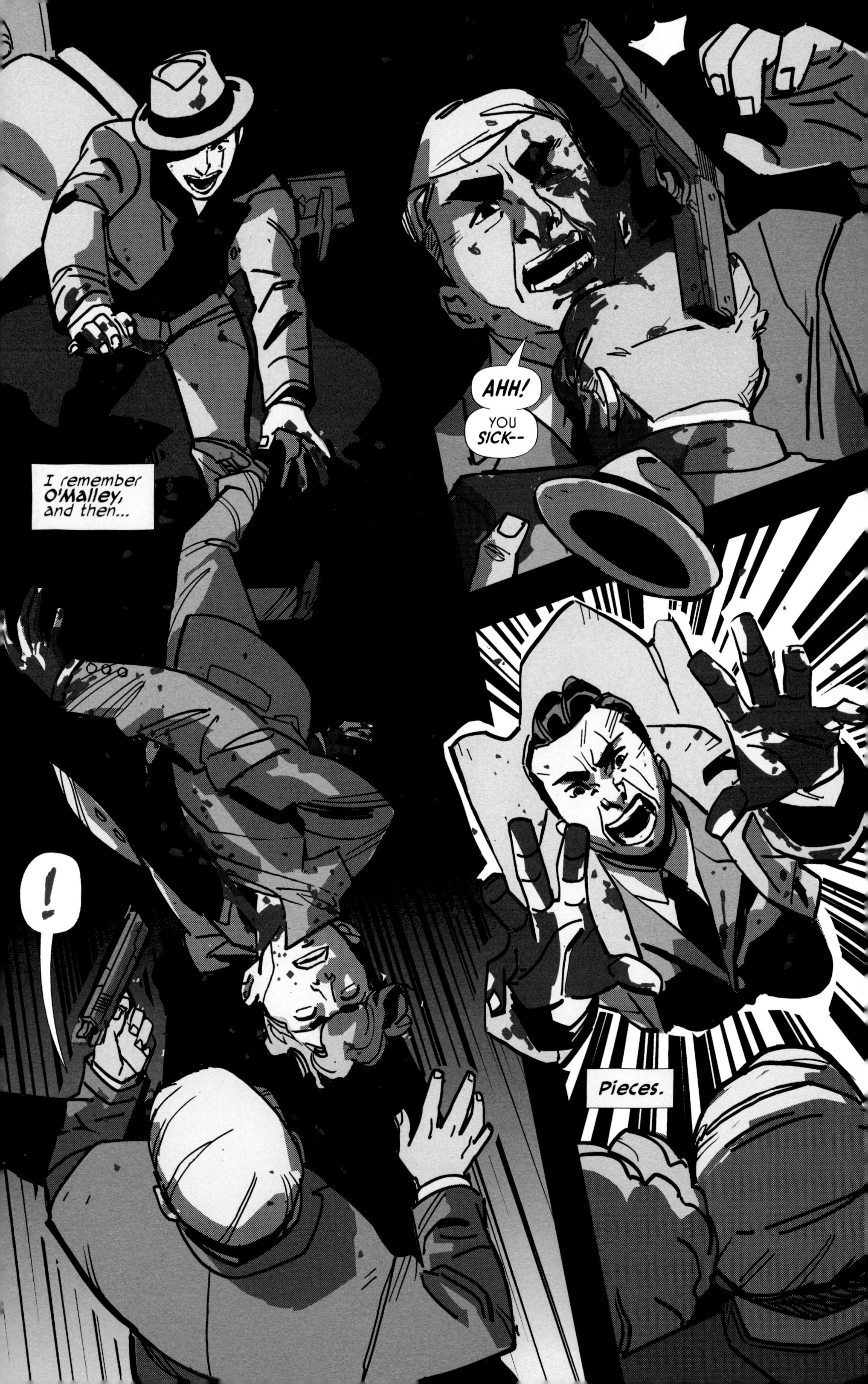
I remember O'Malley, and then...
AHH!
YOU SICK--
!
Pieces.

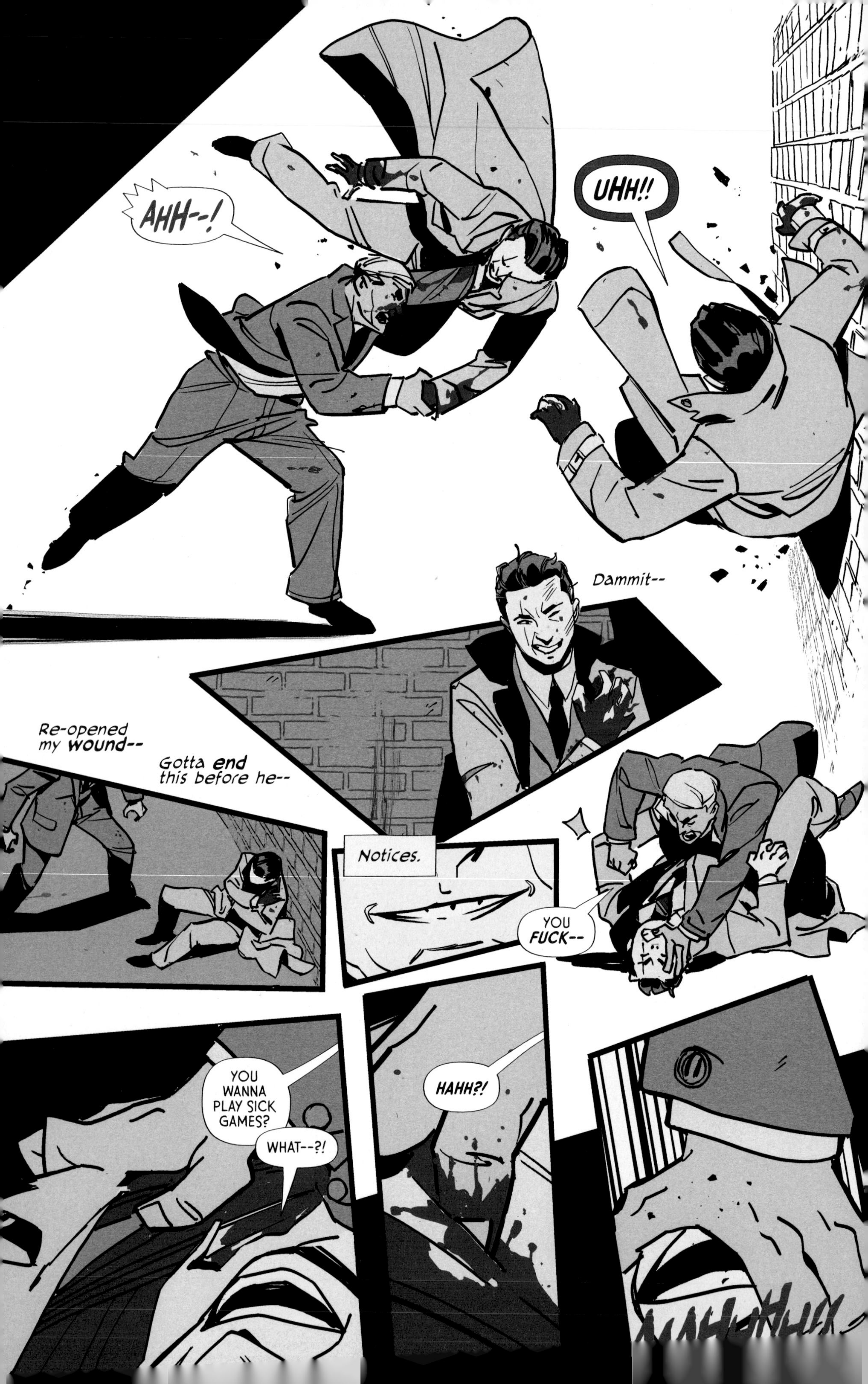
AHH--!
UHH!!
Dammit--
Re-opened my **wound**--
Gotta **end** this before he--
Notices.
YOU **FUCK**--
YOU WANNA PLAY SICK GAMES?
WHAT--?!
HAHH?!

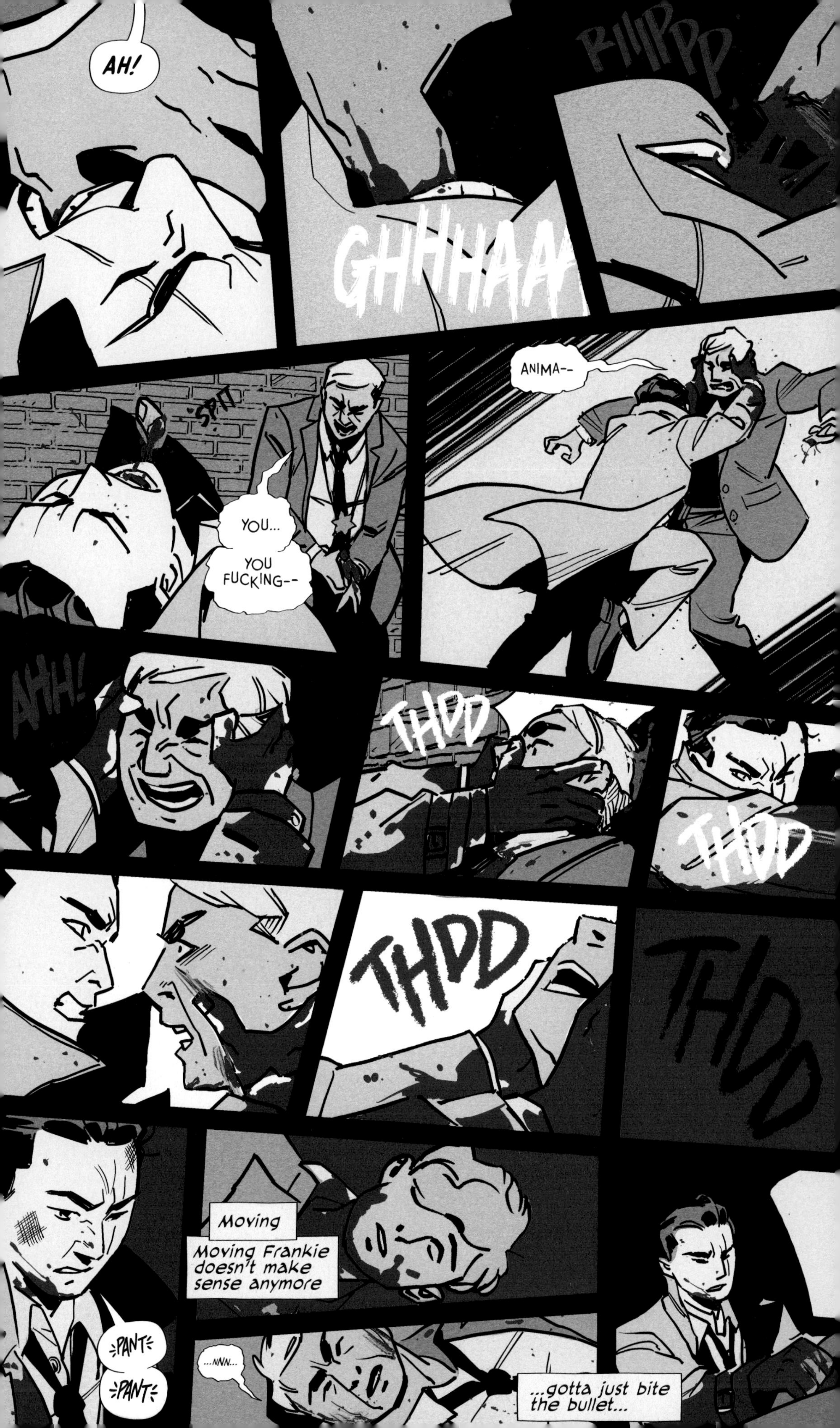
AH!
RIIPPP
GHHHAAA
SPIT
YOU...
YOU FUCKING--
ANIMA--
AHH!
THDD
THDD
THDD
THDD
Moving
Moving Frankie doesn't make sense anymore
PANT
PANT
...NNN...
...gotta just bite the bullet...

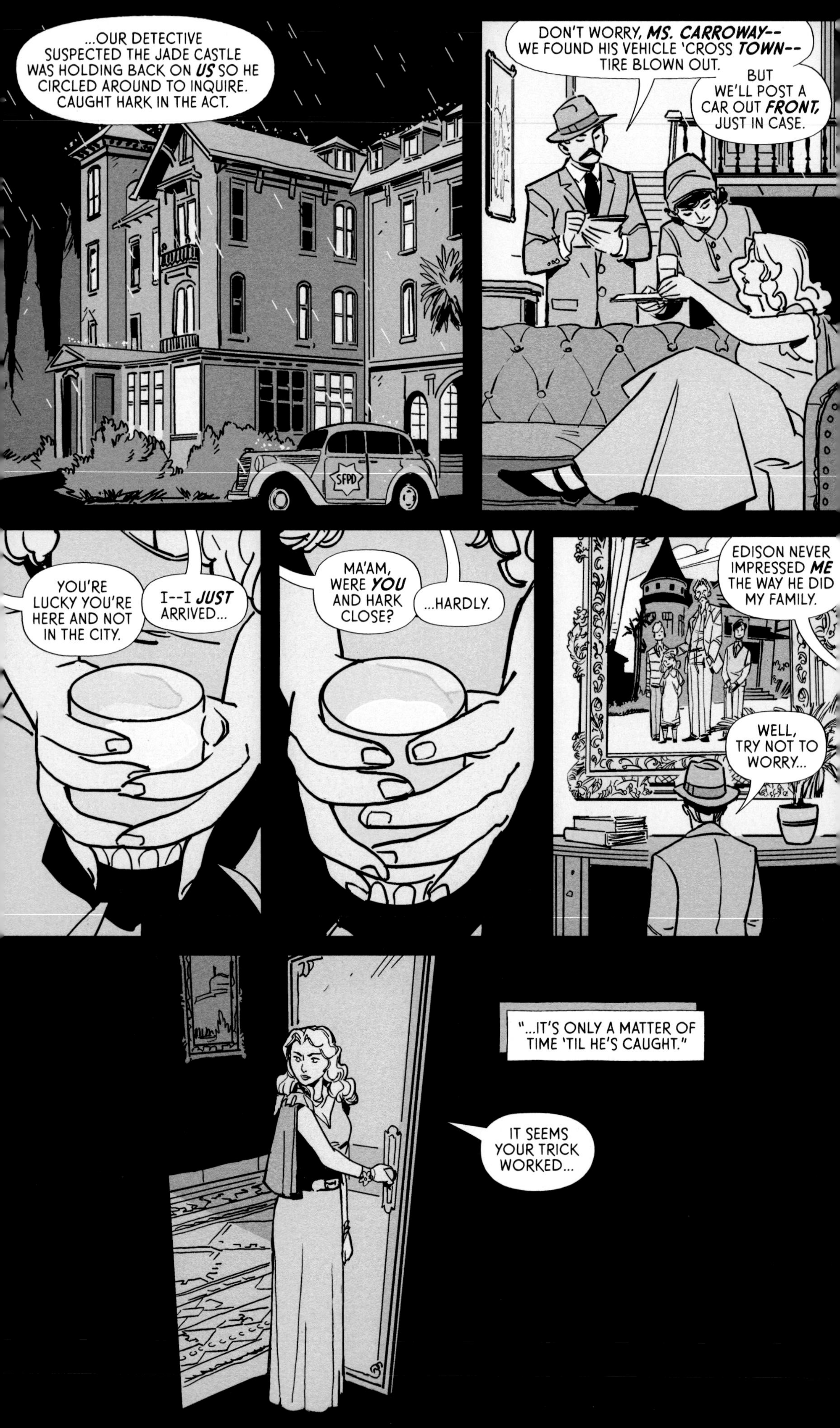
...OUR DETECTIVE SUSPECTED THE JADE CASTLE WAS HOLDING BACK ON *US* SO HE CIRCLED AROUND TO INQUIRE. CAUGHT HARK IN THE ACT.
SFPD
DON'T WORRY, *MS. CARROWAY--* WE FOUND HIS VEHICLE 'CROSS *TOWN--* TIRE BLOWN OUT.
BUT WE'LL POST A CAR OUT *FRONT,* JUST IN CASE.
YOU'RE LUCKY YOU'RE HERE AND NOT IN THE CITY.
I--I *JUST* ARRIVED...
MA'AM, WERE *YOU* AND HARK CLOSE?
...HARDLY.
EDISON NEVER IMPRESSED *ME* THE WAY HE DID MY FAMILY.
WELL, TRY NOT TO WORRY...
"...IT'S ONLY A MATTER OF TIME 'TIL HE'S CAUGHT."
IT SEEMS YOUR TRICK WORKED...

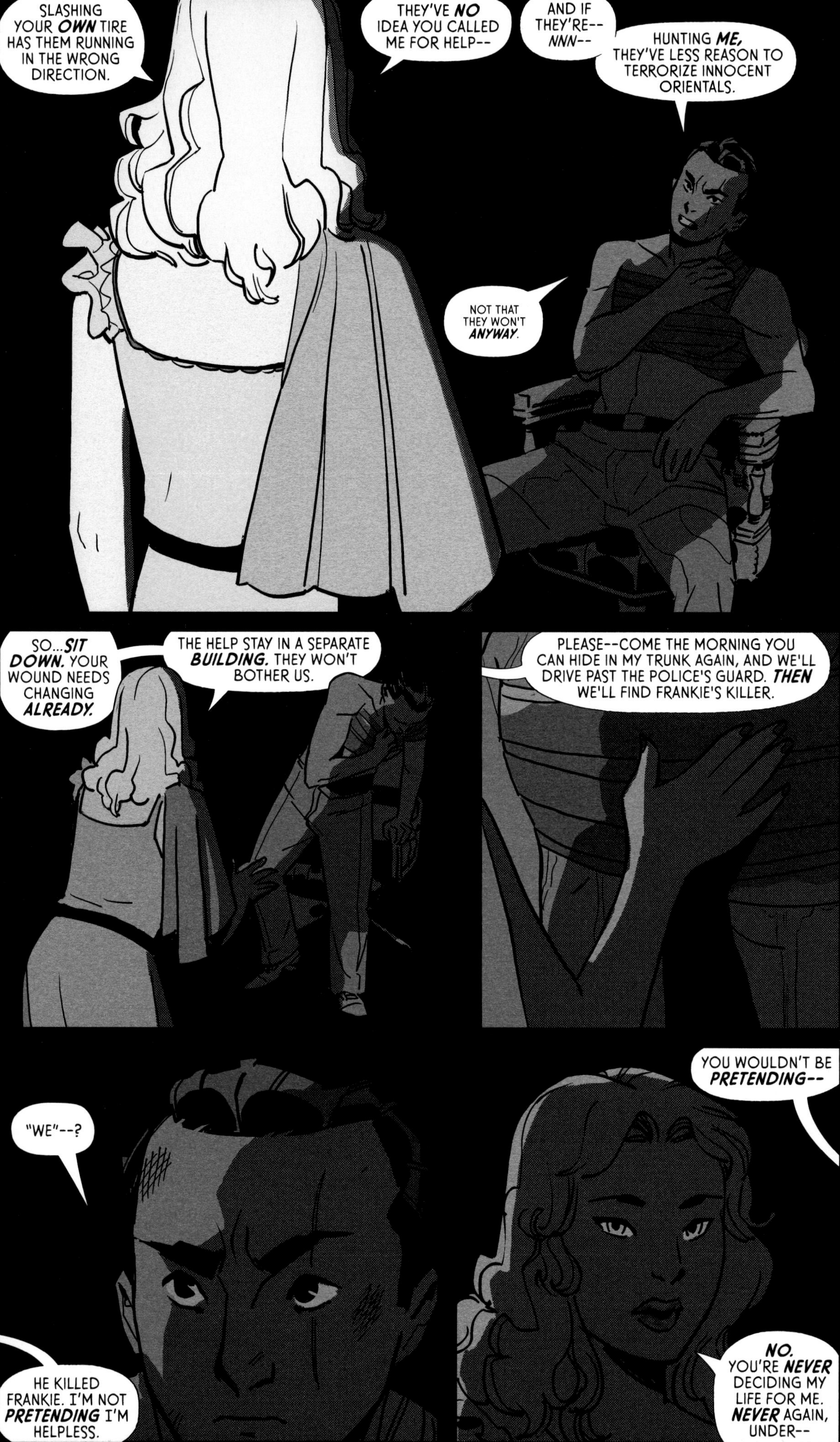
SLASHING YOUR OWN TIRE HAS THEM RUNNING IN THE WRONG DIRECTION.
THEY'VE NO IDEA YOU CALLED ME FOR HELP--
AND IF THEY'RE-- NNN--
HUNTING ME, THEY'VE LESS REASON TO TERRORIZE INNOCENT ORIENTALS.
NOT THAT THEY WON'T ANYWAY.
SO...SIT DOWN. YOUR WOUND NEEDS CHANGING ALREADY.
THE HELP STAY IN A SEPARATE BUILDING. THEY WON'T BOTHER US.
PLEASE--COME THE MORNING YOU CAN HIDE IN MY TRUNK AGAIN, AND WE'LL DRIVE PAST THE POLICE'S GUARD. THEN WE'LL FIND FRANKIE'S KILLER.
"WE"--?
YOU WOULDN'T BE PRETENDING--
HE KILLED FRANKIE. I'M NOT PRETENDING I'M HELPLESS.
NO. YOU'RE NEVER DECIDING MY LIFE FOR ME. NEVER AGAIN, UNDER--

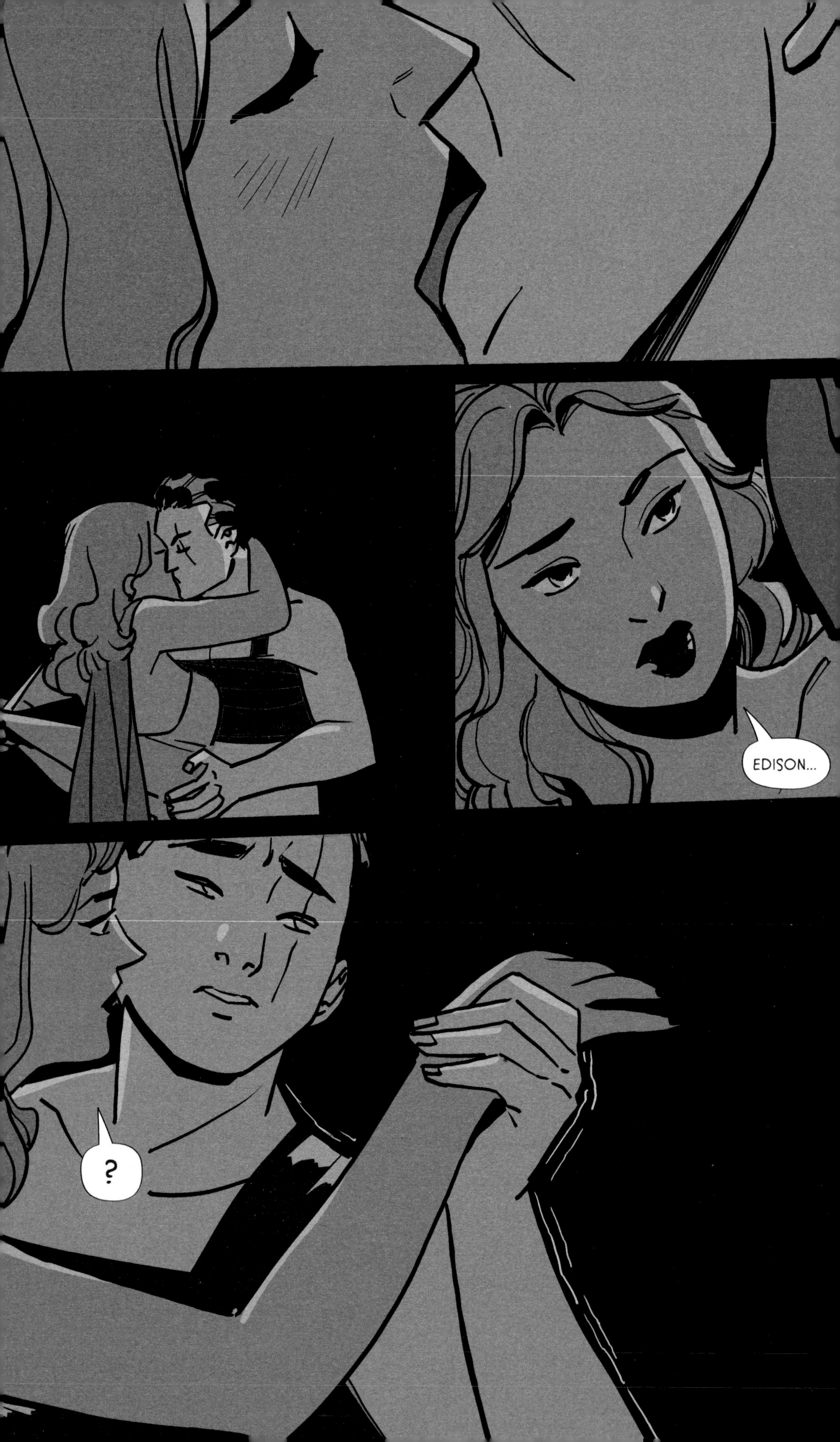
EDISON...
?

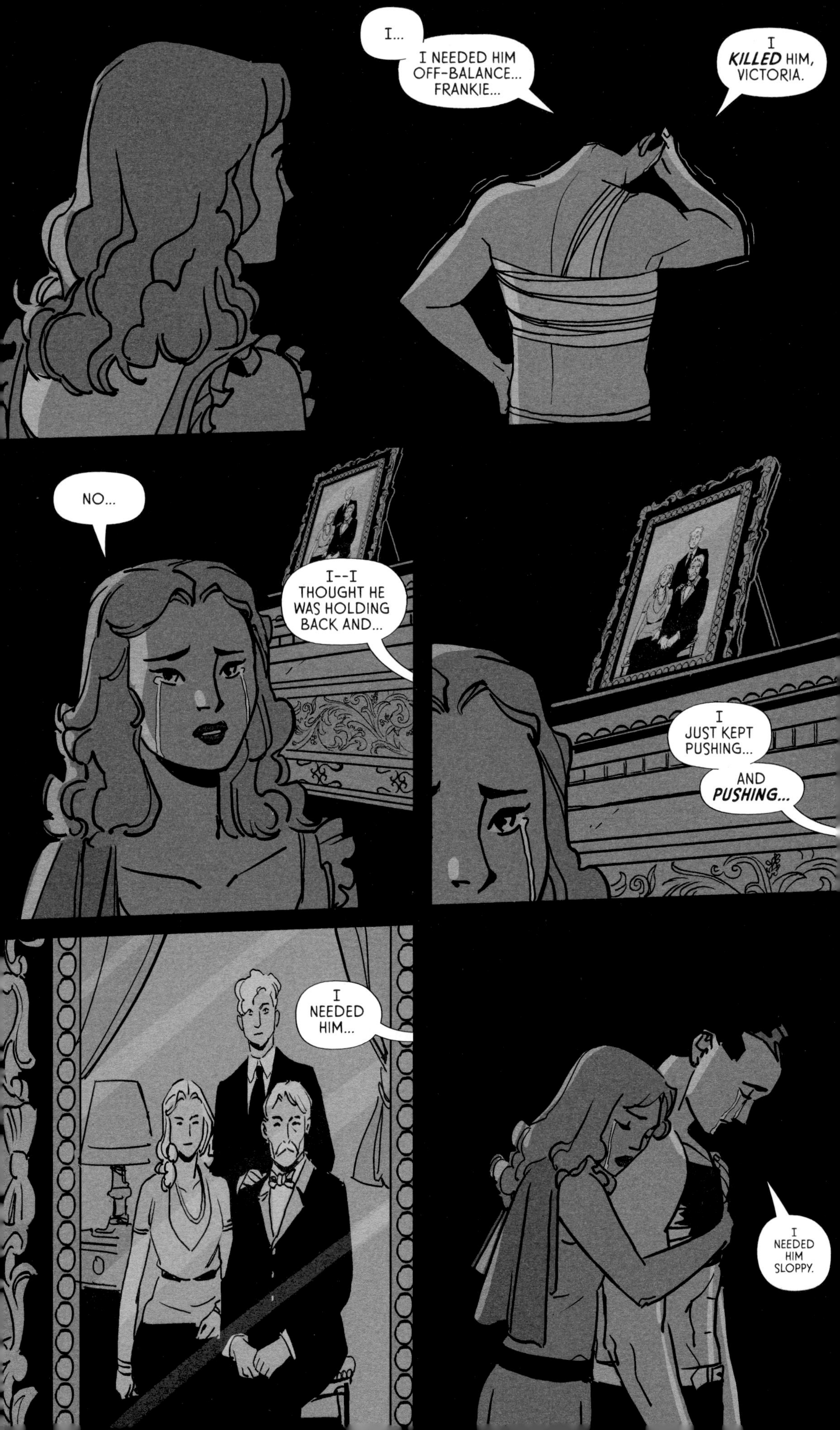
I...
I NEEDED HIM OFF-BALANCE... FRANKIE...
I *KILLED* HIM, VICTORIA.
NO...
I--I THOUGHT HE WAS HOLDING BACK AND...
I JUST KEPT PUSHING...
AND *PUSHING...*
I NEEDED HIM...
I NEEDED HIM SLOPPY.

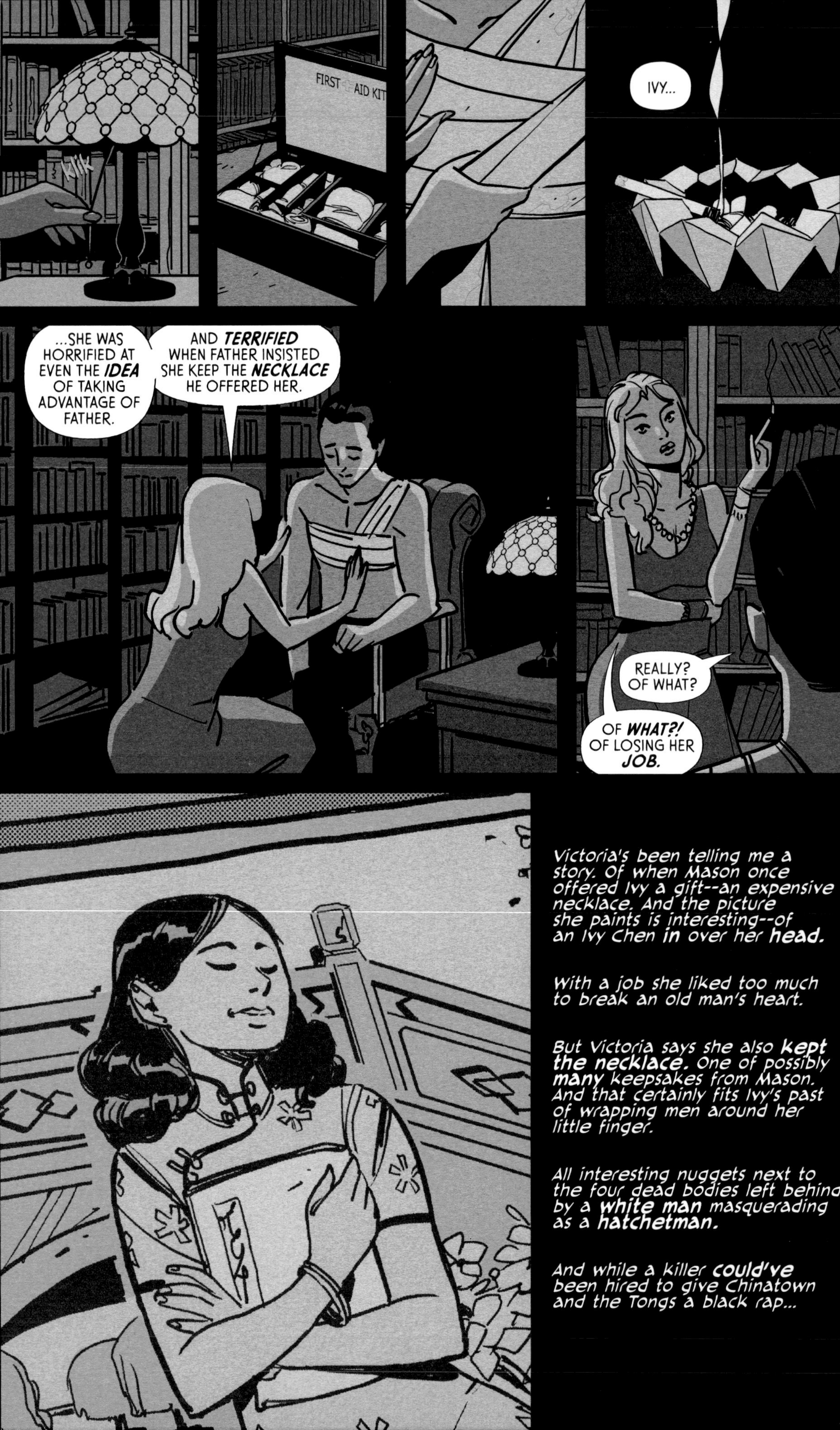
KLIK
FIRST AID KIT
IVY...
...SHE WAS HORRIFIED AT EVEN THE IDEA OF TAKING ADVANTAGE OF FATHER.
AND TERRIFIED WHEN FATHER INSISTED SHE KEEP THE NECKLACE HE OFFERED HER.
REALLY? OF WHAT?
OF WHAT?! OF LOSING HER JOB.
Victoria's been telling me a story. Of when Mason once offered Ivy a gift--an expensive necklace. And the picture she paints is interesting--of an Ivy Chen in over her head.
With a job she liked too much to break an old man's heart.
But Victoria says she also kept the necklace. One of possibly many keepsakes from Mason. And that certainly fits Ivy's past of wrapping men around her little finger.
All interesting nuggets next to the four dead bodies left behind by a white man masquerading as a hatchetman.
And while a killer could've been hired to give Chinatown and the Tongs a black rap...

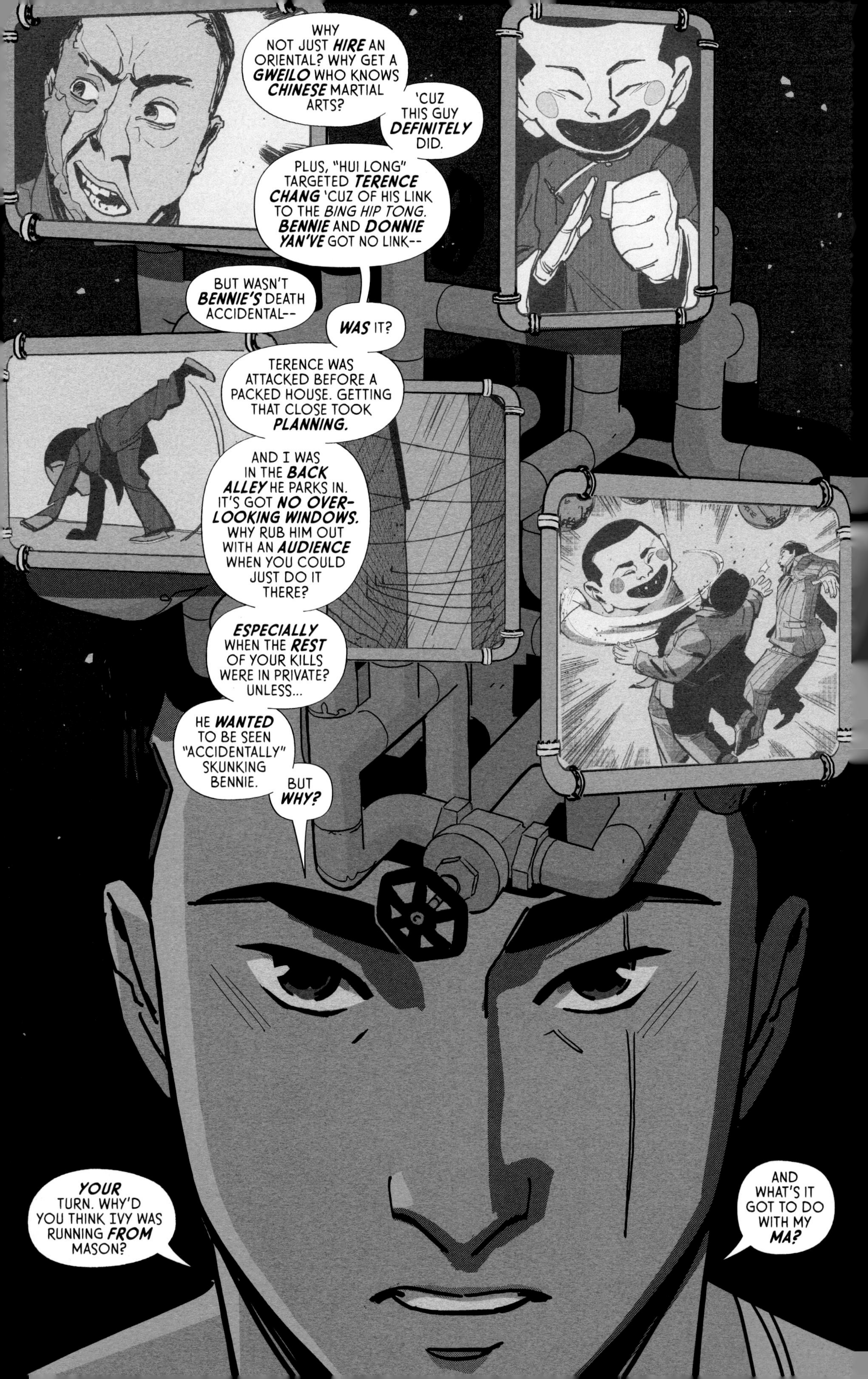

WHY NOT JUST HIRE AN ORIENTAL? WHY GET A GWEILO WHO KNOWS CHINESE MARTIAL ARTS?
'CUZ THIS GUY DEFINITELY DID.
PLUS, "HUI LONG" TARGETED TERENCE CHANG 'CUZ OF HIS LINK TO THE BING HIP TONG. BENNIE AND DONNIE YAN'VE GOT NO LINK--
BUT WASN'T BENNIE'S DEATH ACCIDENTAL--
WAS IT?
TERENCE WAS ATTACKED BEFORE A PACKED HOUSE. GETTING THAT CLOSE TOOK PLANNING.
AND I WAS IN THE BACK ALLEY HE PARKS IN. IT'S GOT NO OVER-LOOKING WINDOWS. WHY RUB HIM OUT WITH AN AUDIENCE WHEN YOU COULD JUST DO IT THERE?
ESPECIALLY WHEN THE REST OF YOUR KILLS WERE IN PRIVATE? UNLESS...
HE WANTED TO BE SEEN "ACCIDENTALLY" SKUNKING BENNIE.
BUT WHY?
YOUR TURN. WHY'D YOU THINK IVY WAS RUNNING FROM MASON?
AND WHAT'S IT GOT TO DO WITH MY MA?

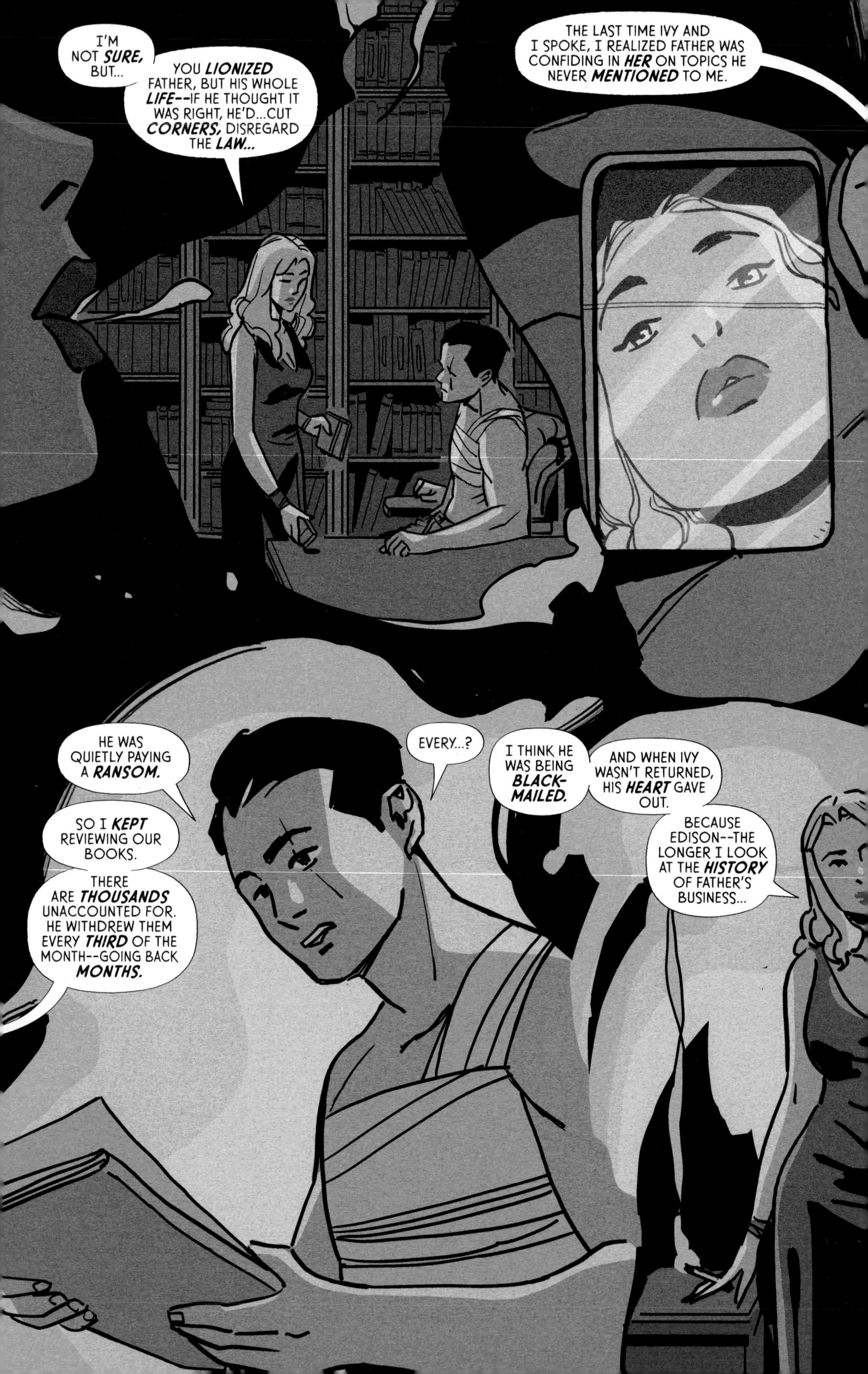
I'M NOT SURE, BUT...
YOU LIONIZED FATHER, BUT HIS WHOLE LIFE--IF HE THOUGHT IT WAS RIGHT, HE'D...CUT CORNERS, DISREGARD THE LAW...
THE LAST TIME IVY AND I SPOKE, I REALIZED FATHER WAS CONFIDING IN HER ON TOPICS HE NEVER MENTIONED TO ME.
HE WAS QUIETLY PAYING A RANSOM.
SO I KEPT REVIEWING OUR BOOKS.
THERE ARE THOUSANDS UNACCOUNTED FOR. HE WITHDREW THEM EVERY THIRD OF THE MONTH--GOING BACK MONTHS.
EVERY...?
I THINK HE WAS BEING BLACK-MAILED.
AND WHEN IVY WASN'T RETURNED, HIS HEART GAVE OUT.
BECAUSE EDISON--THE LONGER I LOOK AT THE HISTORY OF FATHER'S BUSINESS...

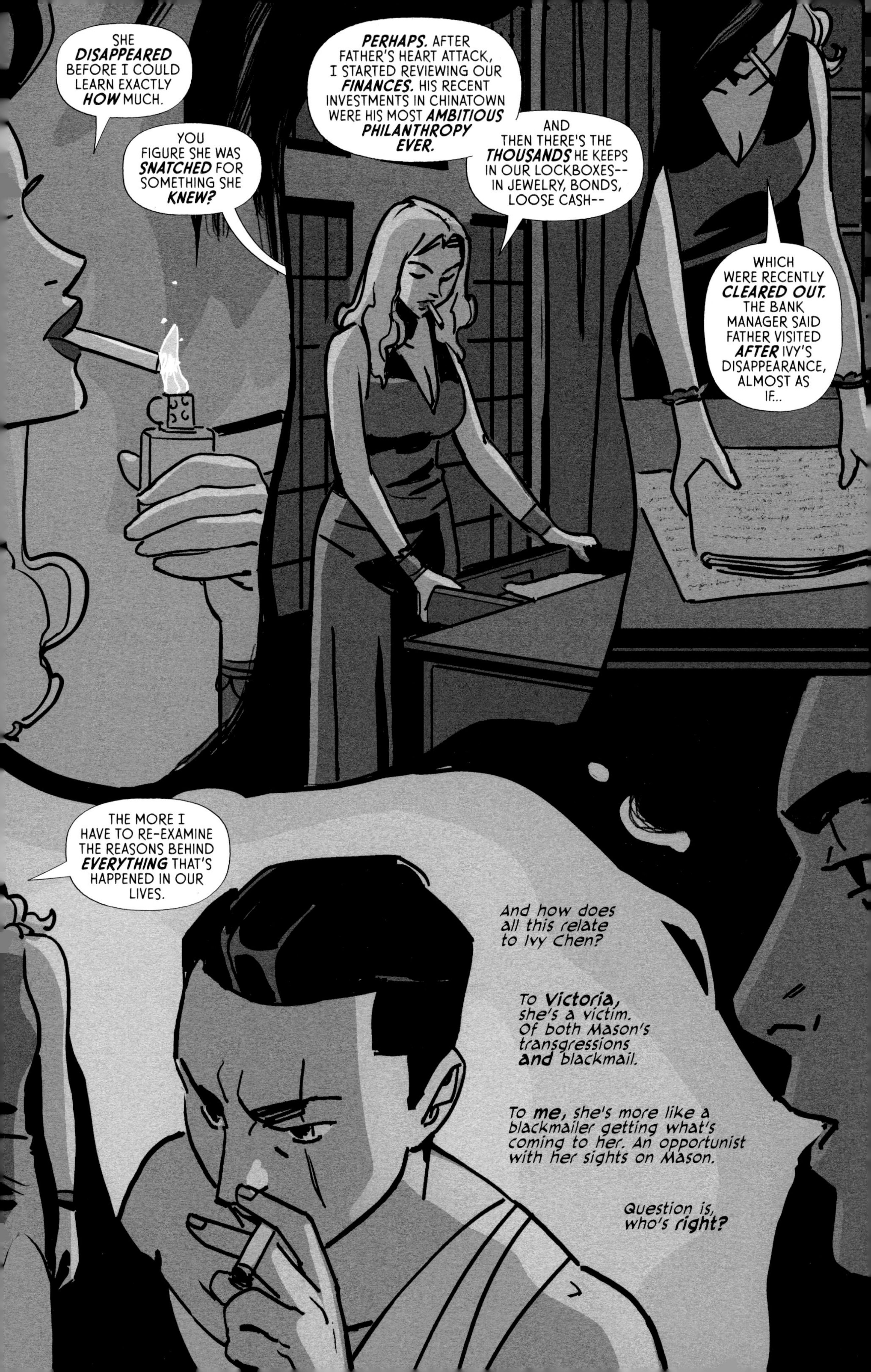
SHE DISAPPEARED BEFORE I COULD LEARN EXACTLY HOW MUCH.
YOU FIGURE SHE WAS SNATCHED FOR SOMETHING SHE KNEW?
PERHAPS. AFTER FATHER'S HEART ATTACK, I STARTED REVIEWING OUR FINANCES. HIS RECENT INVESTMENTS IN CHINATOWN WERE HIS MOST AMBITIOUS PHILANTHROPY EVER.
AND THEN THERE'S THE THOUSANDS HE KEEPS IN OUR LOCKBOXES-- IN JEWELRY, BONDS, LOOSE CASH--
WHICH WERE RECENTLY CLEARED OUT. THE BANK MANAGER SAID FATHER VISITED AFTER IVY'S DISAPPEARANCE, ALMOST AS IF...
THE MORE I HAVE TO RE-EXAMINE THE REASONS BEHIND EVERYTHING THAT'S HAPPENED IN OUR LIVES.
And how does all this relate to Ivy Chen?
To Victoria, she's a victim. Of both Mason's transgressions and blackmail.
To me, she's more like a blackmailer getting what's coming to her. An opportunist with her sights on Mason.
Question is, who's right?

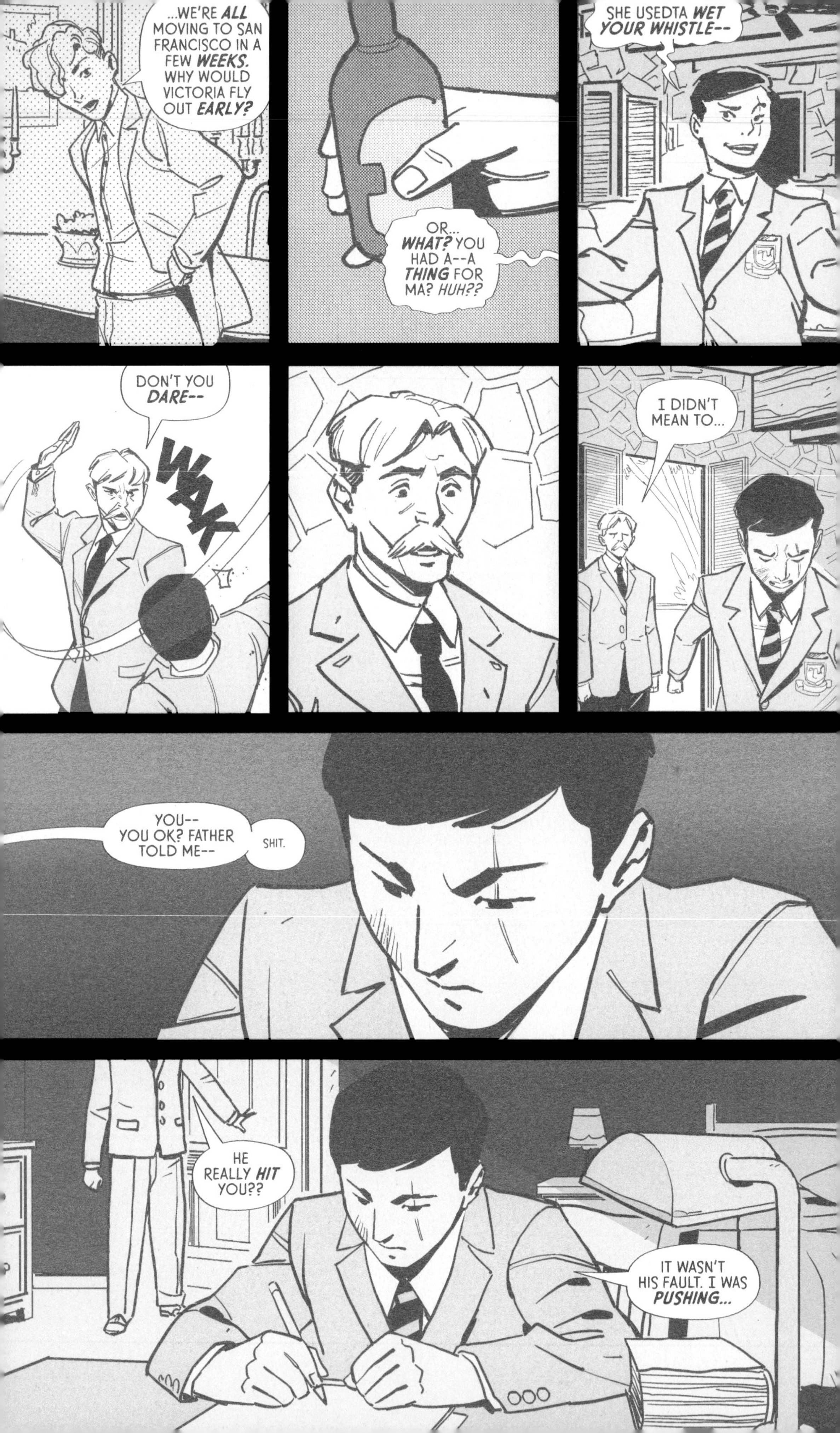
...WE'RE ALL MOVING TO SAN FRANCISCO IN A FEW WEEKS. WHY WOULD VICTORIA FLY OUT EARLY?
OR... WHAT? YOU HAD A--A THING FOR MA? HUH??
SHE USEDTA WET YOUR WHISTLE--
DON'T YOU DARE--
WAK
I DIDN'T MEAN TO...
YOU-- YOU OK? FATHER TOLD ME--
SHIT.
HE REALLY HIT YOU??
IT WASN'T HIS FAULT. I WAS PUSHING...

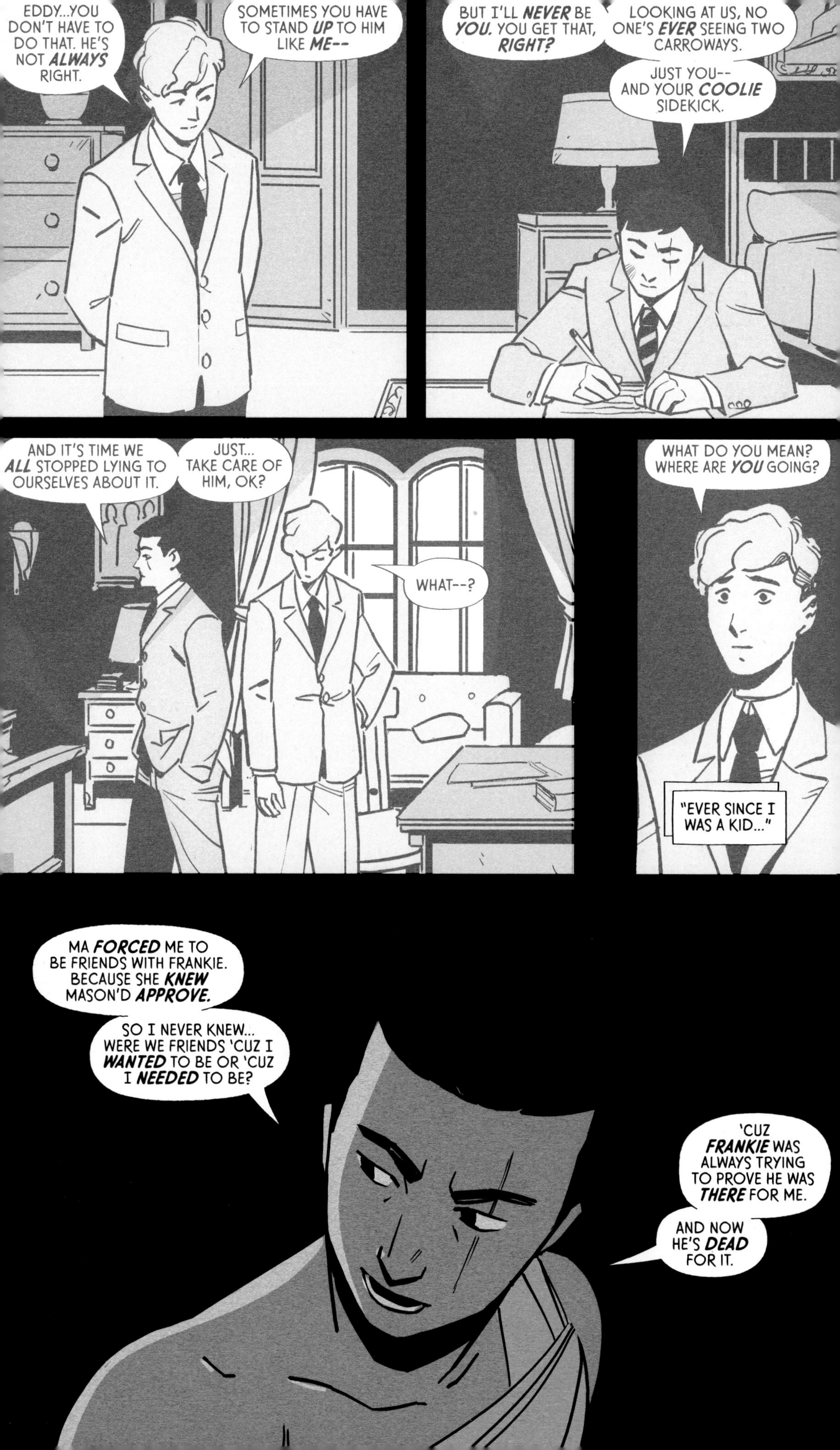
EDDY...YOU DON'T HAVE TO DO THAT. HE'S NOT ALWAYS RIGHT.
SOMETIMES YOU HAVE TO STAND UP TO HIM LIKE ME--
BUT I'LL NEVER BE YOU. YOU GET THAT, RIGHT?
LOOKING AT US, NO ONE'S EVER SEEING TWO CARROWAYS.
JUST YOU-- AND YOUR COOLIE SIDEKICK.
AND IT'S TIME WE ALL STOPPED LYING TO OURSELVES ABOUT IT.
JUST... TAKE CARE OF HIM, OK?
WHAT--?
WHAT DO YOU MEAN? WHERE ARE YOU GOING?
"EVER SINCE I WAS A KID..."
MA FORCED ME TO BE FRIENDS WITH FRANKIE. BECAUSE SHE KNEW MASON'D APPROVE.
SO I NEVER KNEW... WERE WE FRIENDS 'CUZ I WANTED TO BE OR 'CUZ I NEEDED TO BE?
'CUZ FRANKIE WAS ALWAYS TRYING TO PROVE HE WAS THERE FOR ME.
AND NOW HE'S DEAD FOR IT.

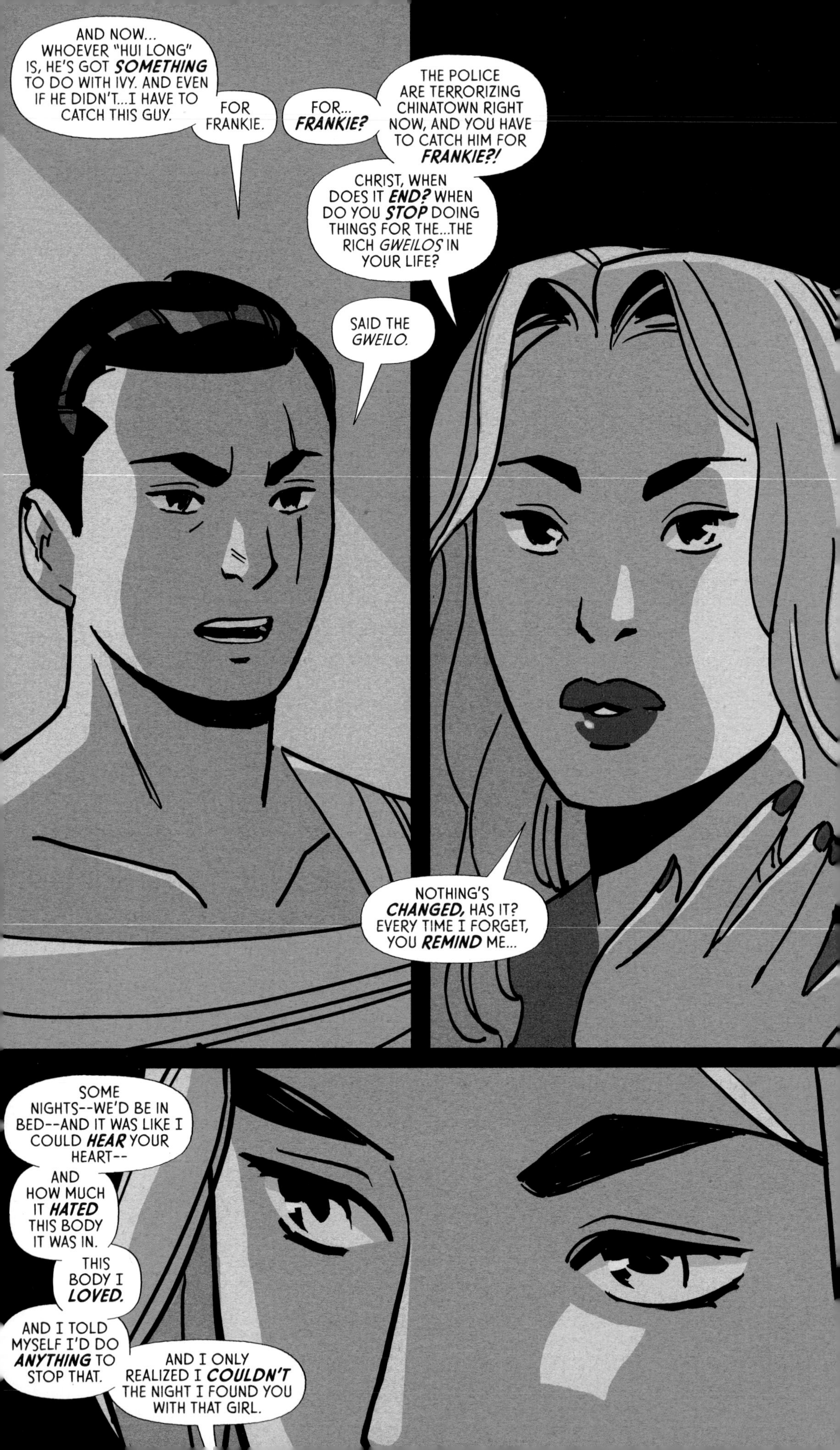
AND NOW... WHOEVER "HUI LONG" IS, HE'S GOT SOMETHING TO DO WITH IVY. AND EVEN IF HE DIDN'T...I HAVE TO CATCH THIS GUY.
FOR FRANKIE.
FOR... FRANKIE?
THE POLICE ARE TERRORIZING CHINATOWN RIGHT NOW, AND YOU HAVE TO CATCH HIM FOR FRANKIE?!
CHRIST, WHEN DOES IT END? WHEN DO YOU STOP DOING THINGS FOR THE...THE RICH GWEILOS IN YOUR LIFE?
SAID THE GWEILO.
NOTHING'S CHANGED, HAS IT? EVERY TIME I FORGET, YOU REMIND ME...
SOME NIGHTS--WE'D BE IN BED--AND IT WAS LIKE I COULD HEAR YOUR HEART--
AND HOW MUCH IT HATED THIS BODY IT WAS IN.
THIS BODY I LOVED.
AND I TOLD MYSELF I'D DO ANYTHING TO STOP THAT.
AND I ONLY REALIZED I COULDN'T THE NIGHT I FOUND YOU WITH THAT GIRL.

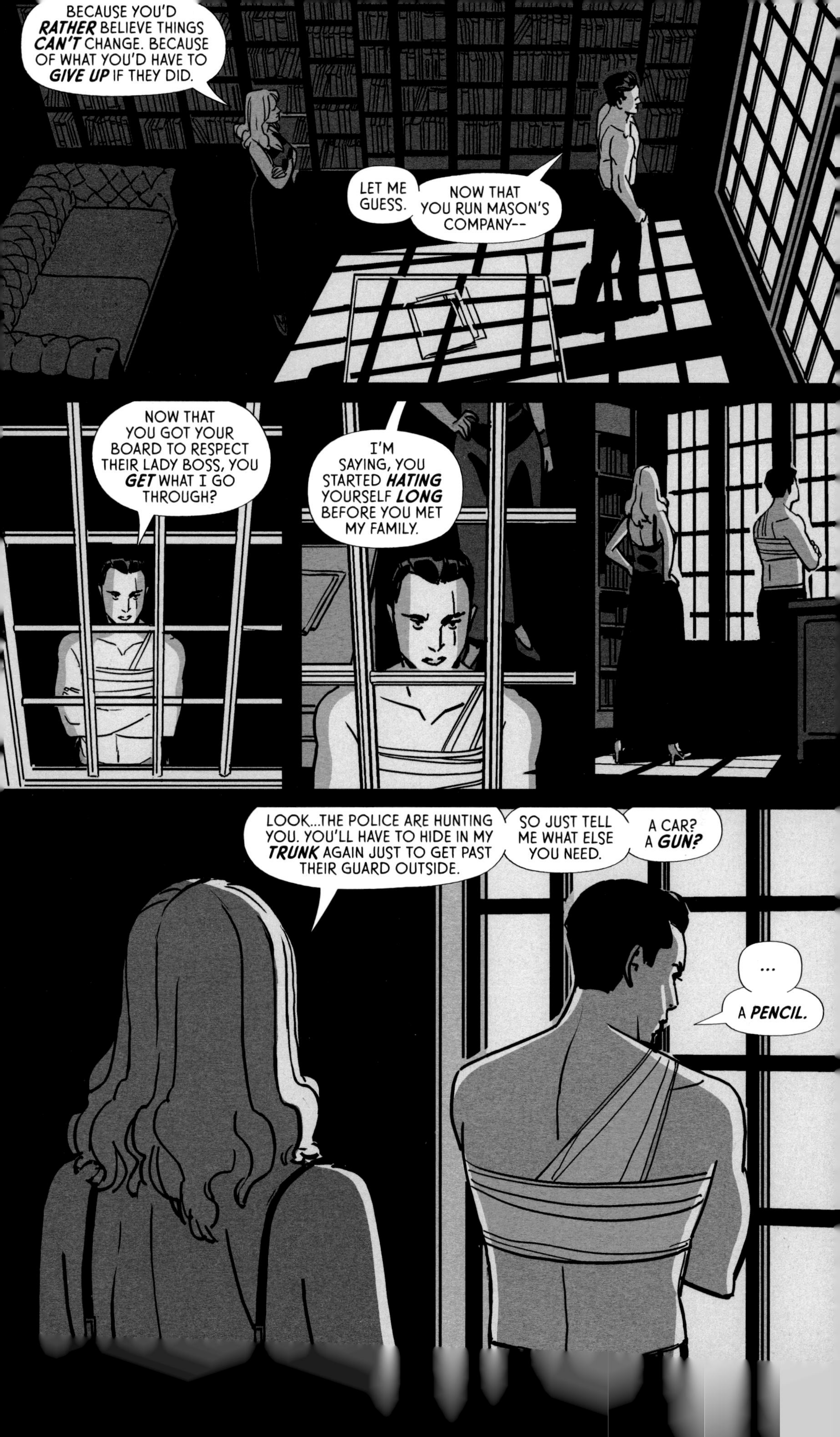
BECAUSE YOU'D RATHER BELIEVE THINGS CAN'T CHANGE. BECAUSE OF WHAT YOU'D HAVE TO GIVE UP IF THEY DID.
LET ME GUESS.
NOW THAT YOU RUN MASON'S COMPANY--
NOW THAT YOU GOT YOUR BOARD TO RESPECT THEIR LADY BOSS, YOU GET WHAT I GO THROUGH?
I'M SAYING, YOU STARTED HATING YOURSELF LONG BEFORE YOU MET MY FAMILY.
LOOK...THE POLICE ARE HUNTING YOU. YOU'LL HAVE TO HIDE IN MY TRUNK AGAIN JUST TO GET PAST THEIR GUARD OUTSIDE.
SO JUST TELL ME WHAT ELSE YOU NEED.
A CAR? A GUN?
...
A PENCIL.

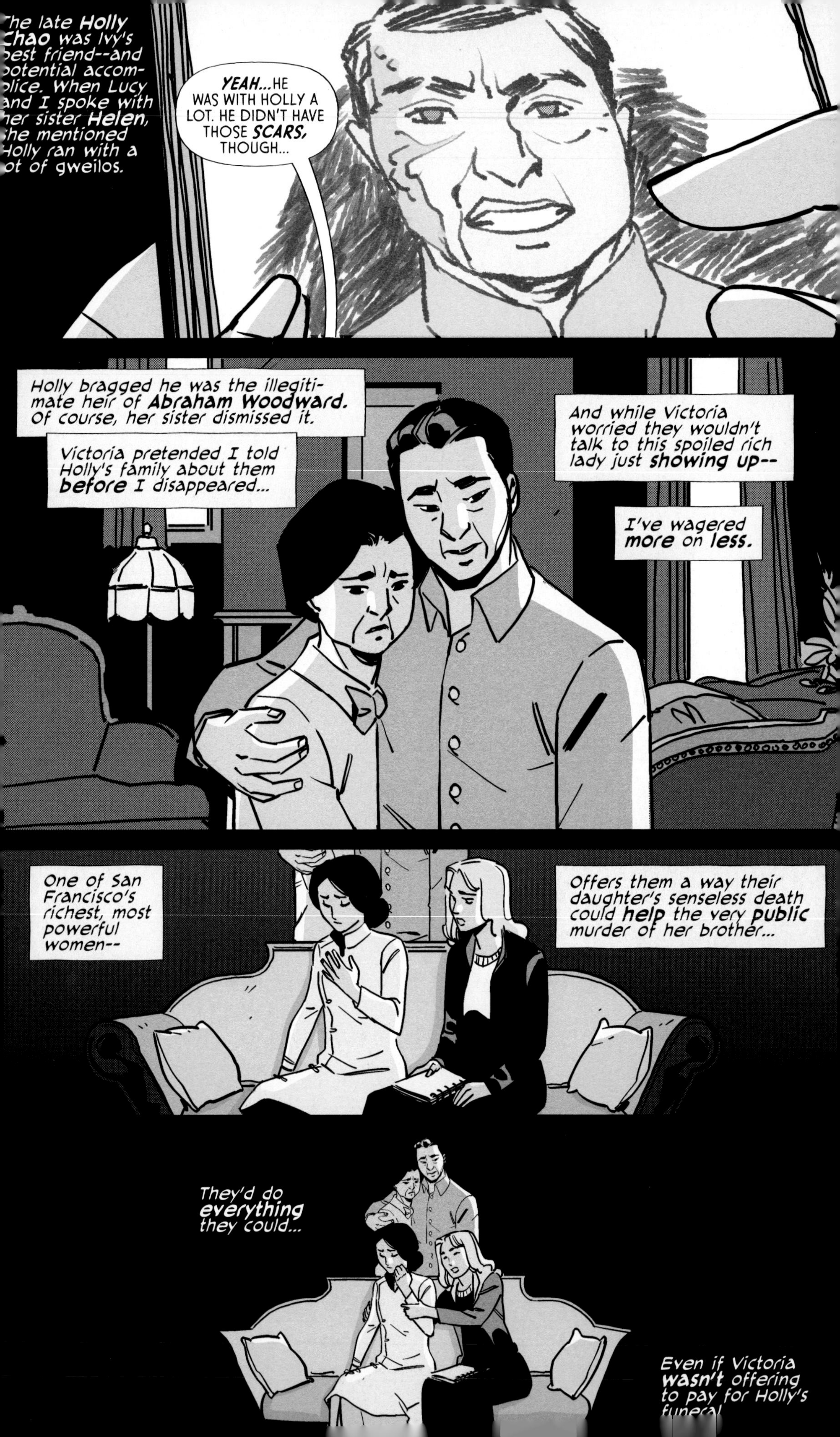

The late Holly Chao was Ivy's best friend--and potential accomplice. When Lucy and I spoke with her sister Helen, she mentioned Holly ran with a lot of gweilos.
YEAH...HE WAS WITH HOLLY A LOT. HE DIDN'T HAVE THOSE SCARS, THOUGH...
Holly bragged he was the illegitimate heir of Abraham Woodward. Of course, her sister dismissed it.
Victoria pretended I told Holly's family about them before I disappeared...
And while Victoria worried they wouldn't talk to this spoiled rich lady just showing up--
I've wagered more on less.
One of San Francisco's richest, most powerful women--
Offers them a way their daughter's senseless death could help the very public murder of her brother...
They'd do everything they could...
Even if Victoria wasn't offering to pay for Holly's funeral

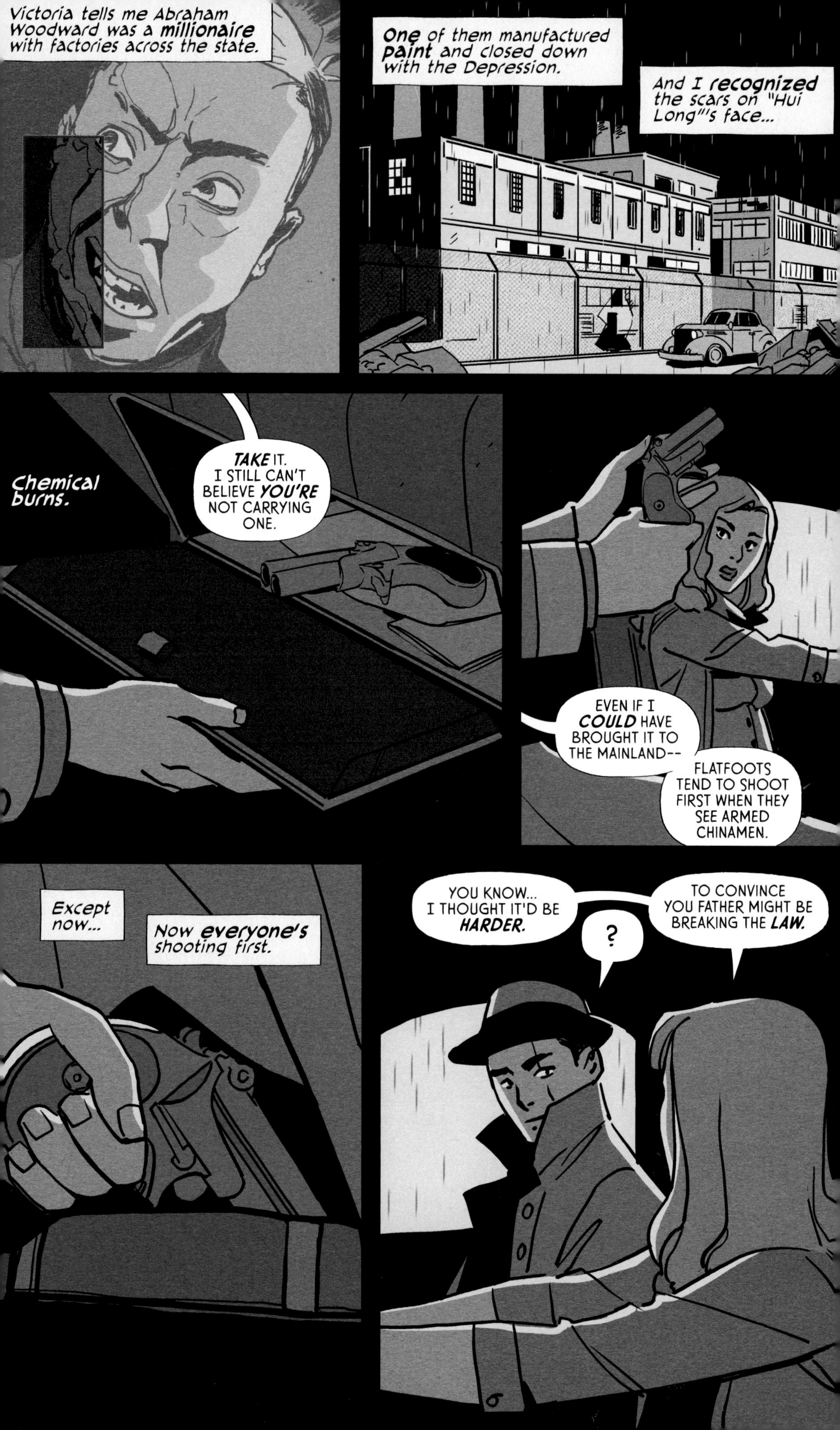
Victoria tells me Abraham Woodward was a **millionaire** with factories across the state.
One of them manufactured **paint** and closed down with the Depression.
And I **recognized** the scars on "Hui Long"'s face...
Chemical burns.
TAKE IT. I STILL CAN'T BELIEVE **YOU'RE** NOT CARRYING ONE.
EVEN IF I **COULD** HAVE BROUGHT IT TO THE MAINLAND--
FLATFOOTS TEND TO SHOOT FIRST WHEN THEY SEE ARMED CHINAMEN.
Except now...
Now **everyone's** shooting first.
YOU KNOW... I THOUGHT IT'D BE **HARDER.**
?
TO CONVINCE YOU FATHER MIGHT BE BREAKING THE **LAW.**

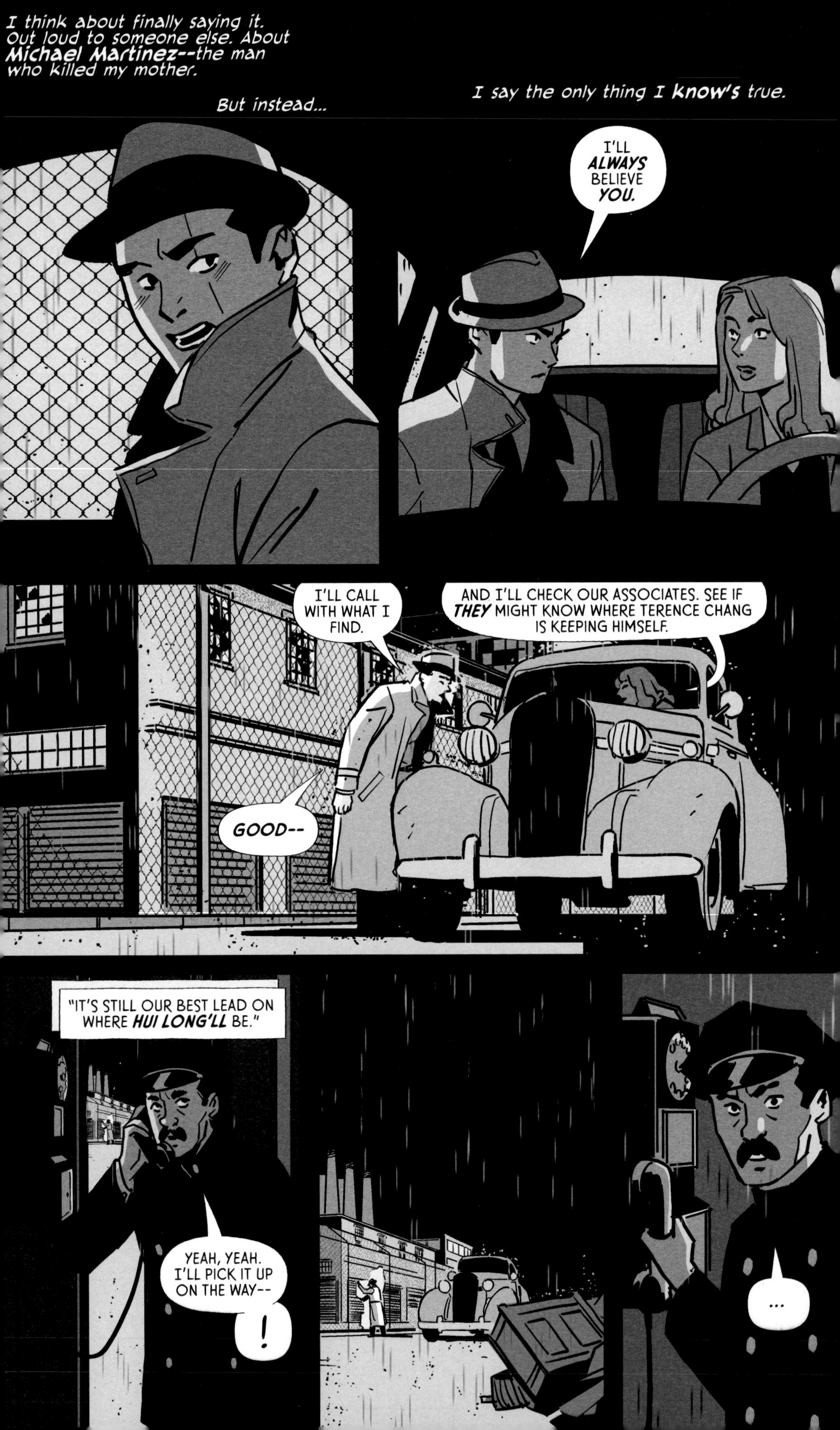
I think about finally saying it. Out loud to someone else. About Michael Martinez--the man who killed my mother.
But instead...
I say the only thing I know's true.
I'LL ALWAYS BELIEVE YOU.
I'LL CALL WITH WHAT I FIND.
AND I'LL CHECK OUR ASSOCIATES. SEE IF THEY MIGHT KNOW WHERE TERENCE CHANG IS KEEPING HIMSELF.
GOOD--
"IT'S STILL OUR BEST LEAD ON WHERE HUI LONG'LL BE."
YEAH, YEAH. I'LL PICK IT UP ON THE WAY--
!
...

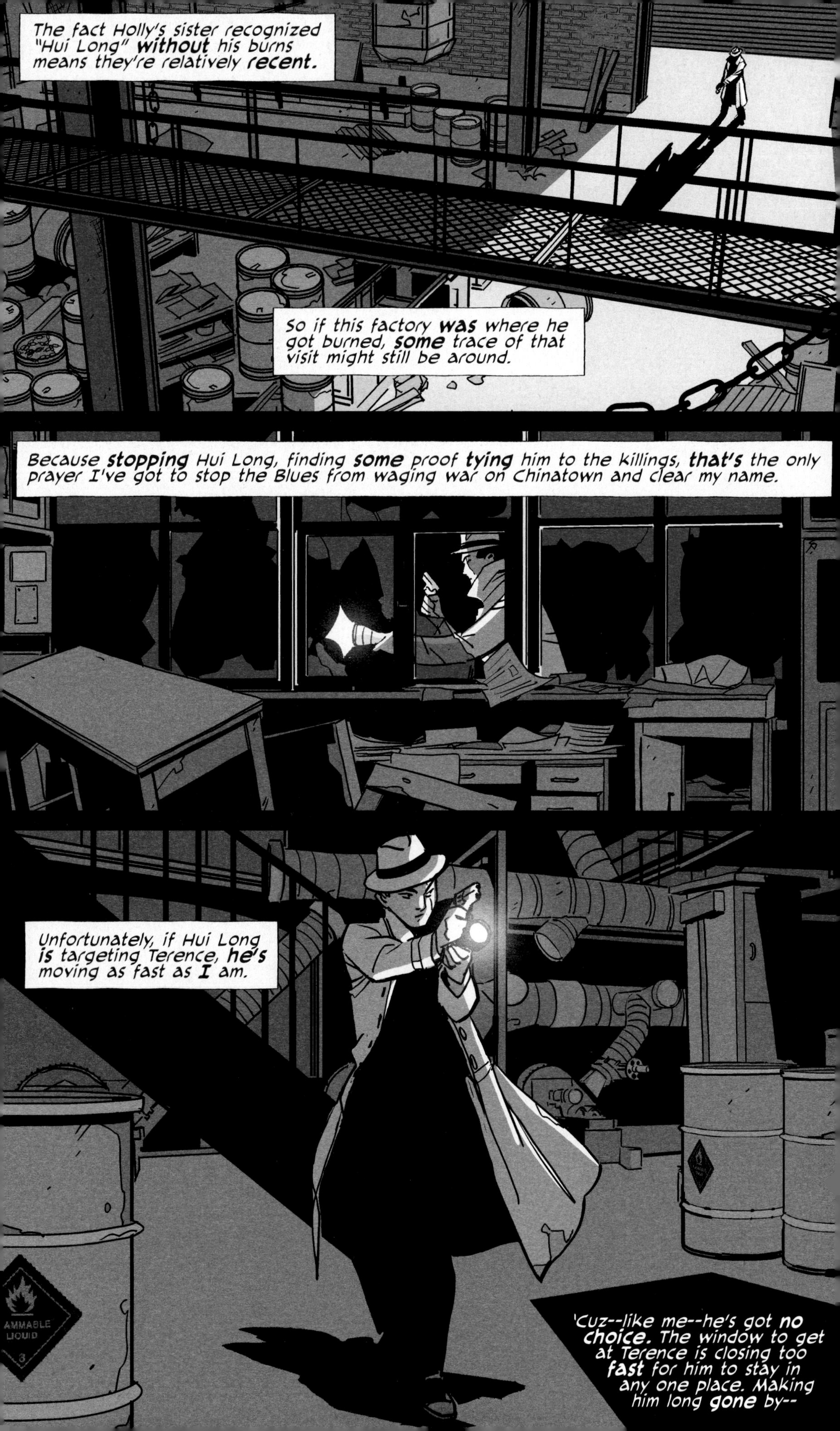
The fact Holly's sister recognized "Hui Long" without his burns means they're relatively recent.
So if this factory was where he got burned, some trace of that visit might still be around.
Because stopping Hui Long, finding some proof tying him to the killings, that's the only prayer I've got to stop the Blues from waging war on Chinatown and clear my name.
Unfortunately, if Hui Long is targeting Terence, he's moving as fast as I am.
'Cuz--like me--he's got no choice. The window to get at Terence is closing too fast for him to stay in any one place. Making him long gone by--

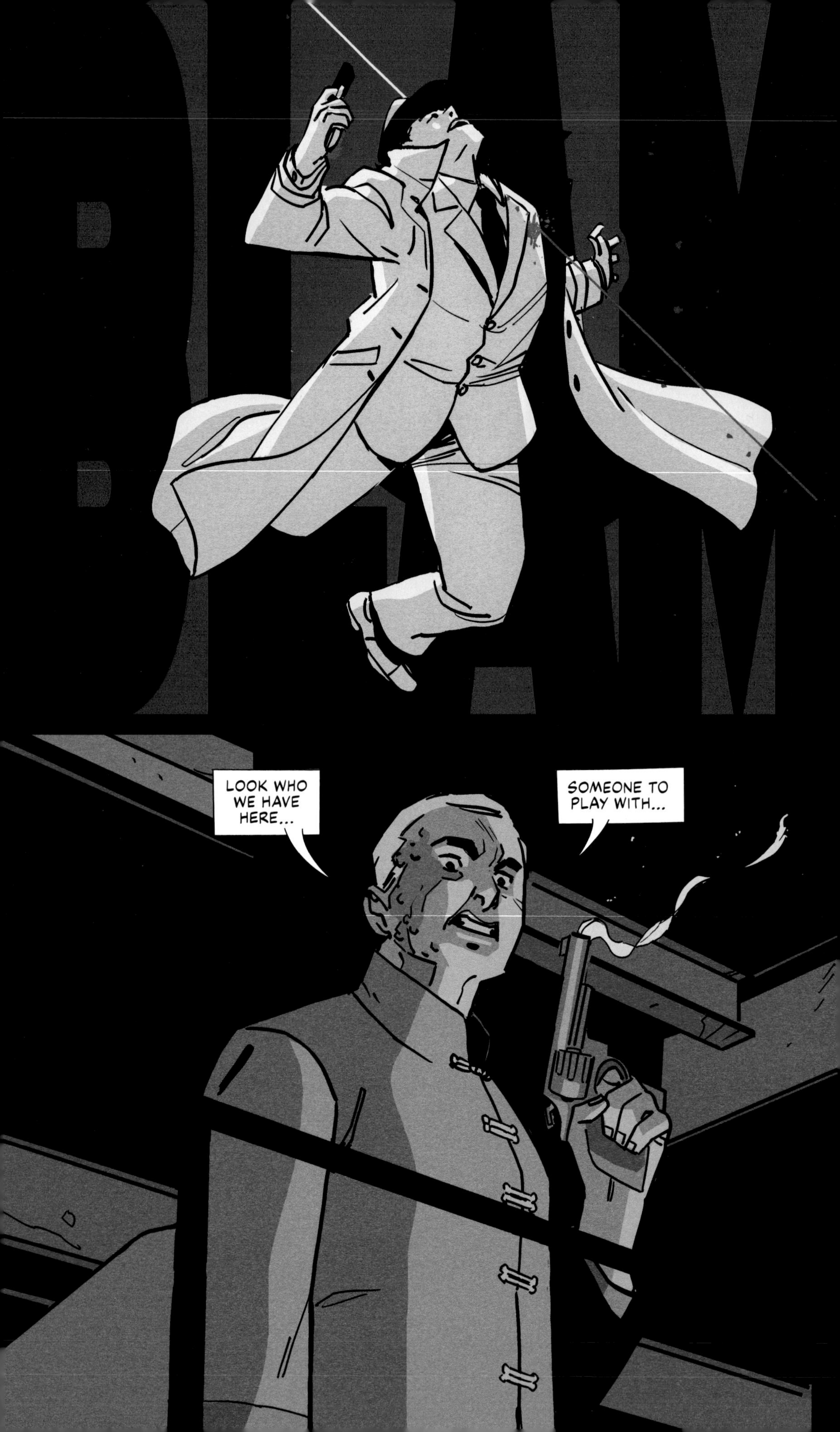
BLAM
LOOK WHO WE HAVE HERE...
SOMEONE TO PLAY WITH...

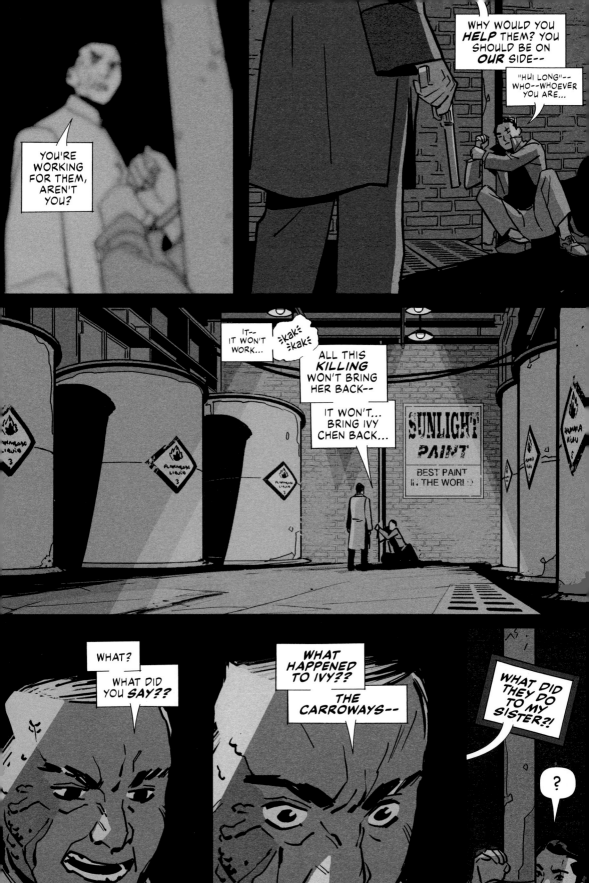

YOU'RE WORKING FOR THEM, AREN'T YOU?

WHY WOULD YOU *HELP* THEM? YOU SHOULD BE ON *OUR* SIDE--

"HUI LONG"-- WHO--WHOEVER YOU ARE...

IT-- IT WON'T WORK...

≤kak≤ ≤kak≤

ALL THIS *KILLING* WON'T BRING HER BACK--

IT WON'T... BRING IVY CHEN BACK...

SUNLIGHT PAINT

BEST PAINT IN THE WORLD

WHAT?

WHAT DID YOU *SAY??*

WHAT HAPPENED TO IVY??

THE CARROWAYS--

WHAT DID THEY DO TO MY SISTER?!

?

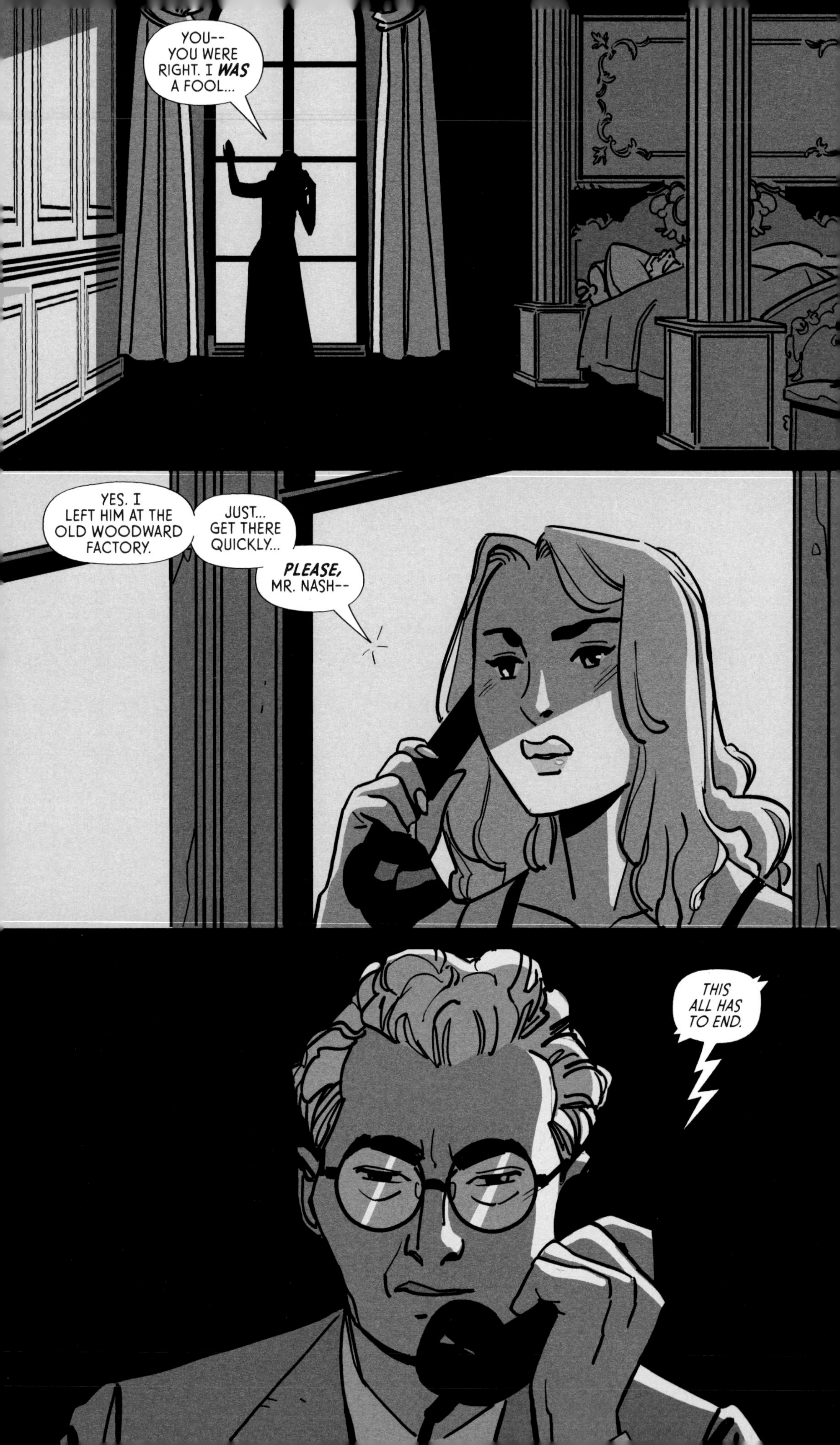
YOU-- YOU WERE RIGHT. I WAS A FOOL...
YES. I LEFT HIM AT THE OLD WOODWARD FACTORY.
JUST... GET THERE QUICKLY...
PLEASE, MR. NASH--
THIS ALL HAS TO END.

CHAPTER SEVEN

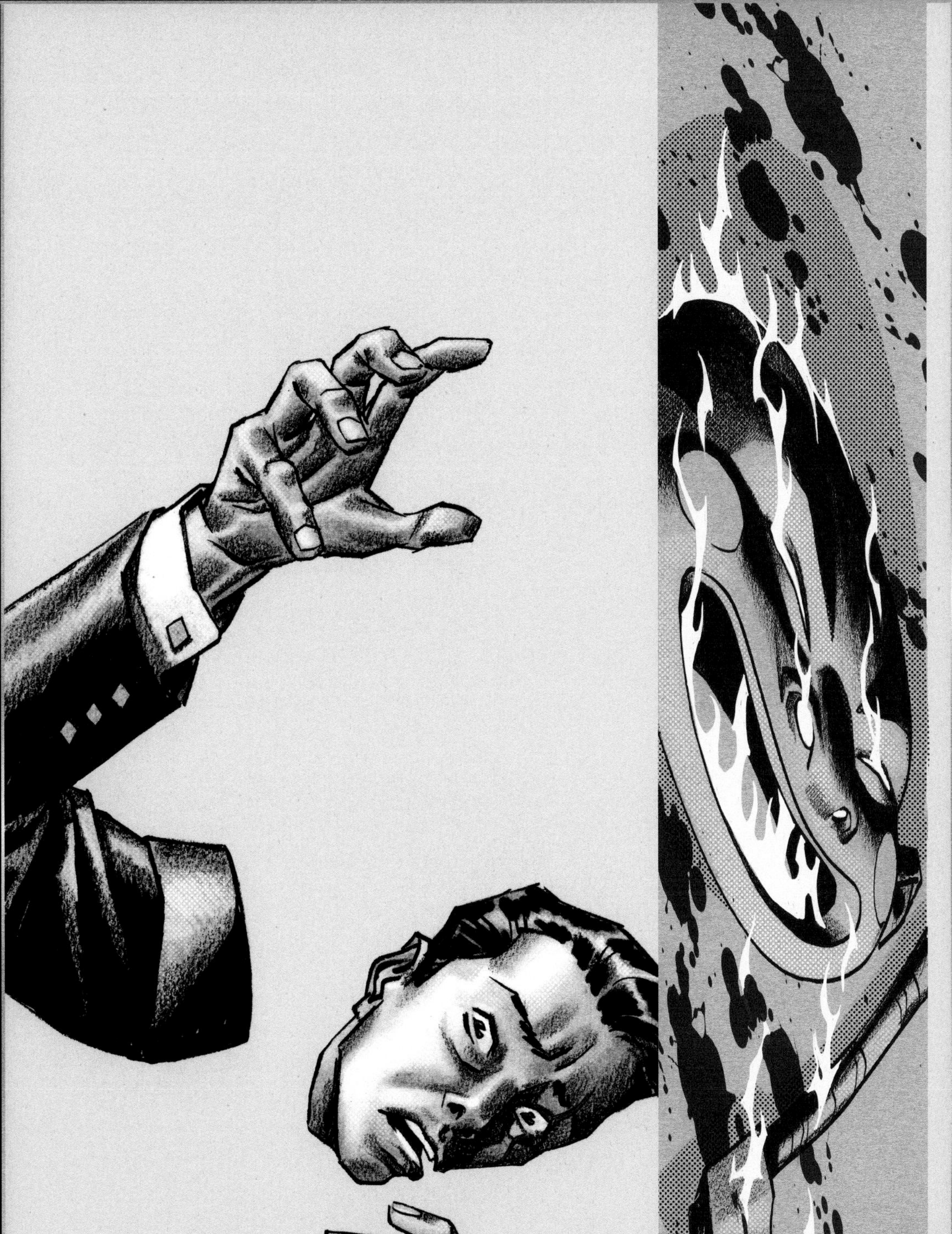

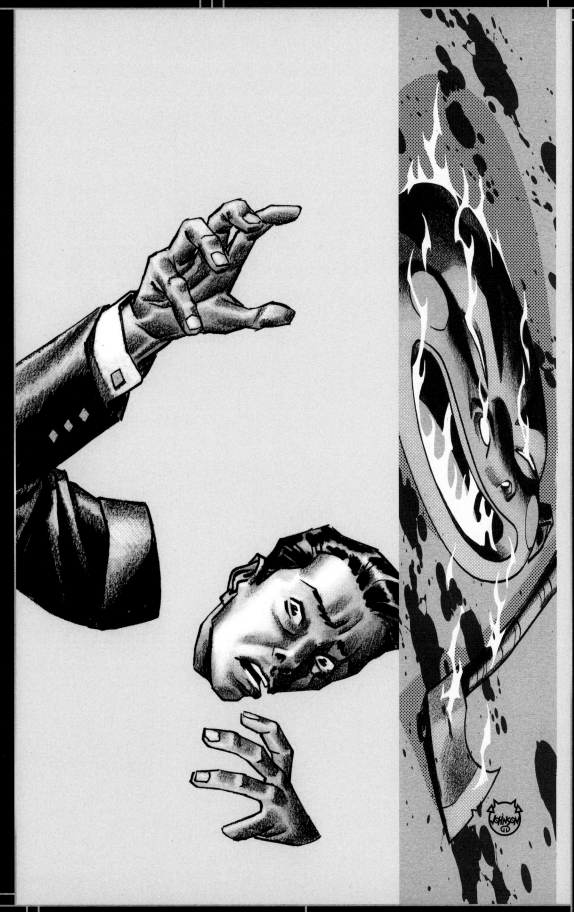

ART BY **DAVE JOHNSON**

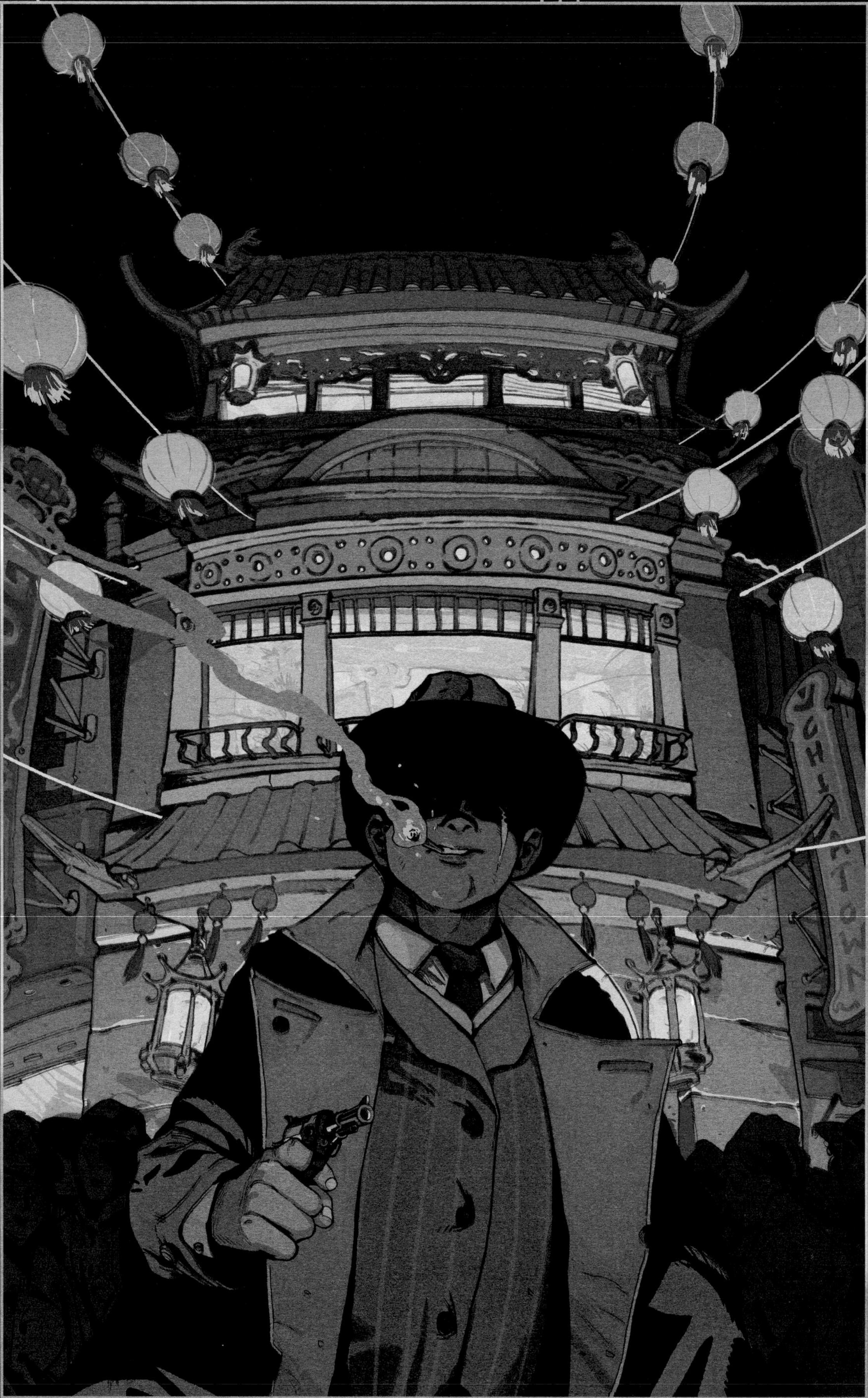

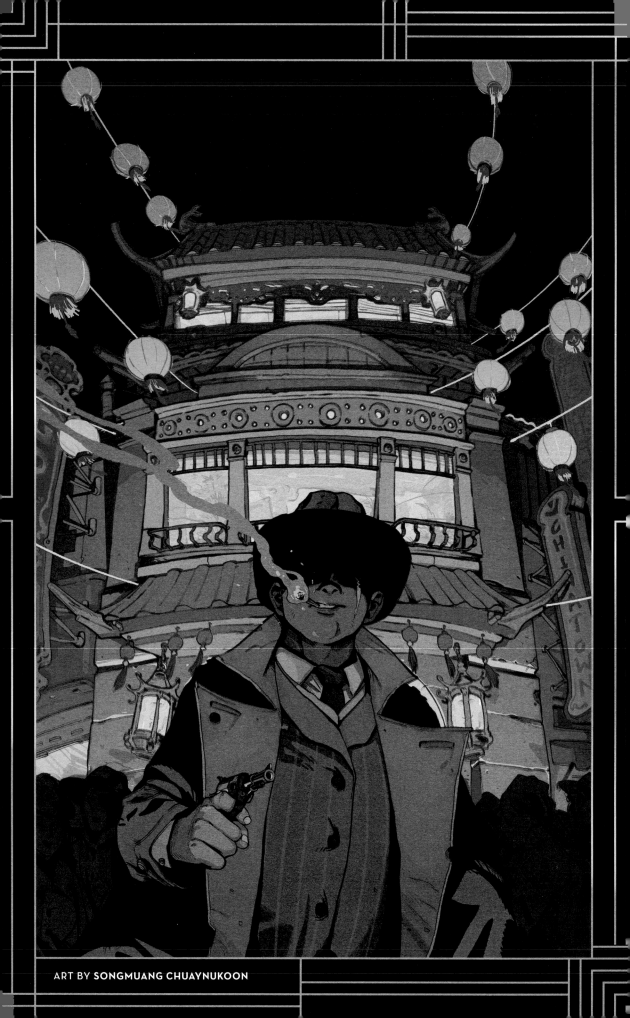

ART BY **SONGMUANG CHUAYNUKOON**

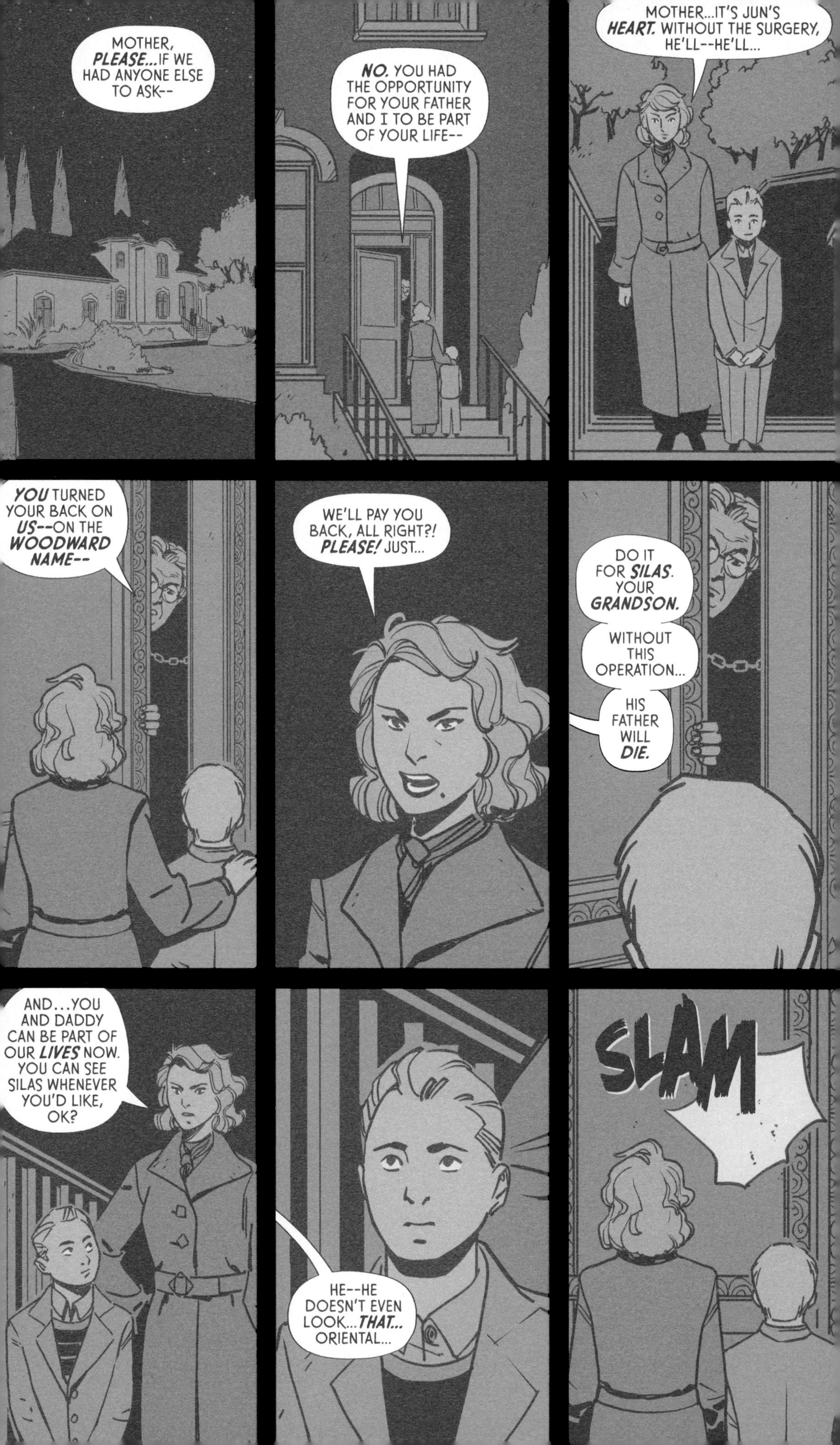
MOTHER, PLEASE...IF WE HAD ANYONE ELSE TO ASK--
NO. YOU HAD THE OPPORTUNITY FOR YOUR FATHER AND I TO BE PART OF YOUR LIFE--
MOTHER...IT'S JUN'S HEART. WITHOUT THE SURGERY, HE'LL--HE'LL...
YOU TURNED YOUR BACK ON US--ON THE WOODWARD NAME--
WE'LL PAY YOU BACK, ALL RIGHT?! PLEASE! JUST...
DO IT FOR SILAS. YOUR GRANDSON.
WITHOUT THIS OPERATION...
HIS FATHER WILL DIE.
AND...YOU AND DADDY CAN BE PART OF OUR LIVES NOW. YOU CAN SEE SILAS WHENEVER YOU'D LIKE, OK?
HE--HE DOESN'T EVEN LOOK...THAT... ORIENTAL...
SLAM

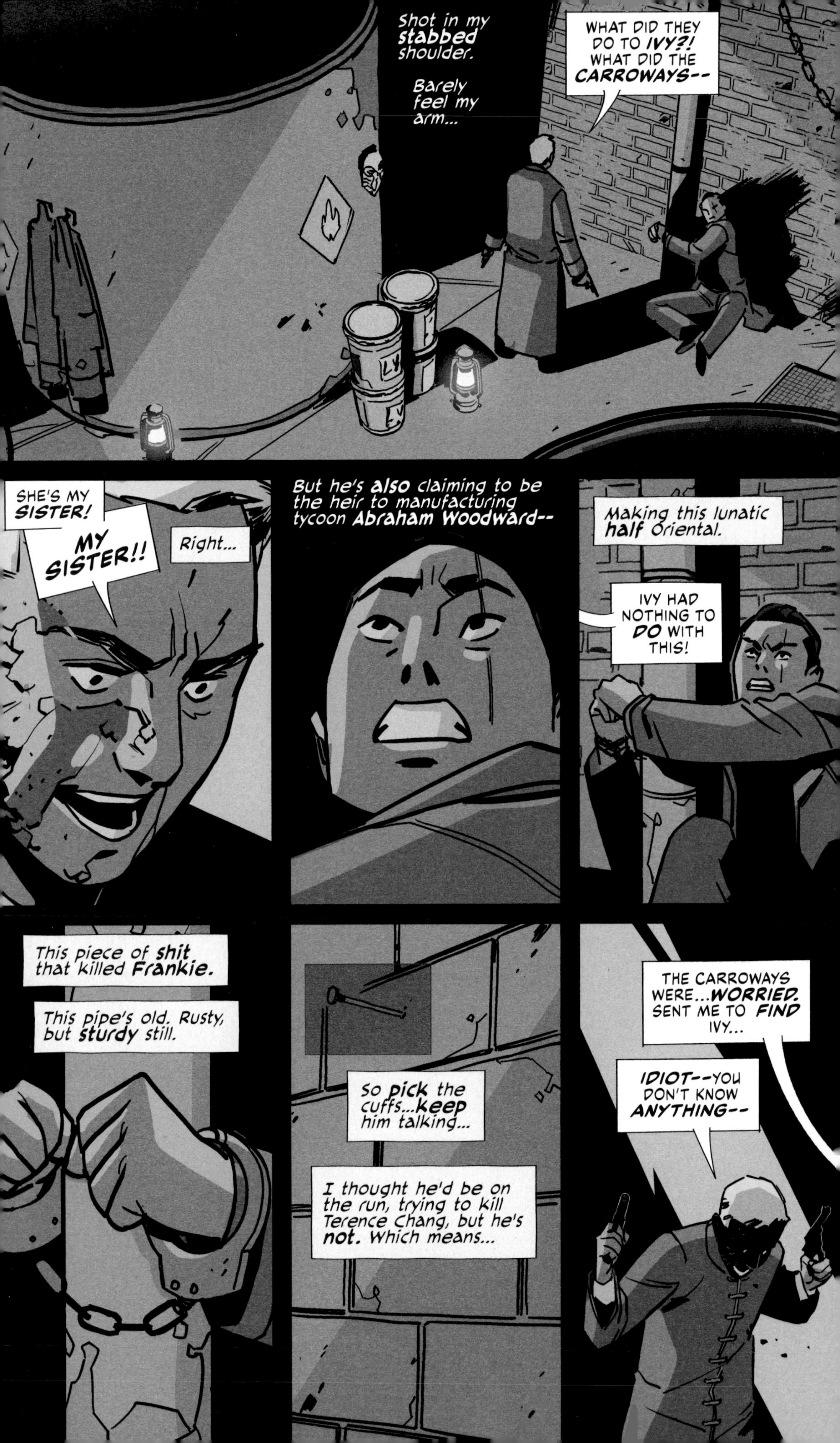
Shot in my stabbed shoulder.
Barely feel my arm...
WHAT DID THEY DO TO IVY?! WHAT DID THE CARROWAYS--
SHE'S MY SISTER!
MY SISTER!!
Right...
But he's also claiming to be the heir to manufacturing tycoon Abraham Woodward--
Making this lunatic half Oriental.
IVY HAD NOTHING TO DO WITH THIS!
This piece of shit that killed Frankie.
This pipe's old. Rusty, but sturdy still.
So pick the cuffs...keep him talking...
I thought he'd be on the run, trying to kill Terence Chang, but he's not. Which means...
THE CARROWAYS WERE...WORRIED. SENT ME TO FIND IVY...
IDIOT--YOU DON'T KNOW ANYTHING--

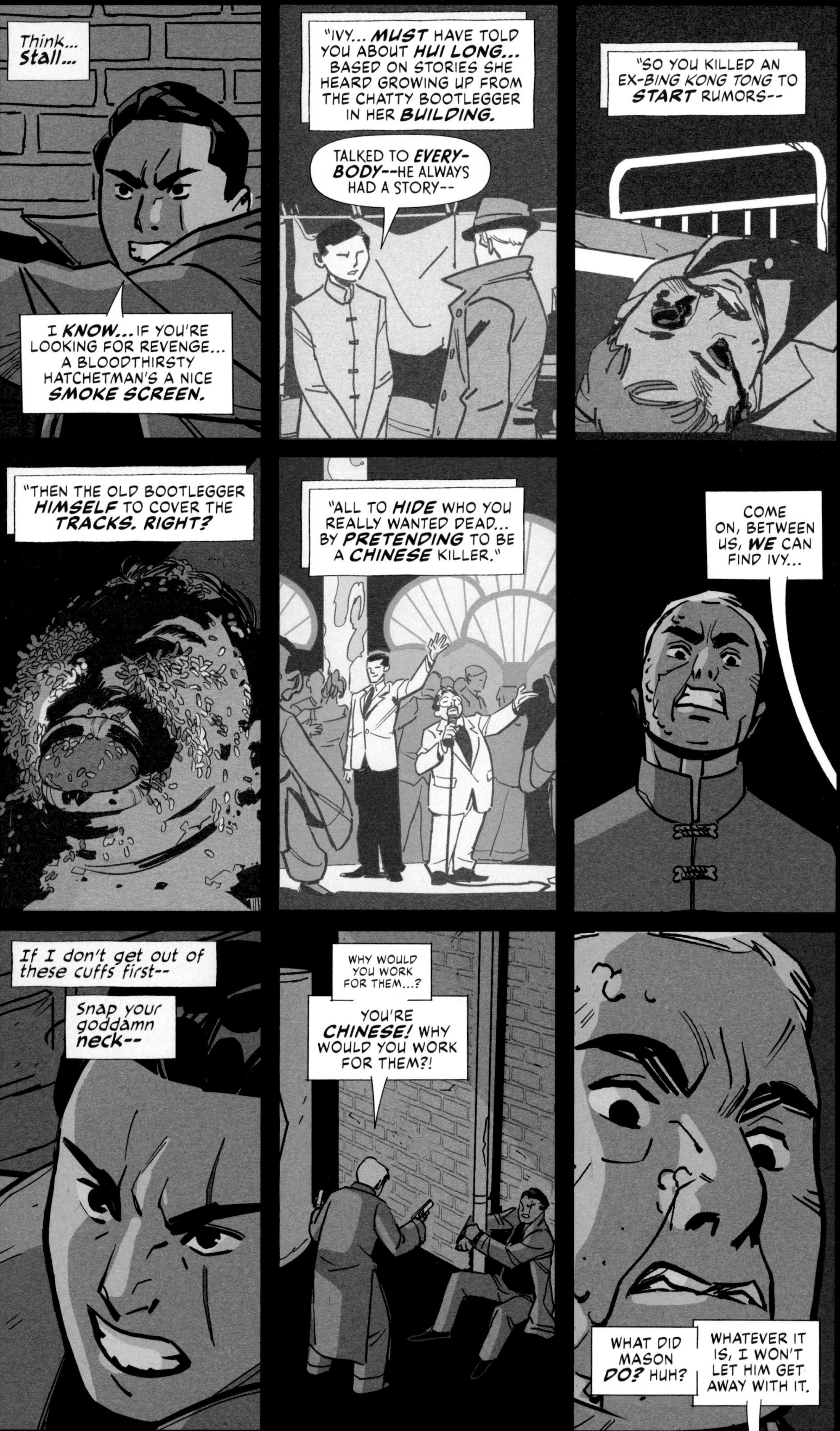
Think... stall...
I KNOW... IF YOU'RE LOOKING FOR REVENGE... A BLOODTHIRSTY HATCHETMAN'S A NICE SMOKE SCREEN.
"IVY... MUST HAVE TOLD YOU ABOUT HUI LONG... BASED ON STORIES SHE HEARD GROWING UP FROM THE CHATTY BOOTLEGGER IN HER BUILDING.
TALKED TO EVERY-BODY--HE ALWAYS HAD A STORY--
"SO YOU KILLED AN EX-BING KONG TONG TO START RUMORS--
"THEN THE OLD BOOTLEGGER HIMSELF TO COVER THE TRACKS. RIGHT?
"ALL TO HIDE WHO YOU REALLY WANTED DEAD... BY PRETENDING TO BE A CHINESE KILLER."
COME ON, BETWEEN US, WE CAN FIND IVY...
If I don't get out of these cuffs first--
Snap your goddamn neck--
WHY WOULD YOU WORK FOR THEM...?
YOU'RE CHINESE! WHY WOULD YOU WORK FOR THEM?!
WHAT DID MASON DO? HUH?
WHATEVER IT IS, I WON'T LET HIM GET AWAY WITH IT.

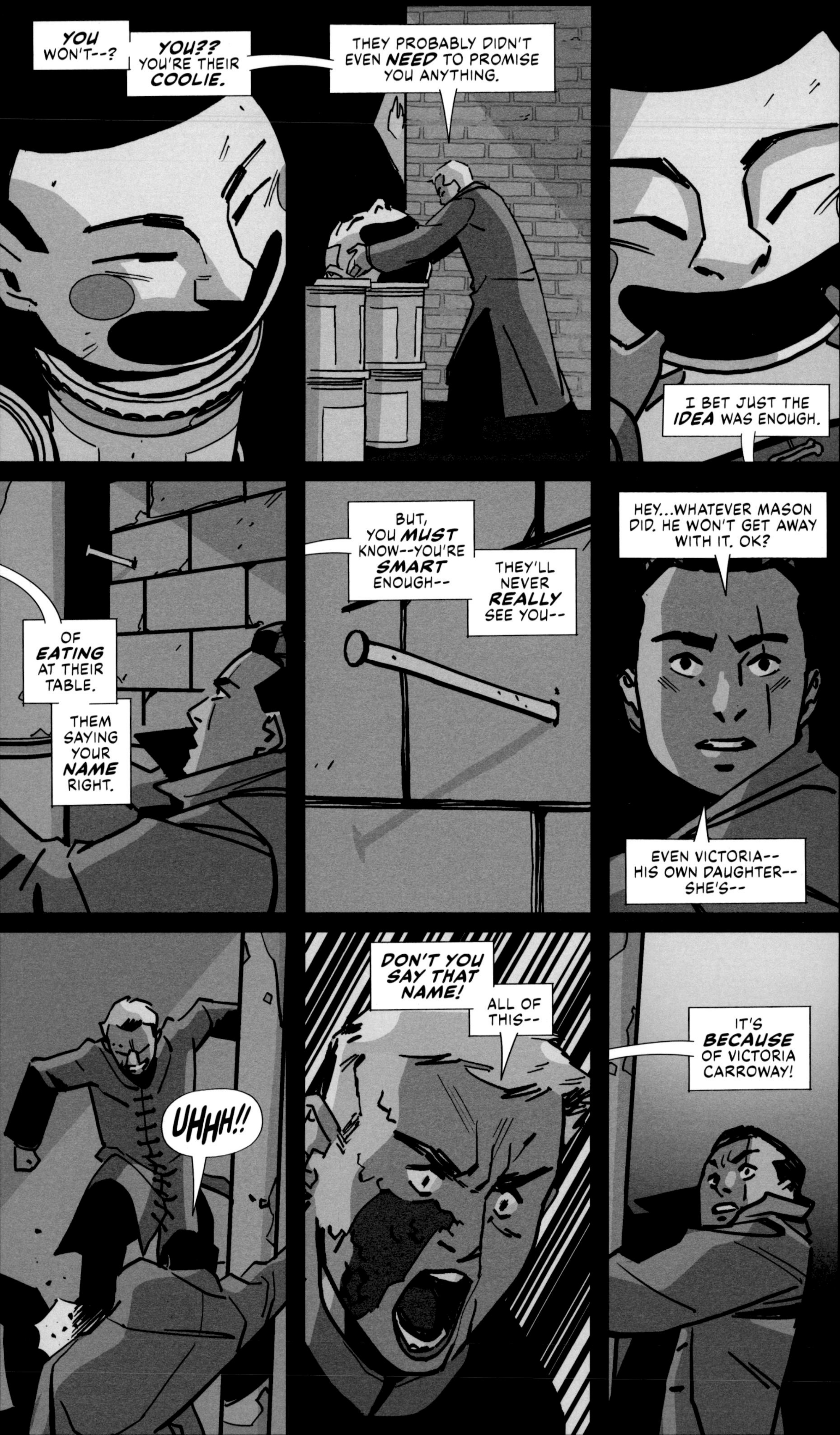
YOU WON'T--?
YOU?? YOU'RE THEIR COOLIE.
THEY PROBABLY DIDN'T EVEN NEED TO PROMISE YOU ANYTHING.
I BET JUST THE IDEA WAS ENOUGH.
OF EATING AT THEIR TABLE.
THEM SAYING YOUR NAME RIGHT.
BUT, YOU MUST KNOW--YOU'RE SMART ENOUGH--
THEY'LL NEVER REALLY SEE YOU--
HEY...WHATEVER MASON DID. HE WON'T GET AWAY WITH IT. OK?
EVEN VICTORIA-- HIS OWN DAUGHTER-- SHE'S--
UHHH!!
DON'T YOU SAY THAT NAME!
ALL OF THIS--
IT'S BECAUSE OF VICTORIA CARROWAY!

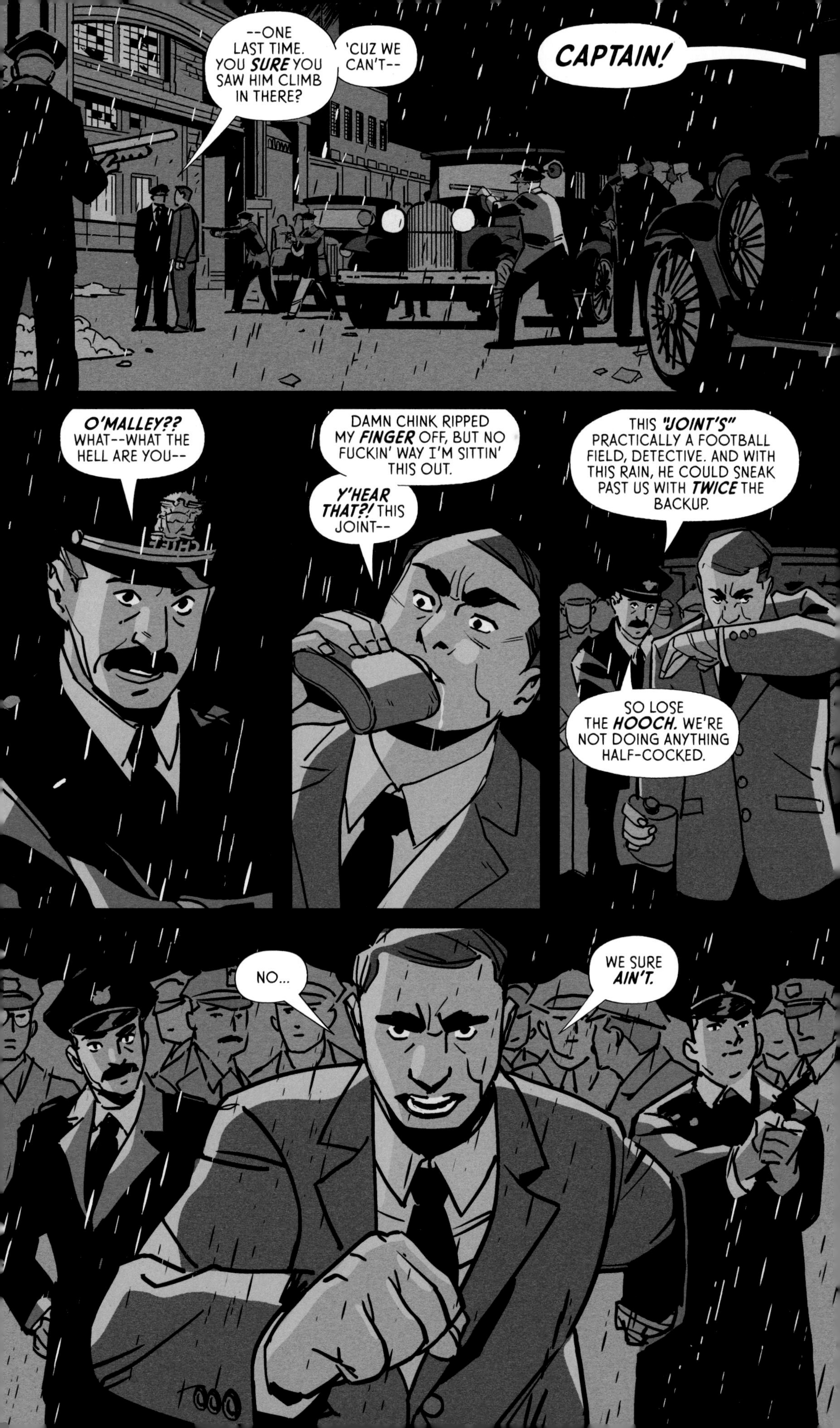
--ONE LAST TIME. YOU SURE YOU SAW HIM CLIMB IN THERE?
'CUZ WE CAN'T--
CAPTAIN!
O'MALLEY?? WHAT--WHAT THE HELL ARE YOU--
DAMN CHINK RIPPED MY FINGER OFF, BUT NO FUCKIN' WAY I'M SITTIN' THIS OUT.
Y'HEAR THAT?! THIS JOINT--
THIS "JOINT'S" PRACTICALLY A FOOTBALL FIELD, DETECTIVE. AND WITH THIS RAIN, HE COULD SNEAK PAST US WITH TWICE THE BACKUP.
SO LOSE THE HOOCH. WE'RE NOT DOING ANYTHING HALF-COCKED.
NO...
WE SURE AIN'T.

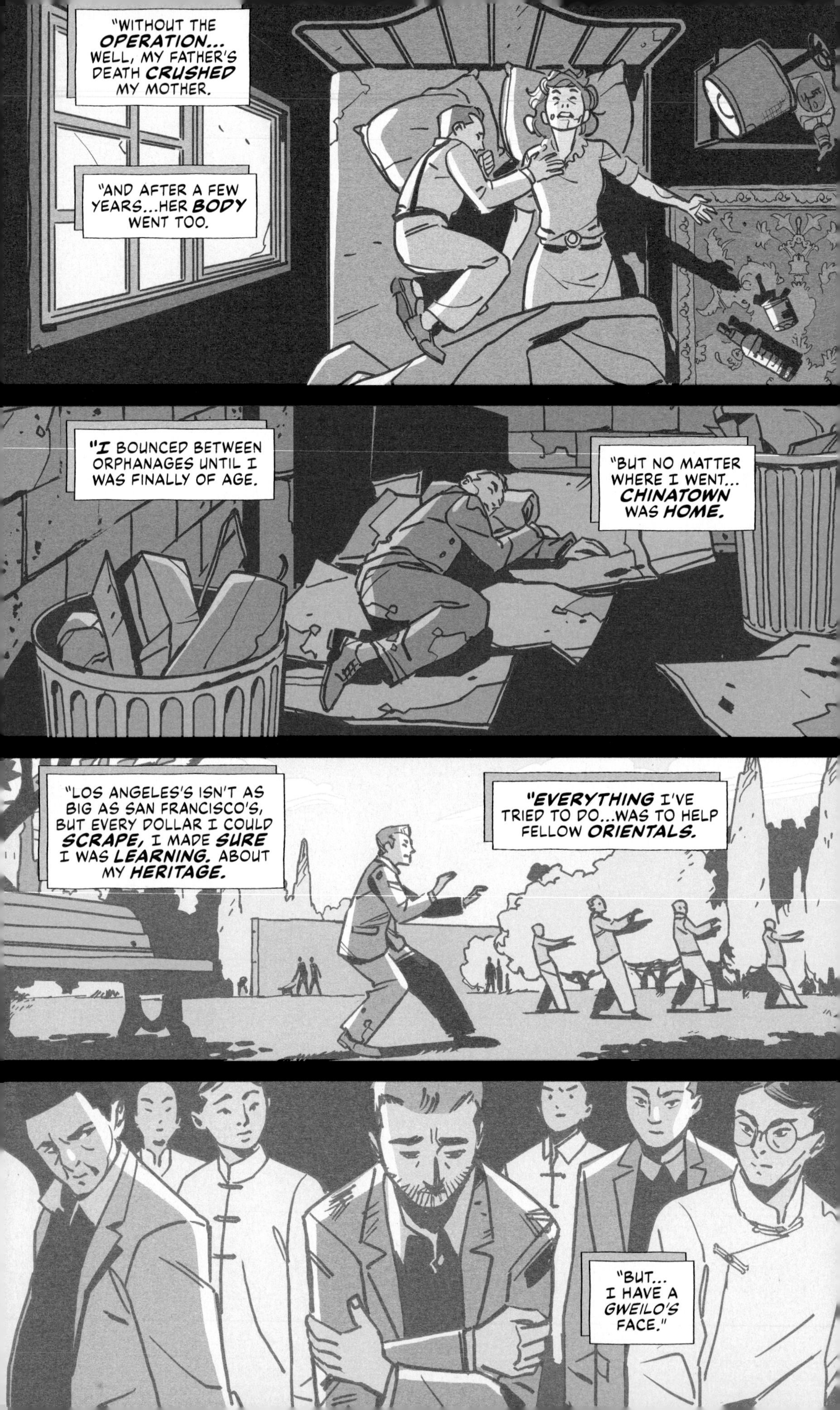
"WITHOUT THE OPERATION... WELL, MY FATHER'S DEATH CRUSHED MY MOTHER.
"AND AFTER A FEW YEARS...HER BODY WENT TOO.
"I BOUNCED BETWEEN ORPHANAGES UNTIL I WAS FINALLY OF AGE.
"BUT NO MATTER WHERE I WENT... CHINATOWN WAS HOME.
"LOS ANGELES'S ISN'T AS BIG AS SAN FRANCISCO'S, BUT EVERY DOLLAR I COULD SCRAPE, I MADE SURE I WAS LEARNING. ABOUT MY HERITAGE.
"EVERYTHING I'VE TRIED TO DO...WAS TO HELP FELLOW ORIENTALS.
"BUT... I HAVE A GWEILO'S FACE."

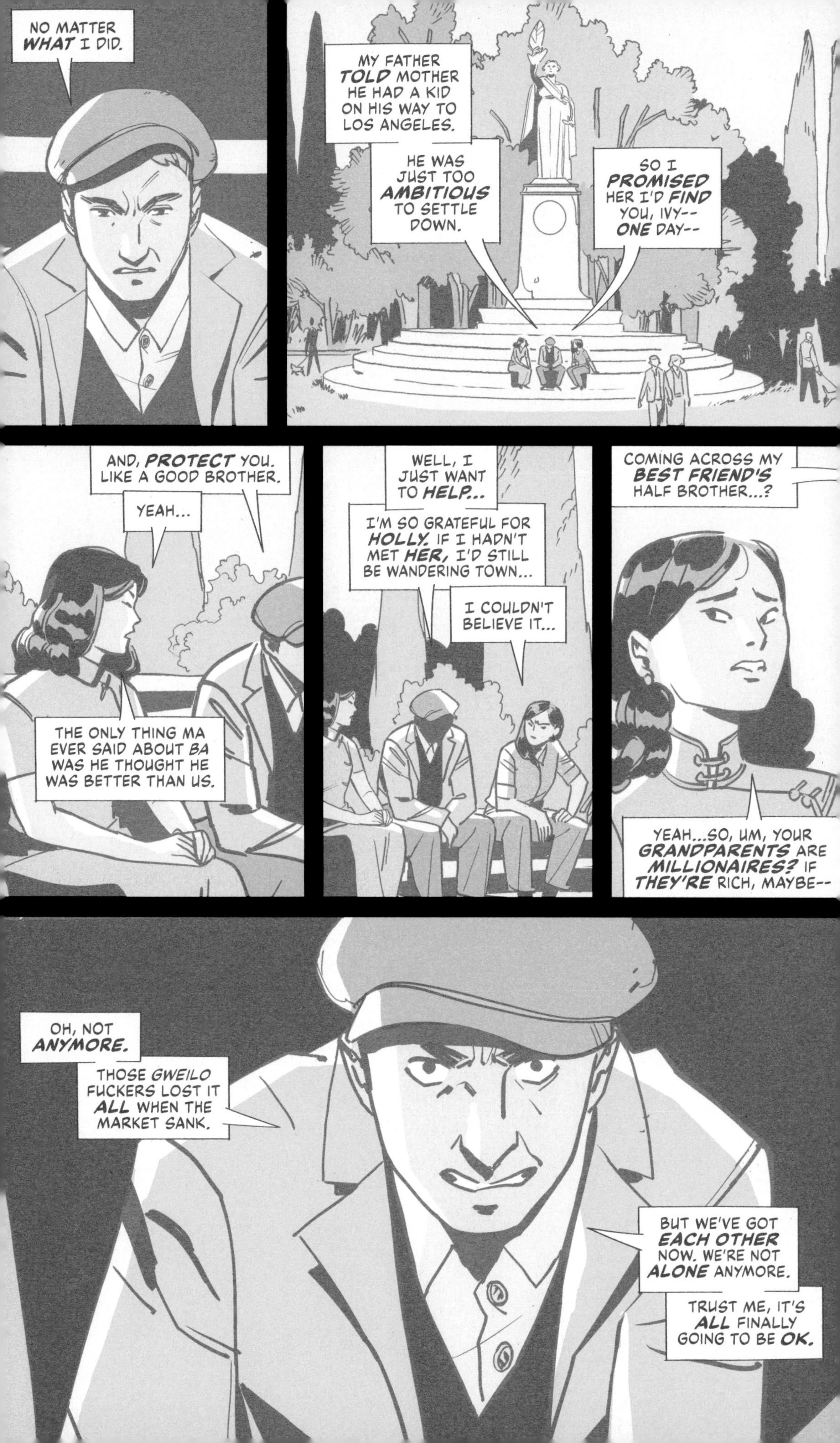
NO MATTER WHAT I DID.
MY FATHER TOLD MOTHER HE HAD A KID ON HIS WAY TO LOS ANGELES.
HE WAS JUST TOO AMBITIOUS TO SETTLE DOWN.
SO I PROMISED HER I'D FIND YOU, IVY-- ONE DAY--
AND, PROTECT YOU. LIKE A GOOD BROTHER.
YEAH...
THE ONLY THING MA EVER SAID ABOUT BA WAS HE THOUGHT HE WAS BETTER THAN US.
WELL, I JUST WANT TO HELP...
I'M SO GRATEFUL FOR HOLLY. IF I HADN'T MET HER, I'D STILL BE WANDERING TOWN...
I COULDN'T BELIEVE IT...
COMING ACROSS MY BEST FRIEND'S HALF BROTHER...?
YEAH...SO, UM, YOUR GRANDPARENTS ARE MILLIONAIRES? IF THEY'RE RICH, MAYBE--
OH, NOT ANYMORE.
THOSE GWEILO FUCKERS LOST IT ALL WHEN THE MARKET SANK.
BUT WE'VE GOT EACH OTHER NOW. WE'RE NOT ALONE ANYMORE.
TRUST ME, IT'S ALL FINALLY GOING TO BE OK.

VICTORIA?? WHAT ARE YOU TALKING ABOUT...?

YOU KNOW, NOT THAT LONG AGO, I WAS WHERE YOU ARE...

AND... WELL...

HEH.

YOU SHOULD FEEL IT...

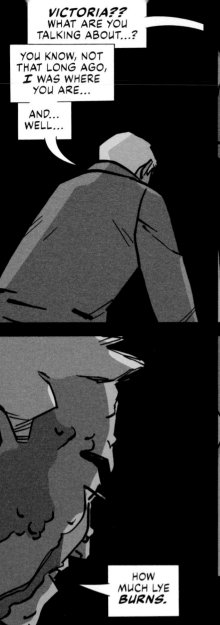

HOW MUCH LYE BURNS.

HEY-- HOLD ON...

THEY LEFT ME FOR DEAD. DONNIE YAN, HIS PATHETIC BROTHER, VICTORIA CARROWAY--

DONNIE SHOT ME IN THE GODDAMN BACK! BUT I GOT AWAY BEFORE...

HEH. THEY MUST HAVE LOOKED SO HARD FOR ME...

BUT THEY DIDN'T KNOW ABOUT MY FACTORY. THE WOODWARD FACTORY...

BUT WHEN-- WHEN I GOT HERE...

HOLD ON, OK? WAIT!!!

IF I JUST ASKED WHAT YOU KNEW...

YOU'D LIE FOR THEM--THE CARROWAYS...

WOULDN'T YOU?

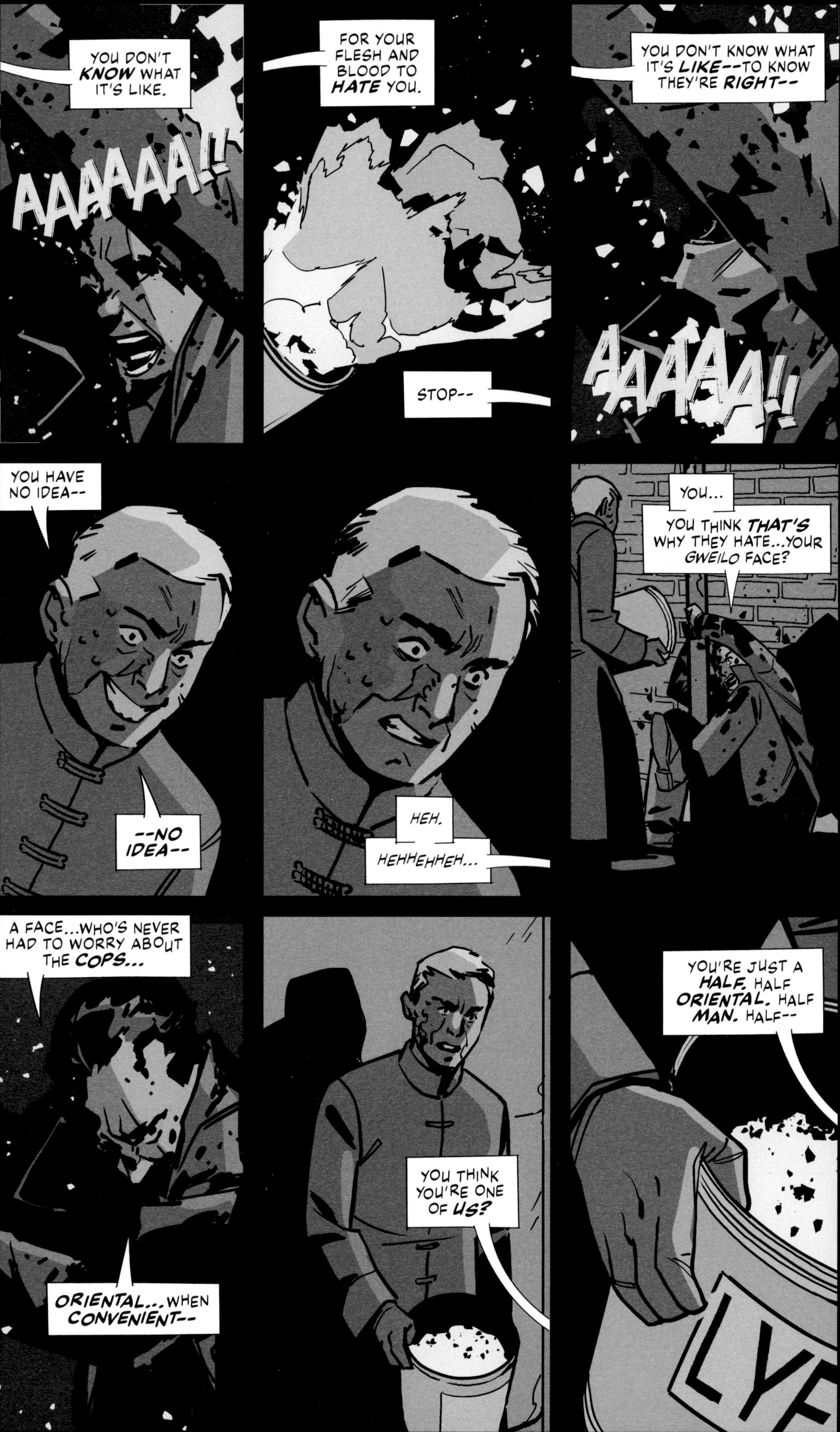
YOU DON'T KNOW WHAT IT'S LIKE.
AAAAAA!!
FOR YOUR FLESH AND BLOOD TO HATE YOU.
STOP--
YOU DON'T KNOW WHAT IT'S LIKE--TO KNOW THEY'RE RIGHT--
AAAAAA!!
YOU HAVE NO IDEA--
--NO IDEA--
HEH.
HEHHEHHEH...
YOU...
YOU THINK THAT'S WHY THEY HATE...YOUR GWEILO FACE?
A FACE...WHO'S NEVER HAD TO WORRY ABOUT THE COPS...
ORIENTAL...WHEN CONVENIENT--
YOU THINK YOU'RE ONE OF US?
YOU'RE JUST A HALF. HALF ORIENTAL. HALF MAN. HALF--
LYE

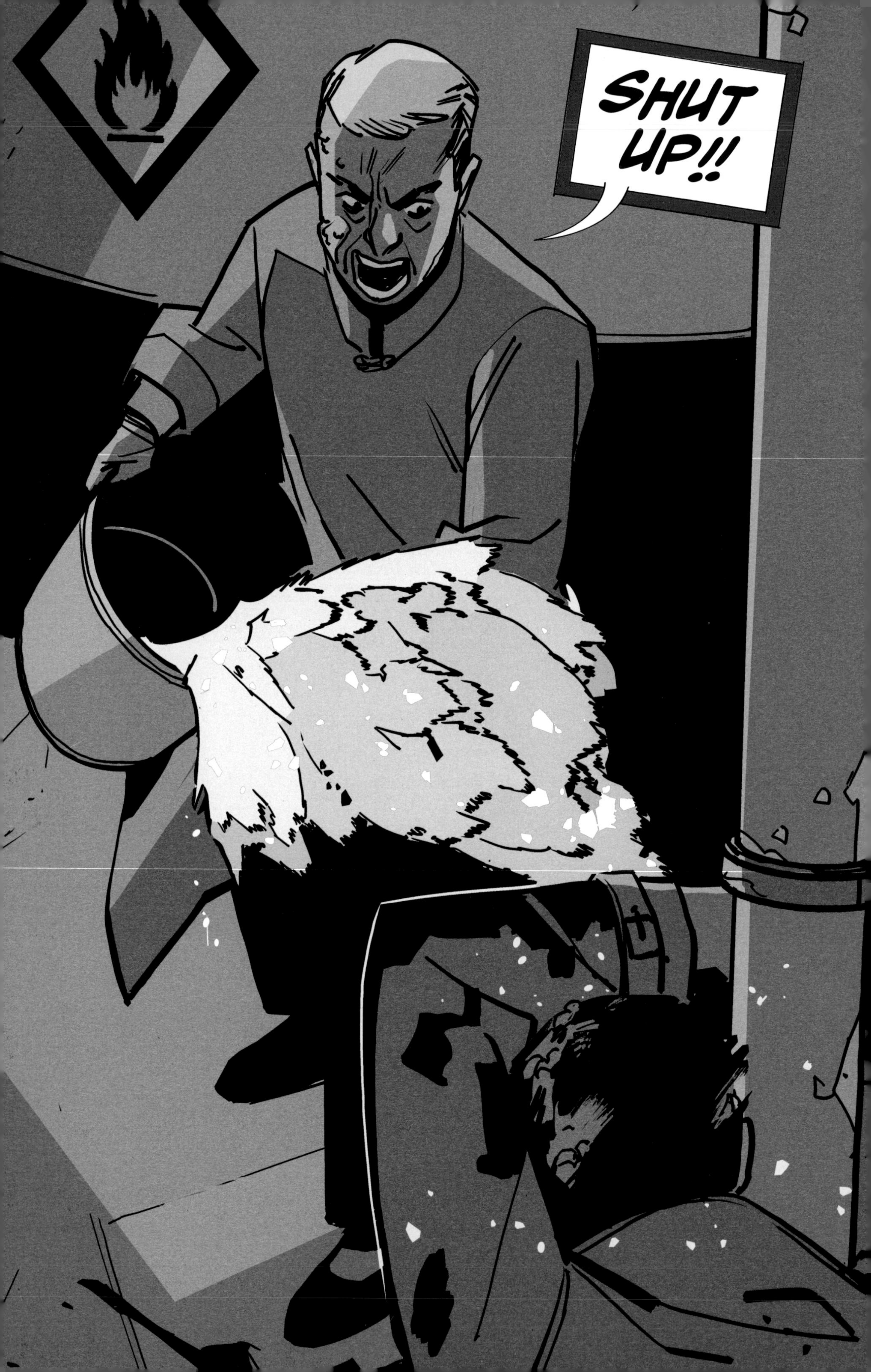
SHUT UP!!

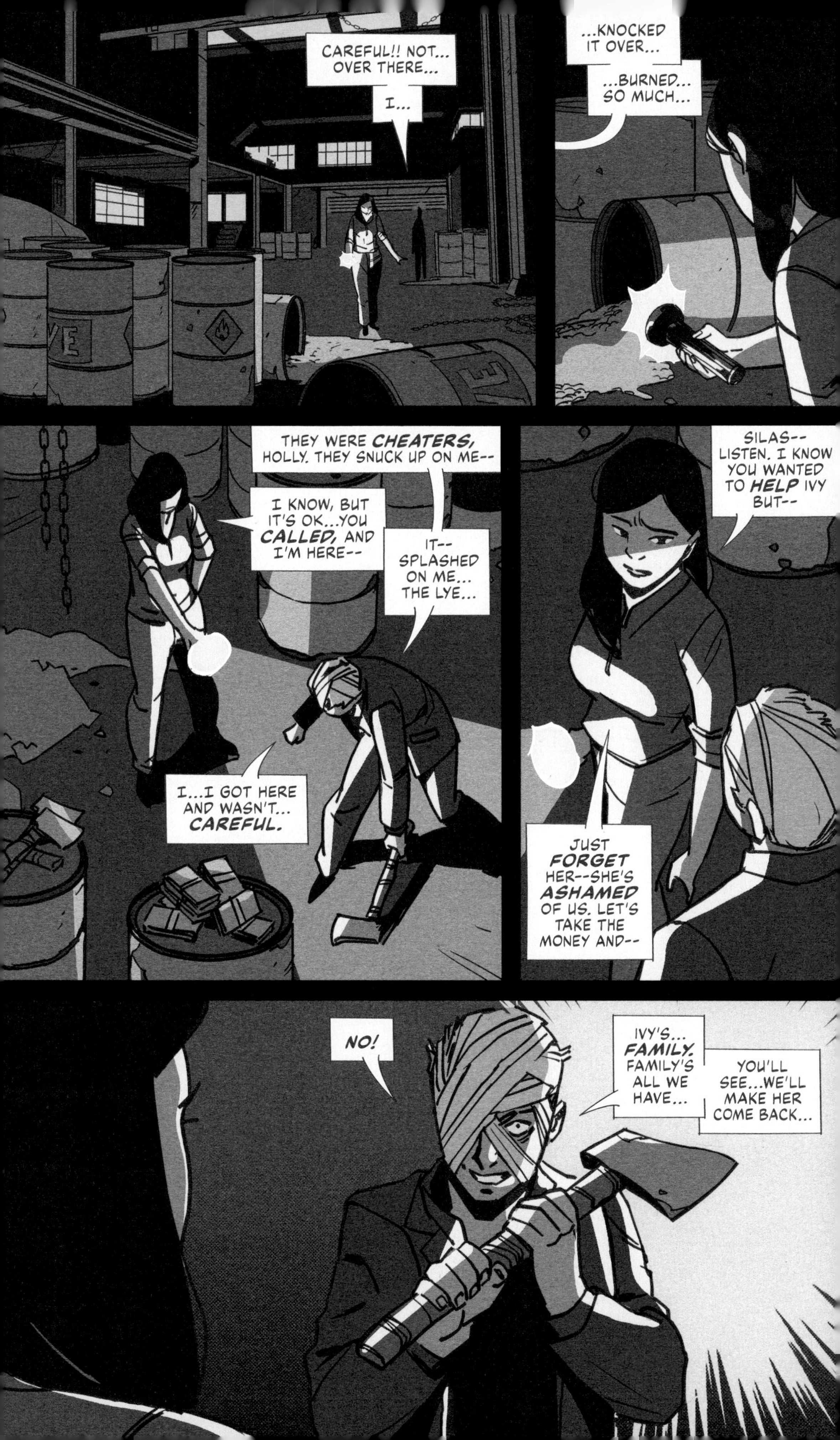
CAREFUL!! NOT... OVER THERE...
I...
...KNOCKED IT OVER...
...BURNED... SO MUCH...
THEY WERE CHEATERS, HOLLY. THEY SNUCK UP ON ME--
I KNOW, BUT IT'S OK...YOU CALLED, AND I'M HERE--
IT-- SPLASHED ON ME... THE LYE...
I...I GOT HERE AND WASN'T... CAREFUL.
SILAS-- LISTEN. I KNOW YOU WANTED TO HELP IVY BUT--
JUST FORGET HER--SHE'S ASHAMED OF US. LET'S TAKE THE MONEY AND--
NO!
IVY'S... FAMILY. FAMILY'S ALL WE HAVE...
YOU'LL SEE...WE'LL MAKE HER COME BACK...

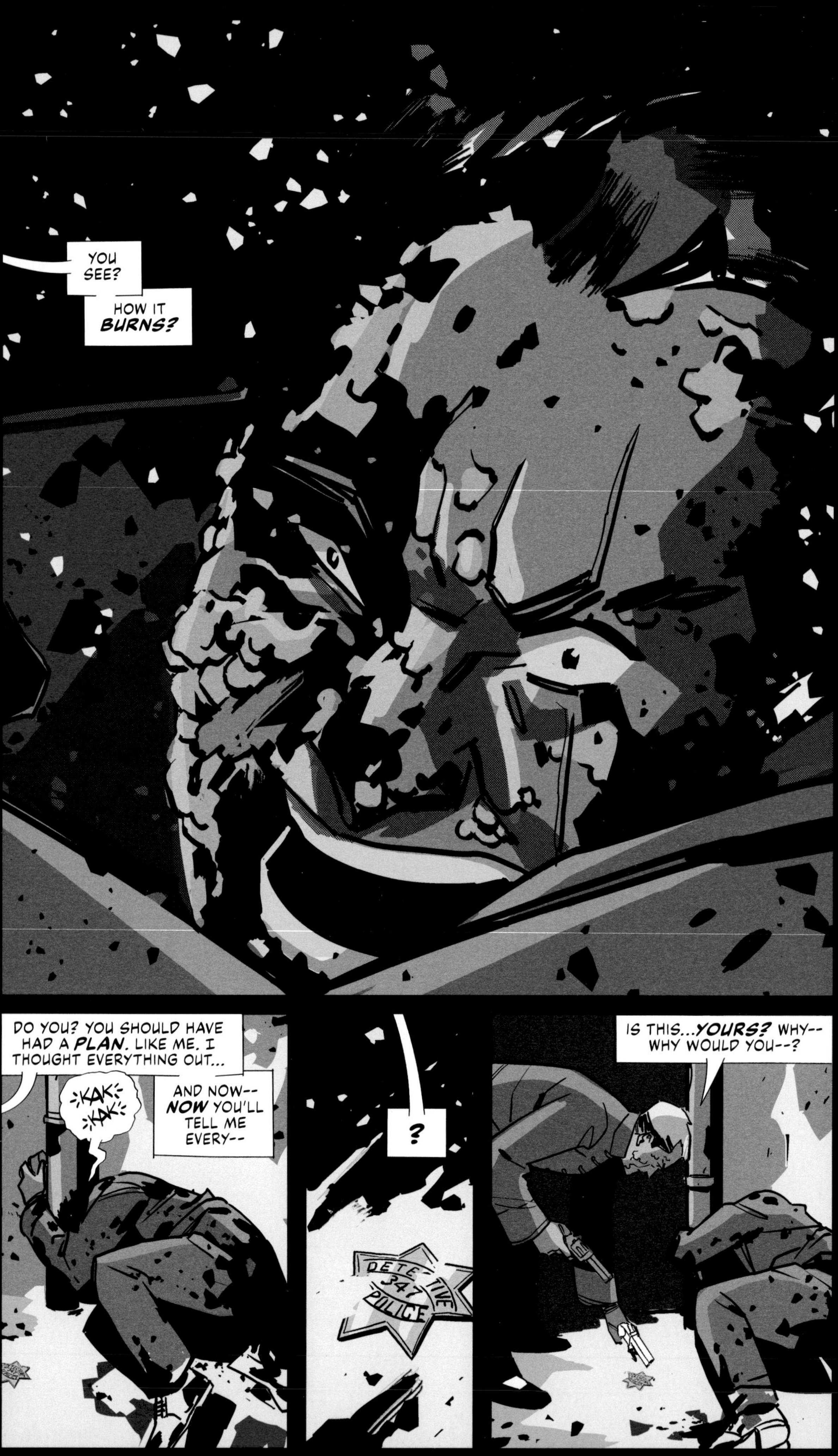
YOU SEE?
HOW IT BURNS?
DO YOU? YOU SHOULD HAVE HAD A PLAN. LIKE ME. I THOUGHT EVERYTHING OUT...
KAK KAK
AND NOW-- NOW YOU'LL TELL ME EVERY--
?
DETECTIVE 347 POLICE
IS THIS...YOURS? WHY-- WHY WOULD YOU--?

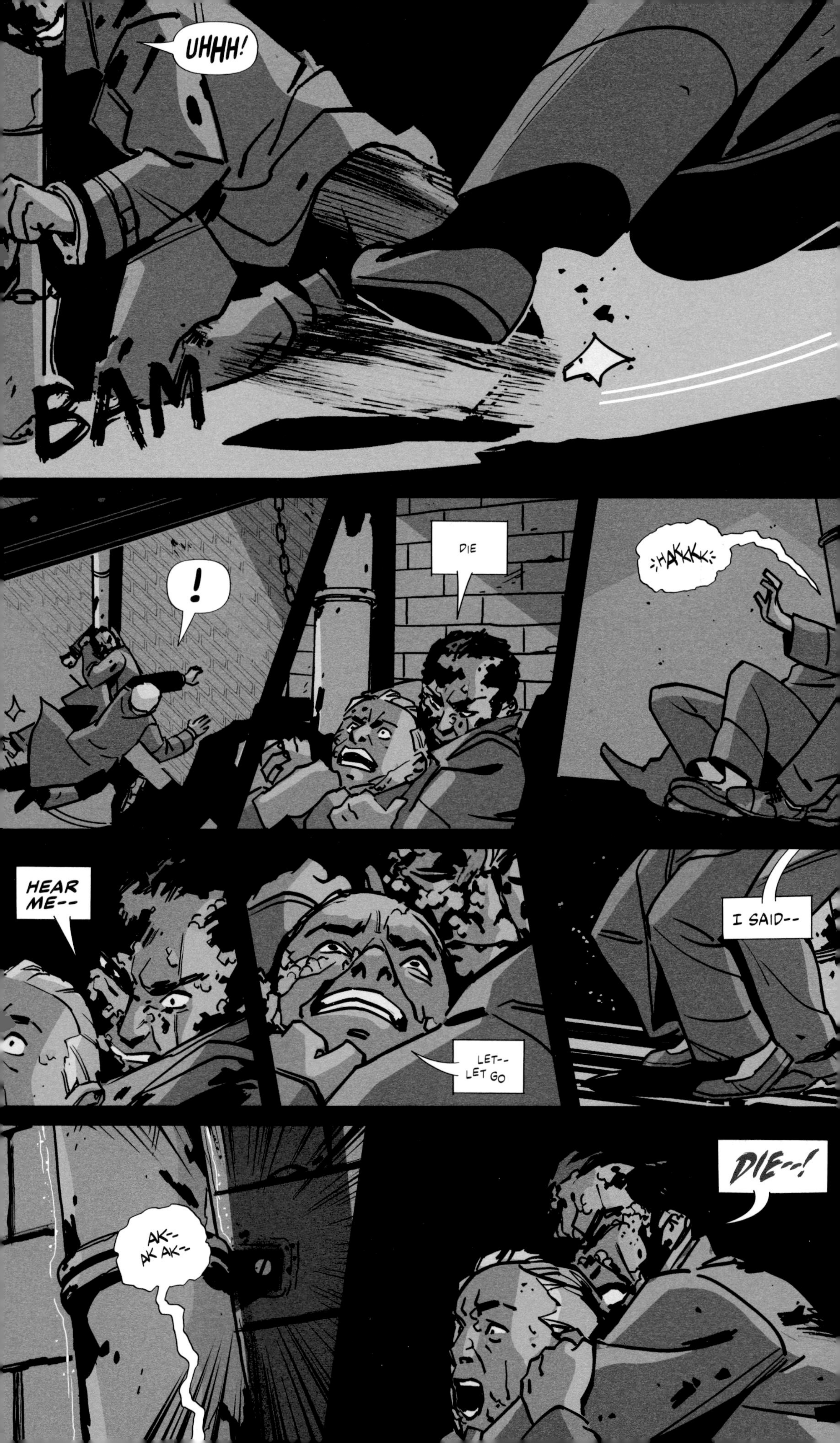
UHHH!
BAM
!
DIE
HAKKKK
HEAR ME--
LET-- LET GO
I SAID--
AK-- AK AK--
DIE--!

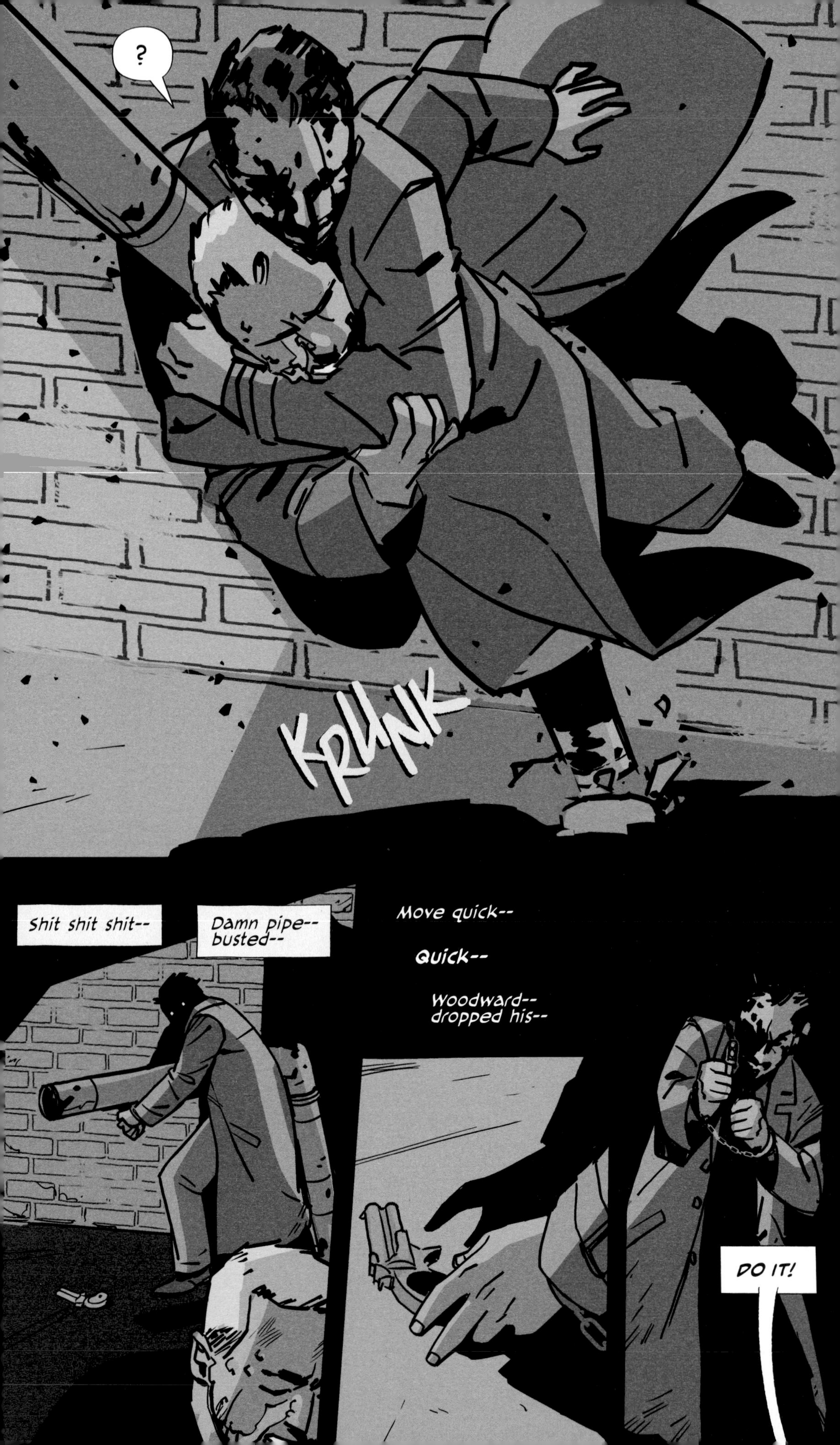
?
KRUNK
Shit shit shit--
Damn pipe-- busted--
Move quick--
Quick--
Woodward-- dropped his--
DO IT!

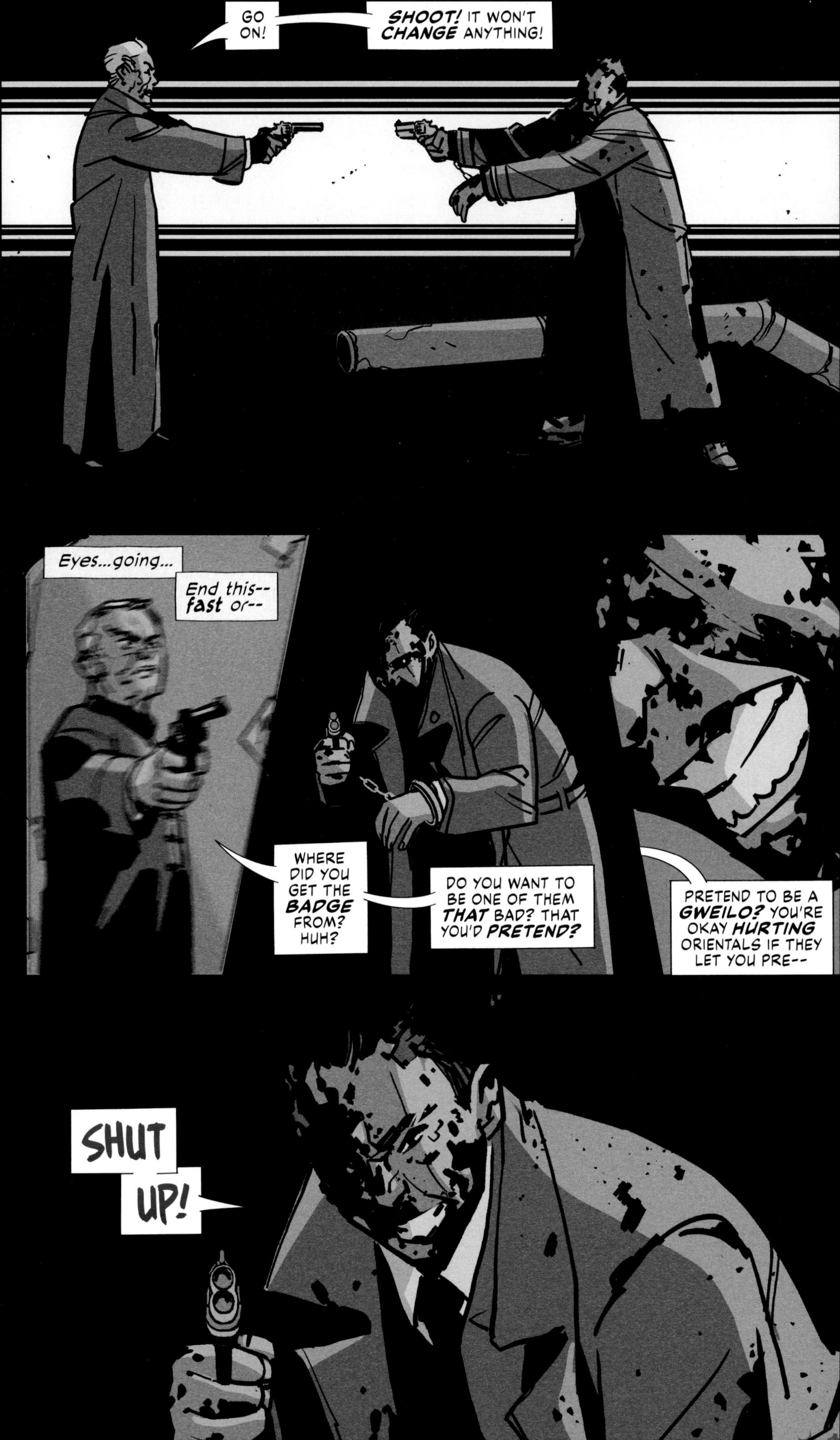

GO ON!
SHOOT! IT WON'T CHANGE ANYTHING!
Eyes...going...
End this--fast or--
WHERE DID YOU GET THE BADGE FROM? HUH?
DO YOU WANT TO BE ONE OF THEM THAT BAD? THAT YOU'D PRETEND?
PRETEND TO BE A GWEILO? YOU'RE OKAY HURTING ORIENTALS IF THEY LET YOU PRE--
SHUT UP!

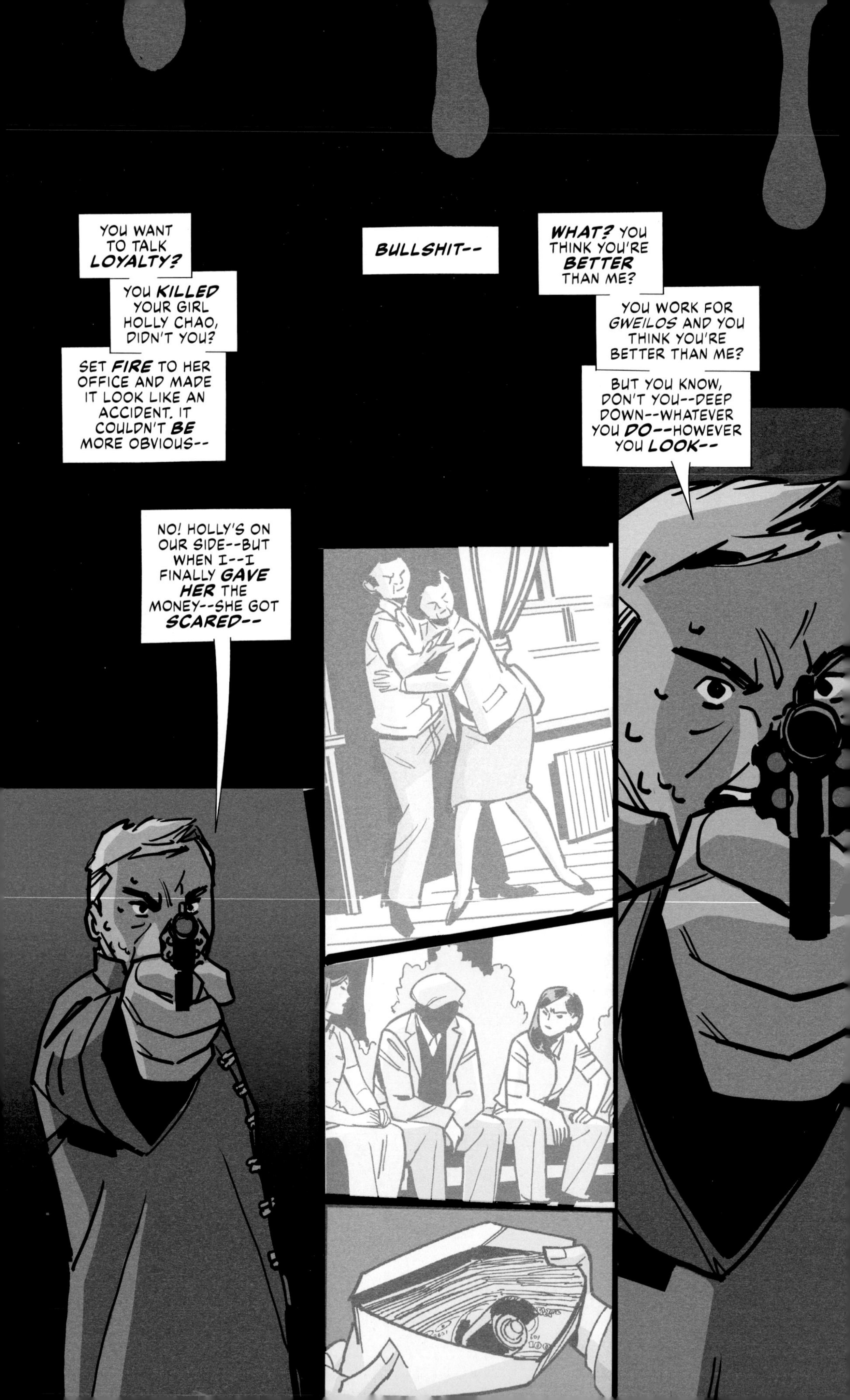
YOU WANT TO TALK LOYALTY?
YOU KILLED YOUR GIRL HOLLY CHAO, DIDN'T YOU?
SET FIRE TO HER OFFICE AND MADE IT LOOK LIKE AN ACCIDENT. IT COULDN'T BE MORE OBVIOUS--
BULLSHIT--
WHAT? YOU THINK YOU'RE BETTER THAN ME?
YOU WORK FOR GWEILOS AND YOU THINK YOU'RE BETTER THAN ME?
BUT YOU KNOW, DON'T YOU--DEEP DOWN--WHATEVER YOU DO--HOWEVER YOU LOOK--
NO! HOLLY'S ON OUR SIDE--BUT WHEN I--I FINALLY GAVE HER THE MONEY--SHE GOT SCARED--

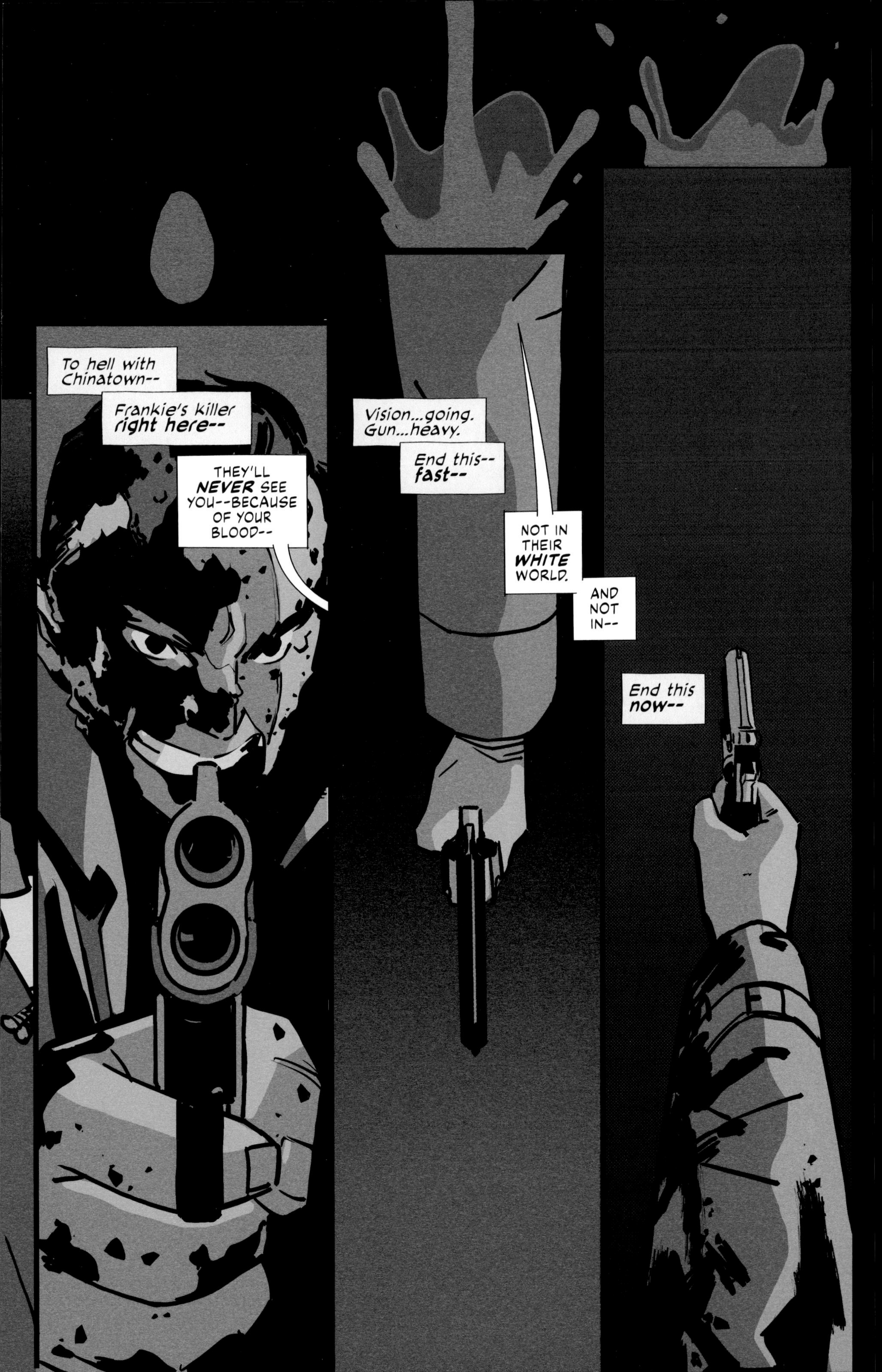

To hell with Chinatown--
Frankie's killer right here--
THEY'LL NEVER SEE YOU--BECAUSE OF YOUR BLOOD--
Vision...going. Gun...heavy.
End this-- fast--
NOT IN THEIR WHITE WORLD.
AND NOT IN--
End this now--

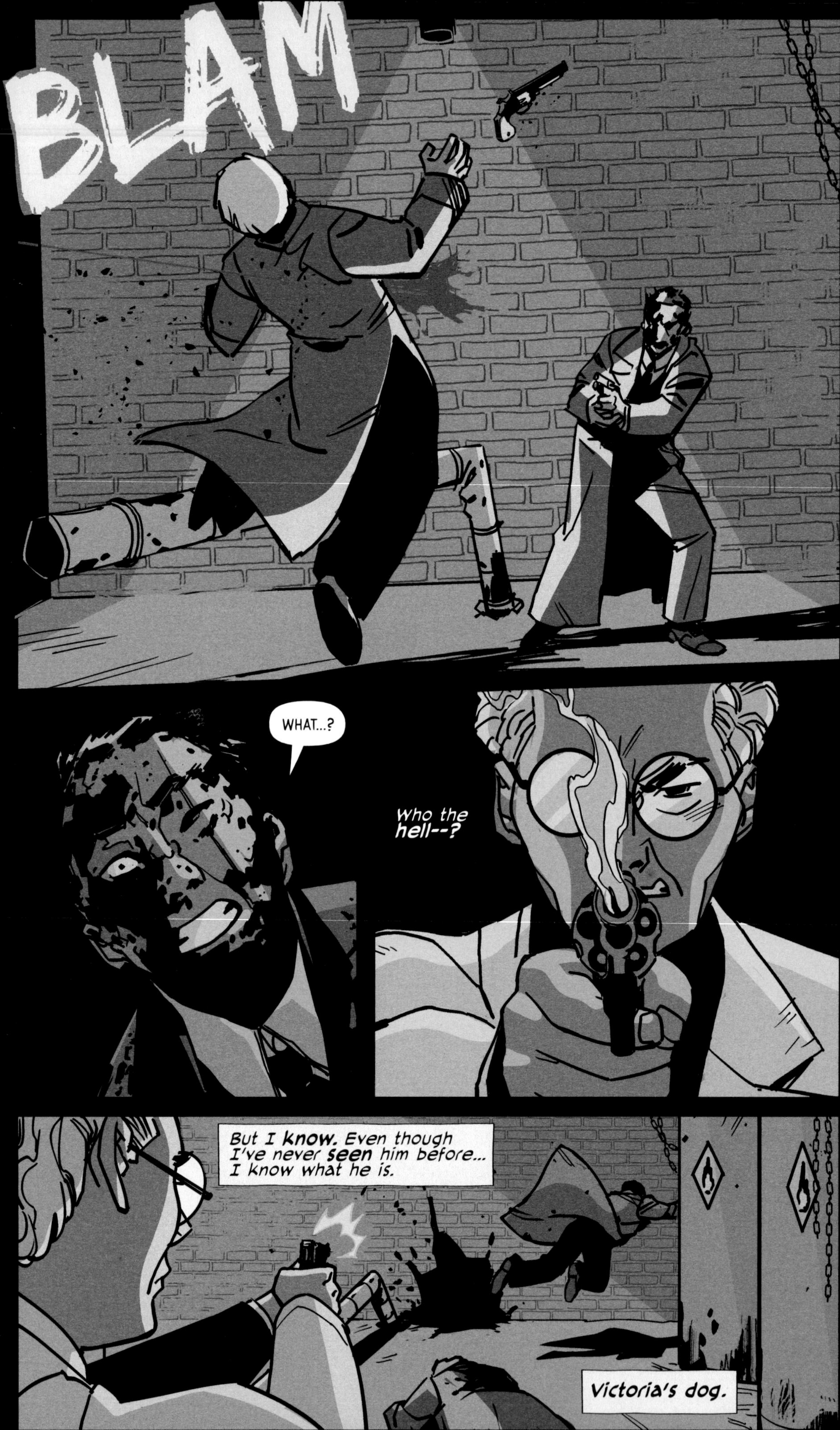
BLAM
WHAT...?
Who the hell--?
But I know. Even though I've never seen him before... I know what he is.
Victoria's dog.

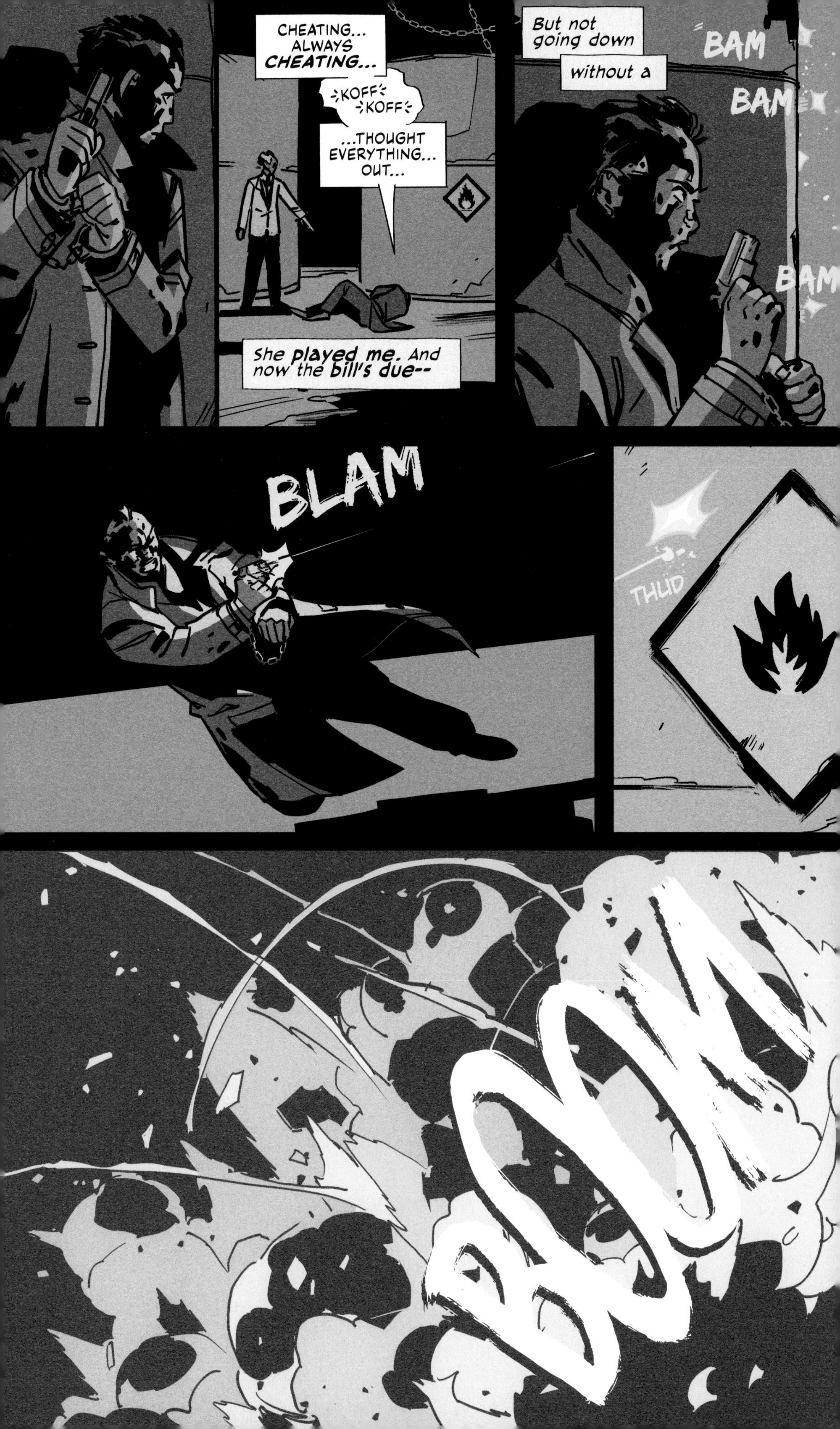

CHEATING... ALWAYS CHEATING...
KOFF KOFF
...THOUGHT EVERYTHING... OUT...
She played me. And now the bill's due--
But not going down
without a
BAM
BAM
BAM
BLAM
THUD
BOOM

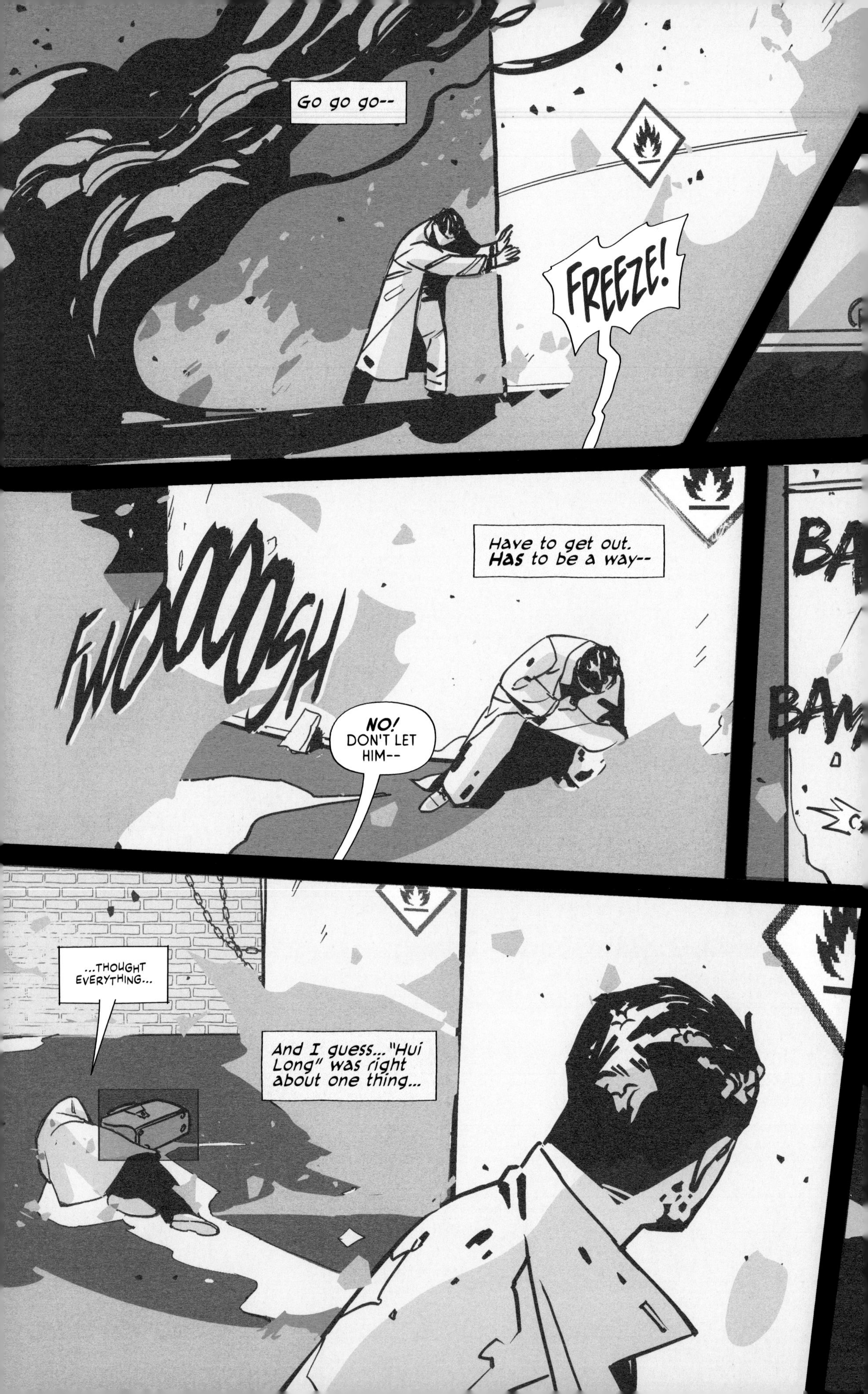
Go go go--
FREEZE!
Have to get out. **Has** to be a way--
FWOOOOSH
NO! DON'T LET HIM--
...THOUGHT EVERYTHING...
And I guess... "Hui Long" was right about one thing...

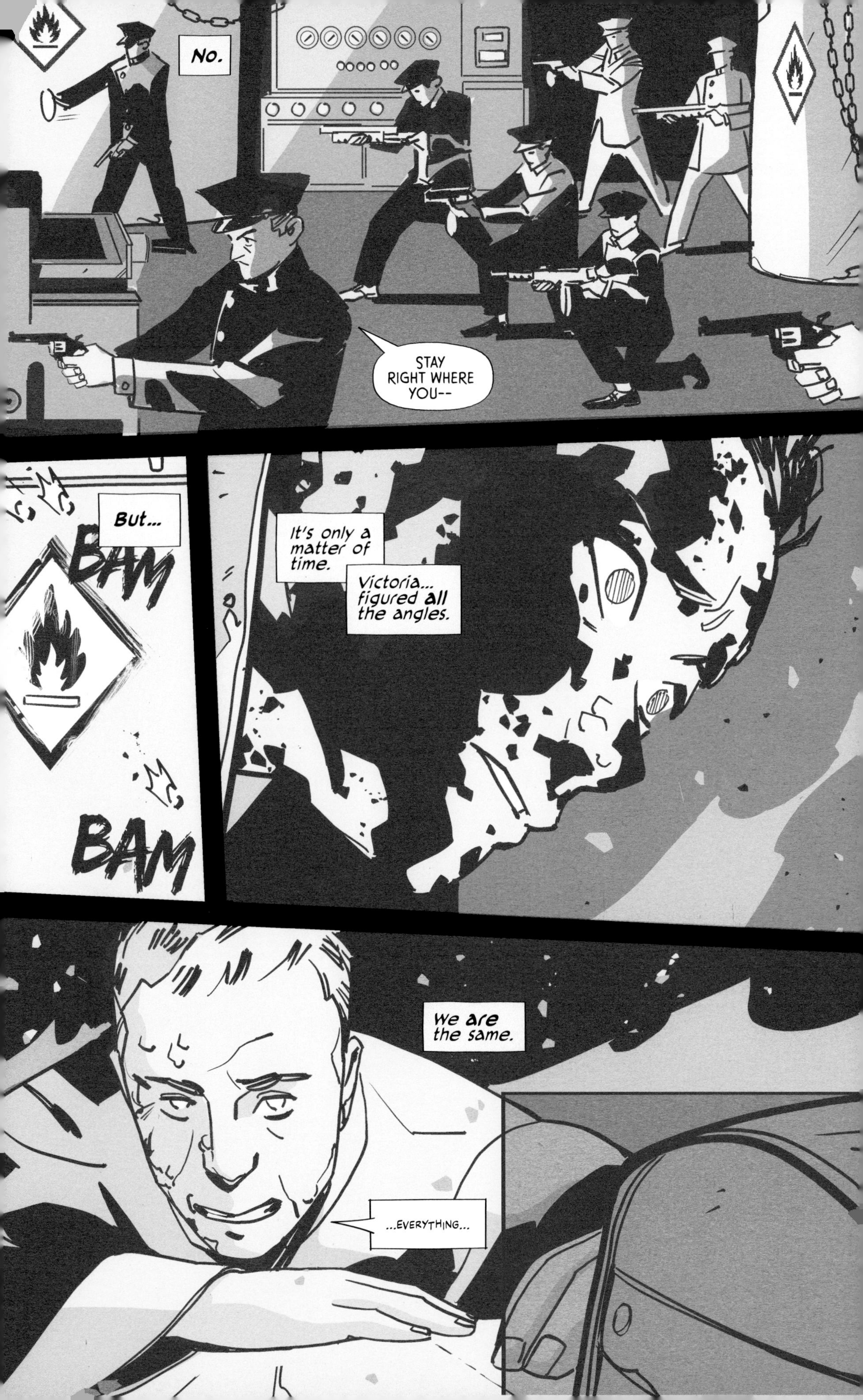
No.
STAY RIGHT WHERE YOU--
But...
BAM
BAM
It's only a matter of time.
Victoria... figured all the angles.
We are the same.
...EVERYTHING...

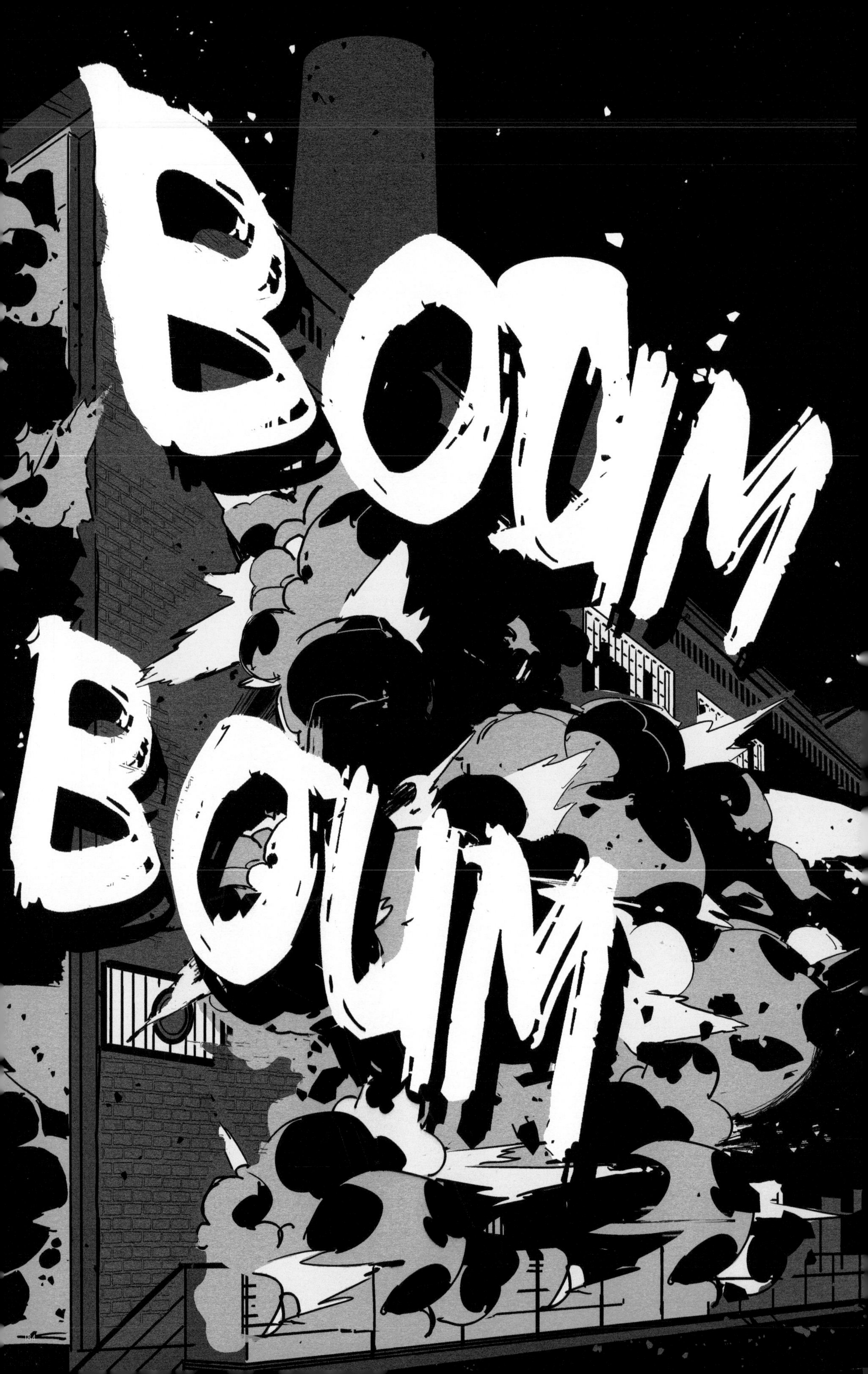
BOOM
BOOM

CHAPTER EIGHT

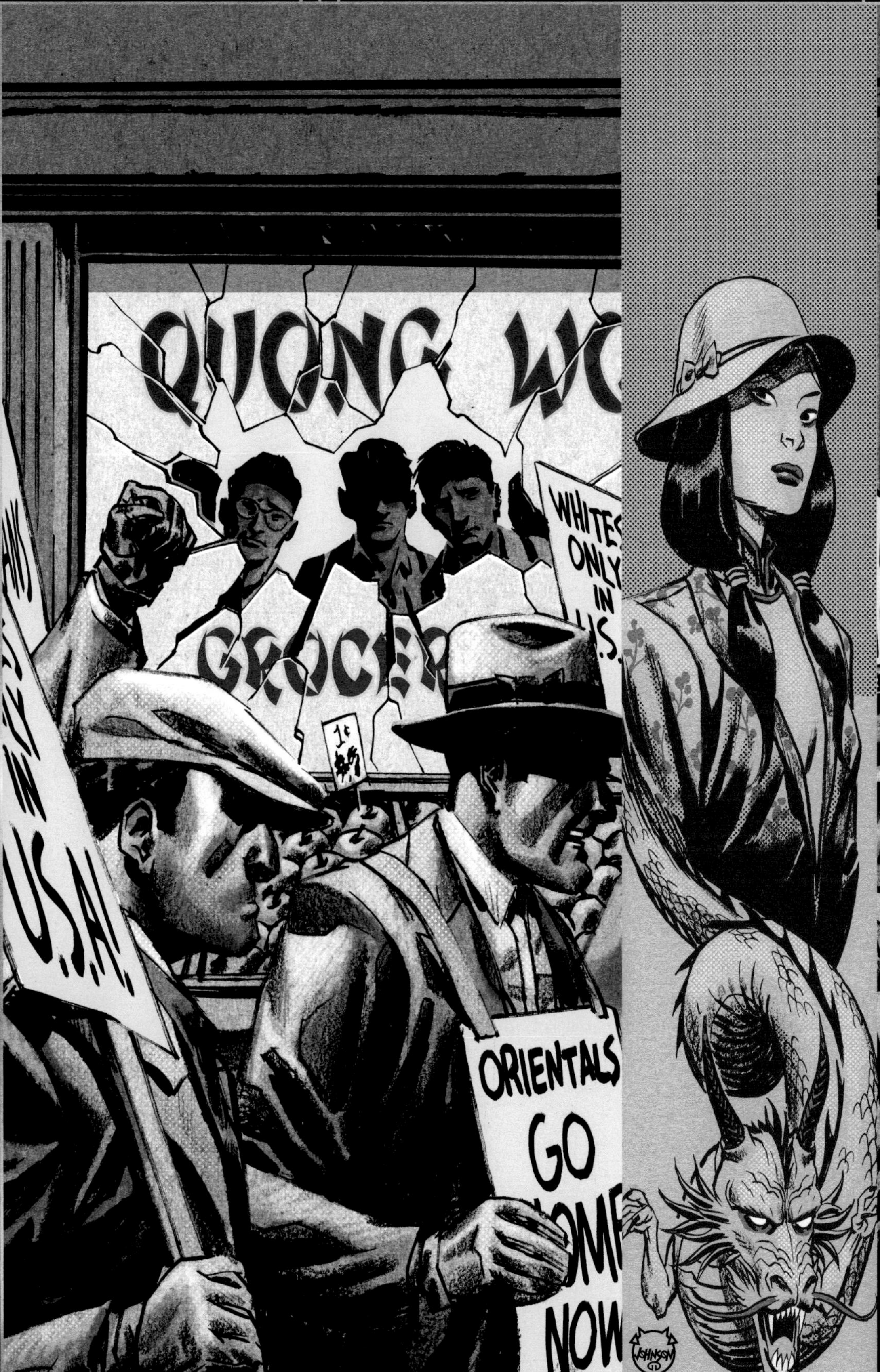
QUONG WO
GROCER
WHITES ONLY IN U.S.
U.S.A.!
ORIENTALS GO HOME NOW
JOHNSON

ART BY **DAVE JOHNSON**

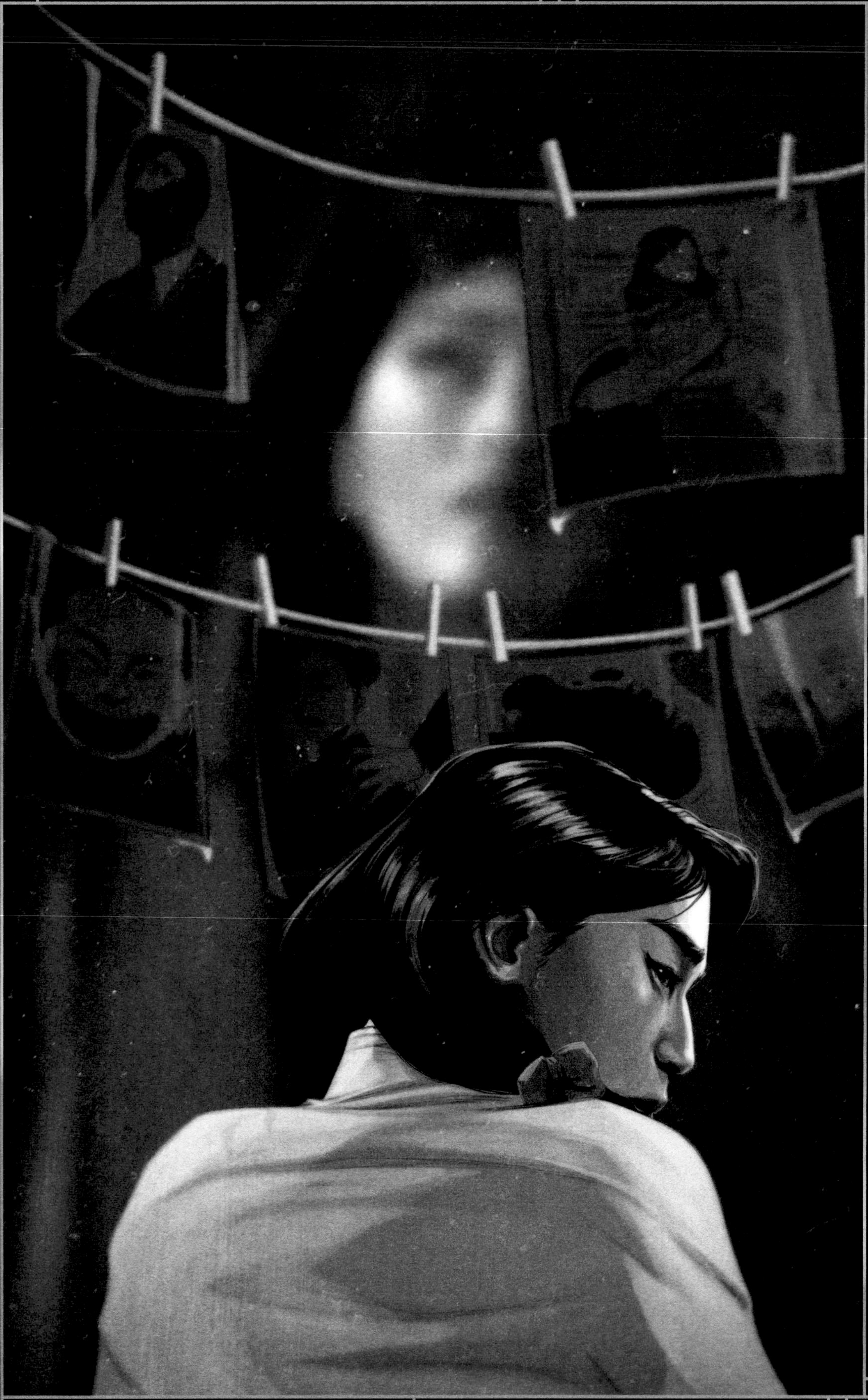

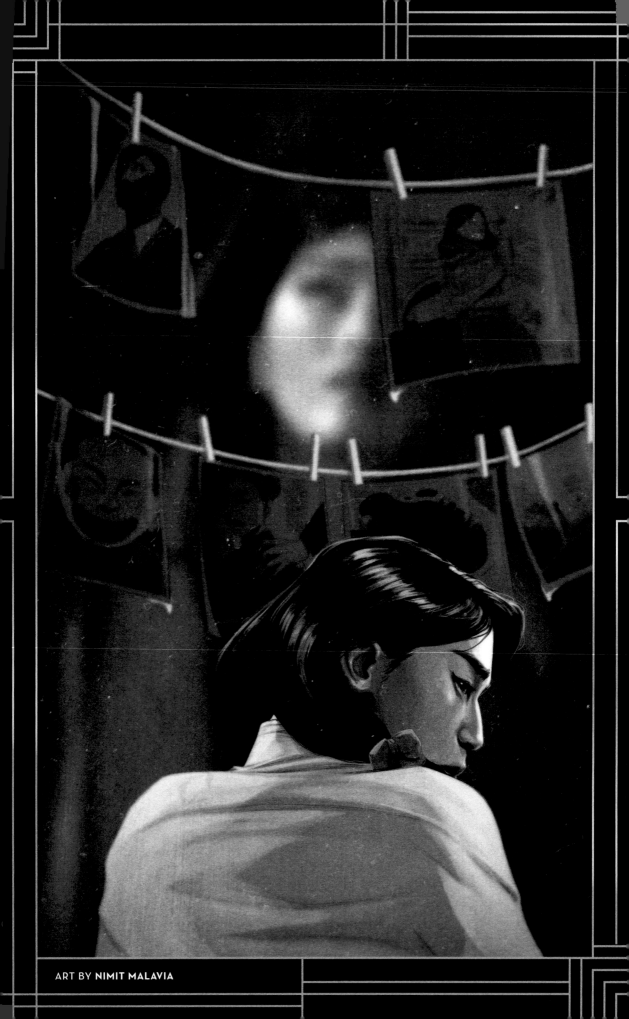

ART BY **NIMIT MALAVIA**

They found shit
smeared on the doors
of two restaurants
down the street.

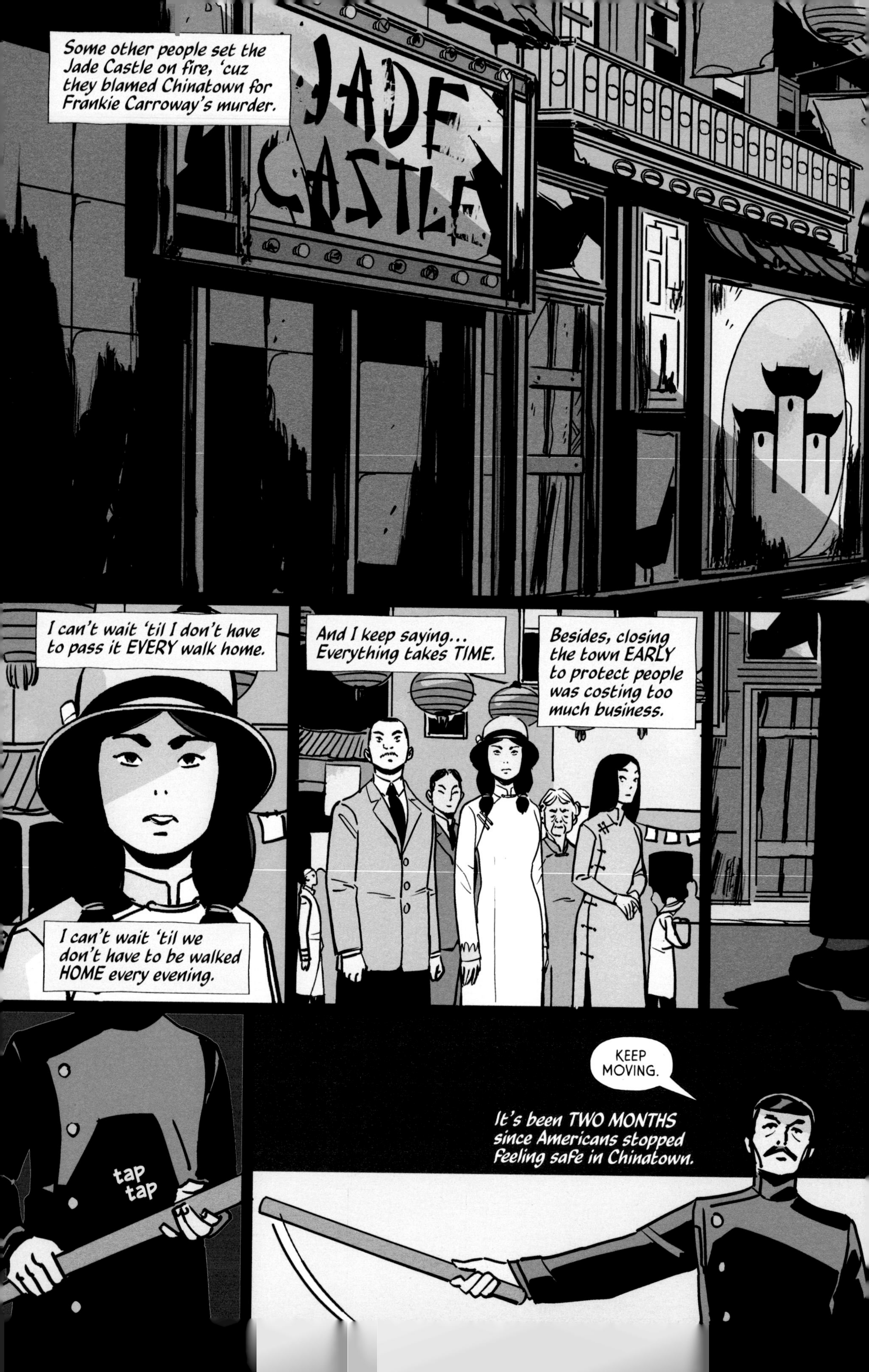
Some other people set the Jade Castle on fire, 'cuz they blamed Chinatown for Frankie Carroway's murder.
JADE CASTLE
I can't wait 'til I don't have to pass it EVERY walk home.
I can't wait 'til we don't have to be walked HOME every evening.
And I keep saying... Everything takes TIME.
Besides, closing the town EARLY to protect people was costing too much business.
tap tap
KEEP MOVING.
It's been TWO MONTHS since Americans stopped feeling safe in Chinatown.

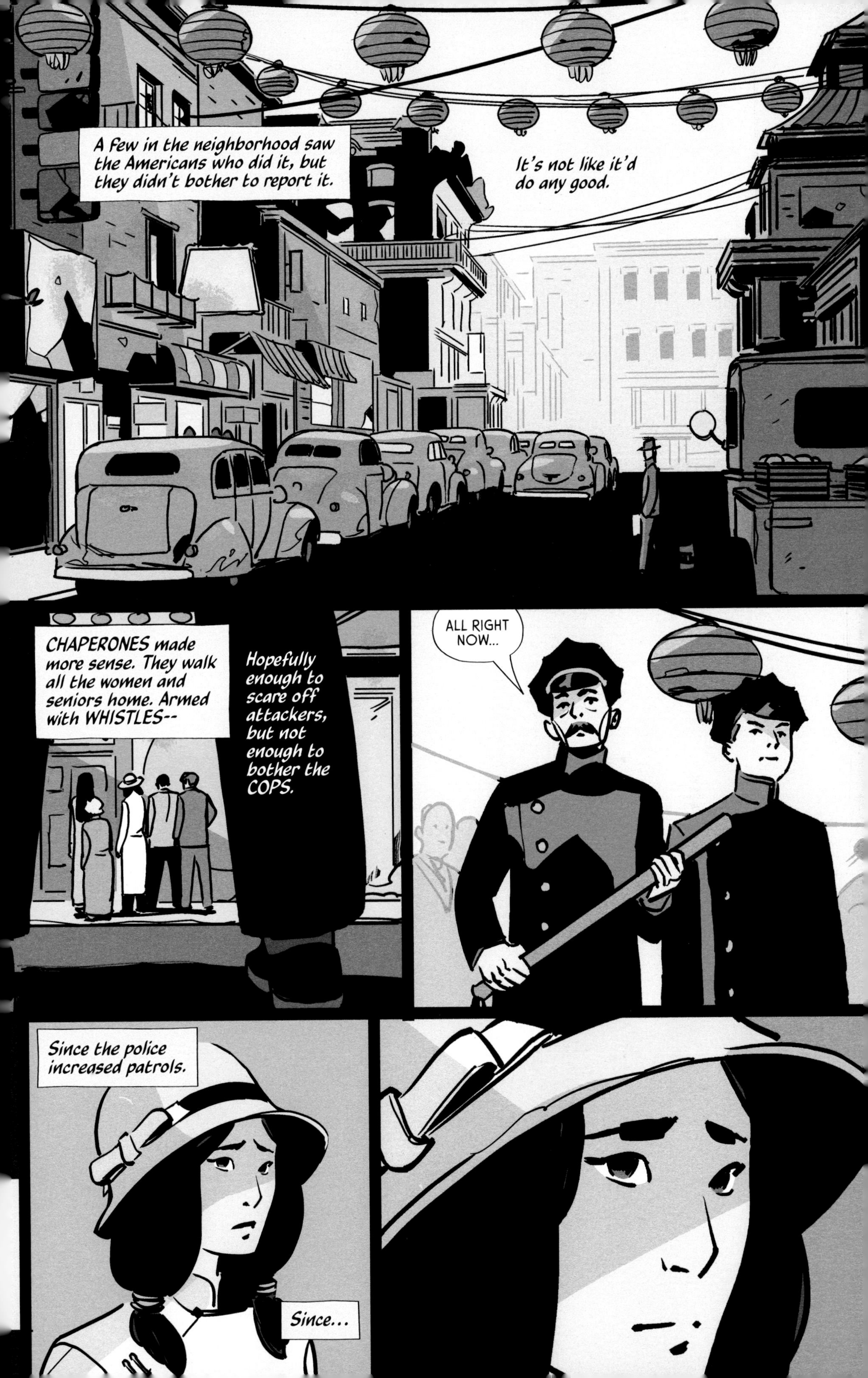
A few in the neighborhood saw the Americans who did it, but they didn't bother to report it.
It's not like it'd do any good.
CHAPERONES made more sense. They walk all the women and seniors home. Armed with WHISTLES--
Hopefully enough to scare off attackers, but not enough to bother the COPS.
ALL RIGHT NOW...
Since the police increased patrols.
Since...

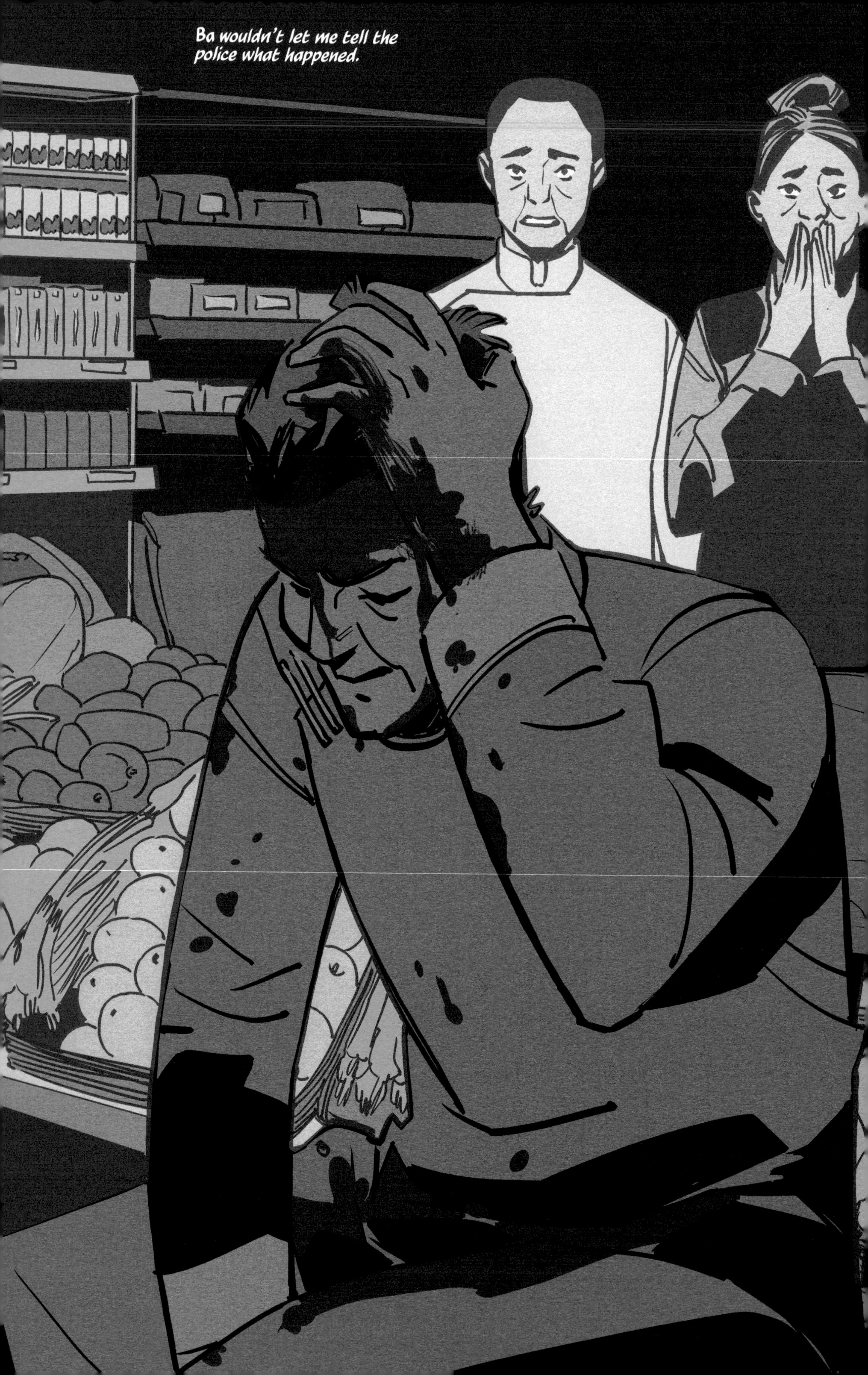
Ba wouldn't let me tell the police what happened.

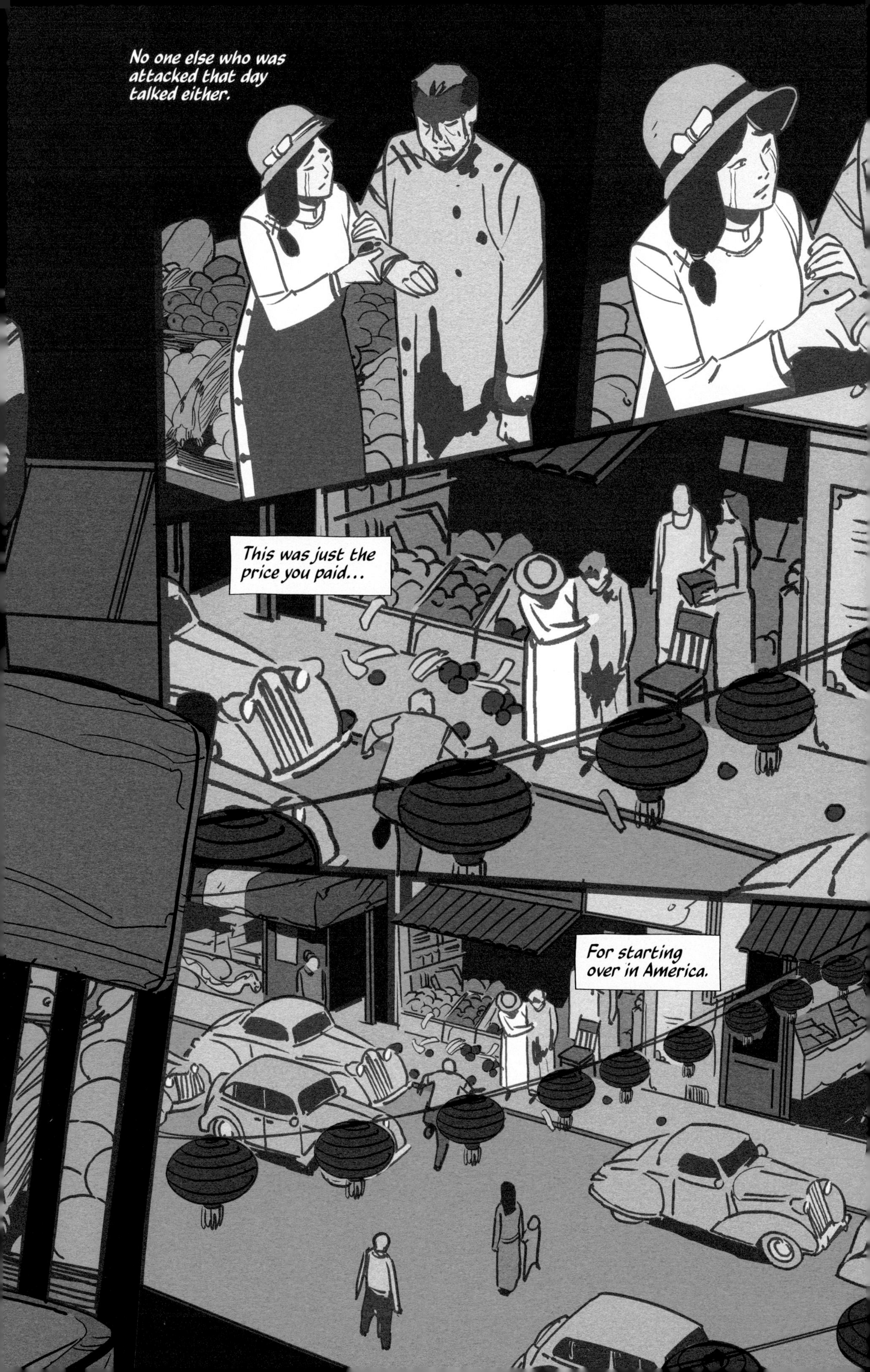
No one else who was attacked that day talked either.
This was just the price you paid...
For starting over in America.

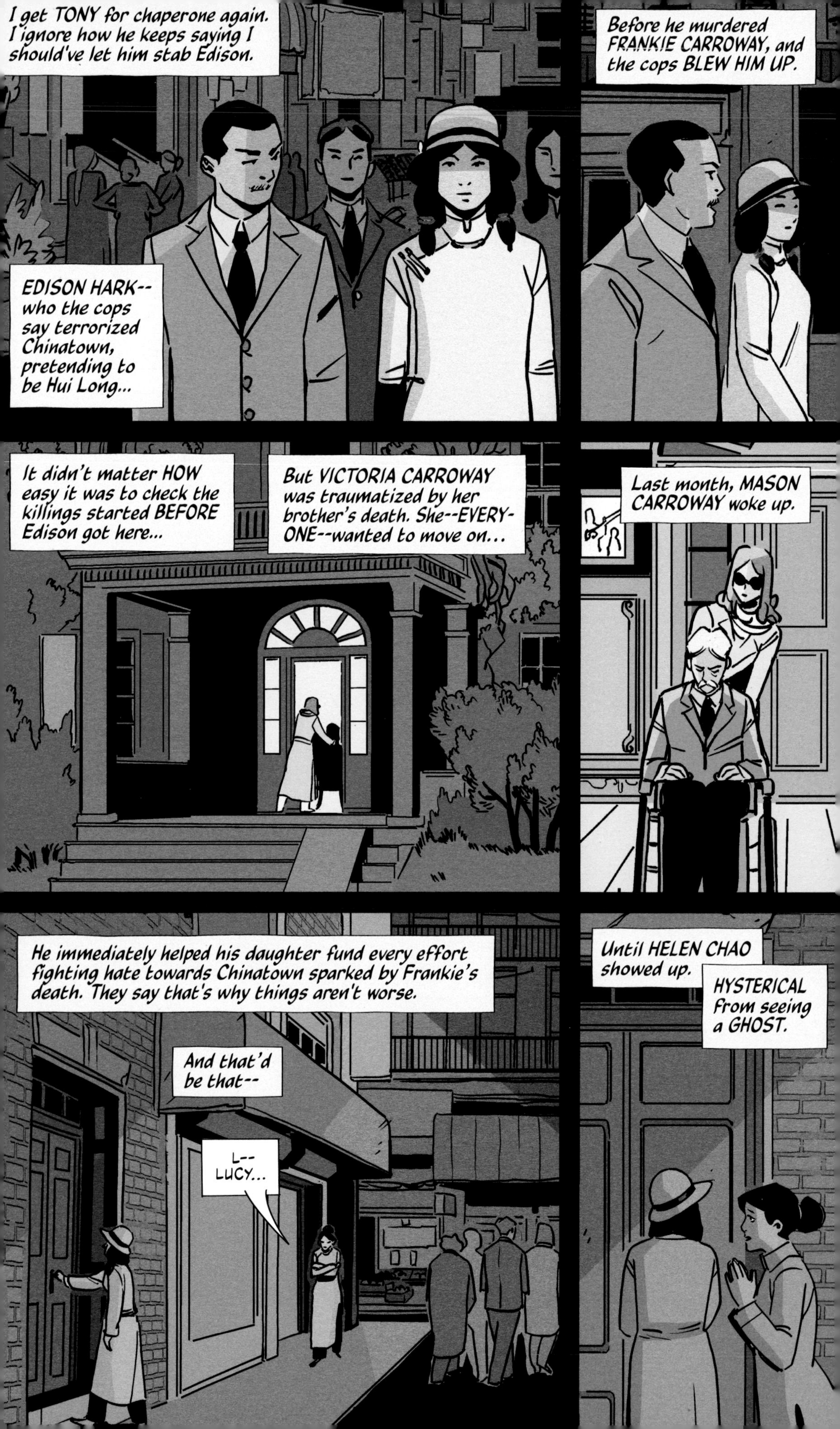
I get TONY for chaperone again. I ignore how he keeps saying I should've let him stab Edison.
EDISON HARK--who the cops say terrorized Chinatown, pretending to be Hui Long...
Before he murdered FRANKIE CARROWAY, and the cops BLEW HIM UP.
It didn't matter HOW easy it was to check the killings started BEFORE Edison got here...
But VICTORIA CARROWAY was traumatized by her brother's death. She--EVERY-ONE--wanted to move on...
Last month, MASON CARROWAY woke up.
He immediately helped his daughter fund every effort fighting hate towards Chinatown sparked by Frankie's death. They say that's why things aren't worse.
And that'd be that--
L--LUCY...
Until HELEN CHAO showed up.
HYSTERICAL from seeing a GHOST.

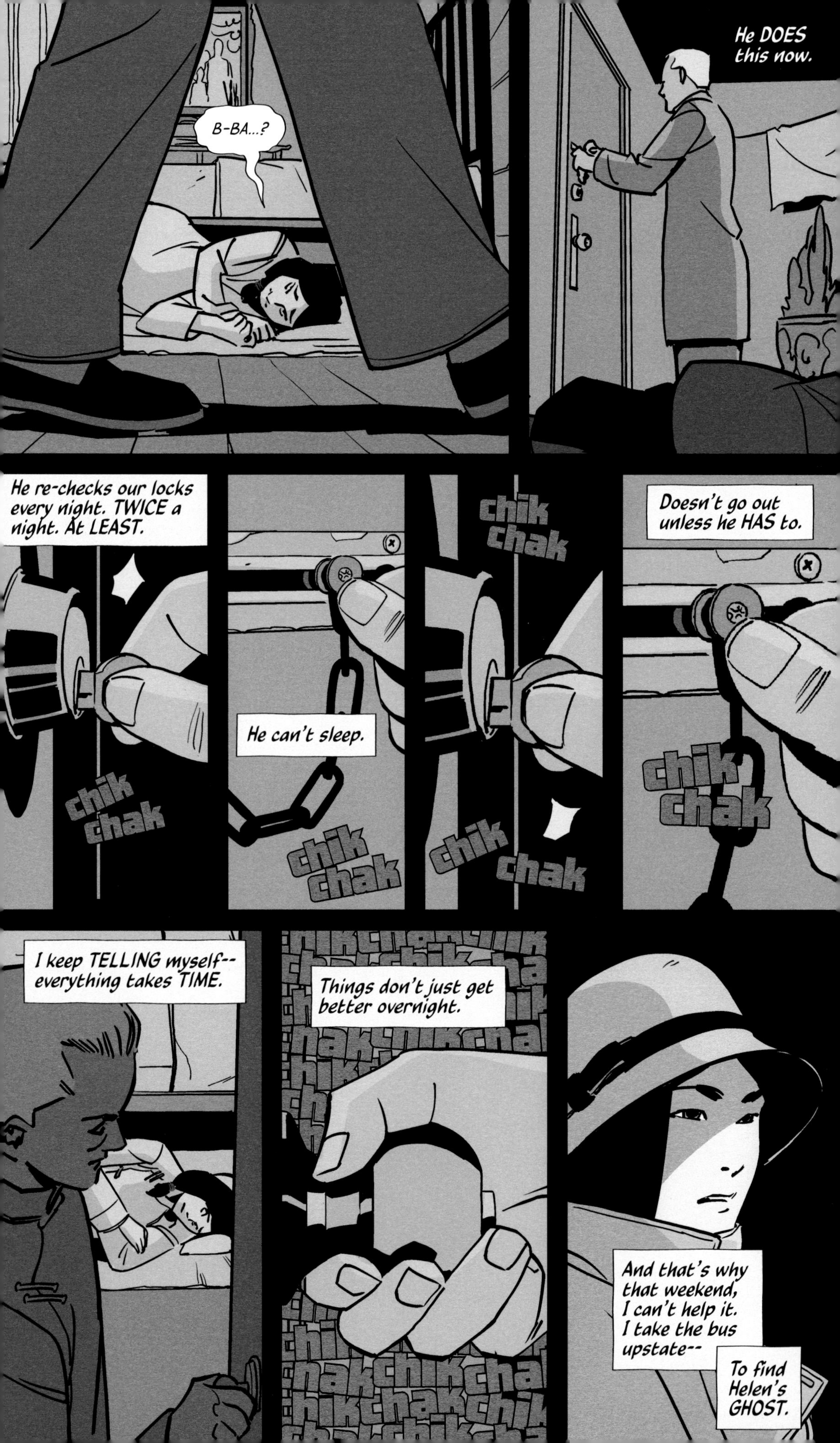
B-BA...?
He DOES this now.
He re-checks our locks every night. TWICE a night. At LEAST.
chik chak
He can't sleep.
chik chak
chik
chik chak
chak
Doesn't go out unless he HAS to.
chik chak
I keep TELLING myself--everything takes TIME.
Things don't just get better overnight.
And that's why that weekend, I can't help it. I take the bus upstate--
To find Helen's GHOST.

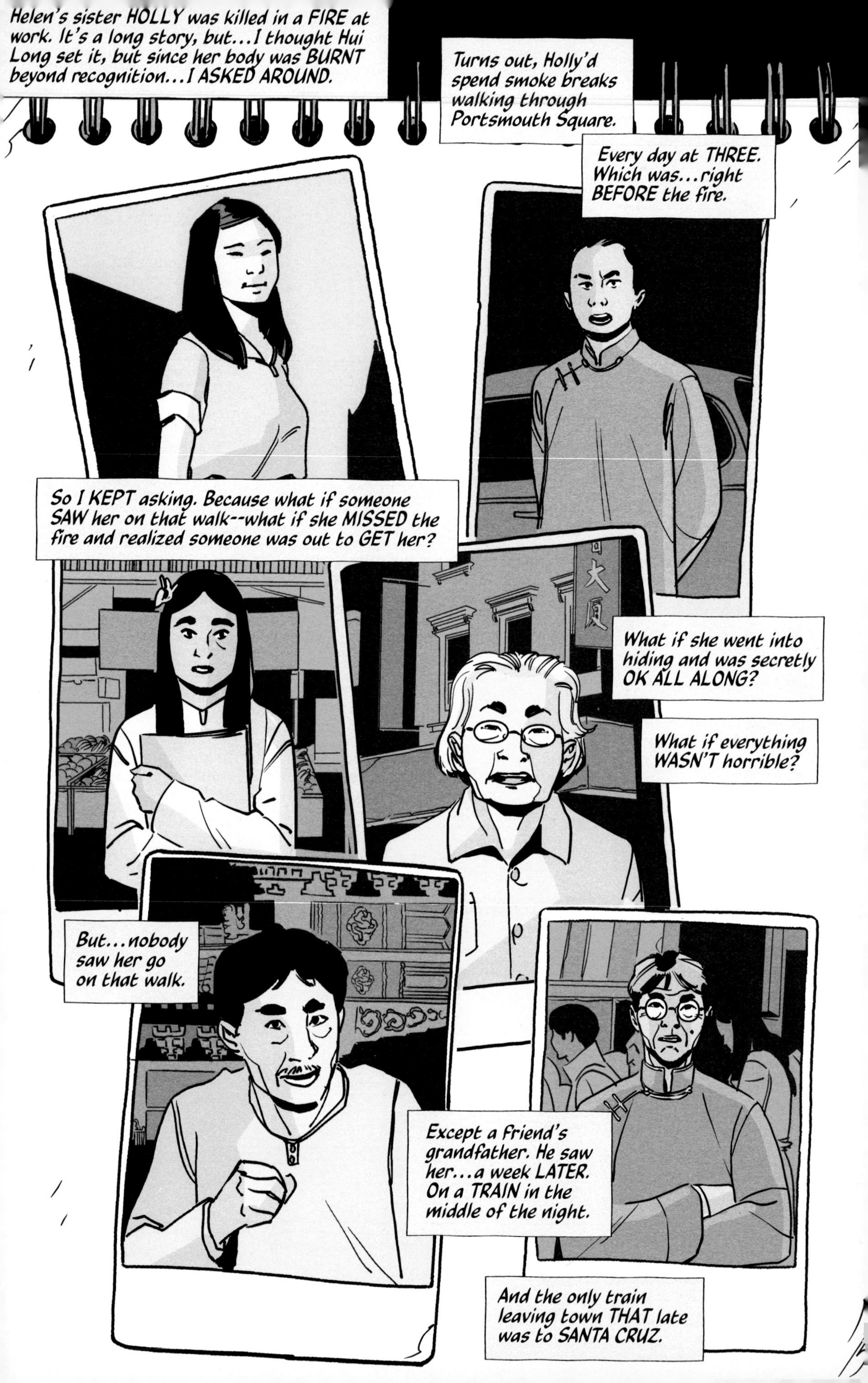
Helen's sister HOLLY was killed in a FIRE at work. It's a long story, but...I thought Hui Long set it, but since her body was BURNT beyond recognition...I ASKED AROUND.
Turns out, Holly'd spend smoke breaks walking through Portsmouth Square.
Every day at THREE. Which was...right BEFORE the fire.
So I KEPT asking. Because what if someone SAW her on that walk--what if she MISSED the fire and realized someone was out to GET her?
What if she went into hiding and was secretly OK ALL ALONG?
What if everything WASN'T horrible?
But...nobody saw her go on that walk.
Except a friend's grandfather. He saw her...a week LATER. On a TRAIN in the middle of the night.
And the only train leaving town THAT late was to SANTA CRUZ.

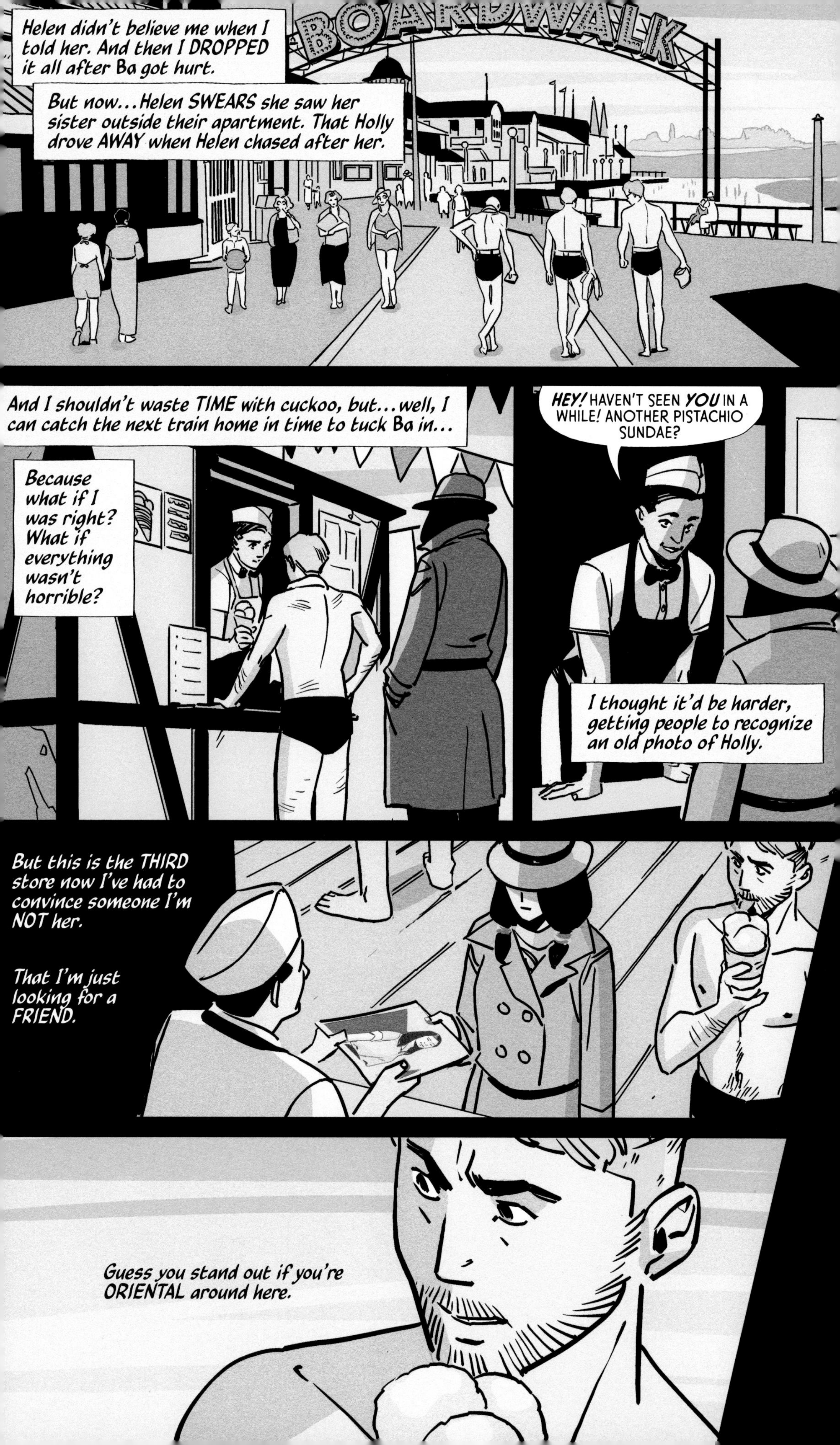
BOARDWALK
Helen didn't believe me when I told her. And then I DROPPED it all after Ba got hurt.
But now... Helen SWEARS she saw her sister outside their apartment. That Holly drove AWAY when Helen chased after her.
And I shouldn't waste TIME with cuckoo, but... well, I can catch the next train home in time to tuck Ba in...
Because what if I was right? What if everything wasn't horrible?
HEY! HAVEN'T SEEN YOU IN A WHILE! ANOTHER PISTACHIO SUNDAE?
I thought it'd be harder, getting people to recognize an old photo of Holly.
But this is the THIRD store now I've had to convince someone I'm NOT her.
That I'm just looking for a FRIEND.
Guess you stand out if you're ORIENTAL around here.

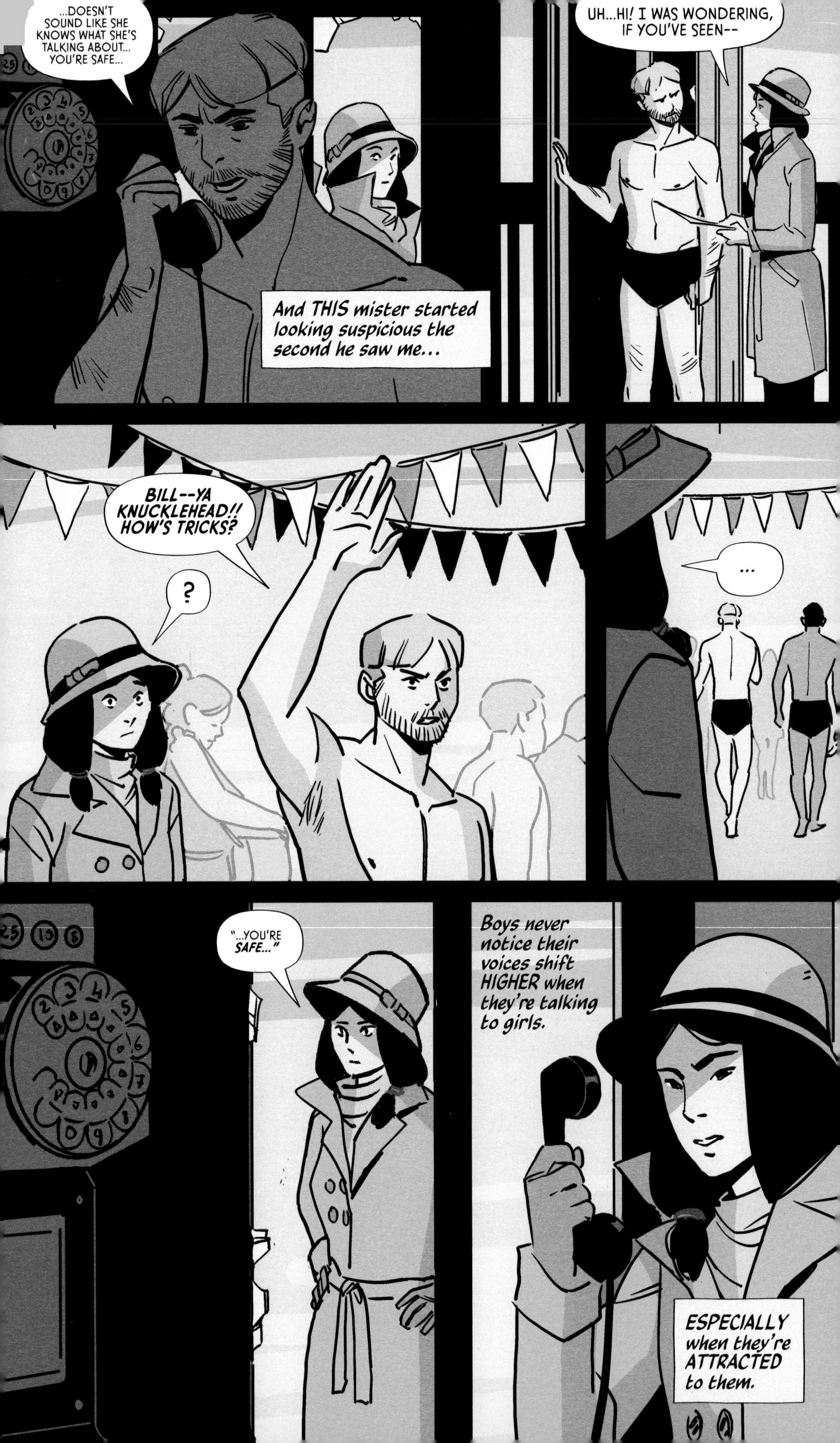
...DOESN'T SOUND LIKE SHE KNOWS WHAT SHE'S TALKING ABOUT... YOU'RE SAFE...
And THIS mister started looking suspicious the second he saw me...
UH...HI! I WAS WONDERING, IF YOU'VE SEEN--
BILL--YA KNUCKLEHEAD!! HOW'S TRICKS?
?
...
"...YOU'RE SAFE..."
Boys never notice their voices shift HIGHER when they're talking to girls.
ESPECIALLY when they're ATTRACTED to them.

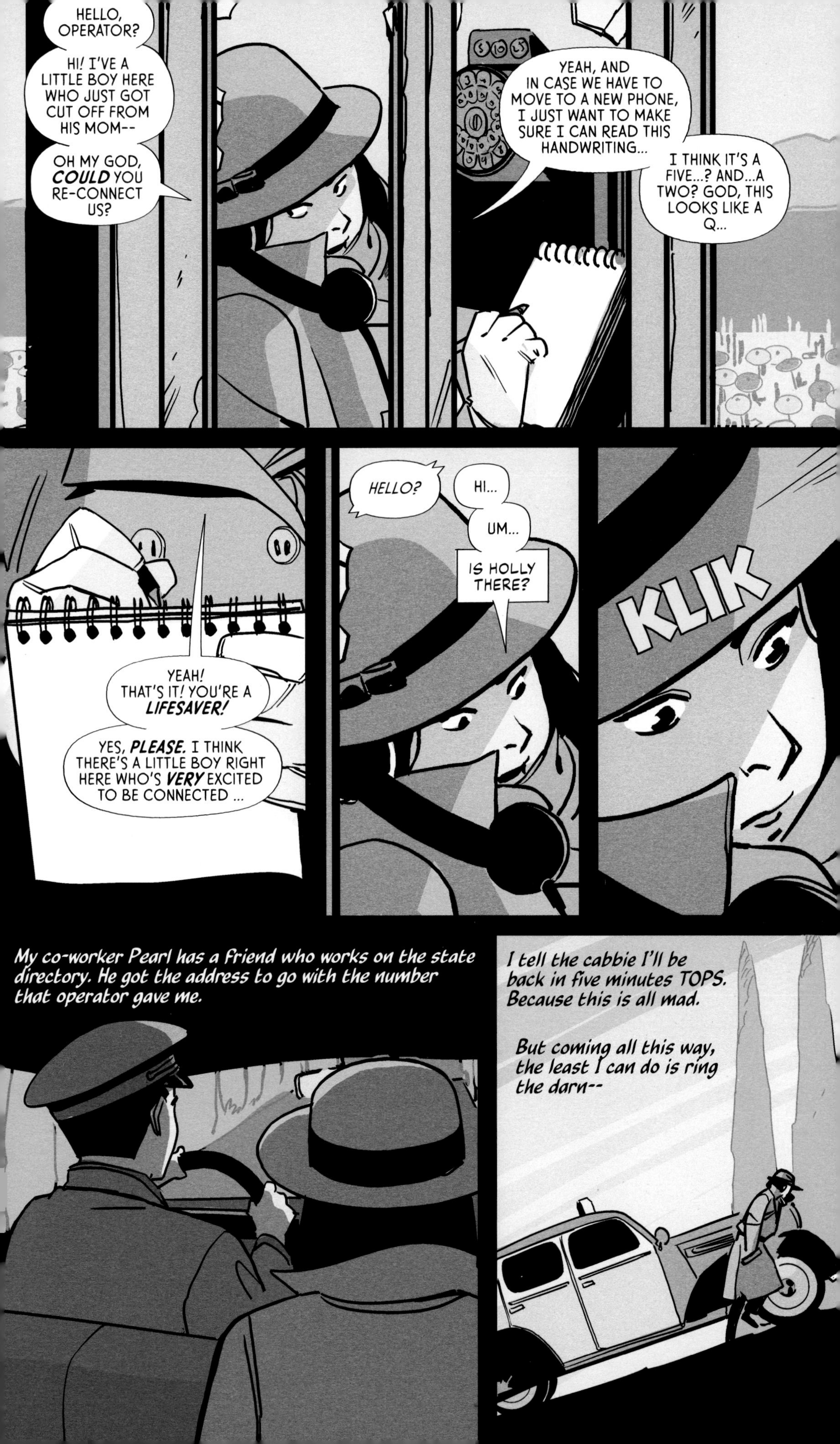
HELLO, OPERATOR?
HI! I'VE A LITTLE BOY HERE WHO JUST GOT CUT OFF FROM HIS MOM--
OH MY GOD, COULD YOU RE-CONNECT US?
YEAH, AND IN CASE WE HAVE TO MOVE TO A NEW PHONE, I JUST WANT TO MAKE SURE I CAN READ THIS HANDWRITING...
I THINK IT'S A FIVE...? AND...A TWO? GOD, THIS LOOKS LIKE A Q...
YEAH! THAT'S IT! YOU'RE A LIFESAVER!
YES, PLEASE. I THINK THERE'S A LITTLE BOY RIGHT HERE WHO'S VERY EXCITED TO BE CONNECTED ...
HELLO?
HI...
UM...
IS HOLLY THERE?
KLIK
My co-worker Pearl has a friend who works on the state directory. He got the address to go with the number that operator gave me.
I tell the cabbie I'll be back in five minutes TOPS. Because this is all mad.
But coming all this way, the least I can do is ring the darn--

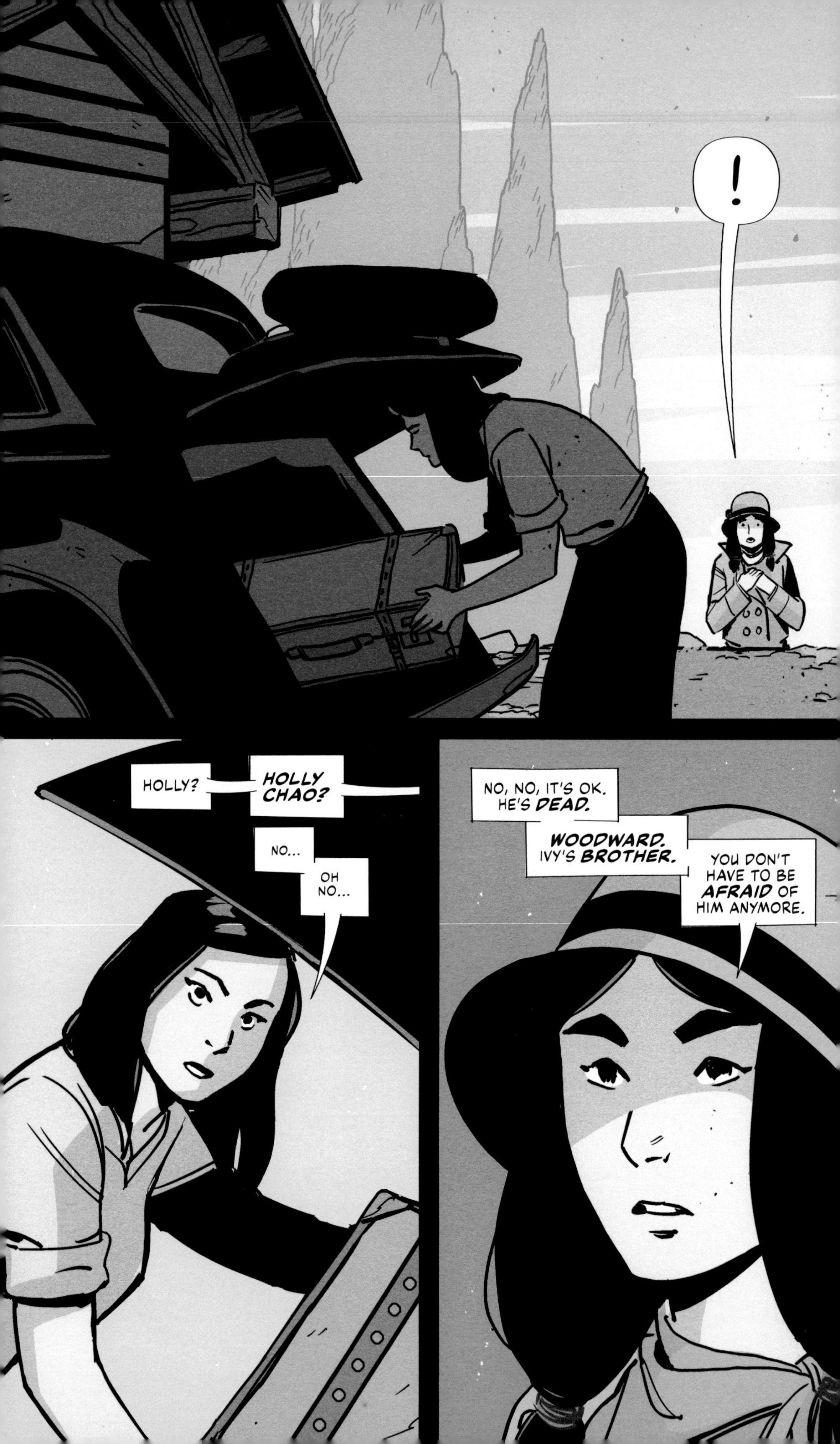
!
HOLLY?
HOLLY CHAO?
NO...
OH NO...
NO, NO, IT'S OK. HE'S DEAD.
WOODWARD. IVY'S BROTHER.
YOU DON'T HAVE TO BE AFRAID OF HIM ANYMORE.

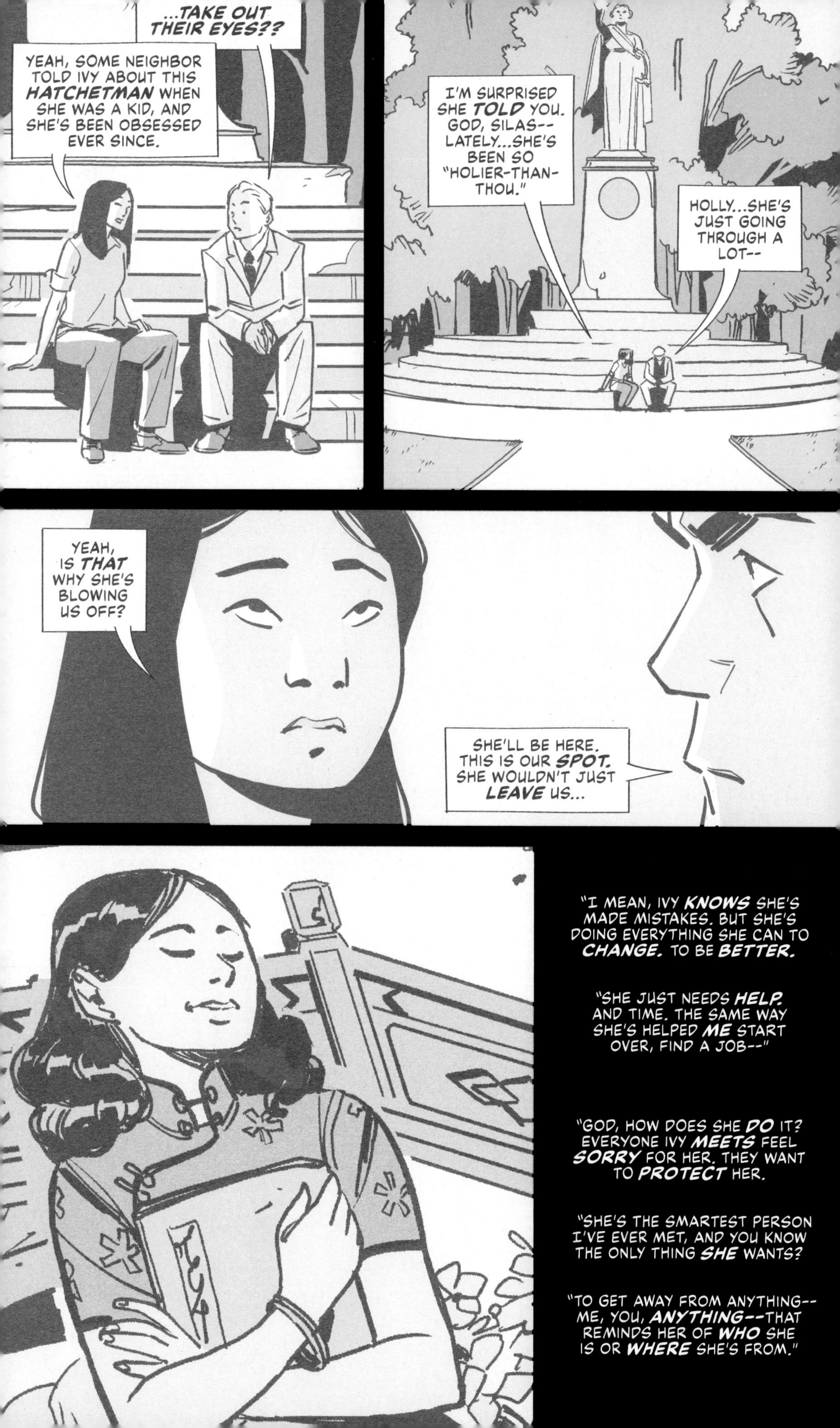
...TAKE OUT THEIR EYES??
YEAH, SOME NEIGHBOR TOLD IVY ABOUT THIS HATCHETMAN WHEN SHE WAS A KID, AND SHE'S BEEN OBSESSED EVER SINCE.
I'M SURPRISED SHE TOLD YOU. GOD, SILAS-- LATELY...SHE'S BEEN SO "HOLIER-THAN-THOU."
HOLLY...SHE'S JUST GOING THROUGH A LOT--
YEAH, IS THAT WHY SHE'S BLOWING US OFF?
SHE'LL BE HERE. THIS IS OUR SPOT. SHE WOULDN'T JUST LEAVE US...
"I MEAN, IVY KNOWS SHE'S MADE MISTAKES. BUT SHE'S DOING EVERYTHING SHE CAN TO CHANGE. TO BE BETTER.
"SHE JUST NEEDS HELP. AND TIME. THE SAME WAY SHE'S HELPED ME START OVER, FIND A JOB--"
"GOD, HOW DOES SHE DO IT? EVERYONE IVY MEETS FEEL SORRY FOR HER. THEY WANT TO PROTECT HER.
"SHE'S THE SMARTEST PERSON I'VE EVER MET, AND YOU KNOW THE ONLY THING SHE WANTS?
"TO GET AWAY FROM ANYTHING-- ME, YOU, ANYTHING--THAT REMINDS HER OF WHO SHE IS OR WHERE SHE'S FROM."

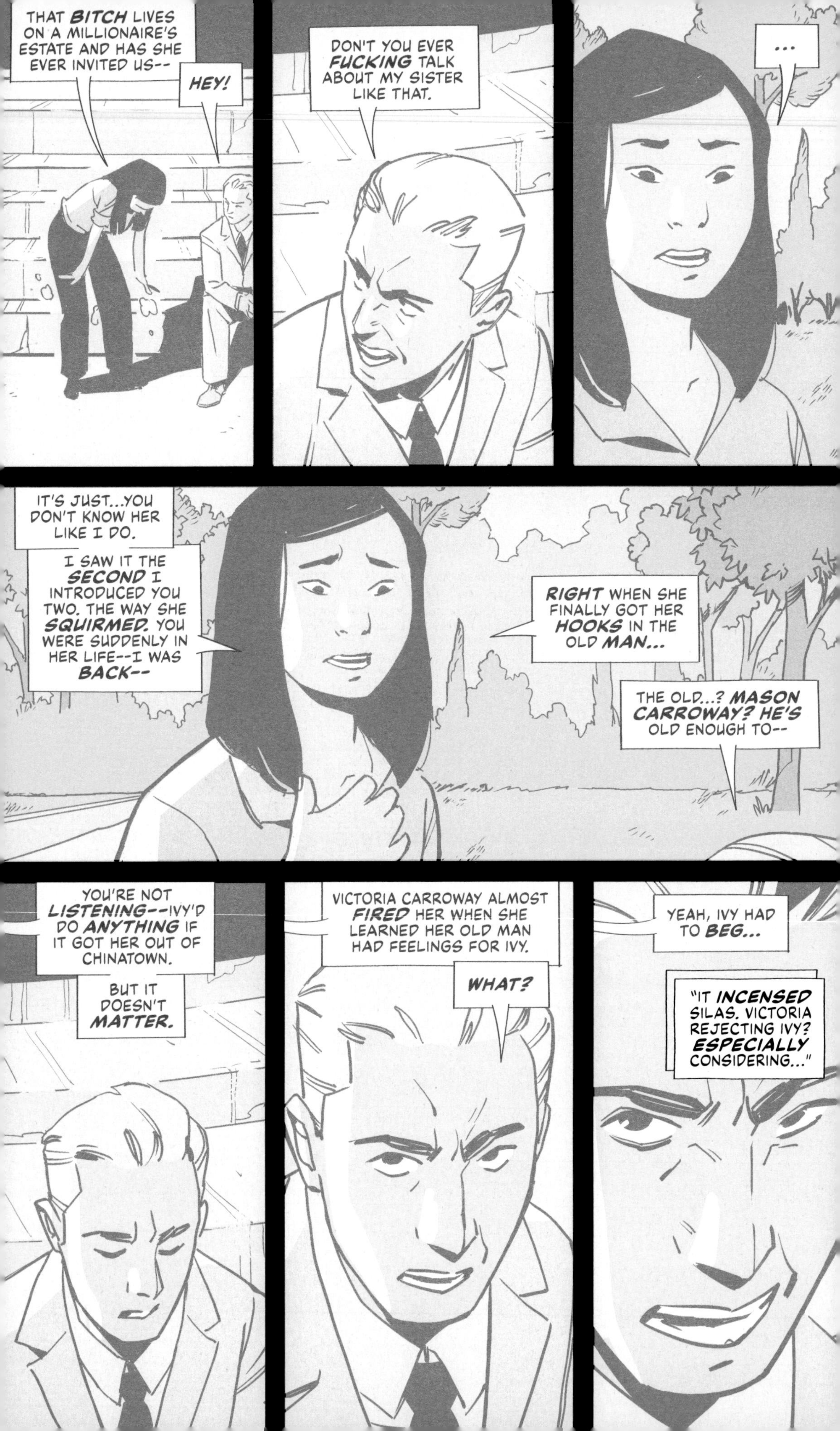
THAT BITCH LIVES ON A MILLIONAIRE'S ESTATE AND HAS SHE EVER INVITED US--
HEY!
DON'T YOU EVER FUCKING TALK ABOUT MY SISTER LIKE THAT.
...
IT'S JUST...YOU DON'T KNOW HER LIKE I DO.
I SAW IT THE SECOND I INTRODUCED YOU TWO. THE WAY SHE SQUIRMED. YOU WERE SUDDENLY IN HER LIFE--I WAS BACK--
RIGHT WHEN SHE FINALLY GOT HER HOOKS IN THE OLD MAN...
THE OLD...? MASON CARROWAY? HE'S OLD ENOUGH TO--
YOU'RE NOT LISTENING--IVY'D DO ANYTHING IF IT GOT HER OUT OF CHINATOWN.
BUT IT DOESN'T MATTER.
VICTORIA CARROWAY ALMOST FIRED HER WHEN SHE LEARNED HER OLD MAN HAD FEELINGS FOR IVY.
WHAT?
YEAH, IVY HAD TO BEG...
"IT INCENSED SILAS. VICTORIA REJECTING IVY? ESPECIALLY CONSIDERING..."

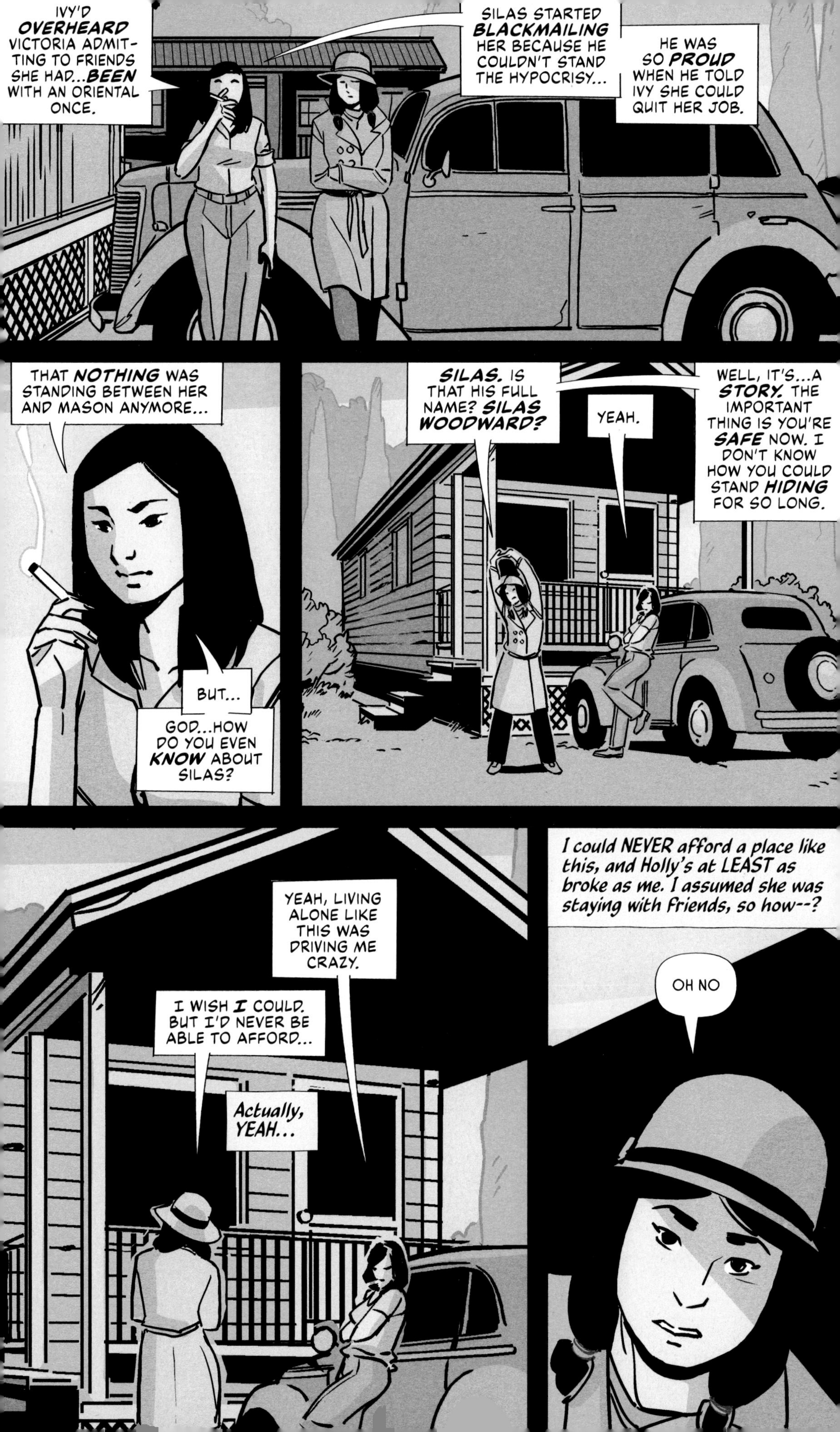
IVY'D OVERHEARD VICTORIA ADMITTING TO FRIENDS SHE HAD...BEEN WITH AN ORIENTAL ONCE.
SILAS STARTED BLACKMAILING HER BECAUSE HE COULDN'T STAND THE HYPOCRISY...
HE WAS SO PROUD WHEN HE TOLD IVY SHE COULD QUIT HER JOB.
THAT NOTHING WAS STANDING BETWEEN HER AND MASON ANYMORE...
BUT...
GOD...HOW DO YOU EVEN KNOW ABOUT SILAS?
SILAS. IS THAT HIS FULL NAME? SILAS WOODWARD?
YEAH.
WELL, IT'S...A STORY. THE IMPORTANT THING IS YOU'RE SAFE NOW. I DON'T KNOW HOW YOU COULD STAND HIDING FOR SO LONG.
YEAH, LIVING ALONE LIKE THIS WAS DRIVING ME CRAZY.
I WISH I COULD. BUT I'D NEVER BE ABLE TO AFFORD...
Actually, YEAH...
I could NEVER afford a place like this, and Holly's at LEAST as broke as me. I assumed she was staying with friends, so how--?
OH NO

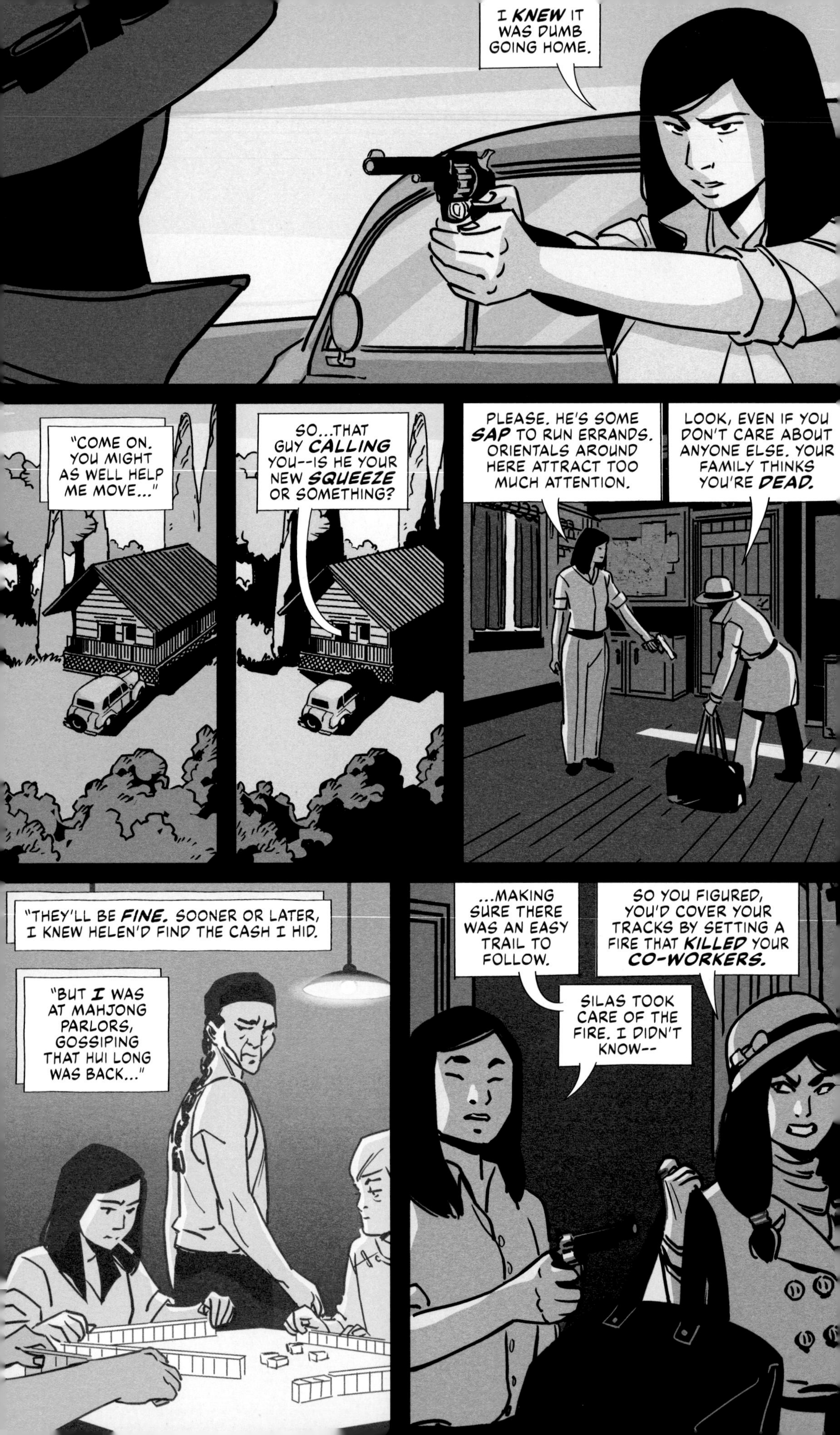
I KNEW IT WAS DUMB GOING HOME.
"COME ON. YOU MIGHT AS WELL HELP ME MOVE..."
SO...THAT GUY CALLING YOU--IS HE YOUR NEW SQUEEZE OR SOMETHING?
PLEASE. HE'S SOME SAP TO RUN ERRANDS. ORIENTALS AROUND HERE ATTRACT TOO MUCH ATTENTION.
LOOK, EVEN IF YOU DON'T CARE ABOUT ANYONE ELSE. YOUR FAMILY THINKS YOU'RE DEAD.
"THEY'LL BE FINE. SOONER OR LATER, I KNEW HELEN'D FIND THE CASH I HID.
"BUT I WAS AT MAHJONG PARLORS, GOSSIPING THAT HUI LONG WAS BACK..."
...MAKING SURE THERE WAS AN EASY TRAIL TO FOLLOW.
SO YOU FIGURED, YOU'D COVER YOUR TRACKS BY SETTING A FIRE THAT KILLED YOUR CO-WORKERS.
SILAS TOOK CARE OF THE FIRE. I DIDN'T KNOW--

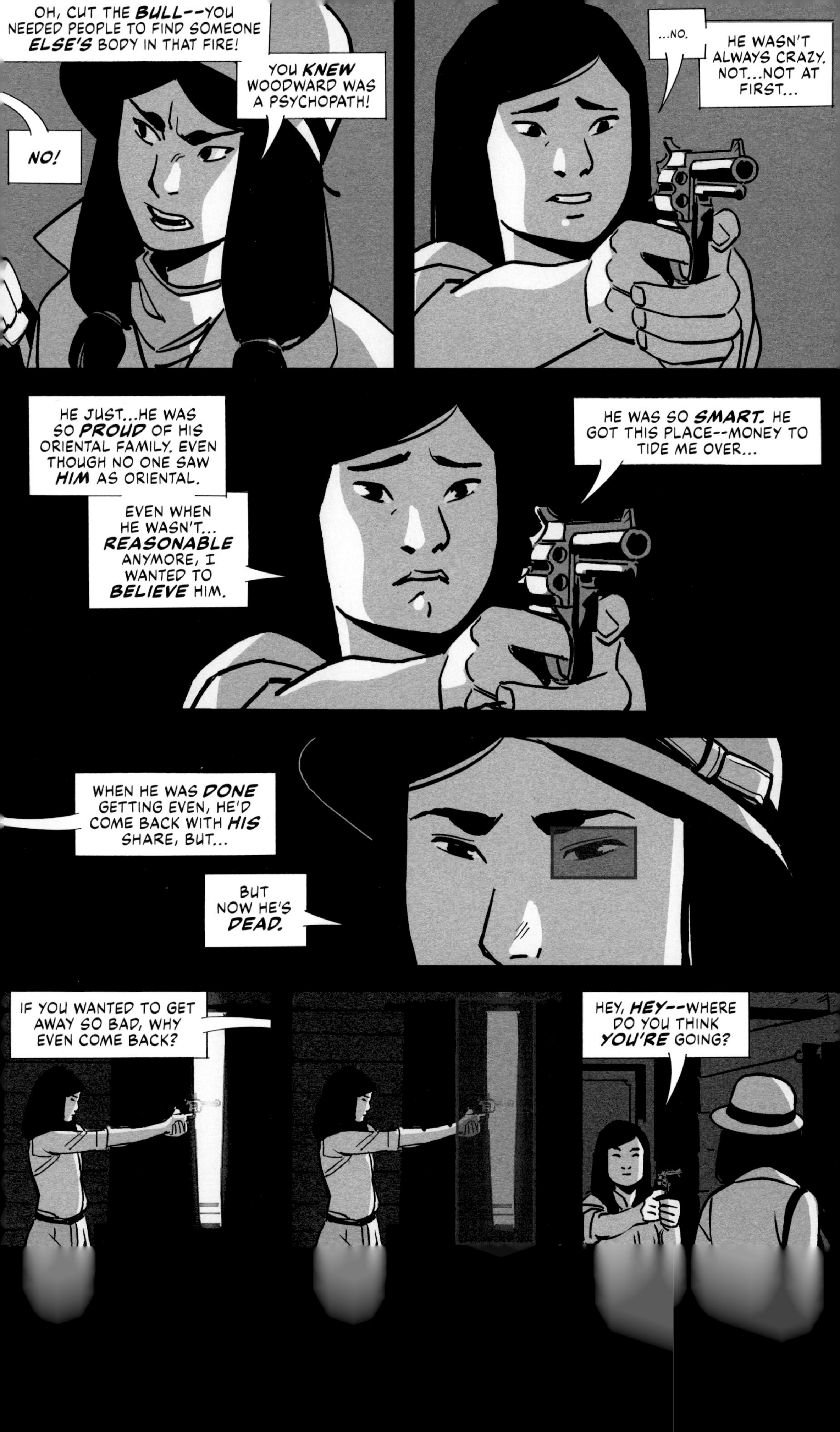

OH, CUT THE BULL--YOU NEEDED PEOPLE TO FIND SOMEONE ELSE'S BODY IN THAT FIRE!
NO!
YOU KNEW WOODWARD WAS A PSYCHOPATH!
...NO.
HE WASN'T ALWAYS CRAZY. NOT...NOT AT FIRST...
HE JUST...HE WAS SO PROUD OF HIS ORIENTAL FAMILY. EVEN THOUGH NO ONE SAW HIM AS ORIENTAL.
EVEN WHEN HE WASN'T... REASONABLE ANYMORE, I WANTED TO BELIEVE HIM.
HE WAS SO SMART. HE GOT THIS PLACE--MONEY TO TIDE ME OVER...
WHEN HE WAS DONE GETTING EVEN, HE'D COME BACK WITH HIS SHARE, BUT...
BUT NOW HE'S DEAD.
IF YOU WANTED TO GET AWAY SO BAD, WHY EVEN COME BACK?
HEY, HEY--WHERE DO YOU THINK YOU'RE GOING?

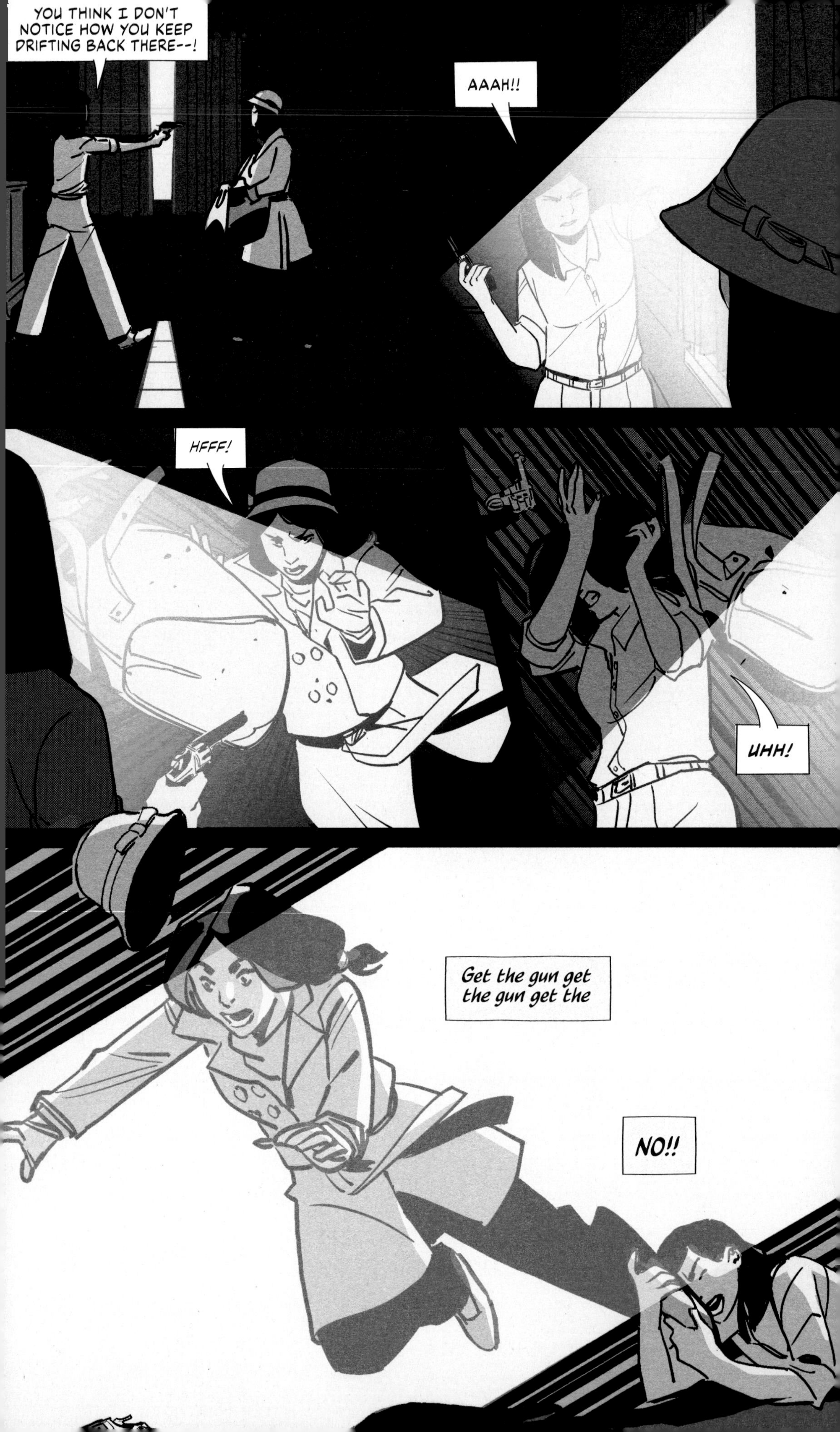
YOU THINK I DON'T NOTICE HOW YOU KEEP DRIFTING BACK THERE--!
AAAH!!
HFFF!
UHH!
Get the gun get the gun get the
NO!!

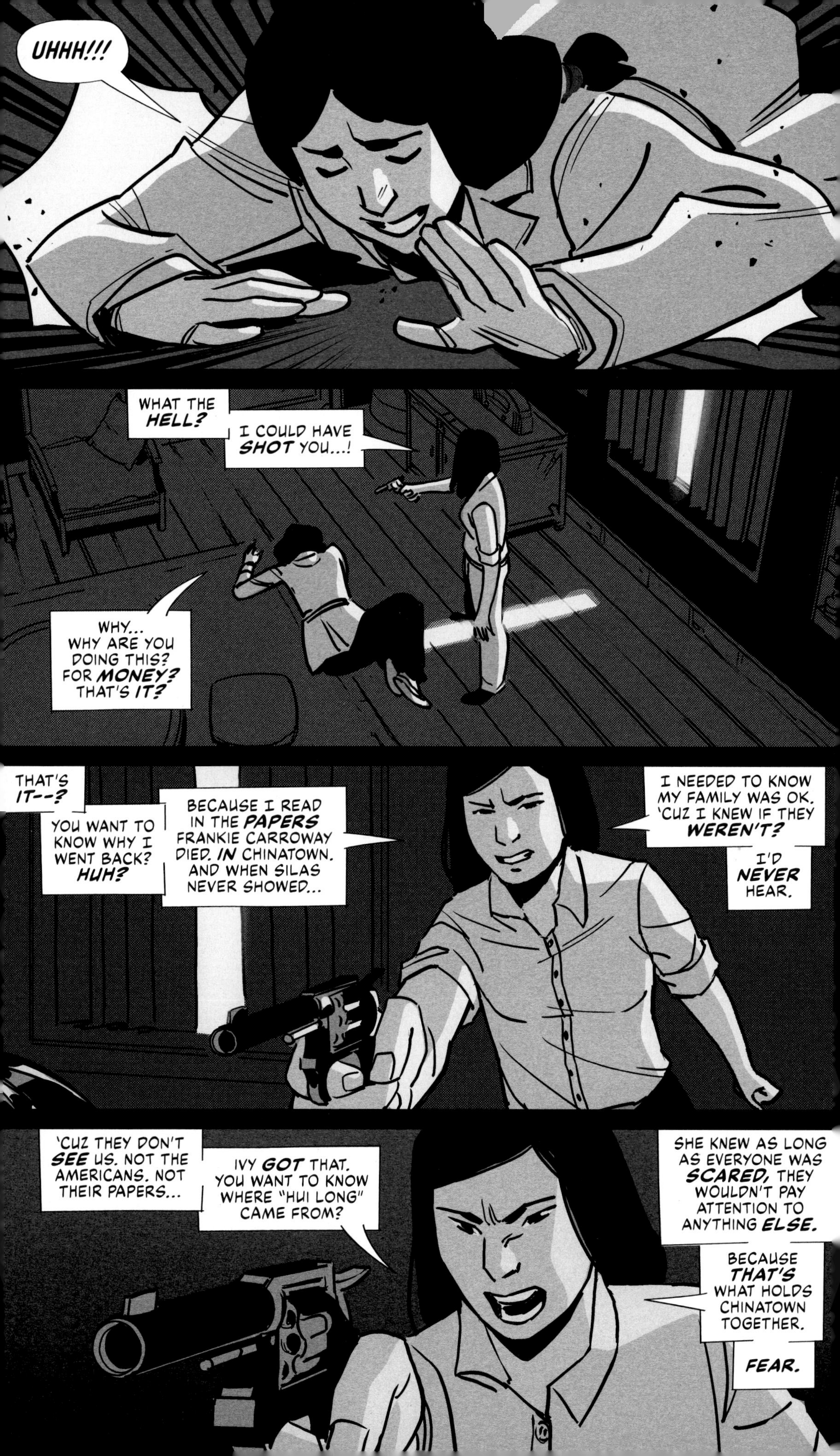
UHHH!!!
WHAT THE HELL?
I COULD HAVE SHOT YOU...!
WHY... WHY ARE YOU DOING THIS? FOR MONEY? THAT'S IT?
THAT'S IT--?
YOU WANT TO KNOW WHY I WENT BACK? HUH?
BECAUSE I READ IN THE PAPERS FRANKIE CARROWAY DIED. IN CHINATOWN. AND WHEN SILAS NEVER SHOWED...
I NEEDED TO KNOW MY FAMILY WAS OK. 'CUZ I KNEW IF THEY WEREN'T?
I'D NEVER HEAR.
'CUZ THEY DON'T SEE US. NOT THE AMERICANS. NOT THEIR PAPERS...
IVY GOT THAT. YOU WANT TO KNOW WHERE "HUI LONG" CAME FROM?
SHE KNEW AS LONG AS EVERYONE WAS SCARED, THEY WOULDN'T PAY ATTENTION TO ANYTHING ELSE.
BECAUSE THAT'S WHAT HOLDS CHINATOWN TOGETHER.
FEAR.

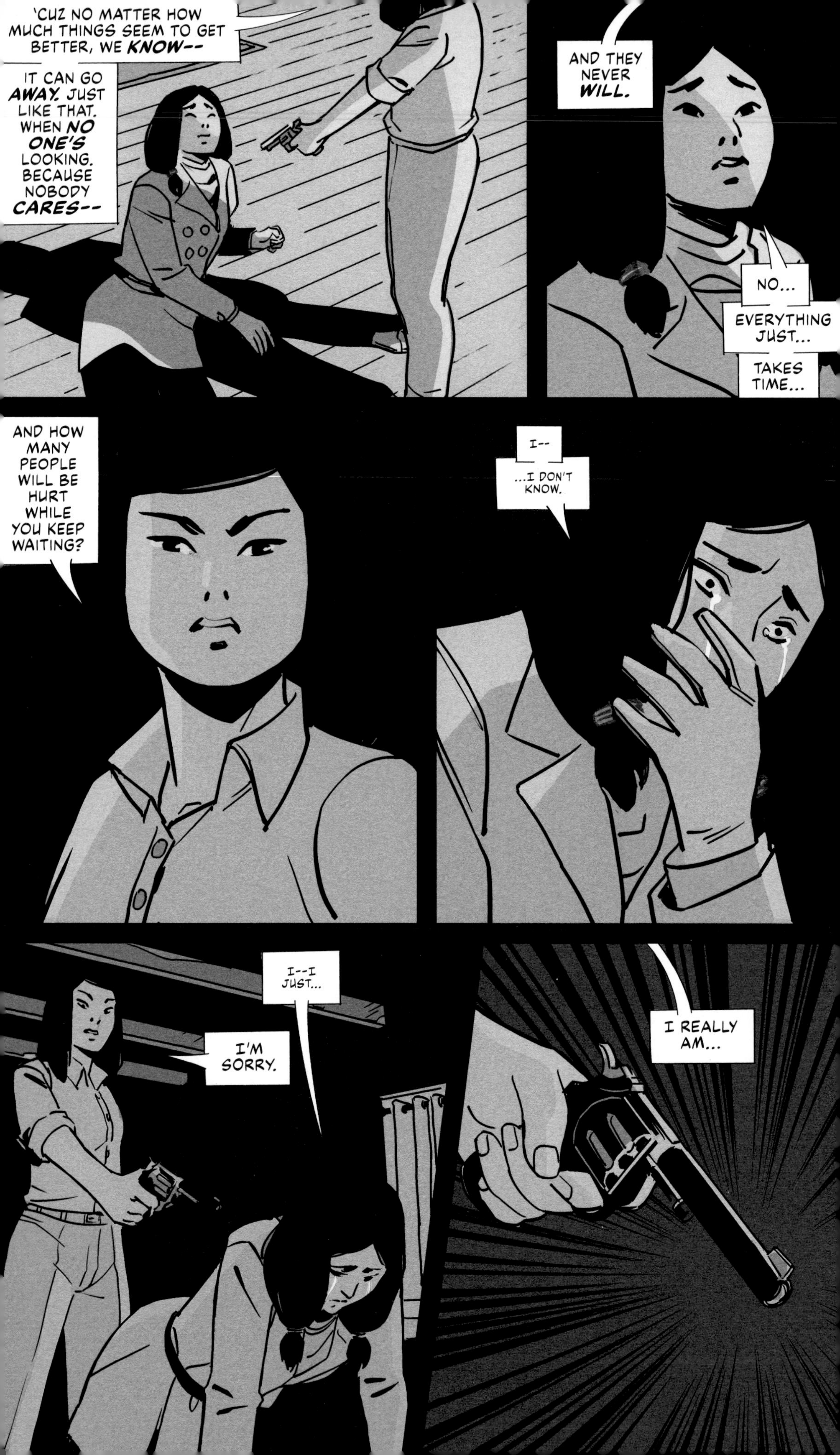
'CUZ NO MATTER HOW MUCH THINGS SEEM TO GET BETTER, WE KNOW--
IT CAN GO AWAY. JUST LIKE THAT. WHEN NO ONE'S LOOKING. BECAUSE NOBODY CARES--
AND THEY NEVER WILL.
NO...
EVERYTHING JUST...
TAKES TIME...
AND HOW MANY PEOPLE WILL BE HURT WHILE YOU KEEP WAITING?
I--
...I DON'T KNOW.
I--I JUST...
I'M SORRY.
I REALLY AM...

SLAM

VROOOOOOOOOMMM

I tell myself Holly walked away because she's not a KILLER.

But she SAID it--she felt sorry for me.

Even though my cab's long gone, it was easy to call another to pick me up. Despite everything, I'm home to tuck Ba in.

chikchakchikchak

And hear him check those locks.

And I've no more lies to tell myself. About things taking time. All I've left from the pit of my stomach...

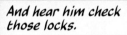

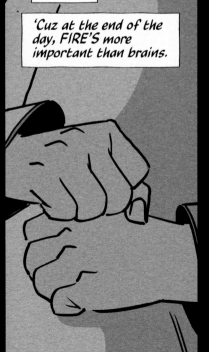

Is FIRE.

'Cuz at the end of the day, FIRE'S more important than brains.

And I don't care that I promised myself LAST WEEK I'd never come back here, I'm here NOW--

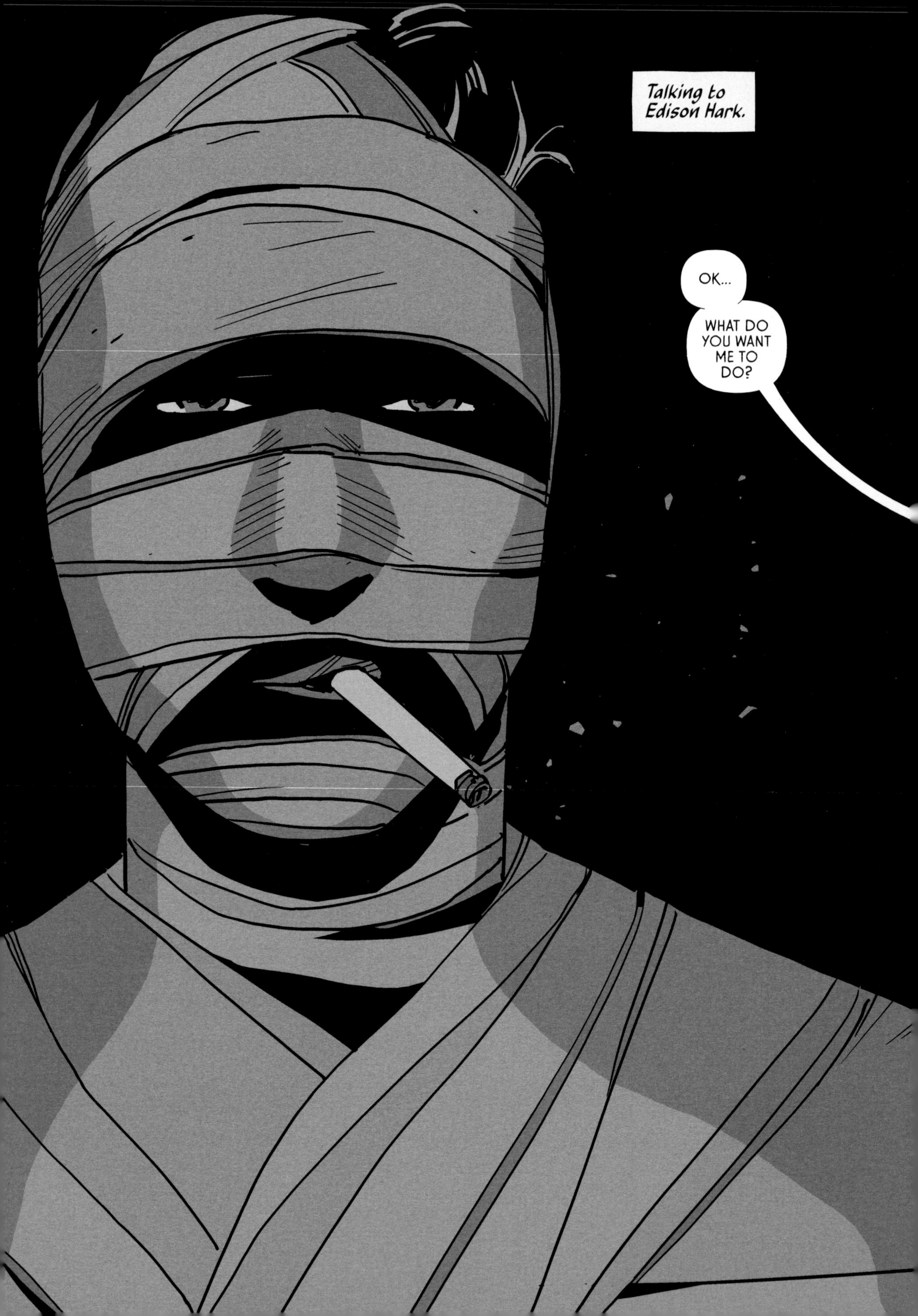
Talking to Edison Hark.
OK...
WHAT DO YOU WANT ME TO DO?

CHAPTER NINE

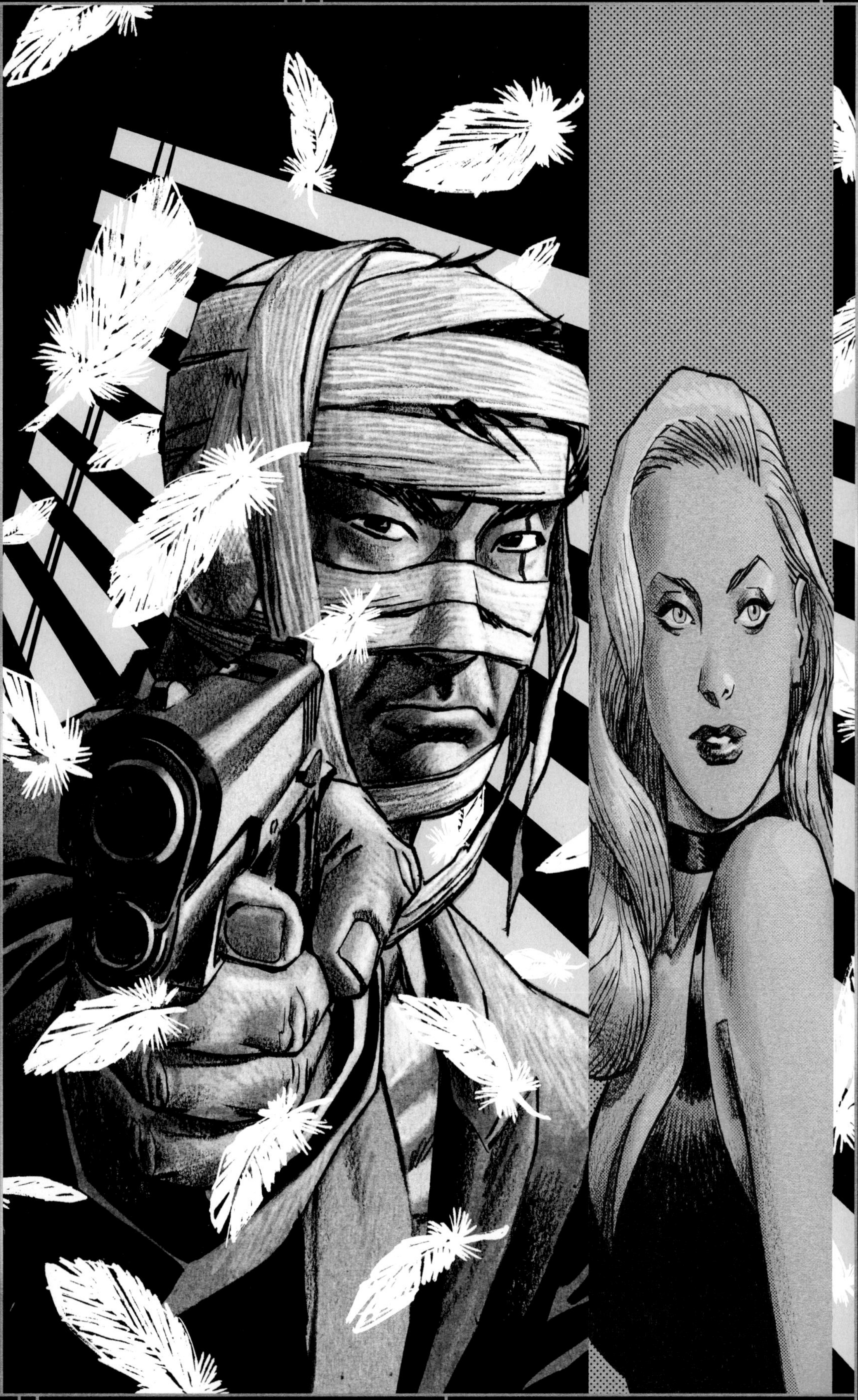

ART BY **DAVE JOHNSON**

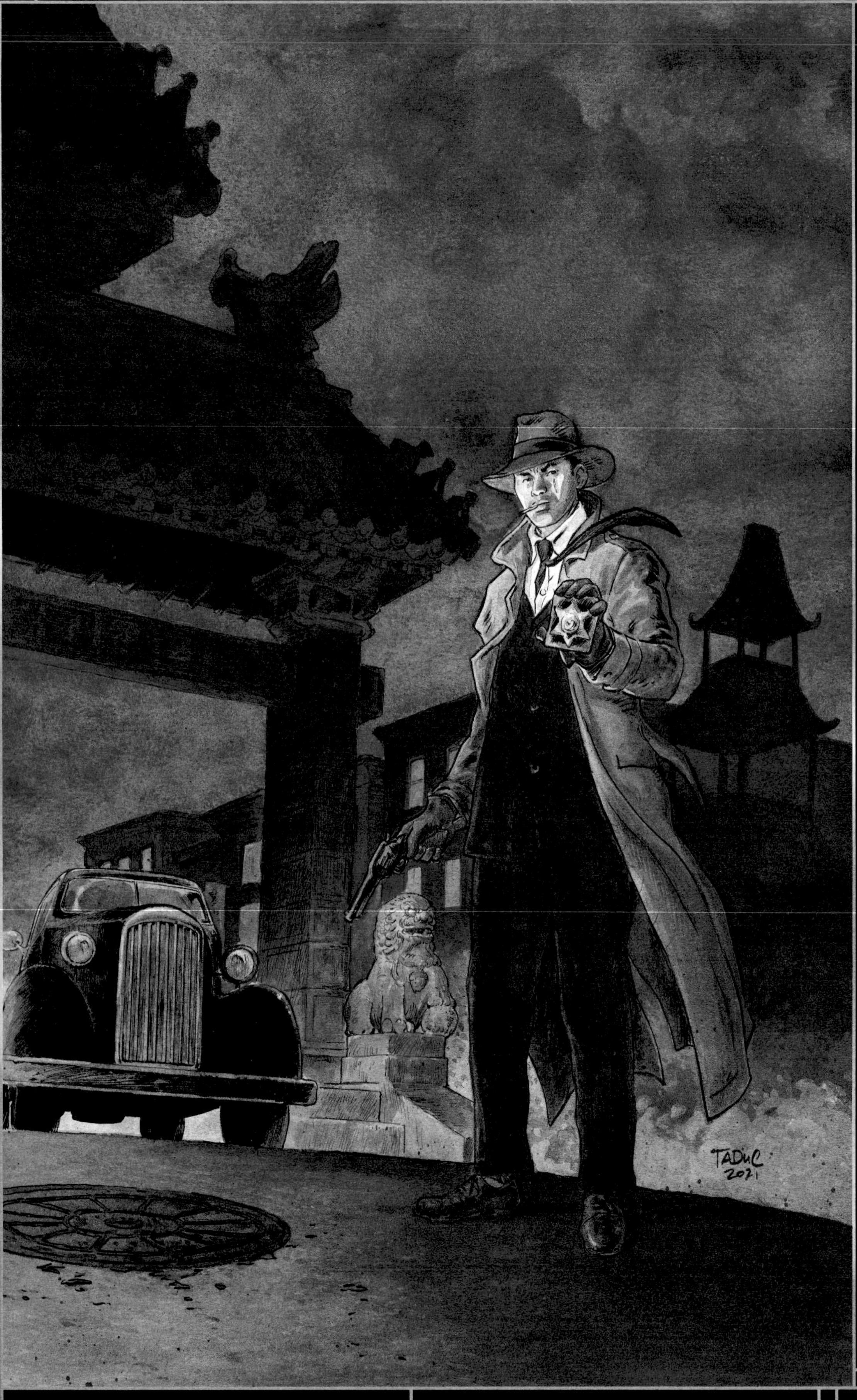
TADUC
2021

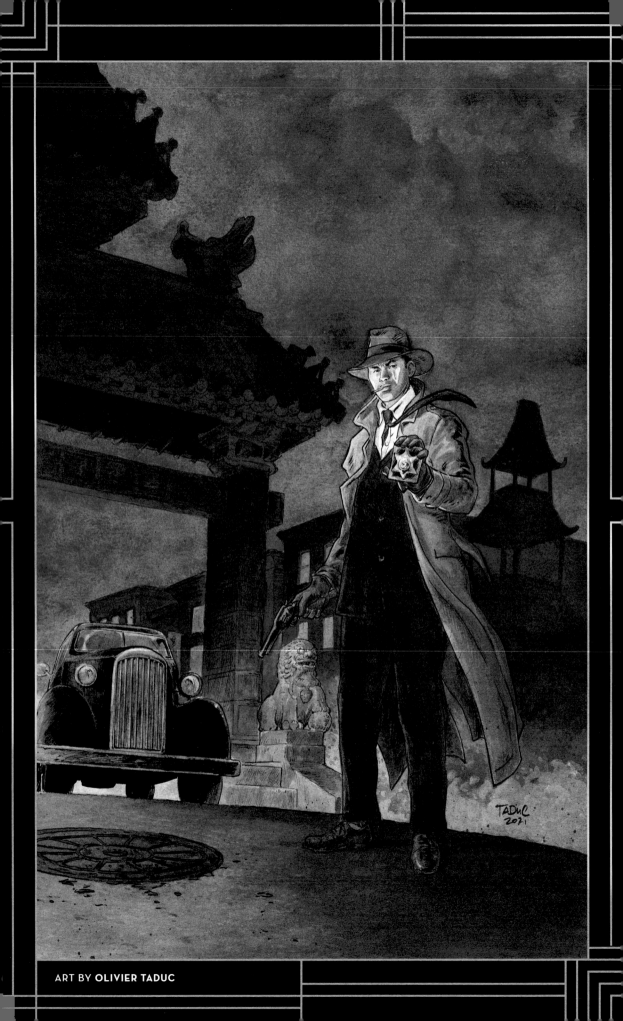

ART BY **OLIVIER TADUC**

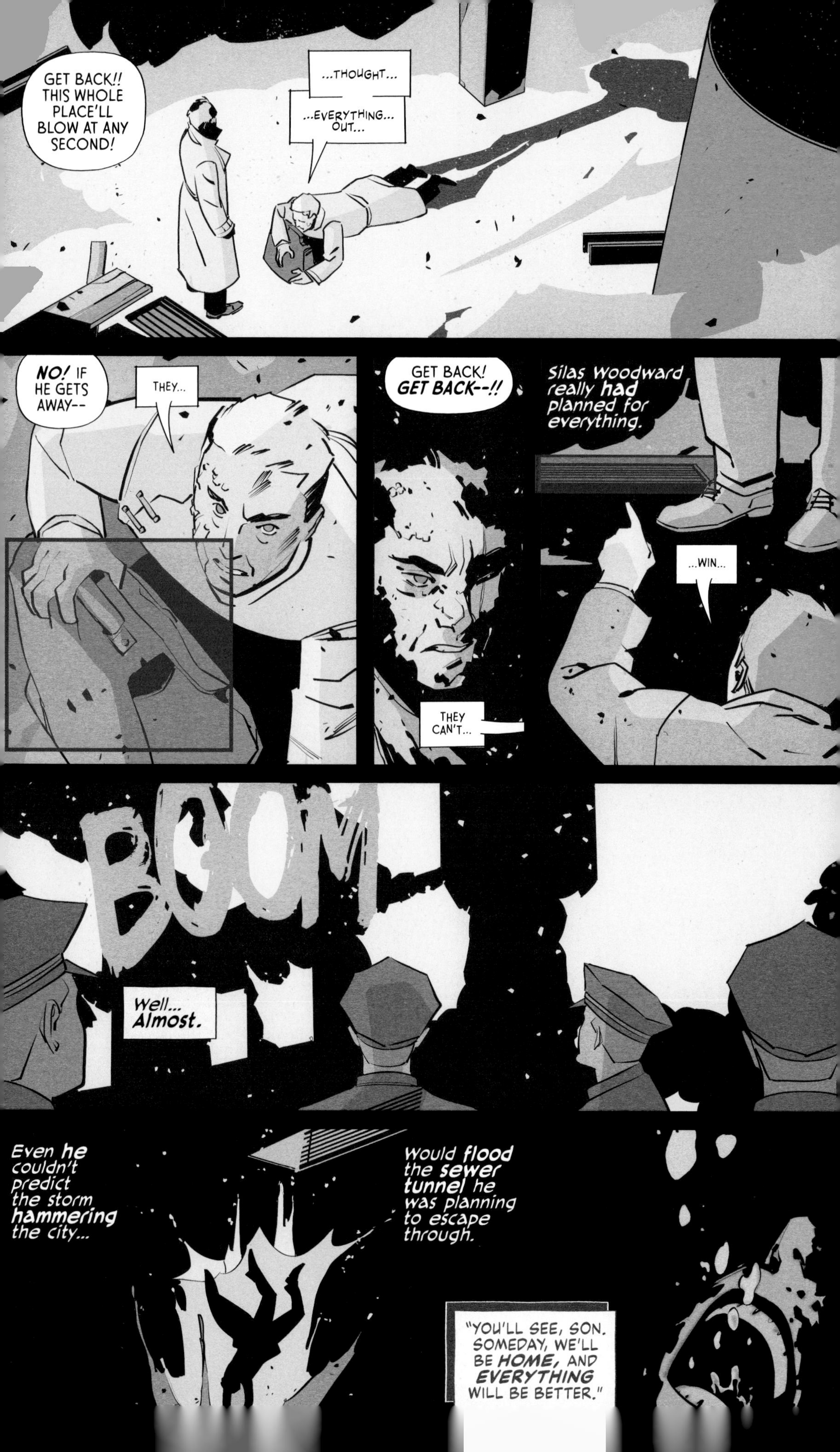
GET BACK!! THIS WHOLE PLACE'LL BLOW AT ANY SECOND!
...THOUGHT...
...EVERYTHING... OUT...
NO! IF HE GETS AWAY--
THEY...
GET BACK! GET BACK--!!
THEY CAN'T...
Silas Woodward really had planned for everything.
...WIN...
BOOM
Well... Almost.
Even he couldn't predict the storm hammering the city...
Would flood the sewer tunnel he was planning to escape through.
"YOU'LL SEE, SON. SOMEDAY, WE'LL BE HOME, AND EVERYTHING WILL BE BETTER."

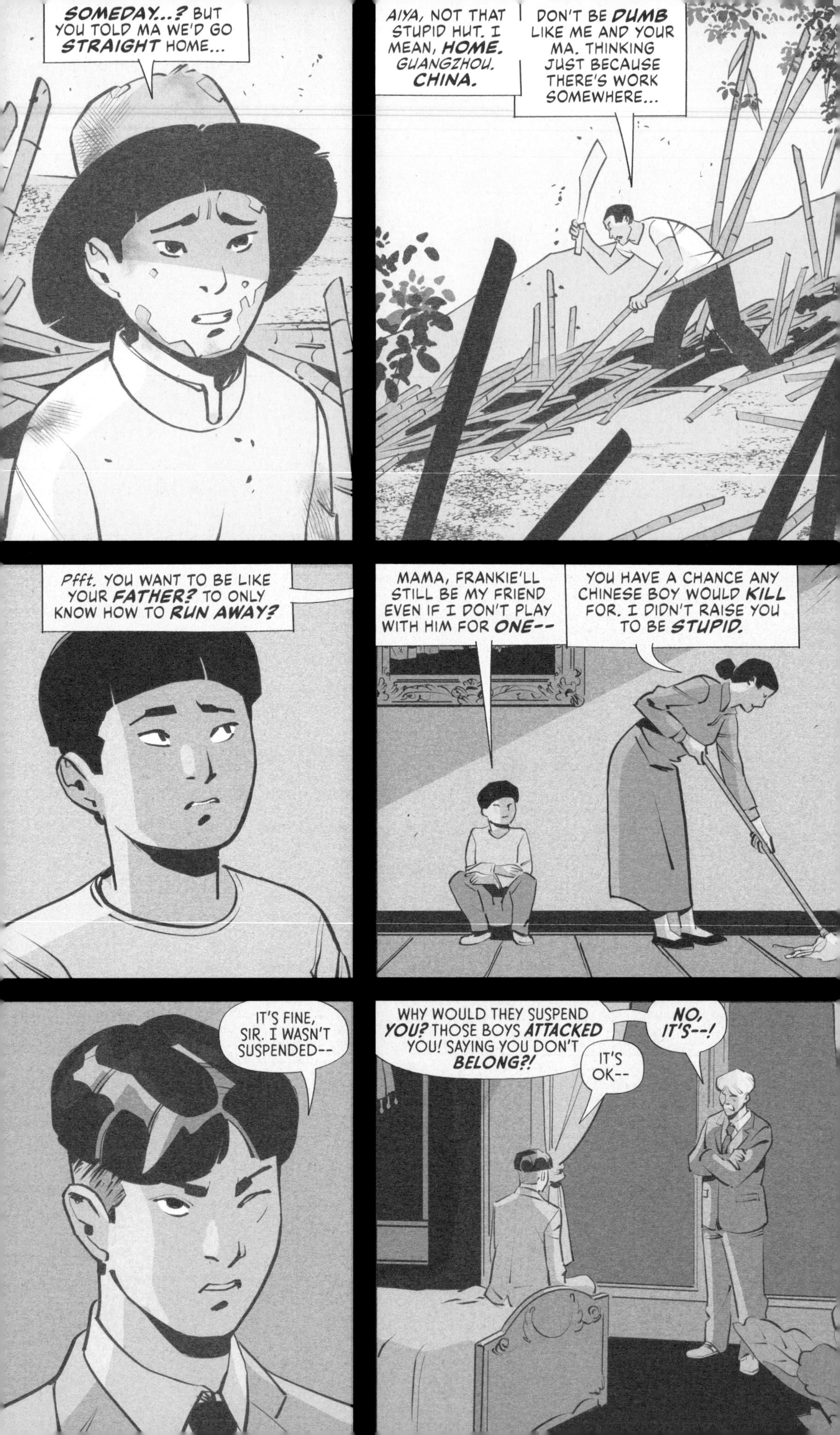
SOMEDAY...? BUT YOU TOLD MA WE'D GO STRAIGHT HOME...
AIYA, NOT THAT STUPID HUT. I MEAN, HOME. GUANGZHOU. CHINA.
DON'T BE DUMB LIKE ME AND YOUR MA. THINKING JUST BECAUSE THERE'S WORK SOMEWHERE...
Pfft. YOU WANT TO BE LIKE YOUR FATHER? TO ONLY KNOW HOW TO RUN AWAY?
MAMA, FRANKIE'LL STILL BE MY FRIEND EVEN IF I DON'T PLAY WITH HIM FOR ONE--
YOU HAVE A CHANCE ANY CHINESE BOY WOULD KILL FOR. I DIDN'T RAISE YOU TO BE STUPID.
IT'S FINE, SIR. I WASN'T SUSPENDED--
WHY WOULD THEY SUSPEND YOU? THOSE BOYS ATTACKED YOU! SAYING YOU DON'T BELONG?!
IT'S OK--
NO, IT'S--!

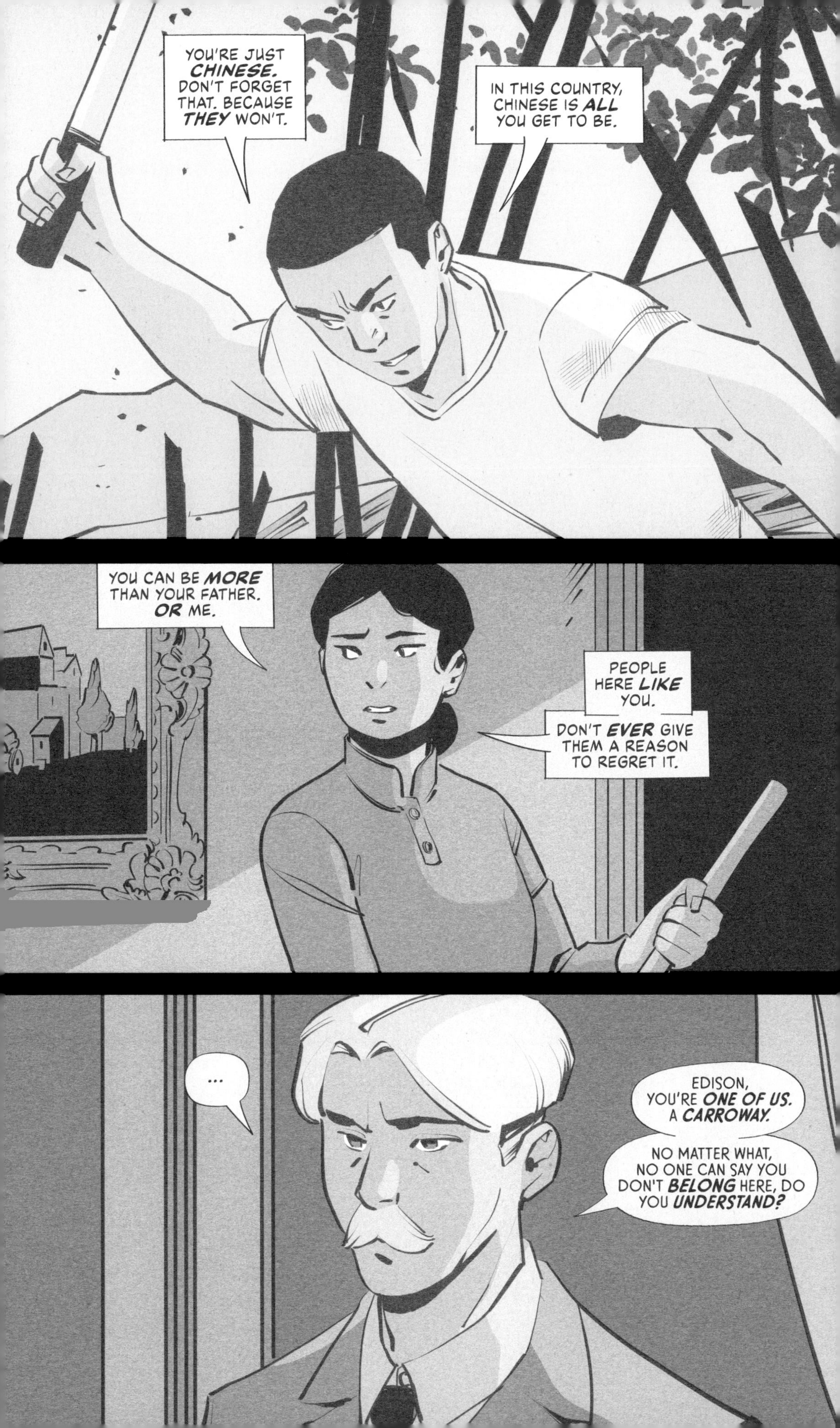

YOU'RE JUST CHINESE. DON'T FORGET THAT. BECAUSE THEY WON'T.
IN THIS COUNTRY, CHINESE IS ALL YOU GET TO BE.
YOU CAN BE MORE THAN YOUR FATHER. OR ME.
PEOPLE HERE LIKE YOU.
DON'T EVER GIVE THEM A REASON TO REGRET IT.
...
EDISON, YOU'RE ONE OF US. A CARROWAY.
NO MATTER WHAT, NO ONE CAN SAY YOU DON'T BELONG HERE, DO YOU UNDERSTAND?

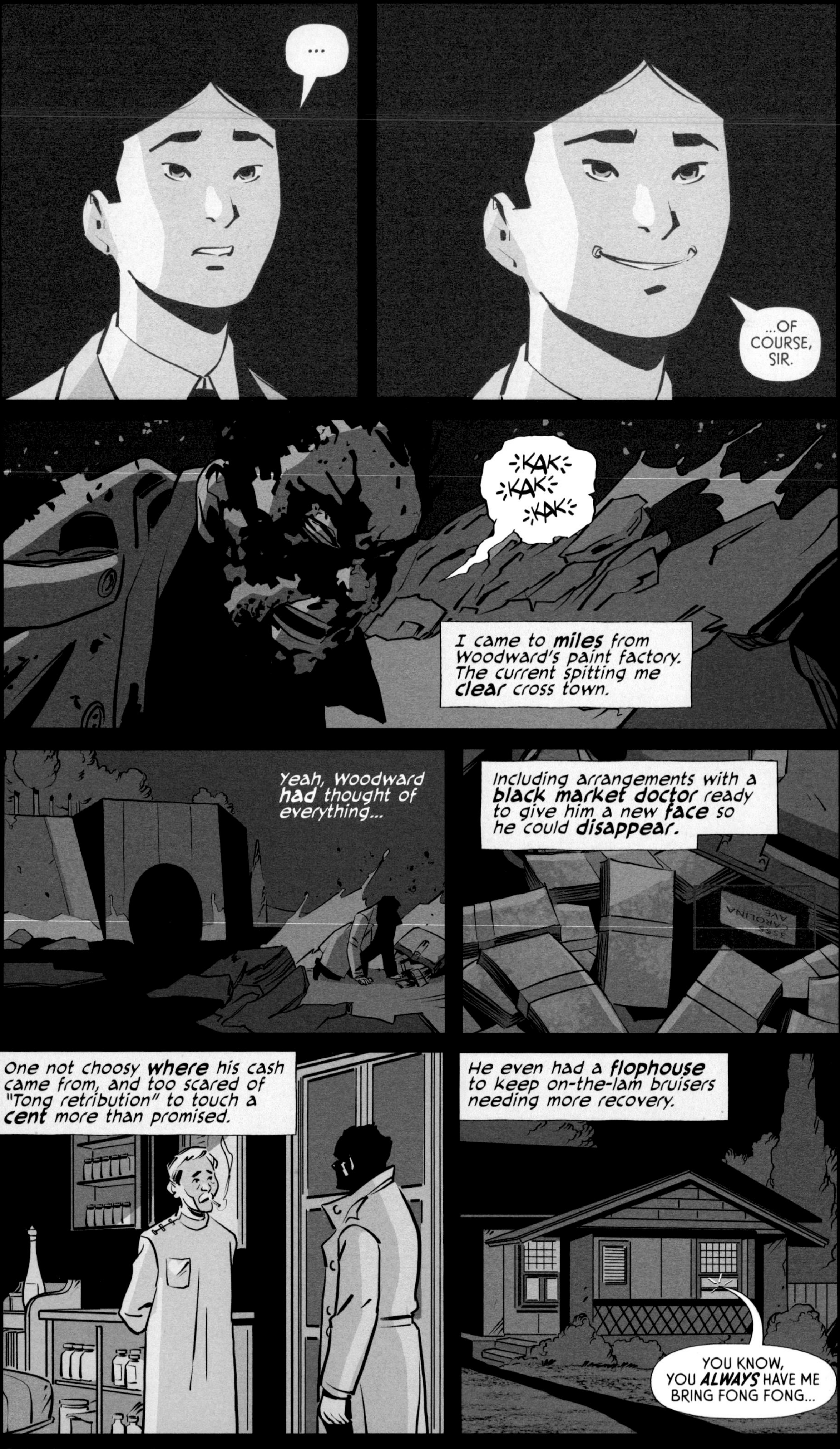
...
...OF COURSE, SIR.
KAK KAK KAK
I came to miles from Woodward's paint factory. The current spitting me clear cross town.
Yeah, Woodward had thought of everything...
Including arrangements with a black market doctor ready to give him a new face so he could disappear.
One not choosy where his cash came from, and too scared of "Tong retribution" to touch a cent more than promised.
He even had a flophouse to keep on-the-lam bruisers needing more recovery.
YOU KNOW, YOU ALWAYS HAVE ME BRING FONG FONG...

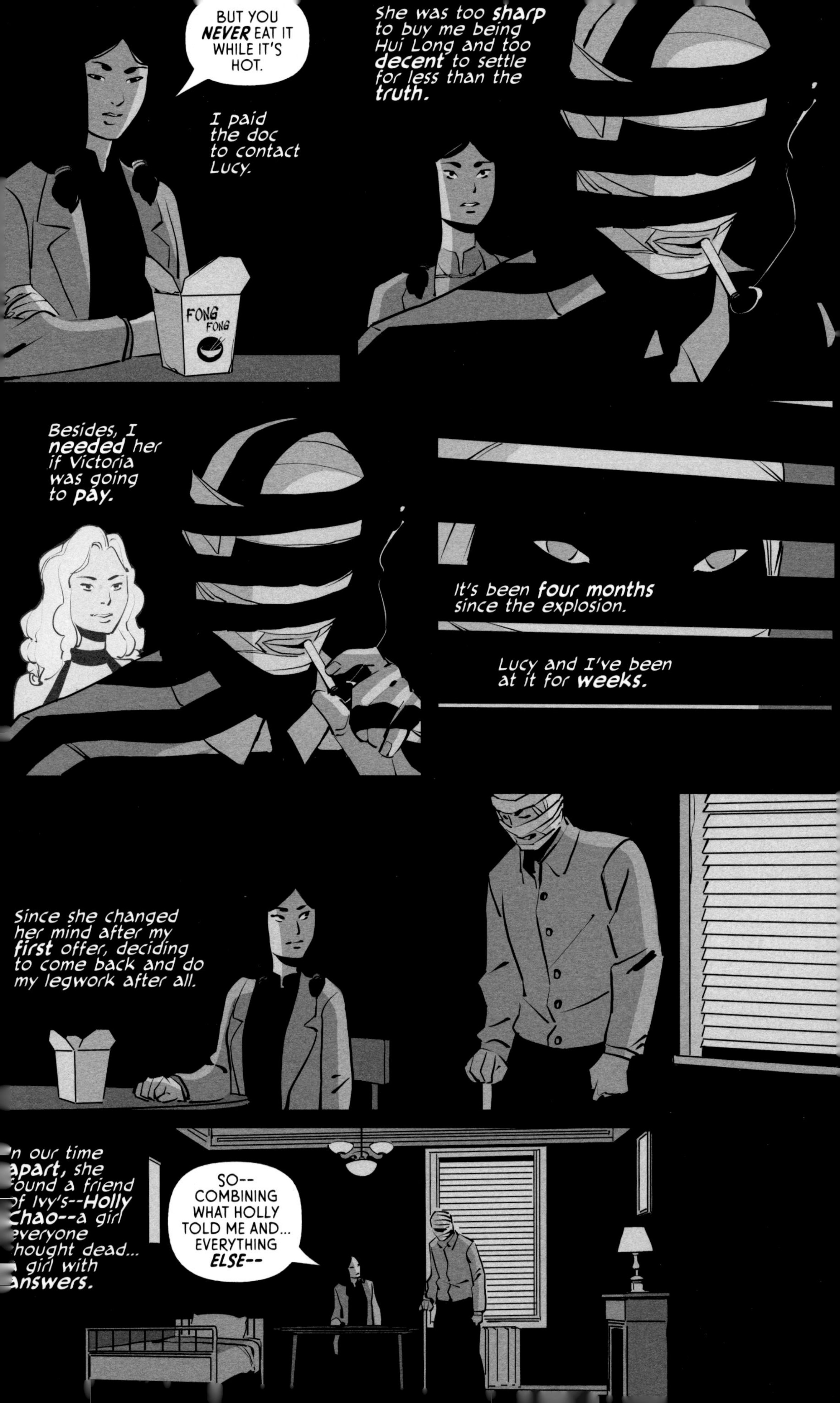

BUT YOU NEVER EAT IT WHILE IT'S HOT.
I paid the doc to contact Lucy.
FONG FONG
She was too sharp to buy me being Hui Long and too decent to settle for less than the truth.
Besides, I needed her if Victoria was going to pay.
It's been four months since the explosion.
Lucy and I've been at it for weeks.
Since she changed her mind after my first offer, deciding to come back and do my legwork after all.
In our time apart, she found a friend of Ivy's--Holly Chao--a girl everyone thought dead... a girl with answers.
SO-- COMBINING WHAT HOLLY TOLD ME AND... EVERYTHING ELSE--

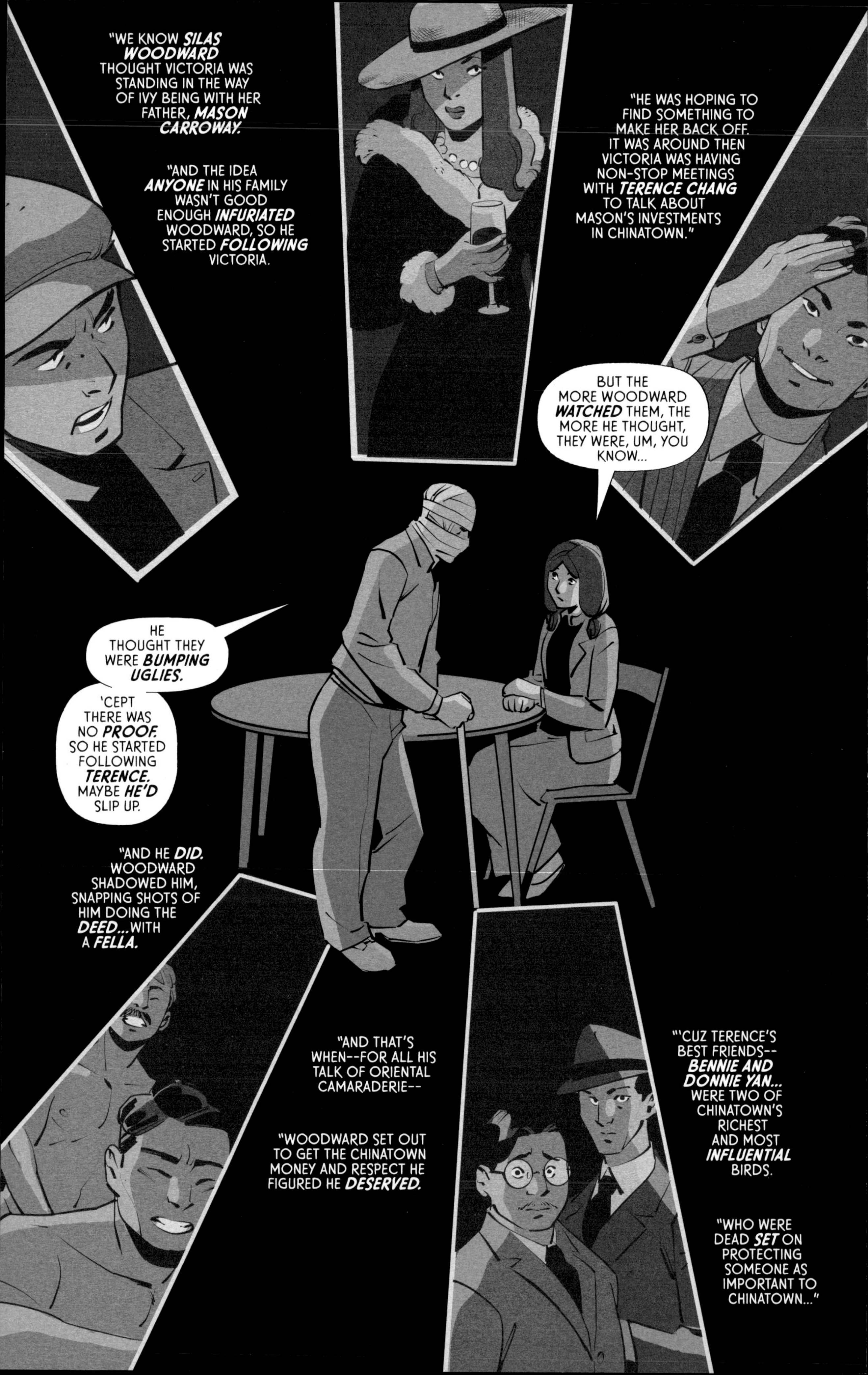
"WE KNOW SILAS WOODWARD THOUGHT VICTORIA WAS STANDING IN THE WAY OF IVY BEING WITH HER FATHER, MASON CARROWAY.
"AND THE IDEA ANYONE IN HIS FAMILY WASN'T GOOD ENOUGH INFURIATED WOODWARD, SO HE STARTED FOLLOWING VICTORIA.
"HE WAS HOPING TO FIND SOMETHING TO MAKE HER BACK OFF. IT WAS AROUND THEN VICTORIA WAS HAVING NON-STOP MEETINGS WITH TERENCE CHANG TO TALK ABOUT MASON'S INVESTMENTS IN CHINATOWN."
BUT THE MORE WOODWARD WATCHED THEM, THE MORE HE THOUGHT, THEY WERE, UM, YOU KNOW...
HE THOUGHT THEY WERE BUMPING UGLIES.
'CEPT THERE WAS NO PROOF. SO HE STARTED FOLLOWING TERENCE. MAYBE HE'D SLIP UP.
"AND HE DID. WOODWARD SHADOWED HIM, SNAPPING SHOTS OF HIM DOING THE DEED...WITH A FELLA.
"AND THAT'S WHEN--FOR ALL HIS TALK OF ORIENTAL CAMARADERIE--
"WOODWARD SET OUT TO GET THE CHINATOWN MONEY AND RESPECT HE FIGURED HE DESERVED.
"'CUZ TERENCE'S BEST FRIENDS-- BENNIE AND DONNIE YAN... WERE TWO OF CHINATOWN'S RICHEST AND MOST INFLUENTIAL BIRDS.
"WHO WERE DEAD SET ON PROTECTING SOMEONE AS IMPORTANT TO CHINATOWN..."

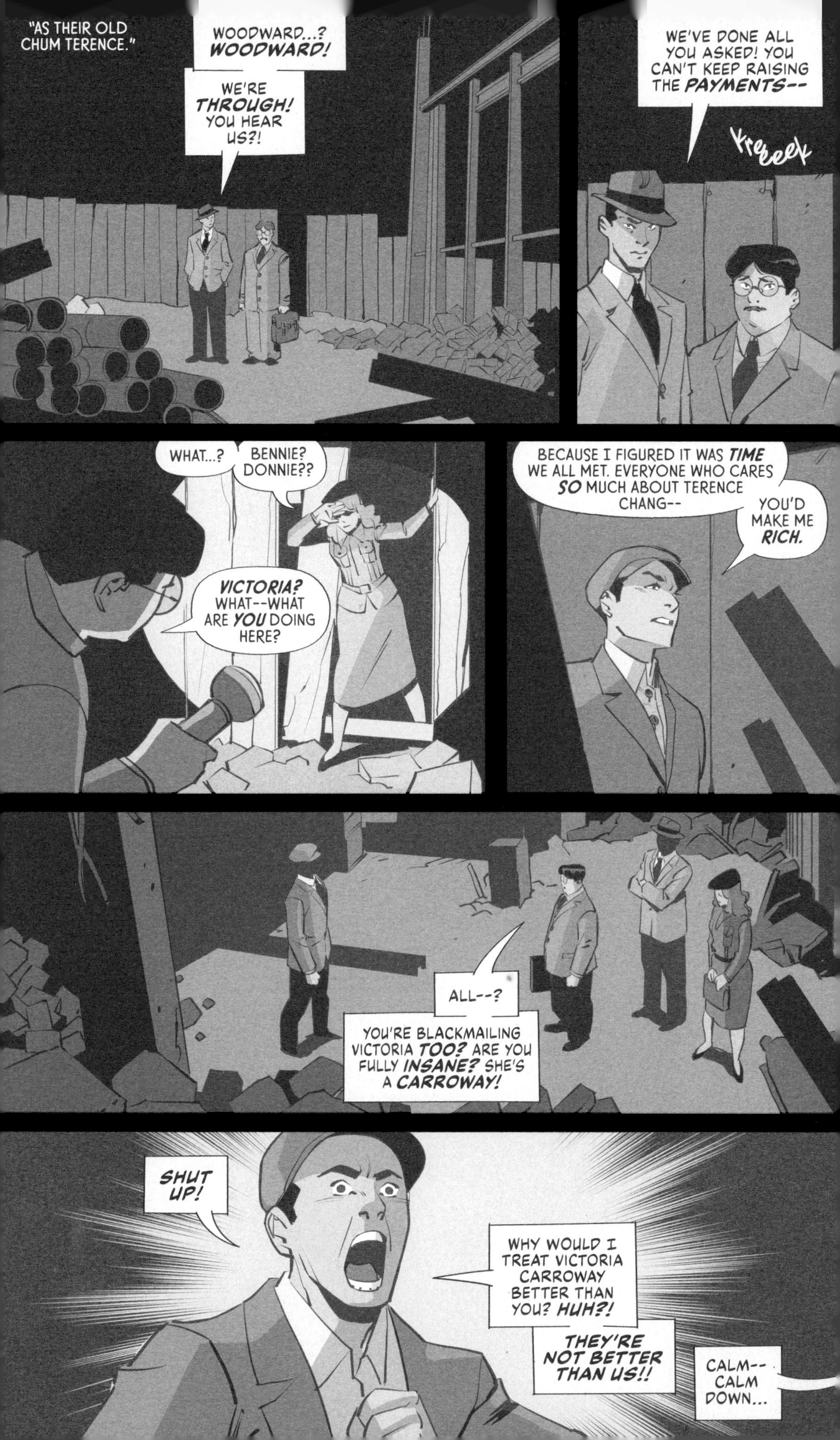

"AS THEIR OLD CHUM TERENCE."
WOODWARD...? WOODWARD!
WE'RE THROUGH! YOU HEAR US?!
WE'VE DONE ALL YOU ASKED! YOU CAN'T KEEP RAISING THE PAYMENTS--
KREEEEK
WHAT...?
BENNIE? DONNIE??
VICTORIA? WHAT--WHAT ARE YOU DOING HERE?
BECAUSE I FIGURED IT WAS TIME WE ALL MET. EVERYONE WHO CARES SO MUCH ABOUT TERENCE CHANG--
YOU'D MAKE ME RICH.
ALL--?
YOU'RE BLACKMAILING VICTORIA TOO? ARE YOU FULLY INSANE? SHE'S A CARROWAY!
SHUT UP!
WHY WOULD I TREAT VICTORIA CARROWAY BETTER THAN YOU? HUH?!
THEY'RE NOT BETTER THAN US!!
CALM-- CALM DOWN...

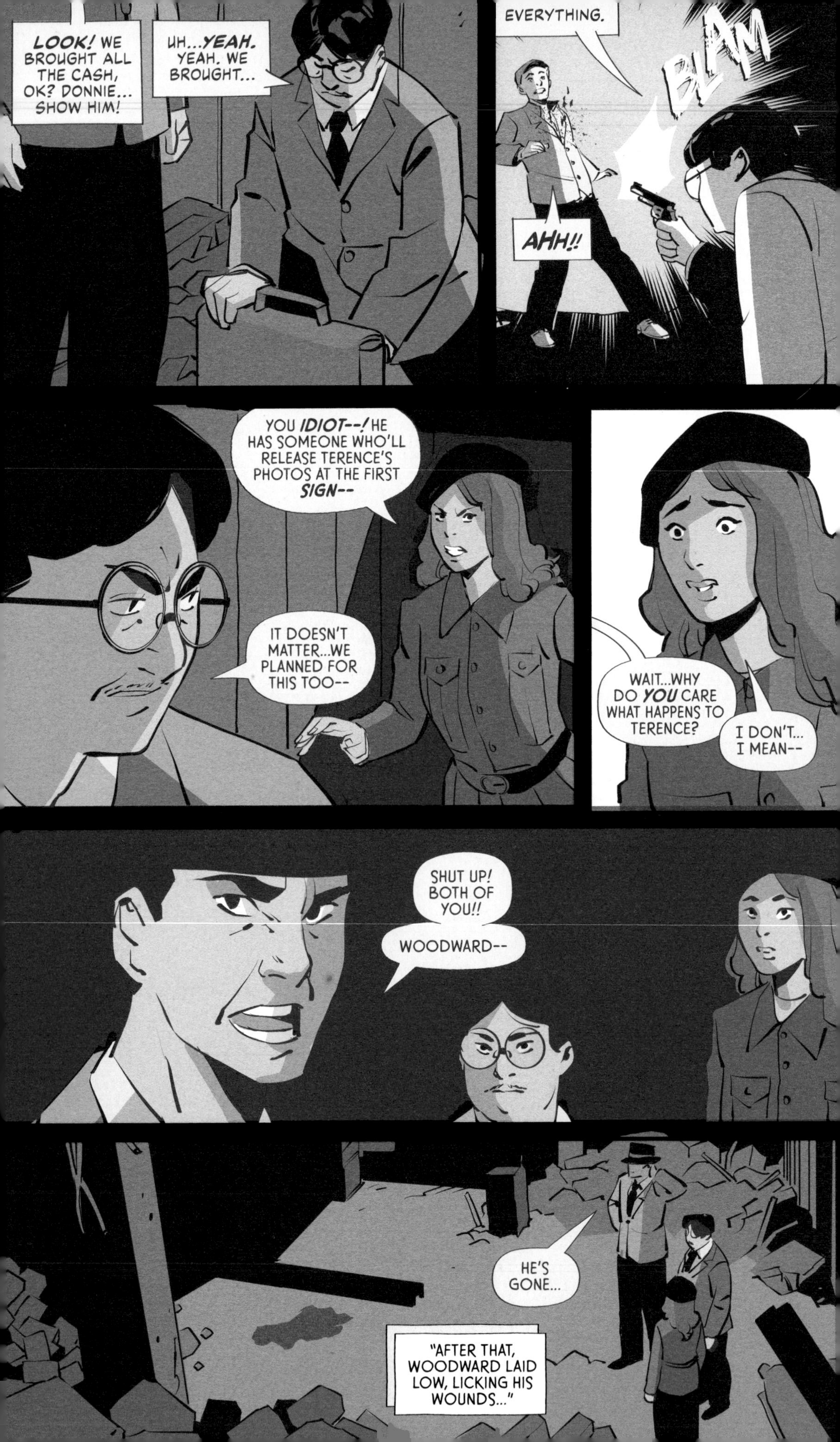
LOOK! WE BROUGHT ALL THE CASH, OK? DONNIE... SHOW HIM!
UH...YEAH. YEAH. WE BROUGHT...
EVERYTHING.
BLAM
AHH!!
YOU IDIOT--! HE HAS SOMEONE WHO'LL RELEASE TERENCE'S PHOTOS AT THE FIRST SIGN--
IT DOESN'T MATTER...WE PLANNED FOR THIS TOO--
WAIT...WHY DO YOU CARE WHAT HAPPENS TO TERENCE?
I DON'T... I MEAN--
SHUT UP! BOTH OF YOU!!
WOODWARD--
HE'S GONE...
"AFTER THAT, WOODWARD LAID LOW, LICKING HIS WOUNDS..."

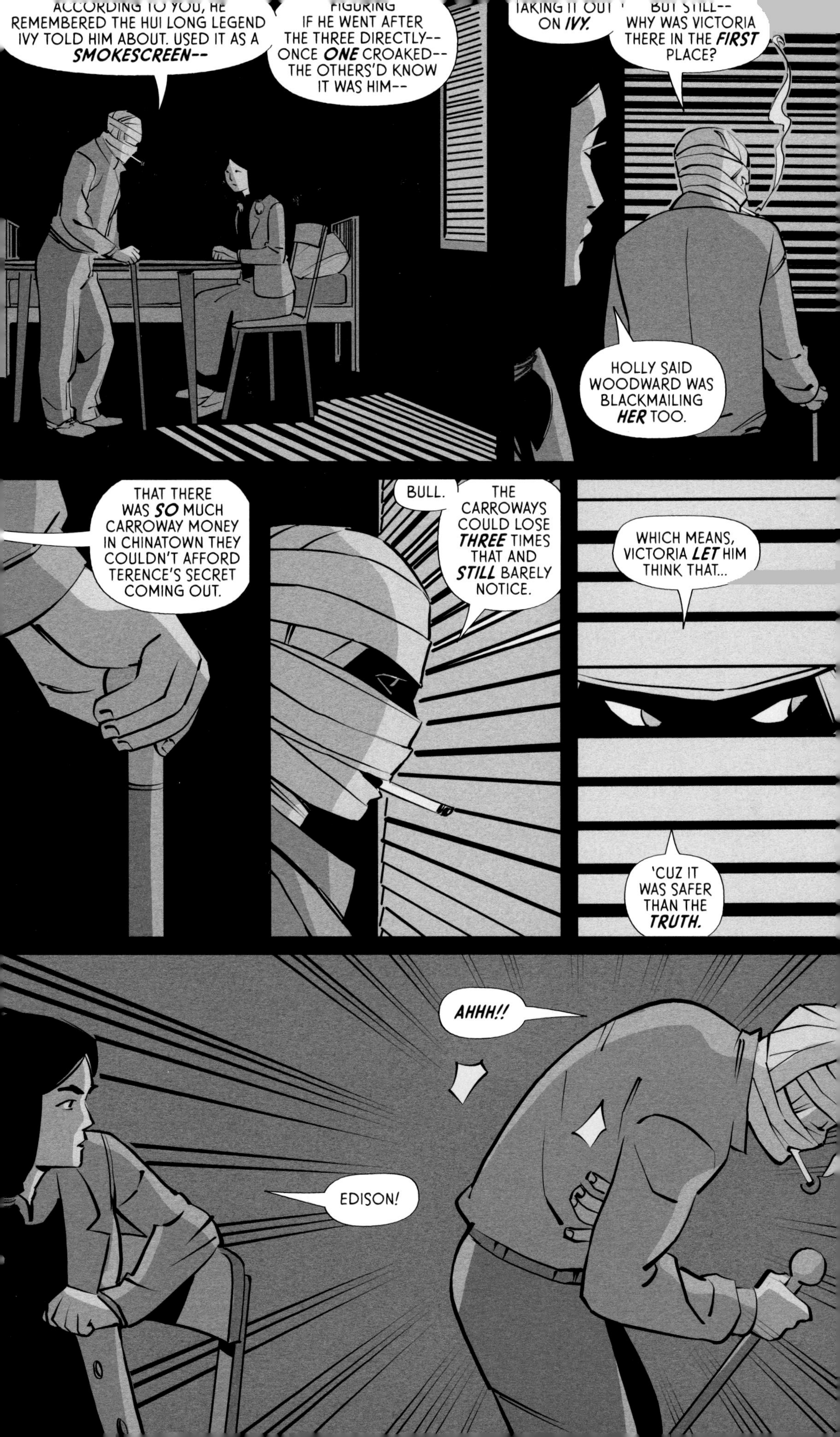
ACCORDING TO YOU, HE REMEMBERED THE HUI LONG LEGEND IVY TOLD HIM ABOUT. USED IT AS A *SMOKESCREEN--*
FIGURING IF HE WENT AFTER THE THREE DIRECTLY-- ONCE *ONE* CROAKED-- THE OTHERS'D KNOW IT WAS HIM--
TAKING IT OUT ON *IVY.*
BUT STILL-- WHY WAS VICTORIA THERE IN THE *FIRST* PLACE?
HOLLY SAID WOODWARD WAS BLACKMAILING *HER* TOO.
THAT THERE WAS *SO* MUCH CARROWAY MONEY IN CHINATOWN THEY COULDN'T AFFORD TERENCE'S SECRET COMING OUT.
BULL.
THE CARROWAYS COULD LOSE *THREE* TIMES THAT AND *STILL* BARELY NOTICE.
WHICH MEANS, VICTORIA *LET* HIM THINK THAT...
'CUZ IT WAS SAFER THAN THE *TRUTH.*
AHHH!!
EDISON!

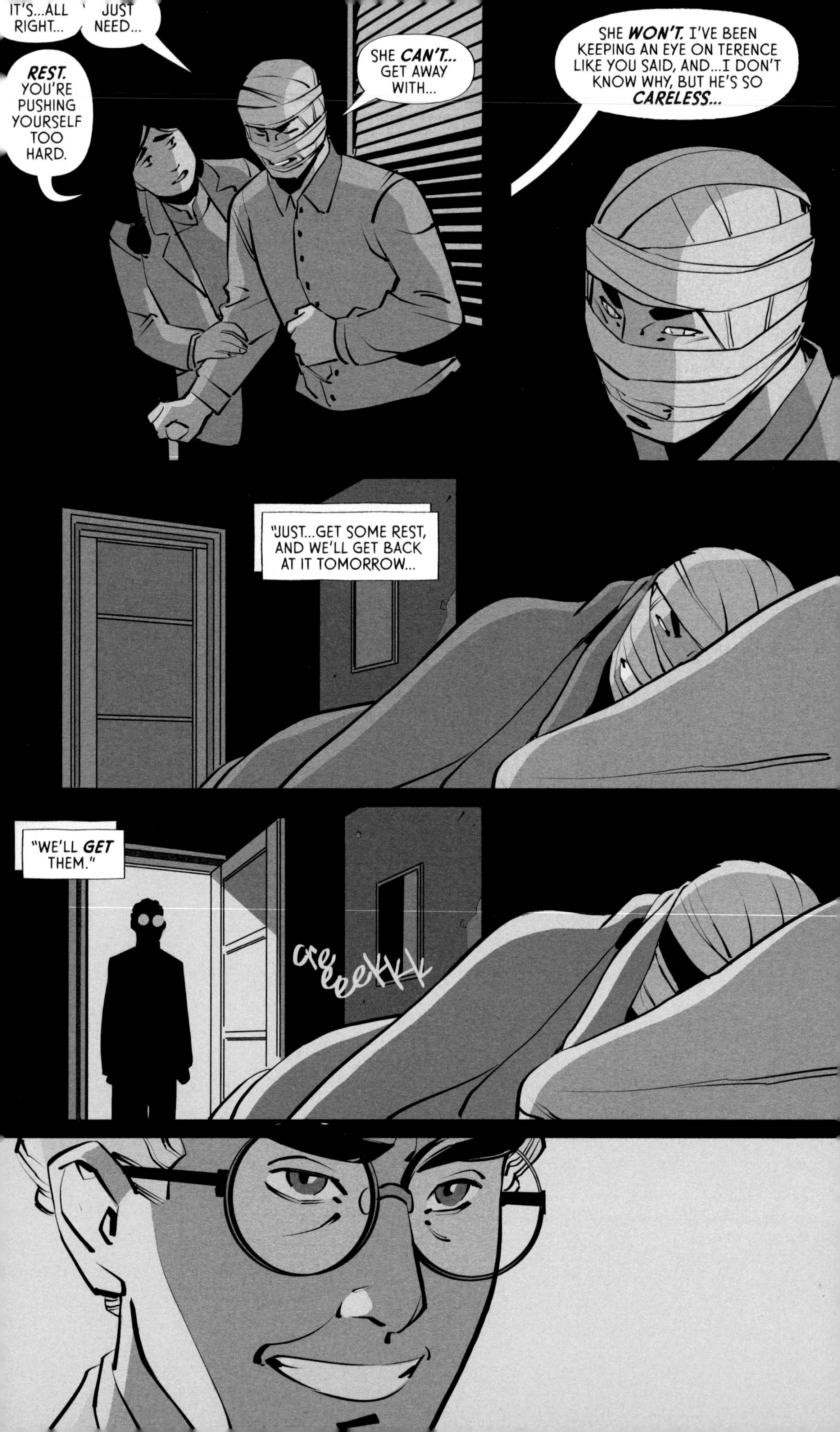
IT'S...ALL RIGHT...
JUST NEED...
REST. YOU'RE PUSHING YOURSELF TOO HARD.
SHE CAN'T... GET AWAY WITH...
SHE WON'T. I'VE BEEN KEEPING AN EYE ON TERENCE LIKE YOU SAID, AND...I DON'T KNOW WHY, BUT HE'S SO CARELESS...
"JUST...GET SOME REST, AND WE'LL GET BACK AT IT TOMORROW...
"WE'LL GET THEM."
CREEEKKK

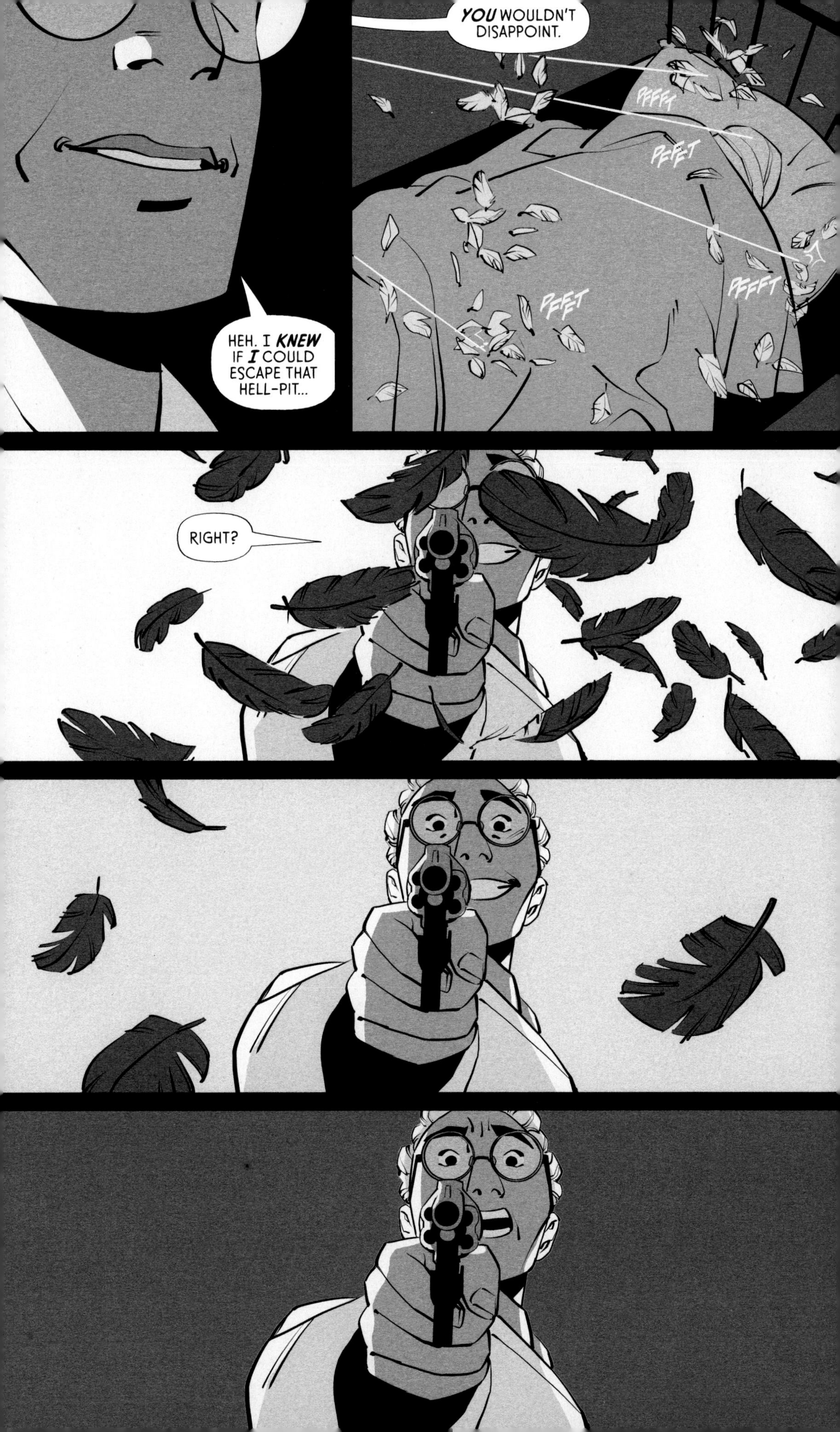
HEH. I KNEW IF I COULD ESCAPE THAT HELL-PIT...
YOU WOULDN'T DISAPPOINT.
PFFFT
PFFFT
PFFFT
PFFFT
RIGHT?

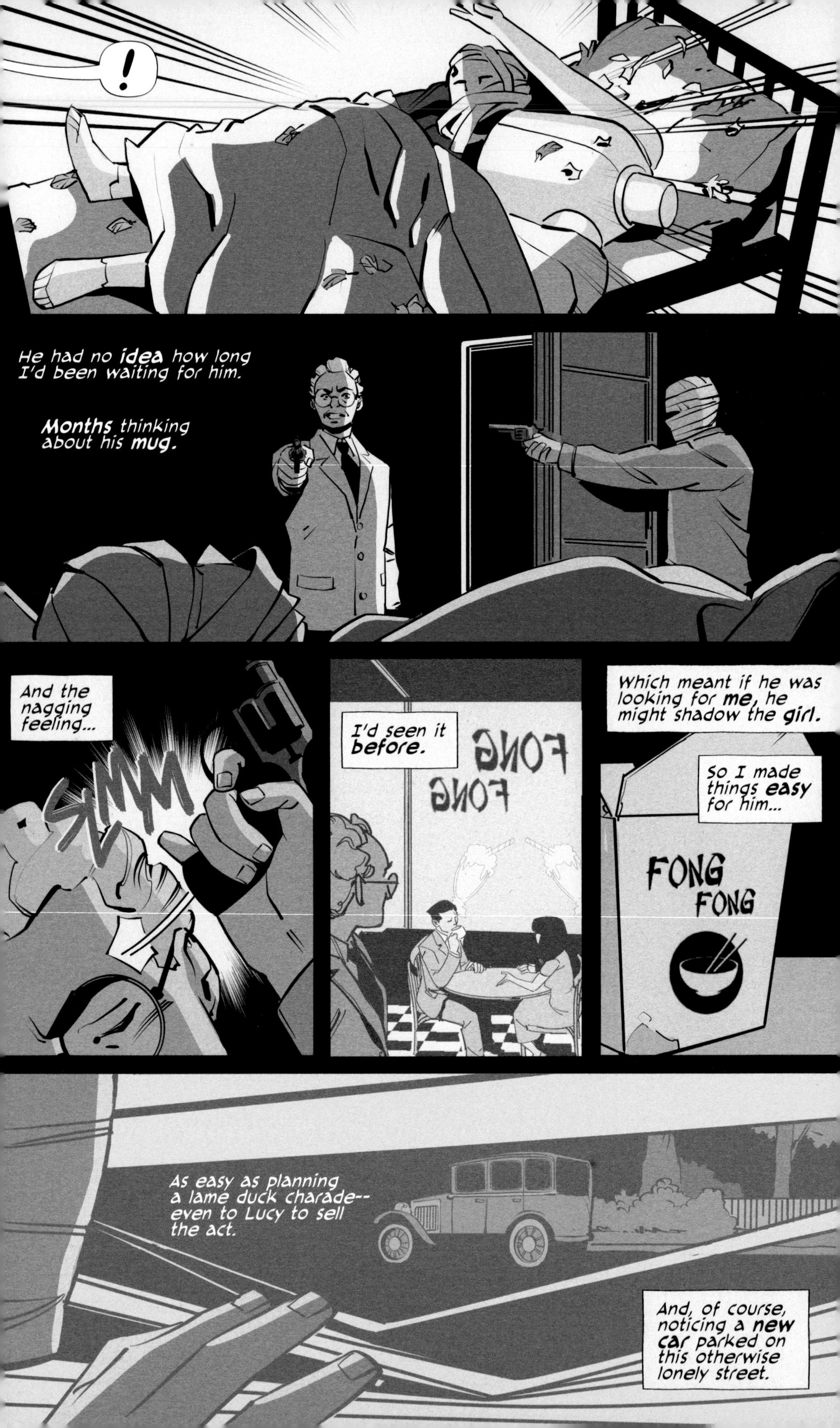
!
He had no idea how long I'd been waiting for him.
Months thinking about his mug.
And the nagging feeling...
SMMM
I'd seen it before.
FONG FONG
FONG FONG
Which meant if he was looking for me, he might shadow the girl.
So I made things easy for him...
FONG FONG
As easy as planning a lame duck charade-- even to Lucy to sell the act.
And, of course, noticing a new car parked on this otherwise lonely street.

AHH!!

BLAM

YOU GOT ME, OK? JUST...⋛AH⋚ GET THAT OUT OF MY FACE...

I'LL--I'LL TELL YOU WHAT YOU WANT TO KNOW.

THAT'S...WHY YOU *LURED* ME HERE, RIGHT?

RIGHT?

TALK--

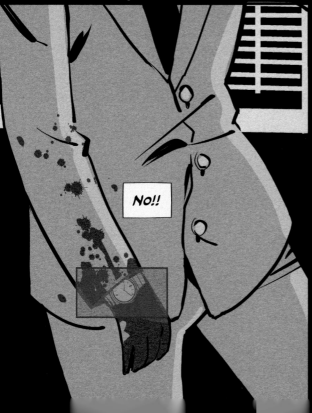

NO!!

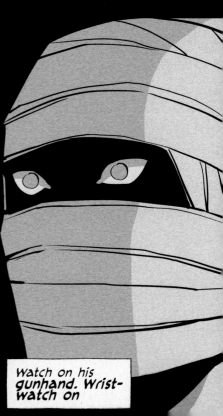

Watch on his *gunhand.* Wrist-watch on

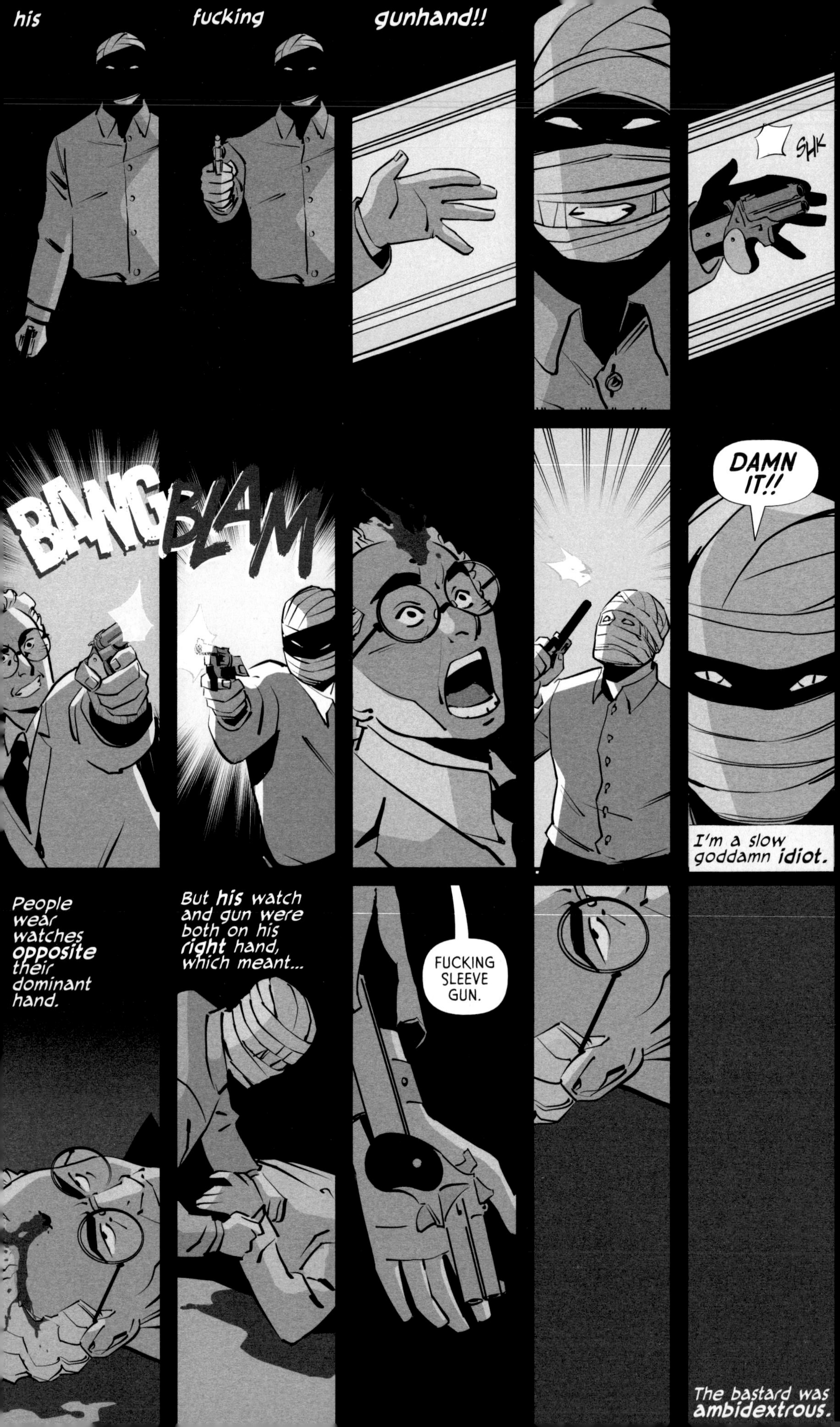
his
fucking
gunhand!!
SHK
BANG
BLAM
DAMN IT!!
I'm a slow goddamn idiot.
People wear watches opposite their dominant hand.
But his watch and gun were both on his right hand, which meant...
FUCKING SLEEVE GUN.
The bastard was ambidextrous.

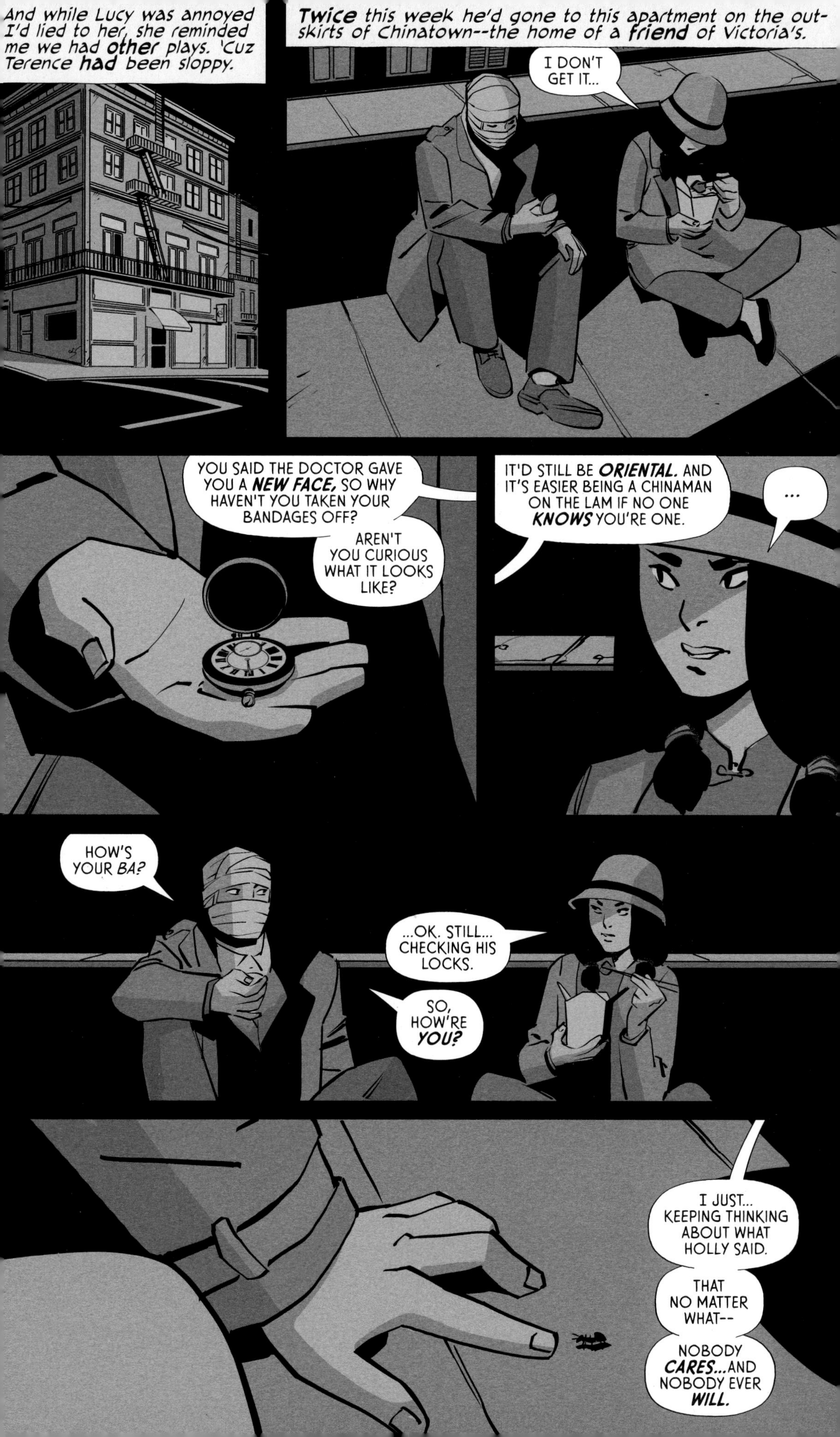

And while Lucy was annoyed I'd lied to her, she reminded me we had **other** plays. 'Cuz Terence **had** been sloppy.
Twice this week he'd gone to this apartment on the outskirts of Chinatown--the home of a **friend** of Victoria's.
I DON'T GET IT...
YOU SAID THE DOCTOR GAVE YOU A ***NEW FACE,*** SO WHY HAVEN'T YOU TAKEN YOUR BANDAGES OFF?
AREN'T YOU CURIOUS WHAT IT LOOKS LIKE?
IT'D STILL BE ***ORIENTAL.*** AND IT'S EASIER BEING A CHINAMAN ON THE LAM IF NO ONE ***KNOWS*** YOU'RE ONE.
...
HOW'S YOUR *BA?*
...OK. STILL... CHECKING HIS LOCKS.
SO, HOW'RE ***YOU?***
I JUST... KEEPING THINKING ABOUT WHAT HOLLY SAID.
THAT NO MATTER WHAT--
NOBODY ***CARES...*** AND NOBODY EVER ***WILL.***

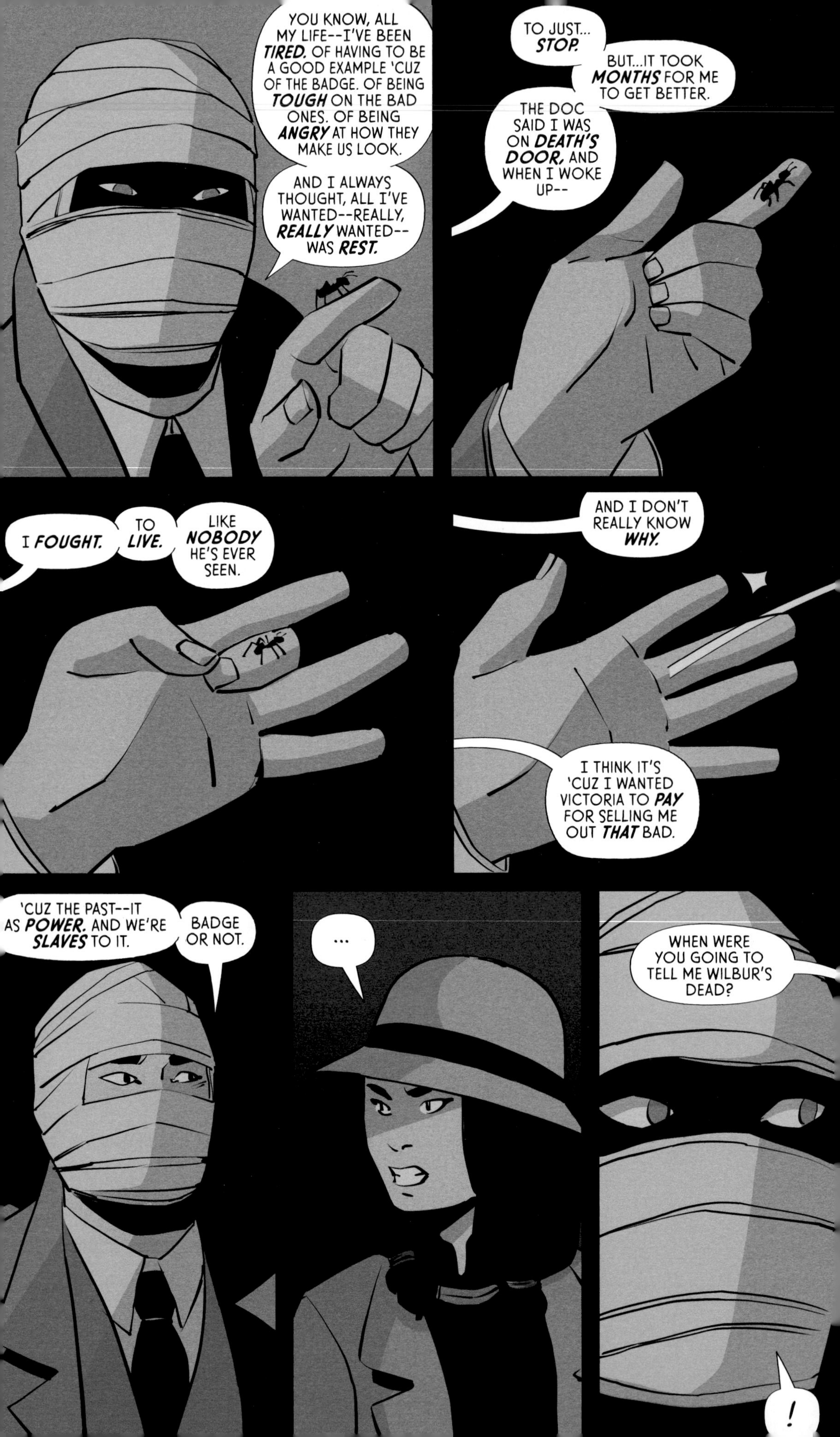
YOU KNOW, ALL MY LIFE--I'VE BEEN TIRED. OF HAVING TO BE A GOOD EXAMPLE 'CUZ OF THE BADGE. OF BEING TOUGH ON THE BAD ONES. OF BEING ANGRY AT HOW THEY MAKE US LOOK.
AND I ALWAYS THOUGHT, ALL I'VE WANTED--REALLY, REALLY WANTED--WAS REST.
TO JUST... STOP.
BUT...IT TOOK MONTHS FOR ME TO GET BETTER.
THE DOC SAID I WAS ON DEATH'S DOOR, AND WHEN I WOKE UP--
I FOUGHT.
TO LIVE.
LIKE NOBODY HE'S EVER SEEN.
AND I DON'T REALLY KNOW WHY.
I THINK IT'S 'CUZ I WANTED VICTORIA TO PAY FOR SELLING ME OUT THAT BAD.
'CUZ THE PAST--IT AS POWER. AND WE'RE SLAVES TO IT.
BADGE OR NOT.
...
WHEN WERE YOU GOING TO TELL ME WILBUR'S DEAD?
!

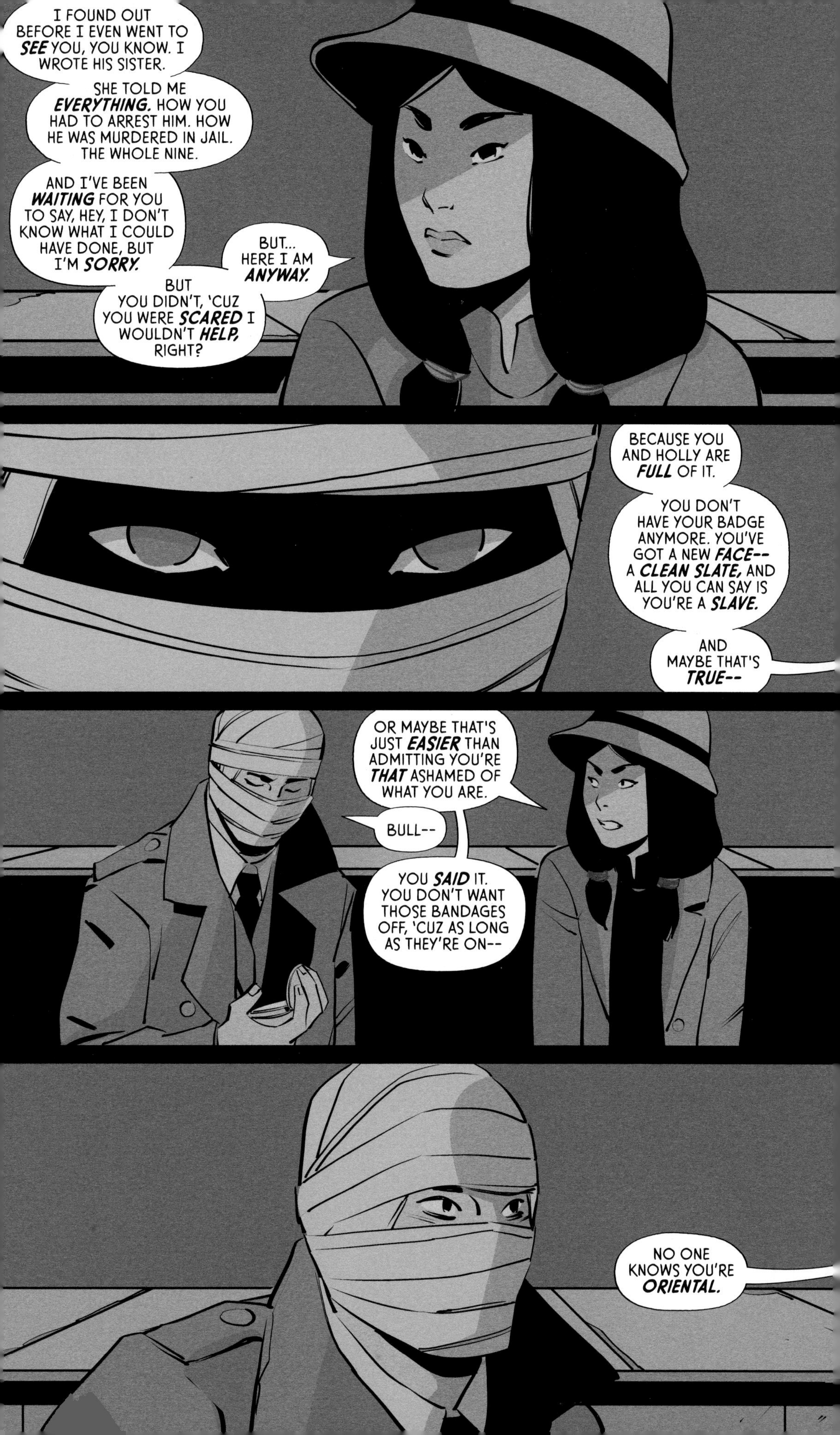
I FOUND OUT BEFORE I EVEN WENT TO SEE YOU, YOU KNOW. I WROTE HIS SISTER.
SHE TOLD ME EVERYTHING. HOW YOU HAD TO ARREST HIM. HOW HE WAS MURDERED IN JAIL. THE WHOLE NINE.
AND I'VE BEEN WAITING FOR YOU TO SAY, HEY, I DON'T KNOW WHAT I COULD HAVE DONE, BUT I'M SORRY.
BUT YOU DIDN'T, 'CUZ YOU WERE SCARED I WOULDN'T HELP, RIGHT?
BUT... HERE I AM ANYWAY.
BECAUSE YOU AND HOLLY ARE FULL OF IT.
YOU DON'T HAVE YOUR BADGE ANYMORE. YOU'VE GOT A NEW FACE-- A CLEAN SLATE, AND ALL YOU CAN SAY IS YOU'RE A SLAVE.
AND MAYBE THAT'S TRUE--
OR MAYBE THAT'S JUST EASIER THAN ADMITTING YOU'RE THAT ASHAMED OF WHAT YOU ARE.
BULL--
YOU SAID IT. YOU DON'T WANT THOSE BANDAGES OFF, 'CUZ AS LONG AS THEY'RE ON--
NO ONE KNOWS YOU'RE ORIENTAL.

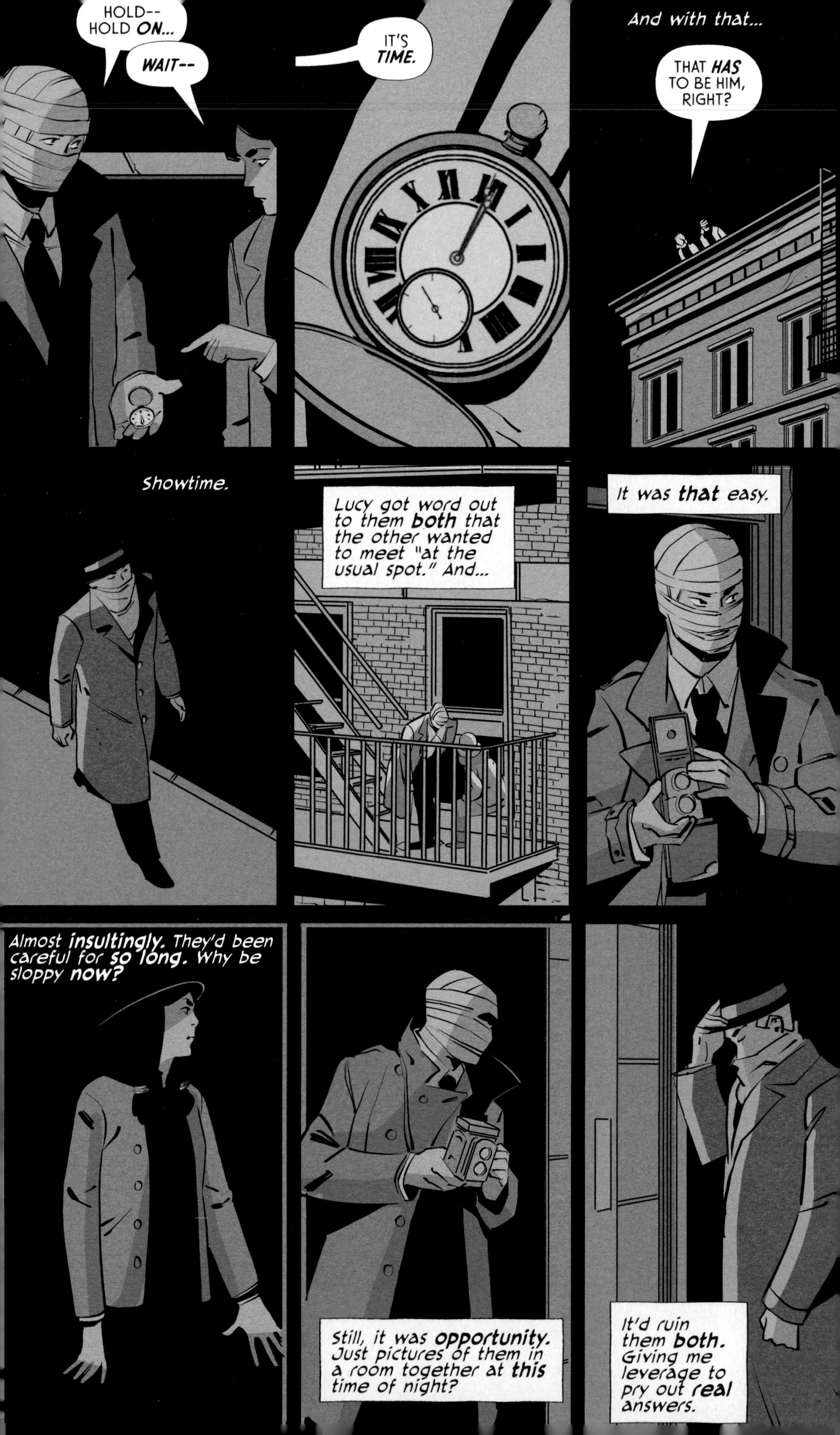
HOLD--
HOLD ON...
WAIT--
IT'S TIME.
And with that...
THAT HAS TO BE HIM, RIGHT?
Showtime.
Lucy got word out to them both that the other wanted to meet "at the usual spot." And...
It was that easy.
Almost insultingly. They'd been careful for so long. Why be sloppy now?
Still, it was opportunity. Just pictures of them in a room together at this time of night?
It'd ruin them both. Giving me leverage to pry out real answers.

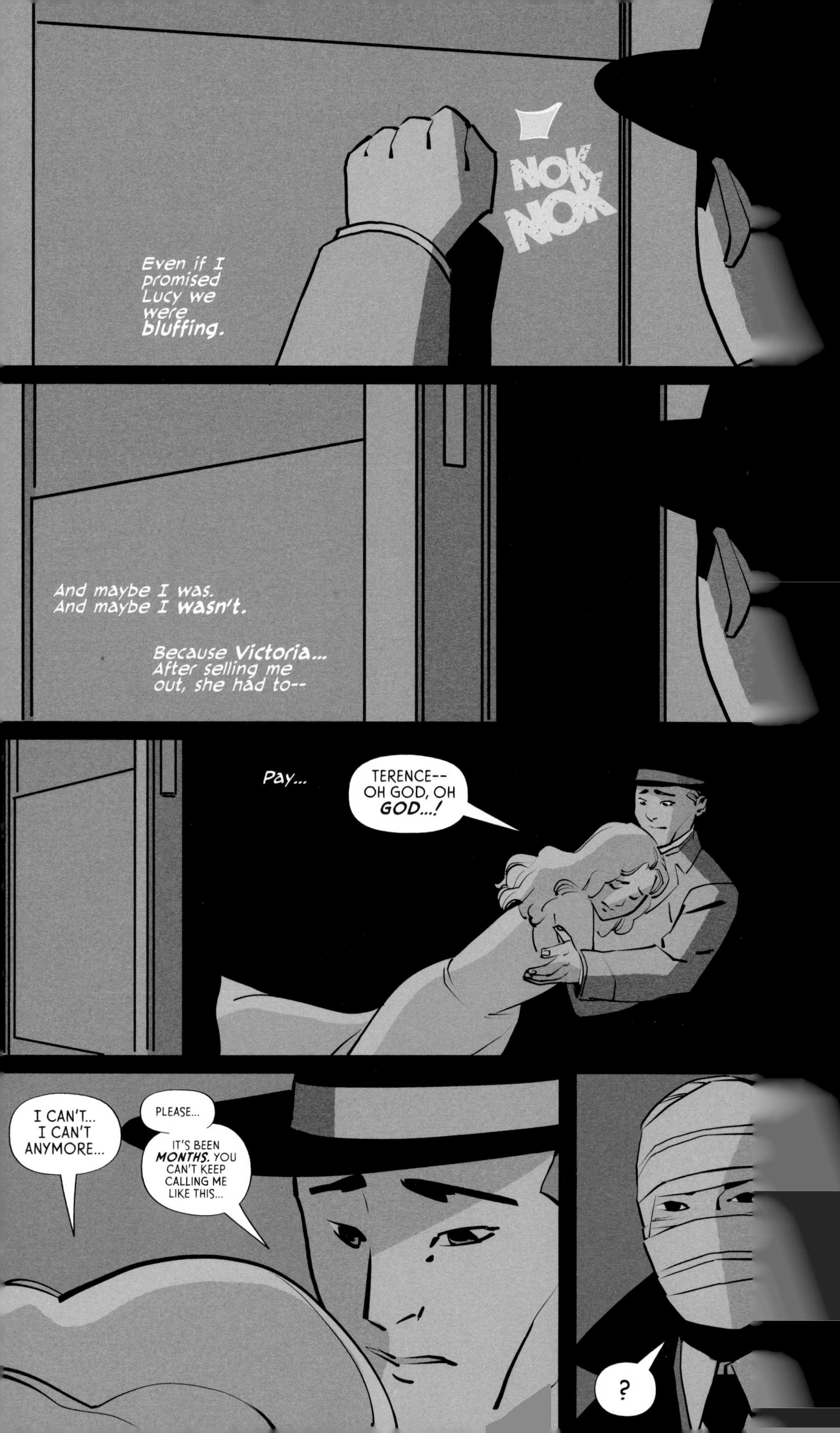
NOK NOK
Even if I promised Lucy we were bluffing.
And maybe I was. And maybe I wasn't.
Because Victoria... After selling me out, she had to--
Pay...
TERENCE-- OH GOD, OH GOD...!
I CAN'T... I CAN'T ANYMORE...
PLEASE...
IT'S BEEN MONTHS. YOU CAN'T KEEP CALLING ME LIKE THIS...
?

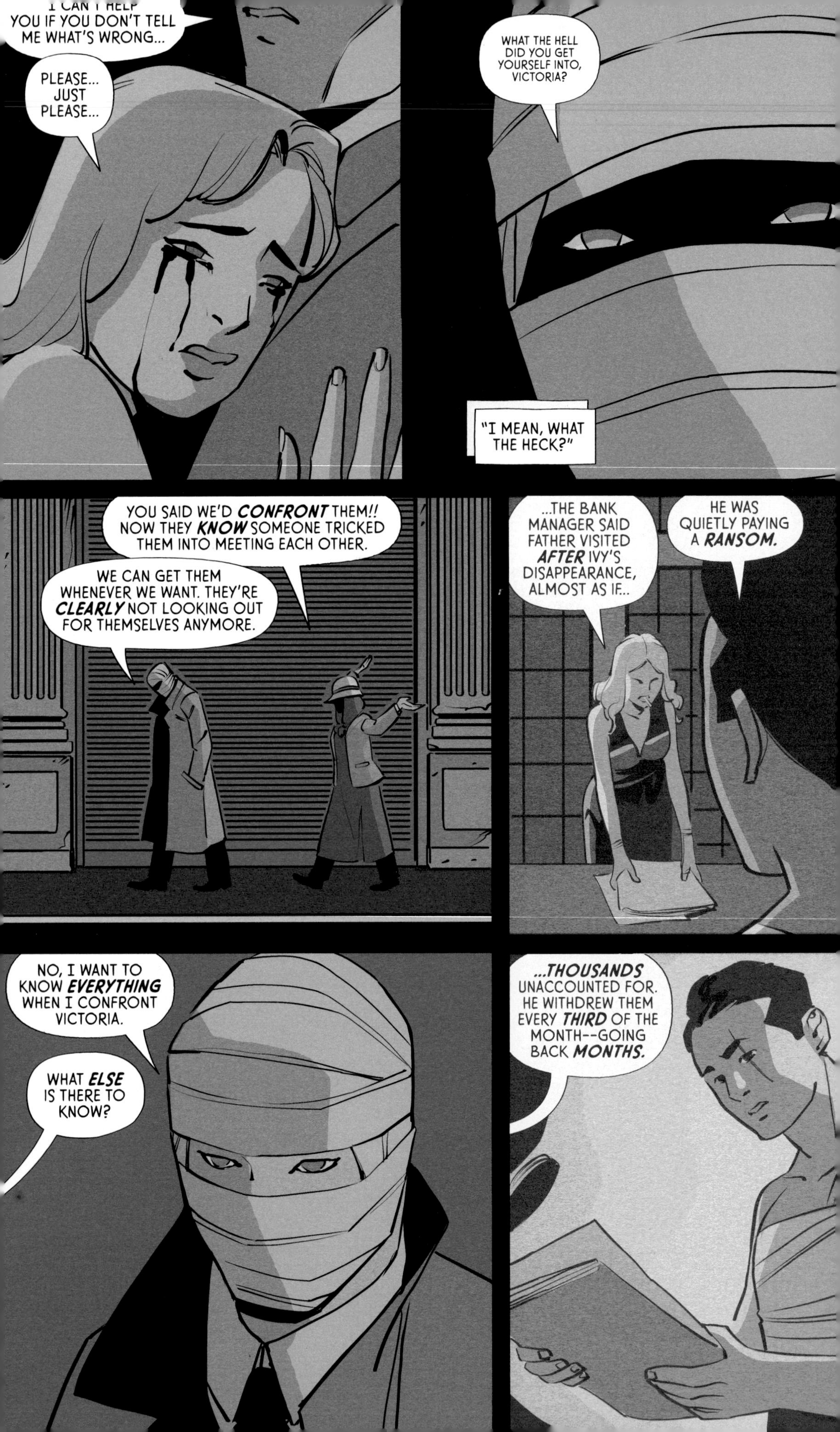
I CAN'T HELP YOU IF YOU DON'T TELL ME WHAT'S WRONG...
PLEASE... JUST PLEASE...
WHAT THE HELL DID YOU GET YOURSELF INTO, VICTORIA?
"I MEAN, WHAT THE HECK?"
YOU SAID WE'D CONFRONT THEM!! NOW THEY KNOW SOMEONE TRICKED THEM INTO MEETING EACH OTHER.
WE CAN GET THEM WHENEVER WE WANT. THEY'RE CLEARLY NOT LOOKING OUT FOR THEMSELVES ANYMORE.
...THE BANK MANAGER SAID FATHER VISITED AFTER IVY'S DISAPPEARANCE, ALMOST AS IF...
HE WAS QUIETLY PAYING A RANSOM.
NO, I WANT TO KNOW EVERYTHING WHEN I CONFRONT VICTORIA.
WHAT ELSE IS THERE TO KNOW?
...THOUSANDS UNACCOUNTED FOR. HE WITHDREW THEM EVERY THIRD OF THE MONTH--GOING BACK MONTHS.

IN A FEW DAYS, IT'LL BE THE *THIRD* OF THE MONTH.

AND LAST WE TALKED, VICTORIA WAS CONCERNED ABOUT MASON'S *REGULAR WITHDRAWALS* FROM THE FAMILY SAFETY DEPOSIT BOX *EVERY* THIRD OF THE MONTH.

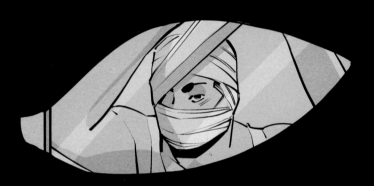

SHE WAS WORRIED HE WAS BEING *BLACKMAILED.*

NOW, SHE *COULD* HAVE SAID ALL THAT TO THROW ME OFF, BUT THEN WHY PULL OUT *ACTUAL* BOOKS TO SHOW ME?

UNLESS... SHE REALLY *WANTED* MY HELP, BECAUSE IT WAS LEGITIMATELY *VEXING* HER.

MAYBE SHE HADN'T DECIDED TO SELL ME OUT AT THAT POINT.

SO *WHAT?* WE'RE GOING TO STOP EVERYTHING JUST ON *THAT?*

AND...WHY EVERY *THIRD* OF THE MONTH? WHAT'S SO IMPORTANT ABOUT THE *THIRD?*

PLENTY, I'M SURE. BUT FOR *ME,* ON THE THIRD OF THE MONTH A LONG TIME AGO, A MAN NAMED *MICHAEL MARTINEZ...*

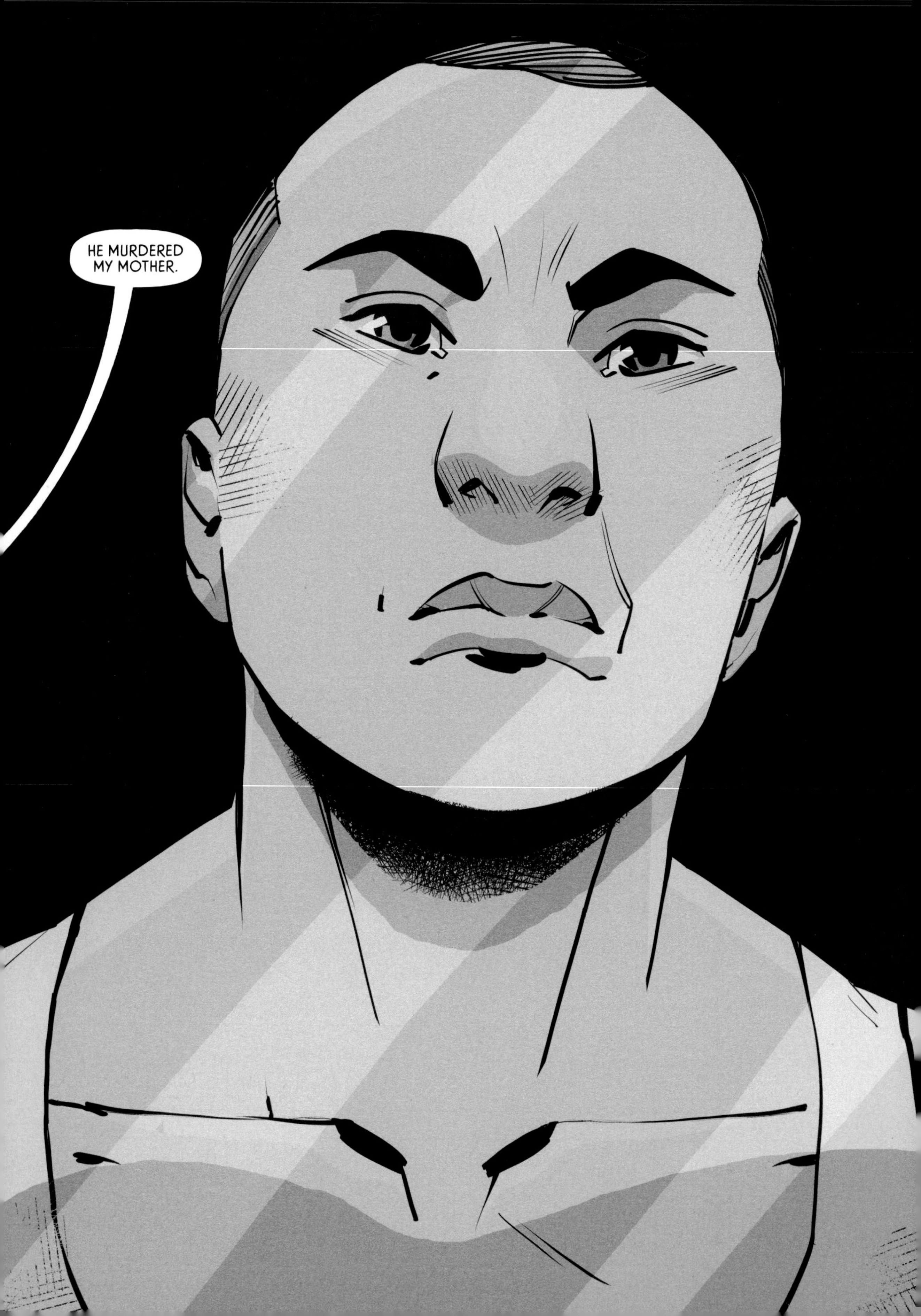
HE MURDERED MY MOTHER.

CHAPTER TEN

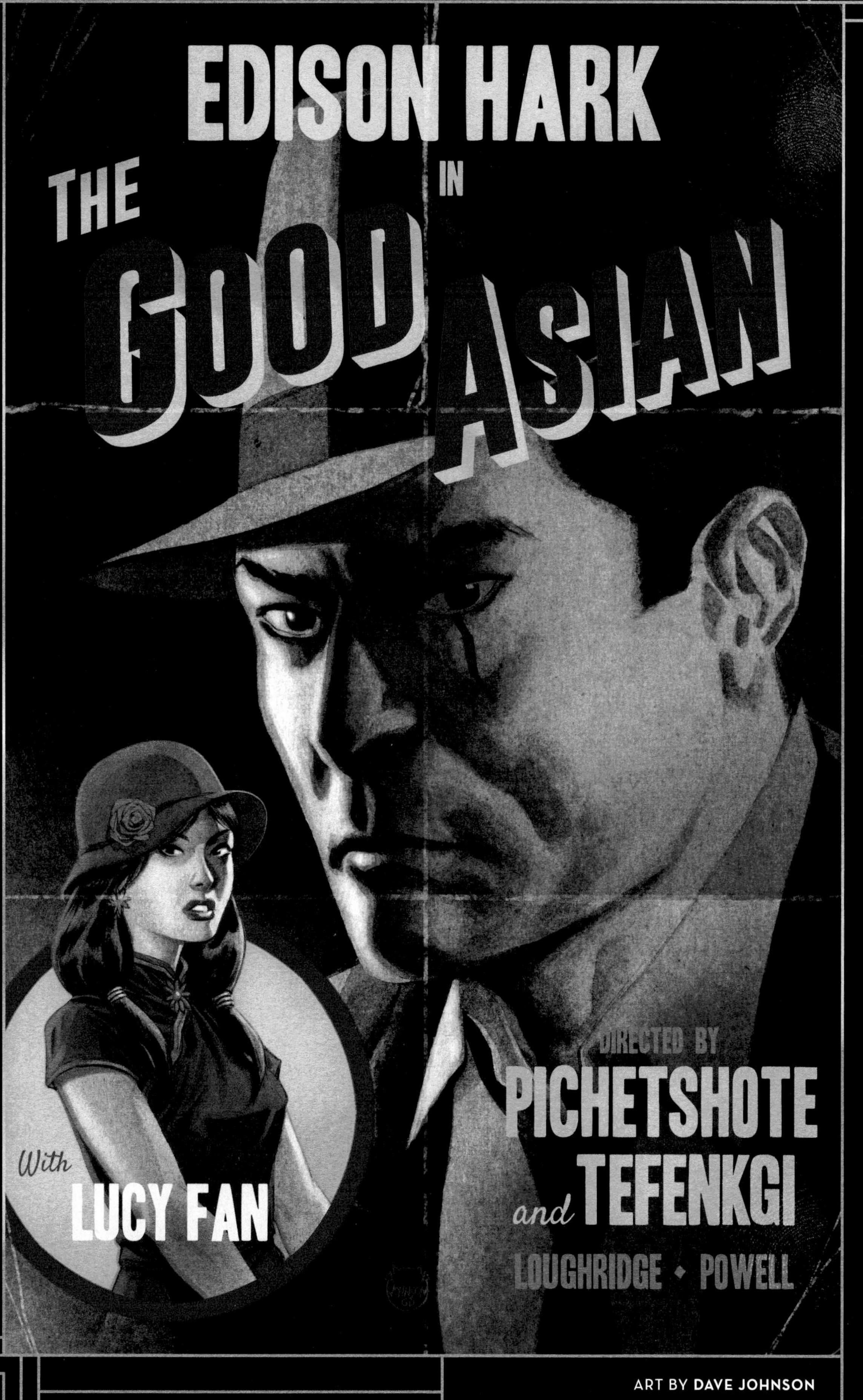

ART BY **DAVE JOHNSON**

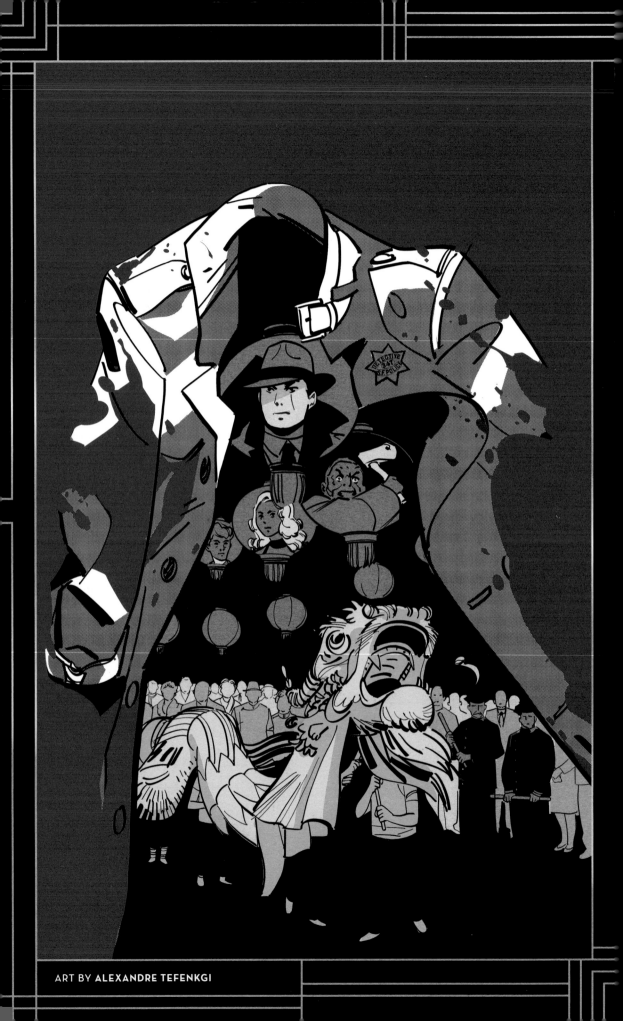

ART BY **ALEXANDRE TEFENKGI**

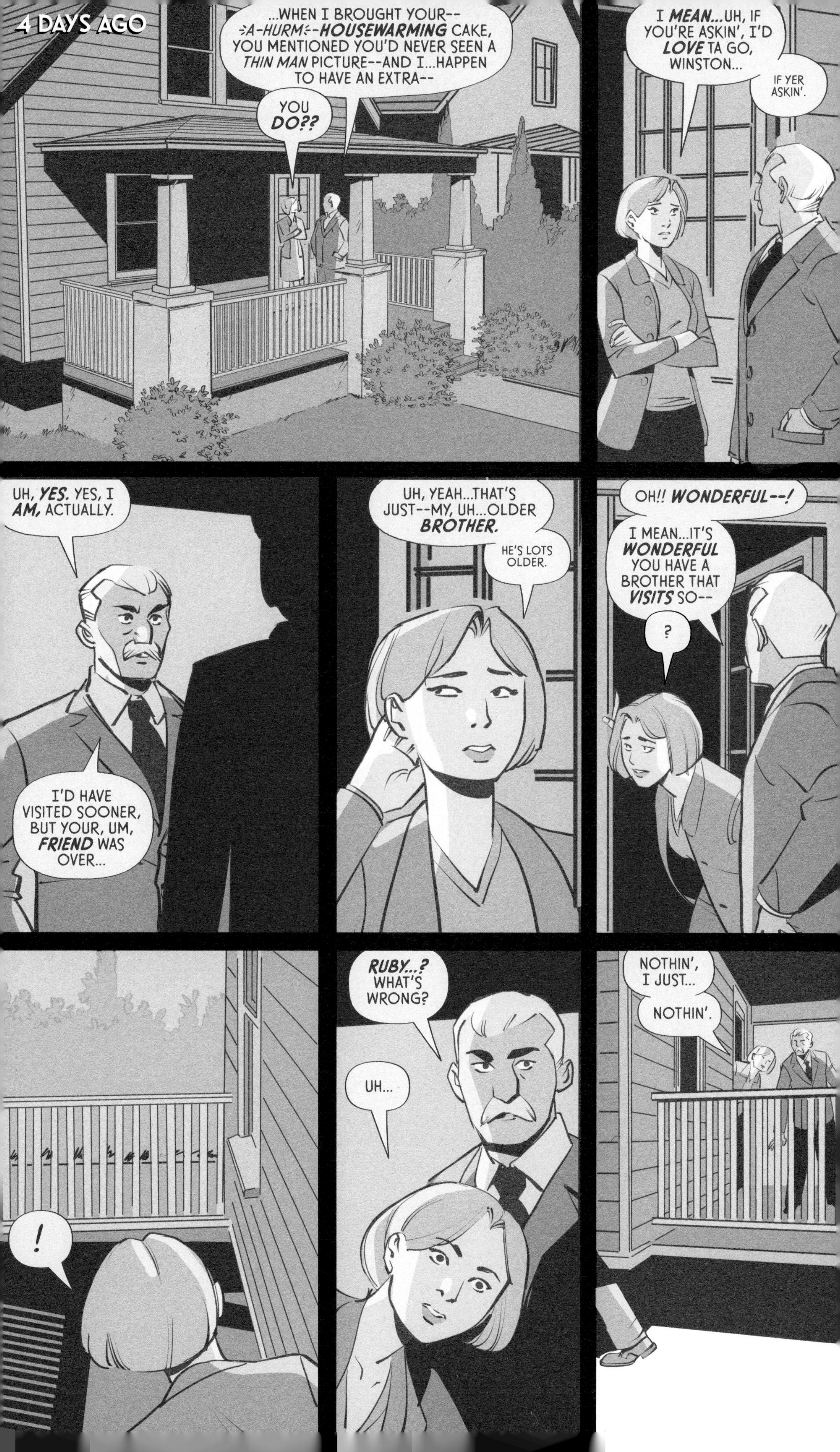
4 DAYS AGO
...WHEN I BROUGHT YOUR-- -A-HURM- -HOUSEWARMING CAKE, YOU MENTIONED YOU'D NEVER SEEN A THIN MAN PICTURE--AND I...HAPPEN TO HAVE AN EXTRA--
YOU DO??
I MEAN...UH, IF YOU'RE ASKIN', I'D LOVE TA GO, WINSTON...
IF YER ASKIN'.
UH, YES. YES, I AM, ACTUALLY.
I'D HAVE VISITED SOONER, BUT YOUR, UM, FRIEND WAS OVER...
UH, YEAH...THAT'S JUST--MY, UH...OLDER BROTHER.
HE'S LOTS OLDER.
OH!! WONDERFUL--!
I MEAN...IT'S WONDERFUL YOU HAVE A BROTHER THAT VISITS SO--
?
!
RUBY...? WHAT'S WRONG?
UH...
NOTHIN', I JUST...
NOTHIN'.

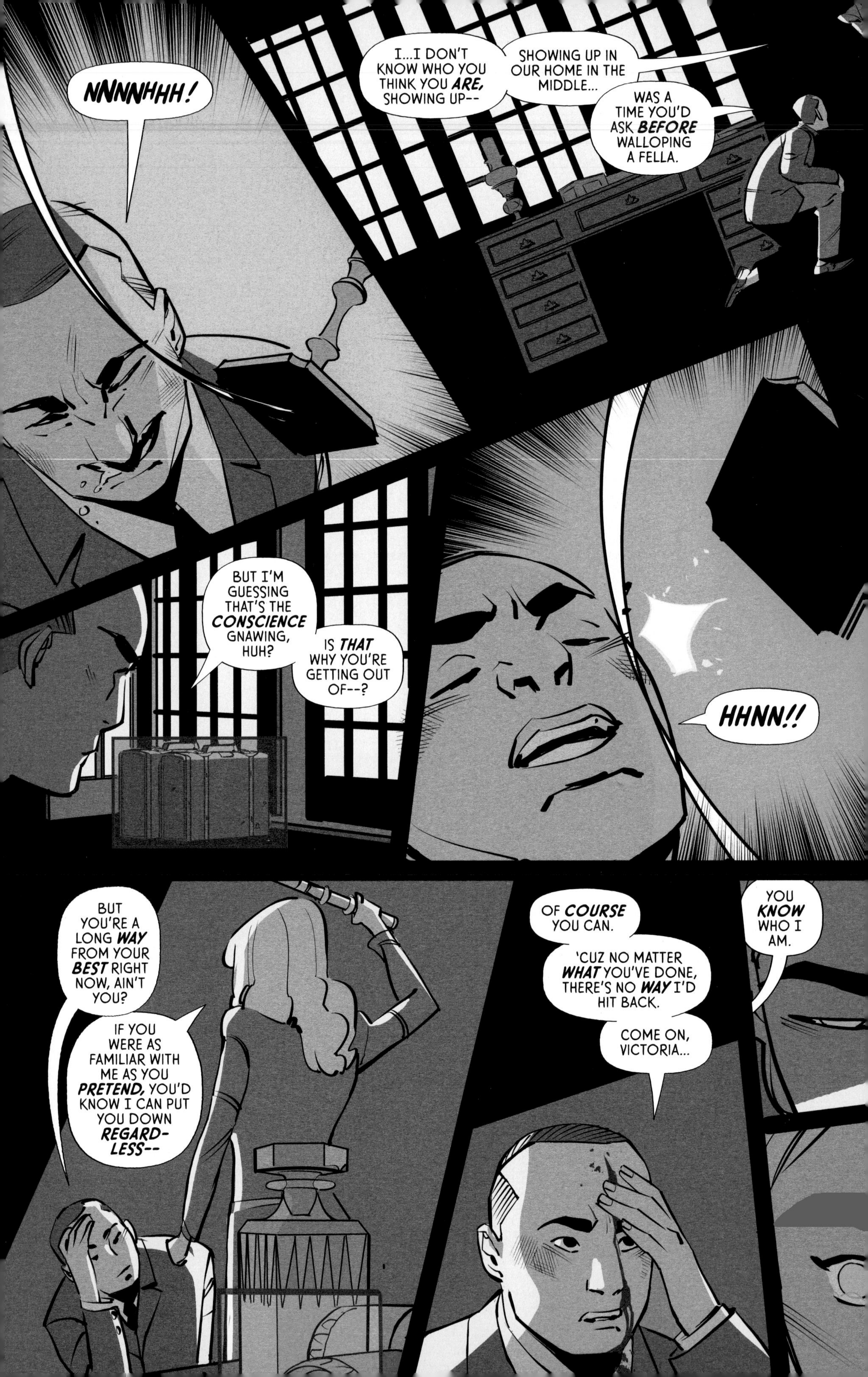
NNNNHHH!
I...I DON'T KNOW WHO YOU THINK YOU ARE, SHOWING UP--
SHOWING UP IN OUR HOME IN THE MIDDLE...
WAS A TIME YOU'D ASK BEFORE WALLOPING A FELLA.
BUT I'M GUESSING THAT'S THE CONSCIENCE GNAWING, HUH?
IS THAT WHY YOU'RE GETTING OUT OF--?
HHNN!!
BUT YOU'RE A LONG WAY FROM YOUR BEST RIGHT NOW, AIN'T YOU?
IF YOU WERE AS FAMILIAR WITH ME AS YOU PRETEND, YOU'D KNOW I CAN PUT YOU DOWN REGARDLESS--
OF COURSE YOU CAN.
'CUZ NO MATTER WHAT YOU'VE DONE, THERE'S NO WAY I'D HIT BACK.
COME ON, VICTORIA...
YOU KNOW WHO I AM.

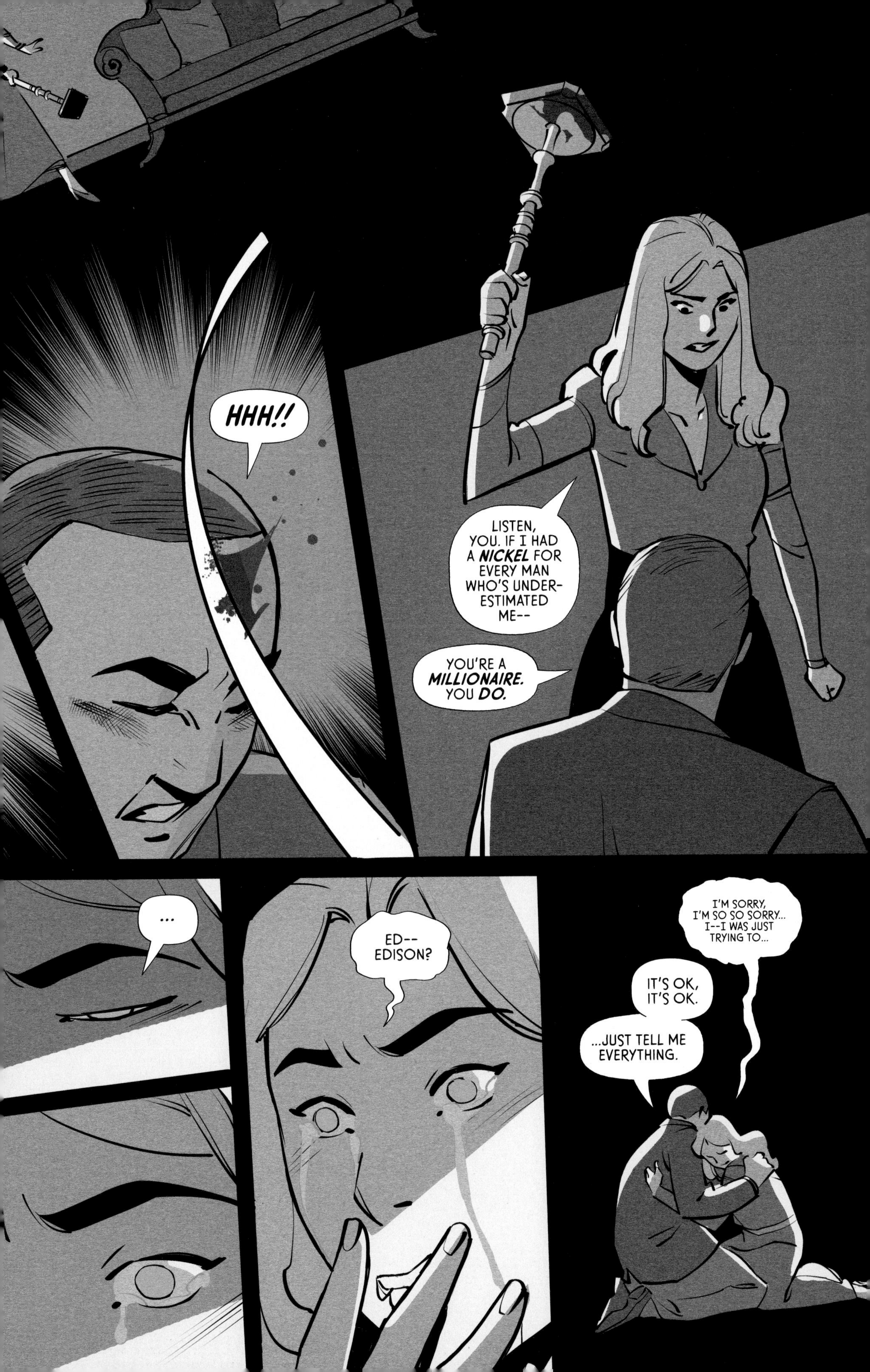
HHH!!
LISTEN, YOU. IF I HAD A NICKEL FOR EVERY MAN WHO'S UNDER-ESTIMATED ME--
YOU'RE A MILLIONAIRE. YOU DO.
...
ED-- EDISON?
I'M SORRY, I'M SO SO SORRY... I--I WAS JUST TRYING TO...
IT'S OK, IT'S OK.
...JUST TELL ME EVERYTHING.

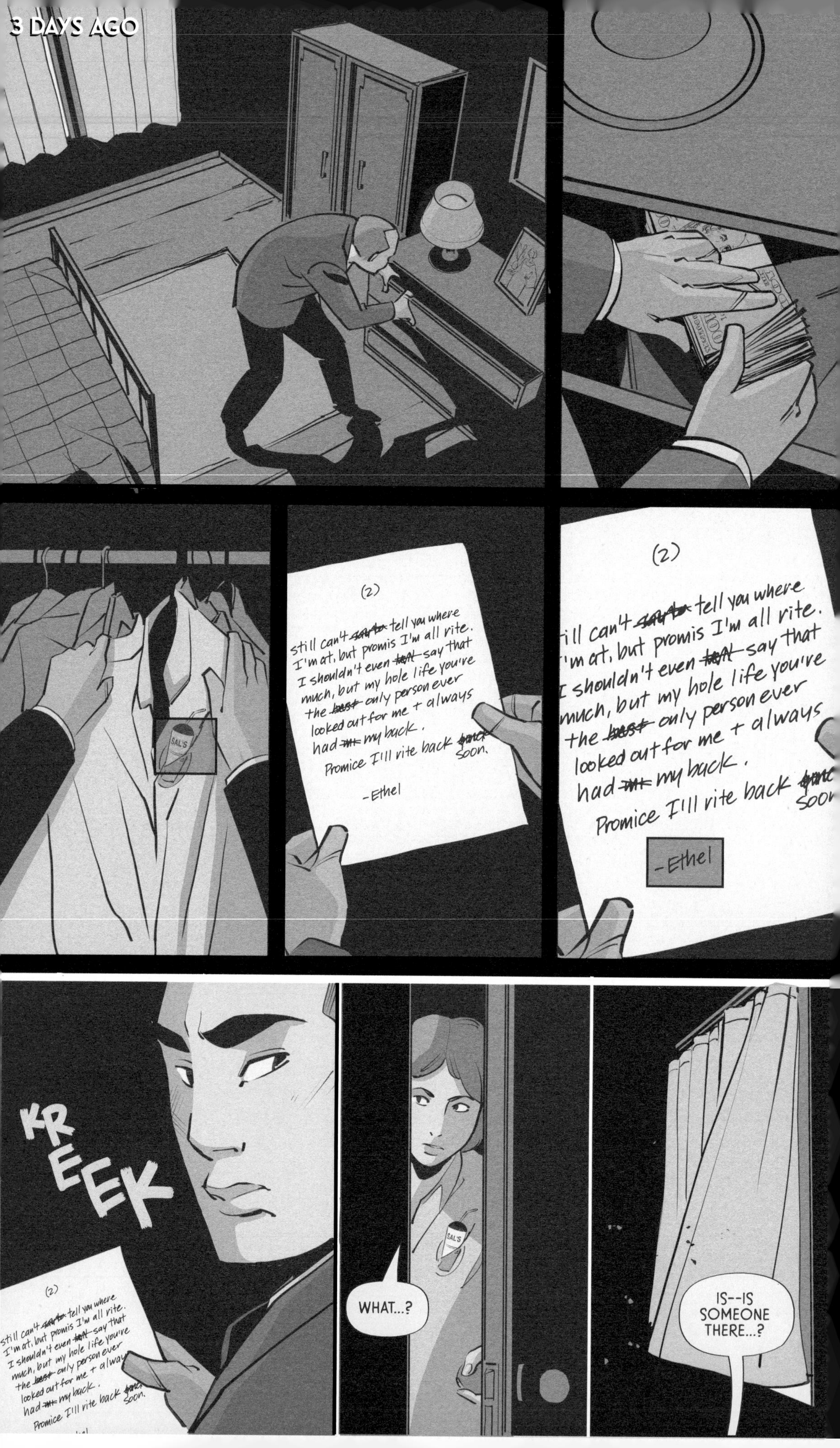
3 DAYS AGO
(2)
still can't tell you where I'm at, but promis I'm all rite. I shouldn't even say that much, but my hole life you're the only person ever looked out for me + always had my back. Promice I'll rite back soon.
-Ethel
KREEK
WHAT...?
IS--IS SOMEONE THERE...?

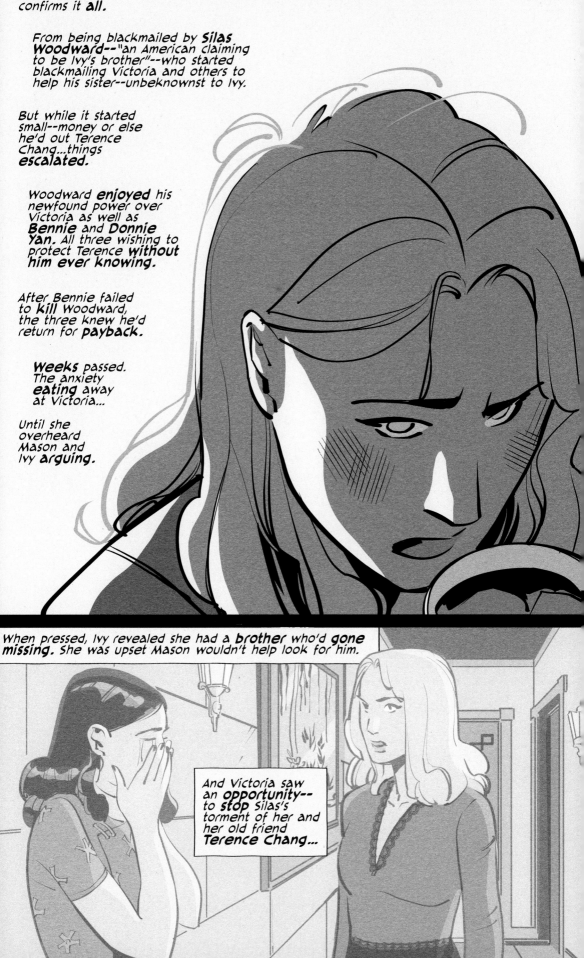

And Victoria confirms it **all**.

From being blackmailed by **Silas Woodward**--"an American claiming to be Ivy's brother"--who started blackmailing Victoria and others to help his sister--unbeknownst to Ivy.

But while it started small--money or else he'd out Terence Chang...things **escalated**.

Woodward **enjoyed** his newfound power over Victoria as well as **Bennie** and **Donnie Yan**. All three wishing to protect Terence **without him ever knowing**.

After Bennie failed to **kill** Woodward, the three knew he'd return for **payback**.

Weeks passed. The anxiety **eating** away at Victoria...

Until she overheard Mason and Ivy **arguing**.

When pressed, Ivy revealed she had a **brother** who'd **gone missing**. She was upset Mason wouldn't help look for him.

And Victoria saw an **opportunity**-- to **stop** Silas's torment of her and her old friend **Terence Chang**...

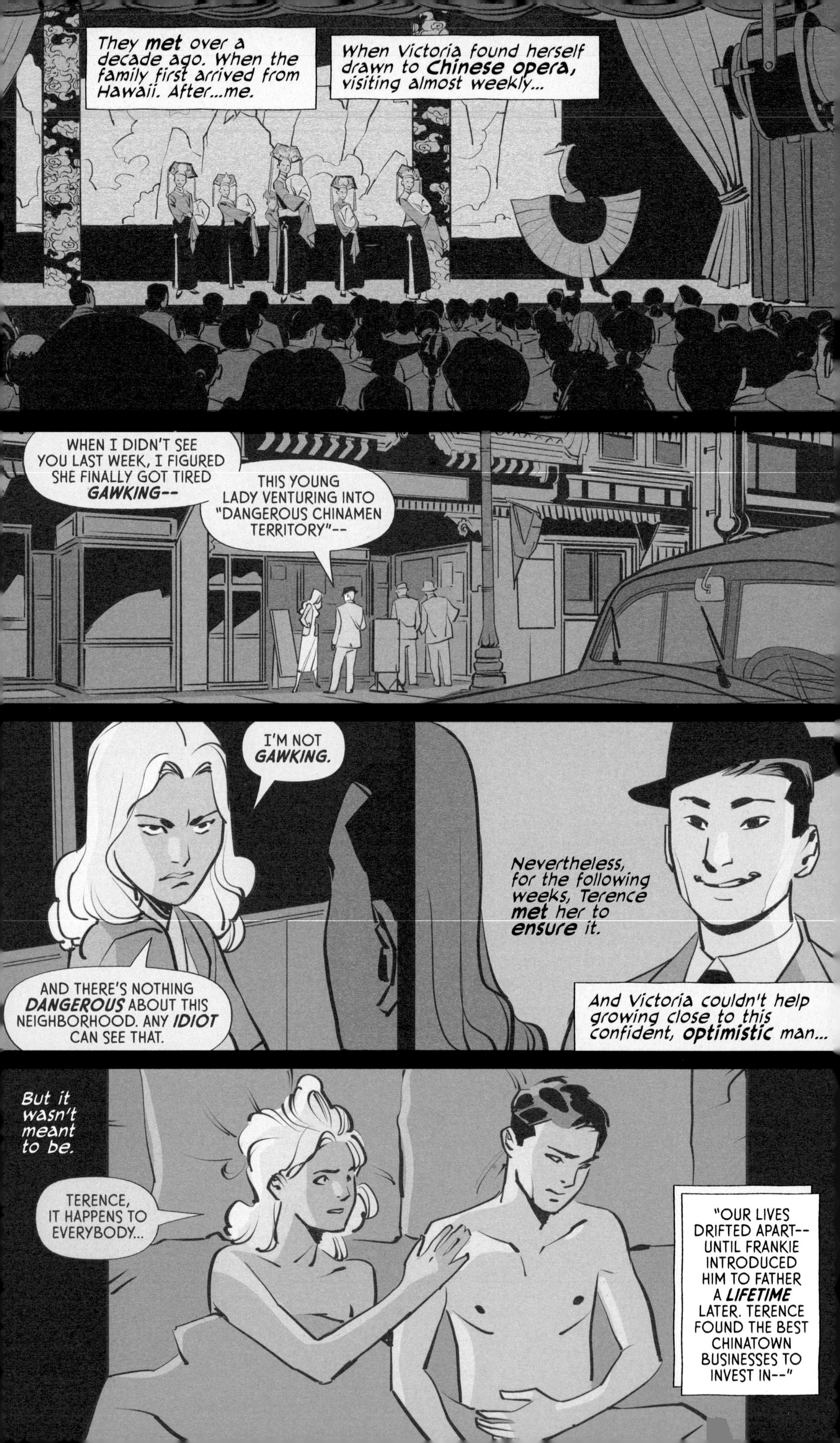
They met over a decade ago. When the family first arrived from Hawaii. After...me.
When Victoria found herself drawn to Chinese opera, visiting almost weekly...
WHEN I DIDN'T SEE YOU LAST WEEK, I FIGURED SHE FINALLY GOT TIRED GAWKING--
THIS YOUNG LADY VENTURING INTO "DANGEROUS CHINAMEN TERRITORY"--
I'M NOT GAWKING.
AND THERE'S NOTHING DANGEROUS ABOUT THIS NEIGHBORHOOD. ANY IDIOT CAN SEE THAT.
Nevertheless, for the following weeks, Terence met her to ensure it.
And Victoria couldn't help growing close to this confident, optimistic man...
But it wasn't meant to be.
TERENCE, IT HAPPENS TO EVERYBODY...
"OUR LIVES DRIFTED APART--UNTIL FRANKIE INTRODUCED HIM TO FATHER A LIFETIME LATER. TERENCE FOUND THE BEST CHINATOWN BUSINESSES TO INVEST IN--"

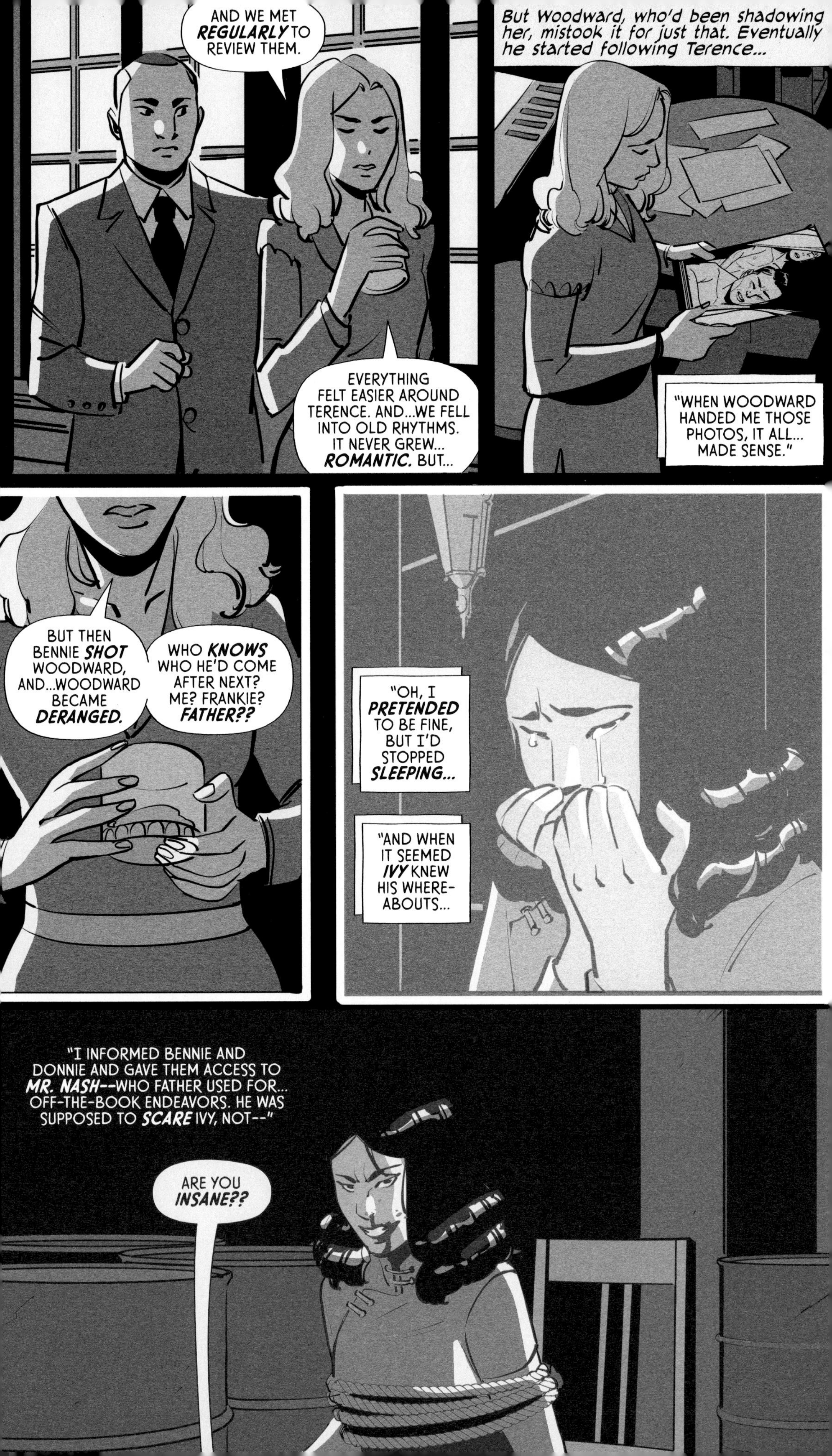
AND WE MET REGULARLY TO REVIEW THEM.
EVERYTHING FELT EASIER AROUND TERENCE. AND...WE FELL INTO OLD RHYTHMS. IT NEVER GREW... ROMANTIC. BUT...
But Woodward, who'd been shadowing her, mistook it for just that. Eventually he started following Terence...
"WHEN WOODWARD HANDED ME THOSE PHOTOS, IT ALL... MADE SENSE."
BUT THEN BENNIE SHOT WOODWARD, AND...WOODWARD BECAME DERANGED.
WHO KNOWS WHO HE'D COME AFTER NEXT? ME? FRANKIE? FATHER??
"OH, I PRETENDED TO BE FINE, BUT I'D STOPPED SLEEPING...
"AND WHEN IT SEEMED IVY KNEW HIS WHERE-ABOUTS...
"I INFORMED BENNIE AND DONNIE AND GAVE THEM ACCESS TO MR. NASH--WHO FATHER USED FOR... OFF-THE-BOOK ENDEAVORS. HE WAS SUPPOSED TO SCARE IVY, NOT--"
ARE YOU INSANE??

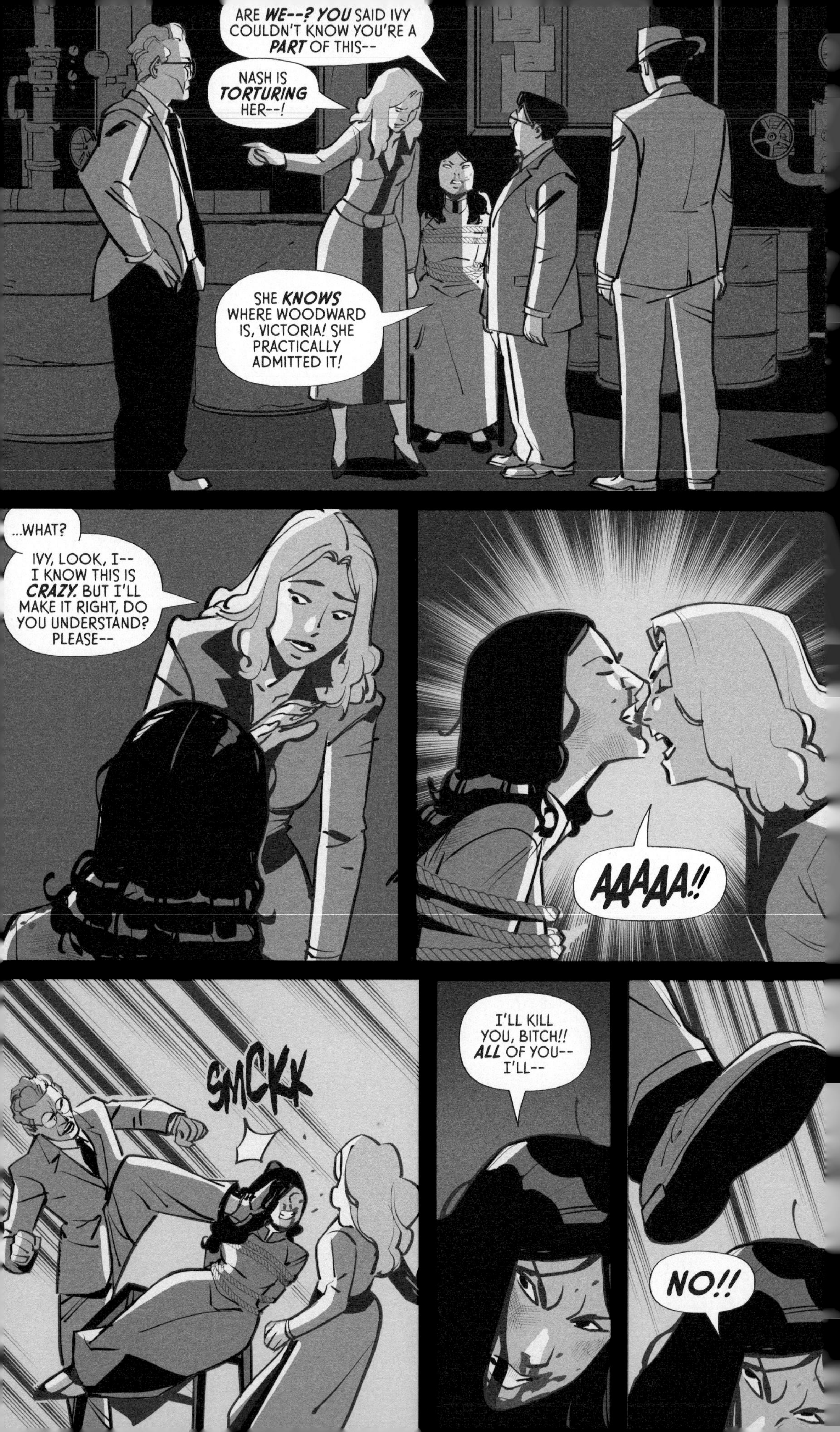
ARE WE--? YOU SAID IVY COULDN'T KNOW YOU'RE A PART OF THIS--
NASH IS TORTURING HER--!
SHE KNOWS WHERE WOODWARD IS, VICTORIA! SHE PRACTICALLY ADMITTED IT!
...WHAT?
IVY, LOOK, I-- I KNOW THIS IS CRAZY. BUT I'LL MAKE IT RIGHT, DO YOU UNDERSTAND? PLEASE--
AAAAA!!
SMCKK
I'LL KILL YOU, BITCH!! ALL OF YOU-- I'LL--
NO!!

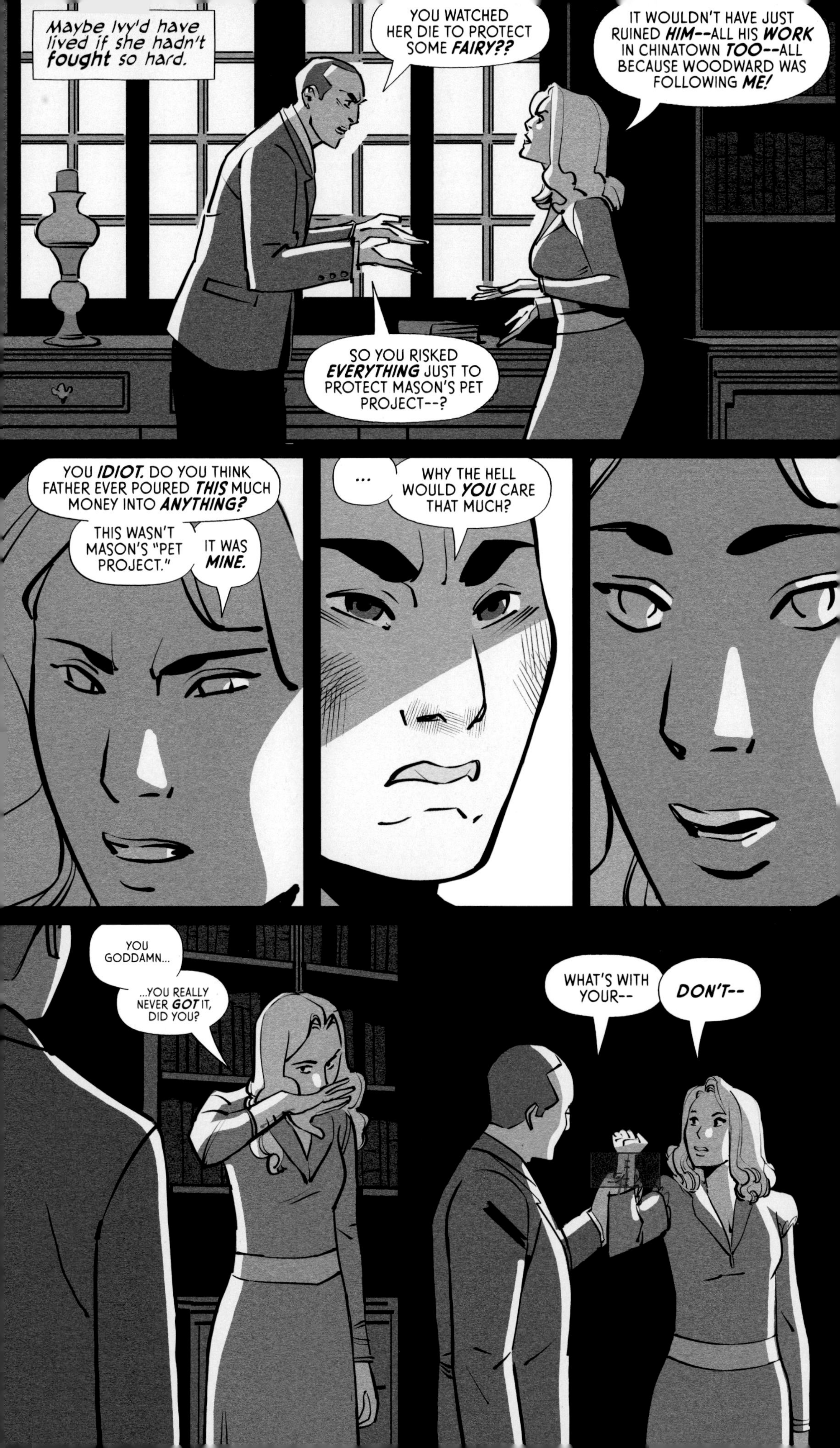
Maybe Ivy'd have lived if she hadn't **fought** so hard.
YOU WATCHED HER DIE TO PROTECT SOME ***FAIRY??***
IT WOULDN'T HAVE JUST RUINED ***HIM--***ALL HIS ***WORK*** IN CHINATOWN ***TOO--***ALL BECAUSE WOODWARD WAS FOLLOWING ***ME!***
SO YOU RISKED ***EVERYTHING*** JUST TO PROTECT MASON'S PET PROJECT--?
YOU ***IDIOT.*** DO YOU THINK FATHER EVER POURED ***THIS*** MUCH MONEY INTO ***ANYTHING?***
THIS WASN'T MASON'S "PET PROJECT."
IT WAS ***MINE.***
...
WHY THE HELL WOULD ***YOU*** CARE THAT MUCH?
YOU GODDAMN...
...YOU REALLY NEVER ***GOT*** IT, DID YOU?
WHAT'S WITH YOUR--
DON'T--

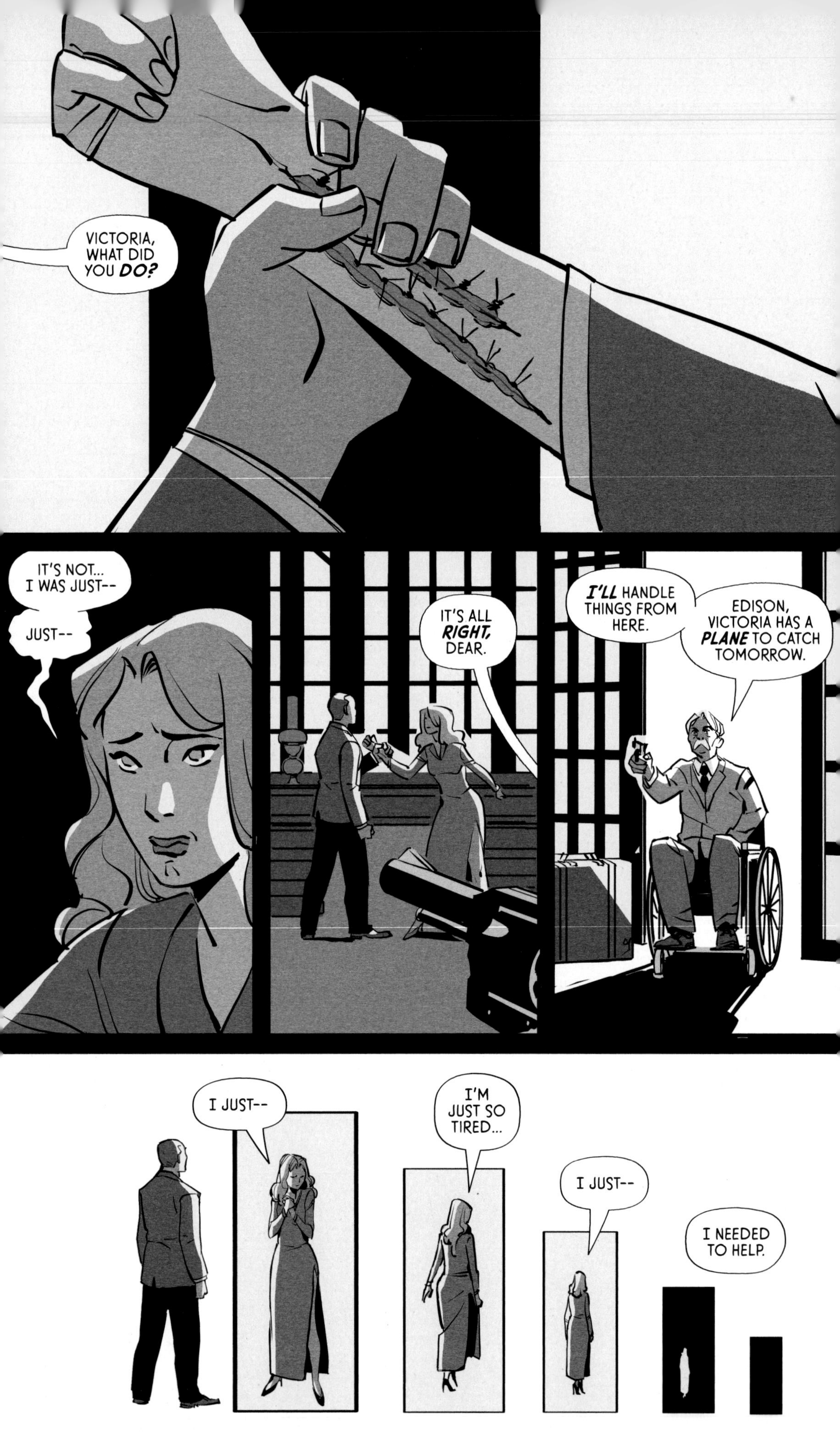
VICTORIA, WHAT DID YOU *DO?*
IT'S NOT... I WAS JUST--
JUST--
IT'S ALL *RIGHT,* DEAR.
I'LL HANDLE THINGS FROM HERE.
EDISON, VICTORIA HAS A *PLANE* TO CATCH TOMORROW.
I JUST--
I'M JUST SO TIRED...
I JUST--
I NEEDED TO HELP.

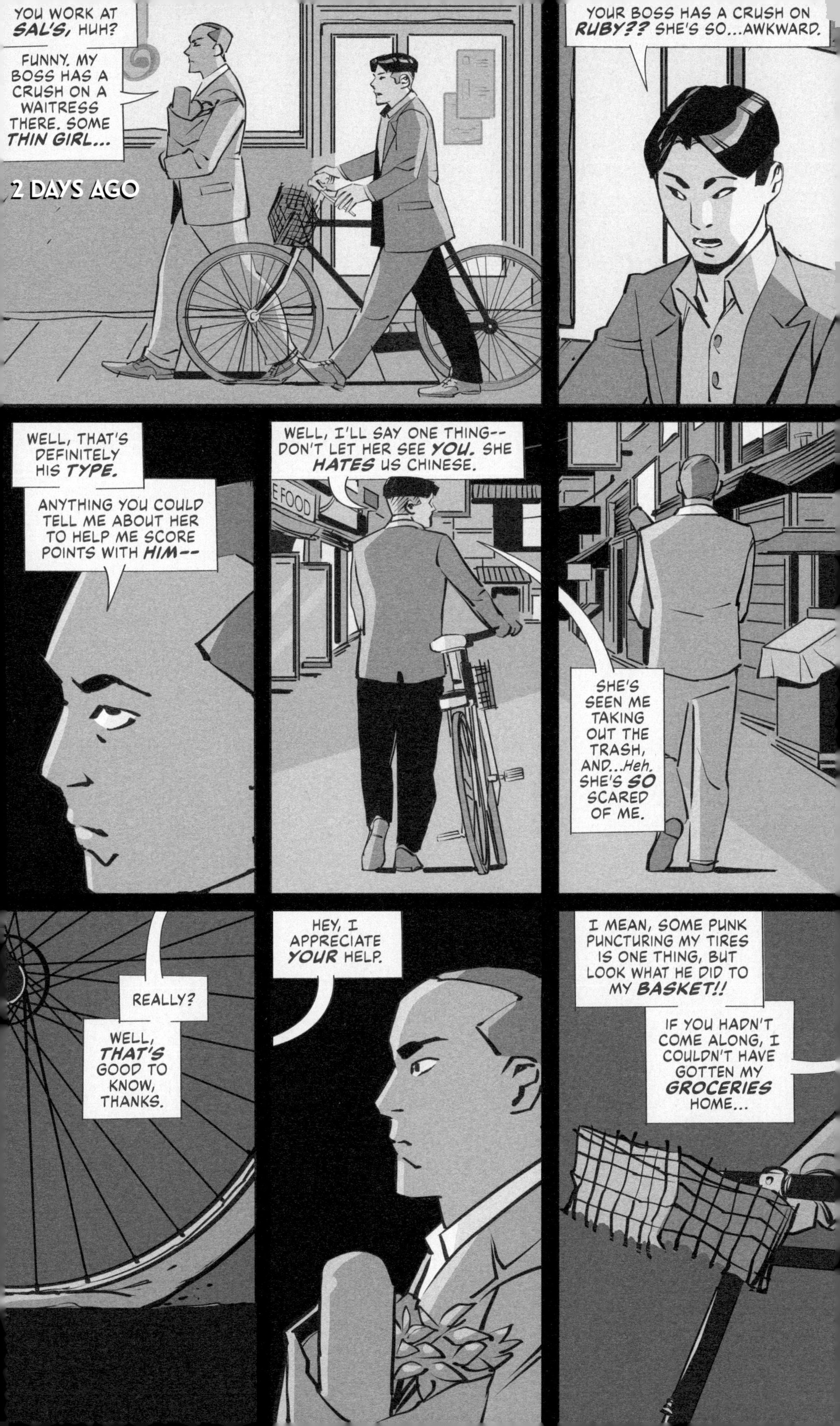
YOU WORK AT SAL'S, HUH?
FUNNY. MY BOSS HAS A CRUSH ON A WAITRESS THERE. SOME THIN GIRL...
2 DAYS AGO
YOUR BOSS HAS A CRUSH ON RUBY?? SHE'S SO...AWKWARD.
WELL, THAT'S DEFINITELY HIS TYPE.
ANYTHING YOU COULD TELL ME ABOUT HER TO HELP ME SCORE POINTS WITH HIM--
WELL, I'LL SAY ONE THING-- DON'T LET HER SEE YOU. SHE HATES US CHINESE.
E FOOD
SHE'S SEEN ME TAKING OUT THE TRASH, AND...Heh. SHE'S SO SCARED OF ME.
REALLY?
WELL, THAT'S GOOD TO KNOW, THANKS.
HEY, I APPRECIATE YOUR HELP.
I MEAN, SOME PUNK PUNCTURING MY TIRES IS ONE THING, BUT LOOK WHAT HE DID TO MY BASKET!!
IF YOU HADN'T COME ALONG, I COULDN'T HAVE GOTTEN MY GROCERIES HOME...

And as a broken Victoria slept, Mason explained--

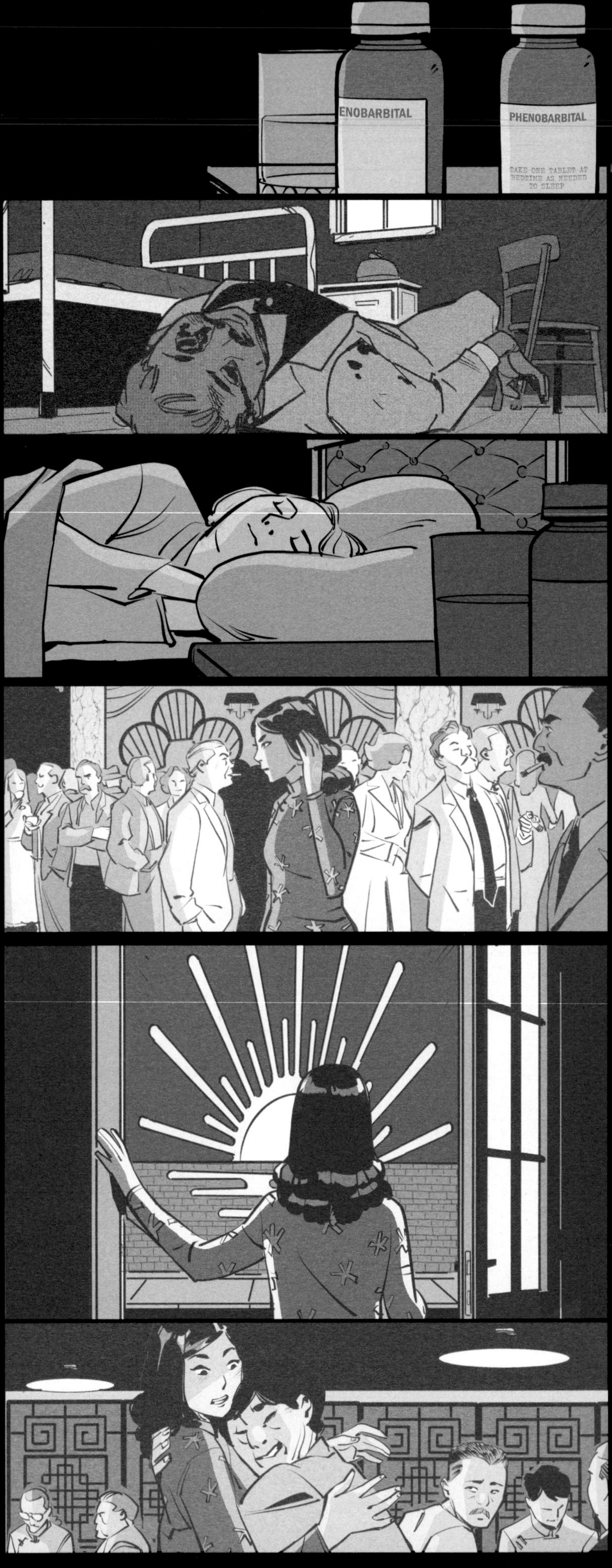

ENOBARBITAL
PHENOBARBITAL
TAKE ONE TABLET AT BEDTIME AS NEEDED TO SLEEP

"IVY DESCRIBED HERSELF AS AN ***OVERLOOKED*** CHILD. THIS 'HUI LONG' WAS JUST A YOUNG GIRL IMAGINING HOW TO ***CAPTIVATE*** CHINATOWN.

"SHE EVEN INVENTED THE ***FLOURISH*** OF REMOVING A VICTIM'S EYES, BECAUSE ALL TONG LEGENDS ***NEEDED*** EXTRAVAGANT TOUCHES.

"BUT WHEN HUI LONG'S ***FIRST*** VICTIM WAS REPORTED TO HAVE THE ***SAME*** FLOURISH IVY ***INVENTED,*** SHE WAS ***UNDERSTANDABLY*** UNSETTLED. AND THE ***ONLY*** PEOPLE SHE TOLD THOSE STORIES ***TO--***

"WERE HER FRIEND HOLLY...AND HER ***BROTHER.***

"WHICH, OF COURSE, ***INTENSIFIED*** HER WORRY.

"YOU SEE, ***MONTHS*** PRIOR, WOODWARD INFORMED HER HE'D COME INTO HIS ***FORTUNE***. SHE COULD QUIT HER JOB AND BE WITH ANYONE SHE DESIRED NOW.

"HOWEVER, WHEN IVY NOW INQUIRED ABOUT HER BROTHER, SHE COULDN'T ***LOCATE*** HIM. SHE RECALLED A JADE CASTLE STAMP ON HIS HAND DURING THEIR PREVIOUS ENCOUNTER.

"UNFORTUNATELY, THAT ***TOO*** PROVED A DEAD END.

"WHICH LED HER TO RECALL HOW HER INTEREST IN HUI LONG STEMMED FROM ***STORIES*** TOLD BY AN OLD NEIGHBOR. SO SHE RETURNED TO THE BUILDING SHE GREW UP IN.

"BUT SPEAKING TO ***HIM*** PROVED FRUITLESS AS WELL.

"LISTLESS NOSTALGIA BROUGHT HER BACK TO THE ***MAHJONG PARLOR*** WHERE HER MOTHER ONCE WORKED--TO DISCOVER ***EVERYONE*** TALKING ABOUT HUI LONG."

"WHICH LED IVY TO GROW FEARFUL...AND, WELL--***OBSESSED.*** I ***BEGGED*** HER TO FORGET IT..."

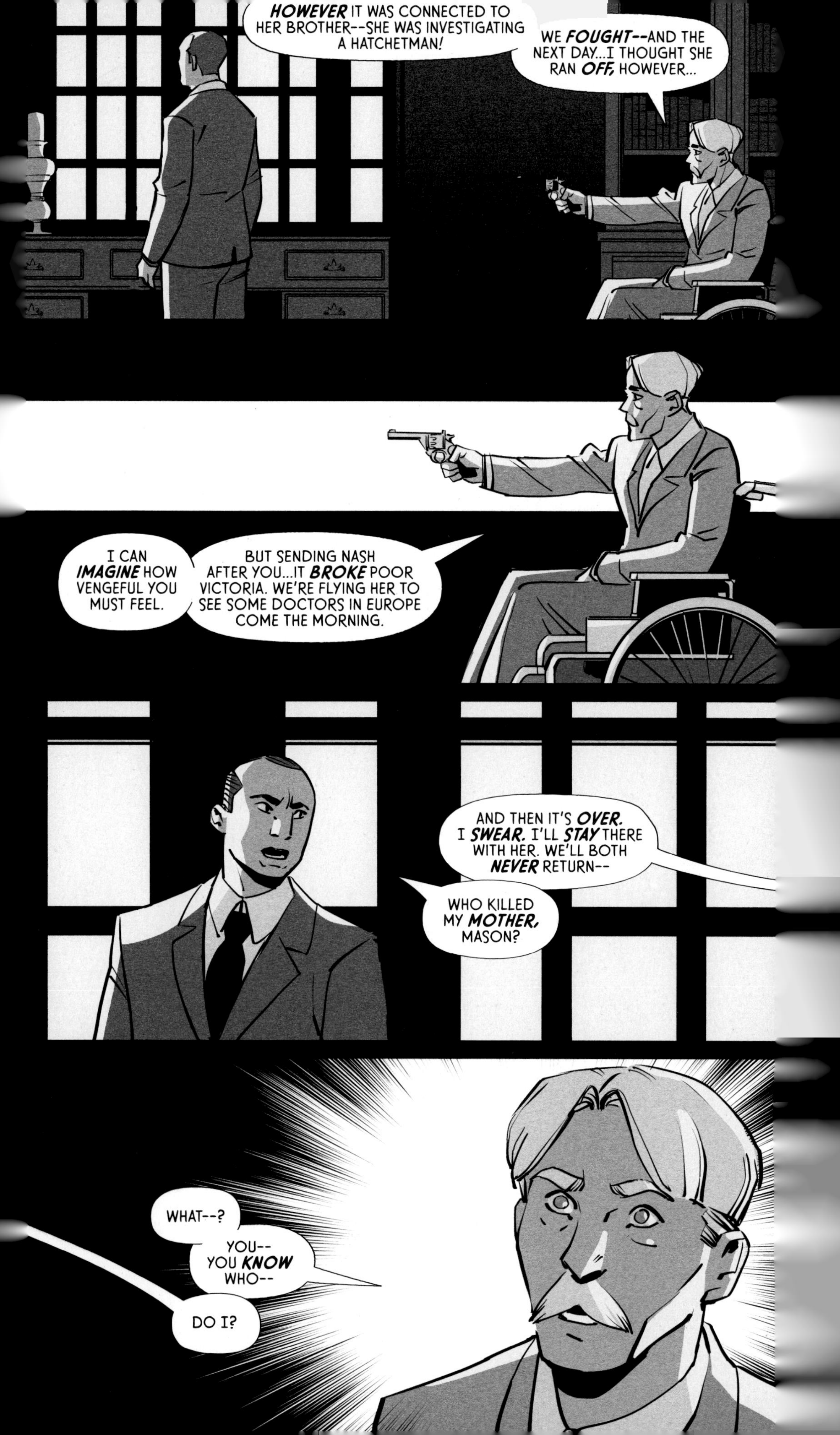
HOWEVER IT WAS CONNECTED TO HER BROTHER--SHE WAS INVESTIGATING A HATCHETMAN!
WE FOUGHT--AND THE NEXT DAY...I THOUGHT SHE RAN OFF, HOWEVER...
I CAN IMAGINE HOW VENGEFUL YOU MUST FEEL.
BUT SENDING NASH AFTER YOU...IT BROKE POOR VICTORIA. WE'RE FLYING HER TO SEE SOME DOCTORS IN EUROPE COME THE MORNING.
AND THEN IT'S OVER. I SWEAR. I'LL STAY THERE WITH HER. WE'LL BOTH NEVER RETURN--
WHO KILLED MY MOTHER, MASON?
WHAT--?
YOU-- YOU KNOW WHO--
DO I?

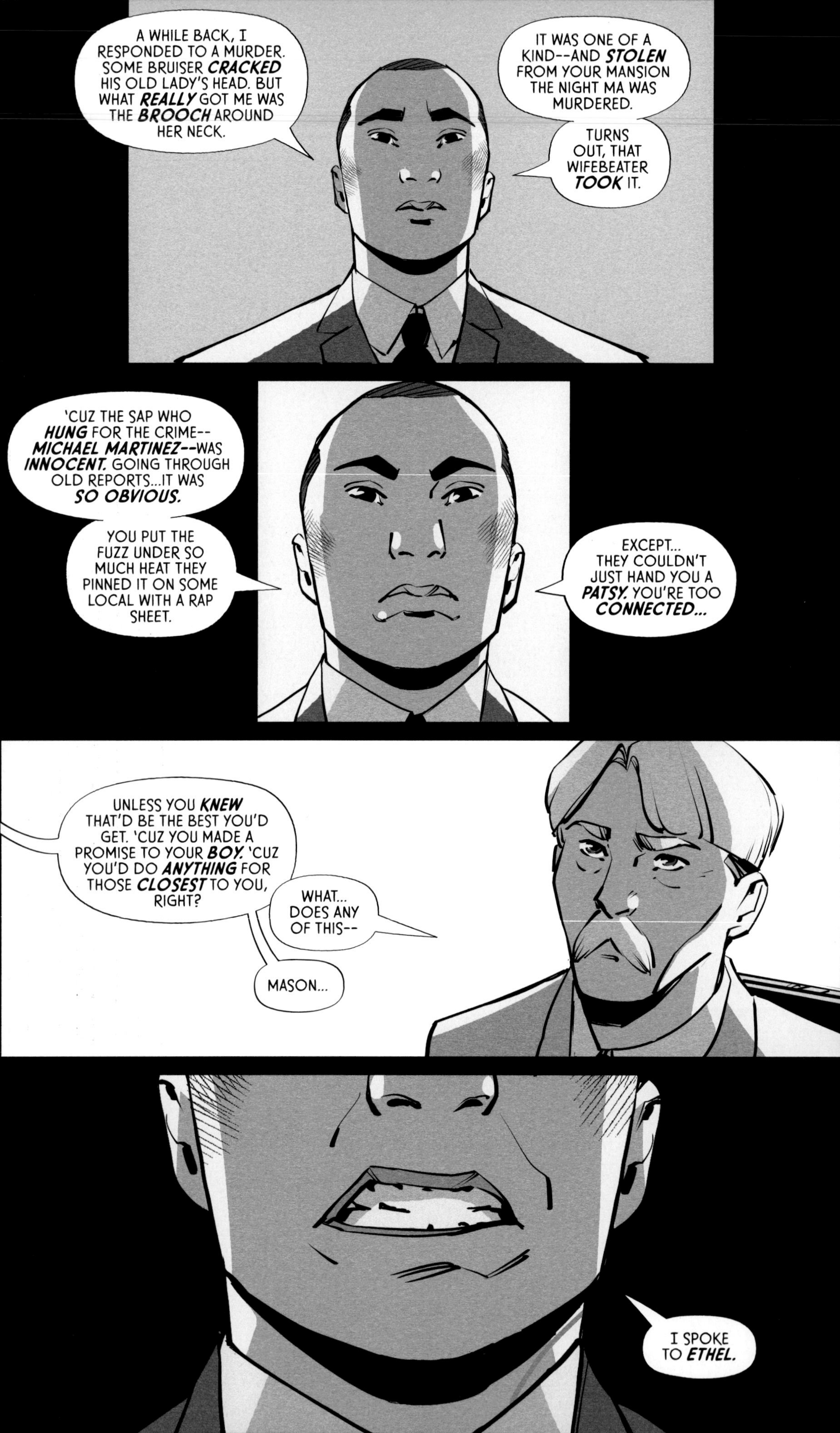
A WHILE BACK, I RESPONDED TO A MURDER. SOME BRUISER CRACKED HIS OLD LADY'S HEAD. BUT WHAT REALLY GOT ME WAS THE BROOCH AROUND HER NECK.
IT WAS ONE OF A KIND--AND STOLEN FROM YOUR MANSION THE NIGHT MA WAS MURDERED.
TURNS OUT, THAT WIFEBEATER TOOK IT.
'CUZ THE SAP WHO HUNG FOR THE CRIME--MICHAEL MARTINEZ--WAS INNOCENT. GOING THROUGH OLD REPORTS...IT WAS SO OBVIOUS.
YOU PUT THE FUZZ UNDER SO MUCH HEAT THEY PINNED IT ON SOME LOCAL WITH A RAP SHEET.
EXCEPT... THEY COULDN'T JUST HAND YOU A PATSY. YOU'RE TOO CONNECTED...
UNLESS YOU KNEW THAT'D BE THE BEST YOU'D GET. 'CUZ YOU MADE A PROMISE TO YOUR BOY. 'CUZ YOU'D DO ANYTHING FOR THOSE CLOSEST TO YOU, RIGHT?
WHAT... DOES ANY OF THIS--
MASON...
I SPOKE TO ETHEL.

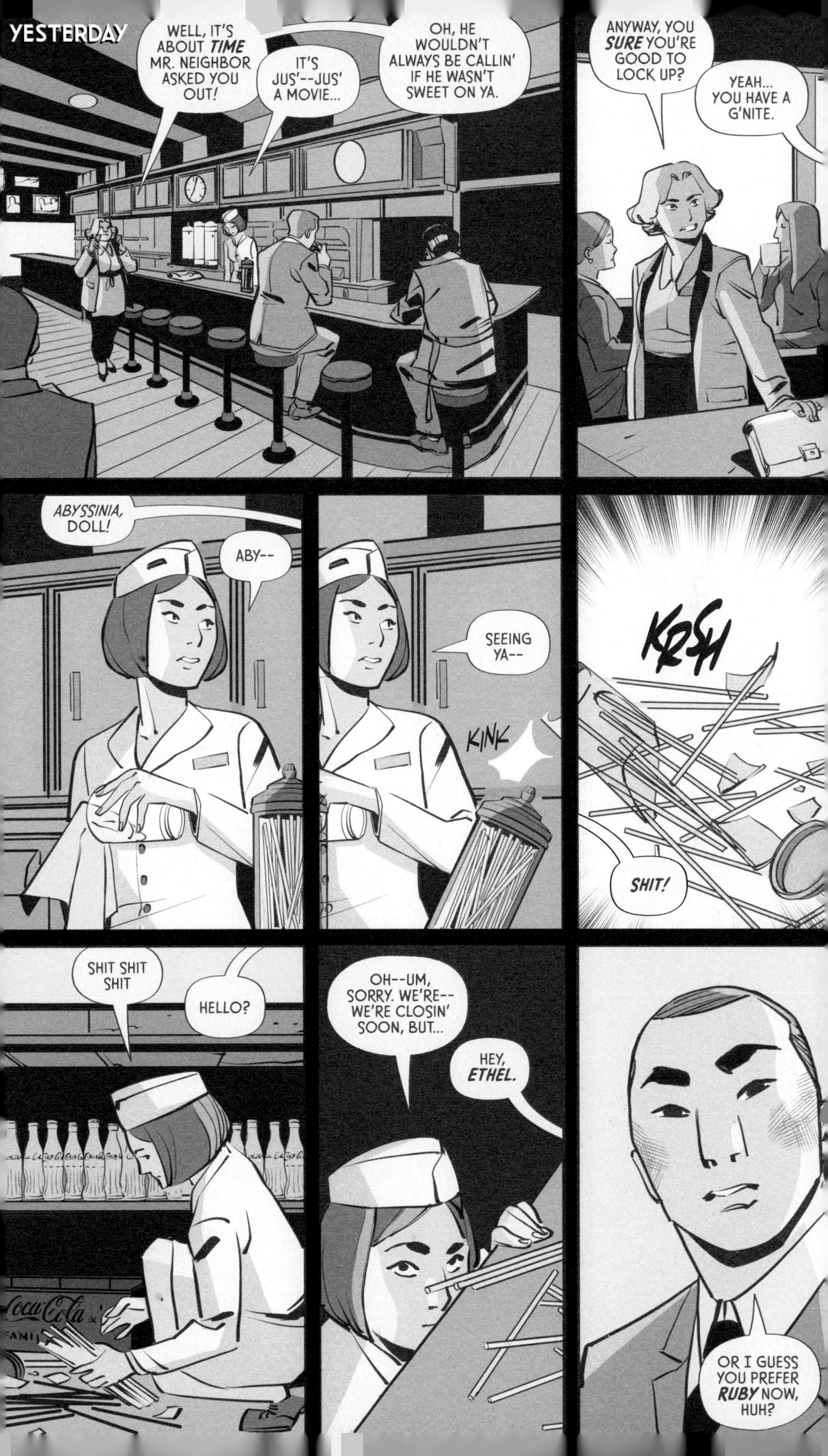
YESTERDAY
WELL, IT'S ABOUT TIME MR. NEIGHBOR ASKED YOU OUT!
IT'S JUS'--JUS' A MOVIE...
OH, HE WOULDN'T ALWAYS BE CALLIN' IF HE WASN'T SWEET ON YA.
ANYWAY, YOU SURE YOU'RE GOOD TO LOCK UP?
YEAH... YOU HAVE A G'NITE.
ABYSSINIA, DOLL!
ABY--
SEEING YA--
KINK
KRSH
SHIT!
SHIT SHIT SHIT
HELLO?
OH--UM, SORRY. WE'RE-- WE'RE CLOSIN' SOON, BUT...
HEY, ETHEL.
OR I GUESS YOU PREFER RUBY NOW, HUH?

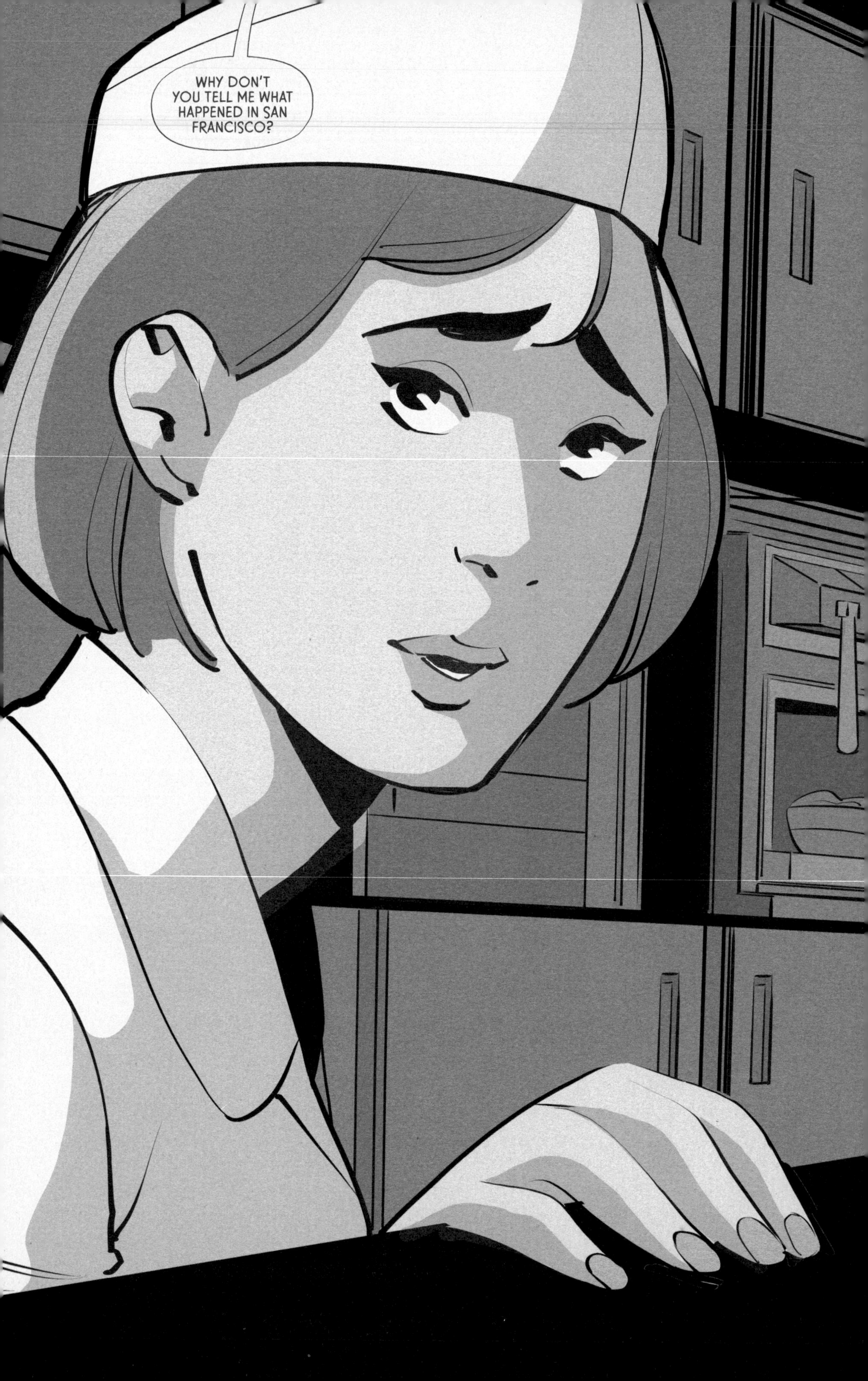
WHY DON'T YOU TELL ME WHAT HAPPENED IN SAN FRANCISCO?

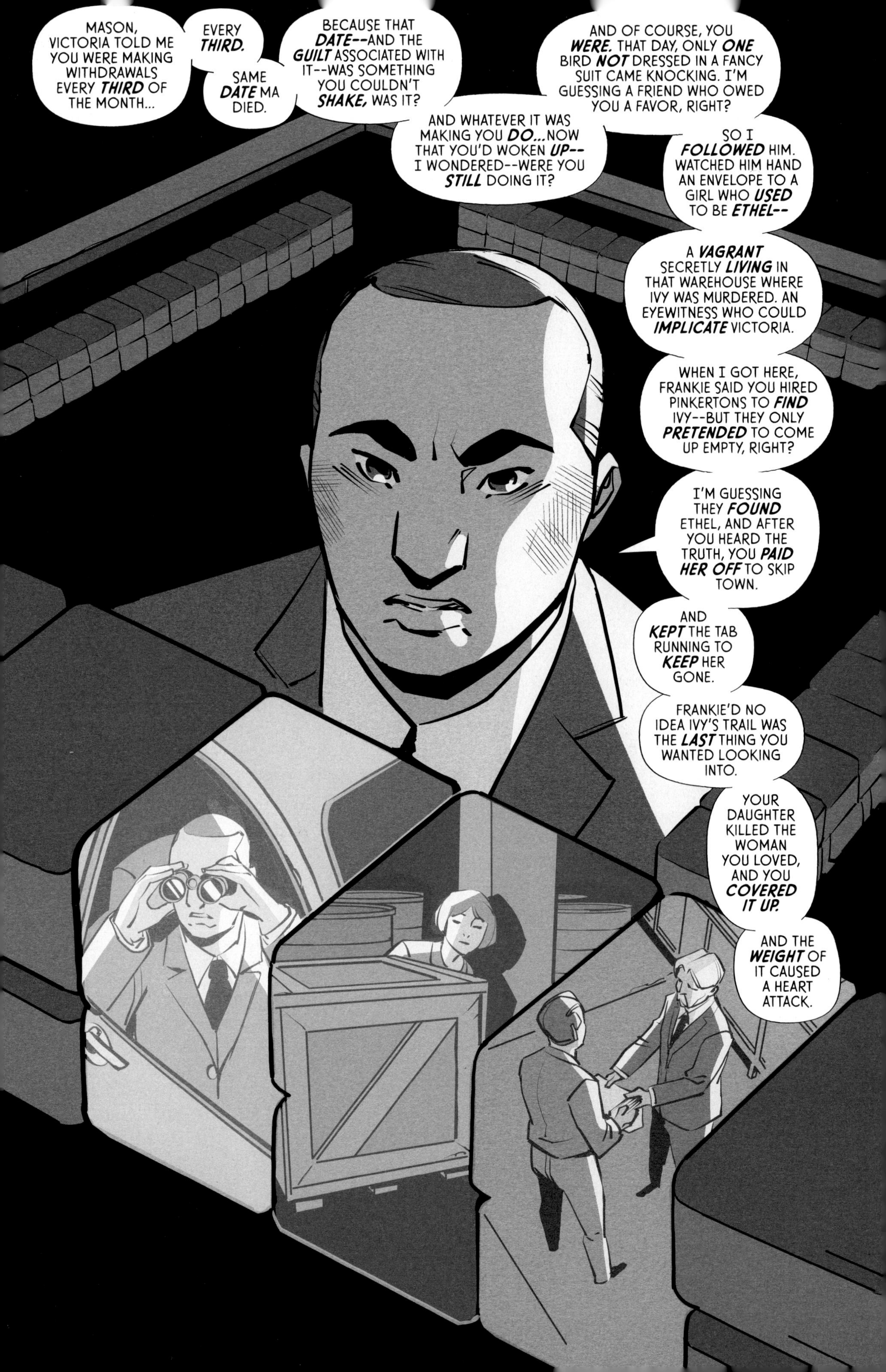
MASON, VICTORIA TOLD ME YOU WERE MAKING WITHDRAWALS EVERY THIRD OF THE MONTH...
EVERY THIRD.
SAME DATE MA DIED.
BECAUSE THAT DATE--AND THE GUILT ASSOCIATED WITH IT--WAS SOMETHING YOU COULDN'T SHAKE, WAS IT?
AND WHATEVER IT WAS MAKING YOU DO...NOW THAT YOU'D WOKEN UP--I WONDERED--WERE YOU STILL DOING IT?
AND OF COURSE, YOU WERE. THAT DAY, ONLY ONE BIRD NOT DRESSED IN A FANCY SUIT CAME KNOCKING. I'M GUESSING A FRIEND WHO OWED YOU A FAVOR, RIGHT?
SO I FOLLOWED HIM. WATCHED HIM HAND AN ENVELOPE TO A GIRL WHO USED TO BE ETHEL--
A VAGRANT SECRETLY LIVING IN THAT WAREHOUSE WHERE IVY WAS MURDERED. AN EYEWITNESS WHO COULD IMPLICATE VICTORIA.
WHEN I GOT HERE, FRANKIE SAID YOU HIRED PINKERTONS TO FIND IVY--BUT THEY ONLY PRETENDED TO COME UP EMPTY, RIGHT?
I'M GUESSING THEY FOUND ETHEL, AND AFTER YOU HEARD THE TRUTH, YOU PAID HER OFF TO SKIP TOWN.
AND KEPT THE TAB RUNNING TO KEEP HER GONE.
FRANKIE'D NO IDEA IVY'S TRAIL WAS THE LAST THING YOU WANTED LOOKING INTO.
YOUR DAUGHTER KILLED THE WOMAN YOU LOVED, AND YOU COVERED IT UP.
AND THE WEIGHT OF IT CAUSED A HEART ATTACK.

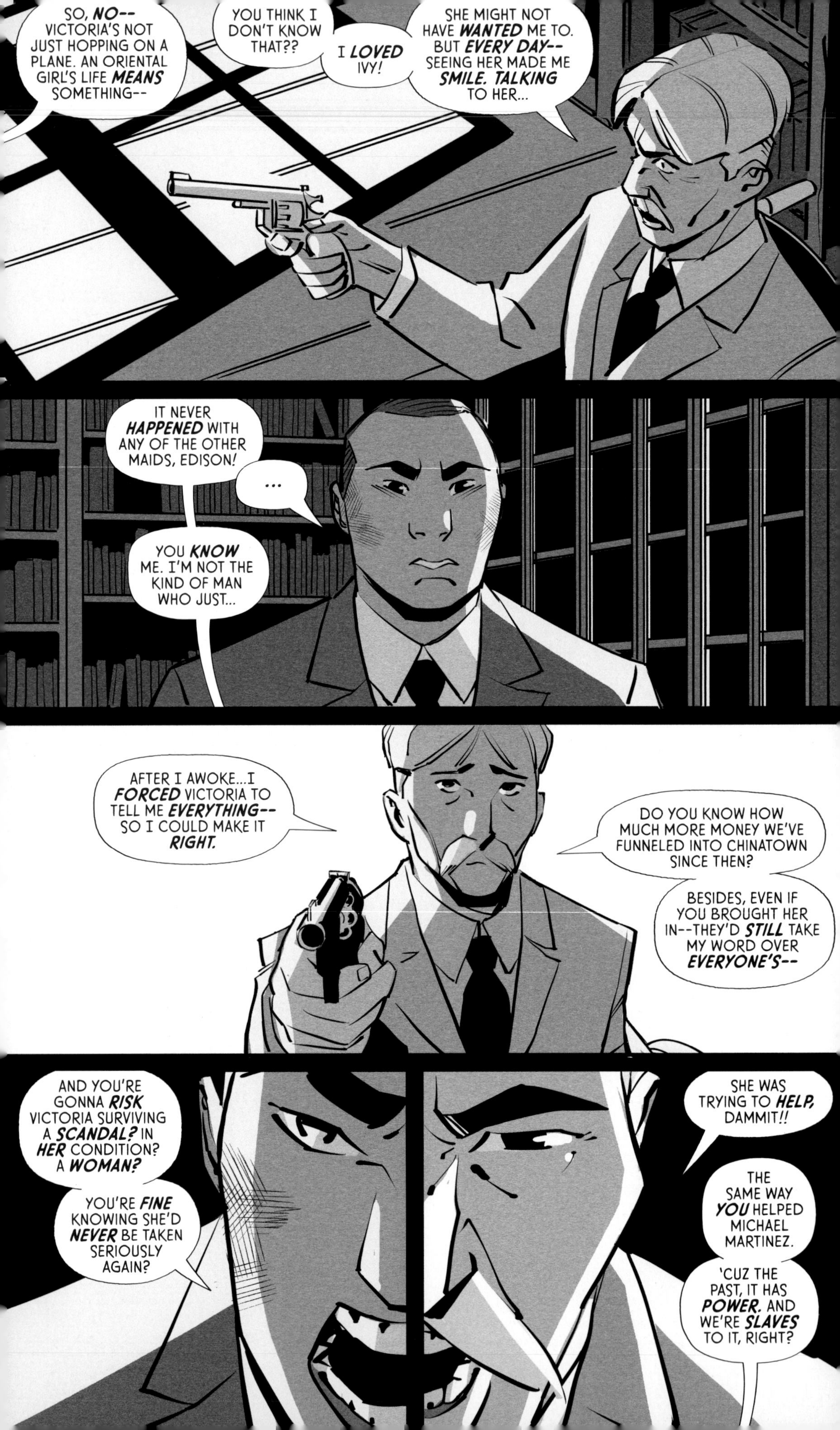
SO, NO--
VICTORIA'S NOT JUST HOPPING ON A PLANE. AN ORIENTAL GIRL'S LIFE MEANS SOMETHING--
YOU THINK I DON'T KNOW THAT??
I LOVED IVY!
SHE MIGHT NOT HAVE WANTED ME TO. BUT EVERY DAY-- SEEING HER MADE ME SMILE. TALKING TO HER...
IT NEVER HAPPENED WITH ANY OF THE OTHER MAIDS, EDISON!
...
YOU KNOW ME. I'M NOT THE KIND OF MAN WHO JUST...
AFTER I AWOKE...I FORCED VICTORIA TO TELL ME EVERYTHING-- SO I COULD MAKE IT RIGHT.
DO YOU KNOW HOW MUCH MORE MONEY WE'VE FUNNELED INTO CHINATOWN SINCE THEN?
BESIDES, EVEN IF YOU BROUGHT HER IN--THEY'D STILL TAKE MY WORD OVER EVERYONE'S--
AND YOU'RE GONNA RISK VICTORIA SURVIVING A SCANDAL? IN HER CONDITION? A WOMAN?
YOU'RE FINE KNOWING SHE'D NEVER BE TAKEN SERIOUSLY AGAIN?
SHE WAS TRYING TO HELP, DAMMIT!!
THE SAME WAY YOU HELPED MICHAEL MARTINEZ.
'CUZ THE PAST, IT HAS POWER. AND WE'RE SLAVES TO IT, RIGHT?

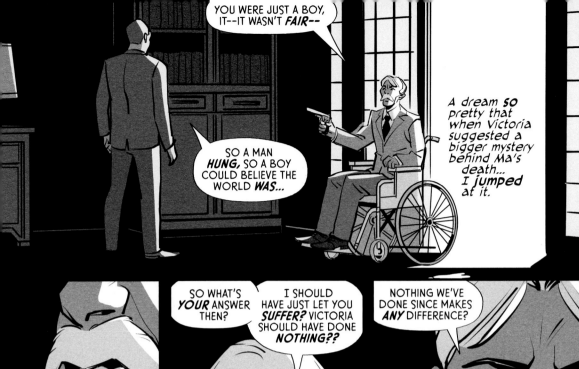

YOU WERE JUST A BOY, IT--IT WASN'T *FAIR*--

SO A MAN *HUNG,* SO A BOY COULD BELIEVE THE WORLD *WAS...*

A dream *SO* pretty that when Victoria suggested a bigger mystery behind Ma's death... I *jumped* at it.

SO WHAT'S *YOUR* ANSWER THEN?

I SHOULD HAVE JUST LET YOU *SUFFER?* VICTORIA SHOULD HAVE DONE *NOTHING??*

NOTHING WE'VE DONE SINCE MAKES *ANY* DIFFERENCE?

BUT REALLY, YOU JUST COULDN'T HANDLE THERE WAS NOTHING YOUR *MILLIONS* COULD DO TO MAKE THINGS *BETTER*--

DAMMIT...

EDISON... ALL THIS HAS ALREADY COST ME THE WOMAN I LOVE...

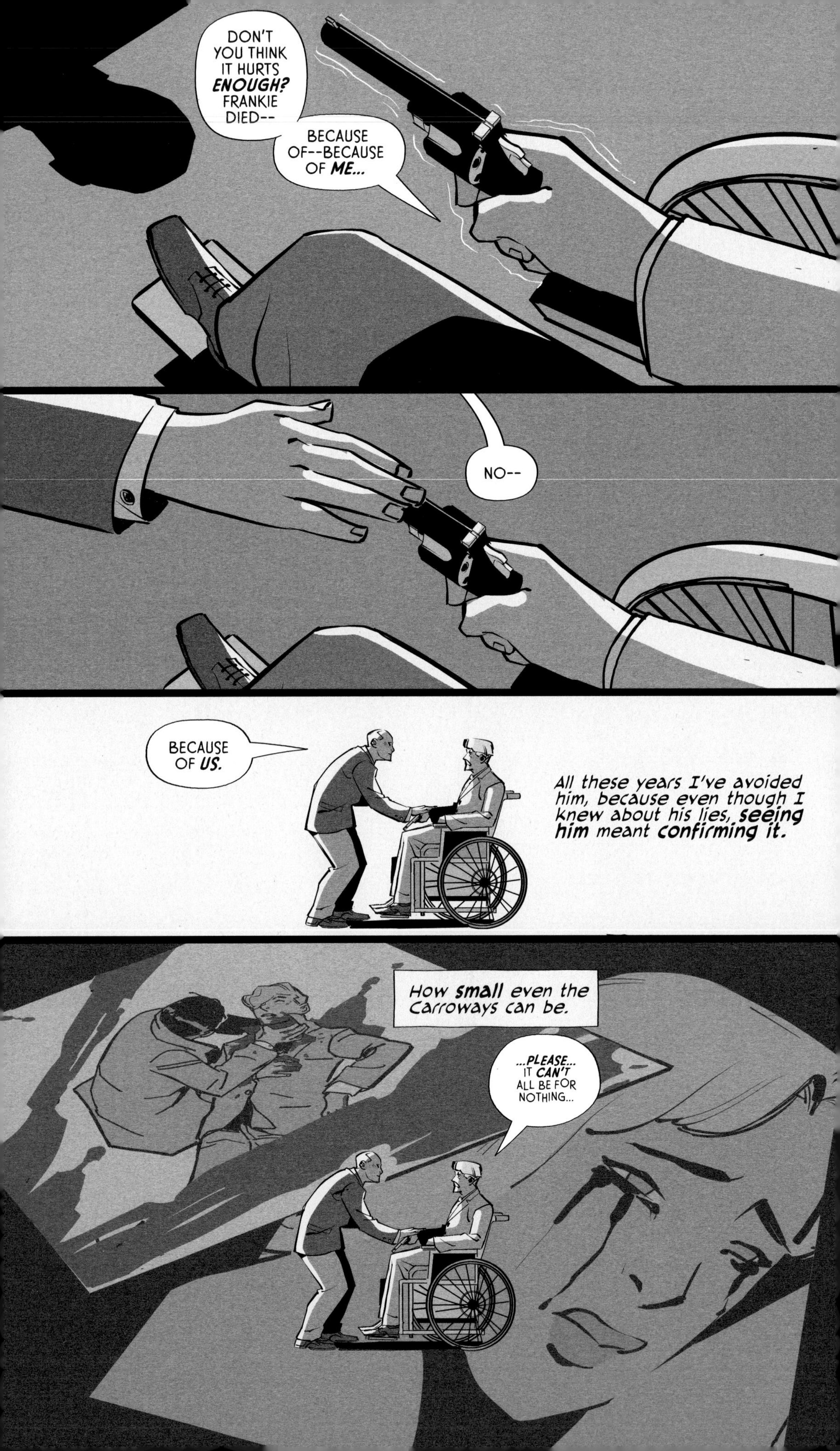
DON'T YOU THINK IT HURTS ENOUGH? FRANKIE DIED--
BECAUSE OF--BECAUSE OF ME...
NO--
BECAUSE OF US.
All these years I've avoided him, because even though I knew about his lies, seeing him meant confirming it.
How small even the Carroways can be.
...PLEASE... IT CAN'T ALL BE FOR NOTHING...

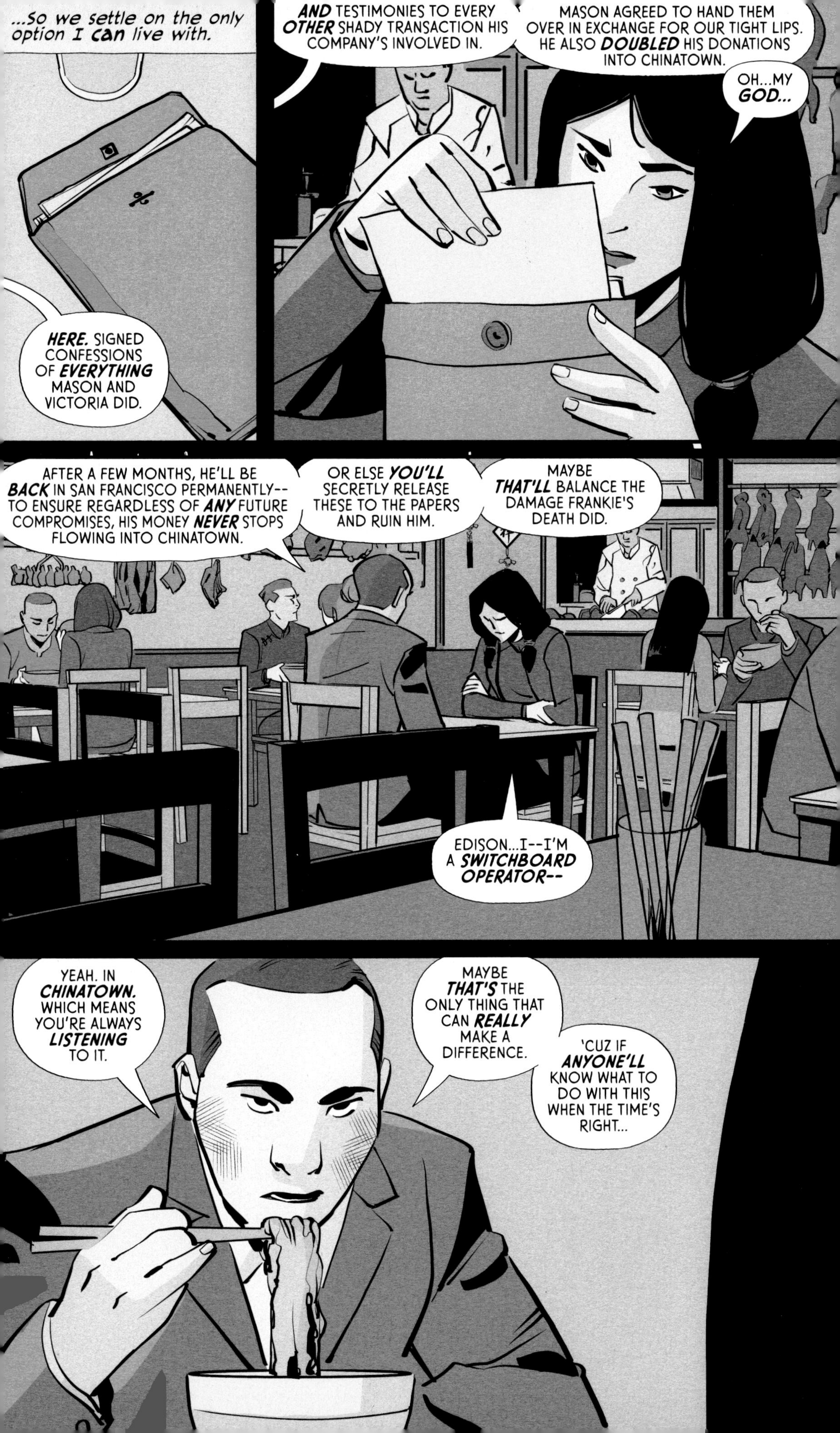
...So we settle on the only option I can live with.
HERE. SIGNED CONFESSIONS OF EVERYTHING MASON AND VICTORIA DID.
AND TESTIMONIES TO EVERY OTHER SHADY TRANSACTION HIS COMPANY'S INVOLVED IN.
MASON AGREED TO HAND THEM OVER IN EXCHANGE FOR OUR TIGHT LIPS. HE ALSO DOUBLED HIS DONATIONS INTO CHINATOWN.
OH...MY GOD...
AFTER A FEW MONTHS, HE'LL BE BACK IN SAN FRANCISCO PERMANENTLY--TO ENSURE REGARDLESS OF ANY FUTURE COMPROMISES, HIS MONEY NEVER STOPS FLOWING INTO CHINATOWN.
OR ELSE YOU'LL SECRETLY RELEASE THESE TO THE PAPERS AND RUIN HIM.
MAYBE THAT'LL BALANCE THE DAMAGE FRANKIE'S DEATH DID.
EDISON...I--I'M A SWITCHBOARD OPERATOR--
YEAH. IN CHINATOWN. WHICH MEANS YOU'RE ALWAYS LISTENING TO IT.
MAYBE THAT'S THE ONLY THING THAT CAN REALLY MAKE A DIFFERENCE.
'CUZ IF ANYONE'LL KNOW WHAT TO DO WITH THIS WHEN THE TIME'S RIGHT...

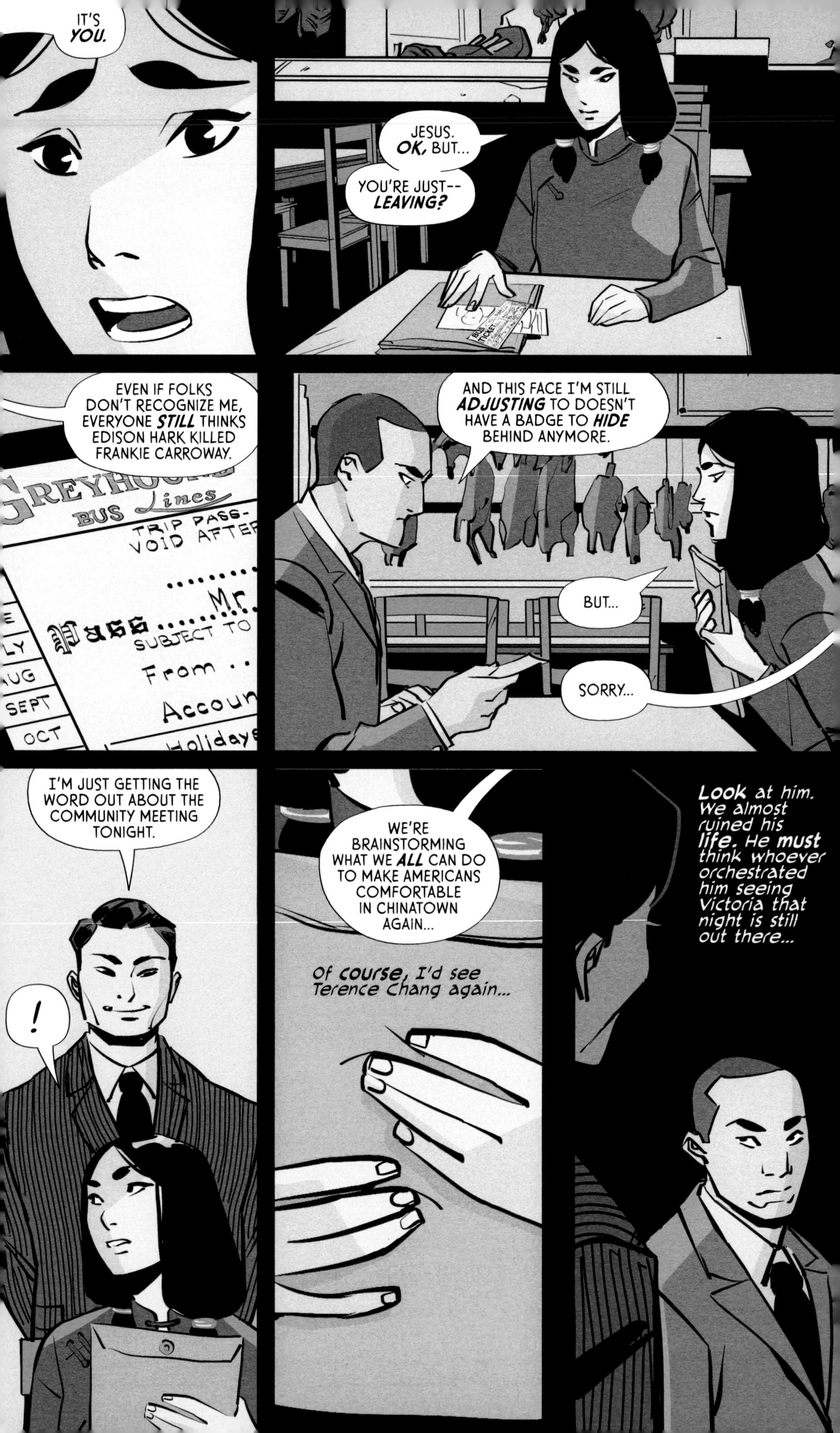
IT'S *YOU.*
JESUS. ***OK,*** BUT...
YOU'RE JUST-- ***LEAVING?***
EVEN IF FOLKS DON'T RECOGNIZE ME, EVERYONE ***STILL*** THINKS EDISON HARK KILLED FRANKIE CARROWAY.
GREYHOUND BUS Lines
TRIP PASS- VOID AFTER
Mr.
Pass
SUBJECT TO
From
Accoun
Holidays
SEPT
OCT
AND THIS FACE I'M STILL ***ADJUSTING*** TO DOESN'T HAVE A BADGE TO ***HIDE*** BEHIND ANYMORE.
BUT...
SORRY...
I'M JUST GETTING THE WORD OUT ABOUT THE COMMUNITY MEETING TONIGHT.
!
WE'RE BRAINSTORMING WHAT WE ***ALL*** CAN DO TO MAKE AMERICANS COMFORTABLE IN CHINATOWN AGAIN...
*Of **course**, I'd see Terence Chang again...*
***Look** at him. We almost ruined his **life**. He **must** think whoever orchestrated him seeing Victoria that night is still out there...*

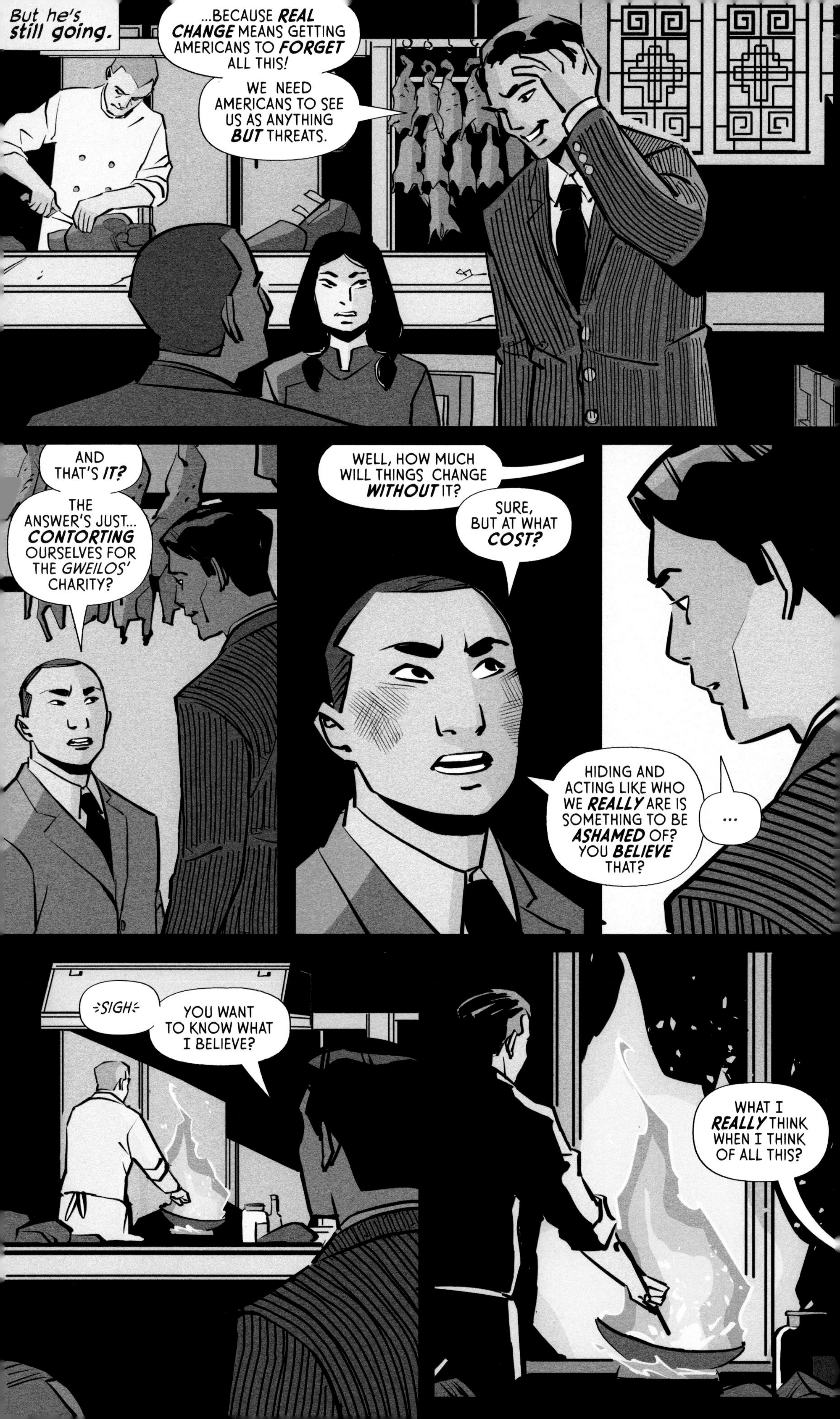
But he's still going.
...BECAUSE *REAL CHANGE* MEANS GETTING AMERICANS TO *FORGET* ALL THIS!
WE NEED AMERICANS TO SEE US AS ANYTHING *BUT* THREATS.
AND THAT'S *IT?*
THE ANSWER'S JUST... *CONTORTING* OURSELVES FOR THE *GWEILOS'* CHARITY?
WELL, HOW MUCH WILL THINGS CHANGE *WITHOUT* IT?
SURE, BUT AT WHAT *COST?*
HIDING AND ACTING LIKE WHO WE *REALLY* ARE IS SOMETHING TO BE *ASHAMED* OF? YOU *BELIEVE* THAT?
...
SIGH
YOU WANT TO KNOW WHAT I BELIEVE?
WHAT I *REALLY* THINK WHEN I THINK OF ALL THIS?

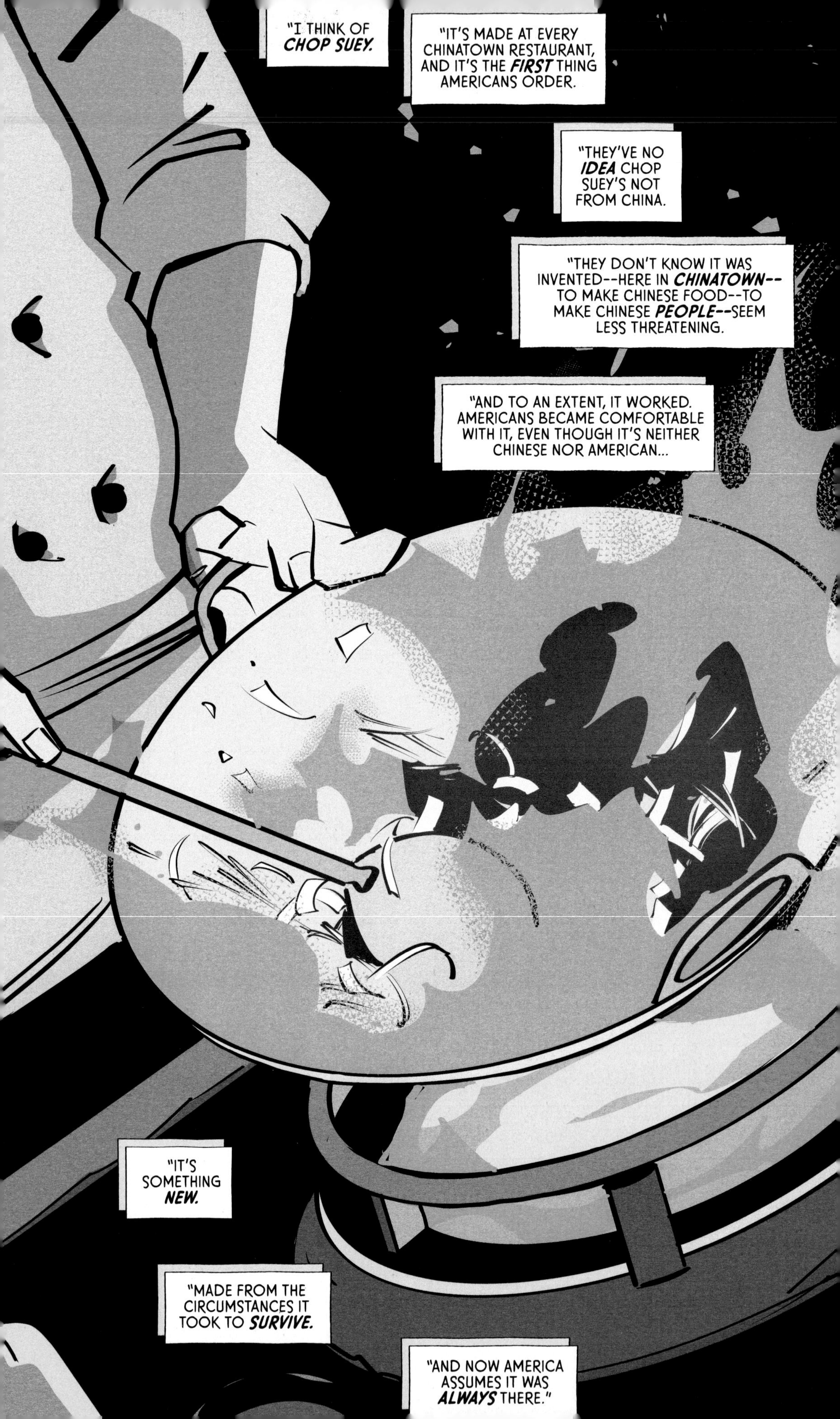
"I THINK OF CHOP SUEY.
"IT'S MADE AT EVERY CHINATOWN RESTAURANT, AND IT'S THE FIRST THING AMERICANS ORDER.
"THEY'VE NO IDEA CHOP SUEY'S NOT FROM CHINA.
"THEY DON'T KNOW IT WAS INVENTED--HERE IN CHINATOWN--TO MAKE CHINESE FOOD--TO MAKE CHINESE PEOPLE--SEEM LESS THREATENING.
"AND TO AN EXTENT, IT WORKED. AMERICANS BECAME COMFORTABLE WITH IT, EVEN THOUGH IT'S NEITHER CHINESE NOR AMERICAN...
"IT'S SOMETHING NEW.
"MADE FROM THE CIRCUMSTANCES IT TOOK TO SURVIVE.
"AND NOW AMERICA ASSUMES IT WAS ALWAYS THERE."

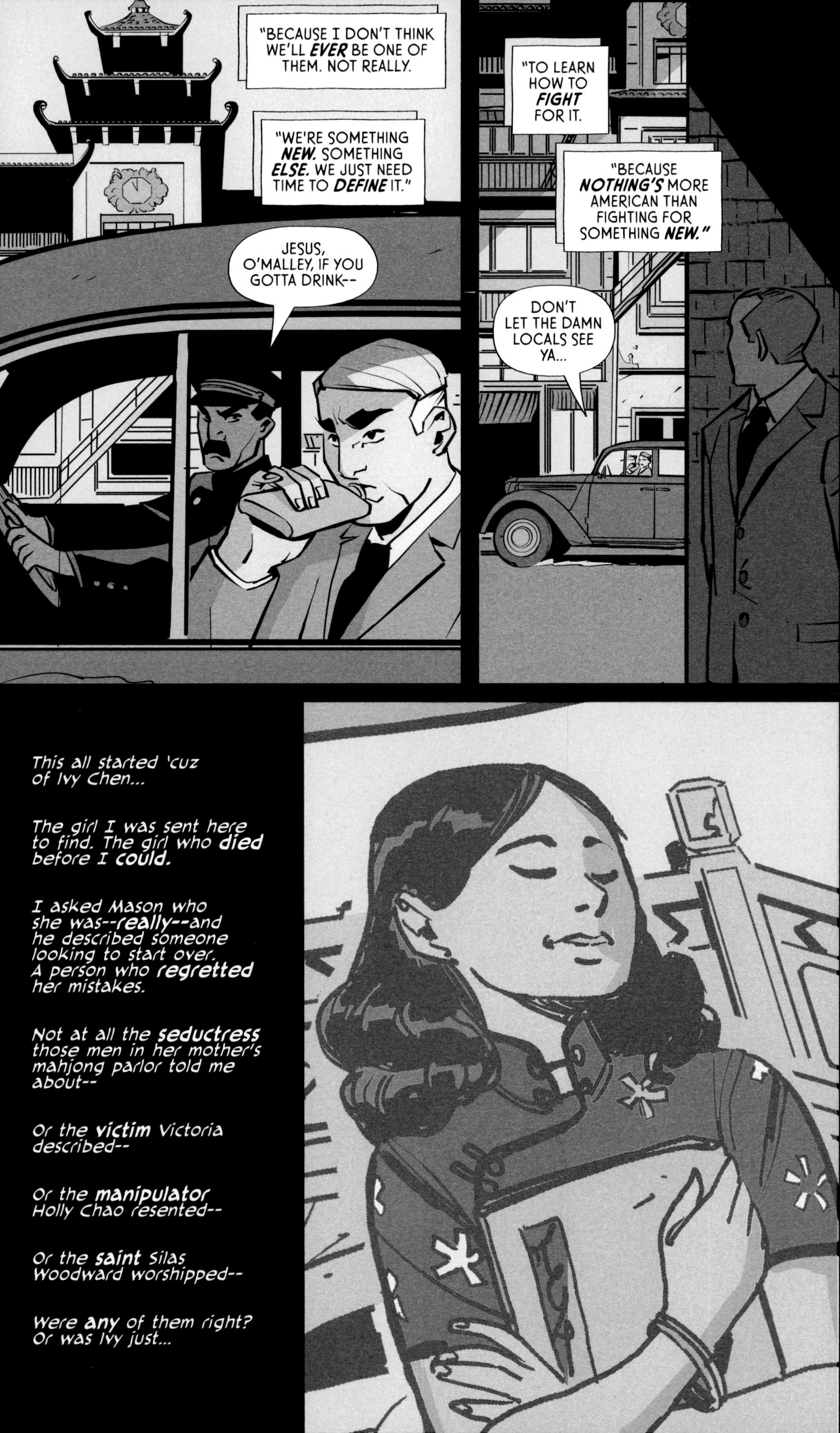
"BECAUSE I DON'T THINK WE'LL EVER BE ONE OF THEM. NOT REALLY.
"WE'RE SOMETHING NEW. SOMETHING ELSE. WE JUST NEED TIME TO DEFINE IT."
JESUS, O'MALLEY, IF YOU GOTTA DRINK--
"TO LEARN HOW TO FIGHT FOR IT.
"BECAUSE NOTHING'S MORE AMERICAN THAN FIGHTING FOR SOMETHING NEW."
DON'T LET THE DAMN LOCALS SEE YA...
This all started 'cuz of Ivy Chen...
The girl I was sent here to find. The girl who died before I could.
I asked Mason who she was--really--and he described someone looking to start over. A person who regretted her mistakes.
Not at all the seductress those men in her mother's mahjong parlor told me about--
Or the victim Victoria described--
Or the manipulator Holly Chao resented--
Or the saint Silas Woodward worshipped--
Were any of them right? Or was Ivy just...

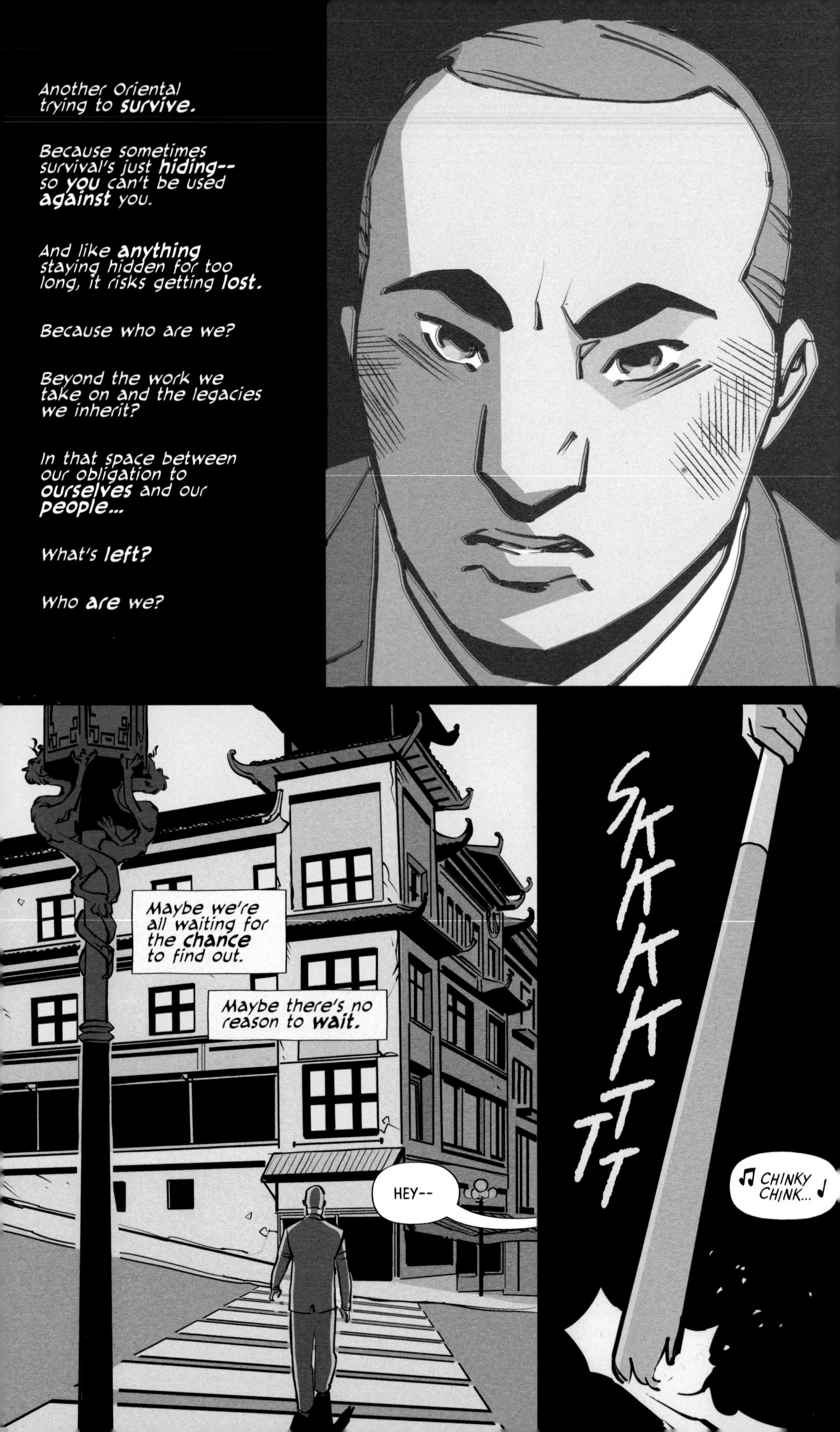
Another Oriental trying to survive.
Because sometimes survival's just hiding-- so you can't be used against you.
And like anything staying hidden for too long, it risks getting lost.
Because who are we?
Beyond the work we take on and the legacies we inherit?
In that space between our obligation to ourselves and our people...
What's left?
Who are we?
Maybe we're all waiting for the chance to find out.
Maybe there's no reason to wait.
HEY--
SKKKKTTT
♫ CHINKY CHINK... ♩

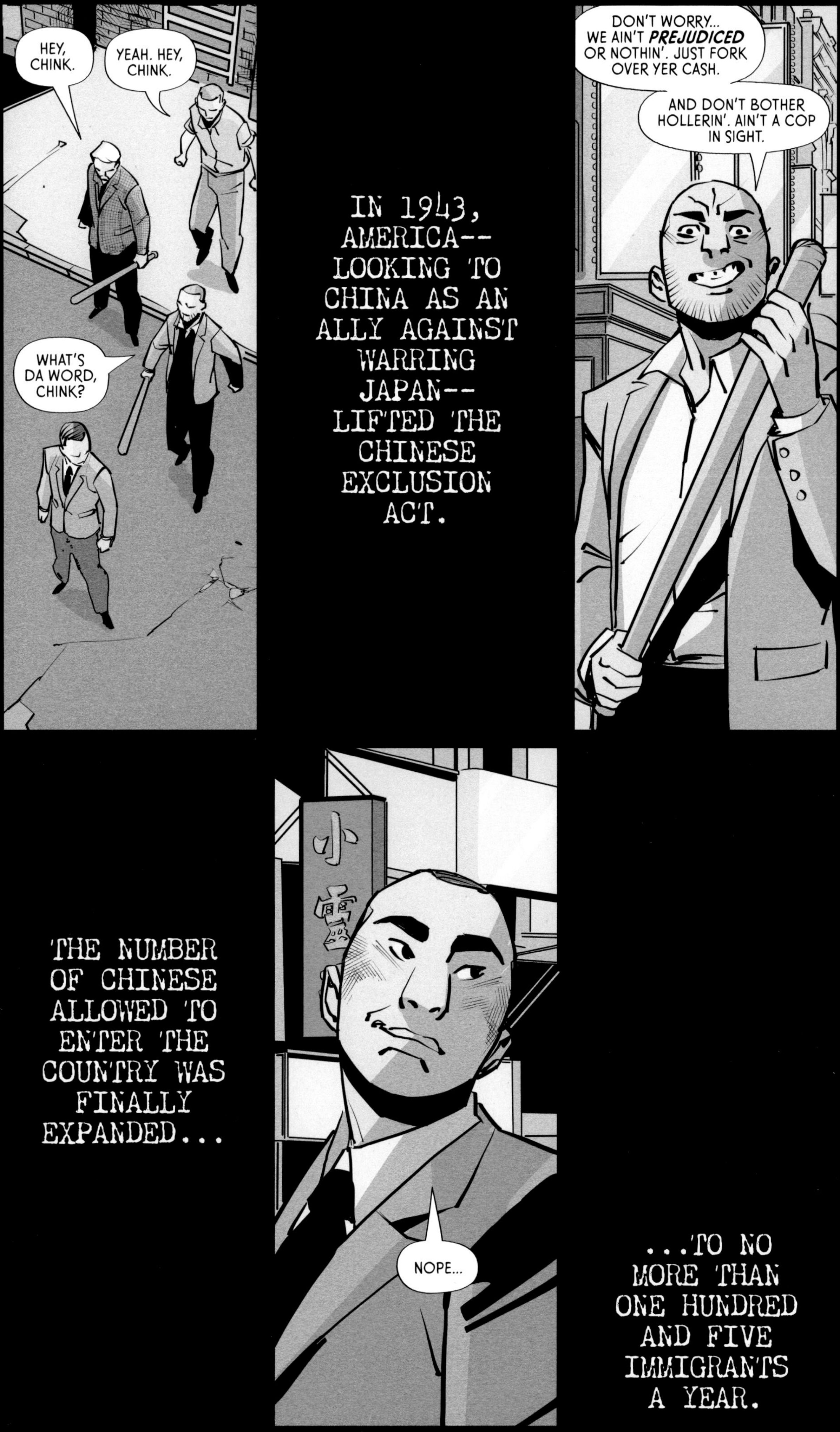
HEY, CHINK.
YEAH. HEY, CHINK.
WHAT'S DA WORD, CHINK?
IN 1943, AMERICA-- LOOKING TO CHINA AS AN ALLY AGAINST WARRING JAPAN-- LIFTED THE CHINESE EXCLUSION ACT.
DON'T WORRY... WE AIN'T ***PREJUDICED*** OR NOTHIN'. JUST FORK OVER YER CASH.
AND DON'T BOTHER HOLLERIN'. AIN'T A COP IN SIGHT.
THE NUMBER OF CHINESE ALLOWED TO ENTER THE COUNTRY WAS FINALLY EXPANDED...
NOPE...
...TO NO MORE THAN ONE HUNDRED AND FIVE IMMIGRANTS A YEAR.

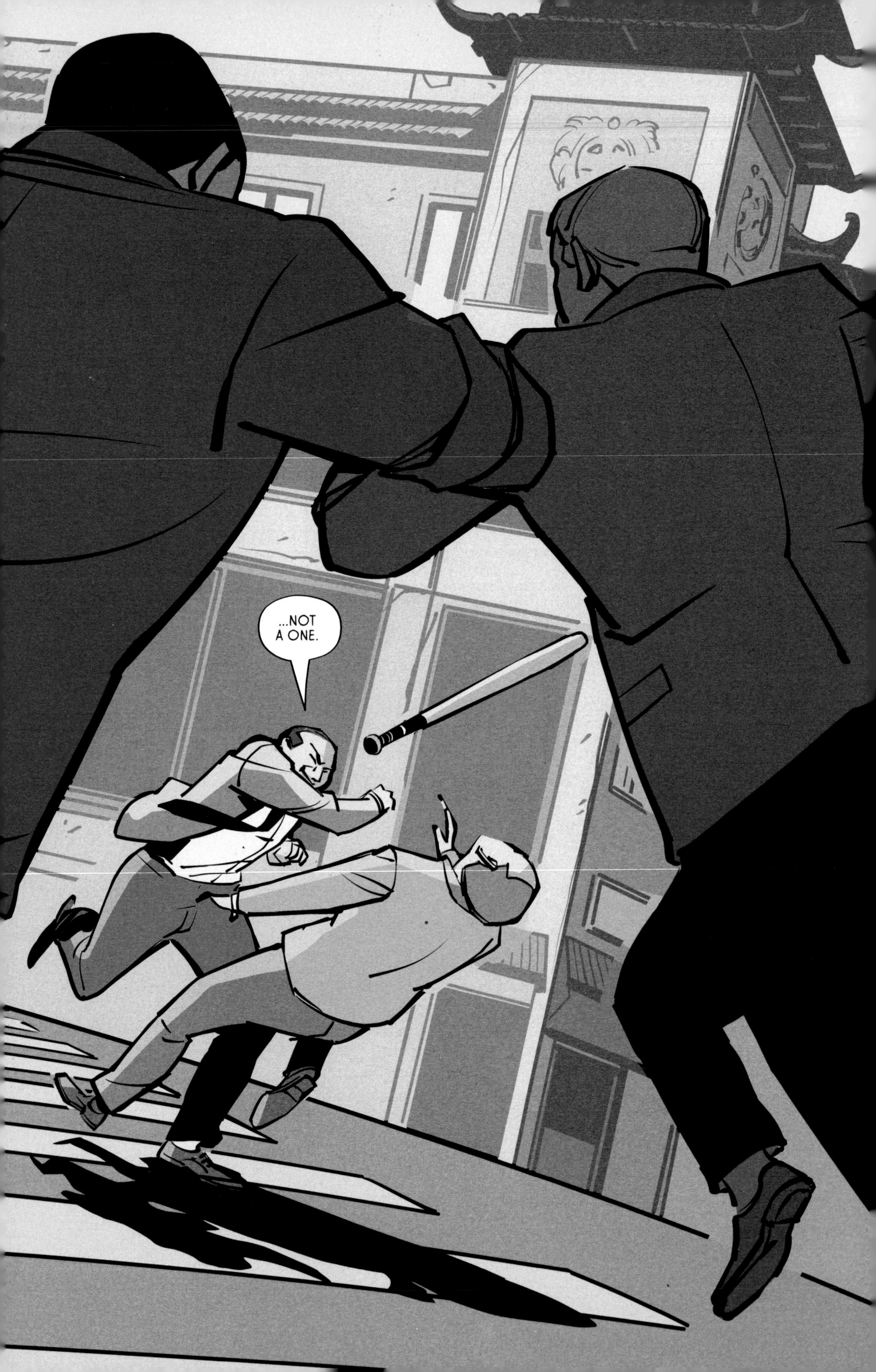
...NOT A ONE.

OTHER LAWS WOULD
CONTINUE RESTRICTING
ASIANS AND ARABS FROM
ENTERING AMERICA
UNTIL THE IMMIGRATION
AND NATIONALITY ACT
OF 1965.

EDISON HARK WILL RETURN.

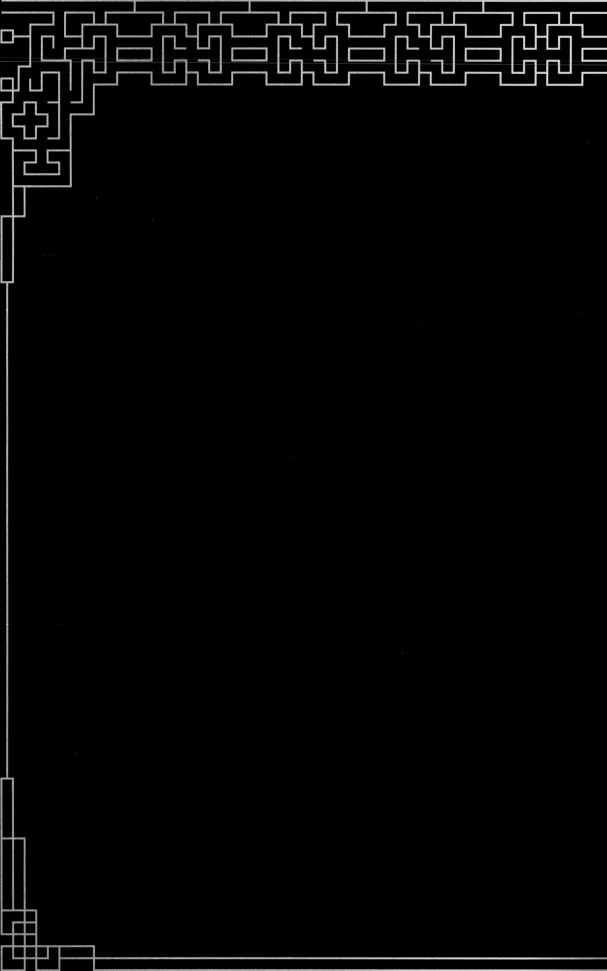

— *Fin* —

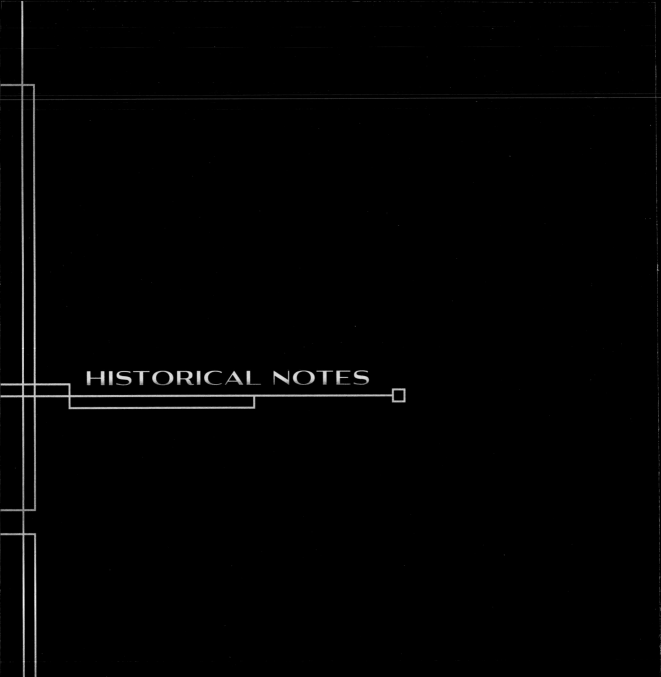

HISTORICAL NOTES

THE CHINESE EXCLUSION ACT AND ANGEL ISLAND

Context. The primary surge of Chinese immigration into the west coast of America began in the 1850s. The jobs were primarily in mining and railroad construction, but the California Gold Rush also played a part, western America becoming known as the "Golden Mountain" to working-class Chinese who came to the state — like their American counterparts — in the hopes of striking gold and sending money home to their families. Many, of course, didn't, but found payment as cheap labor in dangerous, low-wage jobs.

They were perceived to be driving down worker wages, and America... reacted. In 1854, the California Supreme Court ruled people of Asian descent couldn't testify against a White person in court, which meant a white person could escape repercussions from anti-Asian violence. In addition, politicians campaigned on anti-Chinese platforms with anti-Chinese riots breaking out across multiple American cities in the 1870s. All of it culminated in Congress passing the Chinese Exclusion Act in 1882. While the Act was targeted to keep Chinese laborers out, it would affect all Chinese travelers entering the country, allowing entry to only specific categories of travelers (we'll spell out those categories next issue).

This, of course, didn't deter the Chinese from trying to enter the country in the hopes of providing for their families (an estimated 80 – 90% of exclusion-era immigrants were able-bodied men; approximately seven men for every woman). Many saw immigration as their only way to survive. These banned Chinese would become America's first "illegal immigrants," entering the country through the borders along Canada or Mexico.

Just as immigrants crossing the Atlantic went through Ellis Island, the immigrants crossing the Pacific came through Angel Island. Whereas Ellis Island travelers, however, spent anywhere from a few hours to a few days at Ellis, Asians traveling through Angel —

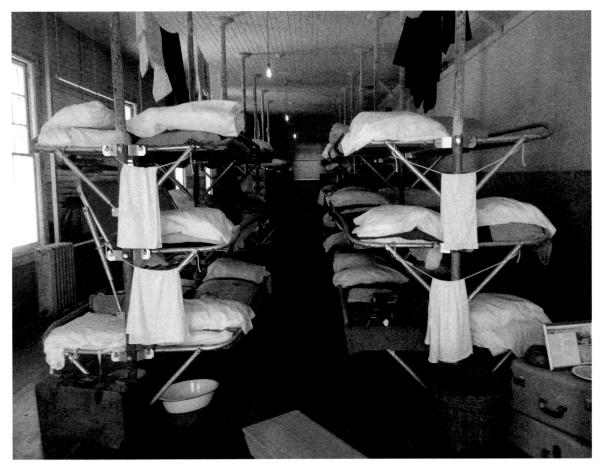

The men's dormitory.

Women's sitting room.

in particular, the Chinese — could spend anywhere from days to years detained.

Background. Angel Island is the second largest island in the San Francisco Bay, roughly 6 miles away from San Francisco, making it four times as far as Alcatraz. It began screening immigrants as early as 1891, where worries about the bubonic plague led Angel Island to be a quarantine station where visitors and their baggage were inspected before they could enter the country. Chinese immigrants in particular were believed to be more diseased than Europeans and thereby considered dangerous and contagious.

While the Immigration Station on Angel Island began construction in 1905, it wasn't opened until January 21, 1910, running up until 1940. Different groups were separated upon entry: Europeans were kept apart from the other races. The Chinese were segregated from Japanese and other Asians. Men and women were split into different dormitories — including husbands and wives who were forbidden to see or communicate until they were granted entry into America.

While Angel Island processed immigrants from eighty-four different countries, an estimated 100,000 were Chinese. Each of these travelers had to prove they belonged to one of the categories of Chinese allowed to enter America or risk deportation. In general, however, Chinese immigrants were detained longer than other nationalities.

Proving these travelers hadn't purchased fraudulent papers in the hopes of entering the country illegally was a process that could be as short as less than a week or as long as two years. The median stay for Chinese detainees was sixteen days. During that time, they stayed in large dormitory rooms, some holding over one hundred people. A person's race and class usually determined the intensity of the examination, which meant fewer white Europeans and American citizens were subjected to inspection.

Inside the dormitories themselves, the beds were crammed together, three metal bunks stacked atop one another. At one point in Angel Island's history, visitors hailing from San Francisco inspected the condition of the grounds. The lavatories were found unsanitary, and the hospital inadequate. Many detainees referred to it as an "island cage," they only being allowed to leave their quarters for meals and a short recreation period. While they waited, some detainees carved and inked their dormitory walls with Chinese poetry expressing their despair. The Angel Island State Park has preserved two of the original buildings, that poetry still etched there. One example:

The insects chirp outside the four walls.
The inmates often sigh.
Thinking of affairs back home,
Unconscious tears wet my lapel.

Examinations and interrogations. Determining if the Chinese travelers could enter involved a series of examinations and interrogations, processes complicated by a dearth of documentation at the time. Records of Chinese births, marriages, and divorces weren't always available. Many Chinese women in America gave birth at home, leaving their Chinese-American children without birth certificates to prove they were citizens. Complicating matters was how hard immigration officials found telling the Chinese apart. For a period, in addition to photographs, inspectors even instituted the Bertillon system to identify travelers — a process developed in the 1880s to identify criminals by measuring their forearms, feet, fingers, ears, heads, teeth, hair, and genitalia.

But what officials relied on most were detailed interrogations of the travelers entering the country. While they would range in length, it wasn't uncommon for these exams to span over a hundred questions, delving deep into the minutia of someone's life.

How many windows are in your house? Who lives in the third house of the first row of houses in your village? What kind of feet (bound or not) does the wife have? Chinese immigrants were expected to answer such questions without any signs of hesitation or suspicious behavior. These answers would be cross-checked against testimonies of their "fathers" or people the immigrants offered to vouch for their authenticity. People living in America were obviously the best kind, which meant travelers without relatives or friends in America faced a considerable disadvantage. If any discrepancies were found between a traveler's testimony and their witness, the inspectors assumed the immigrant was entering the country illegally.

The grounds.

A view of the dormitory through the fence.

Any Chinese-American citizen lacking papers was required to undergo a similar interrogation to re-enter. On top of their testimonies, they could also be judged by whether they dressed enough like an American, how well they recited facts about US history and, of course, how well they spoke English. Unfortunately, until the mid-twentieth century, it was common for Chinese immigrants as well as their American-born children to have little contact with non-Chinese people, tainting the accuracy of any language test.

These interrogations were so extensive that all Chinese immigrants got into the practice of relying on coaching notes, whether or not they were using "real" or "fake" papers. A small business cropped up in China selling coaching books to prospective travelers looking to study up on the most literal type of entrance exam, the topic tested being their own lives.

Exclusion also spawned creative methods of cheating. While visitors weren't allowed to interact with the detainees, some would sneak coaching notes into care packages they left for them — scraps of paper hidden in seemingly innocuous items: Peanuts whose shells were pried apart and glued back together to hide notes inside; oranges which were actually just orange peels carefully wrapped around crumpled up notes and re-glued together. Hollowed out pork buns stuffed with notes. Sometimes these "cheat notes" were even passed along by Chinese kitchen staff feeling sorry for the detainees. Some corrupt immigration guards also got into the action, smuggling notes for a fee.

While the Chinese Exclusion Act would be rescinded in 1943, its creation would impact the lives of all Americans going forward. The Act (and the laws surrounding it) provided America its first example of how to contain undesirable foreigners, initiating the government's first attempts to identify and record them, setting a precedent for the bureaucratic machinery that would eventually create US passports, "green cards," and America's deportation policies.

IMMIGRATION HISTORY TIMELINE

While THE GOOD ASIAN deals primarily with Chinese immigration, it's important to understand America's perception of non-whites, immigrants, and immigration leading up to 1936. Presented below is abbreviated (and admittedly somewhat arbitrary) timeline stringing together some of the most important years, laws, and events which form the story's backdrop.

***1790* - The Naturalization Act of 1790** - Granted "free white person[s]... of good character" from other countries a path to US Citizenship, while excluding Native-Americans, indentured servants, free blacks, and Asians.

1868 - After the Civil War, the **Fourteenth Amendment** granted African-Americans citizen-ship while establishing birthright citizenship for everyone born in the US.

***1870* - The Naturalization Act of 1870** - Extended naturalization to "aliens of African nativity and to persons of African descent" although revoked the citizenship of naturalized Chinese Americans.

***1875* - The Page Act -** While originally intended to bar East Asian forced laborers, prostitutes, or convicts from entry, the ban was only enforced on East Asian women, effectively banning Chinese women from entering the country.

***1882* - The Chinese Exclusion Act -** With the Chinese seen as stealing low-paying jobs from Americans, the Chinese Exclusion Act was passed to prohibit all Chinese laborers from entering the country. The Act was intended to last a decade to stop all Chinese immigration with the exception of diplomats, students, teachers, merchants, and US Citizens.

***1892* - The Geary Act -** Extended the Chinese Exclusion Act and required all Chinese residents carry an internal passport / resident permit. Failure to carry one was punishable by deportation or a year of hard labor. In addition, the Act barred the Chinese from bearing witness in court.

***1898* - *United States v. Wong Kim Ark* -** The Supreme Court case recognizing US birthright citizenship to American-born children of Chinese parents who had a

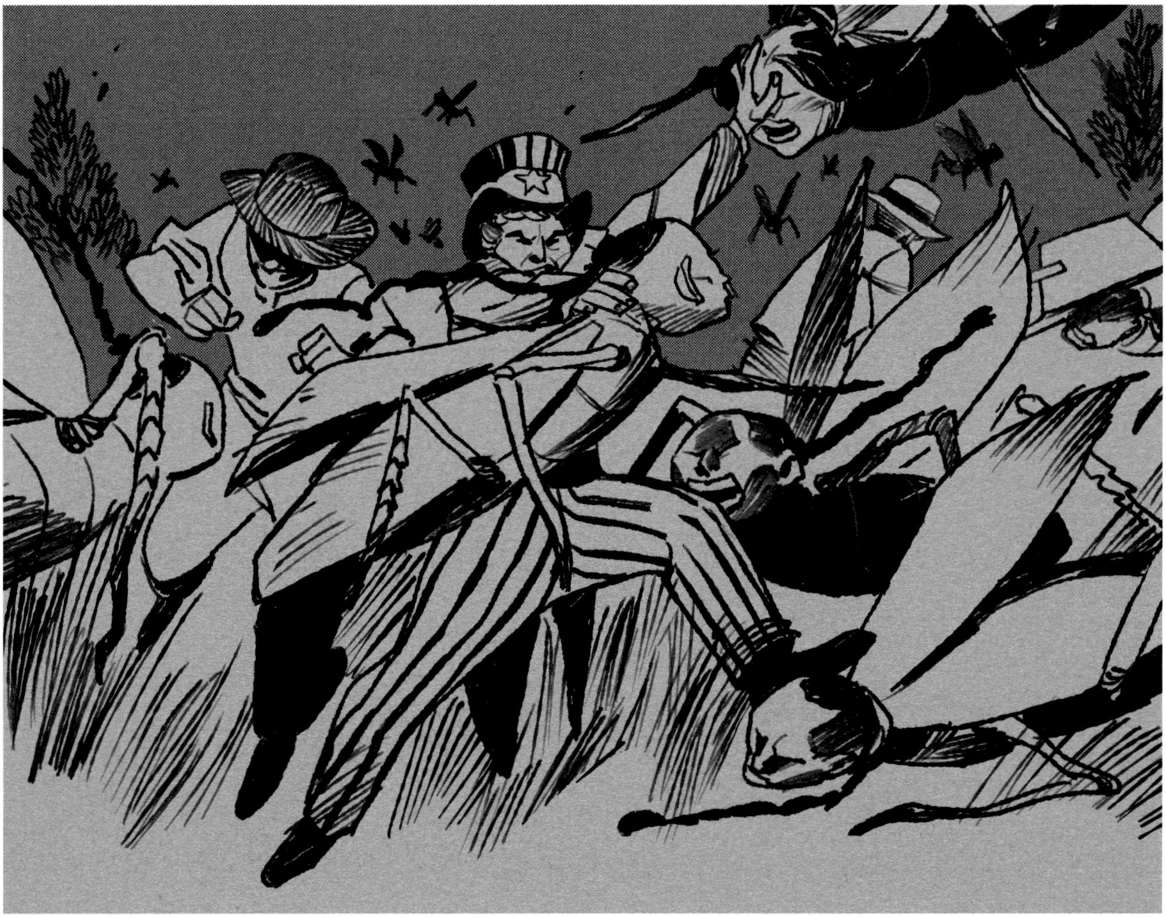

permanent residence in America. This case noted the 14th amendment applied to everyone born in the U.S., even if their parents were unable to become citizens.

1907 - The Gentlemen's Agreement - An informal agreement between the U.S. and Japan specifying how the U.S. would not impose restrictions on Japanese immigration, while Japan would not allow further emigration into America. Those Japanese in the U.S. could send for their families - resulting in "picture brides," a form of arranged marriages - so Japanese men already in the country could marry. After Chinese laborers were banned from America, many Japanese had come to the US, taking the low-paying jobs the Chinese once worked.

1917 - The Asiatic Barred Zone extended the impact of the Chinese Exclusion Act to include all of Asia (Japan was already covered by the Gentlemen's Agreement) and imposed a literacy requirement for all immigrants.

1920 - The Cable Act - While in theory designed to grant women their own national identity, the law tied a woman's citizenship to her husband and decreed any American woman who married "an alien illegible for citizenship shall cease to be a citizen of the United States." As a result, any American woman who married a Chinese immigrant would lose their citizenship.

1922 - *Takao Ozawa v. United States* - The Supreme Court case ruling ethnic Japanese were not considered Caucasian and therefore did not meet the Naturalization Act of 1790's "free white persons" requirements, allowing no path to US citizenship for Japanese immigrants.

1923 - *United States v. Bhagat Sing Thind* - The Supreme Court case ruling that while Indians were considered Caucasians by contemporary racial anthropology, they were not seen as "white" in the common understanding, making immigrants from India also ineligible for US citizenship.

1924 - The Immigration Act of 1924, also known as the **Johnson-Reed Act -** Barred Asians and Arabs from entering America, while setting quotas on the numbers of immigrants from the Eastern Hemisphere and reducing immigration from Southern and Eastern Europe. It also banned those ineligible for citizenship from immigrating, which of course applied to Asians. The act provided funding and legal instructions to courts for deporting immigrants while authorizing the formation of the US Border Patrol. According to the US Department of State's Office of the Historian, the law's purpose was

designed "to preserve the ideal of U.S. homogeneity."

1924 - The Snyder Act - Granted US Citizenship to Native-Americans 148 years after the founding of America.

1930 - Watsonville riots - The Philippines being a US colony at the time, Filipinos were not prohibited from entering America by the Johnson-Reed Act. They and Mexicans migrated to America's West Coast filling jobs previously taken by Chinese, Japanese, Koreans, and Indians. White men decrying this takeover took to vigilantism to deal with what they called the "third Asiatic invasion." Tensions culminated in a 5-day long riot in Watsonville, California where Filipinos were dragged from their homes and beaten; some were thrown off bridges. This violence inspired anti-Filipino riots across other California cities facing similar frustrations.

1929 - 1936 - Mexican repatriation - A variety of small farmers, progressives, labor unions, eugenicists, and racists had called for restrictions on Mexican immigration, feeling they were taking away jobs and blaming them for exacerbating the Depression. President Herbert Hoover, promising American jobs for Americans, slashed immigration by nearly 90% and launched a mass deportation of Mexicans and Mexican-Americans. Roughly 1.8 million men, women, and children were deported, an estimated 60% of those American birthright citizens.

CHOP SUEY CIRCUIT

Although the Jade Castle is fictional, the **chop suey circuit** it represents is not.

In 1936, Charles "Charlie" P. Low opened Chinatown's first cocktail bar — **The Chinese Village**. While locals assumed it'd fail — the Chinese not drinking under moral grounds — white patrons would buoy it, tourists coming for the alcohol but staying for a Chinese singer named Li Tei Ming. And as the bar's popularity grew — reaching standing room only capacity — others copied Low's formula. A slew of Chinese bars popped up, all featuring Chinese entertainment acts, until finally, **Chinese Sky Room** opened in 1937 — America's first Chinese-American nightclub. That led to more copycats and so, the Chinatown nightclub scene was born.

These dine-and-dance venues — now collectively remembered as the chop suey circuit — had a signature formula — food, alcohol, and all-Chinese entertainment, a mix of Chinese showgirls, singers, dancers, acrobats, and magicians. The clubs opened up a renaissance of sorts for Chinese performers. After all, finding work as a Chinese entertainer was hard, their Asian faces being deemed to stand out too much amongst a chorus line or entertainment troop. But with the chop suey circuit's popularity, Chinese dancers became inundated with work — some performing at two or three clubs a night, a few transitioning to work abroad or have their acts recorded for film and TV.

The clubs weren't without their controversy — particularly for the women. Chinese women were raised never to show their arms or legs in public, leading dancers to receive letters characterizing them as loose or whores, telling them they should be ashamed. Recruiting showgirls was so tough most of the women the clubs hired grew up outside Chinatown — from places as far away as Arizona, Hawaii, and the Midwest. They all came to Chinatown following their hunger to perform — and in the process shattered the stereotypes of what an Asian girl should or shouldn't do.

White patrons came to the clubs looking for an exotic flavor. And while owners and entertainers obliged, it was also important they prove they were just as American as their audience. Some acts would start out in traditional Chinese garb, only to tear them off and reveal Western outfits beneath, as their consequent acts prove they could sing and dance in Western styles just as well as Eastern.

These clubs' popularity skyrocketed through World War 2, as servicemen spent more time in nightclubs and bars. Wartime rationing limiting the amount of goods one could buy left Americans with more money for entertainment. And while the end of the war would result in taxation and unionization (as well as a shift in American priorities) that would hurt the clubs' profitability, the popularity of the chop suey circuit nevertheless changed Chinatown, which in 1936 was still recovering from the Depression. It created a club scene completely run by Chinese Americans, transforming the neighborhood into a tourist attraction and turning a people seen as sideshow freaks into local entertainment moguls.

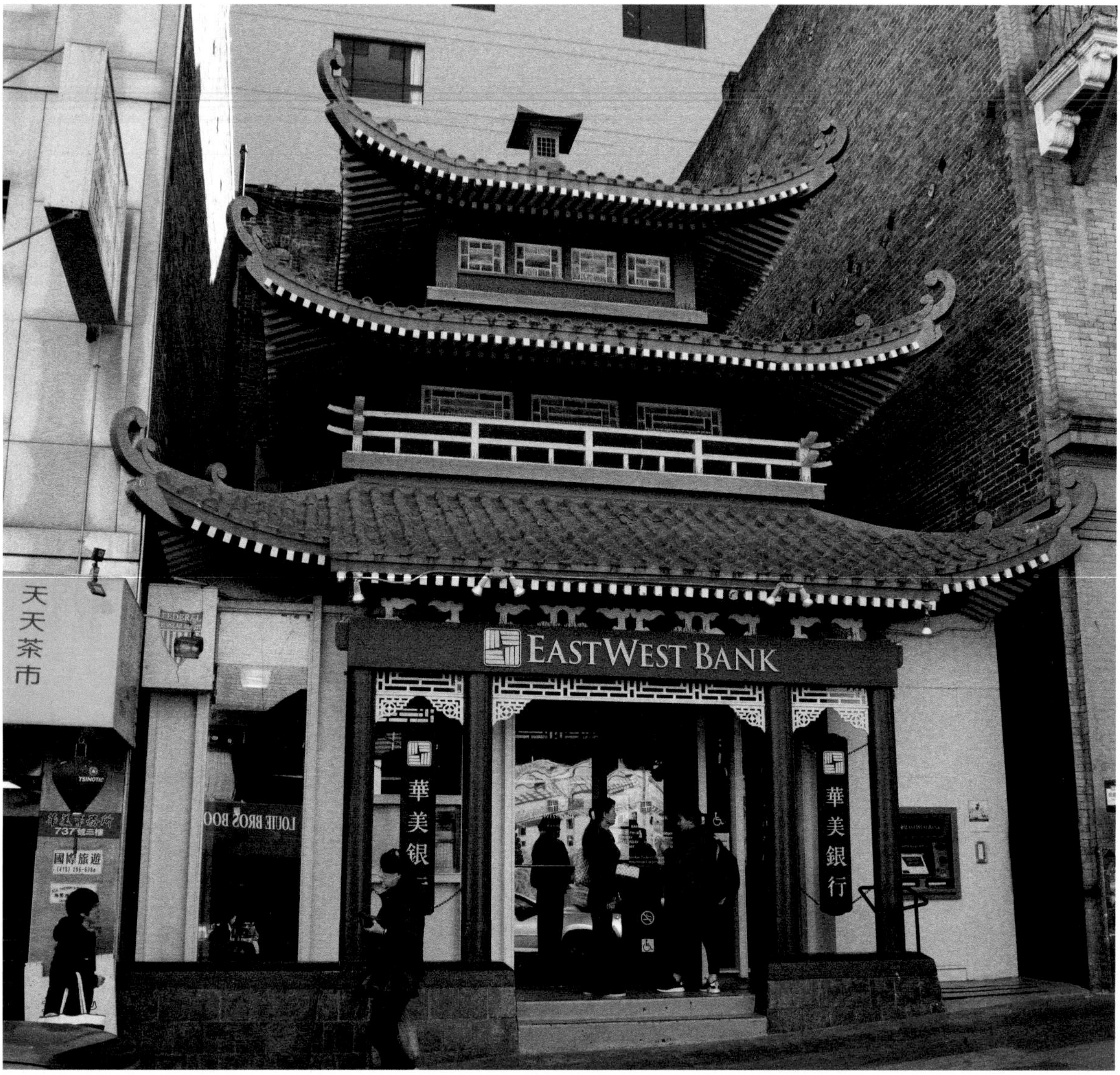
EASTWEST BANK
華美銀行
天天茶市

Former location of the Chinatown Telephone Exchange.

CHINATOWN TELEPHONE EXCHANGE

According to *Bridging the Pacific* by Thomas Chinn, the **Chinatown Telephone Exchange** was established in 1894 at 743 Washington St with three male operators and 37 telephone subscribers. The original, sumptuously furnished location featured chairs of carved teakwood inlaid with mother-of-pearl; windows of Chinese oyster-shell panes; and switchboards of ebony.

After the **San Francisco Earthquake of 1906** destroyed the original building, a new one was constructed in 1909 in a pagoda-like building keeping with the drive to create an "Oriental city." It served 800 phones, and by that point, the staff was all-female. Operators were required to have memorized the addresses and 4-digit telephone numbers of everyone in Chinatown. By 1936, the Exchange had 21 operators for the community's 2,200 phones, which included residents, businesses, and public phones. Callers would ring up, asking to be connected to their aunt / uncle / eye doctor, with Operators expected to know the numbers to be patched through to.

These operators usually spoke two or three different dialects and were all generally of the same age. The Exchange became a social hub, the women not only growing close, but many even having children around the same time. Automatic dialing forced the Exchange to close in 1948, the building now home to an East West Bank (pictured above).

HARK'S REAL-LIFE INSPIRATION

While Hark's psyche and conflicts are the author's creation, the interpretation clings very close to historical precedent, liberally stealing from the life of America's first Chinese detective — **Chang Apana,** who preceded Hark by decades and also served as the inspiration for the 20th century's most famous Asian detective — Charlie Chan.

A recount of Chang Apana's life could easily be criticized as "too comic book-y." He started off as a Hawaiian cowboy, regularly carrying a bullwhip, even as a cop. He was generally considered a master of disguise. He had a scar over his eye given to him by a Japanese leper who attacked him with a sickle. Drug addicts once threw him out of a second story window, only for him to land on his feet and run back in to arrest them. Once, while casing out a suspicious cargo ship, he was run over by a horse and buggy. Another time — without back-up and armed only with his whip — he arrested forty gamblers who he single-handedly lined up and marched to the police station.

These incredible exploits aside... Detective Chang Apana was born on December 26, 1871 in the village of Waipio, his first name a Hawaiianized version of the Chinese name Ah Pung (Chinese names typically listed as [last name] [first name]). While his parents came to Hawaii as laborers, lack of work and homesickness found them returning to China when Chang was only three. But the Opium Wars and the Taiping Revolution had devastated their rural Canton, plunging their home into poverty. And so, when Chang was ten, his parents had him accompany his uncle back to Hawaii, hoping he'd fare better in America than they had.

Chang would eventually become a *paniolo* — a Hawaiian cowboy. Helen Kinau Wilder — the owner of Chang's horses and a champion of social reform — was so impressed she hired him to be an animal case investigator for the newly founded Hawaiian chapter of the Humane Society. While the job only involved investigating animal cruelty, because the Society was technically part of the Honolulu Police Department, it was a position Chang could never have attained without the patronage of the rich white Wilder.

A friend of Wilder's — a Hawaiian Marshall — was likewise impressed by Chang, hiring him to be an officer in the police force. In 1898, Chang became America's first Chinese-American police officer. As part of the Honolulu PD, one of Chang's responsibilities involved arresting Chinese lepers, so they could be deported to the leper colony on the island of Molokai, leprosy at the time considered a "Chinese disease."

Chang also became invaluable during sting operations, becoming one of Hawaii's first undercover cops, since one of the major vices the police were charged with cracking down on was gambling — a favorite pastime for many Chinese.

Chang's most common undercover disguise was posing as a See Yup Man. See Yup Men are Chinese street peddlers dangling two baskets of goods on either end of a shoulder pole. Chang would enter gambling dens pretending to sell goods but actually peeking at the operation so he could tell the raiding cops what to look out for.

Eventually, Chang's considerable exploits received newspaper attention. While the writer Earl Derr Biggers was doing research for his novel *The House Without a Key*, he read of Chang's exploits and inserted a Chinese detective character a quarter way into his novel. That character stole the show, and Biggers' next novel, *The Chinese Parrot,* started a series of books centering around the adventures of Charlie Chan. Biggers eventually met Chang in 1928, giving him credit for inspiring his famous Asian detective. Four years later, Chang retired from active duty after being injured in a car accident.

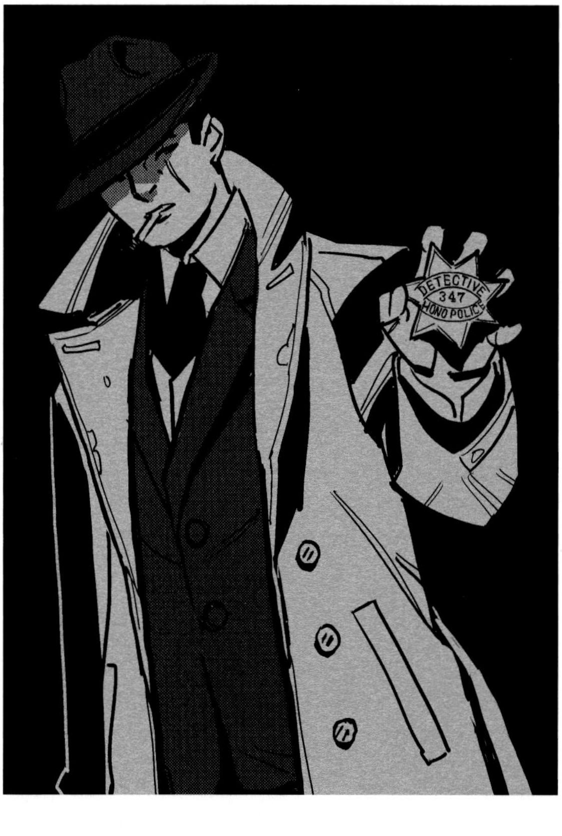
DETECTIVE
347
HONO POLICE

THE MASSIE TRIAL

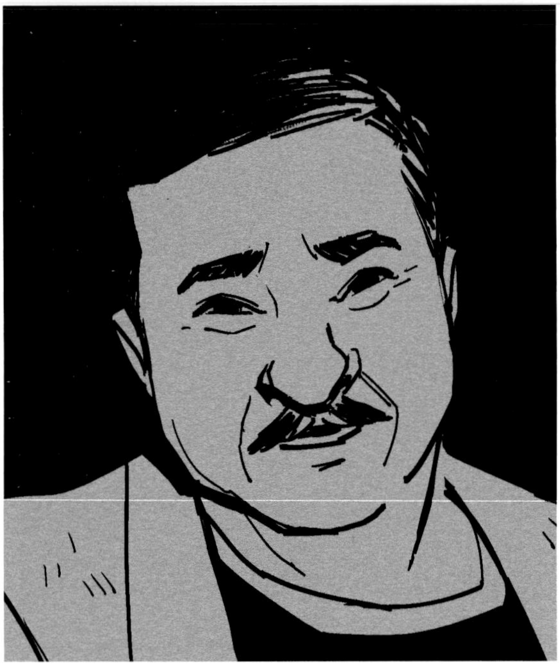

Wilbur Manalao's story is very much inspired by the considerably more explosive Massie trial, one of the most infamous and important legal cases of 1930s Hawaii.

By the 1930s, Hawaii was a playground for wealthy Americans. While the island's overwhelming majority was nonwhite, including its entire low-paid workforce, a small, wealthy white minority – who locals referred to as *haoles* – controlled the economy, living lives of opulence.

Thalia Fortescue Massie was a 20-year-old wife of a rising US Navy officer stationed there. She also hailed from an affluent family, being a descendant to inventor Alexander Graham Bell. On September 12, 1931, she was found one night wandering a deserted Honolulu road, having been beaten, her jaw broken. She claimed to have been abducted while leaving a nearby nightclub, and when questioned, stated a group of Hawaiian men had assaulted and robbed her. While initially she said it was too dark to provide details on the men or their car, hours later, she reported to police not only had she had been raped, but described her assailants as "locals," able to recite their license plate number.

Within hours, the police arrested the alleged assailants. Two were of Hawaiian ancestry, two were Japanese, and one was half-Chinese / half-Hawaiian. And while Massie's story initially seemed credible, it proceeded to fall apart. It was later unearthed that officers taking her statement had fed her information, including the license plate number of the five accused. Additionally, there was no evidence Massie had been raped, while records showed the alleged attackers were involved in a car accident across town around the time of Massie's assault.

Numerous rumors and theories circulated about what really happened that night. Some alleged Massie had not been raped at all. Others believed she was having an affair with one of her alleged attackers. Another theory involved Massie cheating on her husband with one of his friends, it being her husband who broke her jaw upon discovering the infidelity.

These claims enraged Massie's mother, **Grace Fortescue**, who saw them as smears against her family's good name, starting a public campaign to attack the defendants. But due to lack of evidence and conflicting testimony, the case fell apart. After a three-week trial – the court's spectators' gallery frequently jam-packed with an audience – the case against the accused ended with a hung jury mistrial.

According to one account of the proceedings, "bedlam broke loose in the halls of the judiciary building following the discharge of the jury." Some in the Navy viewed the failure to convict the attackers of a Naval wife as publicly shaming their forces. Given that Hawaii prohibited juries to be comprised exclusively of people from only one race, they believed the accused were let go because of racial solidarity. Local paper *The Honolulu Times* covered the events under the headline "The Shame of Honolulu." And while Hawaiians considered the paper a sensationalistic tabloid, the publication eventually circulated to the mainland, influencing the trial's coverage in national news.

In the spring of 1932, *The New York Times* ran almost two hundred stories about the events surrounding the Massie trial. The case was voted by Associated Press editors as one of the top news events of the year – and the most important criminal trial in the country. The Honolulu Citizen's Organization for Good Government was formed with a list of demands including "the sterilization of certain delinquents." The story so dominated mainland America, movie theaters opened their programs with news footage of the ongoing "native uprising" in the islands. *Time Magazine* published a story headlined "Lust in Paradise," describing the islands' "motley population" and the rape of "the daughter of a gallant soldier, the granddaughter of one of the world's greatest inventors," describing how in this "paradise melting pot of East & West... yellow men's lust for white women had broken bounds."

In contrast to mainland hysteria, however, there was in fact no record of a Hawaiian ever raping a *haole* woman by the time of the trial, although there was a history going back centuries of *haoles* raping Hawaiians. Most of these men, if captured, pleaded to reduced charges and received little punishment. In fact, *The New York Times*'s Pulitzer Prize-winning Russell Owen had once been told by one of Honolulu's prominent businessmen that "when he was a boy, attending the exclusive school for white children in Honolulu, he and some of his friends used to find it lots of fun to take some Hawaiian girl out on a dark road at night and rape her."

Massie's mother, Grace Fortescue, became obsessed with getting the accused men jailed pending a second trial. But without new solid evidence, she was told there was no chance of a conviction. Incensed, Fortescue arranged for the kidnapping and vicious beating of one of the accused. Then, she enlisted Massie's husband and two other Navy men to kidnap another plaintiff — **Joseph Kahahawai** — the darkest skinned of the five defendants. The four attempted to beat a confession out of him, ending with one of them shooting and killing Kahahawai.

While they were attempting to dump the body, a passing policeman noted suspicious activity, pulling them over and discovered Kahahawai. The officer immediately arrested all four.

Fortescue and her colleagues were now on trial for murder. For her defense, the socialite hired no less than Clarence Darrow, leading member of the ACLU, bringing the lawyer famous for his involvement in the Leopold and Loeb murder trial out of retirement.

Believing Fortescue and her navy accomplices would not be safe in a jail containing Hawaiian guards and prisoners, the four were imprisoned in a decommissioned ship in permanent dry dock at Pearl Harbor. *Time Magazine* described Fortescue's quarters as a "penthouse, bristling with ventilators to cool the neat single cabins within, each comparable to that on a small liner." With staterooms for cells, the accused murderers of Joseph Kahahawai had "books, cards, and music... electric fans, call bells, and all the conveniences of a modern hotel." The onboard officer's mess hall provided their meals. The four also became overwhelmed with flower deliveries, well-wishers who saw Fortescue as a celebrity wrongly punished for defending her daughter's honor.

Meanwhile, fearing more violence against the remaining four men charged but found not guilty of attacking Thalia Massie, the four were taken in for protective custody, locked up for their own security at Honolulu's municipal jail. If they wanted to eat, their families and friends had to provide the food.

No one in Honolulu wanted to serve in the jury of the trial of Grace Fortescue, fearing they'd inevitably offend someone whichever way they voted. When the trial inevitably did happen, Fortescue and her colleagues were ultimately charged with manslaughter (rather than murder) for the death of Joseph Kahahawai.

The mainland press exploded. Every Hearst newspaper condemned the "Hawaiian rabble" and provided a form for readers to fill out and mail to their representatives urging them "to take immediate action to afford the protection of the United States government to American women in Hawaii... and to force respect in Hawaii for the American flag and its defenders." The volume of mail and cable messages out of Washington, D.C. on the topic was greater than on any subject since the end of World War I.

Meanwhile, members of Congress began calling upon President Hoover to pardon Fortescue and her colleagues. Senators and congressmen lined up to introduce a flood of legislation designed to punish Hawaii. At one point, martial law was even suggested if rioting were to begin.

At a certain point, the Governor hired the Pinkerton's National Detective Agency to further investigate Thaila Massie's attack. They responded with a 279-page report, citing their investigation "makes it impossible to escape the conviction that the kidnaping and assault was not caused by those accused." The White House, however, pressured Hawaii's governor to suppress the report, fearing embarrassment if the five innocent men who had been arrested and tried — one even murdered — were found innocent for a rape that never occurred.

Under pressure from the Navy, Fortescue and her colleagues' ten-year sentences were commuted to one hour served in the high sheriff's office. Days later, the four convicted killers and Thalia Massie boarded a ship back to the mainland, leaving Hawaii as national celebrities.

But the Massie trial would prove a pivotal moment in Hawaii's racial reckoning. The events would lead Hawaiian, Japanese, Chinese, and Filipino community leaders to begin meeting and finding common ground. Meanwhile, prominent *haole* residents in the legal community, press, and politics, abhorred by the events, began speaking out against the arrogance of the long-standing *haole* oligarchy. The combined efforts would start a shift in racial attitudes, and eventually, the politics and laws of the land followed.

REFERENCES

For anyone interested in reading more on any of these topics, the following are some recommended sources:

- *Chinese San Francisco 1850 - 1943: A Trans-Pacific Community* by Yong Chen for a general history of the Chinese in San Francisco.

- *At America's Gates: Chinese Immigration during the Exclusion Era: 1882 - 1943* by Erika Lee is a go-to text about the topic.

- *Island: Poetry and History of Chinese Immigrants on Angel Island 1910 - 1940, Second Edition*, edited by Him Mark Lai, Genny Lim, and Judy Yung features testimonials from detainees who passed through Angel Island as well as people who worked there and the Chinese poems found on the barrack walls, translated into English.

- *Images of America: Angel Island* by Branwell Fanning and William Wong. Photos from the *Images of America* book series is one of the chief photo-references used in the making of this series.

- *Forbidden City, USA: Chinese American Nightclubs, 1936 - 1970* by Arthur Dong who's probably the authority on the subject of America's chop suey club circuit, the book featuring interviews with many of the club's performers. The book is an off-shoot of Dong's documentary on the subject, likewise titled *Forbidden City, USA*.

- *Charlie Chan: The Untold Story of the Honorable Detective and His Rendezvous with American History* by Yunte Huang for more information about the life of both Detective Chang Apana and the origins and enduring popularity of the fictional Charlie Chan.

- *Honor Killing: Race, Rape, and Clarence Darrow's Spectacular Last Case* by David E. Stannard for an in-depth examination of the Massie trail.

- *Carved in Silence* (1987), a documentary by Felicia Lowe about the Chinese Exclusion Act and can be purchased upon any visit to the Angel Island State Park.

- Speaking of which, the **Angel Island State Park** preserves much of this history as well as the original buildings. All pictures shown here were all taken there and running with their permission. Their staff is incredibly helpful and kind, as well as just a google away.

- The CHSA (*Chinatown Historical Society of America*) is located in San Francisco's Chinatown and another fantastic resource for Chinese history. The CHSA has many exhibits chronicling the history of the Chinese in America, including some of the coaching notes passed to Angel Island detainees hidden inside orange peels and peanut shells.

THE GOOD ASIAN
PROPOSAL

The following is the original proposal sent to Image Comics leading to the greenlight of the series. It is presented here in its original entirety, although much of the story would end up changing in the writing — most significantly, the names of almost all the characters.

THE GOOD ASIAN

(A 10-issue series written by Pornsak Pichetshote with art by Alexandre Tefenkgi; colors by TBD; letters & design by Jeff Powell; edited by Will Dennis)

THE LOGLINE: Following a Chinese-American detective on the trail of a killer in 1936 Chinatown, THE GOOD ASIAN is Asian film noir starring the first generation of Americans to come of age under an immigration ban… the Chinese.

THE CONCEPT: EDISON HARK (33) is a burnt-out Chinese-American detective who's built his career on turning in Chinese criminals in his native Hawaii. But when the hunt for a missing person leads him to San Francisco's Chinatown district – where a series of killings threaten to derail the repeal of the Chinese Exclusion Act (the immigration ban prohibiting the Chinese from entering America since 1882) – his investigation will force him to re-examine everything he cherishes, in a murder mystery asking how much obligation we have to our race.

THE PROTAGONIST: After his mother died, young **EDISON HARK** was taken in by her rich, white employer and raised as one of his own. That upbringing imparted him with an appreciation for the law, while a lifetime assimilating in a white world gave Hark an almost Sherlock Holmes-ian ability to read people. The insight would make him a masterful detective. But the department found the best use for him as an undercover officer, infiltrating Chinese opium and gambling dens and turning in perpetrators. While he justified his actions by believing they were for the greater good, a career of turning in his own people has left Hark broken and cynical, believing the Chinese will always be second-class citizens in America. Burnt-out and cynical, Hark is an undercover cop who's become such a good liar, he too easily fools himself.

THE APPEAL: THE GOOD ASIAN is set in an era never before explored in fiction – when America banned Chinese immigrants. Exploring immigration bans, police brutality, and identity politics, the book flips mystery tropes on its head to tells a story about Asian-American identity, all while introducing a tough, sexy, yet deeply conflicted male Asian protagonist. In a post-*Crazy Rich Asians* world, the book explores events unique to the Chinese-American perspective such as **Angel Island,** the immigration center / concentration camp Chinese immigrants were kept before they could enter America; **paper sons,** the unique way the Chinese faked immigration papers; and the fascinatingly singular popularity of **Chop Suey nightclub circuit** in the 1930s.

THE CREATORS: PORNSAK PICHETSHOTE was a Thai-American editor at DC/VERTIGO, his books having been nominated for dozens of Eisners. His hit Image book INFIDEL earned spots on 20+ Best of the Year's lists, including *NPR*, *The Hollywood Reporter*, and *The Huffington Post*, while securing a film option within two issues. ALEXANDRE TEFENKGI is an international illustrator – the co-creator of Image's OUTPOST ZERO in America and *Where are the Great Days?* in France. JEFF POWELL has lettered comics for over two decades, including Kaare Andrews' RENATO JONES, INFIDEL, and the Eisner-nominated *Atomic Robo*. From Image's UNDISCOVERED COUNTRY and FAMILY TREE to DC/Vertigo's *100 Bullets* and *Y: The Last Man*, WILL DENNIS is one of the most respected editors in comics. His work has been nominated for countless Eisners.

THE GOOD ASIAN condensed overview

The year is 1936. **Edison Hark** is a burnt-out Chinese-American police detective working in Hawaii. After a career as an undercover cop selling out his own people, he's come to accept no matter how much he tries to justify his actions, things will never get better; the Chinese will always be second-class citizens. He's called to San Francisco by his white surrogate family, the **Thurstons** – stern patriarch **George Thurston**, repentant eldest **Spencer Thurston**, and overachieving youngest **Victoria Thurston** – only to find George has taken ill. It was Spencer who summoned him to find **May Chen**, the family housekeeper and his father's secret love, Spencer hoping to reunite the two before the old man passes.

Looking for leads, Hark investigates San Francisco's Chinatown district where he finds a community terrorized by cops and yet still believing they're on the verge of acceptance; that America's ban on Chinese immigrants will soon be lifted. And while a younger, more idealistic Hark might have related, everything this cop has seen since has made him too jaded. But the more he uncovers about the missing May Chen, he discovers a ghost of his former self: A cynical woman who also discovered idealism working for the Thurstons. But in her case, was it just an act for their benefit? Answering that question takes on increasing significance as Hark discovers May's path is linked to a killer's – a fabled Tong boss named **Hui Long** – on the loose at a time when Washington is keeping careful watch on America's Chinatowns, as Congress votes to repeal the Chinese Exclusion Act.

As Hui Long's killings escalate, Hark finds himself continually two steps behind him – as he also meets a generation of Chinese-Americans who grew up during the immigration ban, people with a much different perspective on race than Hark had growing up in Hawaii. Despite being inspired by their stories, Hark will be continually forced to believe that the only way a Chinese cop can protect other Chinese is by selling them out. In the process, he'll meet **Terence Chang,** an Obama-esque lawyer rehabilitating Chinatown's public image (who Hark believes is corrupt) and become reacquainted with Victoria Thurston – who Hark dated in high school, their relationship a secret since miscegenation was illegal.

The tension builds when Hark must chase Hui Long with a stubborn Spencer in tow – the killer murdering him to escape. And Spencer's death isn't just disastrous for personal reasons. Realizing news of a dead white man in Chinatown would kill the repeal of the Chinese Exclusion Act, Hark covers up his killing… only to be caught red-handed and blamed for his death.

A fugitive on the run, Hark goes to the only person he can trust – Victoria Thurston. They overcome their considerable baggage to track down Hui Long, in the process unearthing his connection to May Chen: That Hui Long is a smokescreen used by May Chen's *white* half-brother **Raymond Gold**. Gold is using the Hui Long identity to cover his tracks as he murders a cadre of Chinatown VIPs. And in the process of discovering *that,* Victoria uncovers that May Chen is in fact alive and working with her blood-thirsty half-brother. The revelation disheartens a downtrodden Hark; he so desperately wants to believe a cynic could find optimism through the Thurstons like he once did, a part of him believing that perhaps his descent into cynicism was through losing touch with the values George Thurston imparted on him.

It culminates in an epic battle between Gold and Hark. The detective eventually wins, but not before Gold practically carves Hark's face open – grotesquely scarring him. But before Gold can confess his motive, he and Hark are both mowed down by an unseen GUNMAN.

Six months later, and the damage to Chinatown has been done. The repeal of the Exclusion Act has failed; Hark is believed to be Spencer Thurston's murderer; and George Thurston has miraculously recuperated. We reveal a slowly recuperating Hark, one with a new face due to plastic surgery. So disguised, he gets the drop on the Gunman who shot him, discovering the mastermind behind his shooting – and the last person Gold meant to kill – Victoria Thurston.

Confronting Victoria, Hark learns that she and Terence have been having a secret affair. But a year ago, Gold began blackmailing them with pictures. With miscegenation illegal, the revelation would have destroyed Terence's standing, negating his good work. Victoria and other influential Chinatown players planned to eliminate Gold. But the murder attempt failed, allowing him to escape. When Gold finally recuperated, he used the legend of Hui Long – one which his sister May Chen once told him – as a smokescreen to cover his killings. But spotting the erroneous remnants she incorrectly recalled of Hui Long legend in the killings, May Chen realized her estranged half-brother must be involved, leaving the Thurston home in search of him.

But if May Chen went looking for Hui Long, where is she now? Dead, sadly, as Hark eventually deduces Victoria lied about seeing her – because *Victoria* in fact killed her. She confesses: May Chen came to Victoria with the results of her search for her stepbrother, and Victoria, knowing the trail would eventually lead back to her, had May Chen killed, disposing of the body.

But upon learning this, George Thurston still won't allow Victoria to be arrested, vowing to use all his resources to move them out of San Francisco, away from the law. Because no matter her heinous crime, Victoria is still his daughter.

The story ends with Hark harshly realizing that as cynical as he is, he was still idolizing the Thurstons. But his interactions with Chinatown will lead him to an even more disappointing conclusion: that despite believing he chose being a cop as the lesser of two evils to protect his fellow Chinese, he's in fact lived his entire life secretly yearning to be accepted by whites.

With his new face, Hark encounters Terence one final time in the midst of the lawyer trying to gain white support to repeal the Chinese Exclusion Act, and Hark realizes his suspicions of Terence all stemmed from his jealousy of Terence's unshakeable idealism. And while Hark will try to impart what he's learned to Terence – that jockeying for white favor will never truly set the Chinese free – Terence will counter with a cold truth – they also have no hope of equality without it. Hearing the truth in Terence's words, Hark departs, acknowledging for the first time how much Chinatown needs a man like Terence.

But a man like him? Of that, he's less sure. Hark leaves Chinatown an outlaw, bereft of friends and family. But with a new face, a new life, finally his own man…

Curious if America has a place for that.

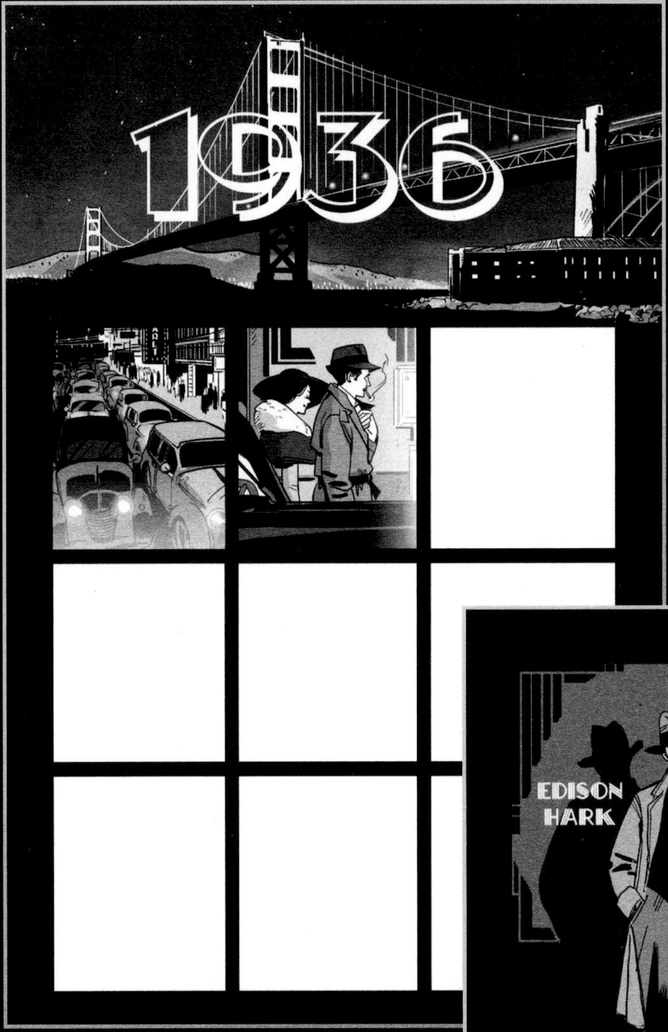
1936

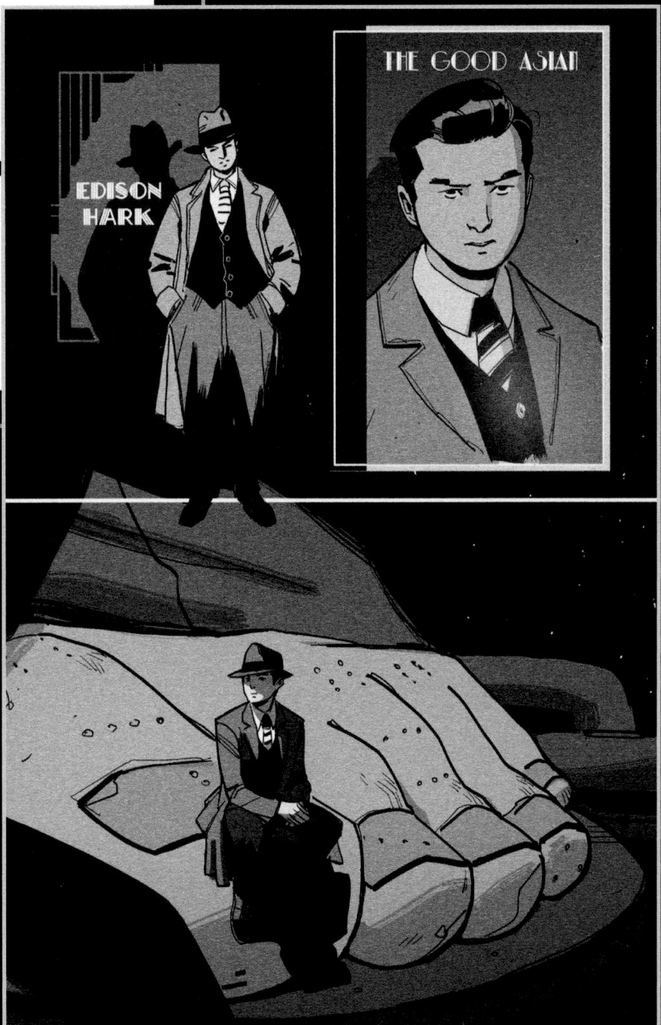
EDISON HARK
THE GOOD ASIAN

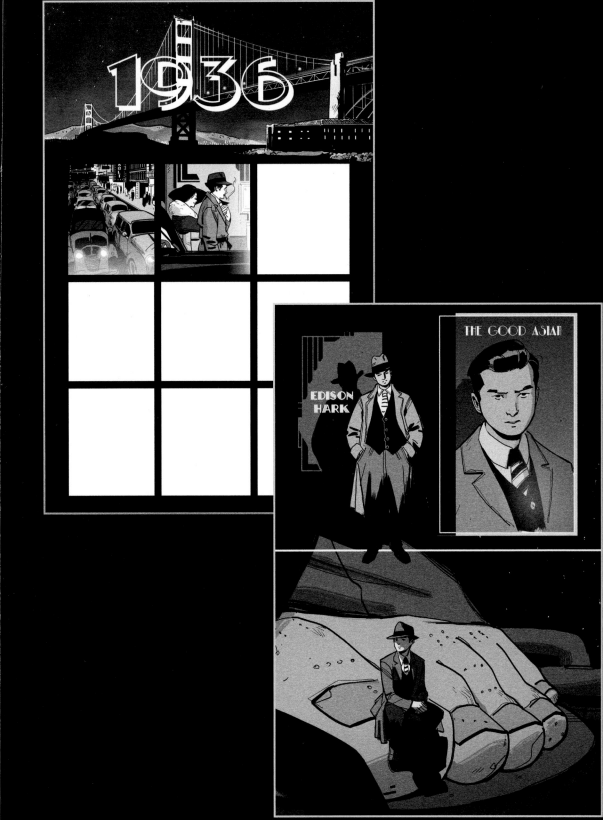

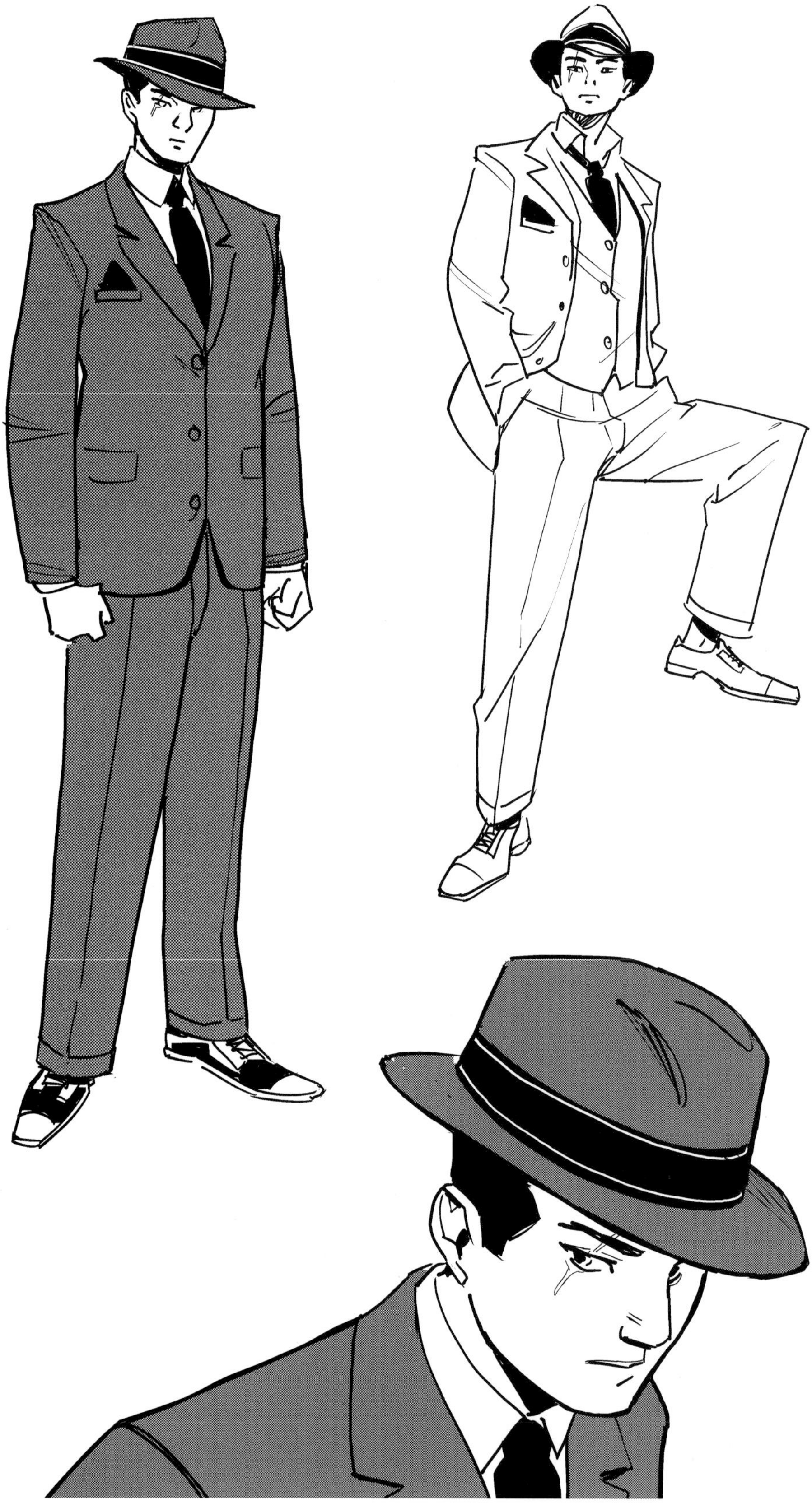

CHARACTER DESIGNS BY **ALEXANDRE TEFENKGI**

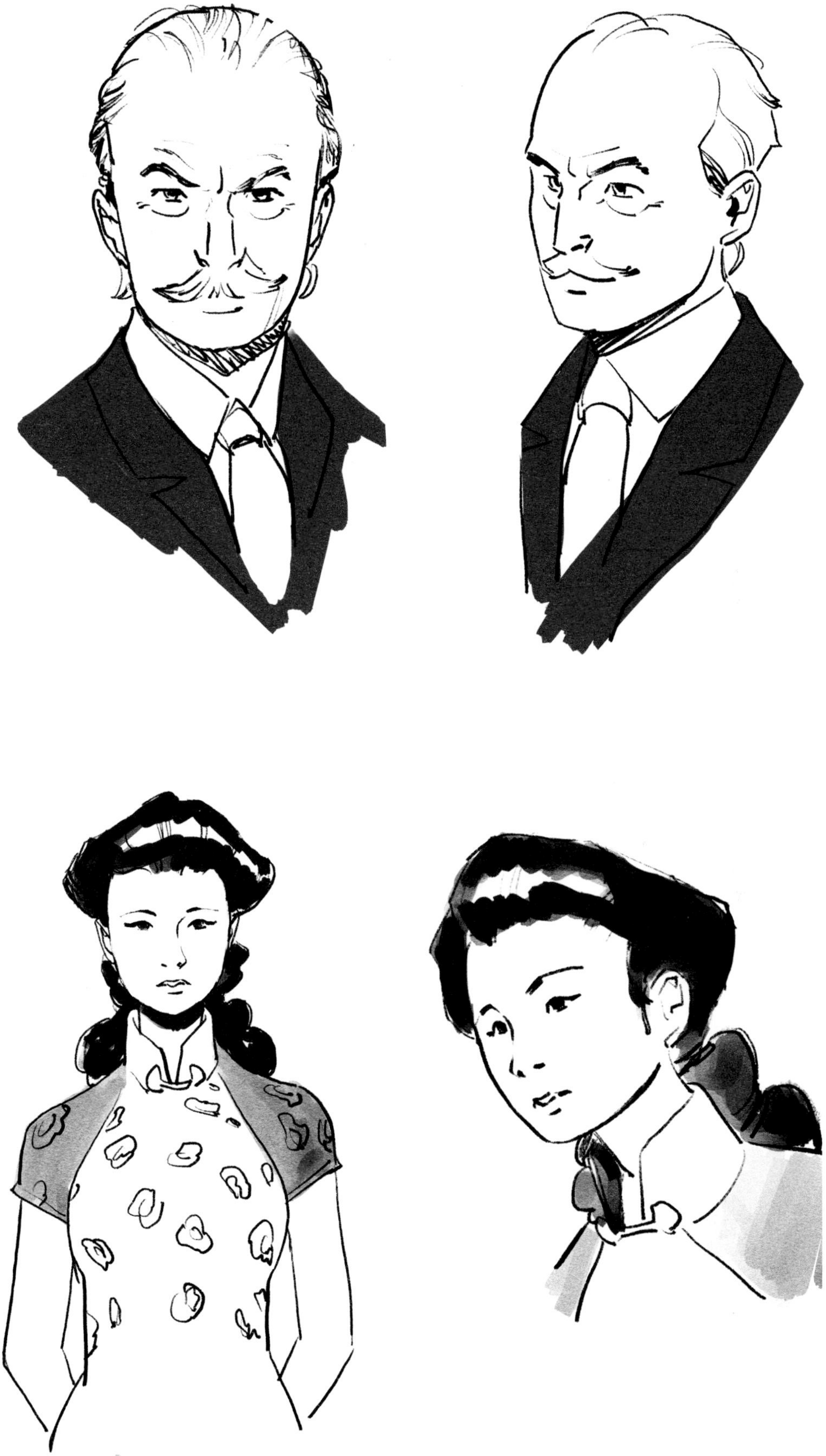

CHARACTER DESIGNS BY **ALEXANDRE TEFENKGI**

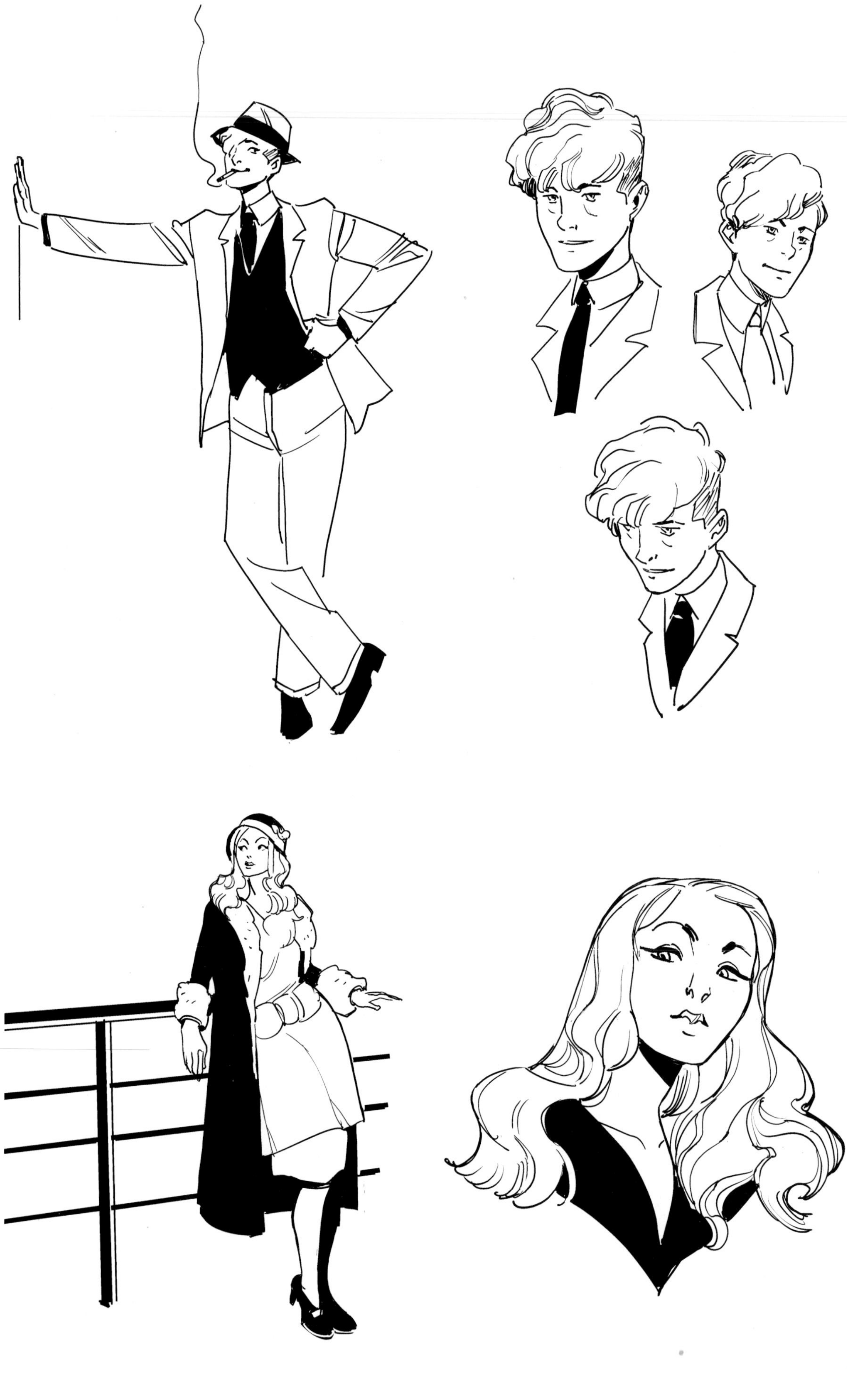

CHARACTER DESIGNS BY **ALEXANDRE TEFENKGI**

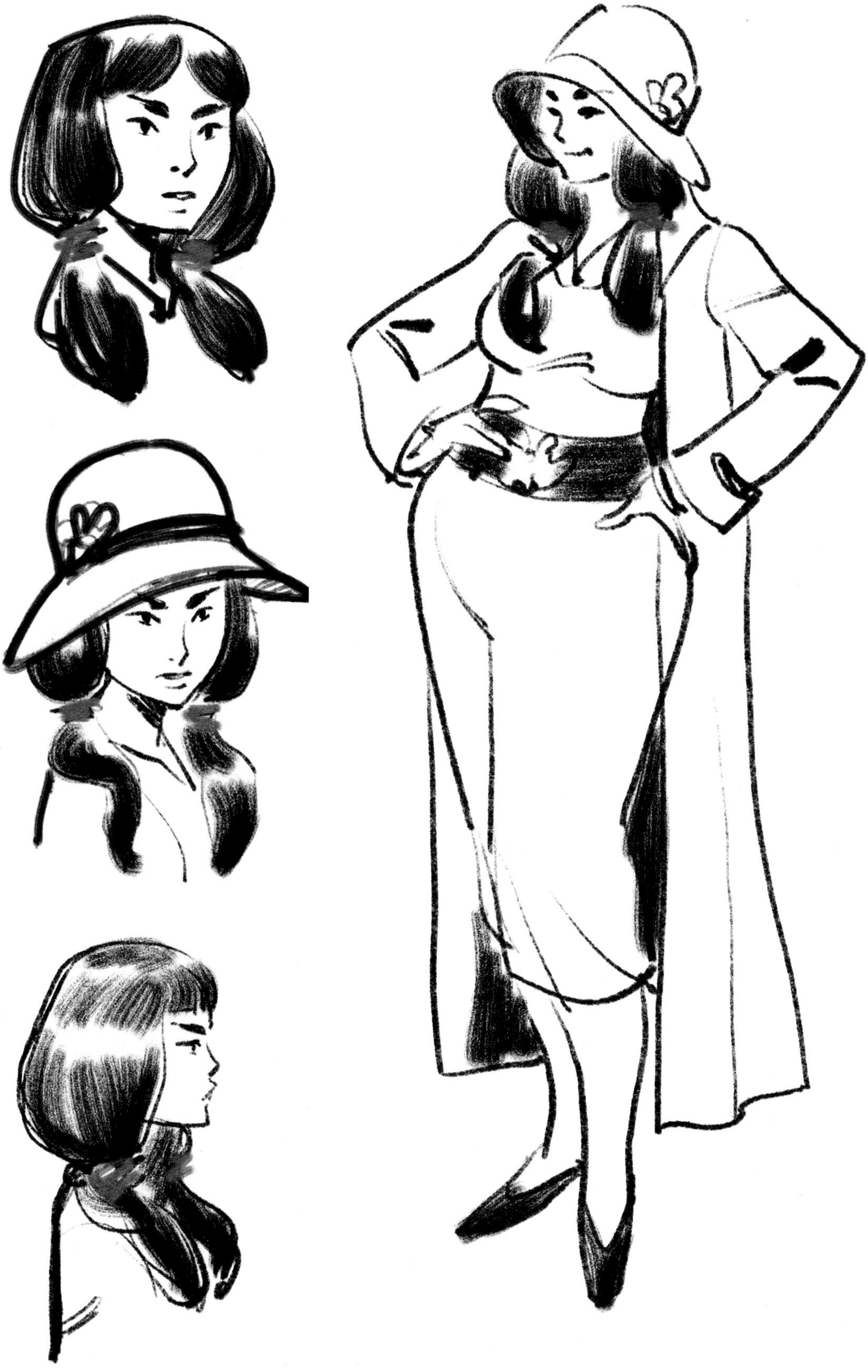

CHARACTER DESIGNS BY **ALEXANDRE TEFENKGI**

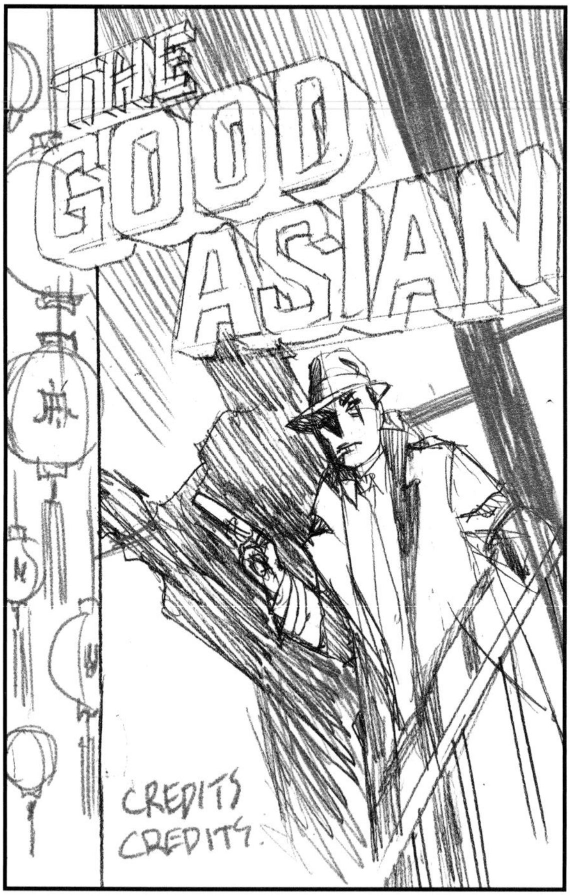
THE GOOD ASIAN
CREDITS
CREDITS

COVER #1 SKETCH BY **DAVE JOHNSON**

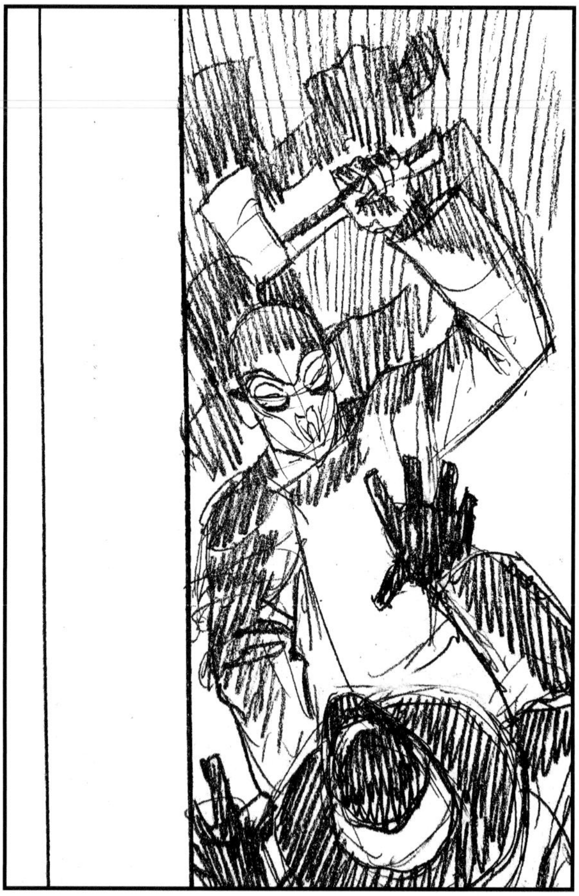

COVER #4 SKETCH BY **DAVE JOHNSON**

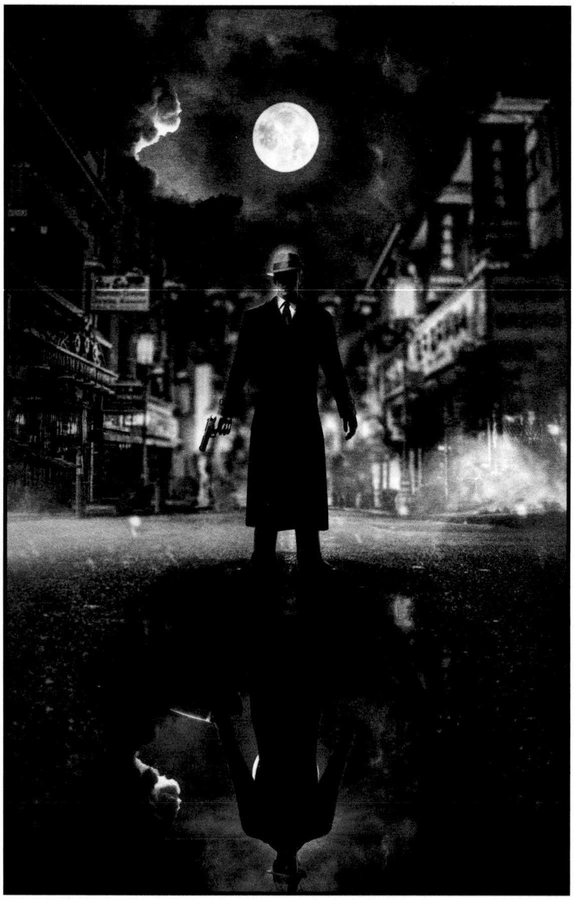

FRANKIE'S / GOLDEN APPLE COMICS
STORE VARIANT COVER BY **YADVENDER SINGH RANA**

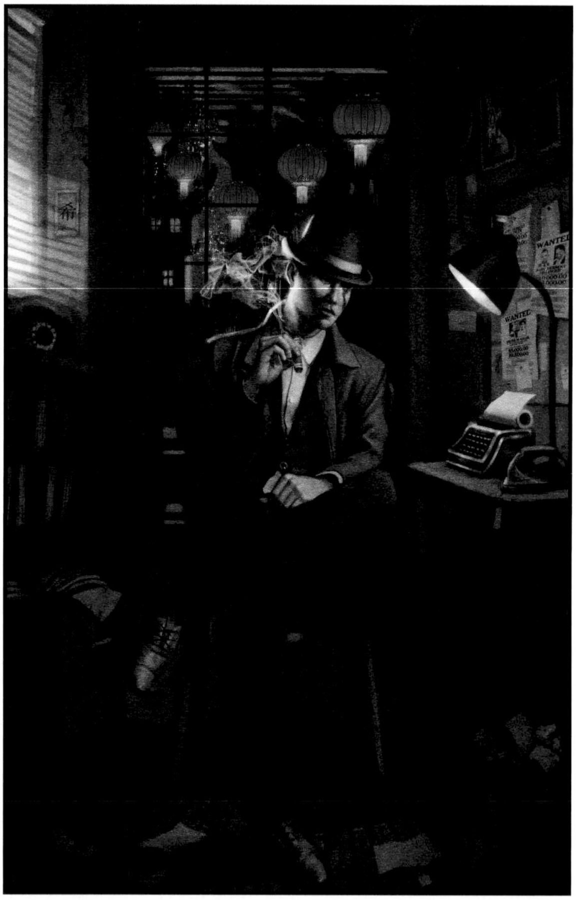

YELLOW SNOW COMICS STORE VARIANT COVER
BY **AARON BARTLING**

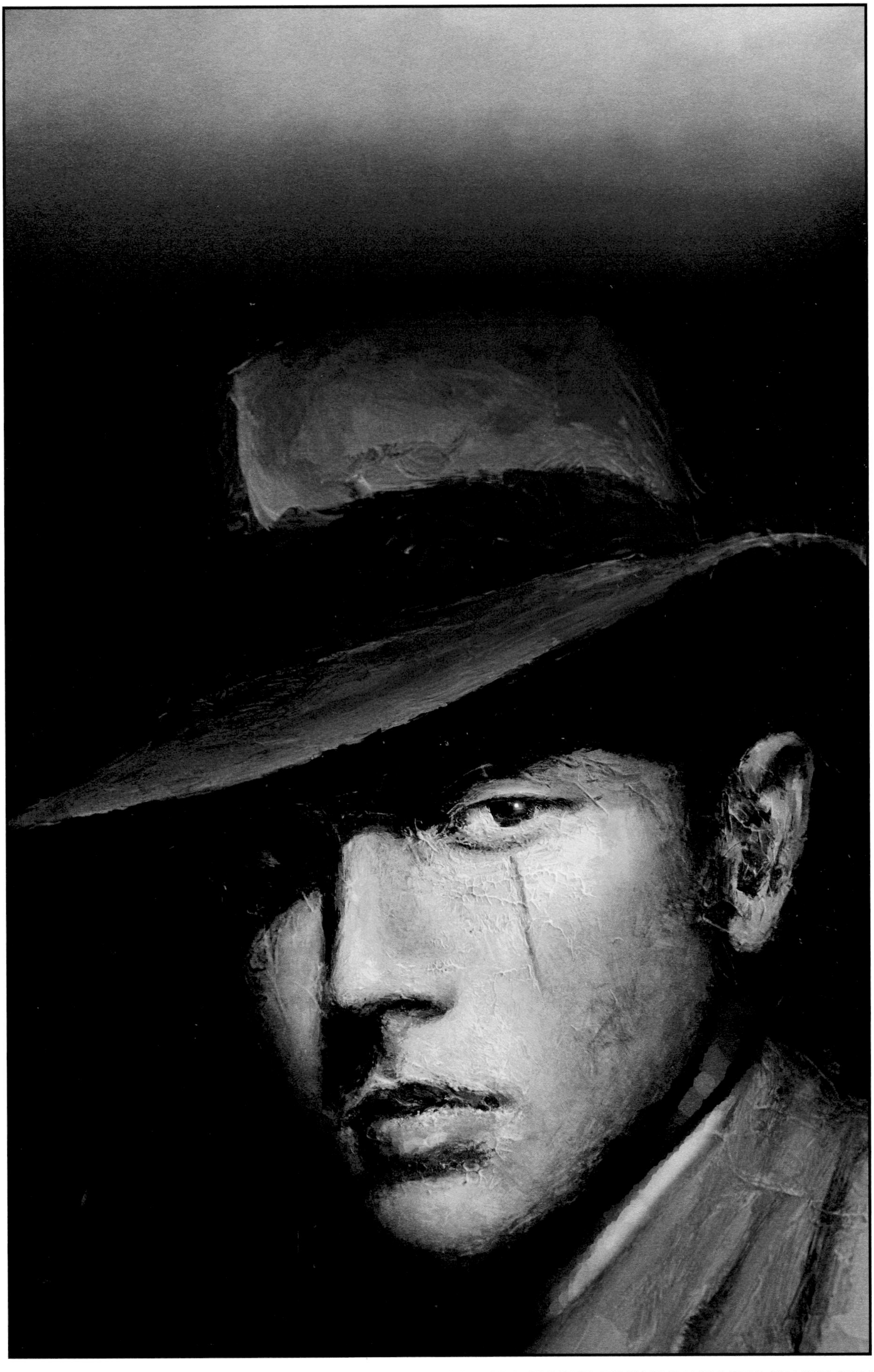

SANCTUM SANCTORUM COMICS & ODDITIES STORE VARIANT COVER BY **MIKE CHOI**

One of the book's early goals was to capitalize on the vast and incredible range of Asian / Asian-American artists working around the globe. Each one contributed a different variant cover for the individual issues, those artists spanning the globe and hailing from many different backgrounds: Some were comic book superstars, while for others, THE GOOD ASIAN marked their American debut. For the first time, the following pages present the early sketches and works-in-progresses before the official illustrations were settled upon.

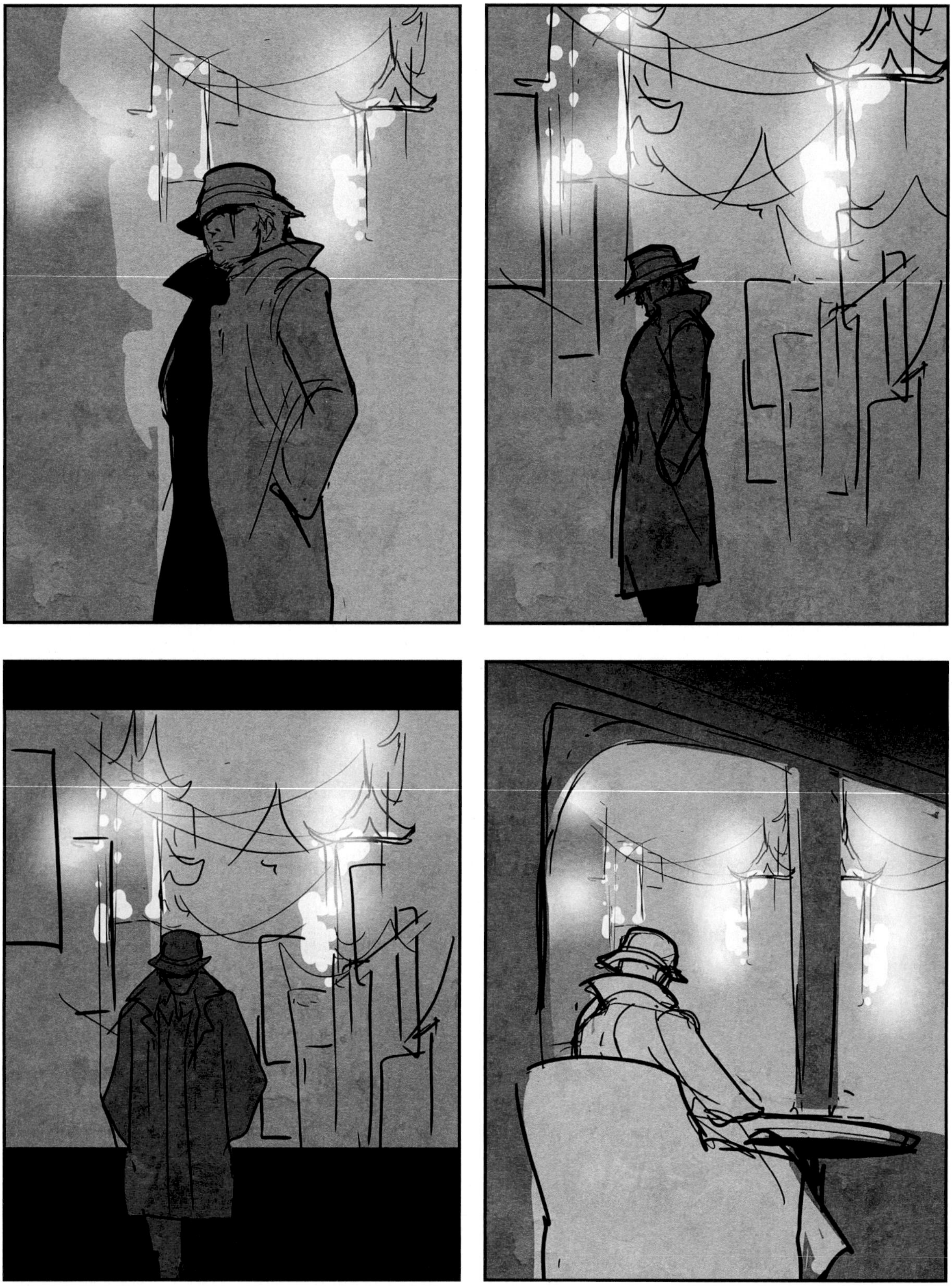

#1 VARIANT COVER SKETCHES BY **SANA TAKEDA**

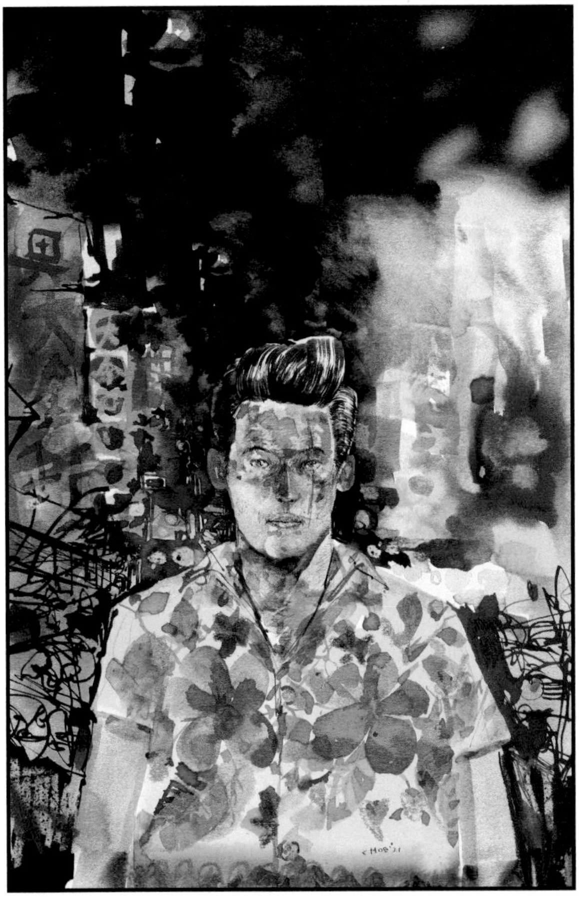

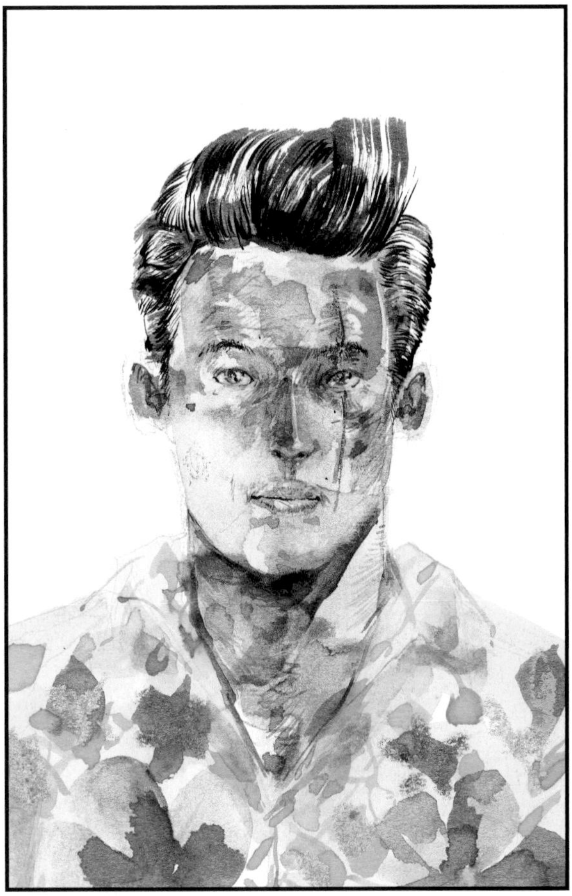

ALTERNATE COVER OPTIONS BY **DAVID CHOE**

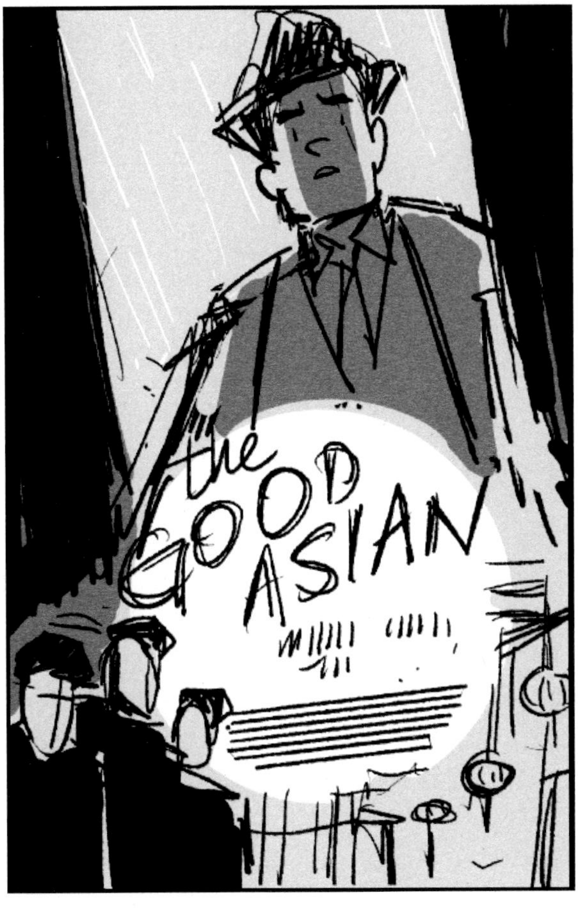
the
GOOD
ASIAN

#2 ALTERNATE COVER SKETCH BY **ANNIE WU**

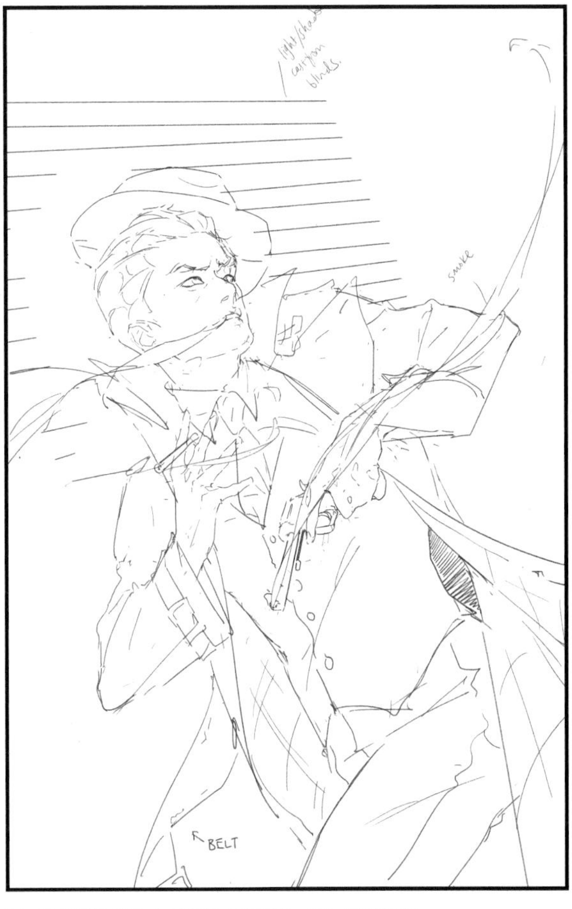
smoke
BELT

#4 ALTERNATE COVER SKETCH BY **AWANQI**

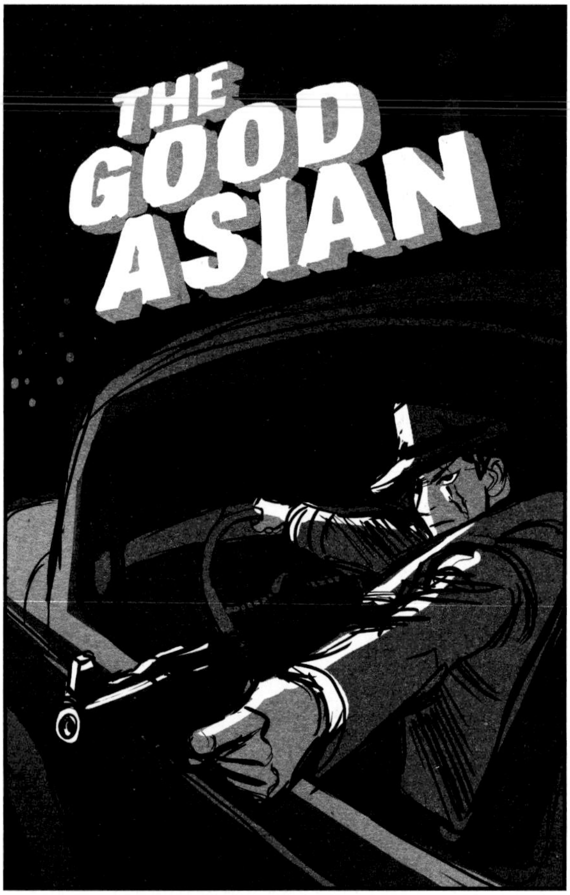
THE GOOD ASIAN

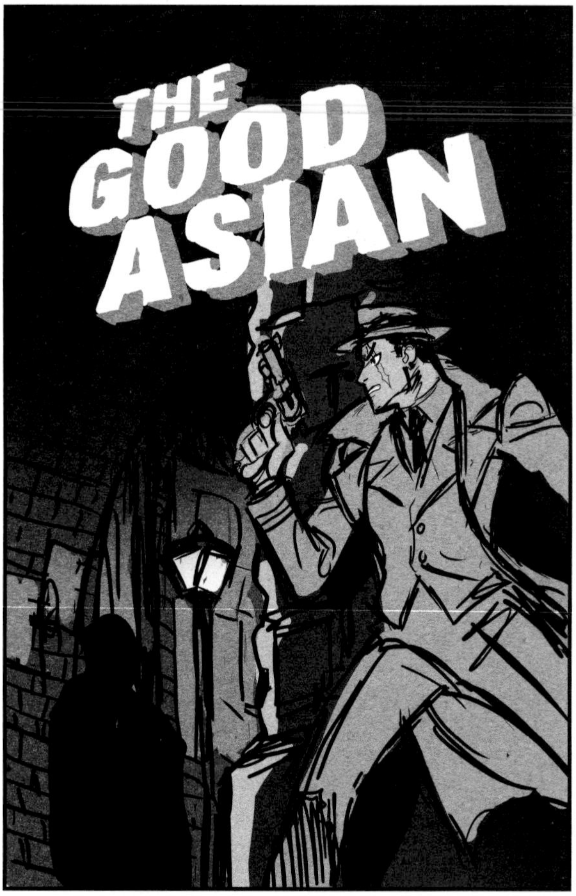
THE GOOD ASIAN

#5 VARIANT COVER SKETCHES BY **AFU CHAN**

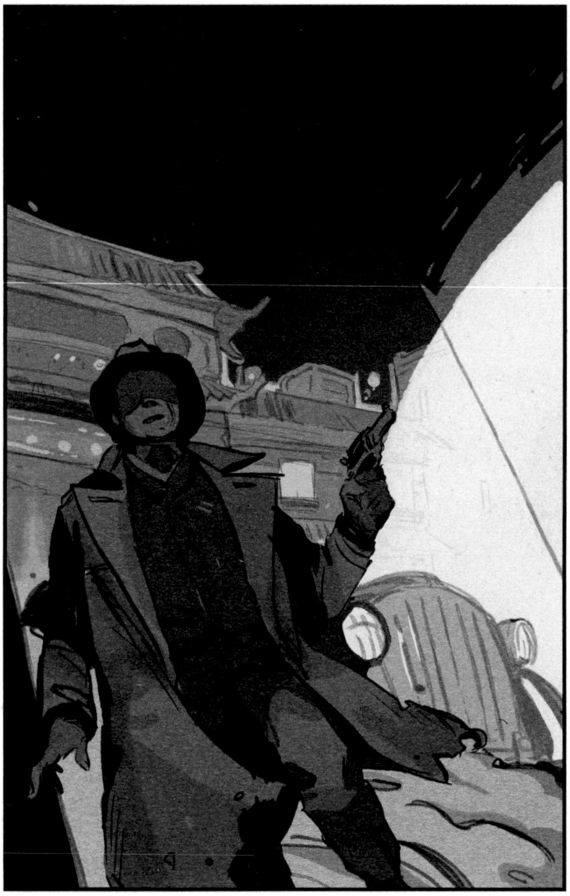

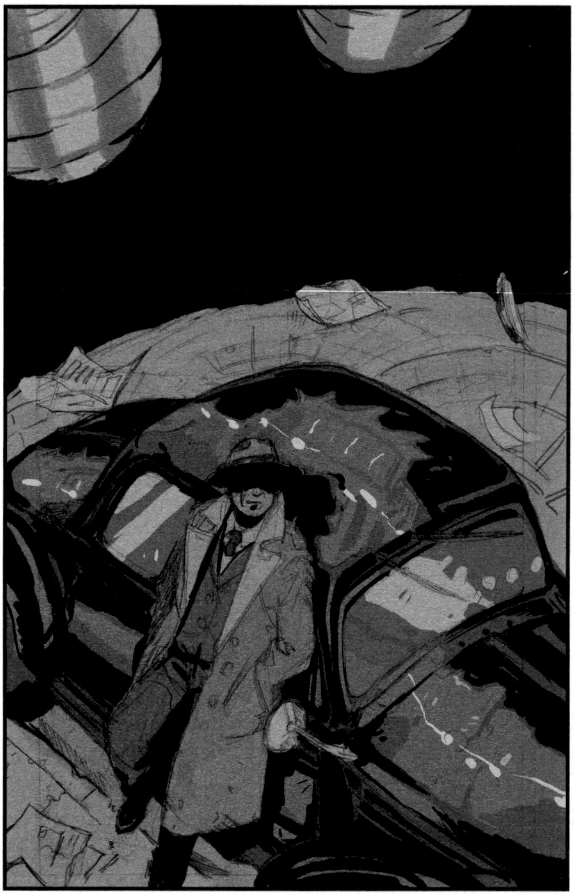

#7 VARIANT COVER SKETCHES BY **SONG CHUAYNUKOON**

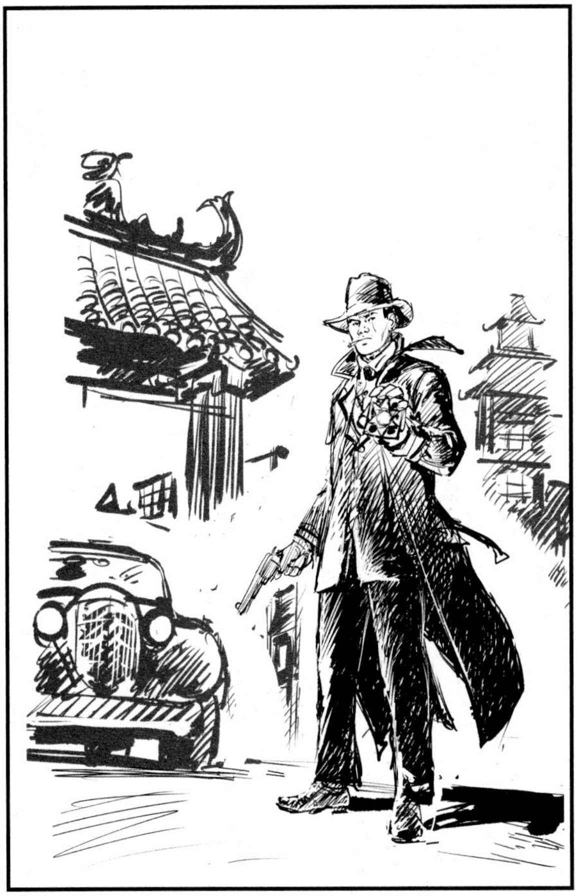

SKETCH

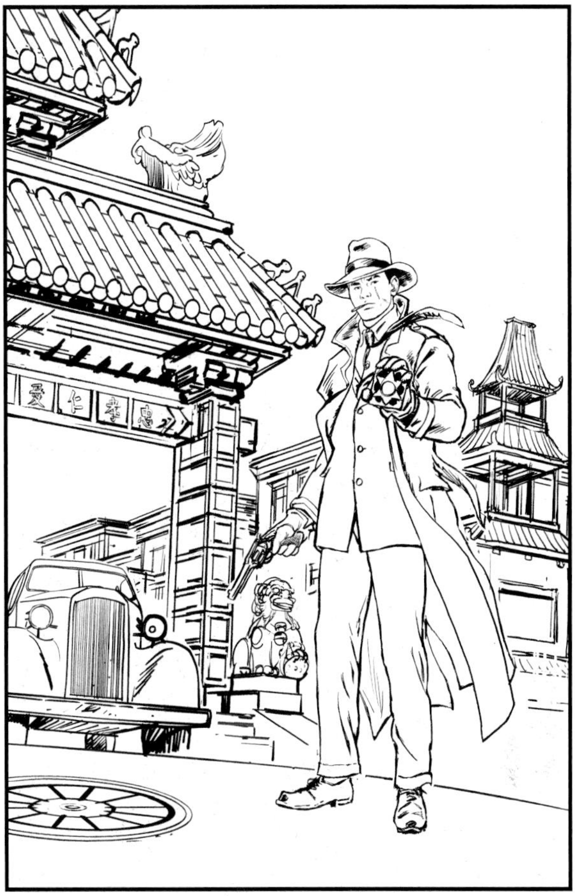

PENCILS

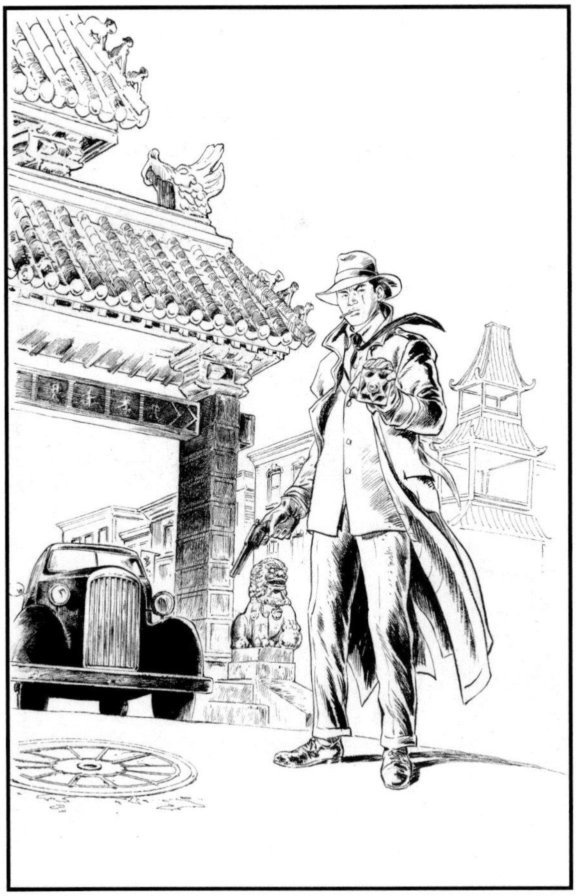

INKS

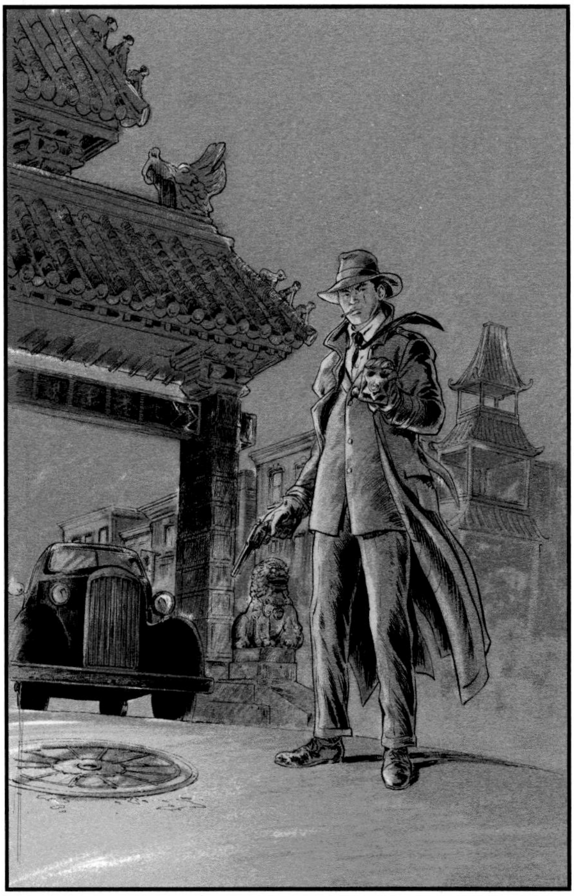

COLOR STUDY

#9 VARIANT COVER PROCESS BY **OLIVIER TADUC**

PORNSAK PICHETSHOTE was a Thai-American rising star editor at DC's VERTIGO imprint, his books nominated for dozens of Eisner awards. Currently writing for television and comics, his TV credits include *Marvel's Cloak & Dagger* and *Green Lantern* for HBO Max. His hit graphic novel INFIDEL was selected for NPR's "100 Favorite Horror Stories of All Time."

ALEXANDRE TEFENKGI is a French comic book artist of Vietnamese-Djiboutian descent. He started his career in the European market working with some of France's top publishers. His first international book is the critically acclaimed sci-fi series OUTPOST ZERO for Skybound Entertainment.

LEE LOUGHRIDGE is a devilishly handsome man, despite his low testosterone, who has been working primarily in the comics/animation industry for over twenty years. He has worked on hundreds of titles for all the industry's major publishers, his talents on display on every iconic comic book character from Batman to Punisher to DEADLY CLASS and more.

JEFF POWELL has lettered a wide range of titles throughout his lengthy career. His recent work includes *The Devil's Red Bride, Scales & Scoundrels*, and *The Forgotten Blade*. In addition, Jeff has designed books, logos, and trade dress for Marvel, Archie, IDW, Image, Valiant, and others.

DAVE JOHNSON may be best known for his minimalist covers on the noir Vertigo series, *100 Bullets*. He has also done a number of covers for Marvel, DC, and Image Comics. He earned the 2002 Eisner Award for Best Cover Artist and has also been nominated for an Eisner in 2004 and 2021. His work on the critically acclaimed *Superman: Red Son* is also a perennial bestseller.

WILL DENNIS was an editor at Vertigo/DC Entertainment for more than fifteen years, specializing in genre fiction comics and graphic novels. His award-winning titles include *100 Bullets, Y: The Last Man, Joker* and many more. He is currently a freelance editor for Image Comics, ComiXology, and DC Entertainment, also writing *The Art of Jock* for Insight Editions.